Praise for

NO LESS THAN VICTORY

"*No Less Than Victory* is a powerful evocation of the war in Europe that will appeal to WWII buffs and the general reader alike. It's a book that's literally impossible to put down until the very end. [Jeff Shaara's] thorough research shines through and the book should serve as a useful introduction to the final six months of the fighting in Europe."

—DAVE M. KINCHEN, Huntington News Network

"[Shaara] breathes life into military history." —*Pensacola News Journal*

"*No Less Than Victory* is a grand achievement, historically accurate yet utterly compelling." —*Booklist*

"Thanks to Shaara's visceral descriptive powers, we ride on a bombing mission with bombardier Sergeant Buckley as his B-17 flies through the flak-filled skies over Germany. With Private Benson, we feel the cold, deprivation and sense of dislocation of the Ardennes. And we sit in an observation post right on the Germans' doorstep as Captain Harroway calls down artillery fire on the enemy." —*Publishers Weekly*

"The Battle of the Bulge was Hitler's swan song on the Western front: a desperate attempt to retake the port of Antwerp. Historical novelist Jeff Shaara starts us there in the forests of Belgium, and takes us through the final six months of World War II through the eyes of the top brass and the average foot soldier, with real and created characters, not only on the Allied side, but the Nazi side as well."

—*New York Post* (Required Reading)

"Jeff Shaara brings history to life." —Texas *Shorthorn*

"[An] incisive portrait of war . . . While battles may be enough for military buffs, it's the dialogue and thoughts of Shaara's characters that make the book a narrative success." —*Bookpage*

No Less Than Victory

No Less Than Victory

A NOVEL OF
WORLD WAR II

JEFF SHAARA

BALLANTINE BOOKS TRADE PAPERBACKS

New York

2010 Ballantine Books Trade Paperback Edition

Copyright © 2009 by Jeffrey M. Shaara
Maps copyright © 2009 by David Lindroth, Inc.

Published in the United States by Ballantine Books,
an imprint of The Random House Publishing Group,
a division of Random House, Inc., New York.

BALLANTINE and colophon are trademarks of Random House, Inc.

Originally published in hardcover in the United States by Ballantine Books,
an imprint of The Random House Publishing Group,
a division of Random House, Inc., in 2009.

LIBRARY OF CONGRESS CATALOGING-IN-PUBLICATION DATA
Shaara, Jeff
No less than victory: a novel of World War II / Jeff Shaara.
p.   cm.
Includes bibliographical references.
ISBN 978-0-345-49793-2
1. World War, 1939–1945—Europe, Western—Fiction.
2. Ardennes, Battle of the, 1944–1945—Fiction.   I. Title.
PS3569.H18N6 2009
813'.54—dc22   2009035940

Printed in the United States of America

www.ballantinebooks.com

2 4 6 8 9 7 5 3

Book design by Mary A. Wirth

TO
MY COUSIN
EDDIE SHAARA

TO THE READER

This is the third volume of a trilogy that tells the story of the Second World War in Europe, through the eyes of a select few of the key participants. As in every story I've written, I feel I should mention that this is not a comprehensive historical account of the entire war. There are lengthy shelves in every library and every bookstore packed with volumes that have tackled the subject in far more detail. My primary goal is to take you back to this time, allowing these characters to tell their story as they lived it. There is no history in hindsight. In World War Two, the men and women who took part were facing the greatest crisis of their lives, a crisis that shaped the future of mankind. Though the historian may analyze that crisis, examine it with the comfortable knowledge of what followed, to the men who fought this war and those who made the great command decisions, there was very little comfort at all. Every day brought new challenges and new decisions for the commanders or a new urgency for the men who carried the rifle. The story here is true, the history accurate, and every event is real.

My research focuses solely on the accounts of the participants, their voices: memoirs and collections of letters, diaries and photographs, and, in wonderfully poignant instances, interviews with living veterans. This book has to be described as a novel, because there is dialogue, the everyday conversations that are not always recorded for posterity. And, much of the story is told from the points of view of these characters themselves, taking you into their thoughts. Even the veterans aren't able to fill in all the blanks.

I understand the risks of telling this kind of story. Many people have their own definite images of these iconic figures. Some of those images have been shaped by Hollywood, which is usually unfortunate. (To a great many Americans, the name *George Patton* conjures up the face of George C. Scott.) In the past, I have had people confront me with a certain level of outrage, one man specifically saying to me: "How *dare* you put words in the mouth of Robert E. Lee!" Fair enough. I accept the challenge. If I dare to put words into the mouths of any of the historical figures in my books, I had better feel comfortable that those words (and thoughts and emotions) are authentic. Otherwise, the characters will be counterfeit, and you, the reader, will know that immediately. Before I write a word, I dig as deeply as I can to find those voices, and the most gratifying success for me is when the writing begins and the story flows freely. It is a wonderful feeling to become that cliché, the fly on the wall, feeling as though I'm just the conduit, telling you what I'm seeing and hearing and feeling. You may certainly disagree with my portrayal of some of these men, and most assuredly, I cannot include every detail of every character's life. But by the end of this book, I hope you have a sense of who these people are, what they accomplished, and why we must not forget or dismiss their accomplishments. And I hope you find this to be a good story. That is, after all, the point.

There is one aspect of this book that is different from the first two volumes of the trilogy. Though I have included German voices before (most notably, Erwin Rommel), by the end of the war in Europe, many in the German hierarchy are dealing with a significant crisis that goes beyond what the war has done to their country. The reality of Hitler's reign can no longer be denied, and each man must confront his own conscience about what Hitler's Germany has become. To portray the Germans as one-dimensional goose-stepping cartoons would do a disservice not only to them, but to you. It is easy to cast judgment on these men today (as, at the Nuremberg trials, it was fairly easy then). But they are important to this story, and I feel that portraying them simply as "the bad guys," while politically correct, would not be authentic.

In a strange twist of coincidence, as I am writing this, I just returned from a brief trip to Washington, DC, where I happened to be when the shooting incident occurred at the Holocaust Museum. That horrifying act was committed by an eighty-eight-year-old Holocaust denier. Toward the war's end, American GIs (and then, the generals) discovered the worst of the Nazi concentration camps. Literally thousands of American and British soldiers witnessed firsthand the grotesque aftermath of the atrocities committed by the Germans. I am appalled by those who deny that the Holocaust took place. The accounts of the Allied soldiers and reporters who were there at the liberations of these camps, the sheer volume of *evidence* is so completely overwhelming that to deny it took place is both comically and tragically absurd. My fear is that the deniers have an agenda, political or social, and that by denying or even excusing what was done to those millions of human beings, their purpose could be to justify it happening again.

If this book is emotional for you, or if, after reading it, you feel you understand a bit more about the war itself, or know a little more about those men who were so responsible for the history of this extraordinary event, then you and I share something. It has been my privilege to tell this story.

JEFF SHAARA
June 2009

CONTENTS

To the Reader ix

List of Maps xv

Research Sources xvii

Introduction xix

Part One 1

Part Two 251

Part Three 325

Afterword 429

LIST OF MAPS

Situation on December 15, 1944 28

Hitler's Plan: "Watch on the Rhine" 35

Situation on December 18, 1944 155

Situation on December 19, 1944 181

Escape from St. Vith 190

Allied Counterattack on Stavelot 197

Patton Pushes to Bastogne 207

The German High-Water Mark—Celles 229

Hitler's Alsace Offensive 240

Situation on March 6, 1945 282

The Allies Cross the Rhine River 316

Situation on April 10, 1945 352

Final Troop Position—May 8, 1945 403

RESEARCH SOURCES

In response to the many requests I have received, the following is a *partial* list of the first-person accounts that document the events in this book.

THE AMERICANS

Colonel Robert S. Allen, HQ Third Army
First Sergeant Jack Alley, Forty-second Infantry Division
General Omar Bradley, Twelfth Army Group
Private First Class Robert Burns, Eleventh Armored Division
Commander Harry Butcher, HQ SHAEF
Private Dick Davison, Eightieth Infantry Division
Lieutenant Al Doherty, 102nd Infantry Division
General Dwight D. Eisenhower, SHAEF
General James Gavin, Eighty-second Airborne Division
Private First Class Irving Grossman, 106th Infantry Division
Major W. M. Hudson, Engineer, Third Army
Brigadier General Oscar Koch, Third Army G-2
Colonel Fred Kohler, 299th Combat Engineering Battalion
Captain Victor Leiker, Ninth Armored Division
Captain Charles B. MacDonald, Second Infantry Division
Major Charles W. Major, Eighty-second Airborne Division
Private George W. Neill, Ninety-ninth Infantry Division
Major Amelio Palluconi, Eighty-second Airborne Division
General George Patton, HQ Third Army
Colonel D. A. Watt, Fourth Armored Division
Private George Wilson, Fourth Infantry Division
The men of the 106th Infantry Division

THE BRITISH

Prime Minister Winston Churchill
Historian (Captain) Sir Basil Liddell Hart
Field Marshal Bernard Law Montgomery
Chief Air Marshal Arthur Tedder

THE GERMANS

Field Marshal Albert Kesselring
Field Marshal Karl Rudolf Gerd von Rundstedt
Albert Speer
General Siegfried Westphal

The following have generously contributed research materials, including memoirs and unpublished private papers and photographs. I am enormously grateful to all.

Paul Adams, Frederick, Maryland
Norma Alley, Norfolk, Virginia
Tom Batchelor, Bradenton, Florida
Tony Collins, Washington, DC
Jim Comer, Denver, Colorado
Courtland Crocker, Austin, Texas
Brooks Davison, Dallas, Texas
Julia Reagan Harmon
Karen Harris, Solvang, California
Joseph W. Hudson, Zirconia, North Carolina
Phoebe Hunter, Missoula, Montana
Jim Kohler, Seattle, Washington
Alan Major, Sarasota, Florida, and the Major/Nicholas family
James McClellan, Magnolia, Arkansas
Terry Misfeldt, Green Bay, Wisconsin
Bruce Novak, Needham, Massachusetts
James G. Ormsby, Leesburg, Georgia
David Palluconi, Fairfield, Ohio
James Pobog, Santa Ana, California
Kevin Shea, Washington, DC
John Smith, Indianapolis, Indiana
Jeff Stoker, Ogden, Utah
John Tiley, Half Moon Bay, California
Robert C. Weikel, Fort Wayne, Indiana
Kay Whitlock, Missoula, Montana
Lieutenant Colonel Pete Zielinski

INTRODUCTION

With the success of the Normandy campaign, which concludes in August 1944, the Allied armies embrace their success with a euphoric confidence that Germany is on its last legs. The English, Canadian, and American armies that have punched their way across France have every right to feel that the victory they have gained is monumental. But that victory does not come without mistakes. The most critical error is the failure to close what is now known as the Argentan–Falaise gap, an eighteen-mile opening in a tightening ring that allows tens of thousands of German troops to escape toward their own borders. Blame for not closing the gap falls primarily on British field marshal Bernard Montgomery, but the British reciprocate by tossing responsibility toward the Allied supreme commander, Dwight Eisenhower. It is a controversy with no simple answer, but the results of the failure are soon made clear. Those German troops will fight again.

As autumn comes to Europe, the Allies rely as much on arrogance as they do on wise tactics. To reward the accomplishments (and placate the egos) of his generals, Eisenhower pushes through changes in the command of his army. Montgomery, who had commanded the combined Allied ground forces at Normandy, is now limited to command of an army group that consists of his own British troops as well as the Canadian First Army. American general Omar Bradley is elevated to equal status with Montgomery and now commands all those American forces that have driven inland from Normandy, whose numbers continue to increase. To soothe Montgomery for the perceived slight to his authority, and to blunt the howls of outrage in the British newspapers, he is promoted to the rank of field marshal. The Americans recognize the gesture for what it is, yet Montgomery continues to press Eisenhower with his own specific agenda for winning the war. To the dismay of the Americans under his command, Eisenhower accepts Montgomery's plan for a massive parachute drop along the northern flanks of the Allied front, an attempt to sweep around the strongest German defensive positions, opening a clear pathway toward Berlin. The attack will punch through the waterways and swampy plains that spread out along the boundaries separating Belgium, Holland, and northern Germany. Critical to the success of this operation is the capture of bridges across five separate rivers, including the bridge at Arnhem, which crosses the Rhine. With the bridges in Allied hands, British infantry and armor will then drive through the doorway held open by the paratroopers. Montgomery is confident that this assault not only will surprise the German defenders, but could also bring a rapid end to the war.

On September 17, 1944, Operation Market-Garden begins. Three divisions of paratroopers, two American and one British, descend from the skies in broad daylight, in the largest airdrop in history. For reasons Montgomery does not explain, the drop zone for the British First Airborne Division is forty miles from their intended target of Arnhem. The delays and difficulties the British paratroopers encounter in reaching the bridge allow German defenses to respond—defenses that are far stronger than Montgomery has anticipated. Worse for the Allies, Montgomery's entire operational plans for the battle fall into German hands when an American officer who carries them in his pocket is captured. Within hours, German field marshal Walther Model knows exactly what Montgomery is trying to do.

Instead of a quick grab of their intended targets, the Allied paratroopers are bogged down in a slugfest they cannot win. Despite Montgomery's efforts to support them with armor and infantry, it becomes apparent that the operation cannot succeed. On September 25, eight days after the operation begins, Montgomery orders a withdrawal. The Allies suffer nearly seventeen thousand casualties, twice as many as their enemy.

Montgomery insists that the operation has been "ninety percent successful" and blames most of the failure on the dismal weather conditions.

No one on the American side agrees with him, especially the commanders of the two paratroop divisions. It is one more rift in the fragile command structure Eisenhower must struggle to maintain.

To support Montgomery's operation, Eisenhower pushes forward the American forces all along the broad Western Front. American general Courtney Hodges presses toward the German city of Aachen, which he captures in mid-October. To the south of Hodges, George Patton's Third Army drives toward the critical industrial region of the Saar Valley. But with the change in the calendar comes a change in the weather, and rain and mud act as effectively to slow the Allied drives as anything the Germans can put in their way.

At a meeting of his generals on October 18, Eisenhower expresses his frustration and begins to understand that their jubilant optimism has dissolved into what might become a bloody stalemate. To the north, Montgomery insists his army can offer no major offensive drive until the first of the new year. In the south, Patton has stretched his supply lines to their breaking point, and his troops are exhausted by the enemy's stubbornness, as well as the difficult conditions offered by the miserable weather.

In the center, as the Americans secure their hold on Aachen, they plan for a continuing advance eastward. But south and east of the city, the Germans have established a defensive position in a stretch of woodlands called the Hürtgen Forest. Before the Allies can safely push farther into Germany, the enemy positions in the Hürtgen must be eliminated. In mid-November, Hodges drives his forces into the forest, anticipating a sweep through the subpar German units that hold the ground. What the Americans find instead is a German defense that has all the geographic advantages, fighting in a morass of thick timber and miserable terrain that completely favors any defender. For two weeks, the Americans slog forward, suffering a staggering casualty count. Hodges responds by ordering reinforcements into the fray, which only adds to the meat grinder the Americans troops are enduring. The "Hell in the Hürtgen" eventually costs the Americans more than thirty thousand casualties and becomes their bloodiest engagement of the war. Though the Americans eventually accomplish their goal, the cost is far worse than anyone could have expected. The euphoria of three months earlier has been replaced by frustration and a hard dose of reality. Despite what many have believed, the Germans are far from a demoralized and disheartened army of misfits and old men. Though Eisenhower continues to urge his generals to maintain some kind of offense, the weather worsens. All across the Western Front, those generals who are veterans of the First World War are drawn back to the memories of a land where winter smothers the armies, where rain becomes snow, where the terrain favors only those who sit low in their trenches and wait for a target.

Still reeling from the cost of the fight in the Hürtgen, Courtney Hodges shifts his various divisions according to their needs, resting the weary veterans, placing the new and inexperienced units out of harm's way. Winter begins to settle down across the front, yet no one is allowed to forget that the Germans are still dangerous, more so now that their backs are up against their own homes. Though no one expects the Germans to launch any major offensive in winter, Hodges strengthens the area north of the Ardennes, where any German attack would most likely appear. Hodges knows, as does Eisenhower, that the loss of the city of Aachen has to be a sore point to Hitler and his generals. Throughout the fall, Hodges's men suffer the worst of the fighting, and so it is reasonable for Hodges to shift those most bloodied units to a quieter sector and allow them to recoup and rebuild. Thus, he sends them south, to the area around Bastogne, along the Southern Front of the Ardennes Forest. Across the greatest span of that miserable terrain, he has placed the new arrivals—the least experienced units in his command, the 106th and 99th divisions—closer to the key intersections at the small Belgian town of St. Vith. With armor support nearby, added protection in the event of some German intrusion through the Ardennes, Hodges has been ordered to keep his primary attention on a renewed drive eastward, toward the all-important Roer River dams. Once the weather improves and the levels of the river drop, Hodges expects to resume a hard offensive alongside Montgomery, while south of the Ardennes, Patton will be turned loose as well, to cross into Germany and seize the industrial Saar Valley. It will be the final drive that will crush Hitler's armies against the Rhine River and then, beyond. With the Russians planning their own major offensive for January, intending to crush Germany from the east, Eisenhower and all of Supreme Headquarters Allied Expeditionary Force (SHAEF) are supremely confident that the end is near.

On the other side, the surprising spirit of the German soldiers results from several factors the Allies do not understand. In July 1944, an attempt is made to assassinate Hitler, but through an astonishing stroke of fortune, the Führer is spared. The consequences for anyone who opposes Hitler are quick and severe, and anyone suspected of disloyalty becomes a target of

Hitler's Gestapo. Thousands of men and women are executed, many more jailed, and thus, any significant energy to oppose Hitler or remove him from power is silenced. Dr. Joseph Goebbels, Hitler's minister of propaganda, makes the most of Hitler's survival, trumpeting to the German people that their Führer is indeed invincible. It is a campaign that inspires the German people more than ever to acceptance of Hitler's leadership.

The disaster in France has brought a change to his army that not even Hitler appreciates. Where once the Germans were ruled by vast army groups headed by field marshals, now, with the mad scramble to survive, the army has re-formed into smaller units under the command of junior officers. These units are far more autonomous than any that have existed before, and so, in the confusion and chaos of a fight in a place like the Hürtgen Forest, German officers who are cut off from rear command have far more ability to make the best fight for the situation they face. Though the generals still hold sway, the average German soldier becomes much more important.

In the east, the Russians have battered German forces to such an extent that even a delusional Hitler is aware that he must have some major breakthrough, some enormous success to turn the tide. He reasons that the weaker enemy is in the west, and that the Americans and particularly the British are culturally and philosophically not so different from the Germans they confront. Hitler believes that a major defeat of those forces will bring the western Allies to the peace table, and that Hitler can easily persuade them to join the greater cause and strike against their common enemy, the Russians. What seems to be perfect logic to Hitler does not sway his generals, but there can be no argument. He forms a plan, a major offensive at a time and place that no one will expect. He is certain that when his plan succeeds, the war will be won. His dreams of a Thousand Year Reich will yet be realized.

PART ONE

Wars are won by people who actually go out and do things.
—GEORGE PATTON

1. THE BOMBARDIER

He was already cold, ice in both legs, that same annoying knot freezing in his stomach. The plane shimmied sideways, and he rocked with it, felt the nose go up, could see the ground falling away, the B-17 climbing higher, steeper. Just in front was another plane, and he could see the tail gunner, moving into position, facing him. They were barely three hundred feet above the ground when the plane in front began to bank to the left, and his plane followed, mimicking the turn. Out to the side, the predawn light was broken by faint reflections of the big bombers just behind and to the right, doing the same maneuver. There were sparks from some of the big engines, unnerving, but the mechanics had done their job, and once full daylight came, the sparks would fade away.

They continued to climb, as steeply as the B-17 would go without stalling, every pilot knowing the feeling, that sudden bucking of the nose when the plane had begun to stop flying. But the bombardier could do nothing but ride. During takeoff, he was only a passenger, the pilot in the cockpit above him doing his job. He leaned as the plane banked into a sharper angle, knew they were circling, still close to the plane in front, more moving up with them. Some were already above, the first to take off, but they had disappeared into thick cloud cover, his own now reaching the dense ceiling, the plane in front of him barely visible. Wetness began to smear the Plexiglas cone in front of him, heavy mist from the clouds. In training, he had been told that the bombardier had the best seat in the plane, as far forward as you could sit, right in the nose, a clear view in every direction but behind. Even the pilot couldn't see downward, had to rely on the planes flying in formation beneath him to keep their distance. But in the dense cloud cover, there was nothing to see, streams of rain still flowing across the Plexiglas, and now, blindness, the clouds thicker still, no sign of the plane in front of him at all.

Behind him to the left sat the navigator, silent as well, staring into his instruments. The blindness in front of them was annoying, then agonizing, the plane still shimmying, small bounces in the rough air, the pilot using his skills to keep his plane at precisely the attitude of those around him. The bombardier leaned as far forward as his safety belt would allow, searched the dense gray above them for some break, the first signs of sunlight, made a low curse shared by every American in the Eighth Air Force. British weather . . .

There had been nothing unusual about this mission, the men awakened at four in the morning, a quick breakfast, then out to the massive sea of planes. The preparation and inspection of the plane had been done by the ground crew, always in the dark, men who did not have the flight crew's luxury of sleeping as late as four. But as they gathered beside their own bird, eight of the ten-man crew pitched in, working alongside the ground crew for the final preparation, while the pilot and copilot perched high in the cockpit ran through their checklists, inspections of their own. Like the other crewmen, the bombardier had helped pull the enormous props in a slow turn, rolling the engines over manually, loosening the oil. He knew very little about engines, had never owned a car, never earned that particular badge that inspired pride in the mechanics, a cake of grease under the fingernails. But oil seemed important to those who knew, maybe as much as gasoline, and the need for plenty of both wasn't lost on anyone. If the ground crew said the oil needed to be loosened up, then by God he would pitch in to loosen it up. After some predetermined number of pulls, the chief mechanic gave the word, and the pull of the heavy prop blades became easier, the slow stuttering of the engines, the small generator igniting the sparks that would gradually kick each of the four engines into motion. The crews would stand back, admiring, their efforts paying off in a huge belch of smoke and thunder, the props turning on their own. Even the older mechanics seemed to enjoy that brief moment, swallowed by the exhaust, the hard sounds rolling inside them, deafening, all the power that would take this great bird up to visit the enemy one more time.

With the engines warming up, the pilot had given the usual hand signal, the order to climb aboard. The bomber's crew would move toward the hatches, and the veterans could predict who would be first in line. It was always the newest man, this time a show of eagerness by the ball turret gunner, a man who did not yet know how scared he should be. As the crew moved toward the hatches, the men who stayed behind had one more job, offering a helping hand, some a final pat on the rump, or a few words meant to impart luck. There were customs now, some of the ground crew reciting the same quick prayer or making the same pledge, to buy the first drink or light the first cigarette. *See you tonight. Give those Nazi bastards one for me.* Some had written names or brief messages on the bombs themselves, usually profane, a vulgar greeting no one else would ever read. All of this had begun at random, but by now it had become ceremony, and the brief chatter held meaning, had become comforting repetition to all of them. There was another ceremony as well. As the crew passed beneath the nose, each man reached up to tap the shiny metal below the brightly painted head of an alligator, all teeth and glowing eyes. The plane had been named Big Gator, some of her original crew insisting that she be endowed with a symbol of something to inspire fear in the enemy. No one had asked if any Germans actually knew what an alligator was, but the flight engineer had come from Louisiana bayou country, and he had made the argument that none of the others could dispute. Not even the pilot had argued. As long as the painted emblem was ferocious, Big Gator worked just fine. This morning, they were embarking on their thirty-second mission, and thus far, only one man had sustained more than a minor combat wound: the ball turret gunner, replaced now by this new man who seemed to believe he would shoot down the entire Luftwaffe.

With longevity came even greater superstition, especially for the ground crew. There was a desperate awareness of the odds, of fate. Thirty-one successful missions was an unnerving statistic by now, rarer by the week. It was the reason for all the rituals, the most religious among them believing that God must somehow be paying particular attention. If someone said a prayer, the same prayer, it might encourage a Divine smile toward this bird that would bring these men home one more time.

The superstitions were reinforced by the number of combat missions they were required to fly, what had become a sore point to every crewman in the Eighth Air Force. Originally, each crewman was expected to complete twenty-five missions, a number that had become some sort of magic achievement. As a man passed twenty, the rituals became more intense, some drawing one more *X* on the wall beside their beds, some refusing the poker games for fear of draining away their luck. Then the number of missions had been raised to thirty, and the grumbling had erupted into unguarded cursing toward the air commanders. But the missions continued, the superstitions adjusted, and the new men, the replacements, seemed not to know the difference. After a time, word had come, some officer knowing to pass along the order and then duck for cover. The number had been raised to thirty-five. The protests had erupted again, but the brass had been inflexible and unapologetic. As the bombing campaigns intensified, the flow of new crews from the training centers was too slow to keep up with the need for more and more aircraft. That was the official explanation. But word had filtered through the hangars and barracks that the number of missions had been raised because so many of the crews were being killed. Experienced crewmen had already begun to grumble that thirty-five might become a luxury, that someone far up the chain of command had already decided the number would continue to rise. The men who had seen so many from their own squadrons fall out of the sky were beginning to believe that they would have to fly as many missions as it would take for them to be killed.

The bombardier's name was Buckley, and at twenty-two, he was no older than most of the ten men who flew the Big Gator. The engineer was the oldest, close to thirty, and looked it, a fierce, big-shouldered Cajun. The rest of the crew started at age nineteen, the gunners usually the youngest, and Buckley thought of the pilot. Hell, he looks like he's twelve. Someone called him Captain Babyface. He's my age, I think. Seems like a good Joe, but who knows anymore? So far so good.

The pilot had come only two weeks before, a replacement for their original pilot who had washed out. It had been one of those unexpected human explosions, the pilot simply coming apart after twenty-four missions. There had been no hint it was coming, no one suspecting a problem, but somewhere over France, on the way toward their target, the plane had suddenly banked and then fallen into a steep dive. Even through the noise of the engines, he had heard the pilot screaming, others reacting violently, shouts throughout the plane. The chaos was complete, something of a fight in the cockpit, the engineer and the copilot wrestling with the man, a terrifying minute that brought most of the crew forward. The navigator had climbed up from the nose to help, but Buckley had to stay put, knowing that he could fly the plane using his bombsight if it came to that. As the terrifying seconds passed, he had stared straight ahead, eyes locked on the ground rising up in front of him, his back pressed hard into his seat. Then the plane had leveled out, someone's sure hands at the controls, and the answers had come quickly. The pilot had started screaming, something about dying, that it was his time. But the man's hysteria had been quieted with a hard crunching blow to his head from the butt of a .45. No one had been eager to take credit for actually cracking a pistol over the man's head. They all knew that some idiot officer at the inquiry, some wet-eared major who had never faced the enemy, might go by the book and try to call it mutiny. But the guy went nutso, Buckley thought. Just fell to pieces. Whoever busted his head saved our asses. Had to be Sergeant Marlette. That damn engineer loves to make out like he's gonna kick asses for no good reason. Good thing, too. If we'd have kept diving like that, the damn wings were gonna come off. Buckley could see that pilot in his mind, a few years older, handsome in that Hollywood kind of way, the pilot who gets the girl. Wonder what they did to him? Court-martial? They didn't tell us anything. The crew had heard rumors, of course, and Buckley thought, it's the same old crap they held over our heads through training: You wash out up here, and they're gonna stick a rifle in your hands and send you to the infantry. I guess I'm supposed to believe that. But if a guy goes crazy in a cockpit, what makes those jackass officers think he won't do the same thing in a foxhole?

He leaned back in his small hard seat, knew that beneath the thin cushion, a half-inch piece of steel had been fastened to the frame. The veterans had learned quickly to buddy up to someone on the ground crew who had access to spare parts, and for a case of beer or a bottle of Scotch you might get someone to slip a piece of extra armor into place. It was unauthorized, the steel considered contraband by the commanders, added weight the plane did not need. But even the new pilot never said a word. No doubt, Buckley thought, the captain's sitting on one of his own. If anything comes up from below, at least the jewels might have a little protection. He might be new, but he's not a moron.

The new pilot, Captain Henry Carlson, had no choice but to settle in quickly with his new crew. In two weeks, he had already flown seven missions, a terrifyingly quick indoctrination. He seems pretty smart, Buckley thought, but he's a little weird. Bad enough somebody called him Captain Babyface, but now, he says he won't get a haircut until he goes home. Calls that his good-luck charm. He survives his first couple weeks, so he decides he won't change a thing. Does that mean he doesn't take showers either? Don't need to know that. That's the copilot's problem.

He stared ahead into the gloom, felt the cold spreading through his legs, the temperature dropping quickly. He reached out, fumbling for the switch that would put the blessed heat through the wiring in his boots and coveralls. At high altitude, the air was numbing, any exposed fingers useless in minutes, even the gloves barely adequate. After a long couple of minutes, he could begin to feel the heat, what there was of it, enough to ease the pain of frozen toes. But still he shivered, his arms clamping tightly around his thick jacket. The overalls took longer to warm up, but even then he knew the shivering wouldn't stop.

It was like this every time, the shivering coming long before the plane actually left the ground. None of them talked about it, no one would risk revealing the secret, would risk the ribbing and the shame of simply being afraid. Buckley had wondered about that, how many of these men were as scared as he was. He glanced behind him, saw the navigator scanning his instruments then writing something on a small pad of paper. Buckley looked out front again, thought, he never says anything during the warm-up, during the climb. Maybe he's as scared as I am. If he's not, he's a fruitcake. I don't want to know that. Just so he gets us out there, gives me someplace to dump these eggs, and then gets us the hell back home.

The heat was increasing in his overalls, and he flexed his toes, the numbness wearing off. He looked back toward the other side, saw the flak jacket hanging on the hook he had made from a piece of the plane's wiring. He struggled to shift in his seat, held by his safety belt, wrapped as well by the thickness of his clothing. Like most of the others, he wore long johns and his uniform beneath the overalls. Over that he wore a thick fleece-lined leather jacket. Once airborne, each crewman put on his oxygen mask and flight helmet. After ten thousand feet or so, the air thinned out enough that any man could black out in seconds if he didn't get his "juice." Buckley had played with that idea in training, thought, how bad could it be? There's still air, right? Hell, there's enough to keep the plane flying. But he found out quickly that passing out gets you a reprimand and, sometimes, one whale of a headache. He put his hand on his mask, tested the flow of oxygen, then reached down beneath his seat. He kept a spare carry-around oxygen bottle there, something every crewman had at his finger-tips. The primary oxygen masks were attached to hoses, and if a man had to leave his seat, the mask stayed put. He nodded to himself. Yep, those lit-tle bottles were somebody's damn good idea. He put his hands against his chest, felt the parachute, thought, I guess this is too. Regulations called for each man to wear his parachute, but most of them did as Buckley did now: released the strap on one side so the chute hung loosely off one shoulder. Despite the fear, it was a defiant gesture, reinforced by the stupidity of peer pressure, a show of swaggering confidence that they wouldn't need the thing anyway. But there was a more practical reason to keep the chute out of the way. It interfered with the final article of clothing, the flak jacket. And bravado be damned, every man wore his flak jacket. He pulled it over his shoulders, saw the navigator doing the same.

Suddenly they broke out of the gray blindness and he saw a dull blue sky, a bright splash of light on the horizon. He let out a long breath, stared ahead, couldn't help feeling impressed, the sky crowded with so many of the big birds, flocks of B-17s in the same arcing turns, formations coming together, a myriad display of triangles, stacking one above the other. They flew in groups of three, one plane in front, the other two behind each wing of the leader. That formation was one of a dozen just like it, thirty-six planes in a much larger pack, clustered as tightly together as they could safely fly. The squadron was only one small part of an extraordinary ar-mada, and he could see most of them now, spread far into the low sunlight.

The great flocks of bombers continued to gather, nine hundred planes arriving from different airfields, taking long minutes to complete their final formation. Like the other crewmen, the gunners, the engineer, and the radioman, Buckley could only wait while the pilots did their jobs. But the training was good, and Buckley marveled at that, knew that whatever made a pilot capable of doing this, of bringing together this massive show of power, he deserved to outrank the rest of them.

The wingtips drew closer, the formations tightening, and he could see other crews, some of the faces staring out through the small, grimy win-dows. There were no waves, no smiles, every man tensely aware that they had passed through the worst of those first deadly moments. In the early dawn, with this kind of cloud cover, with so many aircraft rising up through so much blindness, a disaster could have hit any one of them, the deadly collisions, horrific accidents. Buckley had seen two collisions first-hand, one during training, what he had to believe was someone's grotesque stupidity. The voice had come on the radio, a command to "bank to the left." Buckley's plane had been in formation just behind a pair of others when one plane suddenly veered right, a hard collision that erupted into a massive explosion, blasting two planes and their crews right out of the sky. It was an image he would never forget. Two crews had died, he thought, because someone didn't know left from right. Well, I don't know if that's what happened, but it sure looked like it.

The second collision had come on a combat mission, soon after take-off, the planes not yet in formation. It had been only his third combat flight, and as they climbed up into the overcast, two B-17s impacted right above him, debris crashing against the nose of his plane, flames washing past. Two more crews gone, just like that. It was cloudy, like today, he thought, and someone just ran over his own formation. Guess that happens a lot. Hell of a thing to write home to those families. Your son died because his pilot screwed up. So, what's better? Blown to hell by the enemy? Buckley had seen that as well, on nearly every mission. He had almost become used to it. Almost.

The plane shook and shimmied again. He was used to that as well, endured it, hoped it would pass, that the air would smooth out. The plane closest in front was slightly to the right, and he saw the ball turret rotate, the gunner testing his hydraulics. There was a voice in his ear, the pilot.

"Navigator, we're at altitude, three zero thousand. We're straightening out. The colonel has given us a heading, zero eight five degrees. Airspeed two two zero. Reports say we're looking at a tailwind about four zero. I've heard the old buzzard gets lost once in a while. We're tail-end Charlie on this one, I don't want to lose the crowd."

Buckley glanced back to his left, the navigator staring hard at a chart, pencil in hand.

"Roger, Captain. Zero eight five degrees. Airspeed confirmed. I'll watch him, sir."

Tail-end Charlie. Buckley had heard that before. Of their twelve small formations, they would be that most dreaded last place in line. So, he thought, we get to watch the whole damn show in front of us.

The pilot's voice came again. "We lost one bird. Blue Beauty fell out with a bad engine."

It was inevitable that with this many planes in the air, some would suffer mechanical problems. One out of thirty-six, Buckley thought. Not too bad. Blue Beauty . . . who's that? Yeah, Hobart's the bombardier. Not sure who else. So, they can go back home and read our mail.

The pilot's voice returned. "Gunners, test your weapons. Fire at will, but keep it short. And dammit, watch your aim. No accidents today, right, Granger?"

"No, sir."

The response was meek, an unspoken apology for one very dumb mistake. The week before, Granger, the left waist gunner, had accidentally shot holes in the tail section of a neighboring plane. Buckley nodded toward the navigator, loosened his safety belt, reached for the fifty-caliber beside him. The newer B-17s had been fitted with guns up front, poking out each side of the plane's nose, so that the navigator and bombardier could supposedly contribute to the plane's defense. Buckley pulled back the bolt on the machine gun, watched the brass shell sliding in, the belt of ammo hanging down into a large green box. Before he could grip the trigger the entire plane seemed to erupt in shivering blasts, the gunners behind him touching off a few rounds. He never had gotten used to the shock of that, but he felt for the trigger, aimed at empty air, fired a brief burst, the gun shaking, empty cartridges chattering to the deck. He enjoyed firing the gun, though unlike the trained gunners he never expected to actually hit anything. The skilled specialists on the planes were given a minimum of training with the fifties, and so they caught a fair amount of teasing from the men at the waist, tail, and ball turret, who at least pretended they were marksmen. The engineer worked the turret on top, above, just behind the cockpit, and Buckley knew that no one would tease that crazy sergeant about anything.

He eased back from the gun, looked at Goodman, saw a thumbs-up. Yeah, sure. You can't hit a damn thing either. Just pay attention to your charts.

Davy Goodman was barely twenty, had come out of some New York City neighborhood that Buckley could never imagine. Buckley was from Kansas, the low hill country southwest of Kansas City, where the tallest thing he walked through were cornfields. But Buckley respected that the navigator took his job as seriously as Buckley took his own, and that both men were critical to every mission they flew. Though they had become friends, Buckley knew there was one enormous difference between them.

Goodman carried a different kind of fear, something that went beyond the usual shivering anticipation that accompanied the crew on every flight. They had spoken of it when the beer had flowed, Goodman telling him that if they were shot down, if they survived one of those horrors that had already taken away so many of the crews, Goodman would never surrender, would never allow himself to be taken to a German POW camp. He had shown Buckley a small pistol he carried in his boot. If the .45 at his waist was lost in a parachute jump, Goodman had been very clear what the smaller pistol was for. Buckley tried to dismiss the drama of that, had teased Goodman that he couldn't handle a pistol any better than he could the fifty-caliber. But the navigator would only point to his dog tags. It was there, plainly, for any captor to see. Goodman was Jewish.

Buckley pushed that from his mind, stared out into the sharp light coming above the horizon. In one vast sweep, the bombers had completed their turns, leveling out, heading east. As they moved away from the English coast, the cloud banks had disappeared, and six miles below them the English Channel spread out like an icy pond. He focused downward, saw scattered ships, another distant part of the war, but to the men in the bombers, they might as well have been fishermen.

The sunlight was blinding now, glare on the Plexiglas, and he kept his eyes downward, the formation moving toward a solid strip of land. It was the coast of Belgium. He felt the chill again, and not from the cold. He had been briefed about the target, what they only referred to as Big B, a destination that inspired deep dread in every member of the crew. Once again, they were going to Berlin.

The clouds began to come again, spotty puffs of white, well below them. All around the plane, the sky was streaked with white trails, beautiful, the frosty exhausts from the planes in front of him.

The pilot's voice startled him. "Here come the birdies. Right on time. Three o'clock level. The colonel says more are coming up from behind. We'll have a couple hundred, anyway. Praise Jimmy Doolittle."

Buckley leaned forward, staring out to the right, saw them now, specks against the blue, growing larger. It was their fighter escorts, rising up from the myriad fighter bases across occupied Belgium and northern France. Thank God, he thought. Or Jimmy Doolittle. Might as well thank the man in charge. Maybe, out here, General Doolittle outranks God.

Through the first years of the war, the B-17s had been horrifyingly vulnerable, mainly because the American command insisted on only daylight missions. The British had different technology and different training, and their pilots flew mostly at night. Strategically, the bomber chiefs were pleased by this arrangement, since the bombing missions could destroy enemy targets in a continuous stream around the clock. Since they flew at night, the British rarely equipped their bombers with offensive weapons at all, few of them carrying the fifty-caliber machine guns so prized by the American crews. At night, there was simply nothing for them to shoot at. But the B-17s' machine guns, twelve per plane, had proven to be more of a morale boost than an effective weapon against enemy fighters. The Messerschmitts and Focke-Wulfs seemed untouchable, darting through the vast formations of lumbering bombers like mosquitoes evading the slow swing of a baseball bat. No matter how much practice a gunner had, there was no way to prepare for live attacks by a fighter plane that you could rarely see until he had already shot at *you*.

As the number of bombing missions increased, the losses to B-17 crews had exceeded the most dismal expectations. Every crew had understood that once you were more than a couple of hundred miles from Allied airspace, there was no one to protect you. The fighter planes early in the war had limited range. But then something new and magnificent had come to the Allied airbases. It was designated the P-51, the American fighter that someone had named the Mustang. The P-51 had supplementary external fuel tanks that could be jettisoned in flight, and so it could accompany the vast flocks of big birds throughout their missions. Even better, the Mustang was agile and fast and could outmaneuver and outfight their enemy. Almost immediately, the Messerschmitts had become less of a problem. The attacks would come still, but the German fighters would find themselves engulfed by swarms of this superior enemy. The losses to the Luftwaffe's fighters had become immense, and so, by late 1944, many of them simply stayed away.

As effective as the P-51s were, they could not protect the B-17s from an even greater danger. As the bombers drew closer to their targets, they ran a gauntlet of anti-aircraft fire, the deadly eighty-eight-millimeter, as well as great networks of German flak batteries, firing thick clouds of metal, steel scraps. Every crew in every B-17 knew what to watch for, the first black puffs, that peculiar inverted-Y shape, and very soon the skies around them would be pockmarked with black smoke. Within each cloud, the metal bits swirled and ripped through the air, hanging, falling, a forest of scrap metal the B-17 could not avoid. In tight formations, there was little room for the pilots to maneuver, though many of them tried. All any crew could do was stare out and hope that, once again, the prayers and tricks of fate might let them slide through the curtain of metal with only minor wounds to their bird.

P ilot to bombardier. You awake down there?"
   "Always, Captain."
   "If that guy next to you is doing his job, we'll be at the IP in ten minutes. We'll slow to one five oh, and I'll hand it over to you. You're only togglier on this one, though. Watch the guys in front of us. Hell, you know the drill."
   "Roger, Captain."
   Buckley nodded. Yep, I know the drill. IP. The initial point. That's where all hell breaks loose.
   He had heard the same commands over the past couple of weeks, thought, Captain Babyface sounds like he's reading me the manual. Togglier. I know what it means, sir. It means I don't do a damn thing but watch the lead plane in the group. When he opens the bomb bay doors, so do we. When he drops his load, so do we. All I do is keep this bird straight and level and flip the damn toggle switch, and hope like hell that guy in front of us knows how to use that Norden.
   He leaned forward, put his hand on the bombsight. The Norden was a marvelous piece of technology, a secret the army had tried to protect as much as any piece of equipment of the war. The Norden bombsight was connected by cables to the pilot's flight controls, so that when it came time to make the final run to the target, the bombardier could actually control the plane. There had been talk in training that the Norden was the one instrument that would allow the Allies to win the war, though Buckley seemed to miss as many targets with it as without. But the commanders had stifled any talk that the Norden wasn't living up to its reputation in actual combat conditions. Buckley knew only that it was a machine armed with gyroscopes and electrical motors that somehow gave the bombardier the precise moment the bombs should be dropped, by computing the

plane's speed against the altitude and location of the target. Pretty neat stuff, he thought. This guy Norden had to be some kind of wizard. Buckley reached down alongside the sight itself, felt for the small pistol. Every bombardier was under the strictest orders that if the plane was going down, or if he had to bail out for any reason, he was to shoot the Norden with this pistol, which was loaded with a thermite bullet. The bullet would melt the Norden into a mass of useless metal, thus keeping it out of German hands. All right, he thought, I'm set. He looked toward Goodman, who was scribbling furiously on his pad of paper. Get it right, Davy. My job is the easy one. Any idiot can sit here and watch someone else drop his bombs. At least if we miss, it's not my fault. That's something to be thankful for.

"Flak dead ahead."

Buckley could see the puffs of black himself, far out in front of the squadrons. He had absorbed the briefing, the specific target they were after, some kind of rail yards just outside the Big B. Makes little damn difference, he thought. We either hit them or we don't and if we don't, we blow hell out of some Berlin neighborhood. Nothing wrong with that.

The cold came again, the pounding in his chest, and he could feel the plane slowing. He focused on the planes close by, ignored the other squadrons banking, sliding away to their own targets. Good luck, fellas. He glanced up, the fighter planes in scattered spreads all across the skies above, out of range of the flak. Smart. Get the hell out of the way. Any Krauts show up, you can drop on 'em quick. He put both hands on the Norden, could see that the plane was on automatic pilot, no maneuvers needed, not yet. But there was no target to focus on, and his eyes were up, sharp stares at the puffs of black, a blanket of smoke closer still.

"IP. We're at one five oh. Ten minutes to target. The bombardier has the controls. Use the autopilot unless you need to do something else."

"Roger, Captain."

There was no need for any other response, the pilot's order idiotic. Don't do anything unless you need to do something else. Babyfaced moron. The nervousness was complete, and Buckley flexed his gloved fingers, the plane flying slow and level. He caught a glimpse of the lead plane, thought, only one job left to do. I'm just a passenger except for these next few minutes. He looked down into the Norden, the ground, roads, not much else. He looked up again, frantic motion, found the lead plane again, more smoke, closer, one brief flash of light, smoke swallowing the plane in front, a blast of flak very close.

"Get ready, boys!"

The pilot's voice was cracking, the man as nervous as Buckley himself. Shut the hell up, Captain. Nothing to do now but . . . hope.

The smoke was all around, some of it well below, and he nodded in quick jerks, good, that's lucky. The Germans are undershooting, miscalculating the squadron's altitude. But that'll change. In a few short seconds, it did. There was a burst straight in front of the left wing, and he flinched, reflex, a chatter of metal hitting the plane to that side. He banked the plane slightly to the right, more reflex, a mistake few could avoid. No, keep it level! More smoke came, below again, then two more to the right. Buckley's brain was beginning to scream at him. Pay attention! Watch the leader. He searched the smoke, saw him now, the B-17 not more than two hundreds yards in front. Too close, what the hell? His own plane was catching up quickly, words in his brain, we're gonna run right over the bastard! He grabbed the Norden, pulled back, the nose rising. Buckley held his grip on the bombsight, steadied himself, and fought for control, another blast of flak on the right, the plane bouncing sideways, the right wing rocking upward.

"How you doing down there—"

"Not now, Captain. I've got her."

The plane leveled out again, and Buckley searched for the leader. Where the hell is he? Behind us? He saw the shape now, right above them, the lead plane rolling off to the right, pieces, another burst of fire, thunder in his ears. He held the Norden, fought against the impact of the blast, and the pilot's voice came now, panic, high pitch, "Oh God! She's hit . . . going down! They got the colonel! Not sure we can do this one!"

Another voice now, the engineer. "Knock that off! We're still here. Bombardier, fly the damn plane!"

More voices cluttered the intercom, and the pilot seemed to gain control. "I see parachutes! They're getting out. All right! Shut up! No one talks! Keep the intercom clear! Do your jobs! Radio, can you reach the bird to the right? That's Dragon's Breath, right?"

After a few seconds, the radioman answered, "Yes, sir. Captain Murphy says he'll take the lead, if it's okay with you. He's pulling ahead."

"Yes, yes. Good. Bombardier, fall in behind Dragon's Breath."

Buckley saw the other plane moving out from the right, taking position in front of several others. He knew the radioman was good, but my God, he thought, there must be hell all over the radio. Keep cool, Freddie.

He responded to the pilot now, "Roger, sir. I've got her. We're fine. Just a little bumpy."

"Okay, okay. Five minutes, probably."

The plane bucked again, a hard shock in Buckley's ears, the blast from the flak burst close by, his hands coming up, protecting his face.

Behind him, Goodman shouted, "They hit the nose. A big hole in the glass!"

The Plexiglas had a six-inch-wide gash, down close to his feet, and Buckley saw another crack, one jagged hole right in front of him, the wind blowing into his face.

The pilot's voice came again. "Engine number four is done. Feathering the prop. We're close now."

Buckley fought the wind in his face, thought, shut up, shut up, shut up. The air was driving into him, a low whistling through the Plexiglas, and he blinked away wetness, saw the new lead plane moving ahead, leaving them behind. Watch him, dammit. Three engines. We can't keep up. Okay, fly the plane, jackass. Let's get rid of these bombs.

The bomb bay doors opened on the plane in front of him, and he followed suit, pulled the switch beside the Norden. He heard the doors opening up behind him, the hard hollow rush of air, the plane slowing even more. The flak was still coming in a solid spray of scattered bursts, and he tried to ignore the smoke, kept his eye on the lead plane, his hand on the bomb release. A new burst blocked his view, close, the plane heading straight into it, and Buckley flinched again, jerked the Norden to one side, the plane banking steeply, but the blast had been too close. The plane blew straight through the smoke, the debris from the flak ripping and cracking into the nose. He felt a hard punch in his chest, heard Goodman scream, the rush of wind worse now, blinding him. There were voices on the intercom, a jumble of noise, the earphones ripped away from his head, and he felt his chest, a slice in the flak jacket, but the jacket had worked, breathless amazement, a piece of twisted steel on the deck beside him. He fought the Norden with one hand, his other securing the earphones, and behind him Goodman screamed again. Buckley saw him lean down, grabbing his foot, blood on the deck.

"I'm hit! I'm hit!"

Buckley called out, "Hang on! You'll be okay!" Into the intercom now, "Wounded man up front! I need some help here!"

In short seconds the engineer was there, shouting into Buckley's ear. "Drop the damn bombs! Let's get out of here!"

Buckley was unnerved by the man's panic, saw his face, the handheld oxygen bottle. "Help Davy! He's hit!"

The engineer leaned down, did something to Goodman's foot, and Buckley ignored him, was furious at the older man. You're supposed to be the big rough-ass. Don't tell me my job.

The old sergeant was up again, shouted into his ear, "Bad cut! He's bleeding! Can't stop it! The pilot's been hit too! Cockpit busted all to hell! Get us out of here!"

"You son of a bitch! Get up there and help *them*! I've still got a bomb load!"

The man was gone quickly, and Buckley was shaking, furious, the sergeant's panic becoming contagious. He heard Goodman cry out again, but there was nothing he could do, not yet. He strained to see, too much black smoke, flashes of fire, far to one side a B-17 exploding, pieces, one wing flipping away. There were more flashes now, distant, the others absorbing the punishing terror from the ground. He saw a plane, far to the front, bombs dropping from its belly, his brain reacting, yes! Dammit! Thank God! He waited a long second, one more, one more, then grabbed the bomb release, jammed it forward. Behind him, the bombs fell away silently, and he felt himself lurching upward, the loss of the weight lightening the plane.

He shouted into the intercom, "Bombs away! Copilot, you okay? Take the controls! Let's go!"

"Got her, Bombardier. Good job. Engine two just went, the prop's gone. I've got her."

The plane banked sharply, more smoke, another blast ripping through the fuselage behind him, voices in the intercom, one of the gunners, shouts, nonsense. Go, dammit! Go! He thought of the sergeant's words, *The pilot's hit*. It's all right, the copilot is a good guy. He can get it done. He looked over to Goodman, the blood in a sickening pool on the deck, flowing forward under Buckley's feet. He ripped at the safety belt, freed himself, was down quickly, kneeling in blood, saw a bandage, the engineer's feeble attempt to dress the wound. Idiot. I'll bust that son of a bitch in the mouth.

"Hang on, Davy! Gotta make you a tourniquet!"

Goodman didn't respond, stared at him past the oxygen mask, wide-eyed, terrified.

Buckley grabbed at the first-aid kit, thought, Flight Engineer, you jackass. You didn't think to use the kit? He ripped it open, saw the strip of rubber, the tourniquet, said, "Got it! This'll help!"

He sealed off the wound above Goodman's ankle, tightened the tourniquet, looked to the kit again, saw the syrette of morphine.

"Something for the pain, Davy! Right here!"

He pulled Goodman's pant leg up, above the tourniquet, jabbed the needle into the man's calf. That's gotta help. Okay, now what? Nothing else here. He felt the plane rocking heavily, realized his face was bare. He had left his oxygen mask behind. The dizziness was growing and he cursed aloud, fumbled toward his seat, found the hand bottle, pushed it into his face. Stupid!

He sat for a moment, focused on the Plexiglas, gashes and holes. Gotta get us out of here. The whole damn nose could come apart. He stood, and with his free hand he opened Goodman's safety belt, grabbed his arm.

"We gotta go, Davy! Let's get out of here. You can do it!"

Goodman seemed to understand, reached for his own hand bottle, unhooked himself from his headset and mask. Buckley waited while Goodman put the bottle to his face, then nodded to him. "Good. Let's go!"

The plane rolled hard to one side, Goodman coming down on him, Buckley's head smacking into the bulkhead. Smoke was filling the plane, the smell of burning metal, a hard cold wind, pain in his back. He struggled to lift Goodman, but the man was limp, no effort, more blood on the man's chest, a deep gash through the jacket, sweet sickening smell. Buckley pushed hard, rolled him away, the wound clean through Goodman's back. Oh God . . . Davy. He saw fire now, behind the bomb bay, but heard no sound, just the roar of the wind, the harsh hum of the two remaining engines. Buckley tried to fight the panic, the screams in his mind, saw the fire extinguisher, struggled to reach it. The plane was still in a steep bank, slowly rolled back to level, and he grabbed the fire extinguisher, saw a man on the other side of the flames, the foam covering the fire. In a few seconds the fire was mostly out, charred wires, the hard stink, and Buckley moved out from the nose, the man calling out to him, one of the gunners.

"The copilot's dead! Pilot's wounded bad! That Cajun's flying the plane! The tail gunner isn't answering! I think he's hit too! How's Goodman?"

"He's dead."

Buckley moved through the bomb bay, the narrow catwalk, saw a body, facedown, the copilot, sprawled out on the deck. There was debris through the waist of the plane, rips in the fuselage, but the ball turret was unopened, the man there still inside. He looked to the gunner again, Granger, said, "Man your position. I don't know where the hell we're heading, but we might need you."

He turned away, stared back toward the cockpit, blood on the steps, and he moved forward quickly, climbed up, saw the flight engineer, hands on the controls, the pilot still in his seat, head down, unconscious.

The engineer glanced back at him, blood on his face. "We're not going to make it. Damn eighty-eight shell blew a hole straight through the left wing. Leaking everything, fuel almost gone. How in hell we didn't blow to pieces, I don't know. We're losing hydraulics fast. Two engines gone. Where the hell is your chute?"

Buckley realized now, his parachute was still in the nose. He cursed to himself, backed away from the cockpit, dropped down into the icy wind, saw his chute on the floor, lying in Goodman's blood. He struggled to breathe, realized the portable bottle was running out, took a long breath, held it, thought, it's time to get the hell out of here. He yanked at the flak jacket, tossed it aside, slid his arms into the parachute's straps. There was another blast, deafening, the plane tilting forward, and he looked back, no one, just sky, the tail of the plane gone completely. He held tightly to his own seat, stared at the Norden, tried to reach the pistol, but the plane was spinning now, and he thought, no time to mess with that. Sorry, General.

He was out of breath, fought to see in the harsh wind, grabbed at the emergency hatch to one side, and dove through.

He hit in thick grass, felt a jolt of pain in his knee, rolled over, tried to breathe. Above him, the sky was a chaotic mess of smoke and fire, the sound of popping shells, white trails, B-17s high above. He gasped, but there was no pain in his chest, and he twisted himself, slid out of the chute, tried to bend his leg, more pain in the knee. Damn! Is it broken? He sat up, put a hand on it, probed, felt nothing out of place. Good. Need some of that morphine, though. He caught a glimpse of fire, a plane diving, big, another of the B-17s. Good God, they're killing us. At least I got the bombs out. What the hell difference does that make now? I don't even know if I hit anything.

He knew the Big Gator had gone down badly, had watched it as he hung from his chute, a sheet of flame that blew past him, a swirling mass of metal. There had been other parachutes, and he thought of that now, how many? There were . . . three? I hope to God, maybe more. The gunners, probably. The engineer. No, not him. I'll bet he flew the damn thing right into the ground. He scanned the land around him, trees close on two sides, thick black smoke rising beyond. That's gotta be us. Need to get there, see if anyone else . . .

He saw them now, men running toward him, one with a rifle, another with a long sword. They were civilians. The talk began in a fast flow, all in German, the man with the rifle pointing it at Buckley's head. There was fury in them all, magnified by the words they screamed at him, a chorus of hate. And now another voice, more men coming from the trees: soldiers. Buckley felt a burst of fear, saw one man in a black uniform, surely an officer, and the man was among the civilians now, shouts of his own, but not at Buckley. The civilians were arguing, seemed reluctant to obey this man, continued their shouts, but it was clear the man in the black uniform had the power. After sharp words between them, they backed away. There were parting curses, and Buckley could feel the anger, tried not to look at them. They shouted still at the soldiers, but it was muted, more soldiers coming out of the woods, running toward them, toward this newfound prisoner.

The officer moved close to him, bent low, pointed to his belt. Buckley realized now, I'm still wearing the .45. The officer said something, one soldier putting his rifle under Buckley's chin. Buckley felt the steel, tried to force a smile, raised his hands slowly above his head. The officer grabbed the pistol from Buckley's holster, rolled it over in his hands, admiring. My pleasure, you Kraut son of a bitch. But the words stayed in Buckley's mind, and he still forced the smile, fought to keep from shaking.

The rifleman backed away, and the officer motioned for him to stand, said something Buckley didn't understand. Then one word he did.

"Cigaretten?"

"No thanks."

But the man was not offering, he was pointing to Buckley's pockets.

Buckley nodded, motioned with his head. "Oh yeah, got a pack of Luckies here. All yours, pal."

The officer reached into Buckley's pocket, found the prize, returned the smile now, gave an order to the soldiers, who gathered close to Buckley, the clear signal it was time to move. The officer led them away, and Buckley saw the man light one of the cigarettes. Buckley said in a low voice, "Hope you enjoy those, you bloody Kraut bastard."

The officer stopped, still smiling, said, "Yes, I will."

2. EISENHOWER

I'm sick of hearing about this, Ike. Those damn bomber barons are still spouting off about ending this war by Christmas, and it's bull." Doolittle glanced toward Tedder, stiffened a little. "No disrespect intended, sir."

"None taken, General. Your frankness is necessary. I'm not such a fan of those chaps either. It's an unfortunate coincidence that I do happen to *be* one of them."

Eisenhower knew that Air Marshal Tedder respected Doolittle as much as he respected anyone in the American command. Eisenhower pressed the stub of a cigarette into the glass ashtray on his desk, said, "Jimmy, we need the facts. Hap Arnold wanted you in charge of the Eighth Air Force because he knew you'd energize those boys."

Doolittle looked down for a long second. "I know, Ike. I'm grateful to General Arnold, just like I'm grateful to you. But Hap is one of the problems. So is Eaker. Both of them are right there cheering alongside the Brits. Hell, General Eaker still believes that if you can bomb it, you don't need bullets."

Eisenhower knew exactly what Doolittle was referring to. Ira Eaker, Doolittle's predecessor in command of the Eighth Air Force, had been instrumental in implementing the strategy that established round-the-clock bombing of German cities, the strategy firmly supported by the senior air command in Washington, headed by General Hap Arnold. Many of the bomber barons had insisted, and continued to insist, that the war should be fought almost entirely from the air. Even before the Luftwaffe had virtually disappeared as a major threat to Allied ground forces, the air commands had blithely dismissed ground and sea tactics as a waste of time and manpower. Doolittle's protests had seemed carefully measured, and Eisenhower knew that even with Doolittle's credentials, and three stars on his collar, he would tread carefully with Tedder in the room.

Doolittle continued, "For months now, a bunch of the senior air commanders have been spouting off, telling anyone who will listen that our bombers alone will win this war by Christmas. Have you seen the stateside papers? Well, hell, Ike, you know what's being said over there more than I do. The problem is that the American people are believing this stuff. I keep getting . . . well hell, Ike, what do I call it? Fan mail? I get letters through HQ, farmers in Iowa, shopkeepers in New Jersey. Great stuff. I'm their hero. Nice, I appreciate that. But then they tell me their sons are over here, and by God, with this war sure to end any day now, they know their boys are coming home alive. It's all thanks to *me*."

"You've got to ignore that stuff, Jimmy. You're a damn hero, whether you like it or not. I haven't had a single Medal of Honor recipient come through my office since this war began. Except you. Live with it."

"All right, Ike, that calls for a thanks. So, thanks. I'm *living with it* fine. It's my bomber crews who are being shot to hell. Sending a thousand planes over German cities in broad daylight wasn't my idea. Yeah, I understand it's part of the plan, but for God's sake, bombers alone aren't going to win this war. Can't you at least tell these air people in London to shut the hell up?" He glanced at Tedder again, who held up a hand.

"No apologies, General. I've been trying to get Harris and his brethren to understand the same thing for three years. Ike knows this. They don't seem to have the foggiest idea that the army and navy have a part in this little tiff as well."

Eisenhower flexed a pain in his knee, a stubborn injury, reached for another cigarette. "Look, Jimmy. We're doing all we can to cut down on the bomber losses. The fighter escorts have been a huge help. You know that."

"Of course. But there's another issue. When I took command in January, our fighters were already kicking hell out of the Luftwaffe. It got to the point where two or three hundred of those birds would go out with the bombers and most of them would end up sightseeing. I had to figure a way to make better use of those boys, keep them from spending all day just burning gasoline."

Eisenhower knew that Doolittle's change of tactics was something the fighter pilots had welcomed with raucous enthusiasm. With fewer and fewer German planes willing to confront the Allied fighters, Doolittle had issued an order that the P-47s and P-51s should take the opportunity to do more than just watch the bomber formations. If there was little sign of German fighters, the American fighter pilots were authorized to perform strafing missions, to drop to low altitude and search for targets, truck convoys, tanks, small-scale enemy activity that the high-altitude bombers were not designed to deal with. Eisenhower had welcomed the order as enthusiastically as the fighter pilots. It was a large dose of common sense that he realized had been missing from Eaker's command. Eaker was a good man, as were many of the air barons. But Eisenhower was as annoyed as Doolittle that those commanders seemed utterly devoid of flexibility. Although Eaker had made great use of the fighters as protection for the bombers, the thought of using them as more than escorts had simply never occurred to him.

Doolittle clamped his hat under his arm, the sign he had spoken his piece.

Eisenhower said, "Nothing you've said is out of line, Jimmy. You know more about this air war than any man in Europe, and I want your opinions. Besides, no matter what some of those other people think, you outrank most of them. As far as I'm concerned, you can damn well run the Eighth Air Force any way you want to, for as long as you want to."

"Thanks, Ike."

Doolittle stood, nodded to Tedder, no smile, still formal. "Sir. Thank you as well."

Doolittle was gone now, pulling the door closed behind him, and Tedder stared that way, then said, "Chap doesn't fully trust me. Can't say I blame him."

"You might be my second in command, Arthur, but you're still an air force man. And a Brit. Jimmy's learned that command sometimes requires more than common sense and good tactics. He doesn't like being ass-deep in politics and diplomacy."

Tedder laughed. "Do you?"

"I'm used to it. Well, mostly. But he's right about one thing. You remember those New York papers back in September? Some damn opinion poll said that two-thirds of Americans thought we'd be home by Christmas. *Two-thirds.* And, dammit, I was right there with them. I thought the enemy was whipped completely. I never thought they'd make another fight. We let a bunch of them escape out of France, and I thought they were done for, running home with their tails between their legs. Surely Hitler could see the foolishness of going any farther. The Russians are pushing him just as hard, maybe harder. I didn't expect . . . son of a bitch, Arthur. I didn't expect they'd still put up such a hell of a fight."

"None of us did, Ike. But don't go the other way with this. I know we won't end this by Christmas, but we're not losing either. No commander I've spoken to expected the Jerries to have this much fight left. But consider *why,* Ike. Look where they are. Look *where* they're fighting. I thought we'd march right into Aachen, no problems. Instead, Hodges had one hell of a tussle taking that place. Monty thought he'd trot on over to the Rhine, and the Jerries would scatter in front of him like a bunch of pigeons in Piccadilly. But Hitler built that damn Siegfried line for a reason, and his troops are making good use of it. Defense, Ike. They're defending their own soil now. Every army is a better army when they've got their own families close behind them."

Eisenhower stood, moved to the map, tacked to the makeshift plywood wall. "You're right. I know all of that. One thing the damn newspapers don't understand . . . hell, Arthur, nobody seems to understand. Not Monty, not Patton, not even Bradley. I don't command troops, I command situations. I know we're going to win this thing, no matter how long it takes. Unless he comes up with some odd-assed secret weapon, Hitler can't survive. I'm as confident as anyone, but my job isn't to be a cheerleader. My job is to avoid disasters."

"Large-scale disasters. You can't keep your generals from making mistakes here and there. War is full of small disasters. Look at Market-Garden. Monty comes up with a plan that's so damn complicated, a plan that relies on audacity and luck. And yet Monty is the one man in your whole command who is least likely to pull that off."

"But I had to let him try. It was his damn plan, after all, and it was his sector. And I believed him. It sounded great. A terrific idea. In hindsight, if Patton had been up there, it might have worked. But that's the point. Monty doesn't command this entire front. If he had put together some kind of Market-Garden fiasco that involved this entire army, it could have been a disaster. Capital *D.* That's what I can't allow."

"The bitching's growing louder, Ike. I'm hearing it from London, and I'm hearing it from below."

"Monty? I know. I assume you heard about the cargo ships at Antwerp."

"Just got word this morning. The first ones were finally unloaded."

"Yeah, let's celebrate that. Monty's big damn victory. How do I pat him on the back for opening up that damn port *eighty-five days* after we took the place? We marched into Antwerp in *September*, Arthur. Monty crows like some big red rooster about taking the city, and seems to forget that the Germans control forty miles of waterway between the port and the ocean. He acts like he forgot that a quarter million enemy troops are sitting tucked into their defenses along every mile of the waterway, and they probably aren't going to let our ships just waltz past their guns. Then he sends the poor damn Canadians, who have been beat to hell already, sends them through swamps and mud holes to slug their way straight into the German positions. So, yes, it takes eighty-five days before the port is usable. And now he's blaming the Canadians for the delay, says it was all Henry Crerar's fault. If I were Crerar, I'd give Monty a bloody nose. And worse, the Canadians were so wiped out by the fight, they couldn't stop the enemy from retreating. It was Falaise all over again. Monty should have figured out a way to box the Germans in from behind, pinned them against the water. Instead, tens of thousands . . . hell we don't know how many, but it was a load of them. They escaped, reinforced their defenses in Holland, or slipped back into Germany. And you know as well as I do, we'll be looking at them again one day."

"You spoke to the prime minister yesterday, right? What's he say?"

"You know how Churchill is. He told me a long time ago that I could fire Monty if I thought it was the right thing to do. No problem at all. But yesterday he reminds me in his *cheeky* little way that, oh yes, by the way, if Monty goes, the British troops in the field will probably stage an open revolt, and the British people will call off their end of the war. No problems for us there."

"He's hearing that from Brooke. For the life of me, Ike, I can't understand why the chief of the Imperial General Staff is such a bloody champion of Bernard Montgomery. Monty would never be where he is without Brooke's backing."

"Let it go, Arthur. Monty's not the enemy here. He's just today's designated pain in the ass."

Tedder was up out of the chair now, pacing slowly. Eisenhower knew that Tedder was one of the few high-ranking Brits who despised Montgomery.

Tedder turned toward him, pointed at Eisenhower with his pipe. "He's still crowing about his plan, you know. He's running all over the place telling people that you've held him back. If he'd been allowed to do things his way, he'd be in Berlin by now."

Eisenhower had been through the anger too many times. His jaw was clenched, a familiar headache rising up from the back of his neck.

"Look, Arthur. I can't control Monty's mouth, no matter how wrong he is. He was wrong about Market-Garden and he was wrong about Antwerp. And, yes, he's wrong about Berlin. But he's not the only one making mistakes. You know how tough it's been to bring supplies forward. Bradley had to shut Patton down because we didn't have the fuel for him to keep going. His tanks ran out of gas, or I guarantee you, with or without orders, Patton would have tried to take Berlin himself. It's Sicily all over again. Hodges spends too much time taking Aachen when he could have bypassed the place altogether and moved east. Patton sulks by launching small-scale attacks on Metz, says he has to keep his people from getting bored."

"He took Metz."

"So what? Did Hitler surrender? No, Patton took a ton of casualties and used artillery and gasoline he'll need later. Jake Devers is so eager to keep up with Patton's flank that he leaves a flock of Germans in the Colmar area behind him, so now he's got a major problem to his rear, a potential to disrupt his entire supply line. Hodges got his people bogged down south of Aachen into what Bradley doesn't want to admit is a serious mess. For two weeks, what should have been our grand fall offensive has come apart because we didn't realize that the Hürtgen Forest was full of Germans who decided to stick around and kick our asses. Some of our boys are taking a hell of a beating in that place. It's been raining there for, what? Two weeks? We've got people drowning in mud, while the Germans are digging in for the long haul."

Tedder looked down, and Eisenhower knew what he was thinking. "Go on, say it. I approved every one of these moves. Yep. I trusted my people to make the right decisions. Since we let the enemy go at Falaise, we haven't exactly had a bunch of headline-grabbing *victories*, have we?"

"You can't control the weather, and you can't make every field command. You've got good people . . ."

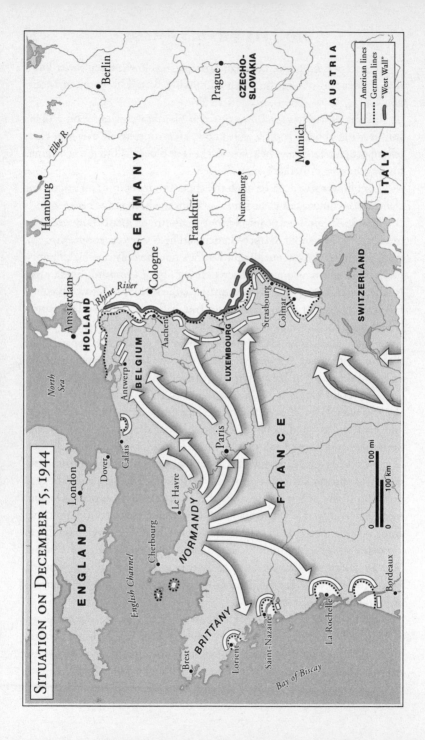

SITUATION ON DECEMBER 15, 1944

"Can that crap, Arthur. The fact is, I agreed with Monty. I thought the Germans were beat, that they had nothing left to fight for, or fight *with*. But hell, that's what the enemy is thinking about *us*. The Germans still have generals who know how to fight a war. They know that we overextended our supply lines, while the enemy shortened his. Our frontline people are exhausted, as much as those Germans who escaped out of France. Now the weather is turning, and who do you think that helps? One of those nasty little rules of war. Bad weather is always an advantage for the guy on defense. And now the guy on defense is fighting to protect his own soil."

Eisenhower paused, massaged the headache, watched as Tedder returned to the chair. Tedder put the pipe in his mouth, smoke rising, the room filled with the sweet smell.

After a long moment, Eisenhower said, "I made another mistake too, Arthur. I thought Hitler might have enough rational good sense to accept that he was defeated. But then, I go back to the president issuing that damn proclamation, all of that *unconditional surrender* stuff. Worst mistake we could have made, and everyone knew it. Played right into Hitler's hands. The German soldier is being told that he's got to fight to the death, because that's what *we're* making him do. Goebbels's job is easy as hell. We've handed the enemy the best propaganda tool possible. Roosevelt has basically told them, *We won't talk to you, we won't negotiate with you. We're just going to shoot you and bomb you until you surrender.* Goebbels is smart enough to remind the German people that, gee, this sounds familiar. Remember the Treaty of Versailles? That's what Germany's enemies are trying to do, make it 1919 all over again. No wonder they're digging in."

"You think we should go into winter quarters, as such? Regroup, rebuild?"

"We can't. The Germans need *time* more than we do. We can't hand it to them. We have to keep up the pressure. But dammit, we have to do it *right*. If Hitler isn't going to quit, I'm betting that some of those German generals know the score. We keep pressing them, it's possible we'll get some wholesale surrenders."

Tedder nodded. "They tried to kill him once, maybe they'll try again."

Eisenhower lit a cigarette. "I don't think so. Everything we've picked up from the Ultra intercepts say that the Gestapo has eliminated anyone who might be a threat. That has a way of keeping a lid on dissent. And those generals are *Germans,* after all. First thing they're trained to do is follow orders."

3. VON RUNDSTEDT

He missed Paris. Outside, the air was thick with icy wetness, a chill he could feel all through his bones. At seventy, he was Hitler's oldest senior commander, but age mattered very little to the High Command anymore, seniority in the army determined more by how truly loyal Hitler believed you to be. He stared at the bleak skies, leafless tree limbs, bent from too much wind, thought, I am senior to everyone, and no one. The only troops I control are those who guard my own door.

He tried to pull himself erect, but his back was stiff, his joints sore, common ailments that had hounded him for more than a year. Will they ever expect me to go into the field again? Even these soldiers will see me as I am, not as I am supposed to be. And what is that anyway? A loyal Nazi, willing to fight to the last breath so my Führer's dreams can be realized? Who believes that anymore, if we ever believed it at all? Even those pathetic sycophants who surround him, Jodl and Keitel, the rest of them, so many cattle at Hitler's trough, spewing out a steady stream of compliments for our Führer's genius. Is that how the army feels as well? They must, most of them. They are still good soldiers, no matter that so many of them are no longer here. How many armies can we lose, entire battle commands swept up by our enemies? North Africa, Russia, France . . . and where shall it happen next? Right here? My command? Of course, if that is how history is to read, then my name shall be included among the great failures. That is, after all, the true reason they brought me back to command.

Behind him, there was a gentle knock at the door. He ignored it, kept his stare toward the window, the bleakness of a gathering winter. A dog appeared, scampering past his window, a brutish-looking mongrel. Farther out in a muddy field, soldiers were calling out, playing some game with the dog. The knock came again, a bit firmer.

"I am not asleep. You may enter."

The door burst open, too much noise, and von Rundstedt turned, was surprised to see Model, heavy boot steps. Behind him, the door closed, von Rundstedt catching a brief glimpse of an apologetic aide. Von Rundstedt tried to focus on the younger field marshal, thought, he *marches* everywhere. Going . . . nowhere.

Model was much younger, a tight-mouthed, exhausting man, the ever-present monocle clamped against his right eye. Von Rundstedt thought of the dog. A fitting comparison. Model did not salute, rarely saluted anyone.

He stared past von Rundstedt, said, "I would never assume you to be asleep at your post, Field Marshal. But I just arrived, and General Zimmerman said you were alone. You should know that we have failed once again to convince the Führer that his plans should be amended. General Westphal is extremely frustrated, and has returned to Italy to advise Field Marshal Kesselring. I have been given instructions that we are to carry out Watch on the Rhine exactly as the plan was presented to us previously. Despite my efforts, and the efforts of several senior commanders, including Dietrich and Manteuffel, no one at the High Command received our suggestions with any flexibility. After long hours of discussion, I was ordered to return to my headquarters and, along the way, to bring you *this.*"

Von Rundstedt saw the thick envelope in Model's hands, knew already what the documents said.

Model continued, "These orders are specific and do not leave any further room for maneuver on our part. I believe the Führer has grown weary of those who question his brilliance."

There was no sarcasm in Model's words. No, he is pure puppet. He will die for his Führer, no matter how stupid the strategy. The old man moved slowly to his chair, sat stiffly, tried to settle comfortably, too many pains. He looked up at Model, who kept the firm stare, already impatient to be leaving, his message delivered. Von Rundstedt had never liked the man, liked him less with every conversation. But Field Marshal Walther Model was in command of Army Group B and, as such, was directly under von Rundstedt's authority. It was the same now as it had been months earlier, when another field marshal had stood before von Rundstedt with obvious contempt, playing the game by the army's rules, pretending that what this old man had to say carried actual authority. Then, it was Rommel, and despite months of arguments and all the disagreements about strategy, von Rundstedt knew that Rommel disliked Hitler and distrusted Hitler's senior staff as much as he did. Hitler knew it too. After Rommel's suicide, word had filtered through the army, rumors inspired by the Gestapo, that Rommel had been considered a conspirator, one of those who had known of the plot to kill Hitler. Whether or not that was true, Rommel was gone now, and von Rundstedt knew the army was weaker for it. *And what does that matter?* he thought. *Generals do not control this army. True authority has not been in our hands for many months. Hitler no longer trusts us. He ignores the men who must actually fight for him. No matter that Hitler himself has never visited his own front lines.* Von Rundstedt took the thick folder, opened it, saw maps, unit designations. He pretended to care, had memorized the absurd plans a month before, took Model's word for it that the High Command had changed nothing at all. He heard Model breathing, could tell the man was anxious to leave, and he took his time with the papers, enjoyed keeping Model waiting. He glanced up at the man, Model averting his eyes upward, and von Rundstedt glanced at a map, too familiar, thought, so now *Hitler must think of this man as his new puppy. And yet he is crude and vulgar with no respect for the army or his place in it. But by damn, Hitler knows he's loyal. I suppose he is. For now anyway.*

Von Rundstedt pushed the folder away, had no more patience for the game. He reached for a bottle of brandy, searched for his glass, but it was gone, already whisked away by someone's annoying efficiency.

"I'd offer you some of this, but you'd have to drink from the bottle."

Model stiffened, said, "In my career, I have broken many an empty bottle. In Russia, a good commander often fueled himself with the only means at hand."

Von Rundstedt leaned back, couldn't avoid looking at the monocle, smiled. *Well, there's something to be proud of, certainly. Drunk generals* are *good* generals. He couldn't help the sarcasm, the unavoidable need to puncture this man's massive ego.

"It seems that lately the Russian generals have a bit more of that fuel than we do."

Model had no humor, seemed to be insulted.

"Do not speak to me of Russia, Field Marshal. It was a glorious campaign." He paused. "There were mistakes in the field. There was disobedience. So much has changed."

Model had been a significant hero early in the Russian campaigns, but that seemed like decades ago now. The old man knew that toying with Model would get nowhere, and his energy was already slipping away.

"Will you please sit down, Field Marshal? All that decorum you insist on displaying is wearing me out."

Model did not move. "I have no need to linger here," he said. "The brandy can wait for another time. Perhaps a toast to our victory when our troops liberate Antwerp."

Von Rundstedt squinted at Model, shook his head.

"Good God. You don't believe that nonsense any more than I do. I might have no choice but to accept your insubordination and your insolence, but lies and duplicity I will not tolerate, not in my own headquarters. You and I are both aware that Hitler's plans are absurd. We do not have the manpower or the supplies capable of maintaining the campaign that has been laid out for us . . . for *you*. It is, after all, your glorious command. But do not dare to insult me with talk of victories, Field Marshal. You and I endured too many hours together designing alternatives. In the event you have forgotten, you and I went to great lengths to convince the High Command that there was a better way, a more efficient battle plan that could trap the enemy in his surge around Aachen. It is a plan that can still work. We have brought the Americans to a virtual stalemate on very difficult ground, and we have inflicted heavy casualties. But the weather is changing rapidly, and any offensive action we undertake now must be precise and focused on a narrow area. Our ability to strike with armor and artillery is limited, and our fuel supplies are insufficient to make a drive beyond what *you and I* have proposed. It is entirely logical that the enemy will expect us to pull back and settle into a winter's rest, and likely he will do the same. His attacks south of Aachen and at Metz are nothing more than exercises for our benefit, to convince us that he is coming still. But I know this land, I know what winter can do here. It is no different now than it was in the First Great War. Any major offensive now will be crushed under the weight of the weather. There are inadequate roads to advance the strength that the Führer has ordered." His voice was rising now, the last explosion of energy. "Hitler lusts for the memories of our great surge through the Ardennes four years ago, how easily we swept aside the French and the British. But that campaign took place in the *spring*, Field Marshal. We have reminded the Führer of that too many times for me to recall. And now you bring me news that he has ignored common sense and military reality once again. But do not dare tell me that, now, you *agree* with him." He paused, saw no change in Model's expression. "There can still be a victory at Aachen. We have the opportunity to cut off a sizable number of American divisions. We can surprise him . . ."

Model pointed to the papers.

"Read the Führer's orders, Field Marshal. The plan is to be followed precisely as he designed it. Our orders are to destroy the enemy by pushing hard and fast on a narrow front through the Ardennes. We shall then cross the Meuse River, and once on flatter ground, the armor shall continue their push and sweep rapidly toward Antwerp. We shall liberate Antwerp in a matter of days. By such a rapid advance, we shall divide the British and American forces, and that will compel the British to resign from the war. We shall supply ourselves with fuel and vehicles by the rapid capture of the enemy's numerous supply compounds and storage facilities. With maximum use of speed and secrecy, this offensive shall catch him totally unprepared. It was explained to me that there is brilliance even in the name of the operation, since the Führer chose *Watch on the Rhine*. Should enemy intelligence learn of it, they will interpret it to mean a defensive posture along the Rhine River. Hitler has thought of every detail."

Model did not change his stare, continued looking straight at the wall. Von Rundstedt glanced at the papers again.

"Field Marshal Model, you lie well. The Führer is fortunate to have such loyal officers as you. And me, of course. Let no one suggest I am not loyal. The Gestapo's files on me are no doubt thick enough." He paused, shook his head, felt a growing hate for this man, such blind obedience to disaster. "After all that you and I worked on, all the maps, the proposals, so much risk of encouraging the Führer's wrath, may I ask what changed your mind? Why is it you now believe the larger campaign will work? I have a great many copies of the proposals we have made, which still bear your sig-

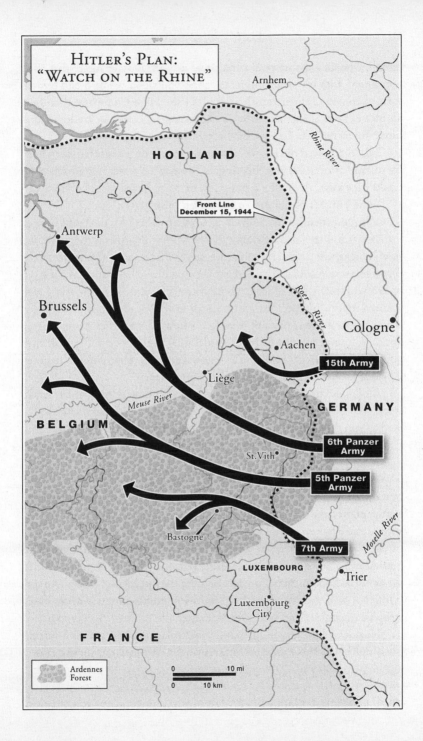

HITLER'S PLAN:
"WATCH ON THE RHINE"

Arnhem

HOLLAND

Rhine River

Front Line
December 15, 1944

Antwerp

Brussels

Roer River

Cologne

Aachen

15th Army

Liège

GERMANY

Meuse River

BELGIUM

6th Panzer
Army

St. Vith

5th Panzer
Army

Moselle River

Bastogne

7th Army

LUXEMBOURG

Trier

Luxembourg
City

FRANCE

Ardennes
Forest

0   10 mi
0   10 km

nature. The Gestapo no doubt has those as well. Do not forget that. But you agreed with my smaller objective, and you stood beside me in our efforts to convince Hitler and those fools in the High Command that their ambitions were at the very least . . . exaggerated. Now you are his champion? You actually believe we shall reach Antwerp?"

Model removed the monocle, wiped it slowly on a white handkerchief. He turned it over between his fingers, seemed to search for any flaw he could wipe away. After a long moment, he placed it back against his eye.

"The Führer's plan does not have a leg to stand on."

Von Rundstedt let out a low laugh, felt an aching for the brandy glass.

"Oh yes, I see. You are doing the *right thing*. So, this is the world we now inhabit, eh? This is the cause we serve? I have worn this uniform for *fifty-four years,* Field Marshal, longer than you have been alive, yes? I have served with many fine officers whose company I did not enjoy, but I recognized *ability.* I respect men who know how to lead troops in the field, who have the fighter's instinct, who know how to crush their enemies. You and I will never be friends, Herr Model, but I respect you. I respect that you are a professional soldier. You know very well what *victories* require. There is no victory to be had with the Führer's plan."

Model did not seem to appreciate the compliment, took a step backward. "There is no argument to be had either, Field Marshal. I have delivered to you the Führer's final decision. There is to be no more discussion."

Model turned away, suddenly exited the room without another word.

"I suppose you are dismissed, Field Marshal."

Von Rundstedt opened a drawer, saw a glass crusted with a remnant of brandy, obviously overlooked by the annoying staff. He reached for the bottle, poured the glass half full, took a quick sip, poured again. He turned toward the window, but his legs ached, a new pain in his back. He sat back in the chair, saw the barren treetops waving, a hard blast of wind. The brandy went down smoothly, the heat welcome, and he thought, Hitler brought me back to this command because they needed . . . what? An old soldier? A scapegoat? And so, I will do his bidding, no matter how catastrophic the result. Do I have a choice, after all?

He downed the rest of the brandy, looked again at the gray sky outside his window. God help us. God help Germany. We shall not survive this.

4. BENSON

I f you puke again, I'm gonna ram this rifle up your butt, you got that?"

"Easy, Lane. He'll be okay. Right, Eddie? You'll be fine."

Benson didn't feel fine at all, leaned hard against the tailgate of the big truck. He reached out, tugged at the flap of canvas, trying to close the gap, shielding them all from the cold windy blast. He turned toward the voice, Mitchell, forced himself to smile, a casual wave of his hand.

"I'll be fine."

Lane was sitting beside him, packed in close. He tried to lean away. "You stink like nobody's momma. You're a damn washout, I know it. Can't even take a truck ride. Stay the hell away from me from now on, you got that?"

Benson didn't answer, felt the cramp in his stomach still, the sour taste of the vomit, stared gloomily out through the canvas flaps. He didn't like Lane, suspected none of them did. Lane was a bullying man, always looking for a target for his inflated anger. It was just bad luck that Lane sat beside him, but Benson's seat at the rear of the truck had not been by chance. He had always suffered from motion sickness, knew that if this truck was on the road for more than an hour, his guts would twist yet again, the same ailment he had suffered in the backseat of his father's Ford. He glanced at Lane, avoided the man's scowl, thought, it's your own damn fault you sat next to me. I'm not interested in following you around, not one bit. You're not even a part of this regiment. Not my part, anyway. He stared out through the canvas again, knew that wasn't really true. No, we're a *team.* That's what the officers keep trying to tell us. We're all part of the 423rd now, no matter that some of us got here three weeks ago. Why does *stupid* seem to qualify you for a rifle company? Just counting to ten is a challenge for this jerk. Why the hell did they have to send him to *this* outfit anyway? He stared out into the cold, engulfed by his silent griping. He tried to ignore the rumble of the truck, the whiff of exhaust, the stirring under his belt.

In the weeks before the 423rd Infantry Regiment had sailed for England, there had been many newcomers, replacing men whom Benson had known well. He had been one of the originals, training with the 106th Division's first base in Tennessee, and then Camp Atturbury, in Indiana. All through those early days, the 106th's three infantry regiments, the 422nd, 423rd, and 424th, had worked themselves into what someone must have thought were effective fighting units. But after months of rumors and speculation, the officers hoping to receive orders on just where they might be put to use, the entire division had begun to endure the indignity of losing an enormous amount of manpower. Entire companies had disappeared, shipped off to destinations no one bothered to explain. Information was carried by rumor, cautionary tales that Benson tried not to believe. As the strength of the division was stripped away, the greatest concern he faced was the fearful worrying of the others who remained, his friend Kenny Mitchell, or their platoon sergeant, that any one of them might be next to go. As the rumors flew, the officers began to speak of the replacement depot, what the troops knew as the repple-depple. Word spread that the 106th was being broken up to supply replacements for other divisions chewed up by the Normandy invasion, or the campaigns since. The men in the rifle companies had no idea if their commanders had protested, or if some vicious controversy was brewing. But generals don't talk to foot soldiers, and Benson only knew that every lieutenant seemed as mystified as the men in their platoons, and just as angry that the 106th was being dismantled, fueling rumors that the division might cease to exist altogether. For the men who remained at Camp Atturbury, there was still an effort to maintain pride in their unit, and the officers never let up reminding them of the meaning of their nickname, the Golden Lions—a snarling symbol of fighting ferociousness that was easy to inject into young recruits. But as so many troops departed, that esprit was drained away as well.

As the summer of 1944 rolled into fall, word flew through the camp that someone in Washington had changed his mind. The 106th would again become a full fighting division. The flow of men now came the other way, replenishing the regiments, refilling the barracks. But it was quickly apparent that many of the new soldiers were not soldiers at all. These men had come because orders had been passed down that staff offices and supply depots from every branch of the service were to be stripped of excess personnel, some of these men coming from various stateside bases, some from air force units. As they repopulated the regiments, they brought along a serious wave of bad morale. Most of the new men had been perfectly content in their rear-echelon roles, many engaged in idyllic busy-work, sleeping in comfortable quarters. Friction was inevitable as the new men moved in alongside the originals on the rifle range, or joined in for the first time on lengthy marches most of them couldn't stop griping about. Many, like Lane, brought a serious chip on their shoulder. Almost none of them had been trained as infantrymen, and few even knew how to fire a rifle. Though the drill instructors had worked feverishly to put these men into some kind of shape, in a few short weeks word came that the 106th was scheduled to ship out to England. If there was to be a crash course in combat survival, it would not come in the farmlands of Indiana. The division crossed the Atlantic, arriving in England in mid-November, but their stay was as brief as promised. Battle-ready or not, by the first week of December, the Golden Lions were on their way to the Continent. As the word passed for the men to board the transports yet again, Benson knew only what the officers told him. They were going to France, and there would be no more training, no more *practice*.

The journey across the Atlantic had been its own slice of hell, the only cheerful note coming too often from the sailors, who bragged longingly of those glorious days when German submarines darted through the convoys, as though every seaman had dropped his personal depth charge on a U-boat. There were very few submarines now, which seemed to disappoint the seamen, though Benson wondered what might happen if an actual U-boat suddenly appeared. These naval *heroes* might experience a little sea-sickness of their own.

The journey across the English Channel had been brief, but not brief enough for some. Many had been told that the North Atlantic was the

roughest water they would ever see, but storms rolled through the Channel as well, and Benson had suffered through hours of seasickness worse
than anything he had gone through in his father's old Ford. The regiments
came ashore at the port at Le Havre, and Benson had fled the transport
ship in desperate need of dry land. But Le Havre was anything but. Benson had tried to feel some kind of excitement that he was actually in
France, but there was no rest, no sightseeing, nothing but awful weather.
The men had marched away from the ports through vast rivers of mud and
sheets of freezing rain. He ignored the ones who spouted off about their eagerness to meet the enemy in battle. The weather soon washed away every
hint of loudmouthed enthusiasm, and the familiar griping had come with
full fury. In Le Havre, they had been ordered to leave their duffel bags behind, some supply officer gleefully announcing that their personal belong-
ings would most certainly be delivered to them very soon. Instead of extra
shirts, underwear, and other gear, the men were to carry only extra pairs of
socks and cold-weather gear that might have been useful had the world
around them not seemed so completely infested with mud. They all wore
the standard-issue clothing, long johns beneath their wool uniforms, a reasonably warm field jacket, and a wool overcoat. But on the march away
from the port, the mud had seeped up into their boots, soaking their pant
legs and oozing into every opening in their clothing. Some of the most
miserable men had fallen out of line, but the MPs were there, and even the
most dedicated shirker discovered there was nowhere else to go.

After several miles of raw soaking misery, the columns had been ordered to pass alongside a line of supply trucks. From the back of the trucks
came vast crates of overshoes, as though someone in a warm supply depot
had suddenly realized he had forgotten something. Their late arrival inspired loud volleys of cursing, the men taunting the supply troops, who
mostly ignored what they had heard too many times before. To Benson's
surprise, the overshoes actually worked, but there was a price. Though they
kept your feet somewhat drier and warmer, they made walking much more
difficult. With this new weight on their feet, the men had resumed their
slogging mud march.

After half a day's agony, the marching columns finally came upon unending rows of trucks, and the officers happily announced that, for now
anyway, the march was over. As the men were portioned out to the trucks,
there had been an eruption of sarcastic cheers, but the drivers weren't smiling, and the men in charge of the convoy had been as grouchy as the driv-

ers they commanded. Benson didn't care. Motion sickness was far better than stepping through knee-deep mud.

The two-and-a-half-ton truck could carry fourteen men facing one another on hard seats like two rows of wool-coated sardines. In Benson's truck, the platoon sergeant rode up front, in the passenger seat, and Benson thought of him now, one of the originals from Tennessee, a perpetually gloomy man named Higgins. Benson had tried to like his sergeant, thought it was a smart thing to do, especially in the beginning, but Higgins didn't seem to like anyone, and though he wasn't particularly sadistic, he held his men to a training schedule that was grim and rugged. Even so, it was hard for the platoon to find fault with him. Higgins had been alongside his men in everything they had been required to do. He might be sitting up there with his feet under a heater, Benson thought, but he had to carry as much mud in his boots as the rest of us. These guys are always cussing about him, but he's never done anything to me I wouldn't do in his place. He can't be much older, and he earned those stripes somehow. In the barracks, after the long marches, Benson had pointed out Higgins's wedding ring, had asked about his wife, whether there were children. Higgins had given him short clipped answers, the message clear: *Mind your own business.* Benson glanced toward the front of the truck. Sure he's grouchy. He wants to get back to his kids. Makes sense to me. I'd feel the same way, I guess. I don't even have a girlfriend, and I'd give up this seat to anyone who wants it. Anybody who thinks joining the army is all about traveling the world hasn't seen this damn place. He glanced briefly at the others, muddy feet and rifles, heads mostly down, breathing in white mist, the cold and cigarette smoke. He thought of the captain, his company commander, Moore. It was a brief overheard comment, Moore talking to another officer on board the transport ship.

We're not going to be much use to anyone if it comes down to fighting.

Benson fought the sickness again, his gloved hands gripping the M-1 pointing up between his knees. *Germans.* Benson looked past Lane to the others, some whose names he still didn't know. He focused on his friend Mitchell, head down, trying to sleep. He's afraid too. I know he is. His momma writing him all the damn time, *Please don't get hurt.* Ken Mitchell was Benson's age, barely twenty, had come from the same kind of small-town boredom that inspired many of these men to enlist.

Benson stared down, thought of sleep, impossible, tried to endure the shaking of the truck, the stink of exhaust. He sat back against the padding of his heavy coat, thought, where the hell are they taking us, anyway? I don't know how to fight a damn war. Germans? What makes anyone think this bunch of GIs is gonna do anything about the Germans?

Benson reached a gloved hand up to his ears, tugged at the wool hat, stretched it as far down as he could. His helmet was no protection from the weather at all, actually made it worse, the steel as cold as the air around him. The plastic helmet liner wasn't much better, but the men had been issued what was quickly dubbed a beanie, a small round wool cap that was their only protection from the icy winds that turned a man's ears to raw red agony. He rubbed his gloves against his ears, his fingers nearly numb. The gloves were thin, and his were wet, no way to escape that. He stuffed them down between his thighs, against the M-1, shivered, glanced at Mitchell, his head bobbing and rocking with the rhythm of the truck. Damn you anyway. Beside him, Lane was silent, but Benson could feel the man's tightness, anger always there. Save it for the Krauts, you stupid moron. That's where we're going, anyway. If the Krauts are as miserable as I am, this war oughta be over in days. How 'bout we all go home to our mommas and give up this stupid game? You promise not to shoot at me, I'll promise not to shoot at you. Bet the generals would love that.

The truck bounced again, and Benson felt his stomach roll over, a stab of misery, fought it. He was angry at himself for his weak stomach, thought, you haven't eaten anything since dawn, so there can't be much else to toss out. There was a narrow gap in the canvas flaps, and he peered out, felt a new swirl of cold pushing through. Behind the truck, the road was a chopped-up mess of pavement and gravel, with patchwork repairs made by the engineers to accommodate so much heavy traffic. Immediately behind them was another truck, and he glanced at the expressionless face of the driver, saw someone next to him holding up papers, a map perhaps. Benson knew that behind that truck were dozens more, maybe hundreds. He wasn't sure of their own place in line, just that the entire division was moving on these miserable roads, heading off into . . . someplace.

He shifted in the seat, heard a grumble from Lane beside him, was readying for yet another confrontation when the truck suddenly slid, the back end fishtailing. Across from Benson, Mitchell raised his head, obviously awake, and groans came from the others. Benson gripped the canvas, saw that what had been ragged pavement was now deep ruts in thick, soft mud. The road had narrowed, and there was fog, the rain heavier, turning to sleet. To the side he could see patches of thick trees, and beyond, fog-bound hills, no more open fields. There's nobody watching us now, he thought. No more civilians. Been a while. We gotta be in the middle of nowhere. There's not even a farm.

As the convoy had passed through the larger towns, there had been many civilians, heavily dressed adults standing with their children, small bundles of brown and gray, all of them watching the unending parade of green machines. There had been some cheers, people holding flags that weren't French, and Benson had guessed they had moved across the Belgian border. Many of the onlookers were waving, weary smiles, as much of a welcome as these people could muster. Benson had seen the driver in the truck behind him tossing something out toward the people, pieces of candy, most likely, or gum. The children had responded with dutiful glee, their parents grateful. Benson didn't know anything about Belgium, wasn't sure what language these people spoke. Wouldn't have mattered, he thought. No time for a chat.

Once they moved out past the towns, the crowds had given way to something new, shattered buildings, entire villages blasted into rubble. The MPs were there, manning the intersections, pointing the convoy in the right direction. Benson had seen them, tough-looking men in heavy coats, and behind them outposts armed with heavy machine guns, mortars tucked behind sandbags. There were armored vehicles, and he had seen several tanks, the round-turreted Shermans, dirty white stars on the sides, and then more armor, different, self-propelled artillery, half-tracks. The countryside was littered with wreckage, more rubble of villages, small homes and farms broken into heaps of stone. There was armor again, or what used to be, black hulks of destruction, tanks perhaps, pieces of ripped steel that could have been anything at all. He had wanted to see more of that, the signs of war, felt a curious excitement, something he could write home about. But fear came as well, churning up the sickness. He tried to hide it, would not let Lane or anyone else mouth off to him about being afraid. He had to believe they all felt it, men like Lane most of all. Until now, the war was training and mindless repetition, grouchy officers and sullen Sergeant Higgins. All the battlefields had been make-believe, fields in Indiana and their too-brief glimpse of England. But now there was smoke, smoldering fires from . . . what? Bombs? Artillery fire? The trucks rolled forward still, and now, as he stared with shivering hands into the bleakness, even the wreckage was gone, replaced by trees and mud and swirls of snow.

He felt a new urgency, intense curiosity, searched for any kind of details, the sickness granting him a reprieve. The road was winding, the truck sliding again, then falling hard into a pothole. He bounced painfully with the rest of them, ignored the curses, thought, it's darker, getting late. The road was hemmed in by tall pines, the truck bouncing high again, a hot curse from Lane. Beneath him, the tires seemed to struggle, spraying brown water back toward the truck behind them. The truck swerved again on the narrow road, someone cursing at the driver. Some of the men who had kept silent began to stir now, a loosening, talk and cigarettes. Benson looked at Mitchell, saw his friend staring back at him, shaking his head, a silent question. Benson shrugged, thought, I don't know either, Kenny. How much more of this are we going to do? Where the hell are we? Maybe we're close, maybe we might actually *be* somewhere. The talk began to come, the men more anxious, some spouting off about the truck, the misery of the potholes, anger at one another, at the sergeant up front. Lane's voice dominated the others.

"They're gonna drop us right into Krautville. You watch. They want to be rid of this garbage outfit, and so they're gonna unload us where we'll make good cannon fodder. I heard the lieutenant talking about it . . ."

Milsaps, another of the new men, responded. "You're so full of crap. You haven't heard a damn thing. I heard they're taking us to a rest area. Captain Moore told the sergeant. They're putting us where we can't hurt anything, and we're gonna start in with the training again. Maybe you'll finally learn to shoot that rifle, Lane. I keep telling you, the narrow part's where the bullet comes out. The big wide wooden part—that goes in your mouth."

"I'll show you where to put this rifle—"

Lane was silenced by a squeal beneath them, the truck's brakes slowing them, then a sliding stop, all the talk ending.

Lane leaned close to him, said, "Open the damn flaps. What's going on?"

Benson pulled one flap in close, the cold rolling over them all, heavy snow falling. The truck behind them had stopped, and Benson saw more trucks behind that one.

Now the sergeant was there, slapping his gloved hands together, his breath in clouds of white fog. "Out! Let's go! We march now!"

Benson felt his heart racing, tried to rise, his legs stiff. He grabbed his backpack, the rifle, leaned out, saw that the woods were nearly dark, black spaces through the trees. He climbed out, pushed from behind by Lane, jumped down into mush, snow on top of more mud. To one side were fat pines, a gathering of thick spruces, the snow dusting them like so many

Christmas trees. Across the road, the ground fell away sharply, and Benson stepped back from the truck, waited for the others to unload, grunts as each man hit the ground.

The sergeant said in a hard whisper, "No talking. There's enemy out here somewhere. The lieutenant says we ought to run smack into the boys we're replacing. Keep an eye out. You see someone, he's one of *us,* you got that?"

There was no need for a response, the men hoisting up backpacks, slinging rifles onto their shoulders, waiting for the next instruction. Benson was shivering, fought it, the coat already growing soggy with the wet melting snow. He looked up past the front of the truck, more trucks, more men, trees and mud and snow. A man was plodding quickly toward him, head low, and Benson saw the face now, the lieutenant.

"Sergeant, we're moving out straight down this road. Four hundred yards, there's a narrow trail that goes into the trees. Someone there will direct you. Stay in line, men, you go wandering off in those woods, you might run into the enemy. You go the other way, you'll roll your asses down that hillside, and I'm not sparing anybody to haul you back up here. Let's move out, Sergeant."

"Yes, sir. Let's go."

Benson fell into line, the lieutenant leading them, the sergeant close behind him. The column was moving with soft, sluggish steps, past a dozen or more trucks that had been in front of them. The drivers were mostly up inside, watching them go past, rude calls, one man shouting out, "Hey, no tip? I got you here without a crack-up. You're lucky. You get to go to sleep in some nice warm foxhole. I gotta do this trip again."

Benson flinched at the volume of the man's voice, no other sound but the muddy slurps of their boots. After long minutes, they passed the lead truck, and Benson saw officers, a cluster to one side of the road, some of them familiar, men in clean snowy coats, the 423rd's brass, others, four men who looked like they'd been rolled in the mud. They crested a hill, and beyond he saw an opening, the trees giving way to a snowy field, churned up by a sea of tire tracks. I guess that's where the trucks will park, or turn around, maybe. The fog obliterated the far side of the field, but he saw shapes, dark smudges against the far trees, saw a jeep coming closer, bouncing high over the ruts. There was more activity, more jeeps, a dark tent nestled into a group of pine trees, larger trucks, but not the deuce-and-a-halfs. Some were kitchen trucks, and he saw a water truck, men moving slowly in huddled misery, doing their jobs.

Lane bumped him from behind, a hard hand in his back. "Get moving, you slug. I wanna get where we're going."

Benson didn't respond, quickened his pace, moved closer to the sergeant. He thought of the rifle on his shoulder, Lane's ugly face, Benson's nervousness focusing into hatred. I know what I ought to do, he thought. Ram this rifle butt into that jerk's gut. Somebody needs to knock his teeth out, he thought. Maybe not in front of the lieutenant, though.

He kept up the march, the road less muddy, hard-packed snow. There were more men standing to one side of the road, heavy coats, helmets low, a voice.

"Halt the march. Make way for the guys coming out."

The lieutenant obeyed, the line behind them slowing, stopping. Benson stared into the dark gaps in the trees, saw them now, heard voices and laughter, shattering the low silence.

"Well, it's the new bunch. Howdy-do, boys?"

"Ski lift is over that way. The lodge is just ahead, big fireplace. About a hundred little barmaids to warm your feet."

"Y'all hoping to see some Krauts out here? Sorry, we done kilt them all."

"Fresh meat, eh? You bring us anything cuddly? I hear the 106th's got mostly girls in the ranks. You're one ugly bunch of broads."

"Shut up that chatter!"

The voice came from behind him, and Benson knew the sound of an officer. The man was there now, two aides trailing close behind him, his authority silencing the talk. Benson recognized him, one of the men he had seen with the brass, older, the coat caked with mud. Across the road, the men continued to emerge from the woods, and Benson caught their smell, thick and musty, heard the slow tramp of feet on the packed snow.

The officer stood to one side, said to the lieutenant, "What's your name, son?"

"Lieutenant Greeley, sir. Company B, Four Two Three."

"All right, Lieutenant Greeley. Your boys are taking over this hillside hole for hole and gun for gun, and you're replacing the best damn fighting division in this army. Take a good look at them. They've earned a rest. You do us proud, you hear me?"

"Yes, sir. We will, sir."

The officer glanced at Benson, then down the line behind him. "You men haven't been under fire yet, have you?"

The lieutenant responded, "No, sir. We just arrived from Le Havre—"

"I don't care, Lieutenant. But you're replacing *veterans* up here. These men fought like hell to take the city of Aachen away from an enemy who fought like hell to keep us out. We were due to move into a rest-and-recreation area, but somebody back at SHAEF forgot to look at a map and stuck the whole damn Second Division out here in the middle of frozen hell. The good news for you is that there's nothing going on here, and not likely to be anytime soon."

There were footsteps, hurrying forward, and Benson saw his company commander, Captain Moore. Moore stopped abruptly, threw up a salute, said, "Sir, I was told you'd be up here. Colonel Cavender is arranging to bring us some dinner."

"Calm your motor, Captain. I just talked to him back there. My men have been perched up on this hill for too many weeks, and we're damn glad to see you. You've got two sections of heavy weapons coming in behind you. That'll give you eight machine guns to go with these rifles. Those boys should know how to get in position, but double-check them, Captain. You won't need to dig too many holes tonight. You'll move right into ours. We're leaving you some eighty-ones, spaced out and dug in where there'll do you some good. No need for us to haul a load of mortars in and out of here. Take your men down this trail until you see my adjutant, Captain Gridley. He'll put your men into position, give you the guided tour. Been pretty quiet for the most part. The enemy tosses a few shells at us the same time every morning. Oh five hundred. Works just like reveille. We've been occupying ground that used to be theirs, so they know the lay of the land. Wasn't my decision, but here we are. And now it's yours."

Benson stared at the older officer, thought, this son of a bitch *knows* a few things.

The officer stepped toward the trail, waved his men forward. "Let's go! You've been bitching about replacements, well, they're here! I'd think you'd be in a hurry to get back off the line!"

"Yes, sir."

"Right, sir."

The men seemed to come out of every dark gap in the trees, ragged and filthy, bent cigarettes hanging from grim faces, rough beards and tired eyes. He caught one man's eye, the man looking straight past him, unseeing, and Benson nodded, a silent greeting that was ignored. There was exhaustion in the man's face, a smear of black on his cheeks, his eyes dull and yellow through the shadow of his helmet. Benson wanted to speak to the man, but he was gone now, moving back toward the trucks. Benson held the man's image in his mind, thought, a *soldier*. That's what we're supposed to be. Behind him, no one was speaking at all, these new men suddenly face-to-face with veterans. Benson shivered again, thought, none of us is a *tough guy* now.

Another officer appeared, emerging from the woods, and Benson saw youth, a lieutenant, a salute for his commander.

"Company D has completed their withdrawal, sir. Captain Gridley is waiting for the replacements."

"Good. Get our men into the trucks as soon as you can. I want to be off this damn mountain before it's too dark to see."

"Yes, sir!"

The young lieutenant began to scramble back along the road, hurrying his men. Benson watched the scene play out, the men of the Second Division flowing out, the woods draining of men, the officer just watching them.

Captain Moore said, "Sir, Colonel Cavender has instructed me to order my men into position only when you give the command. We don't want to hold up your withdrawal."

"The withdrawal's complete enough. Get going, son. It gets dark here at sixteen thirty. You'll be placing your men into those dugouts and holes we left you. It'll be a cold one tonight. I don't expect trouble, but the enemy might sense something's going on here. Keep lookouts posted all night. We've rigged up plenty of noisemakers if anyone goes wandering around in front of us. That means your men too. Keep them in tight for tonight. By morning, you'll see what you've got in front of you." He paused, looked up. "Probably snow all damn night. I told Colonel Cavender to start raising hell with supply for more socks, boots, and anything else they can send up here. Sooner the better. Ask for it before you need it. I think you'll need everything you can get pretty quick." He paused, looked at Moore, then the lieutenant. "Good luck, boys. Keep your heads down."

The officer stepped out alongside the stream of men moving back toward the trucks. Benson watched him go, felt a strange sense of power in the man, nothing empty about his authority. Captain Moore watched him as well, glanced upward, the snow swirling harder through a darkening sky.

5. VON RUNDSTEDT

He was shocked by Hitler, who seemed more like an old weathered tree than a man whose mantle of power was absolute. Hitler seemed to know it too, made his entrance with no flourish, none of the bombast. He seemed instead to be hiding, holding something away from the eyes of the others, a coat wrapped around a quivering left arm. But the eyes were hard, searching, sharp glances toward the faces of the officers, as though he was testing them. Von Rundstedt had seen that before, more so since the assassination attempt. He has changed, certainly, he thought, furious at the betrayal, and just as furious that some of these men might have been involved. We will never know, after all. No matter how brutal the Gestapo has been, no matter how many investigations and executions, Hitler will never again trust this army. Not even Himmler can convince him that the Gestapo was perfectly thorough, that the entire plot was ripped out by its roots.

The plot had erupted in July, a bomb that had killed some, and wounded nearly everyone else in the room. Hitler had been injured as well, but his life had been spared by a phenomenal stroke of luck, the bomb placed beneath a table whose massive wooden legs shielded him from the worst of the explosion. Von Rundstedt knew that some of what he saw now were the effects of those injuries, but there was more to Hitler's physical presence than old wounds. The man seemed to be withering away, betrayed by some physical or mental condition that no one would dare to describe.

Hitler moved close to the long table, self-consciously dragging one leg behind him, was followed closely by General Jodl and the ever-present doctor. He still eyed the gathering of officers but acknowledged no one, no smile, no friendly greeting. We have never been his friends, von Rundstedt thought. He followed Hitler's eyes, glanced around the long room, the faces of men who knew the plans, others who did not yet know why they were there. No one spoke, no private discussions. We have changed as well, he thought. We are more afraid of him now than we have ever been.

Von Rundstedt knew many of the faces, generals and colonels, four dozen men focused almost exclusively on the Führer's efforts to reach his chair. Jodl moved in front of him, pulled the chair away from the table, and von Rundstedt caught Jodl's downward glance. Of course. Every table could have its own bomb.

Hitler sat, his shoulders stooped, curved like a bow. His face had changed as well, and von Rundstedt thought, it is not just aging. He looks sickly, puffy, like a man who drinks too much. The thought pulled his gaze toward Dietrich, one of the principal commanders for the Watch on the Rhine, Hitler's outrageous plan of attack. Sepp Dietrich had once been Rommel's man, at least for a time, a man who shared Rommel's love of armor and, like him, a general who enjoyed ramming his tanks into the face of the enemy. But many of the High Command believed him to be brash and stupid, and his heavy drinking did not endear him to Hitler. All the generals had learned long ago that you did not imbibe strong spirits in front of the Führer. Von Rundstedt looked at the glass of dark liquid, placed carefully by Hitler's right hand. Ah, yes, the doctors at work. Von Rundstedt had often wondered about them, the prissy and proper medical men. They had long ago responded to Hitler's ailments with a steady flow of strong medicines, drugging him to sleep every night, drugging him awake during the day. That is what he has become now, what we see here before us. And yet it is *us* who dare not imbibe the spirits.

The room was mostly full, the senior generals seated around the table, waiting for Hitler to begin. Jodl stood stiffly behind Hitler, ever-present, the puppet of a man von Rundstedt despised. If Alfred Jodl had any real ability as a commander of armies, no one in this room had ever seen it. But Jodl's soul had long been handed over to his Führer, and though his official title was military chief of staff, everyone believed Jodl's job was simply to agree with the Führer's decisions. Jodl has done his job, has flitted about like some butterfly, a soldier who will never hear the guns, adding oil to Hitler's wheels. One must not incur the Führer's wrath, and so we must not incur the wrath of Jodl. Why will Hitler not trust us to do our jobs? Von Rundstedt continued his scan of the faces, so many good generals whose armies had been gutted and blasted from battlefields by so many bad orders that poured over them from behind. Obscene orders. Orders from a madman. The Little Corporal. And here we are again.

Hitler leaned forward on the table, supported by both arms, looked straight ahead at the man across from him, Model, his new favorite. To Hitler's right sat Hasso von Manteuffel, the commander of the Fifth Panzer Army. Manteuffel would be one point of the spear, the armored force that Hitler had chosen to lead the drive toward Antwerp. To Manteuffel's right sat Dietrich, the other spear point, his Sixth Panzer Army designated to drive the right-handed fist through the Allied defenses. Farther down the table sat Erich Brandenberger, the commander of what had once been Rommel's magnificent Seventh Army. The Seventh had been bled viciously in the campaigns that had driven it away from the beaches at Normandy, so many of its veterans dead or scattered throughout other parts of the army. What remained were the men who had escaped through the Falaise gap, pursued and butchered by the Allied artillery and air force. But escape they did, and now they would fight again, though von Rundstedt knew they would never be the same. The Seventh had been rebuilt by scrounging men from other units, home guard militia, the Volksturm, some too old to be soldiers, some absurdly young, schoolboys, all that Germany could spare. The Seventh was the left side of the fist, mostly infantry, that would march close beside Manteuffel's armor to clean up the ragged mess of the enemy on the left flank, the chaotic remnants of the American forces that Hitler expected to be obliterated by the panzers' lightning strike.

Model would command all three wings of the assault, and as Model sat across from Hitler, von Rundstedt had seen the vacant chair to his side. That's for me, he thought. A courtesy perhaps. Jodl is after all, polite. As the others sat, von Rundstedt had hesitated, felt distinctly out of place. This is not my show, he thought. I am here because Jodl probably thought it was *good form* to invite the man who officially commands this entire sector of the war. He glanced at Model, who nodded toward him, motioned to the chair. All right, I'll sit down. Good idea anyway. My damn knees hurt.

Hitler seemed impatient to begin, stared down at a map, details von Rundstedt could not see. Hitler began to speak, a low voice, slow words.

"You are here . . . many of you . . . because I felt it was time to reveal this most cherished of secrets." He held up the map. "You may know some details of *this,* you may have heard that planning was under way for a significant operation. That operation is now to be revealed to you all. We are prepared to make the most brutal strike against our enemies that they have yet experienced. This plan has been fashioned by Field Marshal Model, by his chief subordinates, by myself and my staff. After many weeks of consultations and revisions, this plan is now as perfect as any I have devised."

It did not escape von Rundstedt that his own name had not been mentioned.

Hitler seemed more enthusiastic now, his eyes stabbing through the room, searching out faces. "You shall all be given maps and orders today. Some of you have been kept unaware, and that was by design. This plan is cloaked in the most efficient veil of secrecy we could maintain. I trust you all, but trust can be careless. The enemy will not know of this plan until the artillery begins and the tanks roll forward."

Staff officers began to move through the crowd, handing out maps, sealed folders marked with the names of the recipients. Hitler seemed to enjoy the show, waited for the aides to complete their jobs; then Jodl motioned them out of the room.

Hitler said, "Open your orders."

As the men obeyed, von Rundstedt heard several low gasps, was surprised by that, thought, so, they really didn't know? That is a good sign, certainly. Surprise here means surprise for the enemy.

Hitler leaned back, said, "The plan shall commence at dawn on the sixteenth. Four days from now. You have been ordered to make preparations for operations about which you knew nothing, and yet your senior commanders have succeeded in placing every one of you into position. You have complied with efficiency. That is a statement of your loyalty." He stopped, searched behind him, and von Rundstedt saw the familiar face, tall and lean, broad shoulders, blond hair. The man knew his cue, stepped close to Hitler's back.

Hitler said, "Gentlemen, for those of you who do not know, this is Lieutenant Colonel Otto Skorzeny. The colonel is a hero of the Reich, and one of the most capable and trusted men in our service. I will ask Colonel Skorzeny now to reveal his part of this operation."

Von Rundstedt knew Skorzeny, primarily by reputation. He was a dashing, handsome man, all muscle, blond hair, and blue eyes, with a brutal love for duty. He was, of course, fiercely loyal to Hitler, but von Rundstedt knew that, to Hitler, Skorzeny represented much more than a loyal soldier. He was the perfect Aryan specimen, something not lost on Joseph Goebbels and the Propaganda Ministry. Much had been made in the papers of Skorzeny's daring commando operation that had plucked Benito Mussolini away from captivity, during the earliest days of the fall of Italy. Later, Skorzeny had been a driving force behind the fatal blow to the remnants of the plot to assassinate Hitler. Though the nastiest work had been left to Gestapo operatives, hundreds of late-night executions, trial-less imprisonment, it had been Skorzeny's energy and brutal efficiency that had driven the last nail in that coffin. Skorzeny remained standing behind Hitler, towering above the rest of the men in the room.

"Thank you, my Führer. Within the past few days, elements of a specially chosen force have begun to infiltrate the enemy's position. With great care, we have chosen men who speak perfect English and have mastered American dialects and slang. We have clothed them in American army uniforms, placed them in American vehicles, and sent them directly at the enemy's weakest positions. We have named this Operation Griffin. You are familiar with the mythical bird, the head of an eagle, the body of a lion. Such are these men who are already embarking on their critical mission, a mission to spread contradiction and confusion. Some have been ordered to move rapidly to the Meuse River bridges and capture them, establishing strongpoints that will appear to be a normal American operation. Thus, when the Americans are driven back to the river, we will accomplish two objectives. The retreating Americans will be confronted by machine-gun and mortar positions in the line of their retreat, thus adding to their panic, and more important we will secure the bridges themselves so that their engineers cannot destroy them. Thus will your armies have the means to make a rapid crossing of the river, on the way to their *own* objectives. But there is much more to Operation Griffin. Moving quickly along the networks of roadways in the enemy's rear, my men will kill American military police, who are now charged with directing the flow of traffic at every significant intersection. In their place, my men will direct that traffic to incorrect destinations. We will sever telephone lines, or use those lines ourselves to place confusing calls to various headquarters and outposts. Operation Griffin will be the seed of the enemy's destruction, confusing and deceiving him, so that chaos will ensue. No American soldier will know if the vehicle passing through his outpost is genuine or not."

Hitler seemed delighted, clapped his hands twice, said, "Tell them about the other plan."

Skorzeny was obviously pleased with himself.

"Thank you, my Führer. We have also trained a squad of men to make their way to Paris, with one specific mission in mind. Anytime you can remove the head from the beast, the beast dies. This special squad will use their skills so that they may draw close to the Allied high command. We shall sever its head. Though they will have the opportunity to eliminate a large number of Allied commanders, their primary target is General Eisenhower."

Hitler was glowing, seemed to encourage the same response from the others. Von Rundstedt saw surprised stares, mouths open. Hitler said, "Good, yes? Can you imagine how quickly all our efforts will come to full glory should Eisenhower be assassinated?"

Model looked to von Rundstedt with a forced smile. He wants me to cheer, for God's sake. Von Rundstedt said aloud, "We are grateful for Colonel Skorzeny's efforts. All of Germany is behind you, Colonel."

Skorzeny seemed ultimately self-satisfied, made a curt bow. "Thank you, Field Marshal. I serve my Führer."

Von Rundstedt had said enough, his compliment ignored by Hitler, entirely expected. Thus far, Hitler had not acknowledged his most senior commander at all.

The Führer looked to the map in front of him, his mind already moving beyond Skorzeny's glowing presentation. He leaned forward, looked to his right, said, "Is the Sixth Panzer Army prepared for the attack, General Dietrich? Have you accepted your role in this most historic of victories?"

Von Rundstedt saw unexpected hesitation. "Not completely, my Führer," Dietrich said. "An offensive of this magnitude requires training and preparation—"

"You are never satisfied!" Hitler took a drink from the stinking liquid in the glass, curled his face into a hard frown. He looked at Manteuffel, next to him. "And what of you, General? Are both of my panzer commanders hesitating?"

Von Rundstedt knew Manteuffel to be a solid leader, a small straight-backed man beloved by his troops. He had wondered if Manteuffel might be one bright spark that could give this entire plan some credibility.

Manteuffel replied, "We do not yet have sufficient fuel and ammunition, my Führer. My men are prepared to drive hard toward our objective, but I have not been assured that we will have the support required to secure your victory."

Von Rundstedt worked hard to hide a smile, thought, *a man who tells the truth*. He glanced around, knew the others in the room were pretending to be shocked by Manteuffel's bluntness. He could feel Model shifting in his chair, the prelude to a pronouncement of his own. *Of course, Field Marshal Model will blunt the edge of his most capable commander's indiscretion*.

Model stood, a show of authority, arrogance that von Rundstedt knew too well. "My Führer, I have assured both of these men that when the time comes, all will be ready. There will be no hesitation, and this operation will begin precisely according to your timetable." He focused on the two generals now. "Gentlemen, these are details that have been examined and calculated to the most minute detail. You have known what is expected of you for some weeks now, and you have had ample time to prepare. General Jodl has cooperated with our every request, and even now, support is moving forward. I am certain that there are sufficient allotments of tactical—"

Hitler held up a hand, stifling Model's presentation. "Sit down, Field Marshal." He turned toward Manteuffel again. "General, I have responded positively to your every request. The Fifth Panzer Army has received the greatest share of the armored production pouring from our factories. This month alone, we anticipate that production to exceed twenty-five hundred new tanks, most of them Tigers." He stopped, glanced behind him, Jodl nodding crisply, confirming the number. "Twenty-five hundred new tanks each month, from now on! Is that not sufficient for your army's needs, General? Or yours, General Dietrich?" Hitler sat back again, annoyed.

Neither man spoke, Model answering for them. "There are no complaints, my Führer. This plan will succeed, and I am confident that we have the commanders here to make that happen."

Von Rundstedt looked at both Manteuffel and Dietrich, saw their protests wilting. There was nothing else to say. Hitler suddenly began to change. Von Rundstedt saw a hint of a smile on the man's face, so rare, but he had seen it before. It was Hitler's way of being *fatherly*, of easing their burdens by convincing them that their concerns were dealt with, that all was in safe hands.

"Gentlemen, there is history at work here, history that some of you might have forgotten. We are launching strikes through the Ardennes Forest. Do you not recall that this is precisely what we did four years ago? And those of you who are older, like me, you recall that we used the forest once before. In 1918, we achieved magnificent success on the same ground, using the same tactics. Then, we did not have the benefit of speed that we enjoy now. Then, our beloved General Ludendorff did not have the luxury of panzer armies. In both of these campaigns, the enemy was caught unprepared, and was indelicately removed from the battlefield. This time will be no different." He paused. "You should know that I have been assured by Reichsmarschall Göring that three thousand of the Luftwaffe's finest aircraft will be made available to support this operation from the air. If that seems to be a somewhat grandiose offer on his part, you may be assured that . . ." Hitler laughed now, surprising von Rundstedt. "You may be assured that I do not so much believe the *fat man* anymore when he makes these statements. But I do know that we shall have sufficient air support, artillery support, and supply support. As our thrust shatters the enemy's resistance, we shall have additional infantry and armored support as well." Hitler was fiery now, the old energy von Rundstedt had seen before. "The enemy is weak and will be crushed. The British are exhausted beyond hope, and the Americans cannot stand up to our might. In the past, we have been betrayed by the unwilling, the inept, our efforts hampered by men who thought more of their personal ambitions than their loyalty to Germany. But those men are gone, removed from our ranks. You men here share my vision, and it is you who shall give us victory. It is you who carry the soul of the German people upon your backs. This operation will succeed because *they* believe it will succeed. And so, it *will* succeed. I am entrusting you to do your jobs. On December sixteenth, the final chapter on the Western Theater will be written, and its conclusion has already been decided. This war will yet be won."

Hitler was gone, Skorzeny, Jodl, and the rest of his entourage with him. Von Rundstedt still sat at the long table, the two panzer commanders up and moving, slow pacing. To one side of the room, Model scanned a wide map, seemed occupied by his own thoughts, uninterested in any conversation. Yet still, von Rundstedt thought, he remains here, with us.

There were others there as well, a select few, men who did not seem eager to rush back to their commands. Von Rundstedt watched one in particular, Günther Blumentritt, who had once served as von Rundstedt's chief of staff. Blumentritt commanded his own panzer division now, would be a part of Dietrich's drive on the northern flank of the great assault. He knew Blumentritt too well, could see deep despair on the man's face.

"Speak up, Günther. None of us in this room believes in this plan."

He turned toward Model. "Do we, Field Marshal?"

Model did not look at him, said, "Such talk is treason. You should curb your arrogant disloyalty."

There was no fire in the statement, but von Rundstedt had lost his patience for Model's duplicity. He fought to stand, ignored the pains in his legs.

"You will not accuse me of disloyalty! How easy it is to toss out those words, that grotesque insult! You, who are such a man of integrity and honesty. Where are your loyalties? You are to carry out a plan for what purpose? Does the fatherland require such service from you? Is this the best way you can stand up for the good of Germany? Is that not what is important here? Is that not what we all are fighting for?"

Model moved toward him, haughty and dismissive, and Manteuffel was there, the small man putting a hand on Model's arm. "Calm yourselves. There is no purpose to this. The Führer's plan is now our plan, and it is up to us to carry it out as best we can."

Model threw a sneer at von Rundstedt, pointed at Manteuffel. "You see? That is loyalty! That is the spirit of the German soldier. Not some old man who does not yet know when to give in . . . when to walk away from a duty he is unwilling to perform!"

Manteuffel still held Model's arm, said, "Enough of this! With all respect, sir, we all know what is unspoken here. He merely says the words. Please, be calm. There is only a short time, and I must return to my tanks. General Dietrich must as well."

Dietrich spoke, staring away. "Oh yes. I must return so that I may begin this wonderful adventure." He turned toward Model now. "Would you question my loyalty as well, Field Marshal? My mission, as I understand it, is to drive rapidly through the Ardennes Forest, crushing the enemy who opposes me. In what . . . two days perhaps . . . I am to send my armor across the Meuse River using Colonel Skorzeny's captured bridges, then drive straight through the enemy's fortifications at Brussels, and finally sweep forward to capture Antwerp. I am not to be concerned with my right flank, since we shall sweep past the British so quickly, they will not have time to react. I am not to be concerned about my rear, since the Führer has assured me that there will be ample reserves following closely behind me. I am not to be concerned about gasoline, because what we do not have, we shall capture from the enemy's supply dumps. Excuse me, Field Marshal, but do you have a map that shows the locations of the enemy's supply dumps? Because my tanks have enough gasoline to travel for perhaps a day and a half."

Dietrich looked down, did not expect a response.

Manteuffel stepped away from Model, leaned against one wall, rubbed a bony hand on his chin. "Jodl has convinced the Führer that we have sufficient gasoline to complete our mission. I saw the paper, Jodl's calculations. Marvelous numbers. Jodl was most definite that his mathematics is not to be questioned. I tried to explain that computing the gasoline usage on flat roads in ideal conditions is nothing like consumption on a battlefield. I told him that if this plan is to succeed, we require five times more fuel than they are giving us. Jodl laughed at me, said that I should be grateful the Führer has so much faith in my abilities." He looked at Model now. "None of us is disloyal, Field Marshal. But I know my tanks. And I know what this battlefield will be. The Führer is calling upon history as his guide. The Ardennes Forest has been very good to us, in this war and the last. But in 1940, we drove across those hills in the springtime, across muddy holes filled with French soldiers who did not have the will to fight."

Dietrich interrupted. "Yes! And now, it is winter! There will be waist-deep snow, and the roads are few and narrow. No matter how many tanks I have, no matter how full their fuel tanks might be, I cannot advance into any battle with an attack more than four tanks wide. There is no place for a massed armor assault! The infantry who is to support us is made up of battle-weary invalids, fighting alongside old men and children. Some are refugees from the east, dressed up in our uniforms. Some of them might even speak German, so I've been told. It is make-believe!"

Blumentritt moved closer, said in a soft voice, "We no longer have the training for this sort of operation."

"What do you mean?" asked von Rundstedt.

Blumentritt seemed uncomfortable. He was far outranked by the others. "This army has built itself upon training. In every battle I have witnessed, the well-trained force is the force that holds his ground, that will fight until the enemy loses his will. No matter if they are outnumbered or outgunned, well-trained troops will prevail. When I expressed my concerns about the poor quality of the soldiers under my command, Herr Hitler insisted I not be concerned. He believes that our *soldierly spirit* will prevail."

Model said, "It has to. We have that spirit. I have seen it, so have all of you. No matter what our reverses have been, the German people wish us to continue the fight. The morale of this army is as high as it ever was. I admit . . . I do not completely understand why."

Model had calmed, and von Rundstedt saw the man's gloom seeping past the anger, the energy behind the show of confidence drained away. The old man returned to his chair, nursed the pain in his legs, thought, Model is a man caught in a trap, hard walls closing in on both sides of him. He is angry because he has a job to do that he knows will fail. And he has no choice. Von Rundstedt wanted to speak but held it back, would not embarrass this man. Yet the words rolled through his brain. I feel sorry for you, Walther.

After a long moment, von Rundstedt said, "Do your jobs. That's what Hitler told you. If your soldiers are willing, they have a chance. It has always been so. An army that is unwilling will not fight. This army is still willing. They know nothing of plans and strategies and doubts. They will only do what is expected of them." He paused, thought of the word. *Plans.* "My God, those fools around Hitler so love their plans. That lunatic Skorzeny and his *plans* to kill Eisenhower, his *plans* to capture bridges. We are wallowing in *plans* that are fanciful and absurd in every extreme. Perhaps you are correct, Walther. I should walk away, claim my age is too much of an impairment. Hitler has no use for me anyway, beyond whatever blame he can lay at my feet. None of us here expects to capture Antwerp, none of us believes the British and Americans will beg for peace. But you are right about the German people, and you are right about our soldiers. I have seen it in every fight. This army will do what its Führer tells it to do." He paused, shook his head, looked again at Model. "There is no disloyalty here, Walther. In this room there is only truth. You know what you are being asked to do, and you know that it is quite likely it cannot be done. But you will do it anyway. Nothing we say will change any of that. And there is one more thing that will not change. No matter how successful this *plan,* too many German soldiers will die because they *believe* it when their Führer tells them they can still be victorious."

6. BENSON

The night seemed unending, full dark by five every afternoon, sunrise well after eight, like an afterthought, another screwup by the army. The men of the 106th had struggled that first night, frozen feet and wet wool coats, and if there was any sleep at all, it came from the brutal exhaustion of their journey. Benson had finally found sleep, curled into a tight ball against one side of the muddy foxhole. But as the Second Division's officer had said, the Germans provided reveille. At five that first morning, the artillery barrage came. Now, three days later, it was routine, exactly as the officer had described it.

It had been a shattering surprise, every man stunned by the quaking ground, the hard blasts that numbed their ears. They sat low in their foxholes for those few minutes, what seemed to the new men like hours of hell, engulfed in the unique terror that came with their first experience of incoming shellfire. When it was over, the men around Benson had emerged unscathed, calling out to their buddies. Gradually they rose, emerging from the holes, hesitant, testing the quiet. In some, the fear had given way to maniacal laughter, the GIs realizing that they had survived, that no matter the wreckage throughout the vast stands of trees, somehow they were protected. But the strange hysteria didn't last, word coming along the lines that the company had taken casualties, one direct hit, a shell coming down straight through a makeshift canvas rooftop, the three men in the foxhole obliterated. There were questions, who . . . but the lieutenants had been angry and direct, ordering the men to keep to themselves. Benson had wondered about those men, had made a quick search for those closest to him, no one missing, thought, well, if you're going to go, that's one good way. You won't even hear it. But soon his attention had turned to the woods themselves, damage he had not expected to see. Sergeant Higgins had noticed as well, the word passing that the Germans were using something very different, a kind of artillery shell these men had never seen before. The typical shells they had trained with exploded on impact with the ground, leaving a crater, tossing up muddy debris that a man could escape by staying down low in his foxhole. Those craters were around them now, spread down the wide open hill, dark smears in the snow. But the Germans were using something else as well, shells that exploded above them, high in the treetops, blasting limbs into tumbling debris and, worse, blowing shrapnel straight down. Around the foxholes, pieces of trees jabbed out of the snow, the fresh smell of cut and burnt wood, smudges of black from burning pine needles. The men didn't need the officers to tell them that a foxhole wasn't much protection against that, and with each new dawn there had been more casualties, a dozen men wounded in their shelters, three more men killed by a shell burst that had erupted only a few feet above them.

The airburst shells drove the men to improvise, digging the bottoms of their foxholes sideways, carving angled gashes in the bottom, so a man could hug the ground facing the enemy and feel somewhat sheltered from above. But the idea was drowned by the mud, the sloped earthen walls too soft, more likely just to collapse. By the third morning, when the shelling had come, the routine had taken over, the men huddling up tightly, pulling their knees under their chins, making themselves small, some praying, some, like Benson, crawling deep into their own minds, hands clamped on ears, staring down into darkness, shouting silently at the enemy, *Get it over with.* There was another kind of routine as well, the men who could not keep silent, who screamed, muffled terror from scattered foxholes. Some of those were so engulfed by fear that they never heard the sound of their own voices. The others who sat cramped beside them tried to ignore the screams, but there was a contagiousness some could not resist. Benson had heard it close by, not sure of the man's name, a few others down the ridgeline, a hellish chorus of screams that lasted nearly as long as the shelling. When the shelling stopped, no one sought out the voices, no one would tease or cajole or condemn the man who let his fear strike back the only way he could. In the silence, with ears ringing and debris scattered around them, the men of the 106th could only check on their buddies and begin their day, watching, waiting, resting. There was nothing else to do.

After three mornings of this horrifying routine, Benson had realized, as had some of the others, that the Germans either weren't very good shots or just didn't care about targets. Many of the shells overshot their mark, coming down behind the ridgeline, others falling short, down below, out in the open. But there was mathematics to the shelling. It became clear that the German guns were each launching the same number of shells, four per gun, four guns per battery. It was as though the enemy artillerymen had been given a perfunctory order, a pattern of firing that served no other purpose than to harass the American positions. The shrieks and groans of the incoming shells could be traced from specific directions, what seemed to be beyond the next ridgeline. Benson was growing more curious if those batteries were hunkered down in some fixed position, not bothering to move or adjust, since the Americans had not done much to respond.

H ow long till the sarge is gonna let us have some chow?"

Benson shook his head, swung the ax. "Don't have a watch. Looks like it's getting dark, though. Sun goes down in the middle of the afternoon. Best to work up a good sweat. Maybe keep the cold away for a little longer."

Mitchell ignored the darkening skies, swung again, said, "Yeah, well the first time you come out here to use this trench, you'll forget all about being warm. I tried squatting over the old one, and the snow blew against my ass like I'd been slapped. Can't be healthy for my . . . family."

"If you two jackasses would dig instead of jabber, this latrine would be done by now."

Benson glanced back, saw the sergeant moving close, two more men behind him, their relief.

Higgins said, "All right, back off. I got replacements for you ditchdiggers. You two haven't made a trench deep enough to hide a rat."

Mitchell tossed the pickax up to the flat ground. "Any rat wants to hide in this thing, he's doing it at his own risk. My guts are so torn up, no one'll wanna be near this thing when I let go."

Benson couldn't help laughing, had always enjoyed Mitchell's brand of humor. But Mitchell's condition was increasingly common among the men, the combination of fear and K rations adding intestinal torture to the misery of the muddy cold. Benson had seemed immune, so far, an irony not lost on the men in his squad. As long as his feet were on solid ground, his stomach seemed to leave him alone.

Benson handed his pickax to one of the others, saw the dirty face of Milsaps, no smile, the man accepting the job of latrine excavation with the same resignation that had affected them all.

Higgins said, "You two go back to your foxholes. There's supposed to be some hot food coming up our way by dark. Brubaker, Milsaps, you've got an hour to show these two idiots that a trench is supposed to be dug into the ground. Like a *ditch*." Higgins looked at Benson, then Mitchell, who was already moving away. "You morons."

Benson ignored the sergeant, picked up his rifle, slung it over his shoulder. He tried to keep pace, but Mitchell was moving quickly, puffs of white from his breathing.

"Wait up, Kenny."

Mitchell didn't stop, said, "I gotta get out of these wet socks. The whole damn lot of us are gonna come down with some kind of *fluenza* or something if we don't keep dry. I read about it . . . somewhere. Or worse, there's some kinda crud out here, they say it's worse than trench foot, but damn if I know what could be worse than freezing my ass off in this mud hole."

They tramped through deepening snow, followed the tracks of the others, could see scattered foxholes spread all through the pines. Benson, up beside Mitchell, said, "This is what Maine looks like, I bet."

Mitchell looked at him with a silent question: *How stupid are you?* "Nobody shoots at you in Maine, Eddie boy."

"I bet there's deer out here. Plenty of 'em. You could climb under these short trees, use the limbs for cover. Deer would never know you were there. Probably a pretty good place to kill one."

Mitchell seemed to absorb that, pulled at the branches of a wide spruce, knocking snow off the limbs. "You may be right about that. I hear there's wild boar too. But I'd rather hunt for Krauts. This might be a good way to set up an ambush. Put a thirty-caliber under there, hidden like inside a tent. Nobody could see you at all, as long as you didn't go bumping into the limbs. You're not so stupid after all. Now, do you mind if I have some damn supper? There's at least half a dozen K ration boxes in that hole I been saving for a special occasion."

"What occasion?"

"Easy one, kiddo. By later tonight, we'll have a brand-new straddle trench."

DECEMBER 15, 1944, 5:15 A.M.

The fourth morning's shelling had ended, the ringing in his ears passing. Benson uncurled himself, worked on the stiffness in his knees, rose, one hand easing back the canvas sheet, peered up. Men were emerging, beginning to move, Higgins, rousing them awake, as if any man had slept through the barrage.

Benson looked back into the darkness beside him, put a hand on Mitchell's shoulder, said, "You okay?"

He could only tell that Mitchell wasn't looking at him, the man silent, and Benson thought, damn stupid question. If he was hit, we'd all be hit. He felt the misery, the frozen sogginess in his feet. The slush in the foxhole had turned icy again, but not solid enough, the muddy mess invading his boots. He tried to flex his toes, too stiff, and he cursed, the other two men pulling themselves up, another routine, testing, aching, suffering in their boots.

Benson reached into the dug-out hole in the side wall of the foxhole, felt blindly inside his field pack. "Damn. No more dry socks. You got any?"

Mitchell had stored his pack above the icy slop as well, and Benson could see his movement in the dull shadows, the sound of him rifling through his own pack.

"One pair left. If I could see, maybe there's another one stuffed down in here. I could strike a match—"

"No, don't!" The voice was too loud, panicky, the third man in the hole, Yunis, one of the newer men. "You can't strike a match! The sarge said any light at all—"

"Oh shut up. I don't have any matches to strike. They're all wet. Idiot."

Benson knew Mitchell didn't like the new guy, and when Yunis had been placed into their foxhole, Mitchell had made a grumbling protest. But there was no choice, no one given options on which hole he slept in or who would join him there. Benson didn't particularly dislike Yunis, but the man's voice had a squealing whine that annoyed him, and so he tried to avoid speaking to him at all. It was hard to do in a hole barely long enough for a man to stretch out in, only wide enough for them to lie down close-up side by side. The men who had dug these holes, the veterans of the Second Division, had left them small conveniences that Benson would never have thought of, like the holes punched sideways into the earth halfway up, a makeshift shelf to keep things dry. But nothing was dry now. Each day, the frozen mud thawed just enough to create a deep pool of cold sludge in the bottom of the hole. The sides were soft as well, and Benson understood why the men they had replaced were so dirty. Mud was now a part of everything they did, and at night, when the temperatures dropped, the mud again would turn to ice.

The clothing was adequate during the day, the heavy overcoat offering some protection against the breezy snowfall, which randomly changed from flurries to blinding whiteouts. The foxholes could be covered partially with shelter-halves, sheets of canvas or in some cases plastic, anything the men could scrounge. They were thankful to the Second Division veterans for that as well, the scraps left behind. But inside each foxhole, no matter how well sheltered from the snowfall, there was nothing they could do about the mud. Some men tried starting small fires, gathering small sticks, any sort of kindling, placed on top of some piece of metal, an empty ammo box, a beat-up mess kit, anything that would sit above the mud. The lieutenants didn't seem to care as long as the fires were lit in the daylight. But the efforts were mostly futile, since almost nothing would burn except the wax-coated cardboard of the K-ration boxes, which burned too quickly and spewed out smoke that filled the shelters. Breathing meant uncovering the foxhole, which meant snowfall on the makeshift fire. The results were usually charred cardboard, loud curses, and the hacking cough of men who sucked in too much smoke. The successful fire starters had drawn brief crowds, clusters of men seeking more warmth than the makeshift fires could offer. Though the men kept low, the officers had been right not to be concerned. For the most part, the smoke blew away quickly, the wind-driven snow hiding the precise locations. But Benson remembered the Second Division commander, his words, that this hillside had once been in German hands. If the Germans decided to make real trouble, they didn't need any smoke for their artillery to find its targets.

Benson stuffed his backpack farther into the hole, said, "Keep the socks. I heard the sarge say more were coming up. I'll wait."

"You sure? You know the orders."

"I'll be all right. It'll be light soon, and I'll get up topside and take my boots off."

Yunis had pulled back the sheet of wet canvas, looked upward, said, "No stars again. Nothing at all. Jeez, it'll probably snow again today. How many days is it gonna be like this? There's gotta be some sunshine sooner or later."

"Shut the hell up. Is that all you do? Bitch?"

Benson tried to smile, but Mitchell's cursing had lost its humor. Benson said, "Let it go, Yunis. The weather is gonna clear up when it clears up. Griping about snow isn't gonna make it go away."

"Don't coddle this creep," Mitchell said. "Hell, it's light enough. I gotta go test out the new straddle trench." He grunted, climbed up from the foxhole, too noisy, and Benson wanted to whisper, *Be quiet! Snipers!* But Mitchell was gone quickly, and Benson tested his own gut, nope, not yet. Probably after I eat some more of this . . . whatever it is. Who figures out what we're supposed to have in these K rations anyway? Somebody who never has to eat them.

Beside him, Yunis said, "The snow really helps to see. I been watching those far trees, that ridge over there. The sarge said to keep an eye out on that line, and that narrow gulley to the right. There's brush there, some kind of creek, I think. Could hide the Krauts until they made a move up the hill at us. I heard the lieutenant say there's a road up that way that goes all the way around the hill behind us. The Krauts could show up anytime."

The words came in a nervous babble, and Benson had no patience for it.

"Look, kid. What the hell's your first name, anyway? I forget."

"Arnold . . . Arnie. Arnie Yunis."

"No wonder I can't remember it. Look, the Krauts are sitting low just like we are. The sarge said that we're supposed to sit here and let them know we're on this hillside, so they know they can't just wander up here. It's just the way it works, I guess. They know we're here, we know where they are . . . sorta. We keep an eye on each other and make sure nobody tries anything stupid. The worst thing we have to worry about is some German asshole up on that far hill taking a shot at one of us. Snipers. You get it? So while you're doing all that *watching,* keep your damn head down. Just shut up and relax, okay?"

"Yeah, sorry. I been watching for those snipers. Haven't seen anything over there. But jeez, I don't like the shelling. This whole damn hill shakes when those shells come in. We might get buried alive in this mud hole."

Benson had heard enough.

"I'm going to find the straddle trench." He rapped his stomach with a cold gloved hand. "Maybe something'll happen this morning."

B reakfast is coming up! Stay here and I'll come get you. They're sending trucks, a kitchen. Hot food!"

The voice belonged to Sergeant Higgins, and from across the hill heads popped up, shelter-halves were pulled back, the words echoing through the trees.

"Hot food?"

"Yeah! Breakfast!"

Benson glanced at his backpack, the waxy boxes that held the K rations. Thank God. How much of that stuff can a man eat? He looked out across the hillside, the snow-covered shelters coming alive, revealing their occupants, the thought of hot food putting them into motion. Men began to sit up on the sides of the foxholes, rifles standing up in the snow beside them. Benson looked to the side, a low rise, a thicket of trees, could see one of the machine-gun positions, men stirring around their weapon, their own morning routine. The heavier thirty-calibers were water-cooled, though in this weather no one ever expected that a gun barrel would get hot enough to melt. Benson didn't know enough about the machine guns to understand, but in a hard freeze, there was one problem the gunners had to address, a sight that caused laughter from the riflemen. One of the machine gunners began the routine now, standing upright beside the fat barrel of the gun, his hands maneuvering his pants. Now he began his duty, the stream of urine hitting the gun barrel. The gunners didn't care for the teasing, but it came anyway, the machine guns made ready for firing by a man's pee melting the ice around the barrel. Benson had thought it was yet another one of the army's amazingly stupid rules. If you just fire the gun, won't that melt the water? Maybe it's for show. Those guys just like to impress us by peeing on their guns. He glanced at the M-1. Not you, buddy. You'll work just fine, no matter how cold it is. As long as I keep you clean. He leaned close, mud on the barrel, a crust of brown ice on the clip. Whoops. You need a bath. All right, I'll clean you right now.

There was a steady rumble of sound now, rolling through the trees, the dull roar of motors. More men emerged from the foxholes, began to search the hillside behind them, knew that the ridgeline rolled unevenly away, sank down into small valleys, a narrow stream. But the kitchen trucks would be coming from only one direction, behind them, and some of the men were already ignoring the sergeant's instructions, slipping toward the draw, mess kits in hand. Benson listened to the trucks, thought, no, that's not us. That's . . . over there. Just like before.

He strained to hear, said in a hard whisper, "Hey, fellas! Sarge! It's those trucks again, out there!" He pointed out down the hill and across, to where they knew the Germans were supposed to be. The sounds still came, vague echoes, far in the distance, the noises deadened by the snow cover.

Beside him, the lieutenant was suddenly there, Greeley, another one of those nervous little men, always bent low. He crouched on one knee, pointed along with Benson. "Yep. Same as last night, and yesterday. It's coming behind that far ridgeline, I think. The Krauts have to be moving some equipment up closer, or more troops."

The lieutenant turned away, was gone quickly along the hillside.

Yunis was up out of the foxhole, holding his rifle at the ready, and Mitchell ignored him, watched the lieutenant disappear up over the snowy hill. Mitchell said, "Not sure about him, Eddie. He's a little jumpy."

Benson was focused again on his M-1, pulled an oily rag from his pocket, attacked the dirt.

"Lieutenant Greeley? He'll be okay, I guess. He's as new as the rest of us, but they trained him for this, right?"

Yunis chattered along with him. "Yeah, he's trained. He's a good officer. He'll be good."

Mitchell shrugged, pulled his coat tighter, looked out again at the fading sounds from the far hills. "Krauts are busy, that's for sure. Maybe that's how they keep warm."

Benson examined the gleam on the gun barrel, worked on the rest of the gun, the steps etched in his brain, one part of their earliest training. They all carried a small can of gun oil, an oily rag, and Benson completed the job, felt the clips on his belt, counted, felt the hand grenades on his jacket, more of the drill. He stared out toward the far hill, could still hear the sounds, mechanical rumblings, some farther away, a steady drone, said, "Maybe they're having breakfast, bringing up their own kitchen trucks. I guess a Kraut's gotta eat too."

"You men! Chow!"

No one hesitated, men moving by platoon back through a narrow draw, trudging through the snow like fat dark rats. Benson followed Mitchell, Yunis behind him, the trampled snow leading to the sudden glorious smells. The trucks were down in a hollow, sheltered by thick trees, men already moving away with filled plates, cups of steaming coffee. Mitchell moved faster, and Benson said, "Last in line, again. I guess the lieutenant forgot about us."

"The sarge too," said Yunis. "He was supposed to come tell us."

Sergeant Higgins was already in line, along with most of the platoon. In the distance, through the taller trees, Benson saw more men, another line, more trucks. As he crept forward, he glimpsed the feast, great heaps of pancakes, the mess orderlies stacking them generously onto plates in quick order. There was syrup as well, one man pouring it from a gallon jug, soaking each plate as it passed by. Benson felt the weight of the pancakes on his mess kit plate, held his cup expectantly, headed toward the coffee barrel, the men moving slower, careful, no spilling. Hot coffee was liquid gold, and Benson could smell it, his stomach suddenly aching with hunger. He filled his cup, the steam rising, and he stared at the gooey mountain on his plate, enjoyed the sight, heard some men saying a blessing, offering thanks. It seemed an odd gesture, and Benson looked around him, saw men stuffing pancakes whole into their mouths, not bothering with a fork. Yeah, I guess we should thank somebody for this. He had never been particularly religious as a child, knew that Mitchell's family was far more devout, though you'd never know that from hearing Mitchell swear. He moved back up the hill, away from the trucks, thought, best get back to the foxhole. Eat there. He hurried his steps, careful with the coffee, took a sip, scalding his chapped lips. Okay, this is far enough. He leaned against a tree, set the coffee cup gently on a small stump, scooped up the pancakes with his gloved hand, the wool absorbing the syrup, a sticky soggy mess. The pancakes were barely warm, but it didn't matter, the sweet dough filling him, men around him making odd sounds, all enjoying this strange feast. The plate was empty quickly, and he shoved it down into the snow, rubbed it with his gloves, the snow turning to maple candy in his hands. Hey, there's an idea. He ate some of the snow, bitter, the crunch of mud from the filth in his gloves. Oh well, I'll suck the fingers later. No telling when we'll get *this* again.

He heard a truck, not like the others, clear and distinct, the grinding of gears, a squeal of brakes. It was there now, parked beside the kitchen, men emerging, a sergeant calling out, "Clean laundry!"

Good God, Benson thought. The sarge was right. Socks! The men around him moved that way by pure instinct, no one's socks dry anymore. He saw the lieutenant again, Greeley taking charge of his platoon, other officers coming together, keeping order at the truck. The men were mostly quiet, patient, no one making any kind of ruckus in front of the brass. Benson saw the crates, unloading from the back of the truck, bundles handed out to men in line. He moved with them, a man shoving socks into his gut, no time for words, for thank-yous. He could feel the cold in his feet again, had ignored it long enough. Back to the foxhole, let's get this done.

An officer spoke, and Benson turned, saw the familiar face of the company commander, Captain Moore. Moore waved, said, "Change those socks right *now*. Every one of you! We'll have no trench foot in this outfit, you hear me? No excuse for it. Keep your damn feet dry. I'm already hearing too much bellyaching about this, and I won't have it. The army's got plenty of socks, so use the damn things."

Benson didn't know much about the captain, but there was a hard confidence to the man, and Benson had always thought he seemed like the right kind of officer to command the company. The captain began to talk to other officers, and Benson thought, nothing a private needs to hear. Through the trees, he saw a water truck, moved that way, grabbed at the canteen at his waist, nearly empty. Somebody's gotta keep track of this stuff, he thought. I wonder how they keep that tank from freezing? I guess we could eat snow, but I don't know about that. Tastes pretty nasty. He waited for the line to move, his canteen filled quickly, began to move up the hill again. The captain was still there, talking to an aide, some corporal Benson didn't know. Benson stopped, the question too fresh in his mind. All around him, men were moving back to their positions, cradling their dry socks, and Benson moved closer to Moore, said, "Captain? Sir?"

Moore looked at him, no expression. "What is it, soldier?"

"Sir, we keep hearing trucks, lots of 'em, over that way. Sounds like it could be German convoys, sir. They're moving around a lot."

Moore seemed annoyed, threw a glance over to one side, and Benson saw Greeley, the lieutenant, cringing at his man's impudence. Benson felt suddenly very stupid, and Greeley moved closer to him, the small man snaking through the snow, obviously to shut him up.

Moore said, "It's all right, Lieutenant. Yep, I've heard them too. We called that information back to regimental, and they passed it on to division. After that, I'm not sure if anyone gives a damn. You might as well know what I've heard officially. Stop so many damn rumors. Colonel Cavender has been told that the Germans aren't going anywhere, and what we're hearing is most likely loudspeakers. We've been told they like to do that sort of thing, keep us from getting any sleep, especially at night. They're just trying to scare us. The colonel says as long as we keep our eyes open, nothing's likely to happen. The Germans have nothing better to do than stir up trouble, and I finally persuaded him to let us have a go at doing the same thing. If it'll make you feel any better, Private, I've been ordered to send out some patrols, poke around a little. We'll see if we can find those . . . loudspeakers." Moore looked at Greeley, who seemed to shrivel. "Lieutenant, have you seen Captain Harroway?"

"Who, sir?"

Moore showed the annoyance again. "Harroway, the artillery observer. He's coming up here to set up an observation post as far out front as he can go. He'll need some help, so Company B will put together a patrol, one squad. You'll lead it, Lieutenant. Your job will be to keep the enemy off Harroway's back so he can set up his observation post, and maybe you'll find out what all that racket is over there. You know, those *loudspeakers*. You'll run a phone line up with you, so the observer can connect to his gunners behind us. I'm getting tired of having my coffee spilled on my crotch by that shelling, and we're losing men who haven't done a damn thing but sit on their asses. If Harroway can find at least one of those German artillery batteries, our boys will take them out. They're itching back there for something to shoot at."

Benson saw Greeley's face sag, thought the man was going to cry. Greeley said, "Right now, sir?"

The captain seemed annoyed at the question. "You'll start out at midday. That'll give you enough daylight for the observer to find what he's looking for, and then get your men back here before dark. The enemy's out there too, got his own patrols moving all over hell and gone. He's been real active up in front of the Four Two Two. They've grabbed a few of our boys, so they know it's *us* on this ridgeline now. Probably pissed them off that they let us swap places with the Second Division right under their noses. I'm guessing they'll increase patrols in front of us as well, so keep your men quiet and alert. If you're lucky, you'll pick up a stray prisoner or two. Division wants to keep track of who's over there too." Moore shook his head, said to himself, "Loudspeakers."

Benson thought, he doesn't believe that for a minute. Does sound pretty damn stupid.

Moore continued, "I'll try to find Harroway and send him up your way. Don't play games out there, Lieutenant. I don't want anybody getting lost, and I don't want casualties."

"Certainly not, sir."

Moore moved off, and Benson turned quickly, tried to get away from the lieutenant, but the reedy voice found him.

"Private! Find Sergeant Higgins and tell him I need his squad for the patrol. Since this was all *your* idea, I want to make sure *you're* out there with us."

Benson froze, the order punching him. Yeah, I'll bet you do. Me and my big damn mouth. He turned, a flinch of a salute in his hand, the automatic reflex, Greeley not seeming to notice. Training had taught them that enemy snipers loved to target officers, and Benson knew not to salute the man, not out here. But maybe, he thought . . . just this once. He fought the urge, kept his hand low, said, "Yes, sir. I'll tell Sergeant Higgins."

"And clean your weapon, Private! I'll have no dirty rifles in this platoon! We have orders that the men are to shave and keep themselves clean."

"Shave, sir?" Benson rubbed a hand on the rough wire of his beard.

"Orders, Private. I want this platoon to stand out. The best in the division."

"Certainly, sir. I'll get to it right away."

Benson turned, hugged the rifle hard against his shoulder, moved back up through the draw. If that moron thinks I'm going to tell anybody we have to shave . . . so he can tell all those other idiot lieutenants that his platoon looks spiffier than theirs? And clean up what? The mud? He couldn't help thinking of the training, Indiana, the orders to police the grounds of the drill area. Pick up every cigarette butt, every piece of . . . anything. And Greeley thinks we should do that out here? In six inches of snow? Wonderful, he thought. Truly wonderful. You have to open up your big damn mouth to the captain, and this is how you get paid back. You get to go cross-country Kraut hunting. But first, dress for Sunday school and clean your room.

7. BENSON

Captain Harroway was a small, lean man, sharp eyes, no wasted words. Besides the twelve-man patrol from B Company, the artillery observer had brought his own telephone man, who carried four heavy wooden spools of insulated wire slung across his back. There would be more men accompanying the patrol, another lieutenant, an engineer, who brought his own man as well, a terrified private who carried a metal detector. The private barely spoke, allowed Benson to examine the strange instrument, the private showing it off without pride, more like resignation, as though he would gladly trade it for a rifle. The metal detector had a box at one end, some kind of electronics wired to earphones the man wore beneath his helmet. Opposite the box, connected by a pole the size and length of a broomstick, was a flat disk of metal, what Benson thought looked more like a fancy pie plate than something that could detect mines.

Though Captain Harroway was ranking officer, the patrol would be commanded by Lieutenant Greeley, since escorting Harroway to his observation point would only take them halfway through the mission. The harder job might come afterward, finding a straight line back to the safety of the ridgeline, allowing the telephone man to uncoil his wire, enough presumably to make the connection between the observer and the phone lines on the ridge that led back to the artillery. The patrol included Sergeant Higgins's entire squad from B Company, ten men plus Higgins himself, rifles, and one BAR. Sergeant Higgins had been no happier about forming a patrol than the privates who would follow him. But there was no time for griping. The observer, Harroway, already seemed to know where they were going.

They huddled around him, the engineer standing to one side, as though the briefing by the artillery observer was already too familiar.

Harroway said, "I've been triangulating the incoming artillery as best I can from a fairly high elevation behind us. We have a pretty good idea what hole they're in, just beyond that far ridge. I've seen topo maps, and it's pretty steep up near the road. But down in the woods below that open ground, it flattens out a bit, and that's where we'll start. Once we get in the thicker trees, we'll have to climb, get up to the main road, and cross it without being spotted. The best place for me to see those guns is from above, and I have one hill in mind. Unless the enemy is already dug in there, I should be able to set up a good observation position. I'm certain we have enough wire here to string a phone line back as far as this ridge." He looked at Greeley. "Lieutenant, this is your show. Since you're familiar with this terrain, I'll trust you to lead the way."

Greeley seemed shocked, glanced at the others. "Uh, Captain, we haven't sent out any patrols yet. We've only been here four days, and there hasn't been any enemy activity."

Harroway dropped his head. "I see. Do you know where the minefields are? What the enemy has done to keep us away?"

"Uh, no, sir. Captain Moore had some maps, but we didn't have time to go over them."

Beside Benson, Mitchell made a small grunt, and Benson felt the gloom spreading over all of them. We've had plenty of time to look at a map, he thought. What the hell else has Greeley been doing?

Behind them, the engineer said, "No matter, Captain. The maps are inaccurate anyway. Everything we've been using is off one way or another. Your topo map might be close, but I wouldn't count on it. That's why I'm here. Captain Moore asked me to give you a hand." He looked at Greeley. "If you don't mind, Lieutenant, we'll take the point with the metal detector and make sure we're not walking into any mined areas. And, another thing. You men should avoid walking between closely spaced trees. I don't know about these woods here, but farther up the line, there have been booby traps. The Germans like to make use of the low tree limbs, rig up a trip wire tied across, hooked up to a grenade or high explosive. If you see someplace that looks like it could hide something, you step high and careful, no foot dragging. If there's a trap, you'll have a better chance if you step over it than through it. We have to assume, since the enemy occupied this ground, that when they pulled back, they mined that road. We'll take care of that, Captain, clear a path to get us across. We'll do what we can to get you boys out there safely and bring you back." He scanned the riflemen, his eyes focusing on Benson for a brief second, then Mitchell, the others. "You do your part. Stay quiet, and keep your eyes out front. Look for any movement. We have a pretty good idea where the enemy has dug in, but they could have shifted around. I don't want to wander right into a machine-gun nest."

Harroway nodded, in obvious agreement with the engineer's common sense. Benson waited for something from Greeley, the man who was supposedly in charge. As they began to stir, the men adjusting their ammo belts, a last check of rifles, Greeley looked at Higgins, said, "Sergeant, put men on each flank, and keep them spread out. I suppose . . . I should stay up close to the point. Captain Harroway, will your man string out his wire as we go?"

Harroway's expression didn't change. "No, Lieutenant. We don't know exactly where we're going yet. We don't need to waste wire by wandering all over hell trying to find the right spot. I find a good observation point, it'll be your job to make a beeline back here. My man's done this before, but you'll need to take the shortest route you can. Use your compass."

Greeley nodded furiously. "Compass. Yes, of course." He dug through his jacket pockets, pulled out a small box, studied it. Benson watched Harroway's face, the observer shaking his head, a subtle gesture.

Harroway pointed to the metal detector, said to the engineer, "Lieutenant, that thing working?"

The engineer's private adjusted his headphones, nodded toward the engineer, who said, "We're all set here. Let's go find your hilltop."

B enson was on the left flank, spread out several yards from Mitchell. The others were picking their way through the thinly spaced trees, a formation straight from Greeley's training manual. But this time the training made sense, the men keeping enough distance between them so that any disaster, a mine or artillery shell, or a sudden burst of fire from an enemy position, wouldn't take out the entire squad.

Benson stepped slowly, precisely, his breathing in hard bursts of white, no other sounds but the soft slurping crunch of the snow. He tried to calm himself, focus on his pace, his footsteps, but his heart wouldn't listen, rapid pounding, his eyes straining to see through the tall trees, beyond, searching for anything else, anything that was not a tree. His mind raced as quickly as his heart, and he flinched at flashes of motion, targets flitting in and out of his vision, imaginary shapes, the sounds of the men closest to him magnified, Mitchell's soft footsteps like a drumbeat. Behind him, he could hear faint gasps, knew it was Yunis, the man's peculiar breathing, and the sound rolled over him, high-pitched, Benson's brain exploding with hate for this whining brat of a man. You can't even breathe right. Shut up!

He tried to focus, sweat all through his clothing, wet feet, his fresh socks already absorbing the foot-deep snow. There was pain in his hands, the thin wool gloves wrapped hard on the rifle, too hard, and he loosened his grip, flexed stiff fingers, glanced at the clip, the gun loaded. You didn't forget that. You sure? He thought of the observer, all business, knows his stuff. He's . . . where? Back there somewhere. Keeping an eye on his man with all that damn wire. How much fits on a spool, anyway? He said there's enough. How can he be sure? *Do your jobs.* He glanced to the right, could see glimpses of the engineer out front, and his private, the terrified kid, swinging the metal detector back and forth in a sweeping arc, the round plate close to the snowy ground. Benson wondered just what it was he was listening to, what kind of signal a mine would give the man. How'd you get that job, anyway? Maybe you decided to be an engineer, so the first thing they do is teach you how to be fodder for mines. Trust that stupid-looking broomstick thing. God help him. I hope it works.

Benson stared ahead again, the trees unending, snow blown up in piles against the trunks. To the right a hand went up, Greeley's signal, and Benson froze, silent, straining to hear, to see anything in the trees in front. And then he saw the tracks.

The trees seemed to open for a narrow trail, a trail someone had used to find their way through these woods. There were more tracks now, where men had walked in a spread formation, the snow punched with lines of footprints. The squad was frozen in place, men dropping down, Benson on one knee. He saw Greeley still holding his hand in the air, as though he had forgotten to lower it again. The others were all down low, easing in behind trees. Benson was only a few yards from the first line of footprints, and he eyed a fat pine, on the far side of the trail, crept forward slowly, holding to his hard breaths, trying to keep silent. He paused at the tracks, looked down into the snow, the tread of a boot, perfectly preserved, *fresh*. He felt a surge of panic, dammit dammit, they're out here too. Where? How long ago? The tracks were heading out to his left, beyond the flank of the patrol, and Benson's brain took over, reason through the fear. They're moving away, that way, toward . . . what? Our lines? Maybe we should warn somebody. How? Are we sure they're Krauts? He looked toward Greeley, saw him talking silently to the engineer, the artillery observer joining them, pointing toward the left, in front of Benson. The ground rose up that way, and Benson could see that the tracks followed the contour of the hill, crossing the squad's path at a ninety-degree angle. Greeley stood, looking back toward his men, the engineer already in motion, moving up the hill. On the hillside, the trees were thicker, some of the fat low spruces, and Benson saw Greeley point to him, stopping him, while the rest of the squad moved his way. Benson tried to understand, yes, they're going to swing this way. Hang back, let the point pass me. His brain wouldn't hold the thought, his eyes going down to the boot prints in the snow, perfect, ridges on the soles. Unfamiliar. *German.* The squad moved past him, climbing, and Benson saw Mitchell, the glare, Mitchell staring at him, silent words, a question. *You okay?* Benson responded with a nod, felt calmed by his friend, saw Mitchell gripping the rifle, pointing it out, up the hill, a signal. All right, yes, I know. We have to climb now.

Greeley was still looking back, and Benson saw his face clearly, glistening sweat, wild eyes, turning away now, starting the climb behind the other officers. The man with the metal detector had it up on his shoulder, and Benson tried to understand that, thought, no mines here? It's steep, maybe no place for a minefield. He respected the engineer, the man just as blunt as Harroway, officers who knew their stuff. Why can't *they* be in charge?

Benson was climbing now, hard breaths, felt the uneven footing, saw the tight gaps between the spruce trees, the engineer's words, *booby traps,* picked his way slowly, searched for wire, stupid, the snow too deep, nothing to see. In the narrow passages, he stepped high, saw Mitchell and the others doing the same, thought of a marching band, something from high school, now an odd nightmare, soldiers marching in silence, driven by the beat of their hearts, trying not to die. The trees hid everything now, no open ground, just the slope, sweat soaking him, salt in his eyes. He wiped at one eye with the soggy wool of his glove, useless, blinked furiously, tried to clear his vision. The snow cover was thinning beneath his boots, no more than a couple of inches, much of it trapped by the heavy canopy of the trees above him. He was suddenly hemmed in, a cluster of small young pines, searched for a gap, saw it, shallow snow, *Look for a wire.* He eased up close, stepped high again, his foot coming down softly, a light crunch of snow. Up the hill, he glimpsed a wide swath of small rocks, spread out in both directions, a sloping wall, steeper still. Above the rocks there was nothing, open ground, no trees. It was the road.

He pushed through the saplings carefully, heard a rock tumble to his right, someone climbing. He waited, stared up toward the road, the rocky embankment taller than he was. Others were climbing, more rocks rolling down, hollow sounds echoing through the woods. He took a hard, cold breath, anchored his foot on a flat rock, pushed himself up, had to use one hand, steadying himself, rocks tumbling away under his boots. His boots fought for grip, and he cursed, thought, this has gotta be the junk they built the road with. One boot gave way, slipped, his knee coming down hard on a pointed rock. He cursed, fought the cry, cursed again. His head was at the road level, and he saw the others, all kneeling on the edge of the road, no one moving. He was up with them now, rubbed the pain in his knee, watched as the entire squad gradually emerged up from the thick trees. The officers motioned silently, keeping them down low, everyone holding to the near side of the road. The edge of the road offered no cover, and Benson slid one foot back, feeling where the ground fell away, thought, anybody shoots, I'm going right back down there. The road was several yards wide, and he stared nervously to his left, to the flank, *his* flank, saw that the road stretched on for a hundred yards, then curved away to the right, hugging the hillside. He realized now, there were no tracks in the road. He tried to think, what's that mean? No one's been here. Not us . . . not them. Snow . . . six inches maybe. How long? Hell I don't know. But we're in the wide damn open right here. He looked toward the officers, more talk among them, the road curving away in that direction as well. The artillery observer was animated, pointing up across the road, and Benson understood, yep, let's get off this damn road and up that hill. The man with the metal detector stood, adjusted his earphones, began working again. He was moving slowly across the road, and Benson watched the sweep of the pie plate, left and right, the man focused, precise, listening for what? The private reached the far side of the road, and the engineer was close behind him, waved to the men spread out along the side of the road, motioning them closer. Of course, Benson thought. Cross at *that* place. The safe place. Thank God for metal detectors. He saw Greeley move across, tiptoes, like some idiot bird picking his steps. The others followed, two riflemen first, the engineer, more of the squad, and the man with the coils of wire. They began to climb up off the road, slipping quickly into the trees above, and Benson waited his turn, then followed close behind Mitchell, Yunis behind him, the man's grating gasps even louder. Benson ignored him, happy to be off the road, felt the trees around him wrapping him, comforting, a blanket of cover. The formation took shape again, Benson sliding out to the left, and he saw the observer, Harroway, moving up to the lead, low whispers to Greeley, then to the engineer, and now the observer took the point. Good, Benson thought. We gotta be close to something. That guy knows his stuff.

They climbed with slow rhythm, silence all around them, the trees thinning out, tall again, but there were still the clusters of the fat spruces, and Benson stared at them, glanced at Mitchell, thought, yep, those would be damn good places to hide. He scanned for tracks, nothing large enough to be human, saw smaller trails, thought, a rabbit maybe, or a fox, God knows what else. He moved past a fat spruce, snow on the branches, tried to see through to the open area underneath. He poked the rifle in, finger on the trigger, moved a limb, heard a harsh whisper, Higgins, startling him, the sergeant moving quickly, closing on him from behind.

"Get your ass up this hill! You trying to get blown to hell? You souvenir hunting? Move!"

Benson obeyed, heat on his neck, felt supremely stupid. Mitchell was looking at him, a smile, shaking his head. Benson avoided Mitchell's ridicule, thought, yeah, okay, I'm an idiot. But there might have been a Kraut in there. And, sure, he'd have waited for me to poke my rifle up his nose. Up ahead, the trees thinned, and off to his left Benson could see a white field, trees in the distance, the hillside falling away. The men at the point stopped again, the hand signal, down, and Benson knelt in the snow, tried to ignore the soaking wetness. But he couldn't ignore his feet, the growing misery inside his boots. He had a spare pair of socks in his jacket, but there was no time, and he glanced around, tried to see what the officers were looking at, heard whispering again, thought, they're having another meeting. Officers are good at that. Now one man moved away, low to the ground, quick darting movements, Harroway, and Benson watched him, his own weariness giving way to something new, urgency. After a short minute Harroway returned, a hand signal, pointing at two of the riflemen, waving them forward. Harroway dropped to his knees again, crawled, the others doing the same, the three men disappearing upward through the trees. Benson could only wait, curious, Mitchell glancing at him, a shrug. In short minutes the three men returned, relief on their faces, one of them, Lane, the bully, obviously shaking. Harroway moved close to Greeley and the engineer, a quiet explanation, Greeley glancing around at his men, nervous. Benson thought of moving closer, no, stay here. They want you to know, they'll tell you. Gotta be Krauts, though. What else could it be? He strained to see up the hill, past the trees, nothing, just the snow, low limbs, stumps. *Stumps.* He felt a jolt in his chest. Someone cut some trees down. Why? To see? To see *us*? He pulled himself lower, the rifle ready, his breathing sharp. Where the hell are they? Now Harroway signaled back down the hill, and the man with the wire responded quickly, silently, Harroway motioning to him, *Up.* Harroway led the way, the wire man following, the two retracing the tracks up the hill. Benson's heart was still thundering, and he watched them as far as he could see them. Greeley was slipping slowly back, moving toward each of the men, the men responding to his words by flattening down, low in the snow. Now Greeley pointed to him, waved him forward, Mitchell as well, more men moving up from that side of the formation.

When they were close, Greeley whispered, barely audible, pointing up beyond the crest. "Krauts were dug in all over this hill, but they're gone, at least for now. The captain says he thinks they pulled back, but there's no way to know. But he's got his observation post, and he's setting up. He wants us to stay back, not do anything to draw attention, but I think we need to get out around him, keep an eye out."

Higgins was there now, the sergeant puffing hard. "No, sir. He said stay here. The Krauts are here somewhere. We've got to be damn close to their lines, and there have to be more of them patrolling out here, especially on a hill this size. We should listen to the captain and stay put. He's done this before. We . . . haven't, sir."

Greeley seemed confused, his good idea shot to pieces.

"Then we should get out of here. We're just sitting ducks right here."

Benson saw the engineer moving toward them, realized now that the man had slipped away, was returning from the edge of the hill.

The engineer leaned in close to Greeley, said, "Lieutenant, the enemy is all over that ridgeline across this valley. No more than three hundred yards. Keep your men low, but we can't pull back until the observation point is set up. That's why we're out here. I suggest you crawl up there with no more than two men, rifles, just in case some Kraut wanders by. We can't waste too much daylight before the Krauts swarm all over this hill. There are tracks all over the place on the far side."

Greeley nodded, seemed lost in thought, uncertainty. "All right." He nodded toward Mitchell and Benson. "You two. Keep quiet! Follow me!"

Greeley crawled away, and Mitchell followed, Benson close behind, Mitchell's boots kicking snow in his face. They moved up, winding past the thicker trees. In front of him, Greeley stopped, flattened out, and Benson saw his chest heaving, the man's fear contagious. Greeley looked back toward them, said nothing, pointed with a single finger to the right. It was a foxhole. Benson moved the rifle, but Mitchell was crawling again, and Benson heard the observer's words in his mind. *They pulled out.* No one home. There were more holes, a ragged line stretching away along the side of the hill, some partially covered with tree limbs, the snow barely disguising them. Benson stared at the closest dugout, wanted to see to the bottom, to make sure, but Mitchell was moving away behind Greeley, farther up the hill. Benson tried to control his breathing, put his face down, close to the snow, calming himself. He started to crawl again, more foxholes, one large dugout, logs on top, but there were no tracks in the snow, no one had been here since how long, he thought. A full day for sure. Greeley stopped now, Mitchell moving up beside him, and Benson could see Harroway working in a stand of small saplings, a small shovel piling snow up in a mound. The wire man was working as well, the wooden wheels lying in the snow, a small box emerging from the man's backpack. Mitchell grabbed Benson, startling him, tugging hard at his shirt, pointing out with one finger. Greeley was staring that way, and Benson saw the hillside falling away in a sharp drop, another hill beyond, bare hilltop, coated with fallen trees, but it was not random. The trees were crisscrossed, a makeshift wall, good protection, and Benson could see flickers of movement, men slipping in and out of their cover. Greeley whispered something, and Benson followed his stare, downward, could see the trails in the hillside, many tracks, and down between them a narrow pass, thickets of timber. But there were stumps and cut trees there as well, openings, and Benson saw more men, small dark shapes.

He eased up close to Mitchell, who said, "Krauts! Lots of 'em!"

Benson gripped the rifle hard, felt a bolt of terror, saw Mitchell slide his rifle forward in the snow as though to aim. A voice shouted in Benson's head, no, that's stupid! What the hell? But Benson couldn't help himself, did the same, sighted the rifle at the movement far down the hill. There was no stiffness in his fingers now, no stinging pain from the wet gloves. He tried to see through the rifle's iron sights, but he was shaking, and he fought to keep his eyes clear of sweat, but it was futile. *What do we do now?* He scanned the valley, guessed the distance, yeah, could be three hundred yards, maybe less. They don't see us . . . so, do we attack them? That's idiotic. Captain Moore said find a prisoner. Well, there they are. Hell if I'm going down there to grab one. Not even Greeley is stupid enough to try that.

The valley wound away around the hillside, beyond their view, and Benson searched the openings in the brush, crevasses in the rock, the men there moving idly, oblivious, going about their day.

Beside him, Mitchell said, "There! That black brush! A big gun!"

Benson focused on a blotch of black, men moving out from underneath. It's not brush at all, he thought. It's camouflage! He stared for a long moment, saw another just like it, a few dozen yards to one side, the stick of a protruding barrel just visible. His teeth were chattering, the fear rising, the rifle small, useless, thought, this is more than stupid!

There was a hand on his arm, the face calm, a slight smile. It was the wire man. "Uh, you all can get on outta here now. We're done."

Greeley slid backward, said, "Back up, you jackasses. We're not here to sightsee. The job's done. Let's go!"

Benson hesitated, watched the Germans across the way, and below, the gun crews doing their work. Mitchell was tugging at his pant leg, hard, the message clear, and Benson slid himself backward in the snow, past the observer. Harroway was already dug in, disguised by the saplings, snow piled up to look natural, just one more snowdrift. The wire man moved up close to Harroway, hoisted three wheels of the phone cable onto his back, the fourth held low. He said something to Harroway, a nod between them, and Harroway made a short wave to Greeley, a silent *thank you*, then seemed to disappear into his burrow, already doing his job.

The engineer was using the trees as cover, and Benson thought about taking his place on the flank, but Greeley had given no orders, the squad ambling downhill. Benson watched the engineer, curious, the man's efficient carefulness, thought, why? They can't see us. But there was urgency to the way the engineer was moving, and Benson felt a stab of fear, looked out across the hilltop, the other ridgelines. He was shivering, raw excitement, could still see the Germans in his mind, stupid morons, completely unaware we're up here, what we're doing! He wanted to laugh, felt giddy from the adventure of it, still shivering, moving downhill with more speed, the others as well, saw now that the engineer had stopped, was watching them come, his back against a tree, his hands up, motioning them to stay low.

The crack split the bark of a tree near Benson's head, more cracks, Benson jolted by the sound. Men were dropping flat close to the trees, huddled low.

The engineer was back up, crawling among them, hard whispers. "Don't shoot! Don't shoot! Can't draw any more fire. Keep moving! Get back down to the road! Go!"

Benson didn't understand, saw some of the faces, Yunis, Lane, the others, still huddled at the trees.

The engineer said it again, louder now. "You want mortars to find you? Go! Get out of here!" He began to run, darting from tree to tree, making his way quickly downhill, still waving the men after him.

Benson thought of Greeley, didn't know where he was, the man supposed to be in charge. He searched for the engineer, the man's confidence, felt loyalty to him, the man who seemed to understand everything. Benson was up now, moving quickly, staying close to the trees, mimicking the engineer, pausing at the edge of the open spaces, then quick darts across. There was a new sound, machine-gun fire, but it was far away, no accuracy, the snow popping, trees chattering with the impacts. Benson kept running, could see the engineer again, the man dropping low, behind the cover of a thick pine, waiting for them, waving still, pulling the men off the hill. The engineer held up his hands, gathering the men, and gradually they came together, panting, terrified. The engineer pressed his palms downward, said in a harsh whisper, "Low! Keep down! We're okay! No line of sight now. Too many trees. They can't see us!"

Benson focused on a spruce tree, thought of the tentlike cover, but the shooting had stopped, and Sergeant Higgins was there, close beside him, said, "That was coming from pretty far away. I don't think they hit anybody."

The engineer stared up the hill, the last of the men coming down.

Benson saw Greeley, frightened eyes, a wild animal, falling to his knees, scampering into cover. The engineer crawled up close to him, said, "Take command, Lieutenant! That was sloppy as hell! The Krauts could be anywhere, and you have to keep your men on guard, keep them down. We were standing out like fat pigs up there! Some Kraut must have spotted us from one of those hills across the way, probably that one to the east. I can guarantee you they were about to drop some mortar shells on us, and they still might."

Greeley seemed to fight for control. "What about Captain Harroway? He's alone up there!"

"Harroway knows how to cover himself up. That's his job. You could walk right by him and never know he's there. The enemy probably thinks we're just a patrol, poking our asses around. The way we blew off that hill, they're probably laughing themselves sick, watching how they scared us away. Our problem now is to get out of here before any Kraut patrols decide to come out here to find us. Where's the wire man?"

Greeley was still frantic, said, "I don't know! Was he hit?"

Benson looked back up the hill, saw a man slipping through a cluster of brush, slow, steady steps. Mitchell said, "I'll be damned. There he is."

The man unspooled his wire as he came toward them, calmly doing his job. He reached the thickets, glanced down through the timber.

The engineer said, "You all right, soldier?"

"Fine, sir. Sorry to lag behind, but Captain Harroway would have my butt if I didn't get this here wire strung. Can't leave the captain up there without a telephone. Wouldn't be much point to that."

The words flowed out in a slow southern drawl, and Benson was amazed at the man's serenity.

Mitchell said, "You've done this before then?"

"Oh sure. Buncha times. The captain gets mighty upset if his phone don't work. We kinda take pride in mashing those enemy guns. Pardon me for saying so, sirs, but we need to keep this wire up here, offa that road. It's mostly paved, or else frozen rock-hard, and we probably can't cut across it to bury the wire. Tank treads aren't helpful to phone wire, and the captain gives me hell aplenty as it is."

Benson was enjoying the man's matter-of-factness, but the engineer seemed to find no humor, was staring out toward the far hills.

"You're right. We'll stay up in these trees and head west, until the ridgeline ends. We'll probably be able to drop down, then climb right back to our own position over that way. You have enough wire?"

"Oh, sure, sir. But when each one of these here spools run out, I gotta stop and tie it up to the next one. Make a good connection 'tween the two. Got my tools right here."

The engineer seemed satisfied, looked at Greeley now, and Benson saw the change in the engineer's expression, a hint of disgust. "You ready to lead your men back home, Lieutenant?"

Greeley had gained control, seemed embarrassed. He looked at the others, made a cursory head count, said to Higgins, "Everyone accounted for, Sergeant?"

"Yes, sir."

"Okay, good. Let's keep to these trees, and stay low. I guess we ought to hustle it up. Not much daylight left. Sergeant, you take the point."

The engineer said, "Lieutenant, if you don't mind, I'll take the point with my man. We run into some open ground, or a trail, we'll want to sweep it for mines. I'd keep your men in formation, just like before. We already know the enemy is in these woods, and our mission's complete. We don't need to bump into anyone, especially in the dark."

"Oh yes, of course. Fine. You're up front then. I'll stay back, keep anybody from straggling, make sure the wire gets laid all right."

The men were rising up now, and Mitchell moved past Benson, gave him a glance, a look Benson knew. Yep, I guess the lieutenant's decided he's more valuable in the rear. Hard to argue with that.

They wound their way back through the thicket of trees, and Benson stayed closest to the road, the left flank, kept one nervous eye on the road below him, the wide flat ribbon that followed the hillside. There were still no tracks on the road, no sign that anyone had used it at all, virgin snow. Thank God for that.

Out front the engineer led the way, the metal detector unused now, nothing on this hillside that seemed to concern the man. Below them, the road seemed to rise up, the hillside changing, growing shallow, and Benson saw a hand signal from the engineer, calling the men together. Benson moved close, the others gathering, Greeley there as well, and the man with the wire. Benson saw only one spool now, thought of the man's drawl. So, he made his connection with the wire. I guess he works faster than he talks. Good thing.

The engineer focused on Higgins, seemed to ignore the lieutenant, said, "Sergeant, we're pretty close to our own position. There's open ground up ahead, pretty flat. Hold your men back in the cover, give us a chance to sweep a path. I've seen this place before. We're a little north of your company's position, and the open ground is like a bowl. Our boys are on the far side, dug into the tree line. Up ahead, the main road has a feeder trail coming off this hill to our right. It's just a narrow woods road that goes somewhere out to the north. We have to cross that, so we'd better dig a furrow for the wire." He looked at the wire man. "Can't be helped. You understand that?"

"Sure do, sir. If it ain't paved, no sweat. Done it before. If some of these boys'll cut me a V shape, I'll lay the wire across and slap some flat rocks over it. Oughta work. Snow'll cover the whole shebang right up."

"Good. Give my man a couple minutes to check for mines, clear us a path."

Sergeant Higgins seemed to accept the authority the engineer assigned to him.

"Sir, we'll hold where you tell us, and you wave when you're ready." Higgins looked at Greeley, who seemed to take it all in without comment. Benson watched the lieutenant's face, expected something, outrage, embarrassment. But Greeley just nodded along with the others.

The engineer rose, his man with the metal detector moving with him. The squad followed, Benson closest to the main road, saw the open ground out front, a wide blanket of snow, a ridge farther on, thick with trees. He saw the intersection on the main road, the smaller trail cutting off across the field, just as the engineer had described, barely visible. The hand signal came, *Stop*, and the squad sat low, all of them watching as the metal detector began its sweep. Benson huddled low, felt uneasy, didn't like the open ground, maybe thirty yards just to reach the trail. He glanced toward Mitchell, who was cleaning snow from his rifle. They watched the engineer, who stayed close to his man, guiding, pointing, the man with the earphones doing his work, the wide sweeps back and forth. They reached the narrow roadway, seemed to slow, concentrate on the trail itself, and then they were across, more sweeps. The engineer pulled his man down low, knelt beside him, turned and waved at the squad. Benson let out a low breath, relief, the squad filing out into the field, single-file, following the footsteps in the snow. Greeley pushed his way to the front, taking charge once more, and no one spoke, Higgins falling back, waiting as the others passed, Benson looking at him, the sergeant with no expression, doing his job again, bringing up the rear. The wire man was there, doing his as well, the last coil half empty, and Benson looked up to the ridgeline in front of them, thought, can't go much beyond that. He'll run out of wire. Then what?

They had reached the trail, and Benson could see it was a narrow two-rut road, barely visible in the snow, no tire tracks. Nope, no one's been on that one either . . .

The blast erupted in front of him, men knocked back, falling. Benson was shoved down hard, rocks and dirt showering him. There was a sharp scream, more, a hard cry, men yelling. Benson struggled to pull himself up, rolled over, tried to see, snow in his face, his heart shattering his chest. Some of the men were pulling themselves up, some with rifles raised, wild eyes, frantic, moving quickly but there was nowhere to go.

Benson heard a shout, from beyond the narrow road, the engineer. "Halt! Stop! Stay put!"

The blast still echoed through the hills, hard ringing in Benson's ears, and he wiped at the mud in his eyes. The narrow road was a churned-up mess of black smoking dirt, a man's body, another, pieces. He felt sick, stared, couldn't look away, saw the engineer stepping quickly toward the road, careful, the man watching his own footsteps.

The cries came again, one of the bodies in motion, rolling over in the road, out of control, screaming, the engineer falling on top of him, calling out to the others. "Stay in their footprints! There are mines here!"

The men obeyed, the horror freezing them all so they understood, each man stepping only where the man in front of him had been. Benson looked across, saw the man with the metal detector sitting in the snow, horror on his dirty face.

The questions came now, Mitchell, close to the engineer. "What the hell happened? That thing busted? You killed them!"

"Back off, soldier!"

Benson saw Higgins moving forward quickly, ignoring the footsteps, grabbing Mitchell's shoulder. Higgins knelt beside the bodies, said, "Oh God. It's the lieutenant . . . and who . . . oh mother. It's Brubaker."

The engineer raised himself off the shattered mess that was Greeley's body, said, "He lived for a minute. But too much blood. Took his guts . . ."

The engineer backed away, sat in the snow, his head in his hands.

"I killed them both. Son of a bitch. I killed them both."

Higgins took up Mitchell's anger now, said, "How? That damn machine . . ."

"The metal detector . . . the Germans have been using a new mine, almost no metal, wrapped in some kind of wax. I hadn't heard any reports that there were any out here. I didn't think . . . the trail is old . . . oh hell. God help them. I should have known. I killed these men . . ."

Higgins responded, "What the hell could you have done different, sir? You got a *wax* detector? We gotta get our asses out of this open ground. It's getting dark, and we got no time for bellyaching. If that's our ridge, somebody's watching us."

Benson moved in the footsteps, closer to the bodies, saw blood and blackness, dirt and the stink of explosives. Greeley's face was twisted into some kind of grotesque smile, a wide gash splitting his torso, blood flowing through the melted snow around him. The other man, Brubaker, had lost a leg, the leg itself a burnt stump lying to one side, more blood, too much. Benson felt the sickness coming, spun to the side, dropped to both knees and vomited in the snow. It was contagious, two others doing the same, and he felt Mitchell's hand, the words, "It's okay, Eddie. Nothing we coulda done."

The engineer seemed to take control of himself, said, "We can't move them, not yet. Have to check the area by hand."

He knelt, the man with the metal detector doing the same, the rehearsed training, sliding their arms into the snow, close to the narrow road.

Higgins said, "There's no time for that, sir. We've got to get up to those trees. Some Kraut patrol could be following us, and they had to hear the blast. We're dead out here!"

Benson heard voices, up ahead, in the trees.

"Hey! What happened?"

The uniforms were their own, breathless relief, and Higgins shouted, "Two casualties! There are mines out here! Stay back!"

The men kept coming, a dozen, stepping carelessly through the snow, closer now, one man moving out quickly, an officer.

"We cleared off this field a while back with a flail tank. Must have missed some on the road. Dammit to hell. This field's okay, though."

Benson didn't know the officer, saw dull white captain's bars on his helmet. The captain looked at the engineer now, said, "I know you, Lieutenant. Galen, right?"

"Yes, sir. These men are from Company B, of the Four Two Three."

"Yeah, I know. Captain Moore told me about the mission. You get the observer in place?"

The engineer nodded slowly, and Sergeant Higgins said, "Yes, sir. His wire man is here."

The wire man held up his spool. "Right here, sir. All I need is a wire to hook 'er up to."

The captain called back to his men, who seemed reluctant to get any closer. "Bring two litters up here. There're no wounded, so leave the medics in their holes." He looked again at Higgins, said, "Who's in command here, Sergeant?"

"I suppose . . . I am, sir. That body there is our platoon leader, Lieutenant Greeley."

The engineer pulled himself upright, tried to show composure, said, "Captain, he's correct. I was only accompanying the patrol. My job was to . . . prevent this from happening."

The captain showed no emotion, and Benson saw him glance at the two bodies, shake his head. He put a hand on the engineer's shoulder. "Get hold of yourself, Lieutenant. Sergeant, take your men up into that tree line. Captain Moore's OP is to the left, about a quarter mile down the line, back in a thicket. Somebody'll guide you if you need. Report to him, tell him what happened." The captain moved toward the wire man, looked at the spool. "I'll be damned. Just enough. That crazy Harroway knows how far he can push. All right, soldier, you follow me. I'll hook you up at the communications tent."

"Thank you mightily, sir. The captain'll be pleased to know we ain't forgot him."

The captain moved away, the wire man following, unrolling the spool as he went. Benson was still on the near side of the blasted road, saw Mitchell moving across, between the bodies, stepping through black mud. Well, I guess that's safe. He followed, tried not to look down, the smell overpowering, death and explosives. The rest of the squad came across, some of the men staring away, looking up into the tree line, to safety, some glancing back at the gutted lieutenant, the other man's severed leg, the boot still attached.

Higgins said, "Benson, you and Yunis stay here. Stay with . . . them, until the litter bearers get here. There are animals in these woods. We're not just leaving them out here."

"Okay, Sarge."

Benson looked for Yunis, saw him still out across the road, hunched over, looking sick. The sergeant moved away, led the others up toward the tree line, slow slogging footsteps, each man behind the next, no one with much faith in the captain's reassurance. Benson looked for a place to sit, kicked at the soft snow, cleared an open swath, thick grass and mud. He realized it was snowing again, the sky just as dense and gray as it had been every day they had been there. He ignored Yunis, didn't care if the squirrelly man was sick or not, tried not to stare at the remains in the churned-up road. He didn't know much about Brubaker, would never know now. Brubaker had been one of the new men, maybe friends with the bully, Lane. Lane had been silent throughout the entire mission, and Benson didn't look for him now, didn't care which one of the parade of black shapes he was, the squad disappearing into the trees. He could feel wetness in the seat of his pants, tried to ignore it, his legs too tired to keep him standing. The rifle was upright between his knees, and he felt a light breeze, the snow hitting his face. There was already a light coating on the gash of open ground, the wound in the earth where the two men had died. He looked toward Yunis, sitting as well, the two men staring at each other from across the deadly roadway. Benson thought of the lieutenant, Greeley, not Greeley at all anymore, not a man, just a body . . . meat. He felt sick again, looked away, let it pass, thought, the lieutenant wasn't much of a soldier, no hero, no friend to his men, no leader at all. Doesn't much matter now. He'll probably get a medal, that damn engineer putting him in for it, because he feels guilty for killing him. Hell, he didn't kill him. Mines with no metal. Who'd a guessed that? I guess the engineer should have thought of it. What kind of crazy stupid place is this? He thought of some joke, the usual black humor that swept through the early days of training. Join the army and learn a skill. Find a better way, a smarter way to kill someone. I guess, today, the Krauts won. Their engineer was better than ours. Somewhere out there, some Kraut general is patting that guy on the back for his *good idea*.

It was full dark now, and he looked back toward the trees, wondering, where the hell are those litter bearers? The snow was blanketing the dead men, black stains where the last warmth still rose, a low cloud of steam drifting up from the great rip in the lieutenant's body. The temperature was dropping quickly, and he pulled his coat tighter around him, the wetness all through his pants and his boots, a pair of clean socks still in his pocket. That's the first thing I gotta do, he thought. Well, maybe the second thing. I gotta eat something. I'm hungry as hell.

He heard a familiar rumble coming from the east, far out beyond the hills they had hiked. It was faint at first; then there were singular sounds, steel wheels, the echoes drifting across the bowl of open ground. He stared that way, the noise flowing in from different directions. They're early tonight, he thought. Wonder if it really is loudspeakers, just to scare us? Why would they do that? Some idiot general thinks they're gonna chase us away just because they're showing off that they have tanks? We have tanks too, you know. So, they're over there busy as hell, moving men around. So are we. You need to fake that? Captain Moore doesn't believe it, that's for sure. Wonder what it sounds like out there on that hill, to Captain Harroway? He's right on top of those Krauts in that one valley. Maybe he sees something. Benson thought of the wire man, the private with the deep drawl. Good man, that one. Knows his job. Gotta be from Mississippi or Alabama, someplace like that. Wonder what Harroway's first phone call will be? Once he's hooked up, I guess he'll tell his artillery boys what to do, and we'll start some shelling of our own. God, I'd love to see that, be up there on that hilltop when our guns bust up those Krauts. Hell of a responsibility. I wonder if he can tell where those loudspeakers are, bust those up too. Benson looked out toward the far ridges, too dark to see, the sounds of machines rolling all across the hills and roads to the east. Maybe Captain Moore's right, because if those are loudspeakers, there's gotta be a boatload of them.

8. HARROWAY

After the squad had left him alone, he had sat consumed by the agony of impatience. It was always like that, and Harroway was not one to stare at treetops and pass the time in idle dreaming. It was the worst part of his job, nothing to do but wait for the squad to find its way back home. If they didn't make it, the only way he would know might be the sounds of an ambush or a firefight, sometimes by accident, two patrols stumbling into each other, neither side knowing just what to do. The firing might last until one entire patrol was killed or captured, or until dark, when someone in charge found the guts to lead his men out of the woods, someone confident enough to find his way to his own lines. If there was no sound of a fight, the only other sign of trouble would be a dead telephone, and he might never find out just what had gone wrong.

In these hills, with such poor visibility, the patrols were amazingly dangerous. The Germans knew that as well, but it was their own ground, and they had seemed eager to send out far more patrols than the Americans. Harroway knew that some men from the 106th had already been captured, and so the enemy would know just who it was that held these ridges to the west, would know that the troop movements had been made right under their noses, a fresh division to replace the battle-weary Second

Division. The Germans had increased patrols day and night, but it was the night patrols that were worse for the Americans, mainly because the 106th had never faced the enemy at all, much less in the dark. Often there was no firing at all, the Germans adept at slipping through the lines of foxholes, or sitting low in the timber, a silent ambush that would pick off a man too careless to pay attention to where the trail to the straddle trench was. In the short time the 106th had been in position, all three of the infantry regiments had crawled out to meet the snowy dawn, only to discover footprints in the timber close by, just beyond the booby traps and noisemakers. The Germans seem to know just how close they could come, and too often the Americans had no idea they had come at all. The men who had been on guard duty had endured the inevitable wrath of frightened lieutenants, but it was not always the guards' fault. The Germans knew these woods too well and were very good at night patrols. Worse, for the Americans who had been ordered to patrol in what they thought to be the relative safety of daytime, there was a miserable discovery. The Germans had snowsuits, white coveralls that allowed them to hide virtually undetected even as the Americans moved right past them. There was terror enough for the men on these patrols without being ambushed from behind.

He had been annoyed with the inexperienced Lieutenant Greeley, who didn't seem to understand that he shouldn't haul his entire squad to the crest of the hill. The trees up high were more widely spaced than the thickets in the deeper draws, and anyone who was paying attention could spot movement against the blanket of white on the hillside. We stand out in these woods like preachers in a whorehouse, but I didn't have time to give that lieutenant a tactics lesson. Not all his fault, though. You'd figure someone would have thought of winter camouflage gear. One thing for certain, whoever designed these coats might have been thinking *warm,* but they sure as hell weren't thinking *snow.* Snow is white, you know. Does somebody at supply not understand that? That's because those people don't ever get shot at. Try it sometime, General.

Harroway had done his own job preparing his observation dugout as quickly as it could be done, relying on his own experience, and his wire man, to make sure nothing went wrong. The short one-sided battle didn't seem to have caused much trouble for the squad, no screams, thank God. By the time the shooting had stopped, the Germans seemed to be aiming far below and behind him. But once he was completely alone, Harroway had another reason for vigilance. It was observer's paranoia, wondering always if some German was hidden somewhere close by, watching the whole operation. A smart one would sit tight and allow the patrol to leave, then slip up on the observer and kill him in his hole. No one back at the command post would have any idea why the man was never heard from again. There was just enough of a crunch to the snow to allow him to hear someone close, and in that first hour he kept his carbine upright in his hands, nervously ready. The carbines were smaller and lighter than the M-1, and mostly despised by the field officers who carried them. They were notoriously unreliable and inaccurate beyond short range. But the spotters knew that any enemy soldier they might confront would almost certainly be right on top of them. It was all about defense, about the spotter being spotted himself. Harroway had no interest in trying out his marksmanship on some distant infantryman, and no need to reveal himself in his lonely observation post by attempting a firefight. Like most of the observers, he carried a .45 in his belt. In close quarters, it was a much more reliable way to get out of a jam.

As it grew dark, the phone had not yet begun to function, and so Harroway had nothing to do but scan the maps and, if possible, take a nap. His dugout was just deep enough beneath the soft dirt and snow cover to keep him hidden completely, the saplings he had cut a natural protective roof. He had slid down into as much comfort as he could make, had learned long ago what many of the artillery spotters knew, dig a curved hole to rest your back.

They had tried using wireless radios, but their range was far too short, and the rugged hills and timber country here made that even worse. Harroway had confidence in his wire man, the slow-talking boy from Mississippi. The young man seemed to be able to do his job no matter what kind of trouble the patrol might encounter. Harroway had even offered to help carry the spools of wire, but the young man had an impressively strong back, never seemed to lag behind from the weight of so much wire. Even in combat conditions or the worst terrain imaginable, if it was possible to spool out that wire, the young man with the soft drawl would find a way.

He had tried to sleep, but the silence from the telephone kept him awake. It was a little unusual to have an entire German battery spread out right under your nose, and Harroway knew that once communications was established with the American artillery, it would take very little time to zero in on this wonderful target. The map he carried had been reasonably accurate, a surprise, gridlines showing the valley below him almost precisely where it actually was. All he had needed was someone *back there* he could tell about it.

Harroway had waited a full hour before trying the phone, still listening intently for any sounds of a fight behind him, anything that would cause a delay for the patrol itself or, worse, its destruction. The only sound had been a strange thump, far behind, and he had wondered if it was sound bouncing off the hillsides, probably the echo from a distant mortar round. He had hoped to have the phone operational before dark, but with the sky dead and gray, there was little chance of that. When the snow began to fall, he could only pull his blanket of branches over his head and wait, happy that the snow might cover the patrol's tracks and make his own camouflage that much better. When the hour finally passed, he began testing the phone, anxious, knowing that his wire man might be bogged down somewhere, or still trying to find someone who could hook him up in a communications post. And then, with dull darkness spread over the Germans beneath him, the phone had suddenly come alive.

The first shell had come down far to the right, at the mouth of the valley, and he had called in that adjustment, the second shell dead straight but too long, smacking against the distant ridge, fifty yards above the valley floor. Again, he gave the artilleryman the adjustment, and now he clamped the telephone receiver hard to his ear, waited for the response. The voice came, choppy and erratic, but it was exactly the voice he wanted to hear.

"Roger that, Hawk One."

He waited for the next shell, braced himself for the sound, counted the seconds, *eleven . . . twelve . . .* and now it came, arcing over, the impact thumping into the hillside below him, igniting in a flash of fire. But the impact was too short, the shell exploding up the hill, in his direction. Dammit! They're overcorrecting.

"Big Boy, this is Hawk One. One hundred fifty too short. Try again!"

"Roger, Hawk One."

Harroway took a long breath, counted again, and the shell came over more quickly this time. Now the valley floor erupted, the shell from the 105 coming down precisely on target. He wanted to cheer, knew better, fought the excitement, knew not to shout anything into the fragile phone connection. He rose slightly, heard noises from down below, thought, casualties certainly, medics running around. They don't know what's about to happen. They think we're just dinking around, random, and we got one lucky one. He stared down into the fiery darkness, thought of the Germans still hidden in their holes, the new men scared, the veterans calming them down with their arrogant weariness. Sorry, boys. But there's nothing random about this. I've got your position dead center. He clamped the telephone to his ear again, leaned down, facing the bottom of his dugout.

"Hawk One. Strike. Repeat. Strike. Cut them loose, Big Boy."

"Roger, Hawk One."

Harroway put the phone away, leaned back in the dugout, knew what was coming. He held his breath, perfect silence, the old habit, counting in his mind, *nine . . . ten . . .* and now the air above him was torn apart with streaks of light, a roar of sounds, the valley bursting into fire, bright flashes he closed his eyes to avoid. After a short pause, more rounds came, and he pictured it in his mind, the gunners working with gleeful precision, loading the 105s, heavy shells rammed into the breach of the four guns. No wait, that's six this time. The shells came over again, more streaks of light, and he stared up, counted, six, yes! Wonder who's doing that? Somebody tossed in a couple more guns to help out. Send a Christmas card to that guy.

There was a hard thump from below, one German gun firing, a single response. It was always that way, and he smiled, thought, some officer just got his wits about him. Sorry, pal, it's not your night. From behind him, the next volley came, the sharp shrieks ripping the air, four in quick succession, then two more, the valley erupting again. The smoke began to find him, rolling up the hillside, and he cursed the stink, covered his face, thought, hell of a time for the wind to change. But there was no other response from below, the valley mostly quiet, patches of flame, a brush fire breaking out, the high explosives hot enough to burn through the wet treetops. He stared down, felt the wind in his face, thought, all right, don't need any damn forest fire to light up this hillside. Won't burn up this far anyway. Too much snow. But breathing smoke is no fun at all. I bet those boys down there cleared themselves out a nice piece of open ground under that camouflage, maybe left a few bushes, thick and grassy. Burns like hell. He stood slowly, his head up out of his hole, peered down again, saw movement in the firelight. German troops were scrambling away, some moving up the far hill, survivors from the gun crews or infantrymen who had endured enough. They won't all leave, he thought. Just like us, they've got nice deep holes, and the brave ones will sit and wait until we quit shelling them. Then they'll creep out, like so many rats, checking on what we've done to their wonderful artillery pieces. Scrap metal, Kraut, old boy. Courtesy of Captain Miles Harroway, expert artillery spotter. He smiled at that, tried to imagine the wreckage in the valley floor, the destruction of the German battery. Those were probably Kraut 105s, and they were placed in the dumbest place imaginable. They had a clear field of fire in only one direction, down the mouth of that valley. Unlucky for those boys in the Four Two Three that they happened to be right in the way. And why did the Krauts clear their people off this hill? Where the hell would they be going? Back, I guess. Maybe they were being replaced by new units. Could be that our timing was just right. I bet they were planning to pull that battery out of here too. Harroway had heard too many conversations, his own colonel hearing the reports from intelligence units, that the Germans were almost certain to pull back out of this rugged terrain. No place to spend the winter, and they know we've set up shop as though we like it here. Makes sense they'd give it to us, let our boys get the trench foot and frostbite. Some of those Kraut bastards are probably pretty close to their own homes, maybe have some *fraulein* stashed someplace nearby, or maybe they just want to spend Christmas with their families. Can't fault them for that. Shouldn't have left that battery so damn unprotected, though. Too late now. Can't wait to see the mess down there. Very pretty mess. And if they try to bring up some more guns, I'll give them another happy hello.

God, I love this job.

It was after ten, no stars, but the snowfall was finally letting up. Harroway crushed the empty K-ration box, thought, what was that? Beef stew? Ham something or other? Hard to tell sometimes. Uncle Sam's little surprise for us hardworking officers. Harroway had remembered to bring a healthy supply of chocolate bars this time, was savoring one now, couldn't help thinking of coffee. It was one curse of the forward observer, no coffeepot. He picked up a small envelope, fingered it for a minute, thought of tossing it into the small pile of debris from his dinner. No, I guess I should keep it. You never know. But I sure would like to have a conversation with whatever dumb son of a bitch thought that this powder is supposed to make me believe that it will brew up into a cup of hot chocolate. This stuff has to come from some factory somewhere, where they sweep their floors for sawdust, mix it with brown paint, and then some whiz-bang salesman convinced the army to feed it to *us*. Somebody's going to jail if I ever have any say about it. Don't make me a general unless you want a stink raised. He had tried mixing the powder with melted snow once, in the hope of making something resembling chocolate milk. Drink it? Hell, I could have used that stuff to glue two Krauts together. If I'd have swallowed it, it would have stopped me up for weeks. He still fondled the envelope, reconsidered his thoughts about keeping it, tossed it in the small trash pile.

The cold was settling down on him, the temperature dropping quickly, and he flexed numb fingers. He had already changed socks, but the cold in his boots was relentless, and he reached into his backpack, carefully unwrapped one of the small stubby candles. He glanced up, the makeshift rooftop solid enough, certainly no one perched up anywhere close by who might catch a hint of the glow. A candle could be a luxury, giving off a surprising amount of warmth in a closed space. He fumbled for the lighter, flicked it, then again, lit the wick. The light was blinding at first, and he held a hand close over it, sheltering the light from above. This might be a stupid idea, he thought. But damn, it'll make this place pretty cozy. Nothing else for me to do but sleep, since I won't be able to tell how much damage we did until morning. Even if the Krauts abandon this place, they could open up on us with other batteries nearby. If I'm lucky, I might spot them too, call in some fire again. Might make for another good day's work.

He shifted his back against the soft dirt behind him, thought of his wire man. Gotta get you some stripes, for sure. You've been a private far too long. That'll give you a pay raise, anyway. God, you saved my ass a few weeks ago. Should put you in for something even better, maybe a Bronze Star.

In the Hürtgen Forest, barely three weeks prior, they had accomplished the same mission, seeking out a German gun position buried in cover no aircraft could find, if the weather had allowed aircraft to try. In the worst weather many of the Americans had ever seen, the orders had come for a renewed attack out of Aachen, pushing south and east. It was a strategy that must have made perfect sense on paper. But in the terrain of the Hürtgen, the Americans, particularly the Twenty-eighth Infantry Division, had confronted a well-hidden and strongly fortified enemy, and the results had been horrific, some of the worst casualty counts of the entire war. Harroway had seen too much of that, generals well behind the action who drew neat lines on maps. They're never up here, and by damn, they ought to be.

Then, with enemy troops swarming past his hidden position, his phone line had suddenly quit, and there was no way to know if it had been found by the Germans, cut by shellfire, or simply failed from a bad connection. But then, in a matter of minutes, there was a voice again, his own man, that syrupy southern drawl. The wire man had moved forward, following the phone line by hand until he found a break. The man had hooked up his own phone to it, to find out if Harroway was even there, whether he had been killed or taken prisoner. When Harroway heard the young man's voice, he could only respond in small grunts, since German troops were close by him in every direction. Inevitably, the wire had failed again, but the private kept coming, had followed the wire closer still, finding another break, reconnecting it while he hid inside a makeshift brush pile, allowing Harroway to keep his contact with the artillery. For hours after, he had been able to call down shelling on enemy positions that had now moved behind him, closer to the American lines. The Germans were already digging in, seemed confident that they had safely driven the Americans away. But the sudden rain of artillery fire changed their minds, and soon Harroway had heard a flood of German troops moving around him, pulling back, retreating into their first position. When the woods finally cleared, he had scrambled out of his hiding place, following his own wire in miserable darkness, scampering past blasted timber and the debris of two armies. The wire led him straight into the muzzle of an M-1, a sharp surprise to both men. It was his wire man, no more certain who he was than Harroway was of him. But even in panic, the drawling voice had given the young man away, and after a heart-stopping identification, Harroway had hugged the man, a hard unembarrassed embrace. Yeah, he's earned something, Harroway thought. I'm damn lucky to have him back there. He's probably sitting in the communications post, waiting for me to come home, like some damn golden retriever. All right, kid. Let's wait until the sun comes up and see if I have any other reason to be out here.

DECEMBER 16, 1944, 5 A.M.

He woke to the rumble of engines. The stiffness in his back kept him in place for a long minute, the usual agony of curling up in a tight foxhole. But there was no grogginess, no hesitation, the sounds rolling toward him from the far ridge, the road beyond his line of sight. The candle was still in one corner of the hole, its wick snuffed out when he tried to sleep. He stared up, tried to rise, pushed his head up slowly, carefully, no disturbing the snowy blanket above him. It was still fully dark, and he sank back down, flicked the lighter at his wristwatch. Five A.M. Damn! How'd you sleep so long? Too quiet, I guess. But not now. What the hell is going on over there?

He peered up again, farther, daring to stand, easing aside the thin branches. Across the way, the trucks and other vehicles were moving in a steady stream, and he scanned the darkness with his binoculars, looking for any flicker of light, some telltale hint of just what it was he was hearing. It's four hundred yards across there, easily, he thought. Could be five hundred to that road. Might be time to drop a few dozen rounds on their heads, bust up whatever they've got going on. He heard new sounds, far to the left, beyond the valley down below, back around the curve of the hill. There were more engines, a steady roar, and something new, grinding steel. *Tanks.* He tried to measure the distance, but the hill was deflecting the sounds, and he knew better than to guess. He thought of the road down behind him, the road his own patrol had crossed, thought of the map, lit the candle with shaking fingers. The lighter hesitated, maddeningly, then finally, the small flame, and he held the candle, unsteady, the flame finally igniting the stump of wick. He set the candle down in the soft dirt, grabbed his map, tried to orient himself, the small *x* he had drawn a few hours ago his best estimate where he was right now. The Krauts are moving . . . here, back this way. There's no road on the map, but that's not unusual. Here's the road we crossed. Hell, there are roads all over these woods. Trails. Nothing to drive a tank on. He rose up, peered that way, the direction his patrol had retreated. There were no sounds coming up from that direction, and he let out a breath, thought, well, at least they're not behind me. But that's a lot of activity over there, and they're not being shy about the racket.

The sounds continued, farther away, and he realized the ridgeline across from him was quieting, engines cutting off, the roar growing silent. What the hell? He stared into darkness, nothing, no lights, no sounds, suddenly had the feeling of being utterly alone. He lowered himself slowly, shifted the branches, covering the hole, pieces of glazed snow coming down on him, the crust of ice formed by melting snow from his own heat. He stared at the map, not seeing, his mind racing in confusion. What the hell do I do? My job? Hell, I'd need ten batteries to do anything to that much equipment. But I've got to tell them anyway, let them know that Kraut-boy is up to something pretty serious out here. He grabbed the phone, hesitated, thought of Monroe, the ridicule, costing the man his job. Monroe had been in this same position, suddenly confronted with massive sounds, and he had panicked, calling in artillery on forces that turned out to be his own. The casualties had been minor, but the wrath of the men was not, and Monroe was . . . where? In Antwerp now? Supervising some loading equipment, I think. Calm down, Captain. All you need is some daylight. They have no idea you're here, and it can stay that way. Eat breakfast or something. He thought of the K rations, nope, not now. Look at the damn map, draw their location as best you can. He had the stub of pencil in his hand, tapped at the map, didn't know what to do. And now the candle went out.

He let out a breath, sat in the dark silence, glanced up, no hint of dawn. Relax, dammit. Wait for daylight. You have all the advantages. He suddenly thought of the infantry commander, Moore, right? Yeah, Captain Moore, Company B. Mad as a damn hornet about some jackass up the ladder telling him these trucks out here were fake, that it was just German loudspeakers. Loudspeakers. Somebody back there with a star on his shoulder probably thought that was a pretty clever idea, something he wished *he* had thought of. All you have to do is pretend you have an army out here with lots of *big* stuff, guns and tanks. Lions and tigers and bears. Make enough racket and you'll scare the bejesus out of us poor dumb Americans. Where the hell do these commanders come up with this stuff? But you were right to be pissed off, Captain. The enemy is busy as hell out here, and God knows why. If I'd have had a little more daylight, I might have been able to come up with some good intel, at least. But that wasn't the priority, not this time.

Harroway put a hand on his canteen, shook it slightly, thought, half full. By the time I get back to the CP, I'll be eating snow. Might oughta fill it now. Never know what might happen in the daylight. Germans won't like that I took out their battery, and somebody might want to do something about it.

He had gone through that before, a response to his good work from half a dozen German mortars, laying down a barrage of shells all over the most logical place he'd be hiding. It was the only wound he had received, a mortar fragment going through his hand, slicing a piece off one thumb. No need to stick around any longer than I have to, he thought, and dawn sounds like a good time to get the hell off this hill. Worst part of this job might be making it back to our lines without some trigger-happy idiot on guard duty taking a shot at me. He pulled at the canteen, took a drink, savored it, pushed the canteen back into its canvas holster.

And then he heard the voices.

He froze, every muscle tight, his eyes darting, nothing to see. The crunch of the snow was down the hill in front of him, the voices low mumbles, one sharp whisper, the tones quiet. But the crunches continued, closer, both sides of him, the men moving past, climbing the ridge, more coming up from below. He raised his head slowly, focused on the small dark gap in the branches over his head, one hand sliding slowly out, wrapping around the icy steel of the carbine. There were more whispers, nonsensical sounds, foreign, very close, to one side, and they moved past, another order coming from below, more men streaming along one side of him. He stared up, the carbine moving slowly, one finger moving to the trigger guard, the short barrel pointed up toward the opening. No! You idiot, what are you going to do? It sounds like half a company out there. Just sit still and let them go. Try to guess their number. He wanted to look, try to catch a glimpse, knew better, stayed put, thought of the gear in his hole, where everything was, no accidents, no bumping into anything that might make noise. Did you fasten the canteen? He brushed it with one elbow, felt it secure in place, okay, good. He knew the telephone was beside his left leg, took inventory of the rest, the trash pile, the binoculars around his neck. Just sit still. And stop breathing so hard. It's only a patrol. A big patrol, maybe. He glanced toward the phone, thought, let them get past, then give a call. Somebody needs to know about this, and the artillery boys owe a few favors to the infantry. What's that company commander's name, Moore? Yeah, his guys are green as hell. Don't need any surprises.

He pulled the carbine in tight, tugged at his coat, heard a new round of footsteps, more men coming up the hill. One voice called out, stupidly loud, whispers following, low laughter, the footsteps not as noisy now, the crust on the snow obliterated by so many boots. There has to be a hundred of them, he thought. God, just a quick look. No, don't do it. Patience, Captain. They'll be gone soon.

He allowed himself to take a deep breath, still held the carbine tightly, knew it was ridiculous. Somebody steps on this rabbit trap of a roof, and he'll fall right on top of me. You kill the guy and forty more fill you with holes. *Kamarad.* That's the word. *Kamarad.* Make it loud. Only thing you can do.

There were hard whispers close by, the obvious authority of an officer, the men still moving, another group coming from below. He began to panic, closed his eyes. Too many of them, and they're coming up in formation, probably all along this ridge. Maybe more ridges. And all those damn trucks and tanks, whatever the hell else they were moving up those roads. He flinched, a new sound, a sharp roar coming high above. He waited for the impact, but it was not artillery. There were more, exactly the same, some in the distance, and he understood, a sound he had heard before. They're firing those damn V-1 bombs. Haven't heard any for a few days, but somebody out there decided it's time for a fireworks celebration. They're probably headed to one of the big cities, Antwerp or Liège. Harroway had learned long ago, if you could hear the jet-powered engines on the flying bombs, it meant they were headed somewhere else. Only when the sound stopped did the bomb fall. That's it, he thought, keep going. Sorry for whoever gets to hear them shut off, but they don't usually hit anything anyway, just scare hell out of civilians. The V-1s kept passing over, more than a dozen, and he thought, I've never seen a launcher, never could get close enough, but boy, that would be a dandy target.

The wave of V-1s tapered off, some much farther away, to the south, and he focused again on the troops moving past him. There was silence, a brief calm, but then he heard the whispers again, realized, they're not moving. They're just . . . sitting there. He thought of the German foxholes. Well, this was their hill. Maybe they've come back. He strained to hear, soft sounds of men settling down, sitting, talking, rifles and canteens. Oh good God, I'm dug in right in the middle of their campground. His mind began to race, and he knew that there was nothing he could do right now—that a strange shadow emerging from a clump of brush would draw someone's attention. They still might move away, he thought. Worse thing that happens, I'll just call some fire down on this position right here, maybe a little behind me. That could scare them off, or blow them to hell. The wire won't survive most likely, but at least I can get something accomplished. I didn't expect this. They're supposed to be going home. That's the other way.

The ridgeline across from him was suddenly alive with hard thumps, the air overhead streaking with light. The men around him began to cheer, strange, far too loud, their officers shouting them down. But the thunderous sounds increased, far out on both flanks, the light catching his eye, sharp lines in the dark. Artillery . . . right on time, I guess. It's a little after five, though. I took out the one battery that used a clock. I guess they decided to make up for it. He tried to feel some amusement at that, but the firing continued, much more firing, many batteries, some close, hidden by the ridge, some farther back. The thunder continued to spread, and he gauged the distance, thought, that road, they moved guns up on that road. A whole lot of guns. I took out a battery and they replaced it with . . .

what? A hundred more? His brain was starting to swirl, his mind grabbing the details of what he was hearing. It was part of his job, part of being an *observer.* But the rumbling rolled past him in waves he had never heard before, and he thought, what the hell's going on?

The artillery was continuous now, the echoes rolling through the valleys around him, the rumble driven deep in his gut. The Germans around him were still making noise, but it was mostly subdued, their talk drowned out by the shrieks from the big guns. He heard a brief command, some officer, but the voice was gone, blotted out by the continuing sounds of batteries that were firing as quickly as their men could reload. He heard every variety of gun, the usual 105s, the dreaded 88s, and the larger 150s. There were ungodly shrieks as well, *nebelwerfers,* the rocket launchers, six tubes clustered together that spit out their fire in a hellish scream, no other sound like it, what the soldiers called *screaming meemies.*

He clenched his hands on the carbine, tried to hold the fear away. My God. They're firing every damn gun they have. It was becoming clear now, so much training, strategy and tactics, the great barrages of artillery that always meant more than just roughing up the enemy's positions. And the troops, moving up close, vast formations of infantry, or others, the men who supported their armor, and the Germans always relied on armor. He understood it all now. These Krauts aren't up here to make camp. They're waiting here just long enough for the artillery barrage to stop. This is an attack.

He felt panic, helpless, a blind man who saw too clearly what was about to happen. Somebody's gotta know, he thought. I can give them the infantry's position at least, how close they are. What the hell do I do? Risk the call? Whispering on a phone doesn't work. But I've got to do something. Maybe the artillery will keep the Krauts from hearing me. He looked down at the phone, the ground still rumbling beneath him, the only sounds the waves of artillery fire streaking overhead. He put his hand on the phone receiver, and suddenly the entire box rose up, hung in the air beside him. He stared at it, cold shock, the phone box turning slowly, suspended by the wire, and now he knew what was about to happen. The roar of the artillery was all he could hear, but suddenly the sky opened up above him, his cover pulled away, snow falling on his face. There were shadows and shapes, and now the sudden burst of fire from a machine gun, the blinding flash, sharp punches in his chest, the shock fading into soft darkness, wrapping him in silence, taking him away.

9. BENSON

Sergeant Higgins had them in a semicircle, low beneath a fat pine tree, spoke in clear whispers.

"It seems that we did such a terrific job yesterday, the captain says we're going out again tonight. He says it's our reward. Lucky us. He didn't mention that killing our lieutenant might have been a problem."

Beside Benson, Mitchell said, "How soon we getting a new one?"

Higgins shrugged. "The captain says regimental is working on it. You can bet they'll find us a ninety-day wonder pretty quick. We've got replacements coming in regular." Higgins took a drink from the coffee cup, looked around in the darkness. "I told the captain that we didn't need some shiny new second looey to show us how to walk through these woods. But that's the way it works. They'll want somebody up here pretty quick to replace Greeley, whether he's any good or not. But that's not why he called me back there. Captain Moore wants us to get some night patrol experience. He's given us the day off, and he says some new people are on their way up here to man these positions, get some frontline experience. When they get here, you slugs can pull back behind those kitchen trucks, get some chow, and sit on your asses all day. Just stay off the roads back there and keep out of everybody's way. Since we lost our lieutenant, the captain thinks we oughta hang back and let another platoon dig some holes. I suggested they make another straddle trench. Ours is getting pretty gamy. He actually agreed with me, wants to give the new boys some first-rate shovel time."

Benson huddled low in the snow, impatient for Higgins to finish. He could smell the coffee in the sergeant's cup, thought of the kitchen trucks, those wonderful coffeepots. Well, that's just fine with me.

Beside him, Mitchell spoke up again, his low whisper just loud enough for the squad to hear. "Hey, Sarge, what do they want us to do tonight? We escorting another big-shot artillery guy, or we just cruising for Krauts?"

"Don't know yet. The captain didn't let on any secrets. That engineer won't be with us again, that's pretty certain. The captain said he went back to his unit with his head in his hands. I talked to his private, the guy with the metal detector. Name's Jacklin, or Jerkin, or something. He was pretty down too. Said he's never seen a dead body before. They feel guilty as hell about our guys. Not much I could add to that."

Benson was getting annoyed at the talk, the wind picking up, the iciness biting his face. He pulled hard on the wool cap beneath his helmet, but his ears were stinging, the cold eating all through him.

"Hey, Sarge, can we head back to those kitchens now? Nothing going on up here, and it's three hours until we can see anything."

"Quit bitching, Benson. They'll let us know when breakfast is ready. Nobody leaves this ridge until those replacements get here. The captain would have my stripes if I left these foxholes empty. If you're so damn cold, then crawl back into your hole. The rest of you too. I'll let you know when you can grab some chow." Higgins flicked a lighter, held it low, looking at his watch. "It's getting close to five. Time for our morning wake-up call. Everybody get into cover."

Benson didn't hesitate, slipped away, moved quickly across trampled snow, pulled at the coat, beat his arms across his body, trying to erase the shivers. Damn! How much colder can it get out here? He slid down into the foxhole, curled up as tight as he could, trying to squeeze away the cold.

Yunis said, "Wonder how that artillery observer's doing? Feel bad for that guy. He gets lost or something and he's in it real deep."

Mitchell was surprisingly talkative, said, "You heard all that outgoing stuff after dinner. That battery down in the draw behind us fired off a couple dozen rounds. It wasn't for show. The phone line did the job. That was a hell of a show, and I'm betting he blew those Kraut bastards to pieces." He lit a match, continued, "Five o'clock on the nose. Get ready for it."

Benson huddled low, used to the ritual. Yunis sat on the far side, his face turned toward the dirt, bracing himself. Benson remembered something Mitchell had said the first time they endured the wake-up call. *One of those things lands right in this hole, nothing else matters.* Nope, guess not.

5:20 A.M.

Mitchell was lying back against the side of the hole, his knees stretched out, and Benson could smell the chocolate bar. Mitchell said, "They're late. No reveille. I told ya! That artillery spotter did his job."

Yunis seemed to perk up. "Hey, it's almost five thirty. God. He did it. You know, when our shells went over, I was thinking how exciting it was. Kinda like training. I always did like the sound of the artillery. They shoulda sent me there instead of a rifle unit. Uh, no offense."

Mitchell was fumbling through his backpack. "You're an idiot. It was exciting because they were our shells. Incoming's not so much fun. Or did you forget about that?"

Yunis was silenced, and Benson stared up, starless black. "You've gotta be right, Kenny," he said. "That phone musta worked just fine, and that captain called back for the artillery. Just like it's supposed to work. That's pretty impressive, if he took out that whole battery. We were responsible for that. Got him out there where he needed to be."

Mitchell sat now, and Benson heard the cardboard, knew Mitchell was probably unwrapping another chocolate bar.

Mitchell said, "Yeah, so tonight we get to do it again. That's the army for you. Do a good job, and they make you do it again until you screw up." He paused, looked at Benson. "You saw those Krauts down in that valley. I bet you wish you could have plinked at least one of those helmets. I could have nailed one of them from that hilltop."

Benson knew that Mitchell liked to brag about his shooting. Both men had done well at sharpshooter training. Yunis stayed silent, and Benson thought, I wonder if he's even fired his rifle?

Finally Yunis said, "I was just happy to get off that hill. I don't like getting shot at."

Mitchell began to chuckle, and Benson knew what was coming.

"So, that's why you joined the army? No chance some bad guy might shoot at you?"

There was a pause. Yunis replied, "I told the recruiting fellow I could type, and he said they needed office guys. It made sense to me. I worked for my dad in his store, kept the books. Had some bookkeeping classes in high school, and I type pretty fast. I figured I'd do my part that way. The recruiter told the truth too. The army made me a clerk, put me in an office with three gals working with me. That was pretty fun. Next thing I know, orders come in, and I'm shipped off to Indiana to join up with you fellas."

Mitchell said, "Yeah, ain't we lucky. Just shut the hell up. I don't want to know I'm in a foxhole with a damn secretary. You see any damn typewriters up here? You get somebody killed, Office Boy, and I'll kick your ass . . . or worse."

Benson let the routine wind itself out, his thoughts drifting, his brain trying to distract itself from the chill in his feet and hands. He thought of the engineer, the lieutenant who had seemed so confident, who knew everything about mines and how to move through woods, roads, all of that. Benson realized now, I didn't even know his name. He's gone back to some engineering unit thinking he botched the job, that he got somebody killed. He glanced at Mitchell, the man eating the chocolate with noisy bites. You can kick Yunis's ass anytime you want as far as I'm concerned. But that engineer . . . he's doing it to himself. I can't see how it was his fault . . .

The air was split by a sharp roar, a thunderous impact, the ground suddenly rising up beneath him, the shell coming down close behind the hole. Mitchell fell hard to the bottom of the foxhole, his helmet in Benson's stomach. Benson grabbed him, held tight, heard Mitchell cursing, but more shells came, the ground heaving again, the walls of the foxhole caving in, a burst of fire above them, more shells impacting the high trees. Benson still held Mitchell, felt the man curling up into a ball, and there was no pause, no break in the shelling, more coming in toward the left, men yelling, a call for a medic, someone hit. Still there was no pause, the shelling growing more intense, higher-pitched whines, shrieks, the whistle of shrapnel, slapping trees, timber falling. All along the hillside the shells came down, flashes of fire, hard bursts close by, many more farther away. Men were screaming, as they always screamed, their voices blending in with the sounds of the incoming fire, and Benson wanted to cover his ears, but his grip on Mitchell wouldn't release. Yunis began to yell now, no words, his face buried into the dirt, and Benson ignored him, held his head low, his chin against his chest, felt one thunderous eruption close in front, dirt pouring in on them. He waited for the silence, for the final shell, so used to it now, the game the Germans played, *reveille,* but the sounds were very different, different-sized shells, and many more, ongoing, not stopping at all.

The shelling rolled in over them from a hundred guns, then a hundred more, the entire ridgeline erupting into fire and smoke, the hard stink of explosives, dense smoke swirling around them all. Farther back, the shells came down along the roads, blanketing the kitchen trucks, the men with coffee cups, and to one side the command posts, Captain Moore diving headlong into cover of his own. Other officers had been caught aboveground, were swept away, erased by fire, some wounded, struggling to find cover where there was none at all. Others tumbled blindly into whatever foxholes they could find, coming down on top of men too frightened to curse them. The men who were wounded called for help, but no replies were heard, and those who were suffering, who lay sprawled out aboveground, did not suffer long. The shells came down where others had already landed, no crater offering cover, wounded men blown high, new wounded scrambling blindly, panic, terrified search for escape. The men who had been deep in their foxholes sat in paralyzed terror, the routine they had endured every morning. But then it had been short minutes, now the shelling continued, blankets of fire, the horrifying screech of the German rocket launchers, the piercing shudder of the eighty-eights. Benson could feel the hillside quaking beneath him, some of the shells falling just short, the blasts like so many lightning strikes, bursts of blinding light washing over the foxhole, punching holes in the open field below. More of the shells were bursting high above, shrapnel punching hard into the ground, some straight into the holes, more screams, blood and cries, some foxholes giving way, mud and snow driven down, burying the men in their cover. Though daylight was still hours away, the German artillery brought their own dawn, entire ridgelines erupting into fiery hell, trees shattered, blanketing the men who hid below with torn branches and heavy splinters. In the thickets, the men who manned the machine guns had nowhere else to go, the fire sweeping down on them as well, no protection from the thick canopies of spruce and fir, nothing for the men to do but curl up into their dugouts and wait for the end. For some it was immediate and painless, others enduring the same terror of the riflemen in their foxholes, silent screams, prayers, men deafened and blinded, some paralyzed by the raw terror.

The Germans had observers of their own, and the big guns sought out more than the troop positions. They targeted the American artillery, those batteries nestled into cover behind the infantry. As the men of the 106th absorbed the terrifying bombardment, the German guns opened up on a much wider front, far out in both directions. Two thousand German artillery pieces had begun an extraordinary bombardment along a front that stretched from Bastogne in the south to St. Vith and Elsenborn in the north, and beyond. North of the 106th, the 99th Division was blistered, as was the 2nd Division north of them. To the south, the American Twenty-eighth Division, fresh from their bloodletting at the Hürtgen Forest, felt the German guns as well, while on their flank the Fourth Division, the first men to swim ashore at Utah Beach, found their respite in the forest utterly shattered.

In the command posts all along the American lines, calls rang out, company commanders alerting their colonels, the regiments calling back to division commands. But soon the phones went dead, the wires blown apart by the shells, or the command posts themselves no longer there. On the two main roads through the Ardennes, the two primary intersections at Bastogne and St. Vith, the Americans close to the front began to understand what the generals behind them did not. All the movement in the German lines, all the sounds of trucks and machinery, had a meaning that no one had predicted. The commanders of the American First Army had placed the inexperienced combat divisions, or those divisions that desperately needed rest, along the quiet zone of the Ardennes Forest. Their lines were too thin, their manpower stretched far beyond an effective defensive position. The forest that spread out around them was considered the least likely place to launch an attack, no place for armor, certainly, and with winter swallowing the hills and deep valleys in snow, no place for infantry to make any kind of assault. But still, the shelling came.

DECEMBER 16, 1944, 6:40 A.M.

Mitchell began to slide off him, the hard painful ringing in Benson's ears relentless, blotting out any other sounds. Benson straightened his back, pushed against the wet dirt behind him, dug at the muddy wall that had collapsed across his shoulders. He saw Yunis at the far end of the hole, the man crying, wailing, his hands on either side of his face, a sound Benson could barely hear. Mitchell was moving, trying to unwind himself, picked his rifle out of the mud, turned toward Benson, faceless in the dark, but Benson felt the eyes, felt Mitchell's hand, a light slap on his face, the question, and Benson nodded, *Yes, I'm okay.* Mitchell checked the rifle, struggled to stand, slowly peering out, and Benson pried himself into motion, ice and mud in his clothes, could see Mitchell outlined against the gray, his helmet, the shape of his face. But there was no dawn, not yet, and Benson stared past him, looked at the sky, the darkness gone, a strange glow of light, moving now, waves and streaks, drifting across the sky, revealing the shattered skeletons of trees. The light was not artillery, no blinding bursts, was different, dull and steady, broad swaths sweeping back and forth, coming from the east, from the Germans. Benson stared, fixed, curious, the paralysis wearing off, his brain starting to come alive. What the hell? Those are searchlights.

Men were screaming, Benson's hearing coming back, and he saw bodies close beside them, a direct hit on a foxhole, the men tossed out of the ground like broken dolls. One man was crawling away, down into the open field, plowing his helmet into the snow, dragging a ribbon of one leg behind him. Benson stared for a brief sickening second, saw others moving, one man turning over, rolling, then again, his uniform torn away, ribs, and Benson shouted, "Medic!"

Others repeated the call, and men with medical kits were there, coming up and out of their holes, some slipping close to the bodies, checking, moving away. Benson could see their faces, odd, ghostlike, the searchlights reflected against the thick clouds above, revealing the entire ridge. More men were coming forward, running up from behind, one man helmetless, waving, and Benson recognized him, Captain Moore, pointing out toward the open field, shouting orders, meaningless words. The roar in Benson's ears had changed, the painful piercing ring gone, replaced by something low and metallic. Benson watched Moore, waving at the men on the ridge, the men who had survived, and Moore was closer now, shouted into Benson's face, "Get down! The enemy is on the road! A column of tanks! Watch the woods out there! Watch that open ground!"

Moore moved on, repeating the order, some men responding, dropping down, some staring, as Benson was, paralyzed with the shock of the barrage. He turned toward the new sounds, up the ridge to the left, toward the road, the road they had crossed, out there, somewhere, the artillery spotter . . .

"Get your ass down!"

Mitchell yanked him hard, and Benson fell back, sat down hard onto mud. Mitchell was up again, peering out just above ground level, said, "Grab your rifles! Both of you!"

Benson fought through the mud beside him, his M-1 wedged into the side of the foxhole. He tried to clean it, wiping with his wet gloves, heard shooting up the ridge. He climbed up, shoulder-to-shoulder with Mitchell, could hear the rumble of engines more clearly, the distinct sound of steel tracks. But the sounds came from the right as well, farther away, other roads and trails he had never seen. Down there, the ground was held by other companies of the 423rd, and beyond them, farther south, the 424th. He copied Mitchell, put his rifle up on the ground, pointing down the hill, saw nothing there, no targets, but Moore was back, still shouting, "Get ready! The Krauts are coming! Those are Kraut tanks! Hold here until you get orders to move! Watch that open ground, those far trees!"

Benson stared out across the open slope of the hill, the woods beyond, the low ridge, lit now by the soft glow from the searchlights. Up on the road, there was a hard punch of fire, the impact ripping farther back through the trees, behind the foxholes. He jerked his head that way, but there was nothing to see, the road hidden. He thought of the captain's word, *column*. How many is that? More tanks were firing, blasts in the woods back behind him. Rifle fire began now, familiar *pop*s from M-1s, more, the rattle of machine guns, another hard thump from a tank.

Benson felt a wave of panic, helpless, heard Mitchell screaming, "Get your ass up here! Get that rifle!" Benson looked down, saw Yunis, still curled in a ball, Mitchell grabbing his coat, yanking him hard upright. "Get your rifle up here or I'll break your arm!"

Yunis began to rise, and Benson looked away, would not see the man's fear, not now. Mitchell shouted close to Benson's ear, "Check your rifle! There have to be infantry!"

"It's good. Loaded. I checked it."

Mitchell said nothing, stared out down the hill, and Benson still felt the panic, the churning in his brain. But he knew to follow Mitchell's lead, and so leaned against the muddy walls in front of him, his helmet just above the top of the foxhole, stared out down the slope. The snowy open ground was different now, pockmarked with black, the churning impact from the shelling. He tried to keep his eyes on the far trees, but the fight to his left was increasing, more tank guns, machine-gun fire, the thump of a grenade. The ghostly glow from the searchlights was all across the sky, far out on both sides, and suddenly Mitchell fired his rifle, startling him. Yunis cried out, and Mitchell yelled, "Shut up! There they are!"

Benson felt his heart punching his chest, the cold gone from his fingers, Mitchell's voice driving into him, and he stared again at the trees, saw them now, lumps of white, moving in slow rhythm, coming out of the woods, drifting in a snaking line across the snowy field. More men came behind them, many more, and Benson felt his chest shaking, icy cold, braced the rifle against his shoulder, stared down the barrel. The open hillside was a blanket of motion, and beside him Mitchell fired again. Others were firing as well, the ridgeline coming alive, the rifles and machine guns working, shouts from the sergeants, so much training, all those games in Indiana, now giving way to the horror of *why.* Benson stared at the white figures far out in the snow, the word in his brain, *Germans,* and he felt shaking in his hands, could not aim the rifle, the fear boiling up. He felt wetness in his pants, down his legs, anger at himself, stupid, helpless.

Mitchell shouted, close to his ears. "Shoot the bastards!"

Benson gripped the rifle again, his cheekbone against the stock. He steadied his eye on the rifle's sight, saw a blob of white, the man stepping high in the snow, and Benson aimed at the man's chest, his brain fighting the fear. He hesitated, saw a face beneath a white helmet, the man stepping slowly, deliberately, a rifle held out, pointed forward, and Benson let out a breath, and pulled the trigger.

8 A.M.

He had emptied half a dozen clips, Mitchell even more, the Germans in the field seeking cover, their advance slowed by the withering fire from the men on the ridgeline. The shell holes in the open field made for excellent cover, the Germans bunching up, returning fire, but the Americans had the advantage, protected by their foxholes on the higher ridge, the machine gunners raking the open ground, keeping the Germans from moving forward. Benson was searching through his rifle's sight, no targets, his breathing in heavy bursts, and he heard someone shout, "Hold your fire! Pick a target!"

He wanted to look that way, knew the voice, Higgins, farther up the ridge somewhere, another hole. He's okay, thank God. There was a pause in the rifle fire, both sides content to sit in their cover, but the lull was only in front of him. Up on the road, the tanks had continued to roll past, clear and distinct, machine-gun fire and tank guns blasting their way to the rear. The men were responding there as best they could, bazooka crews and anti-tank guns fighting back. Benson lowered his head, his helmet down below the surface, safe, and he looked that way, the fight a steady chatter, sharp blasts, the sound of tank treads. Down below, in the churned-up field, the Germans were starting to fire their rifles again, some with machine guns, heavier machine guns back on the far ridge. But the German fire was scattered, men protecting themselves by shooting wild, their targets well hidden. To the left, one of the thirty-calibers was working the open ground with regular blasts, and Benson could hear the men, the machine-gun crew, knew their sergeant, the distinctive gruffness in his voice.

"Change barrels. Don't let up. We've got 'em pinned down!"

Mitchell fired his rifle again, and Benson jumped at the sound, more ringing in his ears.

Mitchell said, "They're all ours now! We've got 'em trapped! Can't move forward or backward. Stupid! Marched right out in the open." He yelled out now, "So what you gonna do, Krauts? Wait for dark?" He fired the rifle again.

Benson said, "Kenny! Save your ammo! How much you got left?"

"Hell I don't know! I don't keep count."

Benson looked past him, saw Yunis down in the foxhole, holding his rifle against his chest. The man's eyes were red, tears on his face, his whole body quivering. Benson felt sick looking at him, wondered if Mitchell had even noticed. Benson wanted to feel angry, stared at Yunis, but he couldn't help feeling the cold in his own pants, his own embarrassment.

Mitchell turned, seemed to notice Yunis for the first time. "You son of a bitch! You goddamn coward! Get up here and fight!" Mitchell raised one foot, jammed a boot hard against the man's helmet, pushing Yunis into the mud. "We survive this, I'm going to kill you myself!"

Yunis was crying, the sickening wail again, and Benson turned away, peered up, the *pop*s of rifle fire still coming from the men around him, the Germans responding. There were streaks of fire from the far trees, the heavier machine guns using tracers, the ground churned up in front of the foxhole, someone's sweeping fire. Benson hunched low, checked the rifle, had lost count of the rounds still in the clip, thought, four or five, I think. He put a hand on the clips in his bandolier, six. Is that enough? What happens now? Will they bring us more?

The machine guns had slowed their firing behind him, and he couldn't take his mind from that, the ammo, how much do they have? How much do the Krauts have? He wanted to look back, but the cracks and zips from the German rifles were still coming overhead, no one daring to expose himself for long.

He saw Mitchell aiming the rifle, searching, saw a curl to his lip, viciousness in the man's face. Mitchell was whispering, talking to himself. "C'mon, you Kraut bastards. Let's see you try to run away. That's what you want, ain't it? Get the hell out of here. I see you moving, your helmet . . . just a little higher . . ."

The blast came behind them, no shriek, no sound at all but the impact in the broken trees. Benson flinched again, ducking low, heard the whistle from shrapnel spraying past close overhead. Mitchell was down as well, the cursing fury still there, and Benson heard the word shouted out, echoing across the ridge.

"Mortars!"

More blasts came now, a pattern, steady, distinct, no warning at all until the high-arcing shells impacted. Benson huddled low, nothing else to do. There were no other sounds now, no one firing, the mortars peppering the entire ridgeline. He heard a scream, a brief sharp cry, someone hit, but the voice was erased, the mortar shells falling again. Benson couldn't help staring at Yunis, his hands on his head, the barrel of his M-1 stuffed into the mud. Benson felt rage at the man, useless, suffering like some child, the man with no guts at all. Benson looked up, thought of the Germans in the field, said to Mitchell, "We've got to keep an eye on them!"

"Shut up! Stay down until it stops! They can't advance into their own mortar shells!"

The shelling slowed, one last shell coming down to the left of their hole, a punctuation mark, tossing dirt in their foxhole, something hard, heavy, and Benson saw now it was a boot, a piece of a dead man. Yunis yelped, and Mitchell picked it up, tossed it out, said, "They're killing dead men. That's a waste of ammo, you Kraut bastards."

Mitchell was up again, the brief quiet interrupted by more rifle fire. Benson stood, raised the rifle, his heart racing, white-clad men in the field moving up the hill again. The machine guns started up behind the foxhole, and Benson felt gasping relief, thought, thank God, thank God, they survived. He stared at the Germans as they fell, some tumbling facedown, some rolling in the snow, crawling back to their cover. Mitchell yelled again, "It didn't work! We're still here! Ha!"

He fired the rifle, four shots, the clip popping out with a metallic clink, and Benson searched for targets, nothing, too late, the Germans too well hidden.

Mitchell reloaded the M-1, said, "They thought they could take us out with mortars. It cost them half a dozen men. Go on, Kraut bastard, try that again."

Benson realized now that the fight on the left, along the main road, was slowing. The tanks were there still, but the firing was scattered, mostly bursts of machine-gun fire, nothing else. He heard different engines, trucks, other vehicles, all in motion, the invisible column moving past them, *behind* them. There was a sudden burst of firing far to the right, and it was behind them as well, along another ridge. He turned that way, knew not to rise up to look, nothing to see anyway. There were hard thumps, tank guns, anti-tank artillery, and he strained to hear over the sporadic noise around him.

"Kenny, they're behind us."

"Like hell! Those are our boys, kicking hell out of the Kraut tanks."

Benson knew Mitchell was usually right, but still he listened, another battle growing farther down, distant, in a long ravine that spread out to the southwest.

Mitchell turned that way now, leaning with his back against the fox-hole, staring in silence. After a long moment, he said, "You might be right. Where the hell are *our* tanks? We've got enough artillery back there to stop anything. It's coming. I know it."

The fight seemed to spread out far to the south and west, and Benson focused on the continuous sound of vehicles, close the other way. "Up on the road. Those are Krauts. They're not fighting anymore, they're just . . . moving. They're going past us. Jesus, Kenny, what the hell is going on?"

A voice came from behind them, startling him, Benson raising the rifle. But the helmet was American, and he saw the face, Higgins, the ser-geant rolling, tumbling down into their foxhole, heavy on top of them. Mitchell cursed, but Higgins silenced him with a hard look, different, a look Benson had never seen.

"We have to get out of here. Captain Moore has ordered us to pull back. The Krauts have driven our guys back all along the ridgelines. There's a hell of a lot of armor out there. The captain's CP is gone, blown to hell. There's no communications except the wireless radios, and he's tried to find someone who knows what's going on. He reached D Company, across that road, and they're already pulling out. They can hear fighting farther to the north, toward the Four Two Two. That's all he knows. We're being left behind out here." Higgins paused, out of breath. Even Mitchell was silent, waiting for more.

Higgins looked at the three of them, said to Yunis, "You're not worth a crap, are you? I can tell. You still got a full belt of ammo. Well, if you're not going to fight, divide it up with these guys. Now! Do it!"

Yunis reacted, obeyed, and Higgins looked at Benson, then Mitchell, said, "The machine gunners are going to lay down a heavy fire for about ten seconds. That's all they've got left. When they start shooting, get your asses out of here. Move back, but stay to the left of the kitchens. Krauts are in those woods, all around the road. We need to make our way back as close to Saint Vith as we can. That's gotta be the Kraut objective. Captain Moore's already trying to get there, to hook up with the other company commanders. The wireless sets are working a little bit, and when I left him, he was still trying to raise some of the other guys above the road. These damn woods cut down on the range, but he thinks that everyone knows how important Saint Vith is. Division HQ is back there, and if the Kraut armor is pushing that way, they're gonna need all the help they can get."

Higgins looked up slowly, peered out, ducked again. "Looks like that Kraut infantry is staying put for now. But they're gonna try more mortars, you can bet on that. They see us moving around, they're gonna open up with everything they've got. No screwing around. Get back off this ridge as fast as you can. We'll meet up . . . hell, wherever we can." He paused. "If we can't find a way back to the town, the captain says we may be on our own out here. That's all I know."

Higgins peered up again. "Give me a little covering fire. I think this squad's still got half a dozen guys in good shape. I've gotta pass the word. Give me ten minutes, then expect the machine gunners. You understand?"

Benson nodded, and Mitchell said, "We're ready, Sarge."

Benson raised up, aimed the rifle, Mitchell doing the same, and Benson aimed at a clump of black dirt far down the hill, knew it hid a cluster of Germans. He glanced back at the sergeant, who gave a sharp nod, and now both men fired, Benson emptying his clip. Higgins was up and out of the hole quickly, slithering his way down the ridge. Benson wanted to watch him, make sure he made it, but the Germans responded with fire of their own, a heavy machine gun from the far woods, pops and cracks in the air above. Benson squatted down, and Mitchell said, "He made it. Saw his

boots disappear. I think that's Milsaps and Lane down there, maybe Donnelly. They've been firing pretty steady, so I think they're okay."

Benson felt a strange empty shock, bent his knees, leaning against the
muddy dirt.

"They pushed right past us. We couldn't stop them."

"No time for whining about it. We've gotta get the hell out of here."

Benson looked at Yunis, who seemed calmer now, his head down, staring at nothing.

"What about him?"

The German machine gun had stopped. Mitchell looked up, nothing
to see, bent low again. "What *about* him? He feels like fighting, he can
fight. He feels like curling up in his momma's arms, he can stay here."

"We can't just leave him behind."

Mitchell kicked at Yunis's leg, the man jumping, startled.

"The hell we can't. I'm not carrying him on my back. Hey . . . gutless!"

Yunis looked up, reacting to Mitchell's words as though he had never
seen the man before.

"What? What do you want?"

"We're about to get our asses out of here. Can you run as good as you cry?"

"Easy, Kenny. Look, Yunis . . . Arnie. We've got to get out of here.
Keep your head down and run like hell. Follow us, okay?"

Yunis nodded slowly, but the look in his eyes didn't change.

There was a shout down the line, and the machine guns started now,
short bursts, another one farther away. Mitchell bent low, seemed to coil
like a spring.

"Let's go!"

Benson did the same, a last glance at Yunis, who didn't move at all.
Mitchell uncoiled, was up quickly, crawling, and Benson followed, his
boots slipping on the muddy walls of the foxhole. He was crawling furiously, his knees in wet snow, cradling the rifle in his bent arms. He saw
others doing the same, saw the tree line behind them, broken and blasted
timber, the ground falling away on the other side. The machine guns
stopped, more shouts, and Mitchell rose to his feet, running, bent low.
Benson tried to follow, slipping in the mud, pushed himself hard, his boots
finding the traction. He shadowed Mitchell, the man running in jerking
zigzags, easing past the debris of so many shattered trees. The Germans
were firing, cracks and whistles, but the shots were scattered, wild.
Mitchell was upright, the higher ground behind them, and Benson fol-

lowed closely, stayed with him step for step. The ground still fell away, the men running downhill, gaining speed, some stumbling, losing control, the snow deep, tangles of timber. The hillside rolled into a thick bottom, an icy creek, and Benson felt the ground softer, the snow melting into deep mud. He struggled, the ground sucking at his boots, his breathing in cold hard gasps, and Mitchell stopped beside the creek, tested the icy edges with his boots. Benson put a hand against a small tree, his chest heaving, others there as well, one man with a wound, a bloody bandage on his arm. They stared at each other, searching faces, and Benson saw the sergeant, Higgins, vomiting in the snow, rare weakness. The others gathered closer, waiting for the sergeant's authority, any authority at all, and Benson saw the faces clearly, names in his head, Milsaps, Donnelly, Lane the bully, no bully at all now, just another scared soldier.

Higgins was back on his feet, looking back, searching, scanned the others now, said, "The machine gunners went the other way, I think. Dammit!" He kept his stare on the hill behind them. "The Krauts watched us pull out. So they'll be coming like hell, you can bet on that. We've got to keep moving. They'll probably slow down enough to take a look at our foxholes, see what kinds of stuff we left behind." He turned toward the main road, still hidden by the trees. "Listen."

They all stood quietly, followed Higgins's gaze. There were vehicles in motion still, sounds of a fight to the west and south. Higgins said, "Captain Moore said to get across that road, join up with whoever we can find. I don't think that's likely until dark. The road goes straight to Saint Vith, and if you get lost, use the road to guide you. But stay clear of it."

"Where's the captain, Sarge?"

The voice came from one of the others, Benson ignoring the name.

"How the hell do I know? We've got no radio, and these woods are stuffed with Krauts, all moving west. We might be in a footrace, boys. If they take Saint Vith, well, hell, I don't know what that means. If I knew what was going on, they'd have made me a general. Too much talk. Time to go."

Higgins slogged through the icy creek, the others following. Benson glanced back up the ridge, through the shattered trees, black and broken ground, the stink of explosives still around him. He hesitated, stared at the hilltop they had left, heard voices, German voices, thought of Higgins's words, *They'll search the foxholes.* Benson started to move, tried to escape the image in his mind, Yunis, curled up like a ball, waiting for whatever the Germans would do to him.

10. EISENHOWER

In early December, Eisenhower had spent most of his time on the move, visiting corps and division commands, greeting the troops, most of them already settling into a routine of small-scale assaults, probing and taking advantage of those sectors where the enemy might be weak or unprepared. Since troops on both sides were hampered by the poor weather, air support was either limited or nonexistent, and so the single greatest Allied advantage had been neutralized. Once the weather cleared, the planes would begin their missions again, tactical support for the ground forces that would ramp up the intensity of the Allied drive into Germany. All along the Allied lines, the commanders had begun each day with a weather report, which came to them with dismal consistency. The winter weather was growing steadily worse, especially around the Ardennes, where Hodges had stretched thin his lines with untested troops. Eisenhower had seen the maps, knew that the defenses along the Ardennes were far weaker than he normally would have allowed. But with such bitter cold, and increasing amounts of snow, the Allied command had to assume no one on either side had much to worry about.

On December 16, as the German thrust across the Ardennes Forest blew past the vastly unprepared American defenses, the power of the surprise was absolute. The Germans had so completely disrupted American communications that the highest-ranking commanders had no idea what was happening to their troops. For a full day, three German armies drove westward, cutting off or annihilating the stunned Americans, without anyone in the American command centers understanding just how severe the German assault was. Courtney Hodges's First Army, whose divisions were stretched thin along the ridges and dense woods of the Ardennes, were quickly driven into total chaos. The chaos spread all the way up the chain of command, through Hodges's headquarters, and then higher still, to Omar Bradley, who commanded all American ground forces. Though some Allied intelligence officers had reported the massing of German forces along the eastern edges of the Ardennes, no one among the highest-ranking commanders gave the reports much credibility. It was after all, winter. Since the Normandy landings in June, the Allied forces had waged a steady, if inconsistent campaign to drive the German army back into their own homeland, a campaign that had been mostly successful. Not Eisenhower, not Bradley, not Hodges, had imagined a scenario where the Germans would suddenly turn the tide in the other direction. Despite the various stumbles along the way, to Eisenhower and the generals under his command, victory had been a foregone conclusion. Even as the German forces were driving the bulge deeper through the Ardennes Forest, no one at SHAEF had any idea what was happening, and few command posts near the fighting had any way of letting them know.

SHAEF, VERSAILLES, FRANCE
DECEMBER 16, 1944, 6 P.M.

Eisenhower lit another cigarette, sat back in his chair. Tedder was up, moving around the small office, stopped close to one wall, a makeshift barrier of plywood. He stared at it, smiled, put his hand on it.

"You know, Ike, no one would fault you if you had a bigger office."

"This place is a palace, for God's sake. This was von Rundstedt's headquarters, you know. He used to sit right here, maybe in this same chair. I get the irony of that. It seemed appropriate for me to move in here, especially to the French. But this place is a little ridiculous. Look at the size of these rooms. We could hold banquets in here, and we'd have to shout to be heard. I had them put up that plywood, divide things up a bit. Make these offices a little more practical. A lot more comfortable too."

Tedder laughed, rapped a knuckle against the plywood wall. "Monty wouldn't see it that way. This place would suit him quite well. Without the room dividers."

"I don't give a hot damn what suits Monty. I'd just like him to do his job and keep his mouth shut."

Tedder turned toward him, was filling his pipe from a small pouch of tobacco. "You'll be fortunate if you get one out of two, Ike."

Eisenhower stared at the large map that hung against the far wall. "I'm going to have to hand him some of the American units up close to his flank. Once we begin to push east, the Brits are going to need some strength they don't have now. I have to tell you, Arthur, no one in this command is happy about that. You should hear Patton bitch. But Monty's drive will be crucial, once we get going. I'm expecting a jump-off date in early January, and we can't have any screwing around. If Monty has a few of my boys . . ." He stopped, knew it was another of his intolerable slips, a show of nationalism he had no tolerance for in the others around him. "Sorry. You know what I mean, dammit. If Monty has some *American* support to add to his own, it might encourage him to move a little quicker. With Patton and Devers pushing hard in the south, I can bet you Monty's not going to want to drag his ass behind. Patton knows the job in front of him, and it has nothing to do with Berlin, but I've already heard noises down his way that he thinks he should be the first one in, all that same Messina business again. I'm not having another damn race like they did in Sicily. Patton needs to keep his focus on Frankfurt. As far as I'm concerned, Berlin has very little to do with ending this war."

Tedder seemed surprised. "What do you mean? That would pretty well signal the end, don't you think? I don't care how blindly the German people still support Hitler, if he loses the capital, not even the Gestapo will believe they can still win."

"I'll worry about that when the time comes. I'm much more concerned with driving our people across the Siegfried line. After that, we have some pretty stout rivers to cross, and the enemy won't make that easy for us. Berlin is a word for the newspapers. You ever heard of Ulysses Grant?"

Tedder nodded, smoke rolling up from his pipe. "Quite so. One of your most capable battlefield commanders. Did a pretty thorough mop-up of old Robert E. Lee, if I recall your history."

"Grant understood war. That's why he won. When the time came, he ignored Richmond, ignored the symbolism of a capital city. He knew that if you want to win a war, cities have very little to do with it. You have to kick the hell out of the other guy's army. That's what I intend to do."

There was a gentle knock at the door. Eisenhower put out the cigarette, said, "What?"

An aide appeared. "Sir. General Bradley has arrived."

"Outstanding." He looked up at Tedder. "I invited Brad to come down, have some dinner. I could tell he was itching to get out of his HQ. I can always tell when he wants to talk about things, get something off his chest. Won't do it on the phone. I know him better than that."

"I suspect he also wants to shake your hand."

Eisenhower frowned, said, "I don't want a big deal made out of this. No damn ceremonies." He looked up at Tedder, winked. "Well, maybe a little one. But only after it's official."

The word had come from Washington the day before. Eisenhower had been nominated to receive his fifth star, the highest possible rank in the American military. Despite his own staff's insistence that he don the extra star right away, he had refused, would instead wait until the order came from George Marshall that the nomination had been formally approved. Eisenhower knew that if there was some political subterfuge, some hidden enemy in the Congress who pulled the right string, it would be much easier to add the fifth star to his collar than to remove it.

Tedder tapped the pipe into the ashtray, said, "I'm off then, with your permission. There's some row about gasoline for a couple of the fighter wings, something to do with who gets what. I won't bore you with the details." He clamped his hat under his arm, made a short bow to Eisenhower, was quickly out the door.

Eisenhower heard the voices outside, a hearty greeting between Tedder and Bradley, mutual respect that had often been hard to come by between American and British commanders. Bradley was there now, stood in the open door.

"So, what the hell do I call you now? Your head growing like a balloon? No, I don't suppose so. Not like some. But, Mister Five Star. Nice ring to it, eh?"

Eisenhower motioned him into the office, Bradley shutting the door behind him.

"How about you call me *Ike* until I tell you differently. You hungry? I'm about ready for some supper."

Bradley sat, glanced around the office, shook his head at the plywood walls. "Sure, chow sounds fine. Your mess hall's got a better menu than the one in Luxembourg." Bradley paused. "So, what am I allowed to call MacArthur?"

Eisenhower smiled, knew Bradley had something in his craw. Supper would wait. "Anything you like, as long as it doesn't leave this office."

Bradley seemed to think, choosing his words, but the humor was gone. "It's a knockdown brawl, Ike. MacArthur's screaming at the War Department for every soldier he can get, and they're too intimidated not to oblige him. We've got regiments along our front at two-thirds strength, and the manpower people in the States keep making excuses why we're not getting the troops. Well, no, they're making *one* excuse. MacArthur is getting the replacements faster than we are. That wasn't the plan, never was. Washington expects us to wrap this up before we commit everything to the Pacific. So why do they let him bully them? It's going to cost us, Ike. We start the new campaigns without full strength, we're going to lose people we shouldn't lose. The German is severely weakened, and that's a situation we have to take the best advantage of. Since Normandy, our greatest successes came when the German popped up out of his hole and gave us a shot at him. That's what I'm hoping for now. Every time the German launches a counterattack, we chew it to pieces. But we have to have the people, Ike. The rifle companies have been busted to hell, and you know as well as I do, it makes no difference how many men you can count on a division's payroll, you have to be at full strength on the front lines. We need riflemen worse than we need anyone else. MacArthur needs headlines, and he's got a big damn mouth."

Eisenhower had expected this, but Bradley was rarely this animated.

"I'll send a cable to Marshall. Not much else I can do, you know that."

"Five stars, Ike. Your bitching just got a little more volume added to it."

Eisenhower shrugged. "Maybe. At least now I match Monty's rank."

Bradley smiled, his anger settling down. "I wonder if he knows that a five-star is equal to a British field marshal."

"I promise you he knows it. He already sent me congratulations. Took the opportunity to remind me that he's about to win our bet."

"You made a bet?"

"A while back . . . a long while back, I bet Monty five bucks that we'd have this war over by this Christmas. He asked me if I wanted to go ahead and pay up. I told him there were still nine days left. He'd have to wait."

Bradley sniffed, stared down at his hands. Eisenhower knew how much he despised Montgomery.

"What?"

"Maybe that explains a few things, Ike. Leave it to Monty to drag his ass into battle like a herd of turtles, just so the war would last long enough to win him five bucks."

"Sir! Excuse me?"

The door opened, and Eisenhower was surprised to see his chief of intelligence, the British general Kenneth Strong.

"What's going on, Kenny?"

Behind Strong, Eisenhower saw another man, a British colonel, familiar, part of the intelligence staff. Strong stepped into the room, acknowledged Bradley with a curt nod, said, "Sir, we have received a rather disturbing report. I apologize for the apparent tardiness of this. It seems that at five this morning, the enemy opened up a considerable assault against the American First Army sector. Five separate points across the Ardennes front have been hit."

"A demonstration, probably," said Bradley. "Von Rundstedt has to know that Hodges is stretched pretty thin in that area. But it's hardly a place to launch an offensive."

Eisenhower could see that Strong was clearly concerned. Strong held out a piece of paper, said, "We're not as confident about that, sir. These reports are sketchy at best, and we've not heard any direct confirmation from the forward command posts. The air people can't confirm either, since that entire area is socked in. Fog and snowstorms for a couple days now, not expected to lift anytime soon."

Eisenhower felt an uncomfortable stirring in his stomach. "Do we know the enemy's strength? Any specifics about what kinds of units are involved? How many divisions?"

Strong glanced at his colonel, who said, "Best we can tell, sir, the attack is being made with a considerable amount of armor. We received several reports of a significant artillery barrage early this morning, but after that most of the outposts and regimental commands went quiet. The reports that did get back to General Hodges were, again, sketchy at best. General Hodges did not feel this warranted an immediate response. At least, that's what I was told late this morning—"

Strong interrupted. "With all respects to General Hodges, sir, we've been unable to reach him directly. His headquarters is to the north, and we seem to be somewhat . . . separated. Early reports suggested that the attack drove primarily against General Middleton's Eighth Corps sector." Strong moved to the map on the wall, pointed. "Here."

Eisenhower reached for a phone, waited impatiently for the voice to respond.

"Get General Smith in here, and whatever senior staff is available. Now!"

Strong seemed to wait, and Eisenhower stood, felt the energy flowing, stared at the map, flags indicating the position of the various divisions.

Smith was at the door, Eisenhower's chief of staff moving in quickly. "What's going on, Ike?"

Others were there as well, and Eisenhower said, "Beetle, the enemy is up to something. It could be pretty big."

Strong pointed at the map again, and Eisenhower already knew what the gap between the small blue flags meant. Strong said, "There are suggestions . . . I hesitate to call them reports, that the Germans have sent their Sixth Panzer Army toward Saint Vith, and their Fifth toward Bastogne. Infantry and armored columns are reported all across the sector, but those two towns are primary intersections. It makes tactical sense that if the Germans intended to breach our position there, those two towns are key to their success. I expect further details very soon."

Eisenhower said, "They didn't choose the Ardennes by chance. We're thin there, too damn thin, and von Rundstedt knows it. That's why Hitler brought that old son of a bitch back into command, to run a campaign like this, to hit us hard. We should have known that."

Bradley said, "I'm not too certain about this, Ike. He could be setting us up for a major attack somewhere else, either north or south. My guess is north, since we know he'd love to hand Aachen back to Hitler. The Ardennes is a hell of a place for a winter offensive."

Eisenhower was surprised at Bradley's disagreement, shook his head. "No. We're too strong on both ends. We're weak in the middle. Hodges and Patton are spending all their energy driving east, and there's a big damn gap between them. Those troops spread across the center are just . . . sitting there. And there aren't very damn many of them."

Bradley stared at the map. "But the Ardennes. Jesus, Ike, it's a hell of a place to launch anything. There aren't enough roads through there to support an armored blitz. In those hills, they measure the snow in *feet,* for God's sake."

Eisenhower looked at Bradley, said, "They're not beat, Brad. We may have overestimated that."

Bradley's expression began to change, absorbing the message. Eisenhower looked at the map again. "We were supposed to think the enemy was going backward. I thought . . . hell, we all thought they were headed back behind the Rhine, make their stand there. Maybe that's what we were *supposed* to think." Eisenhower looked at the others, no one speaking. "Hitler seems to be very good at remembering his victories. He did this four years ago, the same damn place, and the French were standing around just like we are now, saying, *It can't be done.* In a month's time, the British were driven to Dunkirk and the French were whipped. Well, we're not going to be driven anywhere, and we're damn sure not going to be whipped. We have armor on both flanks, and I want a call to go out to Patton—and find a way to reach Hodges, even if you have to go through Monty. They are to suspend their attacks to the east and concentrate available armor toward the flanks of the German advance. Move whatever troops we can move and put them into the fight where the threat is greatest. Brad, that's for you to determine. Find out just what the hell is going on up there, and make damn sure everyone knows about it. You're right about the snow. The roads are lousy through there, and unless von Rundstedt has some secret weapon for moving tanks across mountainsides, they can't advance very quickly." He searched the room. "I need some weather reports. Get Group Captain Stagg or some of his staff. Find out how long this crappy weather is going to keep the tactical air people on the ground. That's the key." Eisenhower couldn't take his eyes from the map, the small blue pins that marked the line. "On narrow mountain roads, columns of tanks don't stand a gnat's chance against our airpower. Hitler might have ordered this attack come hell or high water, but an old bastard like von Rundstedt knows it won't work unless the weather keeps us out of the air. So far, he's called it right. Get me some damn weather reports!"

He backed away from the map, saw Bedell Smith standing beside Bradley, both men anxious to go. Eisenhower nodded, said, "Find out, gentlemen. Facts. Troop strength. Who we're up against, where they're going, and how strong they are. If we got caught with our pants down . . . well, dammit, pull them back up!"

Eisenhower pointed toward the door, the room emptying quickly, and he saw Smith put an arm on Bradley's shoulder, Smith saying, "Well, Brad, you wanted the enemy to counterattack. Looks like you've got your wish."

Bradley stopped, looked back at Eisenhower.

"Yeah. I just didn't want one quite this big."

11. BENSON

There had been no sleep, no stopping to reconnoiter. The men had moved steadily west, through patches of snow and heavy timber, staying in the lower ravines, where the creeks flowed past icy banks, soft noises that hid their own or magnified the silence around them. The darkness was oppressive, but the blanket of snow allowed just enough visibility for the men to stay close to one another. Benson had followed the man in front of him, presumed it to be Mitchell most of the time, the men gathering occasionally around the sergeant, a glimpse of Higgins's compass, whispers of where they should move next, what each man might have heard. Higgins did not bully them, and Benson could see that the sergeant seemed as frightened as they were but did not let it rule his decisions. They all knew there were others in the woods, men from both sides, the Americans driven from their cover by an onslaught of German power none of them expected. Higgins had made a priority of finding more of their own, and they had come across a few scattered, terrified men, huddled into hiding, drawn out by the shadows of familiar helmets. Higgins hoped to find more organization too, retreating columns led by field officers, who might know exactly what was happening, how far they had to go, which roads and trails were safe.

Though Higgins relied on his compass, the terrain did not cooperate, and often they were forced to move the wrong way, winding around some deep ravine, the best way to stay in cover. Benson knew, as they all knew, that despite the compass they were most certainly lost, but none of the men had any reason to argue with Higgins about where they were heading.

They continued to find others, small pockets of men who usually let them pass, then a sharp call, English, Higgins quick to respond. There were anxious greetings, every man feeling the safety of increasing numbers. But no officers were among them, not yet, and Higgins spoke to other sergeants, men leading fragments of squads, remnants of platoons. All the while, artillery fire streaked overhead, hard rumbling that echoed through the valleys, the Germans shelling positions far back, driving a massive wedge of power forward across the ragged network of roads. Higgins and the other sergeants kept their men as far from the roads as they could, no one wanting to suddenly stumble into flat open ground in the midst of a German column or, worse, a regiment of German infantry on the prowl for men exactly like these lost Americans. Throughout the night, the noises from the larger roads could be heard above them, the roads carved into hillsides, winding in a haphazard pattern that hid and then magnified the sounds of the rolling machines. They knew the sound of the tanks, the steel treads distinct even on snow-packed roads. But the other vehicles were a mystery, each man imagining the variety, self-propelled artillery pieces, troop trucks and staff cars, armored anti-aircraft carriers, even motorcycles. The noises came in surprising waves, the men slipping around a hillside only to hear some caravan in motion close above them, and so they backed away, staying in their cover, changing direction, trying another way.

By three in the morning, their exhaustion took over, and the sergeants halted them long enough to share whatever rations they might happen to be carrying. Most of the men had backpacks still, and the K rations emerged, canteens passed, whispered thank-yous. Higgins had stopped his own squad close to a creek, some of the men refilling their canteens, Benson among them, no concern now for caution about *bad water,* some long-ago lecture by a lieutenant reading from some manual. Thirst had overpowered the fear of dysentery.

There was other suffering as well, and Benson shared the misery in his boots, socks soaked, kept warm by the slogging march. But the cold was taking a toll, and Benson was relieved that Higgins was tolerant, allowing the healthier men to care for the crippled or wounded. Benson had kept spare socks inside his shirt, another lesson from another lieutenant, a clever notion that a man's body temperature would help dry them. But even those were soaked, this time by his own sweat. The constant movement kept away the astonishing cold, but when they paused, as they did with the K rations, the cold swallowed them, wet gloves and boots chilling rapidly, canteens freezing, men suffering from sneezing fits or coughing, the rasping sound of some new sickness. The sergeants could only respond by moving them again, in case the Germans were close, some patrol perhaps hearing the sounds and sweeping down on them before any of them could react.

There were few heavy weapons among the men Benson had seen, but the rifles were there, nearly all the men carrying some kind of weapon. Among his own squad, there was one BAR, carried by the wide-shouldered Milsaps, a quiet man whom Benson liked. Higgins kept Milsaps in front of their makeshift column, not just for firepower, but in case the heavy weapon wore the man down. Higgins would not let anyone fall back, no one abandoned. At every stop, all the sergeants made quick head counts, and Benson began to feel more respect for Higgins than he had just for a sergeant's stripes. Higgins cared about his men, even men he didn't know, and in the desperate darkness the other sergeants were sharing the responsibility, keeping as many men together as they could. As he trudged through the footsteps of the men in front of him, Benson understood what a leader was.

December 17, 1944, Dawn

It had become light enough to see the treetops above them, and Higgins motioned them to lie low. He signaled to the others to spread out wide to one side, then crawled forward alone in the snow, up a steep incline. Others continued to come up, spreading out along the base of the hill, whispers, pointing, questions. Benson watching the trail Higgins had left, glancing at the men around him. Some were familiar, Mitchell staring ahead, rifle ready, prepared to move quickly if Higgins ran into some kind of trouble. Lane was there as well, frightened, exhausted, the same look on the faces of others, men Benson didn't know, the same look they saw when they looked at him. Around Benson no one spoke, but there were low voices up ahead, up the rise, and every man jerked to attention, rifles ready.

Higgins was there suddenly, slipping and stumbling down through the snow, sliding on his own icy trail, tired relief on his face. "Come on! We found our boys."

All along the hillside, the men began to move, climbing, mostly in single file. The trees were thinning out, tall pines, but above, the ground flattened out, scattered trees, hills beyond. The clearing was a quarter mile across, and nestled in the center were the remnants of a town, shattered buildings, mostly stone, most without roofs, the wreckage of walls. Benson could see now that the village sat in a wide bowl, had heard of this, a scene so typical throughout these hills. This one was small, no more than a dozen structures, all destroyed. The roads ran out in three directions, one climbing the hill out on the far side, and everywhere there were pockmarks of black, the effects of artillery shells. All through the village and beyond, men were in motion, seeking cover, shoving aside debris, creating dugouts and barricades. There was sound too, heavy engines, and Benson saw them now, the great hulks, marked by dull white stars, tanks. They rolled out of the hillside on the left, a solid line of six, the beloved Shermans, and Benson shivered, felt as though they were rescued, heard cheering from somewhere in front. The tanks spread out, seeking some kind of cover in the wreckage of the buildings, jerking to a halt, the turrets all pointing their cannon to the right, down the main road. Benson looked that way, saw open ground, more shattered homes, and beyond, the road climbing up another hill. He searched for Higgins, saw men still staggering up out of the woods, climbing up through the deep ravine, more men than Benson realized were a part of their nightlong march. Some just sat in the snow, too tired to understand what was happening in front of them, why the blasted village was crawling with activity. Benson spotted the sergeant and, with him, another familiar face, haggard weariness. It was Captain Moore. Benson moved that way, others with him, Mitchell close, and Moore looked toward them, scanned the faces, focused on the BAR, nodded.

"Thank God. I didn't think this many of our boys made it. Most of these men are from Charlie and Easy companies. Captain Spence made it, and a few of the platoon commanders. You boys are lucky as hell."

Higgins said, "Where should we go, sir? We're ready to fight."

"You better be. We're not going anywhere else until somebody at HQ tells us to. Colonel Nagle was here a few minutes ago, Cavender's exec, told us that General Jones has ordered us to hold this position. I haven't seen the battalion commander at all. No idea where the HQ command post ended up, if they made it out at all. We've got people beyond that hill to the north, some of Able Company, trying to link up to the Four Two Two, but I don't know what's happening up there. The enemy is up there pretty thick, pushing hard toward Saint Vith. I was told we've got armor support coming. The entire Seventh Armored Division is on its way, but nobody knows when they'll get here. The colonel was pretty pissed, but not much he can do about it."

Moore scanned the village, Benson seeing what he saw. The tank engines had shut down, and their hatches were open, men with binoculars staring out toward the hills to the east. Around them, some of the infantry were moving into the open spaces behind the tanks, using them for cover. Closer to the edge of the woods, a machine-gun crew was crawling into place, one man carrying a tripod, men digging furiously, burying the gun into a good line of fire. Close by, others were moving out beyond the edge of the village, through the trees, digging into banks of snow. He saw a pair of mortar crews, more digging, the men putting their weapons into position, boxes of shells stacked up close by. Through the entire scene were the riflemen, some chopping at the frozen ground with the brim of their helmets or small shovels, a struggle against frozen earth. On the far side of the village, a line of men stretched up into the far woods, some setting up embankments of snow or hauling bits of wood from the tree line behind them, logs and branches. They were building makeshift barricades, poor substitutes for foxholes, but the only cover they had.

Moore seemed to appraise the position, then said to Higgins, "Put your men along the edge of this road, down toward the ravine. Pile up whatever you can and check your weapons."

Higgins said, "Sir, where's the enemy? This seems awfully vulnerable here. The high ground is all around us."

Moore sneezed, wiped his nose with the sleeve of his coat. "If I knew where the enemy was, I'd be a damn general. This isn't a tactics drill, Sergeant. We didn't pick this ground. Orders are to try to keep this intersection open. Every damn village around here sits in the bottom of a big damn eggcup. High ground in every direction. If the enemy brings artillery up to that far ridgeline, we're sitting ducks. But the colonel says they're moving everywhere in this sector, advancing as quick as we let them. They haven't shown any signs of digging artillery in anywhere. Looks to me like they're trying to bust right through us. Some of our field artillery was able to pull back, and they've set up behind us, up in those trees. But it isn't much. Some of our boys had to leave their guns behind, which hurts like hell, but I saw some of the seventy-fives, so maybe we can hold off some tanks."

There were new sounds, jeeps, a column of four rolling down from the wooded hillside behind the village. Moore said, "Now what? That's the exec again, Nagle. And Colonel Cavender. I'm sure this'll be *good* news."

Benson stood silently, watched the men pour forward, clean coats, clean-shaven faces, men who had not slept in foxholes or marched all night through the woods. Moore moved toward the jeeps, and Benson heard the talk, hot and angry. Beside him, Mitchell said, "Sounds like the captain is getting his ass chewed. Sounds like he was just following orders. But this sure doesn't look like a place I wanna be if the Krauts roll over that hill-side."

Moore suddenly shouted, "Then send one of those high-brass sons of bitches out here, and he can see it for himself!"

Benson watched the others, officers reacting to the outburst with quiet words, self-conscious glances toward the men around them, some tugging nervously at their clean coats. Cavender put a hand on Moore's shoulder, leaning in close, discreet words the men around them wouldn't hear.

The officers continued to huddle, the discussion calming, and Mitchell said, "I guess they can't string up a field officer right now. The colonel's letting Moore throw off steam. He's probably as lost as the rest of us."

Higgins was moving through the men, putting them in motion, said, "Keep your mouth shut, soldier. We've got enough problems without you worrying about the officers. Dig in along a line . . . this way. Put your right flank against the trees at the drop-off. If the Krauts show up here, it'll be on that main road, most likely. The captain says they're leading with tanks, not infantry."

Mitchell moved toward a dip in the roadside, and Benson followed, saw rocks, began to dig around them, numb fingers, the wind now slap-ping against his face. The sweat on his face had turned to stinging pain, and he rubbed his fingers through the thin gloves, more pain, his fingertips split and raw. He grabbed a small boulder, tried to free it from the frozen ground, but it wouldn't move, his hands useless, no strength.

Mitchell chopped at the edge of the rock with his bayonet, the icy dirt unyielding. "Dammit! How are we supposed to *dig in?*"

Benson kept probing the roadside, found a larger rock, loose, and Mitchell was there quickly, rolling the rock forward, a shallow depression left behind.

Mitchell said, "Well, there's your foxhole." He began pushing against the snow, forming an embankment, close beside the boulder. "It gets hot, I'm gonna join you behind that rock."

Benson felt guilty, said, "Thanks. My hands are hurting bad. Don't know what the hell happened."

"Cold and wet, kiddo. Used to happen to me on hunting trips. Don't worry about it. The snow'll work. As long as they can't see me, I'm okay."

Around them, the others were working, mostly with snow, adding to the defensive position, makeshift cover from whatever they could find. Benson knelt behind the rock, glanced out to the east, up the road where Higgins had pointed. He looked past the men on his right, down toward the trees, no one there, thought, what if they're wrong? What if infantry comes around us? What happened to those Krauts we were shooting at? The questions were fogging his mind, no answers to clear them away.

Mitchell slid down behind his mound of snow, said, "Sit down, Eddie. Let the officers run the show."

"Yeah, sure."

He crouched on one knee, the misery of the cold spreading through every limb. But he was curious still, focused on the gathering of officers, saw one man with a radio, his hand covering his mouth as he spoke into the handset. The others were staring out across to the far trees, orders going out to men who moved quickly, and Benson thought, the lieutenants, I guess. Or sergeants. He thought of Greeley, the inept lieutenant. *Field officers.* A good way to describe the first guys who get killed.

Benson heard the man at the radio now, the hand uncovering his mouth, no more discretion, frustration in the man's voice. "Sir, there is no sign of them right here. But they've moved into Schönberg, and I have reports of a column to the north, at Hervert. We're doing all we can to pull back and consolidate, but we've lost contact with the Four Two Two, and no one has heard a thing from the Ninety-ninth since this started."

The man paused, and Benson saw disgust on his face.

"Sir, it might be better if you talked to Colonel Cavender directly."

Cavender took the radio, listened for a long moment, then said, "General Jones, with all due respect, General Middleton needs to understand that his order is a little late. The line you are ordering me to hold was overrun by the enemy last night. Those villages he wants us to defend are all in enemy hands." He paused, listening. "Yes, sir. My apologies to the general for his error. Yes, sir, I understand. I haven't heard anything from either regiment. The Four Two Four is well south of us, and the enemy shoved a wedge through the gap pretty easily. As your aide said, sir, we were cut off to the north, so we have no contact with the Ninety-ninth. Yes, sir. We'll hold out here as long as we can. We have retreating infantry still finding us, and this position is getting stronger. One platoon of tanks has come in, and we have a few mortars and heavy machine guns. May I ask, sir, when is the rest of the armor coming up?" There was a pause, and Cavender lowered his head. "I understand, sir. Thank you, sir. Good luck to you as well, sir."

Cavender handed the radio back to his aide, turned to the other officers, another quick huddle, and now he said to Captain Moore, "The corps commander ordered us to hold at all costs along a north–south line the Germans took eight hours ago. Neither division nor corps HQ has any idea what's going on out here. The Seventh Armored Division has been ordered to move up and meet the enemy's advance, but General Jones has no idea when they might actually get here. Maybe hours, maybe tomorrow."

Cavender looked around, shook his head, looked out toward the hill to the east. He pointed, said, "Who's that? Are those our boys?"

There were shouts, and Benson saw movement up along the far ridge, men emerging from the trees, coming down toward the road. They were dressed in dark coats, the helmets familiar, a straggling mass of men gathering in the open, coming off the hill. He raised his rifle, instinct, watched as they came closer. Some began to run, could see the protection of the village, others moved in slow plodding steps. They continued to emerge from the trees on the ridge, and Benson thought, there's gotta be a hundred of 'em, maybe more. The road was a thickening column, a steady flow closer now, and Benson saw up on the hillside wounded, limping men with dirty rags wrapped on legs, bandages on heads, men helping others, supporting them. Others moved with quick steps, rifles in hand, a few glancing back where they had come from. Benson saw one man stumble, holding a bloody wound on his thigh, a medic moving out quickly from the village, kneeling to help. More calls went out, more medics running out to meet the wounded, but the others began to pour into the village, ignoring the barricades, the snowbanks, jogging past the tanks.

Benson heard the voices rising as they passed.

"They're right behind us! They're coming!"

"Go! They're coming! Pull back!"

Officers moved out from the village, a chaos of shouting, some of the officers searching, finding their own men. Some of the men seemed to calm, responding to orders, grateful, moving into line, obeying officers they knew, others falling down beside strangers, still willing to fight. But many more did not stop, pushed through, climbed the logs, kicked through snow, a mad scramble through the wreckage of the village in a steady unstoppable wave.

The medics continued their work, some calling for litter bearers, the worst of the wounded hauled back to some kind of cover. Some still limped forward, but Benson saw one man shoved aside, another wave of men emerging from the tree line in full panic. Benson wanted to go forward, help the medics, saw Moore moving out into the road, grabbing one man, yelling something, and Benson saw the man's face, a lieutenant, terrified, Moore ramming the man with sharp words. The lieutenant seemed to stagger, and Moore dragged him by the coat, back behind the defense, a hard shout, "Get control of your men! We have to hold here! You hear me?"

The man seemed to listen, and Moore released him, the lieutenant responding by running, joining those who had lost control. Moore yelled after the man, put a hand on his pistol, and Benson stared in horror, but the pistol stayed in its holster. Moore ignored the man now, moved away toward more of the refugees, another effort to stop the flow.

Higgins absorbed the scene, some of the men stopping in the ruins of the village, a dirty frightened mob, many voices, officers trying to take control, sergeants grabbing men by the shirt, pulling them down into the makeshift defensive line. Benson looked again toward Cavender, but the jeeps were pulling away, the men in the clean coats moving back up the hill into the trees, back behind the riflemen and the machine-gun and mortar crews, far back from the six Sherman tanks that anchored the entire position. More men were coming down the hill, stragglers, more wounded, the medics still in motion, far out in the open. He fought the need to help, flexed his painful fingers, nothing you can do. He looked to the north, the third road winding away from the village in that direction, disappearing into the woods above. He could see a roadblock, a splotch of black, troops hunkering down, spread out into the tall trees. He realized now, this is the whole thing, the *battlefield*. This is *us,* the Four Two Three, or a bunch of it anyway. Maybe all that's left.

Men were still giving orders, and Benson saw the last of the wounded carried back, the road clear, bloody snow and churned-up tracks. One man suddenly came up from the woods to the right, pure panic, searching, wild fear in his eyes, a high-pitched cry, "We're going to die!"

The man began to run close behind them, and Benson saw Mitchell launch himself up, a shoulder in the man's side, a hard fall, the man's face in the snow. Mitchell kicked the man hard in the side, yelled, "You damn coward! Get up! Fight!"

Higgins was there, grabbed at Mitchell. "No time for this! Let them go! He's useless. Get back in line!"

Mitchell dropped back down, breathing heavily, Higgins standing close behind their small blockade.

After a long moment, Higgins said, "Listen!"

Benson heard it now, the sounds too familiar, steel treads on a snow-packed road, the rumble of heavy engines. He turned that way, looked up the main road, nothing but sound, the heavy roar of engines coming closer.

Higgins said, "Down! Get that BAR up here, behind these rocks!"

Benson felt his stomach churning, the hard beat of his heart, laid his rifle on top of the boulder, saw Mitchell shoving more snow up in front, low curses. For one long moment, the village was silent. He looked toward the Shermans, no motion, their hatches closed, crews huddled low, everyone into their cover. He lay on his side, his helmet against the snow, his hands in a paralyzed grip on the rifle.

Beside him, Mitchell slapped the snow. "Hell of a lot of good this is gonna do."

The first shell impacted in front of them, rocks blowing back past Benson's cover, a blast of snow and dirt into Benson's face. The jolt stunned him, screams to one side, and more shells came in, hard concussion, ringing in his ears. He spat dirt from his mouth, pulled his chin in tight to his chest, saw Mitchell, hands on his ears, rolling over, facing him, hot anger. Mitchell spoke, but there was no sound through the roar in Benson's ears. The ground buckled beneath him, a punch in his side, more shells coming, heavy thumps, tumbling rocks, smoke rolling past. More thunder rolled close by, the Shermans returning fire, and he wanted to see, to know what was coming, what kind of enemy, knew not to look, his brain screaming at him, stay down! He caught a flash of fire, pieces of metal tumbling down, smoking steam in the snow. The fire pulled his eyes that way, and he rose up, saw the flames, one of the Shermans swallowed in a blaze of steel and gasoline. There was machine-gun fire now, *pop*s from rifles close by, more incoming shells whistling past, cracking the air overhead.

Mitchell had his rifle up on the snow, shouted, Benson hearing him, "Kraut tanks! Just tanks! This is no good! We can't stay here!"

Black smoke rolled over them, raw stink, and Benson heard the rumbling of heavy engines close by. He looked that way, saw the Shermans in motion, one backing up, another spinning furiously, churning snow and debris, smashing through the battered wall of a building. Around them, men were rolling aside, frantic, to escape being crushed. He stared, sick disbelief, the five remaining Shermans all moving back, pulling away from the village, from the enemy still coming. Shellfire ripped the ground, and another of the tanks erupted, the turret rising up, tossed aside, a swirl of flame engulfing the men inside. The surviving tanks roared back toward the woods, one of them firing a round, but they were moving quickly, the enemy shells missing their mark. And now the tanks were gone.

The shelling seemed to stop, a strange silence accented by faint bursts of machine-gun fire up on the far hillside. Benson rolled over, looked at Mitchell, who stared out to the woods behind them where the tanks had gone.

"They left us! They just . . . left us!"

The ground was rumbling again, steady, the roar of engines coming closer. There were new thumps, out toward the enemy, smoke in the trees behind the village, and Benson shouted, "The artillery!" Yes! That's it! Our guns will take them out!

Around him, the rifles popped again, Milsaps firing the BAR, the artillery responding to the tanks, the artillery shells coming over scattered, slow, and now the tanks firing again, seeking their new targets, the hillside behind the village bursting into fire. Benson waited for more, but the artillery seemed to slow, then stop, the response to the German tanks meager, weak. Useless. The roar of the tanks continued, the ground vibrating beneath him, and Benson wanted to fire the rifle, glanced up, over his cover, saw the first tanks a hundred yards away, coming fast.

Mitchell yelled close to him, "We have to go! We're dead!"

Around them, men began to rise, some of them running, following the road out of the village, following the escape of the Shermans. Others were shouting, the officers, dozens of men now up out of their cover, a rush toward the trees. Benson heard Higgins, the sergeant, in a frantic dash behind the cover, "Pull back! Let's go! Move!"

Benson pulled his knees up, tried to stand, fear and stiffness holding his legs. He peered up over the boulder, the feeble protection, saw the German tanks two abreast, gigantic, more behind them, black exhaust rising up, the sound monstrous, terrifying. The column stretched back into the trees, all rolling closer, and the first two left the main road, rolled out to the side, spreading out on the flat open ground, turrets sweeping side-to-side, a flash of fire, and another, the shell blasting a stone wall. Mitchell was pulling him.

"Let's go!"

Machine-gun fire sprayed the ground, slicing the snowbank, and Benson pushed his legs in motion, began to run, saw smoke and fire and running men. Some were dropping, cut down hard, the blasts coming again, the German tank guns slicing men in two, fiery rips in the snow, men tossed aside. He ran without thinking, the panic complete, ignored the men around him, passed by the wounded, rips of machine-gun fire in his ears. Some men were pushing past, faster, and Benson stared at the road that led up into the trees, thick with men, too many men, *no*. The blast came, one thunderous eruption, the road smeared with squirming black stains, black earth and shattered men scattered through the snow. His legs kept pumping, trees to his left, the hillside falling away, the place they had climbed that morning. Machine-gun fire cracked past his head, and men were jumping, stumbling down, moving away from the carnage in the road. Benson followed, the tanks closer still, heavy rattle of the machine guns, the tanks firing point-blank into the fleeing men. He jumped down, over a snowbank, was in the trees now, but there was no brush, no cover, and still the tanks kept up their fire. He stumbled, on his knees, rolled over, close to a fat tree, thick enough for cover, but his legs would not stop, and he was up again, the wave of men moving past, pulling him. One man fell hard, facedown, close in front of him, rolling over, blood pouring from his back, spreading through the snow. Benson jumped over the man, panic erasing the image. The machine-gun fire still whistled past, shattering and slicing trees, and he pushed down the hill, rubber legs, gasping searing pain in his chest, another man falling, more screams, relentless, following him, inside his own mind, his own voice.

12. BENSON

The tanks rolled past, two of them, their commanders up, standing tall above their open hatches, oblivious to any threat from the Americans that had scattered away like so many birds. More vehicles came behind, half-tracks, heavy machine guns perched above, manned by crews who were bundled in heavy coats. There were trucks as well, more machine guns, and from the gap in the branches Benson could see the tops of helmets, a dozen or more soldiers in each truck. The column passed in waves of smoke, rattles from the trucks that bounced and jostled their cargo in the uneven mess churned up by the treads of the tanks in front of them. Benson was only a few yards above the road, perched on the embankment beneath a fat spruce. He had a perfect view of the scene, a short parade of enemy power rolling past. Around him there were no more than twenty others, dug into the snow, some, like Benson, using the low canopies of the spruces. He could not stop shivering, his boots soaking through his last pair of dry socks, his coat drenched from melting snow. He shared the shelter of the tree with Mitchell and one other man, a stranger, a straggler from an artillery company. Mitchell held his rifle ready, as though he was preparing to attack the column by himself, and Benson caught Mitchell's eye, shook his head, *Don't do it.* What the hell are you thinking? Benson's rifle stood up against the tree trunk, close enough, but Benson had no interest in putting up a fight, was curled up tightly in a ball, desperate for warmth. He watched Mitchell, saw clouds of foggy breath in a steady rhythm, and Benson thought, he won't do anything stupid. It's just his way. He's pissed off. Like the sarge. Always pissed off. Maybe it keeps them warm.

Benson put a numb hand inside his jacket, felt for the wet socks, held on to a last flicker of faith that this time they might be drying. It was one strange piece of training that had stayed inside his mind, the words rolling past him in the voice of some nameless lieutenant. *Dry your wet socks and underwear against your own skin. The human body has a remarkable ability to provide warmth.* And so they were against his skin, the socks warmer but still soaking wet. That idiot lieutenant. I can't keep any part of my whole damn body warm. How am I supposed to have enough left over to dry any socks? He curled his toes, felt the stinging numbness, shivered again, uncontrollable spasm, saw Mitchell looking at him, concern, nodded, yeah, I'm okay. Mitchell stared out again through the thick branches of the spruce, rose slightly, searching for the best view, and Benson realized that it was growing quiet. The column had passed. There was a long silent moment, no one moving yet, and then, from beyond the tree, the hard whisper. It was Higgins.

"The road's clear. Let's go!"

Mitchell was up and out quickly, a shower of wet snow coming down on Benson from the low limbs above his head. The other man looked up, questioning, and Benson said, "We gotta move. Come on."

"I don't think I can. My feet . . ."

The man seemed to curl up tighter, his eyes closing again, and Benson pushed his shoulder, a hard shove.

"No you don't. I'm not leaving you to freeze to death. Come on!"

He could hear the others, low voices, Higgins there now, leaning low, peering into the cover. "Move it, Private."

"Sarge, this guy's having trouble."

Higgins cursed, launched himself into the canopy of limbs, grabbed the man's coat collar, said, "Help me drag him out. Gotta get him up and moving. I'm not leaving anyone behind. Get up, soldier! You keep moving, you won't freeze!"

The man raised his head, seemed to understand, and Benson pulled with the sergeant, dragged the man from under the canopy. Benson saw

the others now, up and out of their cover, some marching in place, trying
to thaw the misery in their feet, some blowing into hands, puffs of white
steam. With Benson's help, the sergeant pulled the man to his feet, the
man responding, holding them away.

"I'm okay. I can do it. Thanks."

Higgins moved away quickly, stepped down closer to the road, then
came back up the hill, pointed out away from the road, said, "Up this way.
We can keep an eye on the road. We've gotta get far enough west to find
our lines."

They began to move, Benson falling in close behind Mitchell,
thought, what lines? That village was our *lines,* and we got blown to hell.
He thought of the Shermans now, a stab of anger. Damn them. Just took
off like we weren't there. Somebody oughta pay for that. Some officer
probably yelled retreat 'cause he got scared. You're in a tank, you jackass.
Try doing this in wet boots and a rifle and see how that feels. The anger
rolled through him, and he tried not to think about the tanks that had
been hit. He had never forgotten the teasing, back in the States, wiseass description of the tanks as *steel coffins.* Yeah, maybe so. Those Kraut tanks
were a whole lot bigger. Maybe stronger too, bigger guns. Maybe . . . I'd
run like hell too. Especially if my buddy got blown sky-high next to me.

He stumbled, focused on the hillside, watch your step, moron. Don't
need a broken ankle. They were climbing, the steps slow and painful, Higgins keeping them well away from the road below. The hill crested, thinner
trees, and Higgins stopped, held up a hand, turned, waited for the men to
gather close.

"Stay here, stay low. I'm gonna see what's beyond this ridge. This looks
like it drops off pretty steep on the far side."

Benson watched the sergeant go, careful, slipping from tree to tree,
disappearing beyond the crest, and in a short minute Higgins was back,
waving them forward. The march began again, up and over, the woods
spreading out below them, more of the tall pines, no brush, knee-deep
snow, and now Benson could see the village. Like the others he had seen in
this horrific country, it sat low in the bottom of a bowl of hills, narrow
roads leading out into tight valleys. Higgins led them down quickly, Benson's wet boots kicking up snow in front of him as he half slid down the
hill. He braced himself against a tree, slowing his descent, a stab of pain
through his hand, the fingers aching. What the hell are we doing? A damn
village could be full of Krauts. But Higgins was moving on, the others as

well, some limping badly, and Benson pulled the rifle tight against his shoulder, followed them. Close to the first building, the tree line ended in a small square garden, a low picket fence surrounding dead greenery. Higgins stopped, motioned them low, his eyes darting back toward the men, then into the village, searching ahead. Benson realized now, the village was intact, none of the destruction that had blasted the first village off the map. It was also deathly silent.

They followed Higgins into a narrow lane, houses on both sides, frosted windowpanes, thick-hewn wood doors. Higgins's alertness was contagious, each man stepping slowly, stopping at each gap between the houses, peering cautiously around corners. Benson heard his heartbeat, the rifle in his hands now, a quick check of the clip, no time for surprises from an empty M-1. They moved past a larger building, a sign above a wide door, meaningless foreign words, the lane ending at a wider open square. In the snow were heavy tracks, tanks treads and rubber tires, the snow flattened to an icy glaze. Higgins waved them back away from the square into a side street, narrow again, and Benson did as the others did, crouched low beneath the windows. Higgins waved to one side, pointed to an alley to the right, sending several men in that direction with a low whisper.

"Stay parallel to us. Either no one's home, or they know we're here. I think no one's home."

Higgins waited for the men to move away, made a quick motion forward to the others close behind him.

"Spread out, both sides of the street. You see anybody at all, don't keep it to yourself."

Benson stayed close to Higgins, Mitchell as well, and two of the others Benson ignored. The sergeant rose slightly, peeked into a window, and Benson did the same, saw curtains, then an opening, dark interior, furniture, no one moving.

Higgins whispered, "Krauts have been here, for sure. Where the hell are the people?"

Beside Benson, Lane was there, said, "Hey, Sarge, how about we try to find something to eat?"

"My idea exactly. Stay together. We'll do it carefully, each side of the street."

Higgins pointed to a door across the street, the men nodding, pushing inward, the door opening slowly. The men slipped inside, one man standing upright, his rifle pointed in, covering the rest.

Higgins looked back, pointed to Mitchell, said, "I'll stay out here with Lane. You take the other three, go into this one."

Mitchell was at the door, tried to open it, stood back, said, "Locked. They locked the damn door."

Mitchell raised his rifle, brought the butt down hard, the doorknob coming apart. He pushed the door with one boot until it gave way. Benson wanted to say something, *Careful, a trap,* but Mitchell was inside, the others following. Benson was the last one in, keeping his rifle high, pointing at shadows in jerking motions. The house was dark, musty, the smell of old ashes in a fireplace. Mitchell pointed his rifle into a small kitchen, stepped inside, knelt, began searching cabinets, made a low yelp.

"Ha! Try this, boys!"

The other two men moved that way, and Mitchell began to toss glass jars out onto the floor, looked back at Benson, tossed one toward him. It was some kind of fruit, and Mitchell tossed him another. "They left us some chow. Damn nice of them."

The treasure seemed to relax them all.

Higgins was there, said, "The boys over there found a whole ham. At least we can eat."

The festive mood was spreading, men poking into other rooms. Benson stuffed the jar in his jacket, examined the room, a soft plush couch, dark red velvet, a chair, small tables, a gas lamp. There was a photograph on one wall above a thick wood table, and he moved closer, saw a family, the sober stare of one old man flanked by two women, one standing close behind a younger boy. There were smiles from the others, the woman with her hand on the boy's shoulder, a scene of warmth, affection. Benson backed away, scanned the artifacts in the room, a scattering of objects on a mantel over a dark fireplace. There was a porcelain vase, old, and beside it, another photograph in a thick wood frame. Benson leaned close, saw the same old man, but younger now, an army uniform, medals. The mantel was scattered with other bits of the family's life, a crucifix standing upright inside a domed glass box, another small vase, something to hold a small bouquet of flowers. The wall itself was dark, reddish brown wallpaper, peeling, one seam coming apart. Thick wood beams were overhead, low and oppressive, and Benson felt uneasy, guilty, looked around at the others as they rummaged into more of the rooms. Some of the men were becoming playful, one man emerging with a dress in his hand, red and yellow flowers on white cotton.

"By damn, look at this! My gal'd look like a million bucks in this. There's more, too, lots of 'em. Lady shoes too."

Benson realized, *cotton.*

"Hey, cut up some of that stuff. It'll go in our boots, help dry 'em out."

The man looked at the dress, his enthusiasm rising. "Yeah, good idea. Warmer too."

The man's bayonet came out, the dress ripped, sliced into pieces. He handed a few to Benson, said, "Hey, you guys. I'll get some more, make a bunch of small pieces."

From the kitchen, Mitchell said, "Look for socks too. Gals might wear 'em around here. Check every drawer."

The man with the bayonet disappeared into a back room, and Benson stuffed the cloth pieces into his pocket, thought of pulling off his boots. No, not now. There might not be time. The sarge likes to haul his ass out of places pretty quick.

The man emerged from the back of the house. "No socks. Dammit. Just lady stuff, old silky drawers. I ain't wearing lady underwear on my feet. You want any, get it yourself. But damn, you oughta see the beds! Big fat mattresses! They still got sheets on 'em. Those'll do. I'll cut 'em up too."

Mitchell emerged from the kitchen, pockets stuffed with the jars, said, "White sheets? Roll 'em up, bring em along. They could give us some camouflage. The rest of you . . . we're not moving in here. Grab some of this chow. There're some tins of sardines, or something close. Take whatever you can put in your pockets."

Higgins was at the door now, scanning the others, said, "Let's go, boys. No time to hang around."

Benson looked again at the photograph. "Sarge, where'd they go, you think?"

Higgins didn't answer, and behind Benson, one man said, "Oh hell! They're right here! I'll be damned." The man was standing in a doorway, looking down into a cellar, and he said, "Hey! It's okay. You can come out. We're not the Krauts."

Mitchell was there quickly, said to Higgins, "They hid right here in the cellar, Sarge. They look scared to hell. Any of you idiots *sprecken* German?"

Word had passed across to the other house, and more of the men were behind Higgins, curious, some of them already eating whatever they had found. Mitchell was waving the people up from the cellar, said, "It's okay, folks. We're the good guys. Good God . . . look what they got there! It's a damn wine cellar!"

Benson pushed forward, others as well, saw down into the darkness, three white faces staring up at them, wide-eyed terror. He recognized the women from the photograph, and now the old man, much older, standing slowly, and behind him a rack of wine bottles.

Higgins moved through the others, stopped at the top of the stairway, said, "Okay, back up, you slobs. They're scared enough as it is. You're gonna ugly them to death. There's enough wine here to start a riot with you guys, and we can't be having any of that right now."

"Aw, Sarge."

"Hey, come on, Sarge."

Higgins turned, his voice louder.

"Back away! This isn't a damn USO! We need to know how to find Saint Vith. That's a hell of a lot more important than some damn wine."

He turned to the cellar again, motioned with his hand, his voice gentle, patronizing. "Now, you folks come on up out of there. We're gonna take some chow and stuff, and we need to know a couple things. That's it. Nobody gets hurt."

Higgins backed away, and the old man emerged first, stooped, withered face. He seemed defiant, protective, and Benson looked again at the smaller photograph, said, "Hey, Sarge, this guy used to be a soldier. There's a picture. He's in a uniform."

"Well then, he oughta understand what we want. You cooperate, old man, and we leave you be."

The old man searched the faces, the black coats, seemed dismayed.

Mitchell said, "He's looking for an officer. Bet he wants to know who's in charge."

Higgins ignored the comment, was staring down into the cellar.

"Holy mackerel. Would you look at these two."

The women emerged now, eyes holding raw terror, one slightly older, gripping the other's hand. They came up into the room, scanning the uniforms, curious, confused.

Benson said, "They're sisters. Look alike."

The older woman stepped forward, the fear fading slightly, moved in front of the old man, who seemed to object, still defiant, silent. The women had attracted more attention from the others, men crowding in from the street, and Benson could see that both of them were utterly beautiful. There were low hums from the men around him.

Higgins said, "All right. Get a good look. They got ankles and curves and big red lips. Got that? Now get the hell out of here! Start looking in the other houses. No looting, unless you can eat it, got that?"

There were murmurs of protest, Lane, close beside Benson, "Yeah, and what're you gonna do, Sarge? Taste the treats yourself? I say there's enough to go around."

Higgins stared at Lane, a hard hateful glare.

"You get your ass out of here or you'll leave your teeth right here on the floor. You got that, Private?"

Benson eased away from Lane, saw the animal viciousness on Lane's face. Mitchell moved closer, seemed to bow up beside Higgins, eager to join any confrontation that would cut Lane down to size. Around the crowded room, some men began to ease away, some out the door, others closing in, the ugliness among them starting to rise. Lane turned abruptly, pushed his way out, and Benson let out a breath.

Higgins said, "The rest of you. Get going. I'll get some wine from these folks and pass it out later. But I gotta try to find out—"

"You say, Saint Vith?"

The voice came from one of the women, and Benson turned to her in surprise, the others as well.

Higgins said, "English. I'll be damned."

"Not good English. You say Saint Vith?"

"Yeah. We gotta head that way. One of these roads get us there?"

The woman seemed flustered, Higgins talking too fast. Benson said, "Sarge, maybe draw a map."

"Yeah, good." Higgins pulled a small pencil from his pocket, searched the room, opened a drawer in a little table, found a piece of linen. "This'll do." Higgins laid the cloth out flat on a small marble-topped table, drew a circle.

"Here. That's us, this place. Now, over here, this one's Saint Vith. Okay? How do we get from here . . . to there?"

She nodded, understood, pointed to the door, motioned to the left. "Go, six kilometers. Then a road. Turn. Go the other way. Saint Vith."

Higgins pulled his compass out of his pocket.

"Sounds right. We take this road to the left, then we'll come to another road, and we turn right. That what you mean?"

She nodded.

Higgins seemed relieved, looked at Mitchell, then Benson, said, "Six kilometers . . . that's about four miles. You got that? We get split up, find your own way."

Higgins handed the linen cloth to the woman, but the old man stepped forward, took it, thrust it back toward Higgins.

Mitchell said, "Better keep it, Sarge. Krauts come through here and find that, he's dead. I think he knows that."

"Okay, yeah. Hey, *fraulein,* you think we can get some of the wine?"

She laughed, still nervous, said something to the younger woman, who scampered down the cellar steps. Higgins wanted to follow, but the old man stepped in front of him, unyielding.

"Okay, old man, whatever you say. I wasn't gonna do anything to hurt your . . . whatever she is. Daughter, I guess."

The other woman came back up the stairs, carrying a cloth sack, the clink of bottles, handed it to Higgins.

He scanned the contents, said, "Six. That's enough to haul. You gotta save some for the next group who wanders through here."

Higgins moved toward the door, Mitchell following, and Benson looked again at the older woman, not old at all, the beauty in her face worn down by . . . what? He looked again at the photo, the face of the boy, a teenager. He's not here. Maybe . . . not anywhere.

"Good-bye, miss. Thanks."

There was a burst of firing outside, rifles, loud voices. The shots were scattered, rifle fire and machine pistols, now the spray of a machine gun. Benson dropped to one knee, jerked the rifle from his shoulder, crawled to the door, saw men running in the lane, diving into cover, into the house across the way. Mitchell was back, then Higgins, pushing Benson aside, the door slammed behind them.

Higgins said, "Son of a bitch! Krauts!"

Mitchell checked his rifle, was breathing heavily. "They got a couple of us. Stupid bastards were loaded down with crap, and the Krauts came running across that square plain as day. I saw the whole thing. They had to know we were here, probably watched us from one of those ridges. We shoulda seen them coming."

Higgins sat with his back against the front wall, still held the cloth sack of wine bottles in his hand. He tossed them aside with a loud rattle, said,

"My fault. Dammit! We got all damn excited about the loot. Should have posted a guard to watch the roads."

Benson said, "How many Krauts, Sarge?"

Mitchell moved to a window, peered out, and Higgins said, "I don't know. A hell of a lot more of them than us. You hear that machine gun? Where there's one, there's more. We've gotta get the hell out of here."

Benson turned, looked toward the woman, but the room was empty, the cellar door shut. Higgins said, "There's gotta be a back door. Let's go!"

Benson followed, Mitchell taking one last glance through the window, the three men moving quickly through the kitchen. Higgins pushed at a small doorway, cracked it open, said, "Narrow street. I don't see anybody."

The rifle fire continued in front of the house, the machine gun ripping the walls, shattering the window glass, more voices, German. Higgins glanced back at the other two, and Benson saw the fear in his eyes.

"Keep running. Head west . . . that way. If we get split up, remember the girl's directions. Ready?"

Benson nodded sharply, Mitchell saying nothing, and Higgins opened the door wider, moved out quickly. Benson followed Mitchell, saw the lane empty, a row of neat houses, heard firing on the other side. Higgins was far ahead, running hard away from the sounds, Benson fighting to keep up, pain in his feet. Higgins disappeared around a corner, and Mitchell was there as well, a quick glance back, Benson struggling, driven by the fear. He reached the corner, Mitchell moving on ahead, and Benson saw the white fields, trees, the steep hillside beyond. The machine-gun fire was behind them still, the sound of trucks, many voices, *pops* from the rifles. Benson felt his lungs giving out, pain in his chest, Mitchell slowing, waiting, a hard hand reaching out, grabbing Benson's coat.

"Move it!"

They followed Higgins into the snow, the trees close, and Benson pushed his legs, ignored the pain, the trees shielding them now. Higgins stopped, fell down behind a fat pine tree, gasping, looking back toward them, Mitchell moving up close, another tree, his rifle pointed back toward Benson.

"Get up here!"

Benson stumbled, crawling now, the snow in his face, pushed harder, rolled over behind another tree.

Mitchell was watching him, said, "No one followed us."

Higgins, breathing in short gasps, said, "We made it!"

Benson pushed his back up against the tree, tried to bring the rifle up, aiming as the others did, targets that weren't there, but there was no strength in his arms, the rifle lying across his legs. The firing in the town seemed to slow, and there was a dull thump, the sound of a grenade, then another. Smoke began to rise through a rooftop, and Benson heard the voices still, one man screaming, and he looked at Higgins, tried to speak, Mitchell cutting him off.

"Nothing we can do. That's half a company of Krauts. They probably took our guys prisoners . . . the ones that made it." He looked hard at Benson, reading his mind. "Nothing we can do about it. Nothing. We were lucky to get the hell out of there."

"I know. Lucky."

Higgins said, "We better keep going. Could be patrols all over these woods. This ain't friendly ground. We get higher up, we can sit low in some cover, wait till dawn." Higgins held up a jar, part of the booty from the house. "We got some rations at least."

Benson felt the hard lump in his jacket pocket, the jar of fruit, looked back toward the houses, the black smoking rooftop, a spreading fire. He stared, felt a slow twisting horror, thought of the family, the women, terrified, their worst fears coming to pass, and the old man, the soldier, who had seen this all before.

13. VON RUNDSTEDT

Model pranced around the room like an angry bird, stepping past chairs, spinning, hands clasped tightly behind his back. The others sat quietly, had no choice but to wait for the man's pronouncements. Von Rundstedt watched him play out his game, so much anger, so much frustration. He asked himself, when has it ever been any other way?

The only other officer in the room was Manteuffel, the small thin man waiting for the inevitable harangue. Von Rundstedt gave a small silent *thank you* that Dietrich was not there. Manteuffel was at least a man of breeding, carried some decorum. They all knew that Dietrich could be crude and vulgar, and likely would respond to a harsh lecture from his superior with one of his own.

Model stopped, seemed to pounce on an idea. He looked at Manteuffel, said, "How quickly can the Fifteenth Army be brought to bear? The Führer's plan called for them to move in behind your initial thrust and clean up pockets of the enemy who were passed by. We can do considerably more than that, wouldn't you say? We can use the infantry to drive forward, to add power and mobility to your own spear, to enhance the weight of your armor. Infantry do not require effective roads. The enemy is escaping by the hour, and with a large-scale infantry advance, moving in tandem with the armor, the enemy troops can be gathered up more efficiently."

Manteuffel seemed puzzled, looked at von Rundstedt, back to Model. "Forgive me, sir, but is this just now an idea that you find useful? This entire assault has lacked depth, and had we designed this campaign to succeed, the infantry should have moved up with us from the beginning. But surely you know, sir, that the Fifteenth Army is worthless as a fighting force, a shell of what it used to be. It is ill trained, understaffed, and underequipped. How can you suggest such a thing? Would you have us halt our advance and wait while ineffective infantry commanders gather their wits about them? I shall be perched up on those miserable mountain passes until summertime!"

"I am aware of their limitations. But do not forget, General, the Fifteenth Army always figured highly in the Führer's overall plan. You have *not* forgotten that, I hope?"

"I will never forget, Field Marshal. It is one more portion of this folly in which we are all taking part."

Model appeared shocked, part of the game. "It is a good thing that you are so respected. Your panzer army is the tip of the spear in this operation, and you have failed to meet the Führer's expectations. Only by your reputation were you given such responsibility, and only by your *past* reputation shall you remain in command now!"

Von Rundstedt had heard enough of Model's bluster. He motioned a calming hand to Manteuffel, said to Model, "We have all gone far on our reputations, Field Marshal. Unfortunately, the Führer's past reputation is plaguing us far worse than anything your generals have failed to accomplish. I have tired of these dramatics."

Model did not respond with his usual anger, surprising the old man. Model glanced around, seemed to search the room, his eyes settling on the least uncomfortable chair. He sat heavily, adjusted his monocle, seemed to sink into his own uniform.

"No, you are not to blame, General. Neither is Dietrich. I have seen the conditions we are facing, and I know what the roads are like. There is one positive, of course. The Führer got his wish. He was blessed with bad weather. The enemy's aircraft are useless to them, and that in itself is a victory. But the weather does not choose sides."

Manteuffel stirred in his chair, anger of his own. "Is that your explanation for our success? What of our failures? Where are the additional tanks I was promised? Where is the gasoline, those infinite convoys of tanker trucks that were promised to all of us? My tanks have gone as far as they can go without artillery support, and I do not have the gasoline to supply the trucks that bring the artillery. So, I must choose. Advance my tanks or advance my artillery. The tanks are our greatest weapon, and where they have been allowed to wage war, they have obliterated the enemy's positions. The enemy has weaponry that is adequate to stop us, but he does not have those weapons in force where he needs them. So, if the enemy does not stop us, who shall? No, it is not the damnable weather, Field Marshal. It is the *plan*. We are brought to a standstill by flaws in our own strategy, and by the flaws in those who tell us what to do."

Von Rundstedt waved a weary hand. "Watch your tongue, General. It is not always necessary to speak aloud what we know in our hearts."

"Then what, sir? How should I address the task I have been given? I am not *honored* to have been ordered to sacrifice my armor in a place where no battle should have been fought. The timetable laid out by our Führer called for me to be at the Meuse River by now, assisting our engineers in constructing bridges to replace those that the enemy would have destroyed in his haste to retreat. Oh yes, the enemy has most certainly retreated. I have seen it myself. He has pulled away from the most dismal ground I have ever seen, and is re-forming his defenses to meet us. But he is still on *this* side of the river. I am quite certain that General Eisenhower is making considerable use of the Meuse to form a second defensive line, and that those bridges are very well intact. He is using them as we speak to send forward every available American and British unit he can put into motion." Manteuffel turned to Model. "And depend on this, Field Marshal. General Eisenhower is not struggling to find gasoline for his tanks!"

Model stared at the map on the wall, seemed to ignore Manteuffel's outrage. Von Rundstedt had enormous affection for Manteuffel, had heard these same kinds of arguments months before, from another of his favorite generals.

"You very much remind me of Rommel, you know. Always pushing forward, always seeking to crush his enemy. In the end, Rommel failed, but not because of Rommel. He failed because he was not given the support he required from those who sent him to do the job."

Model turned, sniffed at von Rundstedt.

"Forgive me, but this is not a time for reminiscence. There is no romance in this."

"You are quite wrong about that. There *was* romance in this. In the beginning, when all of us were handed our commands. Think about this,
Field Marshal. We were given the finest weapon ever devised, the German
army. We were given technology and tools no one had ever seen on a battlefield. We were superior to our enemy in every way, tanks to submarines,
artillery to aircraft. And so we were given a task. For more than a year, we
accomplished that task with brilliance. There was no theater of the war
that the enemy did not flee. There was no one anywhere, not in London or
Washington or Moscow, who did not fear us. We swept our enemies out of
Paris and Brussels and Amsterdam. In the early days, we defeated every
army placed in our way. That is what we were expected to do, it is what we
expected of ourselves." He paused, took a breath. "So, what happened?
You were in Russia. You made your reputation there, you defeated vast
armies, and then it stopped. Why did you not continue to *roll over* the
enemy as you were told to do, and force him to a humiliating surrender?
Why did Rommel not *roll over* the enemy in North Africa? Why is it that
we are only barely surviving in a quagmire in Italy? How is it that our magnificent army failed to stop the enemy from driving us out of France and
Belgium? Do you believe, Herr Model, that it is the fault of the men sitting here? Might we lay blame at the feet of those generals in the field? Or
perhaps the German soldier was not what we believed him to be. Could
that be it? The British and the Americans are better fighters? Is that what
you believe?"

"Stop it, old man. You are here only because the Führer thought you
might inspire the troops in the west. This is my command now, and I do
not need you wallowing in your own failures."

Von Rundstedt absorbed the insult.

"*Old man.* Yes, you are quite right, Herr Model. I know my place, and
I have done nothing to interfere in your command."

Model seemed to regret his words, shook his head. "I did not come to
your office to insult you. My apologies, Field Marshal." He paused, his energy rebuilding. "Two days ago we achieved total surprise. The enemy was
as weak in the forest as we anticipated. Our initial thrust was overwhelmingly successful. It appeared that we were going to accomplish the fantas-
tic, that the Führer's plan was brilliant after all."

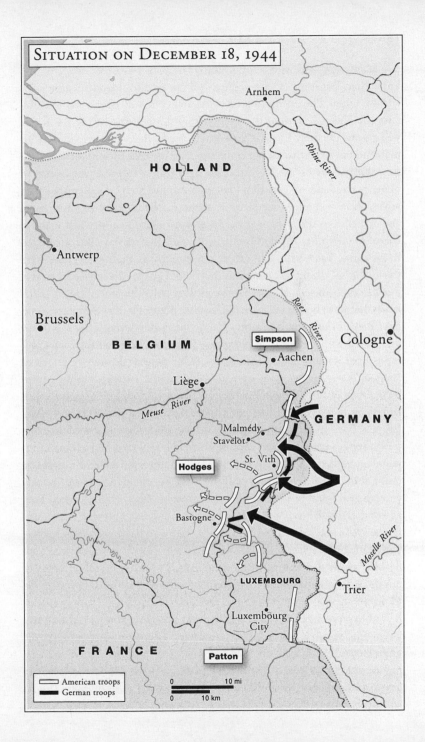

SITUATION ON DECEMBER 18, 1944

Manteuffel said with a soft voice, "The plan was never brilliant. You know that. But it is not yet a failure. We can turn to the north, attack the city of Liège. The enemy forces in Aachen can still be cut off and destroyed. This will prevent the enemy from driving toward the Roer, and will give us the delay this war desperately needs. If the Führer will alter his plan and not insist that we continue the drive toward Antwerp, if we might stop short of the Meuse, we can cause significant damage to the enemy in many places, and we can allow our own supply lines to replenish themselves. *Time* will allow our factories to produce the tanks we must have, and the fuel to drive them. The Americans in front of my army are in chaos. Dietrich has routed his enemy as well. But we have not succeeded in capturing Saint Vith, and we have not captured Bastogne. Those were the linchpins, the critical junctions that would give us the mobility to drive our forces to their goal. The armor must stay to the roads, and it is the *roads* that have been our downfall. Yes, far better infantry support would have helped this plan, but to my south, the entire Seventh Army has not yet moved with the speed necessary to drive the enemy out of Bastogne." He paused, looked at von Rundstedt. "Our only weakness is the lack of support. I was told . . . we were all told that the enemy's supply dumps would fall easily into our hands, that we could sustain ourselves with American fuel and food and guns. That has not happened. It will never happen! Even in chaos, the Americans have been successful in destroying their supplies before we can capture them. I have stood beside tank commanders while, a kilometer away, a million liters of American gasoline erupt into a useless bonfire, only because we could not move quickly enough, we could not strike with a sharpened spear. I have learned long ago that gasoline is not a tool. It is a weapon. It is as important as the cannon and the machine gun. Am I the only one who believes this? Would we have launched any campaign if any significant part of our army was kept back? If we are to continue with our success, if we are to accomplish any of our goals here, we must have replacement tanks and we must have the fuel to propel them. We must have fuel for the artillery, for the supply trucks. It is not complicated. If the artillery moves up in tandem with the armor, we are unstoppable. Instead, there are delays. There are promises from the High Command that no one had any intention of honoring. By not seizing the vital crossroads, by not driving to the river, we will have allowed the enemy to strengthen his flanks, to come up with a plan of his own. It sickens me."

Model looked away from Manteuffel, stared at the map again, and von Rundstedt could feel the gloom from both men.

Model said, "It is not yet lost, General. There is a lesson from Clausewitz I have always embraced. *The point must form the fist.* We have made the fist and we have thrown the punch and we have struck the enemy in a soft place. Clausewitz was saying that we should not worry about the flanks, that if you drive your fist hard enough and far enough, the enemy must respond to the *point.* When I understood how inflexible Hitler was, I tried making the best decisions to allow his plan to succeed. I tried to convince him that if we drive straight and fast, we should not be concerned about the flanks. But he would not agree. He called Clausewitz a fool, out of his time. So, Hitler's plan called for the Seventh Army to move forward while at the same time expanding along our southern flank, to protect us there. Dietrich had to spread out his advance to the north, slowing down the entire attack, so he could guard against enemy forces on *his* flank. By doing that, Hitler has tossed the genius of Clausewitz out the window. We *should* be crossing the Meuse, and instead our mighty army is plodding through a spiderweb of impassable roads, chasing the enemy through the woods like so many cats among a swarm of mice." Model looked at Manteuffel. "I have seen this play before, General. Yes, we have weakness in front of us, a confused enemy who can be driven completely away, who can be destroyed. But right now, the enemy is building up strength on our shoulders, and the Führer is nervous about that. Because we are moving so slowly, his concern is justified. In front of us is General Hodges. I do not know much of him, except that he was not prepared for us. None of his people expected this attack, so I must believe that General Hodges is not a man like . . . well, like *you,* General. But up in the north, there is Montgomery, and he is a man of pride and arrogance, a man with a *reputation* of his own. He will not allow us to sweep past him without making a show of stopping us. And in the south . . ." Model paused, took a few steps, pacing again, turned, faced von Rundstedt. "In the south is Patton. For several weeks now, he has been content to pick and poke at the West Wall, small fights of little consequence. I understood all along, that is by design. He is preparing to drive into Germany, hit us hard as he has done so well before. Eisenhower has probably given him a timetable, and General Patton is pounding the walls in his headquarters for that day to arrive. But now his orders will be changed. And because we did not drive our fist forward with enough skill, the great bulldog will be released from his cage, and if he does not drive east and destroy our defenses along the West Wall, if he does not occupy the Saar, then he will go north and tear a hole in our flank."

He spun, looked at von Rundstedt, a new idea seeming to appear to him.

"Do you know what the Führer said to me? He said that one advantage we will have in this campaign is that the enemy will not be able to react with speed, because President Roosevelt is not a man who understands the battlefield. I did not know what he meant. But then . . . it was Jodl who told me that General Eisenhower must surely get his orders . . . all of his orders from Washington. The Führer believes that the enemy operates on the same principles that guide us. I admit, I did not know how to respond to that. The High Command does not comprehend that General Eisenhower *issues* orders. He does not wait to follow them only after they come all the way from his president."

Manteuffel said, "The High Command has no grasp of anything beyond their lofty offices. They do not know of front lines and ice-covered roads and mud. Their limousines do not run short of fuel, their mistresses do not lack for stockings and cigarettes. Their feet do not freeze and they do not eat moldy bread. And so, they will not understand what we tell them, what we ask of them. They will not hear us at all."

14. BENSON

The fighting had thundered past them all through the night, bright flashes on the horizon in every direction, rifle and machine-gun fire rolling through the darkness. Benson had thought they would keep moving, putting distance between themselves and the Germans in the village, that surely they would team up with other GIs who were stumbling through the forest as they were. But with darkness came the uncertainty and the fear, and Benson had followed the lead of the other two men who seemed far more able, far more confident. Once the darkness was complete, Higgins led them into cover, yet another of the densely shrouded spruce trees. There was frustration with that, Mitchell in particular, the man seeming to itch for a confrontation with the Germans who were driving continuously along the roadways and trails that spread through these woods. They had heard more than one mechanized column passing on some road close by, the sounds distorted and muffled by the terrain, and each time Mitchell seemed ready to launch into a fight that would be far too one-sided. But Benson was starting to understand Mitchell's anger, was feeling it himself. Until now he had no reason to hate Germans, had felt more hostility toward some of the men in his own camp, Lane of course, and the inept Lieutenant Greeley. The Germans had been nameless, face-less, noises in the dark. Even their infantry; the first time Benson had fired his rifle, there was nothing about those men that seemed human, nothing to inspire guilt. But now he could not escape the rising fury at the men who were causing this chaos, the gunners in the tanks whose blasts shat-tered men into bloody pools, the terrible rips of machine-gun fire that tore men apart. There was a sense of helplessness about all of it, stupid and cowardly, every confrontation ending with the Americans dying or run-ning away. This is not why we're here, he thought. Others have done bet-ter, have won battles, for God's sake. Normandy . . . all of it. But we're not doing anything at all. What kind of army is this . . . what kind of soldiers are we that we see the enemy and can't do anything to stop him?

In the silence, he had stared at the dark hulks of the other two, heard low breathing, sleeping perhaps, or just staring, as he was. The fear had faded away for now, and Benson felt something new. In every place, the foxholes, the bombed-out town, the small village, men had been left be-hind. He scolded himself, there was no other way, nothing you could have done, but the guilt was there all the same. It came with the faces, those with the horrible wounds, or Yunis, the worthless soldier, balled up like a helpless child in that one muddy foxhole. There had been too many es-capes now for Benson not to wonder about that, why Benson had escaped, why Mitchell and Higgins, what was different about them? Was it simply random, pure dumb luck? Benson hadn't said anything about it, heard none of that kind of talk from the other two. If they had any guilt at all, Benson saw no sign of it from Higgins, and he would never expect to see it from Mitchell. As the hours passed, they did not talk at all, and in the cold darkness, sleep had been brief and fitful, broken by the agony of the pain in his feet, the frozen fingers, the waves of shivering. He tried to steer his mind away from that, but the thoughts rolled back to the faces, the names, all those who had been overrun, routed, and blasted by the unend-ing onslaught. He had no idea of course what had happened to Lane, if he had been killed in the village or was a prisoner. Does it matter that he was a bullying son of a bitch? If he's dead, is that what justice is? And what of the lieutenant? Benson had to struggle to remember his face, the inept idiot, Greeley. That awful day was a distant memory, the man's gruesome death a horror that might have never happened at all, a gut-twisting episode from the pages of a bad novel.

No, he would say none of this to the others, knew that the nighttime was all about quiet and nothing else. He wanted to ask Mitchell if he thought much about Greeley, or the others, the death and horrific wounds, but he knew what the response would be: no response at all. Mitchell had an edgy grit, would not forget any of this, would carry a grudge about it. Mitchell hated the Germans, and Benson didn't need to understand why. Maybe that makes him a better soldier, maybe he has a soldier's heart . . . whatever that means.

The daylight was spreading through the woods, and Benson tried to flex his toes, flinched from the pain. As he moved, the stiff coat opened slightly, and the cold poured in even more, astonishing, relentless, always worst at first light. He could feel himself stuck to the frozen mud beneath him, pried himself away. Mitchell was closest to him, his back against the tree, and Benson saw the outline of his face, thought, well, Kenny, maybe today you'll get your fight. Maybe this is the day we can kick the enemy in the ass and send him running. I know damn well that if you get the chance, you'll run somebody down with that bayonet. Or maybe we'll just keep running ourselves, like we've been doing.

Benson had become more nervous about Mitchell, wondering if Higgins could continue to control him. Benson was curious about that, why Mitchell deferred so much to Higgins's authority. The man was only a sergeant, had no more training or experience at fighting this enemy than his two-man squad. But Higgins had shown Benson something, that intangible *thing* that inspired other men to pay attention, to follow, to obey. Mitchell seemed to know that as well. Benson knew he could never have controlled Mitchell's temper, his anger at the Germans that might make him reckless. Even in the darkness, there had been opportunity, a patrol moving below them, a small convoy of German artillery moving slowly along one snowy lane. But Higgins had kept him under control.

Higgins made a low grunt, and Benson responded, Mitchell as well. Benson could see enough in the shadows to know Higgins had retrieved one of the jars of fruit from his pocket. The jar was opened, the smell filling the small space, sweet and syrupy. Higgins passed out two more, Benson's stiff hands struggling, the jar lid finally giving way. He slurped it down quickly, didn't notice what kind of fruit it was. The day before, they had learned that the fruit caused more than one problem. There was plenty of time to slip silently behind some tree, to relieve the low stirring in the gut that was plaguing all three men. But far worse was the hunger. The fruit was sugary sweet, and afterward, they were hungry too quickly, the fruit fueling them only for short bursts. Yet there was nothing else to eat. The canteens were filled from the streams, a trickle of water they found in nearly every ravine, the water flowing beneath a hard crust of ice. It was dangerous to drink that, of course, but the threat of dysentery was meaningless now. There was only one priority, to find a safe place, an American position that was not a shambles of wreckage and corpses, where someone was actually in command, where the three men could find some way to eat real food and warm up, trade in worn-out boots and wet clothes, and then find some way to help fight the enemy.

The jars were empty, tossed aside, and Benson peered up through the thick limbs of the tree, searched the skies, no snow, but still the thick gray clouds. They sat in silence for another minute, Benson again massaging the awful soreness in his feet.

Higgins was watching him, said, "If we can find a farmhouse, someplace there might be dry clothes, we'll fix up something in your boots. Even a barn, some dry straw would help. Gotta get your feet dried out."

Benson's boots had come off the night before, sat beside him, a nightlong effort to dry out the insides. His feet had passed the night mostly folded beneath him, wrapped in a dirty mass of white cloth, what had once been a dress. Besides the fruit, it was their only booty from the Belgian family, the dress torn into scraps that might be used to camouflage their helmets should they find themselves hunkered down in the open. But Benson's misery was crippling for all three of them, and as long as there was shelter, the camouflage didn't matter. He massaged through the cloth, winced, said, "Toes are the worst. But I think the boots are dried out pretty good. They're frozen, anyway. Damn, I should have saved more of those socks. They told us to take all we could carry."

Mitchell stared down toward his own boots, his gloved fingers rubbing the stock of his rifle. "Shut up. Those supply idiots had no idea what we'd need out here. Look at these gloves. Holes in every finger. Something a four-year-old would wear. What jackass thought these would keep us warm?"

Higgins pointed to Benson's boots, said, "Try to put 'em on. The gorilla here is getting jumpy. We better get moving."

Benson kept the scrap of cloth around his foot, pulled one boot on, forced the cloth inside, too tight, his toes screaming with the pressure. He took a long breath, knew Higgins was watching, but Benson would not let them coddle him. He glanced at Mitchell, still fondling the rifle, and Benson thought, there's no way the sergeant will leave me behind. Mitchell would kill him first.

Mitchell suddenly looked skyward, said, "Listen."

Benson heard it now, a steady hum of engines.

Higgins said, "Those are planes. It must be better weather. Somebody's flying. Hope like hell it's our boys."

Mitchell crawled out from the tree's shelter, eyed the woods, then stood, a soft whisper.

"Far off. Moving away. Coulda been a few of 'em. I don't know what they think they can see. Look at the fog."

Higgins was out as well, said, "At least they're trying. Maybe just to let our boys know they're up there."

Benson laced up the second boot, crawled out after Higgins, the skies unyielding, no sunlight, just the gloom of thick gray.

Higgins pulled out his compass, turned it in his hand, then tapped Benson on the shoulder, said, "Let's go. The road's that way, we need to keep in that direction."

The sergeant stepped out through the snow, and Mitchell waited for Benson, checking, like a big brother.

Benson stepped past him, tried to ignore the pinched toes, the soreness. "Watch out for yourself, Kenny. I'm okay."

The artillery thundered from the hilltop in front of them, and Benson dropped flat, the others doing the same. The woods were thick, but the shock had passed, and Benson raised up slowly, could see the crest, stumps and cut trees, an opening. The cannon fired again, a hard jolt of sound, and Higgins looked back at them, motioned with his hand, *Forward*. They crawled, the snow soft, no sound, and Higgins turned his head, one hand over the ear facing the gun. Benson did the same, keeping the shock of the firing to a minimum. The gun erupted again, shaking the ground beneath them, and Higgins was moving quickly, reacting to the rhythm of the gunners. He halted, waited, seemed to brace himself, Benson mimicking him, the gun launching another shell. They were very close, and Higgins crawled quickly to a cut tree, knelt, peered up and over, hands on both ears, Benson and Mitchell copying him. The cannon erupted one more time, and Higgins raised the rifle, jerked his hand, *Now!*

They surged forward, up and over the fallen tree, and Benson saw the gun, the short barrel of a 105, and the crew, two men moving around it in a slow-motion routine. They were Americans.

One man was carrying a shell, the loader, staggering to drive the heavy shell into the gun's breach, and Higgins didn't wait, shouted, "Hey! Americans! Hey!"

The men turned, frantic, a pistol coming up, the loader setting the shell down, lurching forward to grab a carbine.

Higgins shouted again, "Americans! Don't shoot!"

They stared back for a moment, and Benson saw dull shock on filthy faces, wide eyes, one man coming forward.

"You pulling us out?"

Higgins didn't seem to know how to respond, and Mitchell said, "No. We're lost."

The man seemed more frantic, stared down the hill behind Benson. "How'd you get up here? That way? There's no road. Where's your truck?"

Higgins responded, "No truck. We walked. Been walking. Got shot up pretty bad, got away from a company of Krauts at a village back that way."

The man wasn't listening, still stared past them, searched the woods.

"How many . . . just you three? We can't stay here. But I can't leave my gun."

Benson moved up close to Higgins, looked past the man, saw the loader standing close beside the 105, the man's carbine still pointing at them, his eyes an empty stare.

The first man seemed to focus on Higgins, said, "I'm Lieutenant Carino. Five Nine Oh Field Artillery. That's Private Woodley. We've been waiting for relief."

Higgins looked at the cannon, said, "Yeah, we know you guys. You're with us. Company B, Four Two Three. We got cut off from the rest of our company. Hell, everybody got cut off, I think. Where's the rest of your unit? You set up along this ridgeline?"

"They're gone. I don't know where. I'm the only one left up here. We need a big truck. The gun's frozen into the dugout. We can't move it."

Benson felt something strange in the man's demeanor, the words soft and automatic. He saw now, the wheels of the cannon buried deep in the frozen mud. The loader finally lowered the carbine, stared at them silently, a hopeful smile now on his face.

Higgins stepped closer to the gun, said, "Who are you shooting at?"

The lieutenant pointed out over the cut trees, the path of fire cleared days ago by his crew.

"The enemy's all over the place. They had artillery positions up on that far ridgeline, and we've had a fix on that. Haven't seen much up there in a couple days. There's so damn many of them, and we're doing all we can to keep it hot, but we can't adjust our fire. We're down to a dozen shells. We need a truck. Either send us some ammo or pull us out of here."

Higgins looked back at Benson, a hint of warning in his eyes.

"Lieutenant, which way did you bring your gun up here? How was it driven in?"

The man pointed down the hill, the far side, and Benson stepped forward, saw the wide trail, the deep tracks in the snow.

The lieutenant said, "My driver left with the damn truck. It got hot here . . . couple days ago. He just drove away. I've got two other men down. We buried them back in those trees, in their foxholes. Took a direct hit. Nothing we can do now but hold out, until you get us out of here. Thank God you're here."

Higgins looked down, said, "Sir, I'm just a sergeant. A squad leader. We got cut off from our rifle company. You're the first officer we've seen since yesterday. The last orders we got were to make our way back to Saint Vith."

The man looked at Mitchell, then Benson, and Benson saw an eerie tilt in the man's stare.

"Saint Vith. That's good. Division HQ is there. We can't leave the gun. My orders . . ."

"Sir, come with us. You can't hold out here. You're right, the enemy is everywhere. These woods are full of patrols. Somebody's bound to come up here and shut this gun up. I don't know how in hell you've kept from being shelled, or why no one has overrun your position."

"They've shelled us, but once the rest of our guns pulled back, the enemy left us alone. If he's on that ridgeline, we're making it hot for him."

"Sir, you and your man come with us. We'll follow the road you came in on. We can get the gun . . . later."

The lieutenant turned, his loader reacting by setting his carbine to one side.

"I can't do that. I have orders to hold this position. Send us some ammo, or pull us out. We'll keep up fire as long as we can."

Mitchell moved close to Higgins, said softly, "We've gotta get going. The Krauts aren't gonna leave this guy alone for long."

Higgins slung his rifle onto his shoulder, said, "Look, sir, we've got to keep moving. I'll tell someone you're up here."

Higgins seemed to hesitate, and Benson watched as the lieutenant moved away, back to his gun. He pointed to the loader, the man obeying, hoisting up the heavy shell, sliding it into the breach. The lieutenant raised his binoculars, staring out toward the only place his gun could target. Benson covered his ears, waited for it, the gun firing again, thunder driving hard through his gut, the loader moving slowly, methodically, picking up another shell.

NEAR ST. VITH
DECEMBER 18, 1944, 10:30 P.M.

The rifle fire streaked past them, and now a wave of machine guns, tracers blinding, cutting past, slicing tree limbs, smacking into rocks. Higgins shouted back toward them, "Get up the hill! Stay low!"

Benson crawled backward, his boots shoving through the snow, the rifle in one hand. Mitchell was still down in front of him, began to fire back, cursing, the M-1 popping until the clip clinked out. But the German fire continued, a spray through the woods above them, pinning all three men flat to the ground.

Higgins yelled again, "Move! No shooting! You're giving us away!"

Benson felt the ground leveling out behind him, crawled more quickly, a pine tree beside him, and he rolled over, breathing hard, the rifle clamped upright against his chest. Down below, Mitchell had reloaded, emptied another clip, the German fire responding. But Mitchell seemed to realize the futility of his one-man fight, and with his silence the German guns slowed, then stopped. Orders were shouted out from below, a new burst of machine-gun fire, and Benson tried to gauge the distance, impossible, the noises ripping through the darkness, still chattering through the trees above him.

Higgins, sliding through the snow close by, shouted down the hill to Mitchell, "Back! Let's go! I'll leave you here, dammit!"

Benson had heard that kind of fury before, the sergeant's voice piercing the dark like a crack of thunder. Benson began to feel the panic, wanted to run, get beyond the ridge, out of the line of fire, but Mitchell was still below, and Benson felt hot frustration with the man's stubbornness, thought, is he reloading? Why? Dammit, let's get the hell out of here!

"Dammit, Kenny! Get up here! Let's go!"

The sergeant curled up against a nearby tree, said, "Shut up! They only know where that idiot gorilla is. If he'll stop shooting . . ."

Mitchell was suddenly there, a crouched run, past them, over the crest of the hill. Higgins rose up, began to follow, Benson doing the same, breathless relief, and Mitchell slid down in the snow, cursing in a steady stream, the others finding cover beside him.

Mitchell said, "Ran out of ammo. No more clips. Sons of bitches! Sons of bitches! They're coming, count on it. I need some clips! Eddie, give me what you've got!"

Higgins grabbed Mitchell, a low hissing whisper, "Shut the hell up! We need to get out of here! They might be coming, but we can't fight them! Not here!"

There was a hard moment, silence, Benson staring at the two silhouettes in the snow. He knew Mitchell's temper, dangerous, but Higgins was holding him by the arms, not backing away. Benson wanted to say something, *Stop this.*

Higgins whispered again, "Let's go, Private. No more fighting here. That was a whole damn platoon, and they had heavy weapons. We can't win this one!" He turned toward Benson. "How many clips you got?"

"Six, I think."

Higgins held out his hand. "Give me two."

Benson fumbled with numb fingers, pulled two clips out of his bandolier.

Higgins again, "Hurry it up! I've got five. Here, dammit. Take his, and two of mine. That's four."

Mitchell had calmed down, his breathing still in hard bursts. "Thanks. That'll do for now. You too, Eddie. Thanks."

The sergeant was up now, and Benson saw only the man's silhouette, knew he was staring back up the hill. Benson turned that way, straining to hear, nothing, and then a low rumble of engines, beyond the ridge.

Higgins said, "They're moving off. We're not worth taking casualties for. If they knew we were only three morons . . ." He paused, the engines a distant hum now, Mitchell back up on his feet.

"I wanted to get that jackass on the machine gun. I could see the tracers. Finally got a bead on him, but the damn clip popped out. I'd have had him."

Higgins began to move, said, "Yeah, and they'd have sent fifty guys up this hill. How many of them woulda had *you*? Let's go."

Benson followed the sergeant, who stopped, pausing again, listening.

"The trucks are heading that way. Let's keep sorta in the same direction. They gotta know where our lines are."

Benson was shaking, thought of the tracers, the slap of the machinegun bullets on the trees. The brief fight was past, but he felt it now, one knee quivering, giving way, the shivering increasing. He stared at Higgins, fell to one knee, said, "Are you nuts? You wanna stay close to them?"

Higgins knelt beside him, leaned close, hot sour breath. "Get hold of it, Private. That was a good road. Has to lead somewhere we need to be. They won't think we're following them. They got trucks, remember?"

Mitchell pulled Benson up by the coat collar, said, "He's okay. Gets a little girlie every now and then. C'mon, Eddie, the sarge's right. We gotta stay kinda close to the Krauts."

Benson felt the hard grip on his collar, slid away from it, felt embarrassed, the fear overwhelming. He forced the calm into his whisper.

"Sorry. Let's go."

They moved down through the snow, through the tracks of many others, trampled pathways now, the sound of artillery off to one side, a distant machine gun. *Close to the Krauts.* Benson stared out through the dark woods, the faint carpet of white broken by the tall trees. When the sun went down, Higgins had kept them moving, and no one had complained. They had run out of food, the precious fruit long gone, and the woods were thinning out, none of the thick spruces to give them a shelter. He tried to keep his brain away from the misery, focused on the trees, stepping carefully, the woods less hilly, open ground where soldiers had been, the snow hard and icy, the sudden obstacle of tank tracks, painful stumbling.

The German convoy had been a surprise, the three men slipping easily down a wide hillside, seeking some trail they could follow. There had been no hint that just below them, a line of trucks were stopped on the road, engines off. But then a voice had called out, a startling yelp of German, someone, a guard perhaps, alert to any noise from the woods around them. The Germans began firing all through the woods, and now Benson realized, they had no idea how many we were, or who. The truck engines had started up in unison, punctuated by fire from the one heavy machine gun, the target that Mitchell so wanted to claim. But the Germans did not seem to want the fight either, the trucks moving away as soon as the shooting started.

Benson picked his way carefully, saw another set of tank treads, black muddy snow, thought, why were they stopped at all? Dinnertime? Maybe they were lost too. At least they had a road to follow.

Up ahead, Higgins slowed, then stopped, waiting, and Benson was suddenly alert, *what?* He saw now, the delay was for him, the other two matching his pace. Throughout the day, Higgins had given Benson every rest he needed, but the lack of food was affecting all of them. When the rags in his boots had been tossed away, they were bloody, something Benson tried not to think about now. The wetness was always there, and he repeated that in his mind, the wetness . . . snow, water. Not blood. Please God. Not blood.

They were moving again, Mitchell falling back behind him, single-file through a tight stand of thin trees. They moved for a few more yards, low, thin branches slapping their coats, and suddenly Higgins stopped in front of him, frozen, one hand sharply in the air. Benson obeyed, another wave of panic, exhaustion, and hunger pulling at him. Mitchell was close beside him now, reassuring, a hand on Benson's back, fingers gripping the coat, pulling Benson slowly downward. Higgins had ducked low, and Benson stared ahead, felt a wave of sickness, sudden, horrible twisting in his gut. He leaned low, scooped out a hole in the snow, put his face down, to muffle the sound. He waited, agonizing seconds, but the sickness passed, and Mitchell grabbed him, a low whisper.

"Not now, Eddie. They're right in front of us."

Benson felt his heart jump, searched the shadows for Higgins, realized he was low against a tree, facing them. Higgins turned past the tree slowly, Benson's brain racing, questions, no explanation from Mitchell, nothing to see. He searched the dark, the small trees mostly behind them, a wide swath of open ground in front. *A road.* Higgins began a slow crawl, and suddenly there was a blast of light, blinding, pushing Benson back, voices.

"Halt! You're covered!"

"Hey, they're our guys!"

"What the hell?"

Benson stayed low, blinded, blinking furiously, held the rifle up in front of him, ready, finger on the trigger. The voices kept coming, and the light was gone now, the darkness a blaze of blue and red ripping his eyes. He stared down, the voices closer, ominous, and he saw a small piercing beam moving across the open ground.

"Hey! You guys! Look here!"

Higgins's voice now, "Four Two Three. Rifle squad. Bruce Higgins, sergeant."

"I'll be damned. Where the hell'd you guys come from? We thought you were infiltrators. Bastards been slipping past us every damn night."

"Back off, soldier. All right, Sergeant Higgins. Who won the pennant for the National League last year?"

There was a strange silent moment, and the voice came again.

"I said, Higgins, who won the National League pennant last year?"

"Hell if I know. I'm not a big baseball guy."

Benson heard the click of a rifle, felt the burst of words coming out of his brain. "Cardinals! I'm from near Saint Louis! The sarge is from out west. He wouldn't know. Cardinals. Musial hit three fifty-seven. Kid's gonna be a star!"

The flashlight beam found Benson, who tried to avoid the light, his eyes still half blind. He caught motion across the open ground, shadowy figures gathering, and a massive shadow behind them. It was a tank.

Close in front of him, another man said, "Outside Saint Louis? Where? I'm from Hanes City. You from near there?"

Benson felt a stab of alarm.

"Sullivan. Sullivan, Missouri. I never heard of Hanes City."

"Good thing, son. I never heard of it either."

Another man stepped close, said, "I'm not sure about this, sir. Krauts have been pretty crafty." He leaned low toward Benson, said, "Look, pal, I'm a Giants fan. Who's their biggest star?"

Benson was frantic now, ran names through his head, Dodgers . . . Giants . . .

"Mel Ott, I guess. Hate the damn Giants."

The man laughed, backed away, and another man spoke, the man with the flashlight, the voice of an officer.

"Get these boys what they need. Feed 'em, fix 'em up, send 'em to my tent. The G-2 will wanna talk to them."

"Yes, sir."

Benson's eyes were adjusting to the dark again, and he could see men in motion, some disappearing back into the woods across the open ground, men up on the tank. Four men were staying close, rifles up on shoulders.

Higgins said, "What the hell was that about? If Benson hadn't been a baseball nut, then what? You'd have shot us?"

"That's about right. Kraut infiltrators every damn place you look. Nice neat GI uniforms, good English, look just like they're supposed to look. Don't know a damn thing about baseball, though. What the hell's your problem?"

Higgins said, "Family's from Los Angeles. Don't have a damn radio. Never took to the game."

Mitchell was beside Benson now, slapped his back, a hearty laugh. "See? I told Eddie he was good for something. You just saved our asses. I couldn't for the life of me remember who won the pennant last year."

Benson began to move with the others, out into the open, hard tracks in the snow, the footing uneven. The voices were blending around him, jokes and low laughter, questions and answers, another hard slap on his back. He felt a swirl of heat, and the sickness came again, his brain spinning in confusion, his knees buckling, the shadows fading away.

He heard the sound of a radio, talking, garbled scratches. The sounds filled his head, warmth and sunshine, the front porch, his father, baseball, *home run,* his father slapping the porch railing, angry, *that damn Mel Ott.* The sunshine was gone now, darkness above him, the stink of medicine, more voices.

"He's awake, sir."

Benson saw the uniforms, the soft light of a lantern to one side. The man leaned low over him, said, "You hear me okay, son?"

Benson blinked, smelled cigar smoke, saw the man's face, older, no helmet, the stub of a cigar in his mouth. The stink was waking him quickly, and Benson said, "Yes, sir."

"Good." The man straightened, and Benson saw a medic moving past, stopping, blood on the man's shirt.

The older man said, "How're his feet?"

"Not too bad, sir. Some pretty rough blisters, but I took care of it. Frostbite not near what I thought. He'll be up in a couple days."

"Good. Damn sick of so much trench foot. You're a lucky man, Private. Too many of our boys getting shipped home because their feet fall apart in this mess. Damn tired of losing people to bad feet. Your sergeant says you boys came in from the Four Two Three?"

"Yes, sir. We were cut off—"

"Yeah, I know. Heard it all from your buddies. I'm Colonel Jayson,

Combat Command B, Ninth Armor, adjutant to General Hoge. This is
Captain Smithers, from G-2. Captain?"

"Doesn't look like he'll be any more helpful than the others. I have to
ask you, Private, did you pick up any information along the way? Figure
out what Germans you ran into? Where you came through? We think the
smaller village you went through was Mützenich. Your sergeant described
it pretty well. It's about the only place that was still intact. We're pretty sure
it's blown to hell now. Every damn place the enemy could use a road, he
rolled right over us."

The colonel interrupted. "Enough, Captain. He doesn't need an intelligence briefing."

"No, sir. Of course, sir. With your permission, I'll report back to G-2."

"Dismissed."

The colonel moved the short cigar back and forth in his mouth,
watched the captain depart. He looked down at Benson again, seemed to
stare right through him, the man's authority pressing Benson down into
the bed.

"Glad you're okay, soldier. These intelligence idiots got us into this
mess, now they're trying to find any way they can to get us out of it. They
want to question every damn GI who floats through here. Don't worry
about it. You know where you are?"

Benson glanced to one side, saw a row of beds, medics moving between them, dark canvas above him.

"No, sir. Sorry."

"Saint Vith, son. Field hospital."

"Really? We made it?" Benson absorbed the man's name now, the
patch on his shoulder. "Did you say Ninth Armor, sir? Really? I heard the
captain say something about the Seventh Armor."

The colonel laughed, hands on his hips.

"Yeah, we're both here, but the Seventh did the job first. Saved this
place from being nabbed right off the bat. We've got people in both outfits
scattered to hell, all the way to Bastogne. Your General Jones got out with
his ass. Can't say that about too many of your other officers. Most of the
Four Two Three is . . . gone. From what we can gather, Colonel Cavender
and a large number of your buddies were captured by the enemy. There
have been a few, like you, who wandered in. But damn few."

Benson tried to grapple with the words, a jumbled flood of memories.

"My God. We were fighting in some wrecked village . . . I saw Colonel Cavender . . ."

"That was probably Radscheid. Let it go, son. Nothing we can do about that now. Those G-2 idiots are still trying to figure out which enemy units we're facing, but at this point all we can do is draw a line in the sand. We've got a hell of a fight on our hands."

"Sorry, sir. There were lots of Krauts, that's for certain. I mean, the enemy, sir."

Jayson nodded, seemed frustrated.

"Get those feet healed up, Private. We need your rifle. We need every damn rifle we can get. The enemy's coming in from every damn direction. I don't know how in hell your sergeant pulled you out of that hole, but the fight's not done. We've got engineers and cooks out there, when we need good riflemen." He paused. "That's all you need to know for now. Your buddies are outside. We're not sure what to do with you boys for now. We've got bigger problems."

Another man appeared, the clean uniform of an aide. "Excuse me, Colonel, message from the general . . ."

The medic was there again, said, "You can handle another shot. Here. This'll put you to sleep."

"Thank you, sir."

"I'm only a corporal, soldier. Save the *sirs* for the big guys."

Benson felt the needle prick, then watched the medic move away, realized the officers were still there, low voices, meaningless now. Benson blinked, bleary-eyed, stared into the darkness above him, a comfortable fog drifting through him. He tried to remember the colonel's words, the authority of the man's voice. Ninth Armor. Seventh Armor. Good. That's gotta be good. Lots of tanks. St. Vith. The sarge did it. Got us to St. Vith. I'll be damned. We're safe. He closed his eyes, flexed his toes, no pain, wonderful, that medic . . . thank you. Tanks. Lots of tanks. Very good. Very damn good.

Sleep was coming quickly, and he didn't fight it, his eyes closing, and he heard the colonel's words again. *Bigger problems.*

NEAR METZ, FRANCE
DECEMBER 19, 1944

He glanced at his watch, ten thirty, looked out at the rain, the entire morning painted by a chilling mist that soaked into every tent seam, every boot. He ignored Harkins beside him, was in no mood for talk. Colonel Paul Harkins had been with Patton nearly as long as any officer on his staff, was as much a friend to Patton as any subordinate could be. But Harkins had come along only because Patton knew a reliable officer might be needed, primarily to handle the communication of orders that would most certainly result from the meeting. The others, including his chief of staff, Hap Gay, were already preparing the Third Army for the specific orders Patton himself was on his way to receive. If Patton needed a good reason for Harkins to be there, it flashed through his mind now. With Harkins on one end of the phone line and Gay on the other, things wouldn't get screwed up.

The roads were mostly bad, what Patton was used to in France. But the driver had been chosen for his skills as well, and Patton appreciated that he seemed able to miss most of the rougher stretches. Their most annoying inconvenience had been the excessive number of MP checkpoints. Even this far from the fighting, SHAEF had issued orders that the roadblocks and outposts be increased in number and in strength. Patton had laughed at that, thought it nothing more than a wave of paranoia washing through SHAEF, inspired by too much faith in the rumors that vast legions of German commandos had completely infiltrated the Allied rear.

As the driver guided the car through the misery of the rain, the checkpoints helped at least to break the monotony. Patton actually found them entertaining. At every checkpoint, he gave the men his own silent inspection, staring at them through the window glass with a stern reproach. These men knew better, had seen enough of Patton passing through their posts to know that neckties were fastened tightly, helmets always on. Even in the misery of the cold rain, the men had stood at sharp attention, rows of stiff backs acknowledging him with respectful salutes. After long seconds of scowling, he would suddenly smile, wave, and the response would come as it always came, the *at ease* that allowed the men to loosen into greetings and cheers, the usual response from the soldiers in the Third Army when he passed by. He knew that once his car had passed a checkpoint, those men were passing the word, telephoning the next roadblock, and he laughed to himself. Fine. Tell the next guy down the road who's in this damn car. I've got no time for bawling out some idiot lieutenant because he forgot his damn tie. Of course, they don't know that. And I do love the cheers.

The weather was as dismal now as it had been for several days, and Patton fought to see through the rain, the road passing by muddy fields, many occupied by small cities of tents, usually supply depots. There were field hospitals as well, where the Red Cross flags flew high, or spread out on the flapping rooftops of the tents themselves, wishful thinking that some Luftwaffe bombardier wouldn't use the hospitals for easy target practice. But enemy aircraft had been scarce, and with the bad weather, no one on Patton's staff had seemed particularly concerned that Patton himself was in any danger in a lone staff car splashing its way through the dismal French countryside.

He scanned a field of trucks, parked in neat rows, nodded to himself. Good. We'll need every damn one of them. For weeks now, a steady stream of hardware had been flowing up to his army from the massive port at Marseille. Patton had long given up on filling his larder by competing with the other commanders for the trickle of supplies that rolled through Cherbourg, and Antwerp was massively overstuffed with ships and their cargo caught up in a spiderweb of bureaucratic and engineering nightmares.

Those supplies were designated for the British mostly, though Hodges's First Army was being supplied through there as well. Patton had never prioritized supply lines the way he had now, a lesson learned in Sicily and, more, in his amazing push across France. He had usually left those details to someone else, what he called his clerk army. But then, when the supplies ran out, when the gasoline stopped flowing to his trucks and precious armor, Patton's fury had been absolute. At first, the blame was aimed at Montgomery, and Eisenhower had been caught squarely in the middle of a different kind of war, Patton fuming that the British were being given first dibs on the limited flow of equipment and fuel. It was a fight Eisenhower didn't need, and Patton understood that. But he also understood that if Eisenhower had sent the bulk of available fuel his way, Patton's army would be the first to drive straight into Germany. There were political realities about that he just didn't want to think about. Montgomery wanted that carrot, certainly, and Patton had envisioned another race, the same kind of race with the British that Patton had won in Sicily. Then, it was for Messina, a major city. This time it could be for *the* major city, Berlin itself. And if Patton won that race, he might end the war. But Eisenhower had pulled him back, and Patton had no choice but to obey. The supply lines were so meager that even if the German army opened the way, Patton's tanks didn't have the fuel to make the trip. It was a lesson learned. Now his primary supply port was on the Mediterranean, far from the chaos of the French and Belgian coasts. The Germans had never bothered to wreck Marseille the way they had Cherbourg. And there had been no time-consuming and costly battle for control of the port, the way Monty had stumbled into Antwerp. Marseille also supplied Jacob Devers's Sixth Army Group, which occupied ground to the south of Patton's right flank, the forces that had invaded southern France in August, two months after D-Day. That landing had been enormously successful, and mostly uncontested. Unlike the Normandy landings, Devers's forces had not been held up by a vicious German defense, and had rushed northward, bringing all of southern France under Allied control. Patton had little affection for Devers, whom he had known for much of his career. But then, Patton had little affection for anyone whose rank was close to his own.

He thought of Hodges, well, there's another of Ike's cronies. Right about now his glorious First Army is kicking up snow trying to get the hell out of the way of the enemy. I thought we were supposed to move forward, not run like hell if we get shot at.

Courtney Hodges had served as Patton's chief of staff in North Africa, though only for a short while. Hodges had come up through the infantry, did not share Patton's love of tanks. But he got his reward, Patton thought. Just like some of the others, he gets a few stars and an army with his name on it because he kisses Ike's boots with plenty of tongue. Bradley should know better than to give that command to Hodges, but maybe Brad has no choice. He's pretty meek around Ike, and I guess it's just his style. I bet they wanted Hodges to stand tall and take some of the headlines, pull some of the attention away from me. But Hodges is never going to be anything more than a slow-thinking, slow-talking Georgia boy, and no amount of wishful thinking on Brad's part is going to make him into Stonewall Jackson. It takes someone with an iron codsack to keep pushing forward without talking about it first. Hodges wants to chat before he makes decisions. Fits right in with Bradley. Maybe all of them. Now his cods are in the frying pan, and sure as hell Ike will want me to get them out. No one else up to the job. Why am I the only one who knows that?

Patton didn't believe the first reports that came out of the Ardennes, had never expected that whatever the Germans were doing in those rugged hills could amount to more than a big noisy show, some kind of rip-roaring Christmas present to build Hitler's pride. I don't care how much Hodges's people have been tossed on their asses, it still doesn't make any logistical sense to launch a major offensive in that part of the front, not with the weather going to hell like this. He was nagged by the thought even now that it might all be a demonstration, lots of firepower to distract the Allies from what the Germans might truly be planning to do. If there was going to be a major offensive in winter, it should have come right here, he thought, straight into my lines. Those bastards are over there in that Siegfried line watching every move I make, knowing every time I shift a unit from one spot to another. They've been eating my artillery and taking casualties every damn day, knowing that it's only a matter of time before I chew them to bits. The best way to defend against a tough son of a bitch standing in front of you is to punch him hard right in the gut. That's what they ought to be doing, punching me square in the gut. If somehow they drove my people back, it would be their greatest accomplishment in years. Every German general would get a boost out of that, and every Allied general would know what it meant, and be damn scared of it. It would mean the Krauts could still put up a fight, a fight that actually *means* something. No matter how much panic they've caused Hodges, no matter how much crying and hair pulling is going on at SHAEF, all the Krauts are doing in the Ardennes is poking a stick into Hodges's eye.

Patton was increasingly frustrated by the orders for him to bide his time, to push his troops forward in limited attacks, gradually shoving the Germans back to the relative safety of their massive defenses along the German border. But Patton's impatience had finally been relieved. The order came from Bradley: Eisenhower's strategy was at last kicking into action. Patton was to drive hard against the Siegfried line and push across, into the Saar Valley. Once he put his people well to the east, German defenses would certainly ease up in the north, allowing Montgomery and the rest of Bradley's forces to advance under much more favorable conditions. The scheduled date for Patton's attack was December 19. But with only three days to go, and Patton fully prepared to resume a glorious drive into the teeth of the enemy, the Germans made their surprise assault in the Ardennes. To Patton's furious dismay, the order came to call off his attack and instead look to the north, shifting his troops in a way that would aid the crisis swallowing up Hodges's troops, a crisis whose magnitude was only now being understood.

He folded his arms across his chest. December 19, he thought. Today. We'd have rolled right over the Siegfried line and left half the Krauts smoldering there in those fat bunkers. I'm so damn sick of looking out across all that concrete. What the hell is the point of that thing anyway? Who could ever believe that a German army, *this* German army, would think it was a good idea to hunker down in big fat concrete boxes, surrounded by tank traps and barbed wire, and fight a defensive war? Who the hell thought that was worth all that labor, all that concrete and steel? Four years ago, those bastards drove straight through the British and French, and either obliterated them or shoved them into the ocean. And yet someone convinced Hitler they should build this line along their own border . . . just in case? The Siegfried line is nothing more than Hitler's people hedging their bets. I guess it makes sense to protect your own borders, but the smart ones over there have to know their history. For centuries, no one's been able to figure out how to build a defense here that actually works. Not in this part of the world, anyway. Hitler must have laughed like hell at the French, knowing his tanks were rolling right on through their big fat defenses. What were the French doing, standing by the roadside selling lemonade? It's all just concrete, and I haven't met a concrete bunker yet that can outthink a good battlefield commander. But I can't prove that today. Dammit, and we were ready to go. Nope, today I have to go to Verdun and sit down with Ike and his boot lickers, and listen to them wring their hands about Hodges getting his ass kicked. I just hope to God Monty isn't there.

They sat around a rectangular table, Eisenhower at one end, Tedder to one side. Devers was there, no surprise, and at the other end, Bradley. Behind them were staff officers, the usual faces, and Patton anchored his own man, Harkins, close behind him. The room itself was sparse and cold, heated by a lone potbellied stove, a makeshift meeting place someone had code-named Eagle Main, one of those peculiarly military practices that Patton usually ignored. He sat facing Devers, thought, this is just a damn meeting. We're not going to change the world, and nobody is ever going to build a monument to this ramshackle building. Why in hell does it need a fancy security name? Has to be Beetle Smith's idea. He's the one who wants to attach importance to Ike's every move, so he can sell this whole idea to Hollywood one day. Beetle will want to be played by John Barrymore, but I bet Monty will put up a fight for that one. Monty ought to be played by Buster Keaton.

Eisenhower's seriousness brought Patton back to the moment, and he realized now that the faces all around the room carried the same look of despair, an infection of gloom that made the room chillier still. Two aides were hammering the top corners of a map to one wall. All faces turned that way, the map hanging loosely.

Eisenhower seemed to pick up the same mood as Patton, said, "The present situation is to be regarded as one of opportunity and not disaster. There will be only cheerful faces at this table. Am I understood?"

There were meager nods, and Patton felt a wave of disgust, the gloom spread even to Bradley. He slapped a hand on the hard wood of the table, said, "Opportunity! Hell, yes! We should let the enemy pour right through that gap until they make it all the way to Paris. Then we can cut the sons of bitches off, and chew 'em up that much easier!"

No one smiled except Eisenhower, who responded, "All right, George, let's not be that damn cheerful. I'd rather we held the line at the Meuse. I don't think de Gaulle would appreciate our strategy if we let the enemy scare hell out of Paris." Eisenhower pointed to the map. "This is what we think we know. The enemy has punched a bulge in our defenses nearly forty miles wide. Fortunately, he has not yet captured Bastogne, though he is driving past on both sides. That may be a conscious decision on von Rundstedt's part, to just move on past and not tie his people up in a knot by bogging down there. So far, there's not much we've been able to do about it. Saint Vith is just as bad, though the enemy doesn't have the place completely enveloped, best as we can tell. Hanging on to both those cities is critical. The road networks fan out westward in such a way that the enemy would have several easy paths toward the Meuse."

Bradley cleared his throat, said, "I have spoken to Hodges on the phone. He's getting a handle on this thing, shifting forces into position, mainly from the north. We're holding out in that direction pretty well, but that was to be expected. We're strongest in that area. Matt Ridgway is moving his paratroop corps down to help out, and as you can see, several infantry and armor divisions are joining the fight."

Eisenhower looked at Devers, said, "Jake, I need you to shore up your juncture with the Third Army, tighten those lines. You already know why."

Devers nodded, and Patton caught the man's look, thought, fine, you want me to do the talking. Patton did not wait to be asked.

"We're already on it, Ike. I've put Walker's Twentieth Corps in line facing east, and Jake's people are moving up alongside. We've already established boundaries and flanks that are pretty well defined, and we're doing all we can to make them secure. Nobody's slipping between us."

Eisenhower absorbed Patton's words. "I agree with you there, George. Walton Walker's the right man for that job. But how quickly will you be ready to push the rest of your people north? You've got to withdraw from contact with the enemy, pull back far enough so they can maneuver without being detected, turn them ninety degrees, and then advance with as much speed as possible. That's a lot of maneuver, George."

The question annoyed Patton, who did his best to hide it.

"I was *ready* the minute I got the order. We're shifting our people now, and we can begin attacking the enemy flank on the twenty-second."

He heard the low comments, saw surprise on every face at the table. Eisenhower said, "*December* twenty-second? Three days? That's pretty amazing, George. How much strength are you talking about?"

Patton was annoyed again, didn't see anything *amazing* about it.

"Three divisions. The Fourth Armored, the Twenty-sixth and Eightieth infantry."

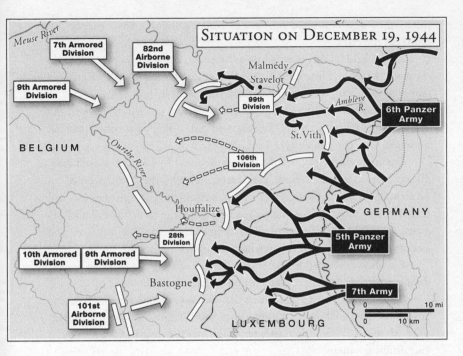

SITUATION ON DECEMBER 19, 1944

Eisenhower looked down, shook his head. "That may not be enough, George."

"If you want me to move the whole damn Third Army, I can do that too. But it won't be done in three days. Seems to me, by looking at your map, Hodges doesn't need help *eventually*, he needs it right now. My three divisions can smack the enemy pretty damn hard, and I guarantee you, whatever Krauts are holding their flank, they aren't expecting me to hit them that quickly with that much power. Isn't that the point here? I would think we would all appreciate that *surprise* works wonders on a battlefield. Judging by your map there, it worked pretty damn well against Hodges."

Patton caught the glare from Bradley, knew he had slid a toe across the fine line of decorum that Eisenhower tried so hard to maintain.

Eisenhower seemed not to notice, rubbed one hand across his chin, lost in thought. He shook his head. "George, I don't mean to cast any doubts here, but you understand the logistical problems of shifting that many men onto a limited number of roads, realigning their supply systems, all the rest?"

Patton held his anger as tightly as he could, one foot tapping the floor beneath the table. He gritted his teeth, said in a muted hiss, "*I know what has to be done, Ike.* We'll do it on the twenty-second."

Eisenhower looked at the others, and Patton saw the wide eyes, the doubt. "Well, then, go to it," Eisenhower said. "Jake, your people can fall in where George's pull away?"

Devers nodded, not nearly as sure of himself as Patton would have liked. Patton stared at him, and Devers caught the look, seemed to straighten, said, "If George can move that quickly, so can we. General Patch is in touch with Walker already. As George said, their flanks are being established, and communication lines are being put in place. The enemy's not slipping past us anywhere along that entire line."

Eisenhower seemed to animate, rubbed his hands together, looked at Bradley, who smiled back, nodded in hesitant approval.

Patton appreciated that, knew that Bradley would side with Eisenhower no matter which way Eisenhower went. Patton looked at the map, studied, asked, "Who's in Bastogne? How much strength. Can they hold out until I get there?"

Bradley said, "Ridgway says the One Oh First Airborne is moving in there pretty quickly, and last night, Middleton reported that units of the Tenth Armor moved in. The German has been a little skittish about marching in there like he owns the place, so he must think we've got more people there than we do." Bradley looked at Eisenhower. "That's a break, Ike. A big break. Same thing's happened at Saint Vith. The panzers look like they're wanting to surround the city instead of just moving right in. Some of our boys there are putting up a hell of a scrap, but I'm not sure who's doing the fighting. The infantry has been scattered all over those hills, and the Seventh Armor is split up to cover every damn road. Hodges has no idea who's in command of the town itself. But whoever's responsible, it's given us a little time to pull some of the scattered infantry units together. Ridgway is moving the Eighty-second Airborne up in support as quickly as he can. Hodges says the Thirtieth and First divisions are in motion, plus units of the Ninth Armor."

Eisenhower held up his hands, the growing hum of talk around Bradley silencing.

"That brings me to another major point. The bulge the enemy has jammed into our front has made communication with General Hodges difficult at best. We can reach him by phone now, but a face-to-face is out of the question." He paused, looked at Patton, as though Eisenhower wanted something from him. "In my position, a crisis such as this offers two options. We can fall back and regroup our forces, forming a stout defensive line, and then await the enemy's next move. Or we can do all we can to stifle that move as it is happening. I believe the latter is the only acceptable option." He looked at Patton, as though asking for a comment. "Do you all agree?"

Patton took the opening.

"Damn right we agree."

Eisenhower did not hesitate. "I have ordered Monty to shift as much of his strength to the west bank of the Meuse as he can spare, to build up that line as an impenetrable defense should the enemy continue his push unabated. I do not expect that to happen, but Monty has done the right thing by accepting my strategy."

Patton sniffed, did not want any of this conversation to shift toward Montgomery.

Bradley said, "Hodges is doing all he can to hold up the enemy's advance. I have confidence that will only improve our situation."

Patton thought, he changed the subject. Brad hates Monty as much as I do. Good for him.

Eisenhower stood, the staffs jumping into motion, the map pulled down, disappearing into a thick roll of paper. Devers moved to the door, never seemed to want to have any kind of informal chat with Patton, and Patton watched him go, thought, he's scared to death. Just get the job done, Jake. Dammit, you outrank me, and you act like you're on my staff. The staffs were filing out of the room now, tight quarters, Patton moving closer to the stove, the heat loosening stiffness in his knee.

Eisenhower moved close to him, said, "You know, George, every damn time I get promoted, every damn time I add a star, the enemy picks that time to attack. Hell of a lack of graciousness."

Patton saw a hint of a smile, said, "That's okay, Ike. Every time you get attacked, I pull you out of the fire."

Bradley was there now. "Hell of a gambit, George. I'd love to see you pull this off."

Patton saw both men looking at him, felt them searching him for some sign of doubt. He pulled his shoulders back, a show of friendly defiance, said, "I'll pull it off. We're already moving. We'll hit those bastards hard. Monty can do whatever he wants to on the other side of the river. Tell his boys to play some cricket or something, because I promise you, Ike, no Kraut will ever get that far."

Eisenhower patted him on the back, and Patton made a short nod toward Bradley.

"Work to do. I better get going."

He moved toward the door, felt the cold rushing in, a slap in his face. Outside, he saw the strange armored car that had brought Eisenhower to the meeting, the response to all the rumors about assassination squads targeting the Allied commander. That's okay, he thought. If Ike sleeps better at night, I suppose that's good for all of us.

He saw his own car, Harkins there, waiting, the driver holding open the door. Harkins said, "It went well, sir. Exceptional, I'd say."

Patton said nothing, moved past him, slid into the car. He waited, already impatient, Harkins moving around to the other side, the doors shutting, and Patton noticed the car already running, the good work of the driver, the car's heater doing its job. He thought of Eisenhower, the grand show of morale, trying to convince the others that what had happened to Hodges wasn't so bad after all, that it was inevitable the bulge could be closed, the enemy tossed back. I know that's true, he thought. Well, I believe it's true anyway. He chuckled to himself, thought, all right George, you've bitten off a hell of a mouthful. Time to start chewing.

A s Patton began the extraordinary task of shifting most of his Third Army northward, one of his primary goals was to secure the vital junction at Bastogne. Before the Germans could occupy the virtually undefended city, the Americans had thrown together a hasty defense, which eventually consisted of the 101st Airborne Division anchored alongside one company of the 10th Armored Division. To the dismay of the Germans, Bastogne was no longer an easy target. Though they kept up pressure on the city, they seemed reluctant to push forward an all-out attack. For the most part, Manteuffel's tanks and the infantry of the Seventh Army slid past, surrounding Bastogne and hemming in the American paratroopers and tank commanders who fought stubbornly for their defenses. Given such stout resistance, Manteuffel considered Bastogne to be more trouble than it was worth, and, knowing how badly his timetable had been shattered, the German general believed his drive westward should be the priority. But Field Marshal Model would hear none of that, and insisted that Bastogne be captured. Once the city fell securely into German hands, the Germans could claim a hold on vital intersections that might eventually aid a defensive action, should the need arise. Patton's move northward was a secret to no one. In their haste to move, many of his commanders ignored protocol and spoke openly on their radios, which provided German eavesdroppers with far more details than Patton would have liked. Though Bastogne was surrounded, the Germans south of the city began to prepare for Patton's arrival. If the troops and armor at Bastogne were to be rescued, Patton's columns would first have to fight. On December 22, Manteuffel's subordinate, General Heinrich von Lüttwitz, who commanded the troops besieging Bastogne, attempted to convince the Americans to surrender the city. Under a flag of truce, the German general sent a staff officer to the American line, with a message, an offer that the Americans give up and thus avoid certain massacre. The aide and his message were brought to General Anthony McAuliffe, the 101st Airborne's commander. His written reply to von Lüttwitz was simple and direct, a single word that would echo through American military lore for all time.

"Nuts."

A t St. Vith, the final blow came from two directions, German tanks and mechanized infantry finally ripping holes in the tattered defenses of the town. Throughout the day on December 21, both sides had made much of their fight with artillery, a duel that caused enormous casualties on both sides. The Germans kept up their pressure, probing small-scale attacks, seeking out any roadway that might collapse under the weight of a few of their massive Tiger tanks. But the American armor, supported by a ragtag defensive line of detached infantry, engineers, and headquarters staff, blunted each German push. By that night, most of the shelling had stopped, a reprieve that allowed both sides to lick their considerable wounds. While exhausted Americans sought to improve their lines, shifting strength to the most vulnerable positions, they believed that darkness had ended the fight, that the Germans would wait for dawn to begin their push again. But the Germans had no intention of spending a quiet night in their tanks. At 10 P.M., they launched a sudden full-throttle attack, and in the chaos of darkness, the Germans made perfect use of flare guns and star shells, illuminating the American positions, and creating perfect targets. The result was a tidal wave of German steel that the Americans could not hold back. By the morning of December 22, St. Vith had fallen, and armored columns from Sepp Dietrich's Sixth Panzer Army rolled into the city from both north and south. With the vital intersection in German hands, the Americans had no choice but to pull away to the west, sacrificing the key position, and once again making a frantic attempt to draw in those troops who had been cut off or driven away, pulling back as much force as they could. This time, the retreat was more organized, the armor and artillery holding back German pursuit as the fragments of makeshift infantry units, supply trucks, and other vehicles fled to the west. For another long and brutal day, the Americans held on to their escape routes, keeping open a narrow peninsula that led toward the Salm River, a dozen miles west of St. Vith, where the newly arrived Eighty-second Airborne had established a stout defensive line. For the ground troops, the weather was more of a benefit to the Allied side. As the Americans around St. Vith slipped through Dietrich's fingers, they were aided by a vicious snowstorm. The men on the march suffered, as they had suffered for more than a week. But this time, the Germans could not press the fight. American artillery provided a harrowing blanket of covering fire, allowing most of the Americans to reach safety at the river. If the Germans were to press their attack and cross the Salm, they would have to face the wrath of hard-core experience. The Eighty-second Airborne had already bloodied the Germans in Sicily and throughout the campaign in Normandy, and were coming off long weeks of rest and recuperation. Whether or not Dietrich expected his panzers to continue their hard-charging drive, the German commanders on the front lines were less enthusiastic about assaulting a position on the far side of a river, defended by one of the toughest fighting units in the American army.

Model and von Rundstedt knew what the Americans did not, that the Führer's great plan had already gone awry. Both Bastogne and St. Vith were to have been overrun on the first day of the attack, and by now the timetable had called for Model's powerful thrust to have already driven across the Meuse. Model and von Rundstedt had expected delays from the poor roads, the terrain, the weather. But they had not expected the Americans to put up such an astounding fight. That fight came from scattered and broken remnants of infantry and armored units, bits and pieces who were not supposed to be fighting at all. From engineers to kitchen crews to army musicians, American units had managed to punch holes in the German wave, slowing them just enough to allow the Allied commanders to adjust. While Hodges shifted infantry and armor divisions into line, Matthew Ridgway had put his paratroopers where they most needed to be. Hitler's dream had met reality. Model knew, as did von Rundstedt, that the great drive toward Antwerp had already been delayed by nearly a week.

As the chaos that had rolled through Hodges's command began to sort itself out, neither Allied intelligence nor the generals in the field were aware how badly Hitler's plan had been gutted by the delay. The key intersections at St. Vith and Bastogne had been far tougher to swallow than the Germans had expected, but between them, where so many American forces had been trampled and scattered across the miserable terrain of the Ardennes, the German push continued. The gap between the two cities was more than thirty miles, and there, in the German center, through small villages and winding forest trails, Manteuffel's panzers continued to drive forward. Hodges was still charged with the urgent job of finding some way to blunt that spear, to stop the German forces before they could reach the Meuse. On every map, the German thrust was narrowing, a deep wedge shoved into the American lines that had inspired a description embraced by the newspapers back home. The campaign that Hitler had named Watch on the Rhine now had a different name: the Battle of the Bulge.

Throughout the campaign, one piece of the German plan had worked to perfection: Hitler's prediction of bad weather, which had eliminated Allied airpower from the equation. But the German commanders knew that even their Führer could not control the weather indefinitely.

16. BENSON

Benson's feet responded well, the bloody blisters healing beneath a thick smear of some kind of ointment. His bed in the field hospital had been needed for far more serious patients, something Benson didn't question. He had seen them, blue hands and lips, bloody rags for shoes, ghastly wounds, some barely alive at all. For a full day he had stayed in the hospital alongside the medics and the few doctors, doing anything he could to help. There could be no boots on his feet, not yet, and so he worked barefoot, warming his feet by the stove that supplied heat to the enormous tent. When the order came to withdraw from St. Vith, Benson's apprenticeship with the medics ended. His feet were healed enough to wear boots, new ones this time. In his backpack were stuffed half a dozen pairs of new socks.

Benson knew very little about what had happened to the rest of the division, though word had filtered through the men about one casualty in particular. As the fighting around St. Vith turned to a full-out retreat, the 106th's commanding officer, General Alan Jones, had suffered a heart attack. To the riflemen of the 423rd Regiment, Jones was mostly just a name, to be replaced quickly by another name, General Herbert Perrin. Far more important was confirmation that the 423rd's commander, Colonel Charles Cavender, was gone, almost certainly dead or snapped up by the Germans.

The 422nd had suffered much the same fate as Benson's own regiment, while the 424th had fared slightly better, many of those men escaping still with some organization, or driven southward, jumbled up with units from the 28th Division west of Bastogne. Though some of the division's artillery had survived, many of the guns were lost, along with their crews. While Benson had recuperated at the field hospital, Sergeant Higgins had made some effort to report the situation of the lone lieutenant, the artilleryman and his loader, the only men in the divisional artillery who actually seemed to believe some training manual's insane propaganda that no gun should be abandoned. But there was little sympathy from above for this one renegade lieutenant when the troops still in St. Vith were working desperately to hold their ground. Benson had seen parades of artillery pieces himself, survivors pulling their guns into the town, and then, beyond, to the west. When the retreat from St. Vith began, those were the men who had the worst task. They were the rear guard, doing as much as they could to hold away the German pursuit in a deadly game of leapfrog, artillery doing their job, then moving past the next unit, which did the same. None of the artillerymen that Benson saw resembled the lone lieutenant.

Unlike the dismal reports coming up from Bastogne, St. Vith was not yet fully surrounded, the German push more like a vise grip than a siege. The road to the west had been kept open, mostly by the extraordinary efforts of Jim Gavin's Eighty-second Airborne, and so, while the armor and scattered infantry made their final effort to hold the town, supply and transport trucks still rolled in. Once the hospital staff were ordered to join the retreat, Benson had been ordered by a doctor there to return to his unit. There was no paperwork, no one sorting through personnel records. The doctor had no idea, and probably didn't care, that for now, Benson's *unit* was Mitchell and Sergeant Higgins. As they rode west into the relative safety of the guns of the Eighty-second Airborne, the three men finally found officers who took charge of them, what remained of the command structure of the 423rd, mostly field officers who had fought their way through the woods and thickets, or wandered with small groups of cutoff troops, until they reached St. Vith. With the supply trucks came boots and fresh uniforms, mounds of dry socks, new gloves and wool hats, and the wonderfully warm overshoes. Once they reached Trois Ponts, the survivors of the 423rd were brought together in increasing numbers, and the ques-

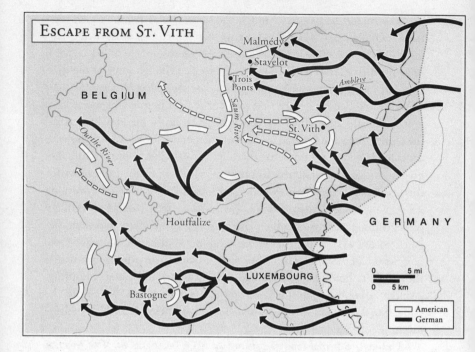

tions had come, men seeking buddies, the few officers locating men from their own commands. For Benson, Higgins, and Mitchell, no one had any answers.

Trois Ponts, Belgium
December 22, 1944, 11 p.m.

"We really don't know what to do with you. I've been told that the army hasn't decided whether the One Oh Sixth should be parsed out to other units altogether. I'm certain no one here wants to see that happen. The major thinks we should ship you back to the replacement depot at Antwerp. But every division in this sector is seriously undermanned, especially their rifle companies, and while the army makes up its mind, we need you to rejoin the party."

The captain was a thick truck of a man, Benson guessing thirty years old, bald head, helmet on the small table behind him. The man paced, seemed no more enthusiastic about his own speech than the men who were receiving it. Benson glanced around, forty men, maybe more, all from the 423rd, a platoon-sized group, most of whom had been a part of the withdrawal from St. Vith. Some were familiar faces, but there were no names, no one he knew well. Other than Higgins and Mitchell, no one had come into St. Vith from the platoon that had once belonged to Lieutenant Greeley.

"You men all get your overshoes?" There were positive mumblings, the captain scanning the room. "Good. I have been told that we are finally going to get snowsuits. White camouflage. For now, pretend you never heard that, since God knows how many of those things will ever find their way out of the depots. Some idiot in supply who never actually goes outdoors thinks all this talk of *snow* is nonsense." The captain paused, seemed to run out of words, thought for a moment. "You're veterans now. Remember that. That's maybe the most important thing right now. Other platoons in my company are being refilled with shiny new replacements from the States, men who couldn't poke themselves in the ass if their bayonet had directions. It took some doing . . . someone at corps HQ owed me a big favor . . . well, you don't need to know about that. But for the time being, you're mine." He paused again. "All right, we're done here. See Lieutenant Fornell, the bivouac next door. He's working on ammo supplies and weapons, making sure everyone has the right equipment. He'll be your platoon commander, organize your squads. There are what . . . four sergeants here? Good. I can't spare anyone else. You know your own men. Until somebody upstairs tells us different, you're a temporary part of the Thirtieth Division. Next week, that could change, and it probably will." He stopped, reached for his helmet, the men beginning to stir. Benson stood, testing the remnants of pain in his feet, and the captain spoke up again.

"Listen. The One Oh Sixth has something to be proud of. If you don't know that, the rest of us do. You took the hardest punch Hitler could throw, and you slowed those bastards down enough so we could do something about it. Hang on to that. The army will figure out . . . well, not for me to say. I've got my orders, and now so do you."

"Excuse me, sir." The voice was Mitchell's, beside Benson.

The captain seemed annoyed by the distraction, said, "Yes, soldier, what is it?"

"Can you tell us, sir, if we are going to fight Krauts again?"

"You damn well better. That's all. Get out of here."

NEAR STAVELOT, BELGIUM
DECEMBER 23, 1944, PREDAWN

The trucks had driven out away from the Salm River, a road slippery with
the snowpack hardened by the troops who were still strengthening the defensive lines along the western bank. This time, the deuce-and-a-halfs had
no canvas covering, the men crushed by the brutal cold, every man bundled tight, faces down, enduring every bounce as they counted the minutes
of the hour-long trip. When they were finally unloaded, they were met by
MPs, hushed instructions to the lieutenant passed to each of the sergeants.
The squads had been thrown together according to which truck the men
occupied, and Higgins now commanded another ten men besides Benson
and Mitchell.

Once they were away from the trucks, they had warmed the numbing
stiffness in their feet by a brief brisk march. They stayed in a narrow road,
moving past vivid signs of the snowstorm that had washed over them the
past two days. The road was in heavy use, and so the bulldozers had
plowed the surface clean, snowbanks pushed high on both sides. But the
road itself was a river of ice, crushed into ankle-shattering debris by the
armored trucks and tanks that had already moved ahead. With daylight
still hours away, the march had concluded at a narrow cut through a
snowbank, the men following their lieutenant and his guide to the hulking shadow of a large farmhouse. Each man had been issued a small, jointed
shovel, and Benson had wondered if this Lieutenant Fornell would issue
that most idiotic of orders, for the men to dig foxholes into brick-hard
ground. But the order didn't come, the lieutenant leading them all into
the house, spreading them from basement to an upstairs attic space. The
luxury of a roof was appreciated by every man, but the wind and cold
found them anyway, no window glass, the house obviously used before,
and just as obviously, it had been in the middle of a fight. Benson and
Mitchell had staked out a space on the main floor, in what had been a
bedroom, where backpacks could be used as pillows. Most of the furniture was gone, and in the shadowy darkness, Benson could see ripped and
trampled remnants of clothing, the bed and other wood furniture long
since used for fuel in one of several fireplaces. But there would be no fire
tonight, nothing to offer a target to enemy gunners. Incredibly, the house
did have one surprising luxury: a working toilet. That caught the atten-

tion of every man in the platoon, and in the dark silence, the men grum-
bled at one another for the excessive amount of time each one took enjoying a porcelain throne.

But not every man enjoyed this particular bit of luxury. Before Benson
could settle down and enjoy an hour or two of sleep, the lieutenant had
come, an order to the sergeants to supply guards to be posted outside. Each
sergeant had offered up two men, and Higgins had come to the men he
trusted most. For Benson and Mitchell, there would be no sleep, no toilet,
and no reveling under the shelter of a hard roof.

They marched in slow, silent steps, flattening a path in the snow close
to the house. Mitchell kept pace beside him, staying in motion only
for warmth. On the far sides of the house, the other guards did the same,
six more rifles and six sets of eyes, a comforting thought as Benson tried to
see any sign of movement across a wide field that spread out in three directions.

Mitchell, slapping his arms against his sides, pulling the coat in tight,
said in a whisper, "How much colder can it get? Where the hell are we,
anyway? That lieutenant . . . not sure about him."

Benson had heard this before, nervous chatter from the man who
never admitted he was nervous.

"I think he's okay. He's been through this stuff too. Damn it's cold."
Benson looked up, saw stars, then looked back to the field. They reached
the corner of the house, saw the shadows of two other guards, no greeting, then turned, paced back the other way. Benson flexed his fingers, kept them stuffed into the pockets of the thick coat. "Just like
home. Clear nights are always the coldest." He stopped suddenly, looked
up again, and Mitchell responded, his rifle slipping quickly off his
shoulder.

"What. See something?"

Benson still stared up, and Mitchell followed his gaze. Benson said,
"Yeah. I see stars. *Stars.*"

Mitchell began to pace again, still thumping his arms around his sides.
"Great. You see stars. Just means it's colder."

Benson caught up with him, scanned the field again, the wide-open
ground showing more light, the first hint of dawn. There was something

new, farther away in the field, thick mounds of black, uneven lumps in the snow. He jerked the rifle off his shoulder, said, "Kenny!"

Mitchell slapped him on the back.

"Just dirt, Eddie. Shell holes. Sun's finally coming up. Those stars are going away pretty quick."

Benson wasn't convinced, studied the dark blotches. From the house, he heard sounds, the men stirring, someone emerging through the shattered front door, the low voice of Higgins.

"Time's up. We're supposed to get moving. Lieutenant's been on the walkie-talkie. The rest of the company is across the road. We're supporting half a battalion of tanks and a slug of infantry moving into the town. Krauts are there waiting for us. Get in here and grab some chow. You got five minutes."

Mitchell led Benson inside, Benson still nervous, glancing back to the field. He caught the new smell, hot chocolate, someone finding a way to boil water, most likely in the basement, the only place a glow of fire would be hidden. The low voices were all around him, men checking their rifles, a BAR man talking to his own sergeant, a four-man bazooka team huddled in one corner, hoisting up their boxes of the tank-killing rockets. Men were coming down the stairs, sergeants bringing their squads into the larger main room, harsh orders to move outside. Higgins was there again, and Benson saw the lieutenant, could make out his face in the low light.

"You boys ready to go to work?"

Mitchell said, "I'm ready to find some Krauts. Sir."

"Keep the big talk to yourself. There's a whole town full of them right up ahead. Get ready to move out."

The lieutenant was gone quickly, outside, and Benson ripped open a K-ration box, fought with the contents, saw a small flame in one corner, another man heating his breakfast by burning the box.

Higgins was there, said, "No time for that soldier. Eat it cold. Then fall in."

The man cursed, was up on his feet, stomped the fire, moved past Benson, said nothing. Benson swallowed something cold and hard, flavorless meat, some kind of stew, moved toward an open window, stared again at the field. The sun was still below the horizon, but he could see much farther now, the black blotches in the field clear and distinct. They were dead cows. He wanted to say something, felt foolish, knew Mitchell wouldn't care anyway. Mitchell had finished his breakfast, tossed the empty boxes in a corner, waited for Benson, who followed him outside. The men were moving quickly, the sergeants pulling them back out into the road, and Benson hustled out, followed the trampled snow, looked to one side, the tracks where he and Mitchell had stood guard. As they moved past the corner of the house, his eyes caught more black, like logs, spread in the snow, a few yards beyond the house. He stopped, saw now that they were bodies, half a dozen, faces upturned, lying in twisted shapes, the helmets German. He stared, more curious than sickened, the faces eyeless, the skin an odd shade of green. Mitchell was beside him, a small laugh.

"I wondered if you knew they were there. We walked right up to them a hundred times. I had a pretty good idea they were Krauts. Our guys wouldn't have been left out here like that. Didn't wanna spook you."

"God, Kenny. They're . . . green."

"They're dead. Let's go."

Benson took a last look, one man's mouth open, yellow teeth, and he forced himself to move, join the others.

Higgins was waiting for them at the edge of the road, and the lieutenant was there, stepping in place, fighting the cold and his own impatience. He pointed, said, "The town's half a mile over that next rise." Fornell moved in closer, weaved the men into a tighter group, spoke in a low voice. "The rest of the company is across the road, in that draw, moving up with us. Can't see 'em yet, but they're there. Another company's along that far ridge beyond. You'll see them soon enough. We're converging on this side of the town, and we're ordered to move in together, if that's possible. So don't shoot at anybody until you know your target." He turned, pointed up the road. "There are supposed to be several more farmhouses up ahead. No reports of snipers, but the Krauts might have moved out here last night. Watch those damn houses, check 'em out as we go by. We can use 'em for cover if we start taking fire from the town."

Benson felt the chill increasing, the nervousness, his teeth starting to chatter.

Fornell continued, "Tanks are already moving up, and there might be armor and artillery coming in on this road, so keep your men the hell out of the way." He stopped, craned his head, staring out past the farmhouse. "Listen." Benson heard them, a cascade of engines far across the field. "That's our boys. Let's go to work. Spread out from the road to the right. Sergeant Jernigan, take your squad to the right flank, anchor the flank yourself."

"Yes, sir."

Benson didn't know Jernigan at all, watched as he led his squad out into the snow. The lieutenant kept up the orders, spreading the men into a thin line of advance, and Higgins was given the final order, would keep his squad closest to the road. The lieutenant moved away, out into the snow, midway along his line of men, made a sharp wave, began to step forward through the snowy field. Benson focused on the engines, louder now, the fear rolling into raw excitement. Half a battalion. How many's that? God, that ought to be a sight. Higgins was just in front of his own squad, moving in step with the lieutenant. Beside Benson, Mitchell kicked up snow with his boots, held his rifle in his hands. Benson tested his feet, numb with the cold, but no pain, another *thank you* to the medics. The men around him were silent, just the soft shuffle of boots through powdery snow, the sound of the tanks still there, moving ahead, passing them by. He looked out across the road, saw the draw, the ridgeline beyond, no sign of the soldiers there, thought, no, you idiot. They're gonna stay hidden as long as they can. Not like . . . us. We're in the wide blue open.

The sun was breaking the horizon to the left, a sharp piercing light along the ridge, the first sunlight Benson had seen since he left Le Havre. Out front, hard thunder began, tank fire, the distinct thump of the Shermans. He couldn't help the fear, the shivering, the pace of the men around him quickening. They crested a low rise, and suddenly the town was there, nestled into a shallow valley. He saw a tower of a church, some scattered wreckage, but most of the buildings were intact. There were bright flashes to the right, smoke rising, the fire from the Shermans increasing, tank gunners finding targets. Above him, a loud shriek, then another, coming from behind, and he flinched, the sound bursting in his own gut, said aloud, "Artillery! Gotta be ours!"

"Shut up. Keep walking."

He felt idiotic, didn't know he had said it aloud, but the whistles and shrieks kept coming, the far side of the town erupting in fire. Benson realized he was jogging, keeping up with the others, all of them caught

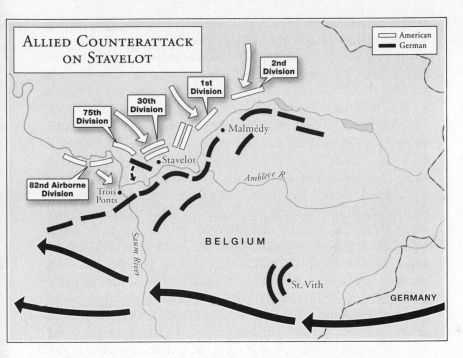

up in the moment, and out front the lieutenant waved them back, slowing them down. Benson forced himself to step slowly, hard breathing, his
heart racing. He had a sudden flash of memory from the training, a film,
some war movie, men charging the enemy in an all-out run. Afterward
an officer had explained to them what kind of shape a man would be in
if he made a charge like they did in Hollywood. *Cannon fodder.* The
officer's words had stuck with Benson then, came back to him now. He
focused on the men around him, the lieutenant, the pace still quick,
Higgins right in front of him, under control. The cold was gone, and he
still fought the urge to run, the energy boiling up, the lack of sleep forgotten, the miserable breakfast. His mind sharpened, staring at the town,
bathed in smoke, flashes of light beyond. He saw now, a river beyond the
town, and across, houses coming apart, artillery shells landing in splashes
of fire.

They reached the first of the houses, most still upright, men hustling
into doors, then calling out, no sign of the enemy, no sign of anyone at all.

Benson was still close to the road, heard engines behind him, spun around, saw the barrel of a cannon coming up and over the ridge they had crossed. It was a self-propelled gun, stopping now, and he saw a sudden flash of fire, the shock of it punching Benson's ears.

"Face front!"

The shout came from Higgins, and the gun fired again, the muzzle blast deafening, the shock punching him in the back. His ears were suffering again, the ringing too familiar, and he glanced at Mitchell, no words, Mitchell's eyes staring ahead, cold slits, fury in his footsteps. They moved past more houses, an intersection, narrow streets, and suddenly Fornell was there, pulling the men together, tightening the formation. The thunder from the big guns behind them was roaring overhead, the ground beneath Benson's feet pulsing, smoke winding in clouds through narrow alleyways that led between the tree-lined streets. Fornell was on the walkie-talkie, nothing Benson could hear, the lieutenant covering one ear, squatting low, trying to hear the voice on the other end. He stood, eyes wide, pointed to an alley, then moved that way, waving the men to follow. Higgins moved up quickly, closer to the lieutenant, Benson close behind him, the others filing into the lane, the sounds of the artillery overwhelming them, a stink of explosives rolling past the houses. Fornell was taking short quick steps, a low crouch, the lane winding, a sharp curve to the right, and he stopped suddenly, Higgins as well, both men dropping low. Benson readied the rifle, nothing to see, the two men in front easing forward, past the corner of a house. Benson moved up close, saw the great hulking monster blocking the lane, the long cannon pointing straight at them. It was a Tiger tank.

Fornell went down, rolled to one side, the others dropping behind him like so many dominoes, many of them still out of the line of fire, not aware what was in front of them. Benson felt paralyzed, hit the cobbled street with both knees, tried to roll away, someone else in his way, no cover for any of them. He wanted to scream, *Move,* waited for the blast, for the waves of machine-gun fire. But there was nothing, silence from the tank, no engine, no guns. Fornell crawled forward, close to the tank, beneath it now, a grenade in his hand. He looked back, directly at Benson, waved him forward frantically. Benson felt weakness in his legs, tried to obey, crawling, the cobblestones catching his hands, twisting, and he was at the tank, ducked to one side, the maw of the eighty-eight pointed past him, over him.

The lieutenant said with a hard whisper, "Slide under. Come up from behind. Grenade in the hatch. I'll go up first. One of us will make it."

Benson thought of the bazooka crew, where the hell are *they*? But the words didn't come, the lieutenant's glare definite, intimidating. Benson felt the grenades hanging at his chest, then crawled under, the stinking hulk of steel close overhead. He could see behind the tank now, another black mass, stopped, frozen. Farther down the lane was an armored truck, machine guns on top. He pushed sideways, rammed tight into the tread of the tank, hopeless cover. But the guns did not fire, no one at the guns, no helmets. He aimed the rifle, searched for movement, any target, and behind him a low voice, moving close, Mitchell.

"Keep going. The tank's dead. Looks like no one's home."

The tank had sealed off the narrow lane, trees and houses close on each side, and so the others began to do as Benson had done, sliding underneath. Mitchell rose up, scampered toward the truck, slipped around to one side, opened the door, pointed his rifle in, did not fire. He waved, and Benson heard the voice of the lieutenant, up above, on top of the tank.

"Halt here! Congratulations, boys. You captured your first Tiger tank."

Men were climbing up, peering down into the tank's hatch, and Benson saw a smile on the lieutenant's face, even Fornell caught up in the moment.

Higgins was beside Benson, who said, "They must have skedaddled. Knew we were coming."

Higgins wasn't smiling, said, "Not likely. No Tiger is gonna run from infantry. Even a bazooka can't hurt this thing." The artillery was still roaring overhead, and Higgins looked back toward the lieutenant. "This ain't a damn party. You think we oughta get moving, sir?"

Fornell stared out, looked past the truck, Mitchell climbing up inside, manning the guns. The lieutenant said, "Let's go, boys. We'll stake our claim on this thing later."

Mitchell shouted back toward the men, "Guns are loaded. Plenty of ammo."

A man popped up from one of the tank's hatches, said to Fornell, "This thing's out of gas, sir. Fuel tank shows empty."

The lieutenant jumped down to the cobblestones. "That explains it. Be grateful for that, boys." He moved ahead, the men following.

Up ahead, Mitchell was out of the truck, said, "Sir, maybe we can turn this thing around, use it ourselves. Nice damn machine guns."

"Leave it alone, soldier. Those black crosses on the side will get you blown to hell. We've still got a job to do."

The artillery fire from behind had slowed, and Benson could hear fire coming back the other way, German artillery from across the river. Fornell moved out past the truck, waved the men forward. Benson moved with him, saw the lane opening up into a wide square, troops emerging from another of the narrow streets. But there was no rifle fire, no sound of machine guns, just the slow, steady thumps of distant artillery. The men continued to flow out from the narrow lanes, and Benson saw another tank, across the square, soldiers gathering around it, climbing up. That tank was smaller, shorter cannon.

Beside him, Higgins said, "That's a Panther. What the hell? The Krauts just shag ass out of here and leave their tanks behind?"

The lieutenant halted the men, moved out toward a gathering cluster of troops, and Benson knew the look of officers, Fornell talking to them, pointing back toward the alleyway. From another side street a jeep appeared, two more behind it, stopping in the wide square. One man stepped out with a map, spread it on the hood of a jeep, the officers gathering.

Higgins said, "This looks pretty good. The brass wouldn't come rolling in here if it wasn't pretty clear. The Krauts must have hauled it across that river. I guess that means we captured this damn town."

Other men heard his words, part of Higgins's new squad, and one man said, "Medals for all of us! That tank'll look good in front of my city hall. Maybe the army'll give it to one of us."

"Yeah, they'll give it to you 'cause you're so damn good-looking."

Higgins kept his eye on the officers, then said, "Artillery fire across the river means we're going across the river. Those damn officers need to finish their meeting."

Benson tried to feel Mitchell's strange rage, to share it, but the momentary lull was a relief. The cold was coming again, the first time he had felt it since the march began. He looked at the sun, barely above the lowest rooftop, felt the glow on his face, tried to absorb that, his breaths in white bursts. The square was lined with quaint old buildings, homes and businesses, one house blasted to rubble, a gaping shell hole in the roof next door, but most of the homes with only minor damage. There were trees lining the wider street, bare skeletons, and Benson thought of the people, no one showing himself. Maybe they're in the basements, he thought. Hope so. Hate to think we're gonna wreck this place. Looks like a nice place to live.

The sound rolled overhead in a hard roar, and Benson ducked, instinct, saw the planes skim past, no more than two hundred feet overhead. More came now, some higher, a formation of five, then five more. Men were staring up, rifles rising, but they all saw, the planes were American. Close by, someone shouted, "P-47s! Go get 'em!"

The planes continued to flow past, and now a new sound, machine-gun fire. One formation rolled up to one side, gaining altitude, then turned in unison, sweeping low again, but farther away. Men were cheering, coming up through the houses onto rooftops, heads and hands poked through upstairs windows. Benson saw men running into a house, followed them, the men scampering up a stairway, some already at the upstairs windows, some climbing farther, Benson with them, a doorway onto a flat, snow-covered roof. He could see the river now, the hills beyond, stared in amazement, the chattering of fire pouring out of the planes, the formations splitting up, single planes heading across the river, a screaming dive, then back up, rolling over, pulling away. The first blast came now, a shock of fire and black smoke, followed by two more, the P-47s swirling over the river like so many angry birds, circling, then with perfect precision, each one swooping down in a hard dive. He watched one, nearly vertical, pulling up at the last possible second, saw the black stick dropping down, the bomb bursting in a cluster of trees, fire erupting, a perfect strike. Now the planes began to pull away, and Benson felt himself shouting out with the men around him, *No, don't leave!* But the planes were not yet through, formations coming together high above, rolling down, skimming the town, low across the river, their machine guns opening up, a strafing run on targets Benson couldn't see. The hills across the river were bathed in smoke, but the Germans were not silent. He could see streaks of anti-aircraft fire, a burst overhead, and suddenly one of the P-47s came apart, the wing fluttering away, the plane a smoking missile, heading down, impacting straight into the river. There was a silent sickening moment, none of the cheering, the only sound coming from the roar of the planes, and the enemy across the river. Benson stared at the water, saw the debris, flickers of fire, black smoke. The other planes were completing their strafing runs, pulling away now, some of them already gone, their mission complete. He heard the sharp call of an officer, the orders coming from inside the house, the men withdrawing. Benson fought to turn away, still stared at the river, the smoke drifting away, much more smoke on the hills across the water.

"Move it, soldier. Show's over."

Benson saw Fornell at the door, realized he was the last man on the roof.

"Sorry, sir. Hell of a thing to see."

The lieutenant moved away, and Benson followed him down the stairs, darkness in the stairwell, his eyes adjusting. He thought now of the stars, the clear night. My God, that's why . . . that's why the planes came. On the street, Higgins was staring at him with a frown, but Benson ignored the sergeant's anger, stared up at blue skies, saw puffs of white clouds, felt the cold again. Mitchell was there, and Benson looked at him, saw a smile, rare.

Mitchell said, "That's what you call air support, kiddo. Things might be a little different now."

STAVELOT, BELGIUM
DECEMBER 23, 1944, NOON

He marched alongside the rest of Higgins's new squad, some of the names becoming familiar. They had moved through the town with a battalion of infantry from the Thirtieth Division, wary of German snipers, seeking out the townspeople, some still hiding in their own cellars. But immediately word began to spread that something terrible had happened at Stavelot, something no one expected. Shortly after their first great push, Stavelot had fallen into German hands. Some of the Belgians in the town had responded to the German occupation with resistance, foolishly taking potshots at the Germans from windows and rooftops. The German response had been sudden and devastating.

Reaching an open field, Benson saw jeeps parked in a cluster, men gathered, more jeeps coming up the road beside him. At the edge of the field, MPs had gathered, directing the men, and Benson saw Fornell talking to one, the man waving the platoon into the field. They moved in silence, curious, the men at the jeeps watching them come. Benson saw dark shapes in the snow, a long row, bodies.

An officer spoke aloud. "Get up here, boys. This is what your enemy does."

Benson tried to see past Fornell, but the lieutenant stopped, seemed frozen in his tracks, said, "Dear God."

The others moved up with Benson, and he stepped past the lieutenant, could see the bodies clearly, heard the single word, soft and low beside him.

"Children."

The officer at the jeep said aloud, "One hundred thirty total. Half of them women and children. There's goddamn babies. *Babies!*"

Benson saw the faces, gaping mouths, hollow eyes, some naked, several women in ripped dresses, old men, and then, the tiny shapes, dark blue skin, bald heads. Beside him a man dropped to his knees, threw up, another man doing the same behind him. Benson felt only numbness, the sickness staying away, and he stepped back away from the others, walked down toward the end of the corpses, more officers there, a man with a pad of paper, writing furiously, low talk from the others. Benson stopped, focused on the last body, an old man staring up, empty eyes, a neat bullet hole in his forehead. He looked at the old man's body for a long moment, absorbed it all, his brain grabbing the sight of the bullet hole, the single word . . . *execution.* He looked down the long row, heard new sounds, more troops coming up the road, officers and MPs guiding them into the field. His own men were backing away, some still sick, the soft sound of tears, and Benson tried to take a breath, his chest cold and tight, his brain winding into a fist. He had never really understood why Mitchell hated the Germans. But he didn't need Mitchell to explain anything. Not anymore.

Though the massacre of the Belgian civilians at Stavelot brought a new reality to many of the American soldiers, another horror was to come. A short few miles to the east, near the town of Malmédy, the advancing Americans made another discovery that revealed the vicious desperation of the enemy they were facing. On December 17, as the Americans had rapidly retreated before the advance of Dietrich's Sixth Panzer Army, one group of Americans had been cut off and captured. Some 150 men of Battery B, 285th Artillery Regiment, were marched out into an open field, and without warning, their captors, men of the 1st SS Panzer Division, suddenly opened fire on them. Some of the Americans managed to flee into the woods, and others who had been wounded survived by pretending to be dead. At least eighty-six American prisoners were killed in what would ever after be known as the Malmédy Massacre. As word of it spread, the resolve of the GIs to crush those responsible was furiously magnified.

O n December 16, the surprise of the German assault had engulfed most of the Americans who stood in the way. By Christmas Eve, with the skies clearing, the overwhelming air supremacy of the Allied forces began to make its own contribution, and the confusion and uncertainty within the American commands had sorted itself out. At the point of the attack, which pushed within two miles of the Meuse River, the once-unstoppable panzers were halted not just by the efforts of Bradley and Courtney Hodges, but by another enemy the Germans could never defeat. Hitler had promised his generals that this magnificent attack would be supported and supplied with every necessity, and in a few short days that promise had proven disastrously empty. As had happened at Stavelot, all across the front, on every road, and in every village where the fights were sharpest, the German advance was finally halted not just by Allied guns. It was halted because their tanks ran out of gas.

The Americans who recaptured Stavelot were content to hold their line at the Amblève River; the Germans dug in deeply on the far side, protected by thick woods and steep hills. By holding that line, the Americans had nailed down the German right flank and prevented the Germans from spreading their advance northward toward the vital city of Liège. Worse for the Germans, with Dietrich's Sixth Panzer Army pressed southward, his troops and their armor were forced onto the same tangle of roadways desperately needed by Manteuffel's Fifth.

The chaotic loss of momentum and the failure to obey Hitler's timetable had suddenly put the Germans on the defensive. In the south, Bastogne was still surrounded and under increasing pressure. But Patton's forces had just begun their hard drive into the German left flank.

17. PATTON

The jeep was moving slowly, blocked on the narrow roadway by a snaking convoy of infantry carriers. Patton forced himself to be patient, knew the drivers were taking these men into a hot fight. For now he had to be satisfied to push them from behind. This time.

He did not expect the resistance the Germans had put up against his forces, strongholds and powerful counterattacks all along the German southern flank. His armor and infantry divisions had driven northward for nearly a hundred miles in what started out as a typical Patton sweep across open countryside, led by his magnificent tank commanders. The first surge had struck the Germans just as he expected, shoving them back across most of the line. Bastogne was well within reach, and he expected word to come quickly that the siege had been shattered, the beleaguered paratroopers rescued. But the Germans had held the line, shifted positions and regrouped, and all throughout the day had been counterattacking with far more power than Patton predicted. Bastogne was still engulfed by a stout ring of German armor and infantry, and Patton had ordered an airdrop of crucial supplies to the Americans trapped in the city, the only lifeline he could yet provide.

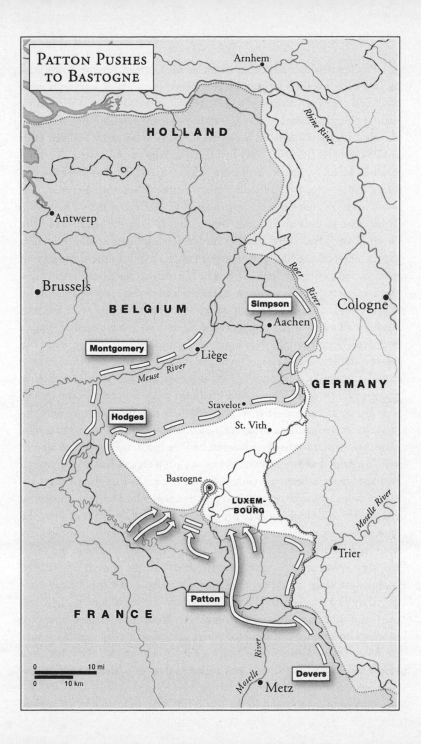

PATTON PUSHES
TO BASTOGNE

Arnhem

Rhine River

HOLLAND

Antwerp

Brussels

BELGIUM

Simpson

Cologne

Aachen

Roer River

Montgomery

Liège

Meuse River

GERMANY

Stavelot

Hodges

St. Vith

Bastogne

LUXEM-
BOURG

Moselle River

Trier

Patton

FRANCE

Devers

Moselle River

Metz

0   10 mi

0   10 km

Patton knew that he was confronting the German Seventh Army, and he had been utterly delighted by that news. He knew the Seventh well, what had once been Rommel's, those troops who had manned the fortifications along the beaches at Normandy. Some of their combat units were the most highly trained and respected in the German army, and yet, even with Rommel at the helm, they had failed to keep the Allied armies off the beaches, failed to prevent them from driving inland. The two-month campaign had resulted in a difficult victory for the Allies, and of course, that was a source of enormous pride throughout SHAEF. But Patton had pride of his own. In early August, ten weeks after D-Day, the remnants of the Seventh Army had failed to slow Patton down in his magnificent gallop through France, the breakout that put Patton's name on the front page of every newspaper in the States. When he learned that the Seventh Army was the third prong of this German offensive, and the one closest to him, he was overjoyed. This fight would surely go more smoothly than the last, since the Allies knew that, by now, the Seventh was only a shell of what it had once been, that the Normandy campaign had decimated even the finest of those combat units. It was common knowledge that the German army's manpower was growing weaker, old men and teenagers, poorly trained home troops. Patton had predicted a deterioration in the enemy that went even further—that what Hitler sent into the field now were the worst dregs the Germans could scrape from their factories and labor camps or, worse, battered refugees from the Eastern Front, men who had simply been used up. And yet for two days now, Patton's forces had been stymied, had not liberated Bastogne with ease, had not bottled up the German infantry in one grand sweeping wave. As he stood tall in his jeep, jostled by chewed-up roads and the slow progress of the trucks in front of him, the frustration dug deep. It figures, he thought. If we'd have blown the German flank to bits, the rest of SHAEF would have had no choice but to let me keep going, maybe drive straight across, all the way to St. Vith or Malmédy, nailing the lid on the entire damn force. We could have swallowed up two panzer armies *and* the Seventh. There's a prize, a big damn feather in my helmet that would shut every damn one of them up, every moron who has ever said something *witty* about all my failings, my stupid mistakes. I'm so damn sick of hearing that. I have to give Ike credit, he's kept a lid on it. Well, maybe a leaking lid. But by God, there's nothing *stupid* about total victory.

He continued to stand in the rear of the jeep, steadied himself against the seat in front of him. His impatience was growing, the progress of the troop convoy far too slow. They were men of the Eightieth Division, reserves moving up to share part of the load of their own units who had gone in before them. Some moron is up there trying to dodge potholes, he thought, or maybe some idiot MP directing traffic by reading a manual. No reason at all we should be moving this slow.

He heard something from Codman, beside him, his staff officer speaking into a radio.

"Well, dammit, bring up the rest of them! Or would you prefer the general lead them himself?"

Patton held back the smile. As one of Patton's senior aides, Charles Codman had the authority to blister anyone's bottom, and he had finally seemed to step into the task. Codman was usually a soft-spoken man, utterly efficient, had been with Patton since the early days in North Africa. Patton enjoyed hearing the man's anger, knew that he had learned well from the master. Codman signed off the radio, started to speak, and Patton held up his hand, didn't want to hear it, not now. He knew what was happening, knew that too many of the field commanders expected a casual waltz through the German lines.

After a silent moment, he said, "They were too slow to put in their strength. Uncoordinated attacks. But not anymore. Enough of this pussyfooting. Some reporter told me that there's a Hollywood producer back in Paris already planning to make a movie about the One Oh First in Bastogne. *Martyrs.* That's the word the jackass used. I ordered that reporter the hell out of my camp. If I could find that Hollywood idiot, I'd throw him in the English Channel. These jerks come over here assuming we're going to fail. But I'll be damned if anyone is going to be sacrificed in front of my command. Those civilians expect miracles every time we hit the enemy, and now they're giving me hell for not delivering one at Bastogne."

Codman laughed, surprising him. "Sorry, sir, but you've spoiled them. And you did expect something of a miracle here yourself."

Very few of Patton's staff could make that kind of observation out loud, and he looked down at Codman, rolled the cigar around in his mouth.

"You're right. Keep your mouth shut about it. We get back to HQ, I want those reporters sealed up in a room. Maybe a big wooden box. No airholes."

He stared ahead, still standing, the jeep lurching slowly behind the covered truck in front. The cigar had gone out, the bitter taste lingering, and he spat it out in the snow, thought, at least we're *fighting* this time. I didn't have to beg Brad to take my handcuffs off. Patton couldn't help thinking of the name, so perfectly etched in his brain, what were now just words on a map no one wanted to talk about. *The Argentan–Falaise gap.* It had been the German Seventh Army's last stand in France, and instead of annihilation, a sizable percentage of those who were able to escape did exactly that. The eighteen-mile gap between the two French towns had been left wide open, and on one side, Patton had been held fast by orders from Bradley that infuriated him still. As the Germans slipped past, they had endured unspeakable slaughter at the hands of pursuing American artillery and Allied airpower, but still, they did slip past. That was a thorn buried deep into Patton's gut. His army had been there, a great bulldog held on a chain, surging forward, teeth bared, prepared to seal the gap from the southern side. The argument with Bradley had been sharp, but Bradley would not yield, and Patton knew that Bradley's inflexibility had come from Eisenhower. Bradley is a better commander than that, he thought, would have seen the opportunity that I held in my damn hands. But across the gap on the north side sat Montgomery, and the British commander could not be swayed, was not prepared to move his troops quickly enough to seal off the Germans in a pocket that would have destroyed the Seventh Army forever. In his long career of frustrations, that was the frustration Patton hated the worst, standing idly by while a desperately beaten enemy simply ran away, through an opening that Patton could have shut down tight, an opening that Montgomery *should* have closed. The orders from Bradley stated it plainly: If Patton advanced, he would be intruding, trespassing into Montgomery's *territory,* the precious boundary drawn by some logistics officer that could not be violated lest Montgomery's feelings be hurt. It gave Patton a sour taste in his mouth every time he thought of it, every time he thought of Montgomery at all.

He was thinking a great deal about Montgomery these days, knew that there had been an ongoing battle of wills at SHAEF. For months after the successes of the summer, Montgomery had lobbied hard to be granted command once again over all Allied ground forces. Montgomery had strongly suggested that the campaigns waged through the autumn had been, in his words, a failure, and that the failure should be placed squarely at the feet of the supreme commander. Naturally, in Montgomery's mind, the only one to rescue the collapsing Allied initiatives was Montgomery himself. Though Eisenhower had often flirted with the idea of replacing Montgomery altogether, in effect, firing him, strong political currents in England made him virtually irreplaceable. Patton knew that Eisenhower's decision was his alone, a point made to Eisenhower by Winston Churchill, who seemed to despise Montgomery as well. But Churchill could not control the morale of the British troops, and Eisenhower knew that Monty was their man. To Patton's intense annoyance, Eisenhower had stuck with Monty. But the latest attempt by Montgomery to reclaim the command he had lost after Normandy was making him no friends at SHAEF. Montgomery continued to insist that the only way to end the war would be his own punch directly across the Rhine River, and the Americans would simply be his support. Beyond politics, there were other major flaws to the plan that seemed obvious to everyone but Montgomery. To cross into the lower Rhine Valley meant first crossing the Roer River, which was blocked by several dams, still tightly in German hands. If the Germans opened the dams, the entire valley southward would be a flood zone, and not even the best Allied engineers had the means to force a crossing through what would become vast swampy lakes. Logistically, capturing the dams would be intensely difficult, requiring a decisive well-timed assault on a broad scale. The attack would also require flexibility and audacity. Though Montgomery was a master of the well-organized set-piece battle, *audacity* was not a description that fit him at all. Any rapid thrust toward Berlin required the kind of all-out bravado of a man like Patton, a comparison Montgomery would never have swallowed.

Montgomery's annoying insistence that he be placed in overall command had continued, the man seeming to be oblivious to the reality that the number of American troops in the field was now vastly larger than the British, a trend that would only continue. It was the simplest rationale Eisenhower had for denying Montgomery's absurd lobbying, and no one but the British newspapers was giving Eisenhower much grief about it. But then, with the Germans so successful at driving a wedge into the middle of the American First Army, Eisenhower had been forced to hand Montgomery an enormous gift.

Soon after Patton returned to his own headquarters, there had been a call from Bedell Smith, Eisenhower's chief of staff, seeming to prepare Patton for a piece of bad news. With the American forces spread so widely apart, Hodges and his primary ground commanders were almost all up on the northern side of the bulge. As well, Bill Simpson's Ninth Army, de-ployed around Aachen, was physically cut off from Bradley's command. Some phone lines were intact, at least for now, but any face-to-face meeting between Bradley and his generals there was a logistical impossibility. As a result, Eisenhower had ordered that Simpson and Hodges be placed under Montgomery's command for as long as it took to drive the Germans back. The pill had been enormous, and Patton had still not swallowed it. Patton's command was left more or less intact, the one part of the army Bradley still controlled. But Patton knew Omar Bradley well enough to know that, sure, Bradley would obey Eisenhower's order, but it would be a mighty blow to Bradley's pride. Bedell Smith's explanation had been cool and logical: Because Montgomery was rapidly spreading a strong British defense behind the Meuse River, it made sense that he should also control the movements and deployment of the increasingly organized Americans who were much closer to him than they were to Bradley. Patton thought of Bradley now. Yeah, I'll bet he enjoyed like hell hearing chirpy little Beetle Smith telling him he was losing half his troops. Or maybe Ike told him. Would have been the decent thing to do. I've seen Brad screw up once in a while, but he can run this show better than Montgomery, no matter what Ike or anyone else says. I'd love for Brad to tell me what he said back to Beetle, but he won't say a word against Ike. Not that kind of man. That's a good thing, I guess. They already know how I feel about Monty. He wants to run the whole damn show, win this war by himself, have his one-man parade through England, get his knighthood, or princehood, or whatever the hell the British do. He's a clever son of a bitch, and if Ike isn't careful, Monty will grab every piece of this war for himself.

Patton's impatience with the trucks in front of him was starting to boil over, fueled by his thoughts of Montgomery.

"Let's go! Get your asses in high gear!"

The shouts attracted the attention of the men in the truck in front of him, men who had already taken their photographs, who had cheered him joyfully. They cheered him again, but he wasn't in the mood for smiles, shouted down to his driver, the ever-patient Sergeant Mims.

"John, I've had enough of this traffic jam. Find some damn command post close by. I need to scream at some people. Doesn't matter who."

EIGHTIETH DIVISION FORWARD COMMAND POST,
NEAR DIEKIRCH, LUXEMBOURG
DECEMBER 24, 1944

"Where is General McBride?"

The lieutenant seemed to quake, staring at Patton with eyes that had never seen the enemy.

"Sir! Sir! Yes, sir!"

"Good God, son, just tell me where he is."

"General McBride is forward, sir. He was angry . . . if I can say that, sir. I didn't mean to suggest the general has a temper—"

"Oh, shut up, Lieutenant. Forward is good. It means he's kicking someone in the ass. If you'd have told me he was in Paris, I'd have to shoot him. Maybe you too. Who's in command here? It's sure as hell not you."

The young man pointed sheepishly to a closed door, said, "Major Hickey is the ranking officer present, sir. He requested not to be disturbed."

Patton looked at the closed door, his brain painting large fat letters across it, *Kick here.* He moved past the lieutenant, who backed away, clearing a wide path. Patton scanned the edges of the door, flimsy, glanced around, the entire house showing its age, run-down, unpainted walls. I gotta hand it to McBride, he thought. He isn't going to put his people up in anybody's mansion. Good. Patton put a hand on the door, tested, and the door opened under the weight of his hand, unlocked. He was mildly disappointed, allowed the door to open completely, saw the back of the major's head perched above a wooden chair, a telephone planted against his ear.

"Forty-eight. Oh hell, make it fifty."

"Fifty what?"

The man turned in his chair, clearly annoyed, saw Patton now, the phone tumbling out of his hand, and he stood with a clatter, said, "Uh . . . cows, sir. Cattle."

Patton rested his hands on his two pistols, stared at the man, the major glancing down at the phone dangling toward the floor, and Patton said, "Doing a little rustling, are we?"

"Sir . . . greetings. We didn't expect you. Uh . . . rustling. Oh, no, sir. Well, yes, sir, I suppose you could say that. Supply made a deal with a local farmer for some beef. The men have been eating . . . well, crap, sir. K rations for days now. I thought we should give them something better."

Patton imagined the scene, a herd of cattle marching into a regimental supply depot.

"General McBride know about this?"

"Not yet, sir."

"He'll approve. Knows how to take care of his men." Patton paused. "This sort of thing used to happen in the Civil War, you know. Union boys were chomping away on a bunch of steaks when Stonewall Jackson attacked them at Chancellorsville. Catastrophe for the Federals. Just make sure there's no German Stonewall out there, watching your boys stuff themselves."

"Most definitely, sir."

"McBride's up front?"

"Yes, sir. Left here about two hours ago. General Summers is back at division HQ. I can get him on the phone for you, sir. The supply traffic is a real bear, and I'm not sure when General McBride will return."

"No, I don't need to talk to his assistant, and yeah, I know about the damn traffic. McBride's a good man. Feisty little son of a bitch. I like that. He give you any indication what he's expecting to do up there?"

"Yes, sir. He has been frustrated with our lack of progress. I believe he intends to relieve at least one regimental commander."

Patton felt immensely satisfied by that response.

"Yep. Feisty." He turned, walked out of the office, stopped just beyond the door, looked back toward the major, who stood stiffly, unmoving. His tie was perfect, his hat in place, and Patton thought, McBride's taught you well. He looked down toward the phone, which dangled loosely, a slow twist in the wire.

"Your man's probably still there. You can talk to him now. You make damn sure those steaks find their way forward. Don't need to fatten up the rear echelon. You got that, Major?"

"Absolutely, sir."

Patton moved through the dark living room of the house, saw several aides standing at sharp attention, men emerging from other rooms, staring at Patton, some saluting. He threw a glance at the terrified lieutenant, who stood at attention against a far wall, blocking a map of the area. Patton thought of examining the map, but the lieutenant was transfixed, immobile. Not worth the bother, he thought. One more word from me, and that kid might piss his pants. Jesus, where do we get these idiots?

"Get your people back to work. There's a war going on, for God's sake."

He stepped outside, cold blue sky, felt a stiff chilling breeze, saw the men staring up, toward the drone of distant engines. He saw them now, a vast fleet of B-17s, the formation spreading out, moving into their bombing runs.

"I'll be damned. The air boys came through."

Codman was beside the jeep, said, "Yes, sir, appears they did. There was another flock earlier, medium bombers. They look to be going in just north of Diekirch."

"How far?"

"The town is three miles or so. The enemy position now lies just beyond, according to General Gay."

"You talked to Hap?"

"Yes, sir. Had him on the radio just now. He says reports are coming in pretty regularly that our boys are starting to break through some of the logjams. The Fourth Armor is on the move again, closing the gap toward Bastogne. We finally got some confirmation that they're up against some of the Panzer Lehr Division."

Patton watched the bombers, the formations spreading out, obviously heading for a variety of targets. The flak was rising up now, flecks of black smoke dotting the skies around them.

Patton focused on Codman. "I knew Panzer Lehr was there. Had to be. Maybe the best tank division in the German army. Some of the SS might be tougher, but I always wanted to go face-to-face with those fellows. Good. Make sure Gaffey gets all the air support he needs. Bombers will play hell with Tiger tanks."

"Already on it, sir."

There was a dull thump high above, and Patton saw it now, a cloud of thick black smoke.

Codman said, "Oh dear God. They hit a B-17."

The plane seemed to float its way to the ground, pieces separating, one wing spinning, slow-motion descent, a trail of fire. Patton felt oddly impressed, thought, hell of a good shot for some Kraut gunner, maybe an eighty-eight. Hope they dropped their bombs. Unlucky bastards.

"Look! There, sir. Parachutes."

Codman had binoculars, was staring high above the falling wreckage, the plane coming down in a trail of black smoke beyond a far ridge of trees.

"How many?"

"I count five. Six. There could be more. Thank God."

Patton moved to the jeep, climbed aboard, stood tall in the back, said, "Good. Can't afford to lose those crews. Planes we can replace. But we need those boys back in the air."

A ll across Patton's front lines, the pressure on the Germans began to take its toll. Despite the effectiveness of German counterattacks, the combination of airpower and added American strength on the ground finally wore down their resistance. Village after village fell to the American advance, German commanders responding the only way they could to preserve any fighting strength at all. They began to withdraw.

Patton's Fourth Armored Division, commanded by his former chief of staff Hugh Gaffey, was still struggling to force a breakthrough into Bastogne. Though only a few miles from the perimeter of the town, Gaffey's tanks continued to meet heavy resistance, and sharp tank battles erupted throughout the farms, villages, and patches of thick woodlands. To the east of Bastogne, nearer the base of the bulge, Patton kept up the relentless pressure. Increasing numbers of American units, the Fourth, Fifth, Twenty-sixth, and Eightieth divisions, were all gaining momentum. Throughout Christmas Day, the Americans pressed on, the Germans conceding ground. Patton knew, with complete certainty, it was only a matter of time.

BRADLEY'S HEADQUARTERS, LUXEMBOURG CITY
CHRISTMAS NIGHT, 1944

"I'm truly sorry, Brad. This must be giving you ulcers. You know I'm behind you on this."

"Knock it off, George. Don't bait me. The damn reporters keep trying that stuff, like if they push me hard enough, I'll explode and give them a nice fat story. The fact is, Ike did what he had to do, and for now, it's the best way to handle it. Monty's got his people fully prepared in case the German breaks through our guys. It's essential that Monty get direct reports of what's going on with the commands in front of him. And besides, it's only temporary. Beetle assured me of that."

Patton felt an explosion of his own, fought to keep the words from igniting the entire headquarters.

"*Beetle* assures you it's only temporary? How . . . can you take that, Brad?"

"I take it because it's the way it is. You surprise me, George, and that's not easy for you to do. You think Beetle is secretly plotting with Monty to stage a coup? You think the Brits are trying to toss Ike out the window and put Monty in command? Face facts, dammit. Of course I didn't like giving up that much of my command. I wouldn't be human if I felt otherwise. But it has to be this way. This war's a long way from over, and the Brits are in this thing right beside us. We're *allies,* George."

Bradley crossed his arms, leaned back in the chair, waited while the orderlies carried away the dinner plates. Bradley held his words, Patton knowing he wouldn't say anything indiscreet in front of aides. The table was cleared quickly, and Patton put a hand on his full stomach, the turkey dinner an unusual treat.

"Nice meal, Brad. Thank you. Glad to hear the men got a fair share of this too."

Bradley seemed to welcome the change of subject, his mood lightening. "Yep. I don't know how many exactly, but supply did a whale of a job putting turkey sandwiches into as many hands as we could. Not much of a Christmas gift, but it's the best we could do. You know, there's a Christmas tree in the staff quarters, and it made me think of something. In the First World War, somewhere on the Western Front, probably right around here . . . both sides stopped fighting to celebrate Christmas. The Germans put Christmas trees on top of their trench works, held up signs saying *Merry Christmas* or something close to that. The officers couldn't approve any kind of truce, of course, so they just looked the other way, both sides. The damn soldiers went out into no-man's-land and actually made something of it, some kind of celebration of the holiday. I heard soccer games were played. Damnedest thing. It only happened once, 1914. The war got a little nastier after that. Hasn't happened at all this time, far as I know. Not anywhere."

The orderlies returned, poured cups of coffee for both men, and Patton could feel a softness in Bradley he rarely saw. Patton touched the coffee cup, said, "Hitler's changed the rules. That kind of war is for old movies and romance books. Can't say I'd have turned my back on any of that, though. It's still fraternization. The enemy's the enemy. I wouldn't trust the

Germans not to pull some crap, open up with machine guns, soccer game or not."

Bradley nodded, sipped the coffee.

"You might be right. But it occurred to me how many times there have been wars in this part of the world. I mean . . . right out there. Thousands of years, probably cavemen beating hell out of each other with clubs right on this same piece of land. In 1918 . . . hell, I remember the optimism. Everybody thought it would be the last time."

"I never thought that. I don't think it now. I know it's Christmas, Brad, but you can keep all that *peace on earth* stuff. It's never going to be that way, not in our lifetimes, not in our children's. My job is to make sure that when it does happen again, there are a lot fewer Germans around to start it. Right now, right this minute, my boys are killing the enemy. Right now. Christmas."

"Doesn't bother you? Not even a little?"

Patton sipped from the cup, Bradley's coffee always bitter.

"Nope. The more we kill on Christmas, the less we have to kill the day after."

Bradley stood, stretched his back, walked around the table, stood facing a curtained window, peered out through the narrow opening.

"No snow tonight. Hope like hell it stays this way." He turned toward Patton, seemed to realize he was still in front of the window, stepped to one side. "The staff raises hell with me about security. German spies, assassination squads still rumored to be around. Can't take a drive without armored cars. Same with Ike. Especially Ike."

Patton couldn't resist. "Any word on assassination squads up Monty's way?"

Bradley laughed, surprising him. "Funny you say that. You heard about Monty's car getting stopped at a checkpoint? Somewhere in the Eighty-second's sector, I think. Some hotshot MP noncom holds him up, asks all those questions the guys are asking . . . baseball, state capitals, all of that. Monty and his driver had no clue what the MPs were talking about, and . . . well, you know Monty. He ordered his driver to ignore all that and move on. Damn if the MPs didn't shoot out his tires. Ike told me about it. I laughed for half an hour." Bradley feigned seriousness now. "Our boys can be a little touchy when it comes to baseball."

"Or Brits."

Bradley shook his head. "That's always the thing with you, right, George? If Ike had split up my command and handed it to an American, Devers maybe, or God knows who . . . you wouldn't have said a word."

"Doubt that."

Patton drank the coffee, knew that Bradley was right. He was feeling restless, the coffee fueling another itch of impatience.

"When is Monty going to put *his* people on the offensive? You know damn well that my boys are getting the job done, and we'll keep getting it done. If Monty would attack from the north, the Krauts would be nailed tight. It could end the damn war."

Bradley returned to the chair, tested the coffee, pushed it away. His mood had darkened, and he hesitated, then said, "I'm not going to have a shouting match with you, George, and this could cause one. A big one. You don't need to know about every damn conversation I have with Ike. But fine, I'll tell you. I've been bitching like hell about this, and Ike's been bitching at Monty. You know what Monty's like. He's saying that he needs to tighten his lines, to *tidy up* his defenses along the Meuse. He doesn't think he can make a decisive move for . . ." Bradley took a deep breath. "Three months."

Patton coughed, slapped his hands on the table. Bradley pointed a sharp finger at him.

"I told you . . . no shouting matches. You can't tell me anything I don't already know, and you can't bitch to Ike any more than I have already. Monty is doing us a world of good by backing up our boys along that river. Just by being there, he might have kept Hodges from retreating too far, and we might still need British guns to keep the other fellow from crossing over."

Patton was dumbfounded, a fog of fury in his brain. He held on to his temper, slow words.

"Brad. The Krauts aren't going to make it to the river. We're putting so much pressure on them right now, they don't dare stretch out their lines that far. If Monty was to hit them . . . with our boys . . . *your* boys, for God's sake . . . hit them at Malmédy, or even farther east, we could cut off the whole damn Kraut position. We could slice this whole *bulge* right off, like cutting off a wart!"

Bradley stared down, said slowly, "Monty says that he is concerned that the other fellow is going to hit us hard in the north again, try to break through toward Liège. He also believes the enemy is regrouping for a new push westward. He expects the panzers will make a major push across the Meuse within forty-eight hours."

"And I expect Santa Claus to drop a grenade into Hitler's crapper!"

Patton rose up, impossible to sit, paced the room. The words were a hot jumble in his brain, and he stared at Bradley, saw forced calm, Bradley not looking at him.

"It's a good thing you're my superior officer, Brad. A damn good thing. If this was my show, there'd be hell to pay right now in Monty's HQ! Ike or no Ike. This is the stupidest damn—"

"*Sit down!*"

Bradley's sharpness was a surprise, Patton caught off guard, his anger tempered by a hard glare from Bradley.

"You're right, George. It's a good thing you're my subordinate. You have one job right now, and you're doing it, and doing it well. Breaking Monty's nose wouldn't do anybody any good at all. Certainly not Ike, and certainly not those boys out there whose Christmas dinner was a stinking turkey sandwich!"

"Monty's dead wrong, Brad."

"You think so? Then prove it. Kick the other fellow hard in the ass, and keep kicking him until von Rundstedt pulls his people back into Germany. Capture and kill as many of the enemy as you can. And get your people into Bastogne!"

BASTOGNE, BELGIUM
DECEMBER 26, 1944

The breakthrough came late in the afternoon. Three tanks from Hugh Gaffey's Fourth Armored Division pushed through a gap in the German position and rolled into Bastogne, met by a desperately grateful Anthony McAuliffe. Though the Germans could have resealed the gap, the pressure from American armor continued, aided by a massive fist of airpower, hundreds of sorties flown by P-47s and light bombers. With the flow of tanks came trucks, ammunition, and supplies for the desperate men of the 101st Airborne, and the tank crews from the 9th and 10th Armored Divisions who had stood beside them. By nightfall on the day after Christmas, Bastogne had been relieved and was firmly engulfed within Patton's front lines.

18. VON RUNDSTEDT

He led them past the huge pines that flanked one side of his head-quarters, a natural camouflage against any Allied fighters. But there had been no raids, the anti-aircraft gunners usually occupying their time with card games, hidden low in their bunkers so the officers would not see. Beyond the small town, more guns had been placed, field artillery, protection against a ground assault that of course had not come. It was the work of an efficient staff officer, his aides protective of him still. He enjoyed having the artillery close by, though as yet no gun had been fired. He took the time to walk among the artillery, as though it mattered, inspecting the men whose crisp salutes always greeted him. It had been a very long time since anyone in Berlin had saluted him at all.

It was frigidly cold, the snow a hard blanket cut by pathways. Von Rundstedt allowed Guderian to lead the way, a three-man parade, cloaked in heavy coats. The staffs had stayed behind, typical when a man of Guderian's authority had come to visit. They had come to accept that these kinds of briefings were rife with high-level details, meetings that Berlin must have thought were important. Von Rundstedt allowed the game to play out, knew it was part of the job, what little job he could actually perform. At least, visitors gave him something to do.

It was typical of Guderian to lead the way, though von Rundstedt outranked him by far. It was just his way, a display of arrogance that Guderian had earned. Von Rundstedt had to respect the man, even if he didn't particularly like his brusque manner.

Heinz Guderian could legitimately take credit for the army's development of the panzer divisions as a primary tool, and the army's reliance on that kind of power had given Germany most of its successes. Even before the war began, Guderian had championed the necessity of a superior armored force that could drive swiftly and mightily through the enemy's lines of defense. The tactic had worked in Poland, had worked in France, and for a while had worked in Russia. But Guderian had none of the soft touch of the men who wished to stay close to Hitler, and though the Führer maintained a grudging respect for what Guderian had accomplished, on two occasions, after some angry disagreement between the panzer commander and his Führer, Guderian had been relieved of his command. In July, after the botched assassination attempt on Hitler's life, Guderian had seemed to sense opportunity and rose up to become one of the principal prosecutors of the conspirators, a brutal show of perfect loyalty that Hitler was certain to appreciate. Though Guderian no longer led tanks into battle, his ongoing loyalty had landed him in the post of the chief of the General Staff, a title that seemed to conflict with the authority of both Alfred Jodl and Wilhelm Keitel. It was one more method Hitler used to shape the theatrics that engulfed the men around him, overlapping authority, keeping his subordinates at odds with one another. It was Hitler's way of exercising perfect control, since every major conflict would have to be addressed by the Führer himself.

Von Rundstedt knew that Guderian was not the simpering toady that Keitel was, that Guderian used his position to go out into the field, to visit frontline positions, to see the tactical situations for himself. Von Rundstedt suspected that those trips had one more purpose as well: to allow Guderian to escape the backstabbing intrigue floating around Hitler's inner circle. And so today he had come to von Rundstedt, to find out just what had happened to wreck the Führer's brilliant plan.

The third man in the procession had been a surprise visitor, a rare civilian, Albert Speer. Von Rundstedt had not spent much time at all with Speer, the man who seemed closer to Hitler than anyone in the High

Command. That Speer was on such intimate terms with the Führer had inspired mistrust toward him from the soldiers in Hitler's circle, but Speer's greatest enemy was Martin Bormann, the man who claimed the official title as assistant Führer, allegedly Hitler's second in command. That title impressed no one but Bormann, and von Rundstedt knew that Speer's rise in influence must have been at Bormann's expense, which could only breed trouble for both men. It was one more reason von Rundstedt despised going to Berlin.

Speer was a tall, handsome man who had been a part of Hitler's regime since 1933, something of a wunderkind to find such a special place in Hitler's circle of social intimates. Speer, an architect by training, had endeared himself to Hitler by providing the plans and scale models for Hitler's dream of a complete renovation and reshaping of Berlin. He had offered plans for stadiums and palatial structures in other cities as well, to accommodate the Führer's grand ambitions for the future of Germany. Hitler's dream of a Thousand Year Reich included the construction of massive monuments that would suit that kind of legacy. Over the years, Speer had designed those monuments, enormously oversized structures that would eventually transform Berlin into a showplace of pure might. Speer's designs were not especially creative, and his architectural skills had been criticized by noted architects in other countries, who dismissed his work as rigid and unimaginative. But he had styled his architecture to the eye of his master, and the hulking blocky structures were far more impressive for their sheer size and grandiosity than for any tribute to Renaissance artistry. Hitler clearly saw himself as a *Renaissance* of his own. In the quiet times at headquarters, it was the scale models of the various structures that captured Hitler's attention. With military matters tossed aside, the Führer would spend hours among the models like a small boy obsessed with his toys, the toys that, one day, Speer would actually build.

Over the past year, Speer's responsibilities had changed somewhat, the architect now charged with the task of designing and expediting the production facilities necessary for Germany's prosecution of the war. He had become the authority over armaments manufacture, labor, and factories, which put him at odds with men like Gestapo chief Heinrich Himmler, who saw labor as something to be squeezed out of the slaves toiling to starvation in the camps. Speer considered that an enormously inefficient waste of manpower, believing that laborers, no matter their ethnicity or level of freedom, should be fed and housed and given the strength and training to make them far more productive. The SS camps were, to Speer, perfect examples of military inefficiency. Men worked slavishly until they died, and so were replaced by more men, who did the same. It was maddening to Speer's organized mind that Himmler saw no value in teaching the laborers special skills, training them to manage the work of others, or building a hierarchy that, even in the camps, could increase the output and efficiency of the labor being performed. So far, Himmler's ways had prevailed, but Speer's power had grown, and his grasp of organization and the efficiency he brought to German factories and production lines had produced results Hitler gleefully appreciated. Von Rundstedt knew that Speer was walking something of a tightrope, that Hitler's favorite boy might suddenly find himself the target of someone's plot, the sort of intrigue that seemed to swirl around Hitler every day. The political paranoia was the primary reason von Rundstedt would never have accepted any position where he had to sit at Hitler's right hand. The left hand could always be holding a knife.

Von Rundstedt had no special feelings about Speer one way or the other, but if Speer had accompanied Guderian, there had to be a reason. Von Rundstedt had to assume that anything he said would be carried back to Hitler word for word.

Guderian led them to a large concrete bunker, a pyramid without a top, the snout of the eighty-eight protruding skyward. The gun's crew emerged quickly, stood in a neat line, snapped their salutes.

Guderian seemed to enjoy the show. "You may return to your post. If I was not so loyal to my tank crews, I would enjoy commanding you. The eighty-eight is a marvel of engineering, the most feared weapon in the artillery's arsenal. But you know that, don't you?"

The men smiled, obvious pride, and von Rundstedt nodded his approval toward their lieutenant, who ordered them back into the bunker. Guderian moved away, glanced around, no one within earshot, allowed von Rundstedt and Speer to move close, turned and faced the old man.

"We have suffered a setback at Bastogne, is that true?"

Von Rundstedt rubbed his chin with the cold leather of his gloves, said, "I should think this meeting should include Field Marshal Model. He can speak much more precisely on the frontline situation."

"If I wanted to talk to Model, Model would be here. What of Bastogne?"

"The enemy was able to break through our best defensive efforts. We knew we would be confronting General Patton's forces in the south. He is not a man who will accept defeat for long."

"So, you respect Patton?"

"Don't you? I believe that General Patton has modeled much of his strategy from the lessons he learned from you, General. You should be flattered."

Guderian seemed to consider the compliment, and von Rundstedt smiled to himself, thought, yes, his ego enjoys a good stroke now and then.

Guderian moved past the momentary glow, said, "The Führer expects your forces to reclaim the city. He expects this to happen immediately. He is not so enamored of General Patton."

Von Rundstedt thought for a moment, sifted through the myriad sarcastic responses. He fought that temptation, said, "It is my belief that Bastogne was an opportunity lost. It was General Manteuffel's feeling that the city should be bypassed in exchange for the speed his tanks could offer in their drive westward. In hindsight, General Manteuffel erred in not securing Bastogne earlier in the campaign. But the goal was to send his armor forward and not be so concerned with the flanks. I believe that is a principle you understand well, is it not, General?"

Guderian pondered the words, a hard scowl on his face.

"You would mock my strategies then? You would dare to place blame at *my* feet?"

Von Rundstedt forced shock into his expression.

"Most certainly not! You misinterpret my meaning. I have always appreciated your philosophy of battle. To paraphrase what you have often said yourself, *Speed eliminates concern for flanks.* If we had been able to achieve such speed in this campaign, I have no doubt it would have been a success."

The scowl faded, and after a moment von Rundstedt saw a hint of a smile.

"Nicely stated, Field Marshal. You have managed to compliment the Führer's plan, while you lay failure at the feet of others. Perhaps I underestimate you."

Von Rundstedt did not respond, the opening for Guderian to continue.

"Bastogne must be recaptured. Those are the Führer's orders. Your *first* orders. I have had a lengthy conference with the Führer, and he is aware that the weather did not aid our forward movement. I have tried to con-

vince him that the enemy's ability to move vast numbers of tanks and artillery in the path of our advance is a problem."

"You are a master of understatement, General."

Guderian ignored the comment, continued. "The Führer believes
more than ever in the fighting spirit of the German soldier. He is less enthusiastic about the spirit of his generals."

Von Rundstedt let the comment pass, thought, when has it ever been
different?

Guderian paused, seemed troubled, glanced at Speer, who so far had
said nothing at all.

"The Führer is of the opinion that, despite the delays, our campaign
has had the desired effect. The enemy has been considerably softened
across the entire front. What is required now is one sharp blow, one strike
to open the gates across the Meuse River. This operation will yet succeed.
We must not rely solely on technology. The Führer believes that our past
reliance on the tools of war has been detrimental to our success. To state it
plainly, we were not provided with a strong armored reserve or additional
artillery because this army should not require it. We must have faith in our
troops to carry out their Führer's orders."

Von Rundstedt felt paralyzed, his mouth opening slightly, felt the cold
in his chest, the three men standing in frigid silence. Guderian looked
away slowly, and von Rundstedt rolled the words over in his mind,
thought, you must have exploded when you heard that. No one could believe such foolishness, certainly not a man who knows the value of armor.

After a few seconds, Guderian said, "The Führer is no longer interested in hearing complaints from you and Field Marshal Model about the
lack of gasoline. It was your job to capture the enemy's fuel depots, and
thus the failure lies with those men who did not take advantage of opportunity."

Von Rundstedt looked at Speer, who was staring at the ground, who
seemed to share Guderian's unease. So, that is the message, he thought.
That is why Guderian has come, to inform us that the fantasy of victory is
yet within our grasp.

Looking at Speer, he said, "Has Herr Speer accompanied the general
to confirm that the Führer's orders were properly communicated? Are you
here because you are a reliable witness to this absurdity?"

Speer seemed surprised by the question.

"It is not my place to offer opinions of the Führer's strategies. I felt I should visit the headquarters where so much is being decided. I assure you, Field Marshal, I am not here to spy on General Guderian's performance."

Von Rundstedt smiled at the word.

"A fine performance it was. So, Herr Speer, are you in agreement that it is not tanks or guns or rockets that will decide this war? It is our beloved private with his bolt-action rifle who will carry the day? Never mind that the enemy is pouring hundreds of new tanks and artillery pieces through the seaports he has taken from us. Never mind that our soldiers have suffered mightily at the hands of the *enemy's* technology. Never mind that when it was promised to us, our own technology did not materialize. Tell me, Herr Speer, why is that so? Where are the tanks that were promised us? Where was the Luftwaffe's vast armada of planes to sweep the enemy from the skies? Where are all those secret weapons the Führer has been speaking of? That is your department, yes?"

Speer reacted slowly, no anger.

"I cannot respond to your questions, sir, because I do not have the answers. I can assure you that the factories are operating at maximum capacity, despite the enemy's best efforts to bomb them to oblivion."

Von Rundstedt laughed, couldn't help himself, shivered in the cold.

"The enemy bombs our factories every day and every night and you expect me to believe that they are unharmed?"

Speer shook his head.

"I am not saying that at all, sir. We continue to suffer significant destruction, however, repairs are made rapidly to every damaged production line, and we are continuing to produce the materials you require. I did not make promises about numbers. It is not my job to do so."

"No, I suppose not. My apologies to you, Herr Speer."

Guderian seemed to lose patience. "I am aware that when the two panzer armies were slowed by enemy resistance, we required, at that precise moment, reserve armor which we did not have available. With some difficulty, I have explained that to the Führer. It is not a point he will consider. It is a familiar argument to me, and one that is . . . frustrating. But we have our orders now, and you will carry them out."

Von Rundstedt mulled over the words, had a sudden burst of clarity.

"You are giving those orders to *me*. I am expected, of course, to pass them along to Field Marshal Model." He laughed, shook his head. "I am no fool, General. I am being given a task that we cannot complete, and so, I will be the one who is labeled with failure. The Führer has great affection for Herr Model, and very little for me. Yes, I understand my part in this. If Herr Model were standing in the streets of Antwerp at this very moment, the bands would play for *him*. However, since he is not, the orders to repair this situation have come to *me*. Very clever. Very clever indeed."

Guderian seemed increasingly uncomfortable, turned away, seemed to search the trees.

"I will now inspect the troops in this sector. I will test their morale, and report on their fighting spirit to the Führer."

Von Rundstedt held out his hand toward Speer, who seemed suddenly miserable. Speer took the hand, a firm shake, and von Rundstedt thought, perhaps I am wrong about him. He sees precisely what is happening. And it appears he does not like it at all. Very good, young man. I respect you for that.

"It was pleasant having your company, Herr Speer. You may certainly visit this headquarters anytime. General Guderian, you may inspect anything you wish while you are here. I am certain that you will find the spirit of this army to be exactly as your Führer expects it to be. I am returning to my office. I am too old to suffer the cold."

DECEMBER 27, 1944, LATE EVENING

More than ever before, the old man knew he was merely an afterthought. The reports continued to come, someone in Model's headquarters informing him of the day's fighting only when it seemed to be convenient. But the reports from Bastogne had been exactly as he expected. The renewed attempt at capturing the city had been a meager effort, the troops in that sector beaten back decisively by the American forces Patton continued to shove into the area.

But the final report of the day had brought meaning that no one, not even the most optimistic general, could misinterpret. With the Allied pressure coming from both north and south, the point of Model's westward spear had been narrowed to a single striking force, the Second Panzer Division, whose men still performed with the fighting spirit that Hitler had predicted. The Second had reached the town of Celles, Belgium, still pressing forward toward the Meuse River, preparing for a direct confrontation with British tanks that defended the river crossings. But the panzers had not been prepared for a sudden attack on their right flank by units of the American Second Armored Division, supported by infantry from the American Eighty-fourth Division. The results of the fight had been a ca-

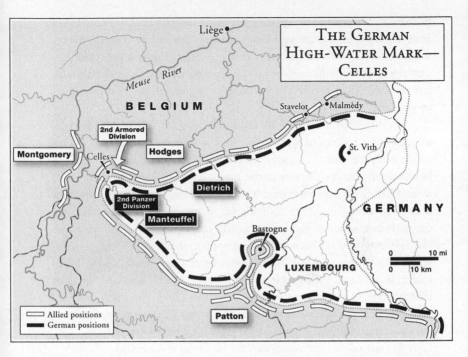

THE GERMAN
HIGH-WATER MARK—
CELLES

tastrophe for the Second Panzers, who lost half their men and most of their heavy armor. No other German support could reach the area, and thus the point of the spear had been thoroughly crushed.

Von Rundstedt stood at the map, staring, no longer seeing, had studied too many maps now, details his brain would no longer absorb. He felt that peculiar pain in his chest, but it was not his heart, no illness. It was far deeper than that, a hard shocking pain to a soldier's instinct when a victory does not come. There *could* have been victory here, he thought. No matter the foolishness of the plan, when we launched this campaign, this army had the fight in them, would still do whatever we asked them to do. Every general knows that no matter the mapmakers and the numbers on paper, when you put men and tanks into motion, when you put men to killing other men on a battlefield, anything can happen. No strategist can predict every outcome. But now . . . no matter what kind of illusions float through Berlin, we have an outcome.

So what happens now, old man? Can Model rally his troops, find the gasoline and the armor to replace what he no longer has? Does he still believe this is a fight he can win? Guderian does not believe that, no matter the ridiculous speech he was ordered to give, no matter the orders he carries here from his Führer. How must he feel about that? A brilliant strategist, serving his supreme commander as an errand boy. Or worse. A propagandist.

Von Rundstedt reached for a bottle of cognac, nearly empty, thought of drinking it without a glass. What does it matter, anyway? But his instincts took over, decorum always, and he reached for the glass, poured the bottle empty. Across the office, the map seemed to loom over him like some kind of shroud, unavoidable. The glass was in his hand now, not nearly full enough, and he sat back in the chair, his eyes blurring. He downed the cognac, no pleasure in the soft burn. The pain came again, the raw and unavoidable shock from the reports of the Second Panzer's disaster. You knew this moment would come, he thought. Model knew, Manteuffel, all of them. So why is it so difficult? Am I to be satisfied that all of us were *right,* that this was the inevitable conclusion? There will never be any pride or any vindication in telling Hitler that he was wrong, that he is *always* wrong. And yet, if he had been right . . . just this one time . . . perhaps this war could have ended well for us, for all of Germany.

He had kept his aides away, did not need anyone to update the map, to redraw the thick lines showing troop movements, colored pins showing the positions of the enemy. It no longer matters, he thought. What matters, and what will always matter, is that on this day, we reached the end. We were turned back, and we do not have the means to change that. No matter what Hitler believes, no matter what any of them believes, we have lost any momentum we had, any superiority. He looked again toward the map, thought of the name of the town, *Celles.* A place no one will ever care about, no one of us will ever see. It holds only one meaning. It is two miles shy of the Meuse River, and it is as far as we were able to go.

19. EISENHOWER

He had been pushing for a meeting with Montgomery, and—with Bastogne secured, and the German western thrust well contained—it seemed an opportune time. But Monty would not come to Versailles, insisting that his guardianship over Hodges's army meant diligence, the kind of watchful eye the British field marshal could not exercise by taking himself away from his forward headquarters. So, Eisenhower would go to him.

The weather had turned again, snow and ice on every road, travel for the supply and troop convoys miserable once again. It made sense that if Eisenhower was going to travel anywhere beyond the outskirts of Paris, the only way to move was by train.

He rode in a small private compartment, the train nothing like the luxurious rolling headquarters used by other generals in other wars. Though he had his privacy, there was little time for relaxation. The staff had loaded him up with every report he had sought, troop movements and orders, Bradley and Devers keeping him fully briefed on action in their sectors. There were newspapers as well, British, with headlines that annoyed him every time he glanced at the bold black print. Montgomery's newly acquired control of the American First and Ninth armies had made an enormous splash, the papers seeming to believe that it was a first step toward Monty's eventual dictatorship over the entire Allied operation. He stuffed the papers beneath the stack of yellow legal pads, scribbled writings of his own that meant more to him than anyone's news in London. He knew the reception to Montgomery's new authority would be handled like a fat ripe plum of propaganda, and it was hard for him to object officially. The British people had been suffering under severe shortages, and the casualty counts were an ongoing nightmare for British families. Eisenhower appreciated that any good news, even *this* kind of good news, was a positive thing.

The train was crowded with MPs, a platoon of top-notch security personnel chosen to safeguard the commanding general. The rumors of assassination squads had continued, and from the frontline troops to the rear command centers, reports filtered up the ladder that Germans in American uniforms were still running rampant through Allied-held territory. The edginess of the guards at the myriad roadblocks was becoming a hindrance to the movement of anyone not traveling with an entire convoy behind him. The stories still came to Eisenhower's desk, outraged inconvenience for senior officers who might have forgotten the capital of Illinois. Montgomery's bullet-ridden tires had been the most dramatic tale, and Eisenhower smiled every time he thought of it. But on every roadway and country lane, the roadblocks were infected with an edgy panic that some jeep carrying a squad of German spies would slip past, depositing a handful of grenades or machine-gunning the guards. Whether anyone ever succeeded in reaching the supreme commander was not as important to the MPs and frontline outposts as what was happening right in front of them. Eisenhower couldn't fault anyone for that.

The MPs had patrolled cautiously all through the train, searching for the bravehearted assassin who might find the way to climb aboard. It didn't seem to matter to the officer in charge that the train would not stop at all along the way. Eisenhower tried to ignore the security, sat quietly in his own compartment, could hear footsteps above him, guards tramping on the roof of his car. He looked out toward the clouds of blowing snow, said aloud, "All right. This is enough stupidity for one day."

He moved out into the corridor, aides responding from the next compartment, and Eisenhower said, "Get those MPs inside. Give 'em some coffee and make sure nobody's dying of pneumonia. The only way any spy is leaping onto this train is if he's blown in here by the wind. By then, he'll be stiff as a board. You got that?"

"Sir, General Smith insists—"

"Yeah, I know. Beetle's reading too many murder mysteries. Get the MPs inside. Now."

"Yes, sir."

Eisenhower moved back to his compartment, an aide appearing behind him, carrying a tray.

"Sir, we have some lunch prepared for you. We weren't certain if you would be sharing lunch with Field Marshal Montgomery."

Eisenhower lifted the white napkin covering a large croissant, a mound of dark red ham beside it.

"This is a hell of a lot better than anything Monty will give me. I'll take it. You did *check* it, right?"

"Sir?"

"For poison. Those assassins are a crafty lot."

The man seemed suddenly alarmed, pulled the tray back. Eisenhower took it away from him with a mild jerk.

"Give me that. You people need to stop this nonsense. How long until we get to Monty's HQ?"

"Uh, we're about twenty minutes out, sir."

"Go up front and double-check that. I want enough time to settle my damn lunch before I have to deal with Monty. I don't need to be belching into his face. Not by accident anyway."

E isenhower took the man's hand, felt himself holding only a light squeeze, as though the man's fragility was still a concern.

"Freddie, it's good to see you."

"Thank you, sir. Up and about, no problems, I assure you. Monty is rather the nursemaid, though. Insists on a curfew much like his own."

There were patronizing laughs all around, and Eisenhower understood the meaning of that. The staffs were overly accommodating to anything Freddie de Guingand would say, this time laughing too hard at his mild joke. Eisenhower knew that Montgomery had established his own strict routine by going to bed at nine thirty every night, leaving the late-night work to his staff. As his chief of staff, de Guingand had always suffered the brunt of the labor, and he had served extremely well as the go-between who soaked up the distrust and animosity between Montgomery and most of the higher-ranking Americans, particularly Eisenhower himself. Other than Arthur Tedder, de Guingand was the British officer Eisenhower most enjoyed conversing with. The man's sudden collapse had been discreetly described as a nervous breakdown, which had unnerved everyone, since de Guingand was such an important cog in the British machine. But Montgomery himself seemed almost unaffected by it, barely altering his own routines at all. If Montgomery showed few outward signs of relief to have his chief of staff back at work, every one of the American generals had sent profound best wishes for de Guingand's health.

Eisenhower scanned the room, the British officers holding teacups, a momentary mood of relaxation that Eisenhower rarely saw around Montgomery. But Montgomery was not yet there. De Guingand seemed to sense the momentary lapse in conversation, said, "Sir, Monty will be along shortly. He's attending to some personal matter. Please don't give it any significance."

"No problem, Freddie."

"Tea, sir?"

"No. Just relax. He can keep me waiting. I'm used to it."

Eisenhower knew the cause of de Guingand's uneasiness. It was one more routine Montgomery enjoyed. If he could not be the very first man into the room, arranging the maps and paperwork to suit his own plan, then he would be the very last. Then and only then could the meeting begin. Eisenhower knew better than to be annoyed by it, would never scold the British commander for what was, to most of the Americans, a show of rudeness. But Monty could play his games, since today, Eisenhower needed him to be in a good mood.

He appeared now, beret affixed, the ever-present sweater, the casual appearance typical. Eisenhower refused to be affected by that, knew that the only man who insisted on neckties at every occasion was George Patton. If Montgomery was using his casualness as a show of disrespect, Eisenhower simply didn't care. There were far more important things to worry about.

"Ah, there you are! Good to see you, Ike, old chap. We've given the Hun quite a blasting, eh? A great deal more work to do, of course. I was just conferring with your General Hodges. His lines are finally coming up to shape, though I must admit, several of his divisions are somewhat slow to move. Can't be helped, I suppose. This weather is a challenge, wouldn't you say?"

Montgomery stood facing him with his hands on his hips, and Eisenhower could only nod, did not expect this much sheer exuberance. He pointed to the long table, said, "May we sit?"

"Oh, most certainly! Take your seats, gentlemen. Let's get to the point, shall we?"

Eisenhower wasn't certain what point Montgomery was referring to, knew it would come soon enough. Montgomery waited for his own staff to arrange themselves, the chair at the far end of the table left empty, Monty's own place. He moved that way, stood behind the chair, appraising the others, seemed satisfied, then took his seat.

"We'll be ready for them, Ike. Working like the devil to whip our boys into shape, convince them of the threat. Can't fault your people for not quite pulling the rope, as it were. Hodges had his hands full, and some of his boys took a terrible licking. Takes time to bring those units back up to speed, you know. He's also got quite a handicap with some of his newer people. Marvelous how you've managed to recruit so many new troops, marvelous indeed. You're drawing from what seems to be a bottomless well. Training a bit lacking, but that will come in time. It took me a bit longer than I'd hoped to convince General Hodges of the danger. A few challenging fellows under his command. This fellow Ridgway . . . tough nut, that one. Paratroopers are harder to rein in than most, I suppose."

"I'm not here to appraise anyone's leadership, Monty. I need you to press the enemy, and press him hard and fast. Brad believes we're staring straight at an opportunity here, and I don't want to see this one get away."

Montgomery seemed to ignore the meaning, too many failures that could only be placed at Montgomery's feet, failures caused nearly always by a lack of speed, what Patton called *audacity*. Eisenhower knew that the man was far too prickly to absorb the blame that so many in the American camps were aiming at him.

After a brief silent moment, Montgomery said, "I am doing all I can to put your people into line. The reinforcements have helped, no doubt. But we must be ready for the inevitable."

"The inevitable what?"

Montgomery looked down, and Eisenhower detected the annoying smirk, that hint of dismissal for Eisenhower's knowledge of strategy.

De Guingand seemed to sense it as well, the arrogance that was a sore point for every American commander. De Guingand said, "Sir, we believe that the Huns are readying a strike near the Malmédy–Stavelot line, possibly intending a major push toward Liège. General Hodges has been most cooperative in shifting strength in preparation for the attack we believe will come in a matter of days."

The man's tone was apologetic, and Eisenhower knew the words had been carefully chosen.

"Sorry, Freddie, but I am not as convinced of the inevitability of the enemy's movements. We have no information that the enemy is preparing any kind of large-scale assault. Quite the opposite. If we press him and press him hard, he will withdraw. He is dangerous still, but he has suffered horribly for the ground he has gained. If he is capable of any significant offensive operation, we should not allow him the time to regroup. On this point, I agree wholeheartedly with General Patton. The best defense is to attack. If we do not attack, and soon, then we are allowing the enemy to dictate our strategy. Whether that means attack or withdrawal, I do not intend to grant him those kinds of options. I spoke to Air Marshal Tedder yesterday. He phrased it quite well, I thought. *The enemy has stuck his neck out.* Imagine a chicken poking its head through a fence. As rapidly as possible, we should sever that head. Brad agrees, and has ordered Patton to continue to push northward from the area around Bastogne. Rather than waiting for General Hodges to *receive* an attack at Stavelot, I would much prefer he make an attack of his own and drive southward. The deep thrust into our lines has placed the enemy at an enormous disadvantage. Every salient has a vulnerable point, and it is usually at the base. We have an obvious opportunity. I should like you to agree with me on this one, Monty."

There was silence in the room, no one touching their teacups, eyes on Montgomery. After a long pause he looked up, his eyes not meeting Eisenhower's.

"Are you ordering me to attack the enemy's salient?"

"I suppose I am."

"When?"

Eisenhower knew the smell of a trap, had already been over the strategy with Bradley. Bradley understood Montgomery as well as anyone, and Eisenhower knew that if the timetable was left up to Montgomery, he might require weeks of preparation. If the order was immediate, the kind of order Patton would leap at, Montgomery would simply claim it could not be done at all. Eisenhower let out a breath, looked at de Guingand, thought, dammit, I'm tired of this crap.

"January third. You said that Hodges has his people in place, and I know he'll be ready."

Montgomery seemed prepared with a response, stared past Eisenhower again, as though he was figuring out the strategy on the spot.

"I suppose, if pressed, we can ready an assault. This weather might play the dickens with the roads, though . . ."

Eisenhower had lost patience, saw the hint of concern on de Guingand's face, Monty's chief of staff seeming to know exactly what was coming. Eisenhower said, "The enemy used this crappy weather to his advåntage. We were caught completely by surprise. If these stinking snowstorms continue, he won't be expecting us to do anything. If the snow quits, the air boys can lead the way. Either way, we have to make the first move."

Montgomery seemed to ponder his options. "Ike, I'll tell you what. If your man Hodges feels he is ready to make a move, I'll not stand in his way. But the maps show me that the opportunity is straight into the Hun's face. With the troop positions we have now, including the reinforcements, we can strike eastward and drive the enemy straight back where he came from."

De Guingand spoke up now.

"Sir, if I may clarify."

"Certainly, Freddie."

De Guingand looked at Eisenhower as though he was carefully asking for a favor.

"Sir, we have our greatest strength in a strong position opposite the enemy's deepest penetration, just east of the Meuse River. It would be tactically reasonable to strike from that position. Preparation for an assault would be minimal. I do not believe the timetable would be a challenge."

Compromise. The word echoed through Eisenhower's brain. He knew that Montgomery's stubbornness could not simply be ordered away. *If I tell him to move down from the north, he'll find a thousand reasons why he can't. But he won't say it here, not to my face. All the bitching will come tomorrow, after I'm gone.*

Montgomery was scowling, nodded grudgingly, said, "All right then. If you insist we make this assault, then Freddie's idea is the most sound. We can hit the enemy from the west, and if we are fortunate, we shall push him back to where he began."

"The *gap* between Stavelot and Bastogne is less than thirty miles." Eisenhower paused, let the word sink in. "Patton will continue his drive northward. It would be very beneficial for the morale of this army . . . this entire army, that the enemy not be allowed to *escape.* Do I need to explain this?"

De Guingand responded, "Certainly not, sir. That is our goal as well."

You're a good chief of staff, Eisenhower thought. You know when your boss needs to keep his answers to himself.

Montgomery turned, scanned the wide map on the wall, seemed lost in thought. The teacups chattered, the staff relaxing, and Montgomery said, "This is a perfect example of the need we have to unite this army under a single ground commander." He looked at Eisenhower now, wagged one finger in the air. "The perfect example. All sides of this attack can be best coordinated through one headquarters. Without such control, there is the potential for failure. I appreciate the strains you are under with a command as cumbersome as this. I completely understand. That's why my idea should be reconsidered. A single field command, right here, could relieve you of the burden for the disposition of so many ground troops."

Eisenhower closed his eyes for a brief second, had not expected Montgomery to open this wound again.

"You are assuming that if *you* are not placed in command of all ground forces in this theater of the war, we are destined for failure."

"Frankly, Ike, I am inclined to believe that the best course of action, given the threat the enemy still poses, is to shelve this talk of a general attack. With the weather so poor, and my certainty that the enemy is preparing to hit us again, we should consider withdrawing westward, behind the Meuse, and in the south we should pull back far behind the Moselle. Only then can we establish an impenetrable defense and await better campaigning weather. Reinforced with fresh troops, we could then launch the final unyielding thrust, driving the Hun all the way back behind the Rhine. Berlin could be ours in a matter of weeks."

Eisenhower was stunned, saw de Guingand shifting nervously in his chair.

"*Withdraw?* Are you serious?"

Montgomery seemed surprised at the question.

"I always seek the best for my men, Ike. Always have. In this case—"

"There will be no damn withdrawal." Eisenhower was losing the battle with his own temper, thought of Patton. If I tell Georgie to retreat back to the Moselle, he'll drive a tank straight into Monty's headquarters. "And I do not want to hear any more talk of failure. You will launch your offensive assault on January third."

Montgomery shrugged.

"Those are my orders?"

"Yep."

O n January 3, the Allies launched the next phase of the campaign. Despite Montgomery's pessimism, the Germans mostly responded by backing away. But the fights were not all simple and one-sided. West of the snow-covered Ardennes, the German rear guard gave ground with grudging steps, striking out sharply at the Americans who pushed forward, increasing the casualty count on both sides.

Though Hitler would not approve any requests from his commanders for a general retreat, the German officers in the field understood the odds against them. All across the front, tanks and trucks empty of fuel were abandoned or destroyed, many of the soldiers pulling back by whatever means they could find. Across the same ridges and snow-filled valleys where the Germans had so crushed their unprepared enemy, they now flowed back in the opposite direction.

In the area of Alsace, where Patton's Twentieth Corps and Jacob Devers's Sixth Army Group held the line against the enemy at Hitler's West Wall, Hitler had ordered a new offensive, designed to strike into American positions well south of the bulge. Hitler's plan was to draw strength away from Patton's northward push; possibly, if the Germans could penetrate deeply enough, Eisenhower would be forced to shift enough strength to that area to slow the progress in the Ardennes. Eisenhower ordered Devers to pull back and consolidate his lines, greatly strengthening his ability to hold the Germans away. But that area was also manned by the French First Army, led by officers who reacted with outrage that Eisenhower would order them to withdraw from French territory. Word was sent quickly from Alsace to Paris, to the man who had proclaimed himself leader of France. As the French people and their army had come to expect, their leader would not accept such a blow to French pride without vigorous

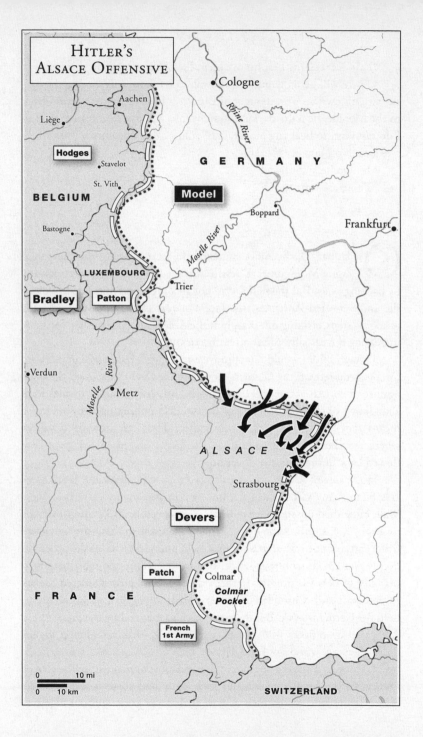

HITLER'S
ALSACE OFFENSIVE

Cologne

Aachen

Liège

Rhine River

Hodges

Stavelot

St. Vith

GERMANY

Model

BELGIUM

Boppard

Frankfurt

Bastogne

Moselle River

LUXEMBOURG

Bradley   Patton

Trier

Verdun

Moselle River

Metz

ALSACE

Strasbourg

Devers

Patch

Colmar

Colmar Pocket

FRANCE

French
1st Army

0   10 mi
0   10 km

SWITZERLAND

protest. That protest would come in a meeting Eisenhower could not avoid. Charles de Gaulle loudly announced that he was going to Eisenhower's headquarters.

In what Eisenhower considered to be a lightning bolt of coincidence, his staff received word that he would have another visitor as well. Winston Churchill had decided he needed a brief look at how things were shaping up at SHAEF.

SHAEF, VERSAILLES, FRANCE
JANUARY 3, 1945

De Gaulle was even taller than Eisenhower had remembered, a head taller than his gloomy interpreter. The uniforms on both Frenchmen were impeccable, a variety of decorations and official badges that made Eisenhower curious. But there was no chance he would give in to de Gaulle's always present arrogance by asking just what the medals were for. De Gaulle had not been on a battlefield leading anyone since the Germans had crushed the French more than four years earlier, and even then he had ranked far below France's military leaders in the field. Eisenhower waited for de Gaulle to take his seat, a slow, deliberate perch, thought, I guess if he's the boss, he can award himself any honor he decides he's earned. It must be a pain in the ass every time he takes off his coat.

Churchill sat to one side, engulfed by a fat leather chair. He had spoken only a polite and smiling greeting to de Gaulle, and then had seemed to decide this conversation was Eisenhower's alone. Once de Gaulle began to speak, Churchill kept completely silent.

The interpreter never smiled, as though the task was far too mundane to require much energy on his part. But unlike so many confrontations before, this time Eisenhower sensed a surprising vulnerability in de Gaulle. Since he had claimed his place at the head of the French government, de Gaulle had tried forcefully to insert himself into the Allied hierarchy. But the Frenchman had been purposely left out of the specific planning for the Normandy invasion, Allied intelligence well aware that his headquarters in Algeria was leaking secrets to German operatives like water through a sprinkler head. De Gaulle had been furious that he had not been consulted prior to the invasion, as he had been furious with the general practice at SHAEF to pass along most other strategic information after the events had actually occurred. It required very little imagination on anyone's part to conclude that Eisenhower not only distrusted French security but—after so many confrontations with de Gaulle's self-importance—had very little use for de Gaulle himself.

Eisenhower had dreaded the meeting, of course, but de Gaulle was offering something different this time, charm, a friendly smile that didn't seem to fit the man's face. Eisenhower appreciated the gesture, even if it was purely superficial.

"General Eisenhower, I must apologize to you. It was a mistake for me not to have congratulated you in a more timely fashion for you receiving your fifth star. I understand that in American military history, that places you among the very elite. You should be quite proud of such an achievement, such recognition by your government."

"Thank you. It was a most pleasant surprise."

De Gaulle held the smile, seemed to wait for some compliment to come back the other way. Eisenhower searched his brain, couldn't think of one.

De Gaulle continued, "Pride in one's army is an essential part of any nation's spirit. Your nation has much to be proud of, and by yourself, you are responsible for much of that. The reward is just. It is so much the same way in my country. Pride in our army is critical, especially since, for much of this war, we have borne the burden of the German curse. My people have suffered greatly. We are grateful to our allies for your efforts. I feel quite strongly that the tide of this struggle has turned in our favor. Everywhere I go, the French people are receiving their liberation with tears of great joy."

Eisenhower understood completely where de Gaulle was going. "Strasbourg is among those cities."

"Yes! I am pleased you understand. I was distressed when I heard the reports that you would have us abandon so much we have gained. The people of Strasbourg would suffer horrible circumstances should the Germans be allowed to regain control. I fear retribution would be bloody. The *Boches* have no morals. I am not telling you what you do not already know."

Eisenhower stood, walked to the map that spread out over one of the plywood walls. He glanced at Churchill, who peered up at him from under the brim of his hat, no expression at all. Eisenhower picked up a stick pointer, felt suddenly ridiculous, like some schoolmaster educating the ignorant. *Dammit, the French know this map better than I do. I shouldn't have to explain this.*

"General de Gaulle, it was most unfortunate that the French First Army could not secure the Colmar pocket." He stopped, wanted to say so much more about that, but he could already feel an icy silence in the room. Beside him, Churchill made a short low grunt. Eisenhower thought, fine, I've put myself in a damn minefield. Now get out of it. "I mean to say of course, that it is unfortunate that the French and *American* armies could not drive the enemy from that area. The enemy's strength there has been a patch of thorns we have had to devote considerable resources to contain. Had the enemy chosen to do so, he might have struck out from Colmar in a way that might have produced a second bulge, and caused us a serious problem. However, by staying put, he has kept his advantages to himself. The German holds a strong defensive position. With this new assault coming at us across the Siegfried line, Hitler is no doubt anticipating that we will respond by drawing strength away from the Ardennes. We cannot do that. Thus, it is militarily sound that we withdraw those troops under attack in Alsace to a far more defensible position, to contract our lines, and allow the German to destroy himself against *our* defenses. I understand that Strasbourg lies outside of the new position I propose, and I understand your concerns for the safety of the civilian inhabitants."

"Perhaps you do not, General. I cannot allow my army to participate in the abandonment of the city. Strasbourg has been a symbol of French greatness for generations. We have rescued the inhabitants from the boot heel of *Boche* occupation in the past, and now we have done so again. If I allow this retreat, the French people will lose faith in their government and in their army. They will also lose faith in yours. If you intend to follow through with the order to withdraw all across the Alsatian front, the French First Army will be forced to operate independently. We will defend the city ourselves, and deal with whatever horrors the enemy thrusts upon us."

Eisenhower felt the heat rising in his brain, tapped the stick pointer against the palm of his hand.

"Despite how you may feel about this strategic decision, General, I do appreciate your zeal for protecting your people. I share that. I am attempting to protect *all* our people against a German breakthrough that could damage everything we have gained in the Ardennes. If you order your commanders to ignore this strategy, you will force me to allow just what you propose. The French First Army will become independent. I have no doubt that the German response will be to swarm out of Colmar, push hard through Alsace, and surround Strasbourg with considerable energy. Your army will become quite a prize for whatever German general can claim it. They will make every effort to cut you off from our protection, and their highest priority will be to sever all your lines of supply. I fear greatly that the citizens of Strasbourg will suffer a fate as unfortunate as any of your people have thus far. Their city will become a battlefield, and most likely will be reduced to rubble. I do not insult the fighting spirit of the French soldier, General. But the Germans will understand immediately what you have done, and they will appreciate the opportunity you have offered them. They will respond with as much force as they can muster."

De Gaulle had stopped smiling, looked away from the map, glanced at Churchill, who still did not speak.

After a long silent moment, de Gaulle said, "If my country loses this fight in the way you describe, my government will lose the support of the French people. It is that simple. If my government does not survive, there will be anarchy, and that will destroy France. That will produce serious consequences for you as well. You have long maintained that you are our ally. Such friendship promises mutual support. If the French people no longer choose to support your cause, there could be *difficulties* for you in the future. Supply lines might be the least of your challenges."

Eisenhower moved back to his chair, sat, one hand across his mouth, rubbing slowly. He looked at de Gaulle, the man utterly serious. Dammit, he's right. The room was silent for a long moment, and Eisenhower avoided de Gaulle's stare. He glanced toward the silent Churchill, thought, you're not helping at all. A minute passed, interminable silence, and finally, Eisenhower reached for the phone on his desk, waited for the voice on the other end, said, "Get me Devers."

The response was annoying, too uncertain. "Well dammit, find him!" He hung up the phone, looked again at the map.

"I have decided to order General Devers to withdraw the northern portion of his lines to the positions we have already planned. I will instruct him to maintain the city of Strasbourg within our lines, and furthermore, I will cease the withdrawal of any additional troop strength from his sector. By now, we should have sufficient manpower in the Ardennes sector to complete that campaign successfully. As long as we can prevent a German breakthrough in Alsace, Strasbourg will not be . . ." He fought for the right word. "Sacrificed."

The smile returned to de Gaulle, Churchill still maddeningly silent. De Gaulle stood, snapped to attention, seemed to touch the ceiling with his hat. He made a short bow, said, "The French people have great admiration for your military skills, General. The French army will continue to serve you with gallantry. Alongside our allies, we shall destroy the German plague."

The meeting was obviously over, and Eisenhower stood as well, took de Gaulle's enormous hand in his own. Without another word, de Gaulle turned and left the room, his interpreter close behind. Eisenhower sat again, felt the heat in the room, looked at Churchill, tried to be annoyed, but there was no anger, Eisenhower so often disarmed by the short squat figure who watched him with a hint of a smile.

Churchill said, "Quite the politician, eh? You, I mean, not that French rooster. But he had you, both hands firmly on your tenders. You did the wise and proper thing."

"I'll hear bitching from Devers about it, but as long as I don't pull any more people away from him, he'll be all right."

Churchill shrugged.

"I don't know much about all that. Your department. My department concerns politics, though if you keep up this sort of thing, you'll be gathering votes yourself." He paused. "You are probably curious why I decided to drop in on you. I know whenever I plop myself into your affairs, it has to be a distraction, and Lord knows, you have plenty to worry about. But I thought you should know what I'm hearing from our *other* allies. Right now, my ears are full of blather from Joe Stalin's minions, telling me that it is our obligation as allies to keep up as much pressure as we can on the enemy. The Russians are planning an enormous offensive that, if it works, should go far toward ending this thing."

Eisenhower had heard talk of the Russian operation, including messages he had received from Washington. He opened a drawer to one side, reached for a bottle, held it up for Churchill to see.

"Brandy. Yours, I believe."

"Of course it's mine. All brandy everywhere is mine. I insist, though occasionally I do allow others to share it. I was wondering when you were going to get around to offering me some. I am deeply grateful you didn't give any away to that Frenchman."

Eisenhower pulled two glasses off a shelf behind him, poured

Churchill's twice as full as his own, the usual tradition. He took the glass to the prime minister, thought, no need to make you move out of that chair.

Eisenhower returned to his desk. "I was hoping you'd chime in, you know, offer me a life preserver."

"Why? You handled de Gaulle perfectly."

"I'm not cut out for all this international sensitivity. I leave that to General Marshall, the rest of them."

Churchill laughed.

"Dear boy, I'm not cut out for sensitivity at all. Still, I manage. I think often of your President Roosevelt, Teddy, the first one. *Walk softly and carry a big stick.* Magnificent, brilliant. But, you have to know when to use that stick, whether to pat the other fellow on the back or bash out his brains. With de Gaulle, you wielded the stick exactly as you should have."

Eisenhower appreciated the compliment, held up the brandy glass, a silent toast. He took a sip, the rough burn unpleasant, not what he needed. His mind focused again on the Russians. "Has Stalin given us a D-Day for his offensive?"

Churchill shook his head, downed half the glass.

"Course not. The Russians are never so forthcoming."

Eisenhower was annoyed, had been through this before.

"Why the hell not? They demand every detail we can give them about our strategic operations, and they don't reveal a damn thing about their own. Clearly they don't trust us. It pisses me off. We are allies, after all."

Churchill held up a hand, stopped him.

"You pulled a grand political stroke with de Gaulle. But Uncle Joe is a different beast entirely. And, I think *beast* is the proper description. The Russians don't understand us at all, never have. They think we talk too much. They're surprised as all hell when we actually tell them our plans without lying to them, and they're appalled that we provide accurate information on things like casualty counts for our newspapers. But, they also think of us as a necessary inconvenience to a war *they* have to win. And make no mistake, Uncle Joe believes this war to be his private domain, a fight to the death between Hitler and him. It's personal. We are merely their assistants, sometimes helpful, but never to be trusted or depended upon. They saw the entire Normandy campaign as a convenient distraction, as though we temporarily stuck a thorn in Hitler's side. The Western Theater of the war is a back-alley stage show to them. Once I understood that, I understood Stalin's ways. They're not about to tell us anything important, certainly not anything as significant as the start date for their new offensive. But in the end, does it matter? Once the Russians jump off, Hitler will have his hands full. More than full. Hitler bit the tail of a tiger when he invaded Russia. Thank God for stupid mistakes."

On January 8, Hitler finally gave the order to his commanders in the Ardennes that allowed them to withdraw. But the order was a formality far more important to Berlin than to the men in the field. Throughout the month of January, as blizzards rolled again through the Ardennes, the Americans continued their push, punching the Germans slowly backward, until, on January 28, German forces fell back to the positions they had held prior to December 16, to the safety of the defensive works they had held when the Battle of the Bulge had begun.

The Russian offensive began on January 12, a massive surge all across the Eastern Front, with a primary strike into the German defenses in southern Poland. Hitler had no choice but to weaken his forces in the west, pulling what remained of Sepp Dietrich's Sixth Panzer Army eastward, a desperate attempt to hold back a Russian wave that was overpowering. Within eight days, Russian troops had shoved their way through Poland and reached the German border.

With Dietrich's tanks gone, the American commanders in the Ardennes kept up their pressure, striking hard at Hitler's West Wall, what the Allies called the Siegfried line.

Though Eisenhower was enormously pleased by the shift in momentum, and the successful actions of all of his commanders, there continued to be one burden he had no choice but to endure. On January 7, Field Marshal Bernard Montgomery opted to give a press conference, responding to the enthusiastic wishes of so many reporters who had been kept mostly in the dark during the chaotic fighting in the bulge. To the furious astonishment of the American commanders, Montgomery worded his statement to indicate in perfectly certain terms that he had saved the day. In typical Montgomery fashion, nearly every part of his report to the press explained the campaign in a way that left no doubt that Montgomery himself deserved the credit for turning the German tide, and in fact had probably saved the entire American army. It was one more bundle of dynamite added to Montgomery's explosively poor relationship with his allies, Eisenhower included. Thus, it was a grateful Eisenhower who received the reports that Winston Churchill had wisely attempted to defuse the controversy by addressing Parliament. Churchill's speech was specific and unambiguous.

The Americans have engaged thirty or forty men for every one we have engaged, and they have lost sixty or eighty men for every one of us. This is the greatest American battle of the war and will, I believe, be regarded as an ever-famous American victory.

With pressure on Germany's borders increasing on both fronts in the ground war, the air war continued to be relentlessly one-sided. When the weather allowed, the intensity of the Allied long-range bombing campaign continued, nearly every German industrial center targeted day and night. More than once, Eisenhower had wrestled with the moral gravity of that, knowing that the obliteration of factories was never precise, that incendiary bombs had already reduced some German cities to ash and rubble, and that the cost in human terms had to be staggering. The amazing tonnage of bombs raining down across Germany's industrial facilities had long convinced the bomber barons in England that bombing alone would defeat the enemy, would blast away Germany's ability to wage war. But somehow, through the continuous destruction, the factories managed at least some level of output, even if the production numbers were far below what Hitler demanded.

The greatest impact of the bombing campaign against Germany's ability to produce gasoline became clear in the Ardennes, witnessed by the enormous quantity of German military machines abandoned from a lack of fuel. Thus the bombing campaign would continue. Eisenhower had never believed the grandiose claims of the bomber barons, but he made no argument against the continuation of the strategy, no matter how many German civilians might be dying in the process. It was, after all, a war against a kind of enemy the world had never seen, not in his own lifetime, and perhaps long before. In too many examples the soldiers had witnessed for themselves, the Germans had shown a stunning lack of regard for human life, and had repeatedly ignored what the Allies considered to be the basic rules of war.

In a retreat from the Ardennes that was both dogged and desperate, the Germans left behind much more than slaughter on a battlefield. There was slaughter in the villages, civilians butchered by mostly renegade soldiers, exacting revenge on the Belgians or anyone else who might have aided the Americans in any way. As had happened at Stavelot, American troops pushed through the bowl-like towns vacated by fleeing Germans, only to find rows of murdered civilians, mostly unburied. To many of the GIs, the German was still a faceless enemy, but as the horrors increased, that face assumed a shape that inspired revenge the Allied commanders had never expected. Captured German prisoners seemed suddenly to disappear, many reports filtering back to company commanders of those prisoners shot while trying to escape. Though senior officers worked earnestly to prevent it, the Americans, Brits, and Canadians had learned to fight with the same viciousness as their enemy. Some officers simply turned their backs as a new brand of justice was handed out by GIs in a way no one back home would ever read about in a newspaper.

Eisenhower and his generals, particularly the West Pointers, had been carefully educated in the rules of war, rules that were carried down from the days when gentlemen faced one another with muskets while audiences of onlookers cheered. But this war had changed everyone's ideas about what was humane. As they advanced on their enemy, GIs were witnessing the results of slaughter and barbarism, the execution of prisoners and the astonishingly inhumane treatment of civilians, the vicious disregard of those rules that, by 1945, seemed a relic of some naïve past. The soldiers had become engulfed in the horror that no one could warn them about, no training could prepare them for. As they began their push into Germany, the war was no longer some adventure for the heroic and the stouthearted. There was evil in the world, and the face of that evil had become more than the newsreel photo of the screaming German dictator with the disheveled hair and the short black mustache. The GI who carried the rifle knew now that the evil was right in front of him, hidden in a bunker, kneeling behind a machine gun, manning an artillery piece. With the Battle of the Bulge behind them, the GIs cared little about secretive Russians and arrogant Frenchmen, about generals and governments. The war was now about them, and the enemy they had to destroy.

PART TWO

The best way to defend is to attack and the best way to attack is to attack. At Chancellorsville, Lee was asked why he attacked when he was outnumbered three to one. He said he was too weak to defend.

—GEORGE PATTON

20. BENSON

The 106th had been put back into action, though the division's rifle-toting infantry was only a single regiment, the 424th, the one regiment that had avoided mass capture in the Ardennes. The undersized 106th was now attached to the 99th Division, its former neighbor during the chaotic battles of December. The Ninety-ninth had suffered enormous casualties as well, but most of that division's structure was still in place. Until the decision was made to rejuvenate the 422nd and 423rd regiments with fresh replacements, the veterans of those units who had survived would become part of the 424th.

Benson had accepted the new orders with the same shrug of indifference that most of the veterans felt. Despite the early training in the States that emphasized unit loyalty, those cheerleading officers who instilled the rah-rah enthusiasm for their unit's symbols, the veterans had learned to appreciate loyalty of a different sort. Benson was no different. When the new assignments came, he had been nervously grateful that Higgins was still his sergeant, and that Kenny Mitchell would remain in the same squad. By now the others in the squad had become somewhat familiar, mainly from their shared experiences during the brief push into Stavelot. But others were there as well, men who had been listed as *missing in action,* no longer missing. As the officers sorted through the mess of reorganizing the 424th, stragglers had continued to appear, some of whom Benson had known from their first days in action. The officers encouraged the sergeants to seek out men they had known before, and Higgins had obeyed. Among the orphans was one of those men captured on that one awful day in that one small village. The man whose obnoxious bullying had given Benson so many hours of misery had suddenly returned. George Lane had been held by the Germans for at least two weeks, but with the collapse of German momentum, he had managed to escape, along with scattered pockets of troops all across the Ardennes. Many of those had never returned, some stumbling into German patrols, blown up by mines and booby traps, or lost in ways no one might ever know. But a fortunate few had trickled through the American lines, singly or in small groups. They had survived mostly off the spoils scrounged from dead soldiers whose uniforms no longer mattered. K rations had become a treasure, stale bread and cans of sardines retrieved from frozen corpses with desperate relief.

When Lane first arrived in the new encampment, Benson didn't recognize him, the man's face thin and deathly pale, even the newly issued uniform hanging loosely on the man's bones. Lane's attitude had changed as well, his voice quieter, his demeanor tempered by weeks of so much astounding horror. It was the same with all of them. Higgins was still the man in charge, who seemed to know more and understand more about what was happening around them than any of the officers who flitted in and out of the encampments. Benson had not worried about the sergeant as he had some of the others, wondering if anyone else was suffering through the same plague he was, wide-eyed sleepless nights, the nightmares, blood and bodies and running desperately to survive some unidentifiable beast. Mitchell had revealed nothing, no sign of weakness, no hint he wasn't still eager to kill Germans, and so Benson kept his nightmares to himself.

On February 3, the orders had come, passing through the regiment like a shock wave. The word came down to the mostly new lieutenants that they were being called upon to do it again. Nobody really knew what *it* was, beyond advancing eastward, assuming a position along the area just west of the Siegfried line, the place where, on December 16, much of the German assault had begun. The shock of being called back into action seemed to affect the entire regiment, rumors and low talk, an unmistakable dread that flowed mostly from the veterans. Most of the riflemen of the 106th had seen the same horror that every combat soldier sees, but there was a difference from the soldiers in the other divisions like the 30th and the 2nd. They had fought the same enemy, had absorbed the same unstoppable thrust, some units striking back with far more effectiveness and skill than the 106th. No cheerleading from the young officers could erase the stain that many of the men around Benson felt deep inside, buried in that place where each man tried to hold to his own courage. Like the others, Benson knew that they had been beaten, a thorough thrashing at the hands of a relentless enemy. No one spoke of it officially, no reprimand had come from the army. To many, it was just fate, the 106th in the wrong place at the wrong time. The senior officers far to the rear had said nothing at all, and Benson wondered about the brass, the men who gave the orders and then disappeared into their comfortable headquarters. Do they describe what happened to us as the enemy's *good strategy*? He had heard talk of that, that the 106th had been the victim of excellent planning, the Germans attacking in a weak spot, the thinly stretched lines of a fresh division that had never seen combat. But Benson felt it, saw it on the faces of the others. These men had met the enemy, and the enemy had prevailed. When the new orders came, no one felt confident that the Germans they would confront again had suddenly become weaker. The officers put a positive face on the new deployment, that they were going to get another opportunity, what their new lieutenant called their *redemption*. It was Higgins who had stopped Mitchell from knocking out the man's teeth.

The cold had not changed, but the uniforms and coats were new. They had snowsuits now, wonderfully white camouflage, though already, one wave of warm weather had stripped away much of the snow, the daylight sunshine turning the hillsides to pools of half-frozen mush. But the thaw had slipped again into the deep hole of winter, snow-covered roads now sheets of ice. Benson had seen it for himself, tanks suddenly sliding to one side, burying deeply into the slush of a snow-filled ditch. Once they were positioned forward again, the men had struggled one more time, as they had struggled weeks before, chopping through frozen ground to dig their foxholes. Once again they were the front line, once again the holes swallowed them with mud and misery. Little else had changed, except for the complete lack of Germany artillery attacks. Even as the men marched forward into the forest, along chewed-up pathways and ice-covered trails, the Germans had offered no response at all. But the woods and valleys around them were far from silent. American artillery had moved up in heavy support, some of the same units from the 106th Division that had barely salvaged their guns from the desperate defense of St. Vith. The tank destroyers had come as well, a much greater force than had been attached to the infantry before. Benson had passed by one platoon of the Wolverines, which seemed at first glance to be just more tanks. But unlike the Sherman, whose armament was no match in a duel with the German armor, the Wolverine carried a three-inch cannon that had one purpose: to penetrate the armor of the vastly superior German machines. As they marched past, Benson felt a strange mix of relief and pride. We have better weapons now, he thought, and more of them. And we're advancing. This time, it means they'll be waiting for *us*.

NEAR LOSHEIMERGRABEN, GERMANY
FEBRUARY 7, 1945

Benson huddled low in the muddy hole, his boots covered by the bulky overshoes. Above him, streaks of fire lit the early-morning sky, the new routine, a barrage of artillery from American guns, aimed at targets the infantry had not yet seen. Beside him, Mitchell huddled low as well, sat with his hands over his ears, his mouth wide open. It was a new piece of training, word handed down that an open mouth during an artillery barrage would lessen the likelihood of hearing loss. Benson's mouth was open as well, no reason to ignore what seemed to be someone's rare dose of common sense. The thought flashed through his mind, Yunis, the useless soldier, the man left behind weeks ago in their retreat. If he was still alive, he wouldn't have any problem with his ears. Since he never stopped screaming, his mouth was always open.

Benson tried to ignore the shivering vibrations in the ground around him, knew the shelling would last for thirty minutes. Like clockwork, it ended abruptly, the echoes still rolling through the hills. He looked up, a hint of light gray in the sky, heard men emerging from their holes, a new day beginning. Benson stood slowly, peered out, nothing at all but thick fog and tall thin trees. To the right was a deep ravine, and the officers had brought word that the remnants of the 106th would serve as the First Army's far right flank. Benson looked out that way, the ground falling away sharply toward a bowl of fog. He knew only what Higgins had told him, that somewhere *right out there* was an outpost of their neighbor to the south, the Eighty-seventh Division. The Eighty-seventh was the left flank of the Third Army, a wonderful boost for the morale of the men around

Benson who had learned to hate this endless forest. The Eighty-seventh belonged to Patton, and Benson had wondered about those men, how different they might be. Rumors had flown, talk of men wearing neckties in
foxholes, of Patton's legendary fury, levying cash fines on men who removed helmets, throwing officers into the stockade for little or no reason,
just to emphasize his own authority. But others had different feelings
about Patton. If the men of the 106th spoke little about Courtney Hodges,
the man who was still their most senior officer, they talked a great deal
about Patton. Benson felt the same as many of the others around him.
Now that they were fighting beside Patton's men, they might become better for it. He had been supremely curious about that, wanted to go down
into the ravine and speak to those men, couldn't help feeling the odd mys-
tique about someone who took orders from Old Blood and Guts. It was a
common topic now that no one shared with the new lieutenant. Would
Patton have allowed the Germans to bust us in the mouth and then keep
going?

He looked at Mitchell, saw the K-ration box coming out of Mitchell's
backpack, felt his own hunger, and now, above them, the voice of Higgins.

"No, you jackass. There's a kitchen truck back here. Came up early last
night. Save the K rations. We've got hot food. Let's go."

They crawled out quickly, followed Higgins back through the trees,
slow going, thick mud holding fast to the overshoes. Benson saw the others falling into line, Higgins leading them up close. The smells from the
truck were disappointingly mild, and Benson saw a steaming container of
oatmeal, one man with a large ladle. There was bread as well, dark and
dense, but the one luscious smell found him now, the coffee. They filled
their plates, moved away, back toward the ridgeline.

Mitchell, ahead of him, waited for Benson to move alongside, said,
"My mother made the worst damn oatmeal in the world. You could wad
that stuff up and make fish bait out of it. Didn't even need a hook. If the
fish ever ate it, they'd choke to death. I promised myself I'd never have to
eat that crap ever again. And lookee here. God, I love the army."

Benson wanted to laugh, was never sure if Mitchell was kidding, no
smile escaping to betray the man's mood.

Behind him, Higgins said, "Eat quick. This stuff gets cold, it turns to
concrete. We're moving out pretty soon."

Benson saw other men from the squad gathering, the inevitable questions.

"Where we going, Sarge?"

"They pulling us out?"

Higgins shook his head, the usual look of disgust.

"They didn't give us new uniforms and equipment and send us out here just so we could have a damn reunion party. We've got work to do in front of us. The enemy's moving around out there, and the whole regiment has been ordered to push forward. That's all I know."

Higgins stuffed a piece of bread in his mouth, moved away toward his own foxhole. Benson did the same, trying to swallow the oatmeal, which was already cold. Mitchell beat him back to the foxhole, jumped down, retrieved his backpack, said, "I got eight damn boxes of K-rations. Swapped my cigarettes for a few cans of C rations too. You don't have to have brains to learn from your mistakes. You better load up the same way."

Benson jumped down, opened up his backpack, felt a measure of satisfaction. Yep. *Brains.*

"Well, for your information, I scrounged up about twenty chocolate bars to go with the K rations."

"Good. You'll have something to offer any *frauleins* we run into. We get cut off, you'll try to survive on candy bars and I'll have actual food."

Benson's balloon deflated, and he thought, dammit, why are you always right? Mitchell reached out, slapped Benson's helmet, the closest thing to outright affection he ever showed. To one side, the rest of the squad was checking their equipment, and beyond, the rest of the company up and around, doing the same. They had a new captain now, a short, squat stump of a man named Horne, who had been a part of the 424th from the beginning. He was the only veteran officer on their part of the line, and Benson saw their platoon commander, the new lieutenant, Williamson, standing tall, watching them prepare.

Mitchell leaned low, said, "That guy's a wiener. I just know it. So damn full of his own authority, and he's never seen any of this before. *Ninety-day wonder* is too generous."

Williamson had introduced himself to his new platoon with a proud burst of self-congratulations by announcing that he was a West Pointer. To most of the men, West Pointers were a good thing to have *back there,* the generals who called the shots. But out here, Williamson seemed too eager to believe that his elite training alone would drive the enemy away. Benson appraised the man, standing erect, hands on his hips, two pistols in his belt.

Mitchell said, "He thinks he's Patton. I guaran-damn-tee you he heard about the general's two pistols, had to have the same thing for himself. To hell with him. You and me, we stick close to the sarge. I learned that lesson already."

It was a rare compliment coming from Mitchell, and Benson searched for the sergeant, saw him a few yards away, checking his ammo belt, counting to himself. Benson took the cue, did the same, a dozen. Good. I hope that's good, anyway. He tossed the backpack up to the hard ground, retrieved his rifle, scanned it for mud, felt for the four grenades hanging from his jacket, beneath the heavy coat. He took a deep breath, tried to calm his stomach, the same tight ball he felt every time anyone talked about seeing the enemy. Out across the ridgeline, the daylight had barely broken the fog, the trees endless, fading into a ghostly gray.

"Guess I'm ready to go."

Mitchell climbed up out of the hole, sat on the side, did his own check, hoisted the backpack onto his shoulders, then stood. The men were gathering, the sergeants taking charge, and Mitchell said, "I guess we're all ready. Wonder what in hell they're making us do?"

The rifle fire was scattered, mostly to one side, the men slipping low through the trees. Far out in front Benson heard a machine gun, short bursts. But there was nothing aimed at them, no whistles or cracks or slaps against the trees. They had gone about a quarter mile, and through it all Benson kept his eye on Higgins. The sergeant watched the lieutenant, Williamson, who stepped through the wet snow with a pistol in his hand. The lieutenant held them up with a sharp hand signal, turned toward them, settled his back against a tree. He slid around, stared ahead, nothing to see, fog and more trees, motioned impatiently to Lane, the man designated to carry the walkie-talkie.

Lane stood close, and the lieutenant took the heavy green box, spoke into the mouthpiece. "Boone Two. Boone Two."

The walkie-talkie crackled, too loud, Benson flinching. The lieutenant cursed, fumbled with the volume knob, listened to a voice on the other end, responded.

"Roger, Boone Two. No reception from Willy yet. Hogan Four needs to keep up on our right."

The conversation ended quickly, the lieutenant seeming pleased at his assertiveness. Benson had learned that each platoon was identified over the walkie-talkie by the name of its leader. Boone and Hogan were lieutenants as well, their men spread out through the woods on either side. Williamson returned the walkie-talkie to Lane, slipped out from behind the tree, waved the men forward. The fog was swirling past them, a cold wet mist, the woods blind. The rifle fire was still far away, and nothing more came from the machine gun. Benson probed the knot in his stomach, kept himself abreast of Mitchell, his eyes focused to the front, searching the soft gray, felt himself shaking. His eyes searched every dark place, every tree, any sign of movement, a rifle barrel, a helmet. The fear was growing, rolling up inside him. He gripped the rifle with stiff fingers, angry at himself, wanted to say something to Mitchell, felt his legs growing stiff as well. His breaths came in short bursts, and he stopped, his legs heavy, immobile, his eyes scanning frantically. His brain began to speak to him, right out there, a flash of something! He jerked his head to the side, snow and more fog, another flicker of movement, gone now. He wanted to raise the rifle, saw a small bush, and beyond, nothing at all. The men around him were still moving, slow deliberate steps, no one reacting at all, nothing to see. They kept the proper space between each man, the good work of the sergeants. Benson watched them moving away, and he tried to move his legs, a block of ice in his chest holding him paralyzed, the shivering growing worse, uncontrollable now. The fear had consumed him, and he started to cry, one part of his brain furious, yelling at him to get control. He lowered his head, wouldn't let Mitchell see, felt utterly ashamed. Why are you doing this? You coward! Stop this! There was a hand on his arm, startling him. It was Higgins.

"Come on, kid. Keep moving."

He nodded, couldn't talk, wouldn't look at the sergeant, felt humiliated, forced his legs into motion, followed Higgins closely, moved back into the formation. No one spoke, the silence broken only by the distant fire, the soft muffled footsteps, and the sudden crackle of the walkie-talkie.

"Dammit! Shut that thing up!"

Benson knew Mitchell's voice, the hot harsh whisper. Up front, the lieutenant was fumbling with the walkie-talkie again, pretended to ignore the fury of the men behind him. He knelt beside a tree, spoke into the mouthpiece.

"Boone Two. This is Williamson Three. Are you still inside the trees?" The crackle came again.

The lieutenant suddenly straightened, said quietly, "Yes, sir. Roger, sir. Williamson Three out."

He handed the walkie-talkie to Lane beside him, glanced back at the men closest to him, the men who might have overheard, and Benson realized, somebody just told him to shut the hell up. He wanted to laugh, the fear giving way to something else, uncontrollable, the lieutenant's expression as funny as anything Benson had seen. He lowered his head, the low laughter escaping, felt men moving closer, Mitchell there.

"What's the hell's the matter with you?"

Benson couldn't speak, Mitchell's description of the lieutenant rising up in his mind, *wiener,* the laughter starting to overwhelm him, quivering hysteria, and he clenched his arms in tight, tried to control it, keeping the laughter silent.

Higgins was close to him, leaned low, said, "What is it? You going nuts on us?"

"What's this man's problem, Sergeant?"

Benson knew it was Williamson, fought for control, the laughter fading, aching in his chest, spasms, tears coming again, nothing funny, more crying, infuriating.

Higgins said, "I'll take care of it, sir. We're okay here."

"I won't have any slacking off. No stragglers. You got that, Sergeant?"

The lieutenant moved away, and Higgins gave Benson's shoulder a hard shake. "Get hold of it, kid."

Benson glanced at Mitchell, saw painful concern.

Mitchell said, "I got him, Sarge. He's just scared. We're all scared."

Benson had calmed, the strange hysteria passing, and he said to Higgins, "I'm sorry, Sarge. It's just . . . the lieutenant. He's just such a . . ." The word wouldn't come, and Benson looked at Mitchell, expected him to end the sentence.

But Mitchell was no part of the joke, was staring ahead, the others already stepping forward. Mitchell said, "It's okay, Eddie. I'm having a tough time too. Stay close, we'll be all right. It'd be better if somebody starts shooting at us. Keep us from thinking."

Benson pondered that, stared out into the fog, nodded.

"Yeah. I hadn't thought of that."

"Just don't go all loony. Might need you to pull my ass out of a jam."

"Yeah, sure. Sorry."

Mitchell seemed to wait for him, and Benson saw men behind them, another platoon, another company, another wave. They stopped, held up by their own lieutenant, keeping distance from the men in front of them, the good training. Benson felt guilty, stupid, thought, what the hell's the matter with me? The shaking was gone, the cold knot loosening, and he checked the rifle, flexed his numb fingers, began to move again.

The mortar shells came in to one side, sudden blasts that severed a tall tree, a hard scream from a wounded man. Benson dropped flat in the icy snow, more shells falling behind them, shouts from men he couldn't see, the loud crack of another tree coming apart. The silence came, the pause, and there was a distinctive *pop,* then another, out in front, and he heard Higgins, "Let's go! Forward! They're right in front of us!"

The blasts came again, the mortar shells coming down farther behind them, and Benson was crawling, furious motion, moved to a tree, the others doing the same, some gathering in clusters. The *pop*s came again, and Benson understood. It was the German mortars, the only sound you could hear until the shell arced down and impacted. He watched Higgins, saw him peer up slightly, white-covered helmet, then back down. Higgins began to crawl forward, Benson watching, waiting for some sign.

A whisper from Mitchell, "What's he doing?"

Benson ached to look, Higgins still moving forward, out of sight, silence, and now the *pop* again. Higgins's rifle suddenly opened up, and quickly others joined him. Benson rolled around the tree, rifle up, searching. He saw them now, a low shelter, a white canvas tarp. Men were moving away, Germans, running, and beside him Mitchell was firing. Benson searched frantically for a target, any movement, a flicker of dark, and he fired the rifle, and then again. All through the woods, the men around Williamson began to rise up, a mad scramble forward, the mortar crews scampering away. Higgins was already beside the mortars, flattening out, searching the woods beyond, other men coming up beside him. To the left, a machine gun erupted, streak of fire going past them, too high, more rifle fire, straight ahead. Benson flattened out, no cover, Mitchell on his knees, quick shots from the M-1, the empty clip clinking out, Mitchell down, reloading.

"They took off! Dammit, I missed!"

Voices came now, more of the Americans in the woods to the left, machine-gun fire that way, the thumping blast of a grenade. The men around

Benson continued to move forward, Williamson waving to them, the lieutenant up close to the mortars, examining them, their prize. The men seemed to let down, good cover in the German mortar position. Benson heard the low excited chatter, some men still searching beyond for some sign of the enemy. The machine gun to the left was silenced, loud voices out that way, more scattered rifle fire. Benson drifted away from the cluster of white-clad soldiers, felt uneasy, the fear again. He moved out to the right, to one side of the mortar position, still the fog, silence, saw slices of black in the snow, an uneven line dug out through the woods. And then, a flicker of motion. He stared, frozen, saw it again, wanted to say something, tell Mitchell, but the men were behind him, focused on the mortar, others still firing their rifles, seeking targets beyond, nervous chatter, loud cursing. Benson raised the rifle slowly, his heart cold thunder, caught the outline of a helmet, then another, *a foxhole,* one man peering up at the gathering around the mortars. *They don't see me.* Both men started to climb up, one holding a machine pistol, pointing it toward the cluster of men. Benson aimed, no thinking, pulled the trigger, the rifle jolting him, the man falling. The other man was up and out of the hole, began to run, clumsy, stumbling, and Benson fired again, then twice more, the man collapsing in the snow. Behind Benson men were reacting with surprise, hints of panic, bursts of rifle fire at unseen targets, voices directed toward him. He ignored the commotion, his brain locked on the ground in front of him, and he stared at the black slits, rips in the ground. He crouched low, the rifle pointed forward, searching for movement, nothing. He was close to the fallen men now, and one of them began to move slowly, a hard groan. Benson stepped closer, the man a few feet away, an oozing black trail in the snow behind him. The German's helmet fell off, and Benson saw the dirty face, turning toward him, the eyes wide, low desperate grunts, the man still trying to crawl away. Benson aimed at the man's head and fired once more.

He stood alone, silence in his brain, the rifle aimed, his finger on the trigger, still ready. The silence opened up now, cold air in his lungs, movement behind him, the voice of Higgins.

"Holy Christ. Any more?"

Higgins moved past him, searching, slipping up quickly on the other foxholes, but they were empty, their occupants already pulling away. Benson said nothing, felt others moving up close to him, a hard slap on his back. Lane, close to his face, "Well, get your damn trophies!"

Benson didn't understand.

Lane said, "Well, hell, if you ain't gonna do it, I damn sure will!"

Lane moved to one of the bodies, rolled the man over, other men doing the same to the second German. They were ripping through the uniforms, snatching off insignia, rifling through pockets. One man held up a piece of paper, said, "This one's got a letter. All German gibberish."

The man stuck the letter in his pocket, the others chattering about their finds, and Williamson was there, booming voice, "Back off, men. No looting. We've still got work to do. Nice job, soldier."

Benson realized the lieutenant was talking to him, and he had no energy to respond, turned away, had seen enough of the bodies, of the men grabbing for loot.

Higgins walked toward him, holding up the machine pistol, said, "No one's keeping this. Can't shoot it, it'll draw fire. Anyone gets captured with a Kraut weapon's gonna get clobbered for it." The sergeant didn't wait for any approval from the lieutenant, heaved the pistol far into the woods. There were mild protests, but the men knew that Higgins was right. The sergeant moved up close to Benson now, a cold stare, measuring, said to Williamson, "I told you, sir. He's fine."

The lieutenant moved away. "Make sure you get his name. I want some medals for this platoon. That's one for sure. Let's get moving."

Higgins glanced toward the lieutenant, no change of expression, and Benson felt queasy, wanted to move away from the dead Germans.

Mitchell, behind him, no smile, said, "Good going, Eddie. You might have saved our asses."

"I don't want a medal."

"The looey? Ignore that moron."

Higgins moved past the men admiring their German emblems, stuffing pockets with their prizes.

"You idiots shag your asses forward. And just remember, any of you gets hit, the Krauts are gonna tear your crap apart the same way." He looked at Benson again. "You sure you're okay?"

Benson felt like crying again, but there were no tears, no energy in him at all. He watched the others moving away, following the lieutenant, saw men huddled at the mortars, disabling them, saw the cold stare from Mitchell.

"I guess so, Sarge. We better keep up."

Higgins seemed satisfied, stepped through the snow, a last glance back at him.

"Good job."

Benson followed him, Mitchell beside him. Mitchell said, "Reload. You shot up most of your clip."

"Hell of a thing, Kenny."

"Hell of a good thing, kiddo."

They had reached a wider roadway, more troops moving together, the advance easier now. The woods had thinned considerably, though the hills and valleys still rolled out in front of them, a patchwork of snow and black earth. They had heard the tanks from a long way off, word coming through the walkie-talkie that American armored units were moving tank destroyers in ahead of them, more of the precious Wolverines. On the road, Williamson had spoken to a tank commander, and the tankers had been cooperative, the heavy machines slowing, moving at the pace of the infantry. No one needed to hear the instructions from Williamson to understand that the armor offered a stout screen of cover against any Germans who might be waiting ahead. More tanks and tank destroyers were arriving, some spreading out onto flatter ground, some allowing infantry to ride up on the steel. On the road, the jeeps were coming up, officers ordering men back down, no encumbrance needed for any armored vehicle that might suddenly need a quick maneuver. Benson was content marching behind a Wolverine, didn't mind the stink of diesel. The vehicle offered cover, certainly, but even better, the exhaust was warm.

They had been in the road for nearly a mile, the roar of the tank destroyers drowning out the sounds of what might be happening off in the distance. There had been some fierce German resistance, small pockets mostly around the farms and villages, rear-guard patrols whose only job was to slow down the American advance. Often it was a single sniper, one carefully aimed shot at a tank commander, carelessly standing tall in his turret. If a tank suddenly went out of commission, it could send a whole company of infantry scattering into the woods. By the time the officers gained control and pushed a patrol into the village, the enemy would be gone. There were other dangers as well. In their retreat, the Germans had mined many of the roads, had left booby traps and trip-wired grenades.

Even with engineers leading the way, the blasts had echoed back along the line. Benson had felt the thumping vibration beneath his feet, some machine up ahead suddenly erupting into black smoke. The column had halted, nervous officers pushing the men reluctantly into the snowy field, preparing them for some sudden surprise thrust from the Germans that had not yet come. The open fields made every man nervous, and Benson had seen why. The Germans had placed trip wires haphazardly, seemingly at random, grenades buried in small holes beneath the snow. One blast had lifted a man several feet in the air, a spray of red fire where the man's legs came apart. The medics were there quickly, but the sight backed many of the men out of the field, whether their officers approved or not. Despite the armor that led the way, Benson was as jittery as the men around him, moving in slow cautious steps, eyes downward for any sign of disturbed earth, anything out of place, any hint of a wire. Any bush or low brush was given a wide berth, as were the sudden trails of souvenirs, German helmets and rifles, some standing upright, their bayonets jabbed into the ground. The sergeants were furious in their warnings, but there were always the fools, a sudden thumping blast echoing behind Benson, someone's grab for a trophy getting him killed. They were passing scattered farmhouses now, and few objected when they were ordered off limits. Benson stepped past one now and understood why. The medics had gathered, moving around a row of litters in the front yard, some dragging out the remains of a squad of men who had swarmed through the house in search of some ridiculous treasure, and had obviously stumbled into a well-hidden bomb. Benson thought of the house in that one village, where Lane had been captured, the family hiding in their cellar. We took their food, and never thought the place could have been booby-trapped. He looked at the house as he moved past, blown-out windows, a wisp of black smoke rising through a ragged hole in the roof. I guess somebody's checking the cellars, but I bet these folks are long gone. They were right in the middle of the war. Still are. He glanced back at the litters in the yard, the bodies of the GIs covered with dirty cloth. For what? Wine? Trinkets?

Williamson moved through his men now, a needless reminder to keep their eyes and their movement forward. Benson saw his face, the man clearly bothered by the sight of the carnage, by the fear of more. He looked straight at Benson, a flicker of recognition.

"Keep to the road! Any one of my men tries that stupidity, any one of you picks up any booty, and I'll have you in the stockade!"

The threat was meaningless, but the men did not react, most very happy to stay close to the growling tank destroyer. Benson watched the lieutenant return to the front of the line, thought, just where the hell would that stockade be out here?

Benson was feeling hungry, knew it had to be midday, the fog mostly gone, low blankets of white only in the lowest valleys. Mitchell was beside him, Sergeant Higgins somewhere behind, tending to someone's injury, a sprained ankle, some annoying delay. There had been bitching from some of the others, but Benson had said nothing at all. Weeks before, Higgins had saved his life because he wouldn't leave Benson behind. If he wants to do that for someone else in the squad, fine.

The tank destroyer suddenly stopped, a single belch of black smoke blowing over the men, coughs and curses. Benson heard voices, the crackle of a radio, and Williamson moved forward, joined the voices up in front of the Wolverine. Now the sounds came, loud and low, sweeping overhead. Benson caught the reflection of silver, a vast swarm of planes, and the men dropped low, but Benson already knew, said aloud, "P-47s!"

He tried to see where they were heading, a few rising up beyond some of the far trees, then swooping down behind a hill, only to rise up again. The machine-gun fire came now, strafing runs, another formation coming in low behind him, wonderfully frightening. He eased around the Wolverine, one hand on the steel treads, saw the hillside more clearly, the planes moving about in all directions. There were bursts of fire from the hillside, hidden anti-aircraft guns, but not hidden well enough. More planes roared up from behind, their machine guns chattering. Benson was searching for the targets when suddenly there was the tinkle of metal on the tank destroyer, men yelping, some shouting out.

"I'm hit!"

"Take cover!"

Benson squatted close beside the steel machine, heard the strange ringing sound, saw bits of brass, bouncing, plopping down onto the icy roadway. He looked up, the plane already gone, more coming up behind, making their runs, and Benson felt relief, laughter, reached for the brass, a scattering of spent shells, fifty-caliber, from the guns of the P-47s. He held one up, called out behind him, "It's okay! It's ours!"

The others were figuring it out now, men grabbing the unique souvenirs, cheers erupting. The crew of the Wolverine had opened their hatches, watching the show as well, more than a dozen of the fighter planes swarming all across the rolling hills in front of them. Some were making bombing runs, the hills erupting into blasts of smoke and fire, more strafing from the deadly machine-gun fire. And just that quickly they were gone.

They had passed by the clusters of mostly broken anti-aircraft guns, the bodies of their crews scattered around them, or gone altogether. The smoke still rolled up out of the targets, and all across the low hills, the soldiers continued their march, slow and methodical, lead scouts moving out front to the low-slung hillside that stretched all across their advance. Benson could see more than brush and earth, could make out the concrete bunkers, flat walls topped with earth or camouflage, German bunkers dug right into the hillsides. As he moved closer, he saw the slits cut all through the massive slabs of gray concrete, like so many narrow black eyes, hollow and empty, watching them come. But there was no firing, the gun ports empty, and he watched as the lead squads clambered quickly up and over, some disappearing into narrow passageways between the hulking structures. There was some rifle fire, far to the right, but in front nothing at all, the entire company easing forward in anxious silence, searching for any sign the enemy was still there. Benson stepped in rhythm to the men around him, saw a man up on top of a bunker, holding a satchel charge, easing along, and Benson thought, that's what I'd do. Drop a handful of grenades into every one of those openings. Take no chances. His brain was spewing out words, the nervousness shared with the men around him, and now more men began to appear up on top of the enormous concrete slabs, hands in the air, what seemed to Benson to be careless exuberance. There was a voice behind him, the company commander, talking on a radio, a jeep coming up quickly, and Williamson called out, gathering his platoon. Benson responded, the men still eyeing the massive concrete walls, so close now, and Williamson held the walkie-talkie, stared back toward the jeep, seemed to be waiting for an order. The walkie-talkie crackled, Williamson listening with wide eyes, then he waved his hand, still holding the pistol, pointed toward the bunker.

"Advance! All clear!"

Benson began to move with the others, the tank destroyers and tanks moving out to one side, following the main road, some word passing through that the engineers had blown openings through the bunkers that the armor could use. He began to climb the low hill, saw Higgins drop down into a trench, then back up again, and Benson could see the trenches spread all along the base of the hill. He stepped down through crushed and broken barbed wire, some engineer's good work, then climbed back up out of the trench. The concrete wall was close in front of him now, more than ten feet high, the gun ports above his head. To one side, he heard a series of thundering blasts, and the men reacted, dropped low, Benson pushing up close to the cold concrete. The smoke rose up several hundred yards away.

Williamson called out, "That's ours! The engineers are blowing gaps in the tank traps! Here! Come this way. There's an opening."

The men obeyed, began to file up between two steep walls, a flattened footpath, part of the bunker's design. Benson waited for the men to move through, and up in the wall, in a narrow slit right above him, a man's head appeared, a happy shout, "You boys come on in! The Krauts done skedaddled! We've got this place to ourselves!"

All along most of the West Wall, the Germans had made a good fight of it, making good use of the enormous defensive advantages, the bunkers heavily armed and manned with troops grateful to be out of the open woods. Though the armies had struggled over this line for several weeks, particularly along Patton's position in the south, ultimately the Germans could not sustain their defensive shield with the diminishing manpower and matériel they could bring to the fight. Despite Hitler's stubborn reluctance to give any ground at all, Model and von Rundstedt understood that no concrete wall was mighty enough to hold back what the Allies were pushing their way. The German commanders continued to insist that the army should be pulled back completely, that their best opportunity for a successful defensive fight lay along the east banks of the Rhine, but Hitler would not concede so much German territory without first making a stand. And so the Allies could not be content with their conquest of what SHAEF called the Siegfried line. The enemy was still dangerous, and even though the Allied armies were continuing to drive them farther back into their own territory, no village was safe, no fence line or cluster of forest could be ignored. The war was not yet over.

21. EISENHOWER

The new headquarters building was what any small-town American would describe as a *little red schoolhouse*. It seemed an odd choice to some of his staff, but Eisenhower had no interest in anyone's opinions of how his office should present itself. He had grown weary of palaces and mansions, and if some of his senior commanders continued to insist on surrounding themselves with someone else's artifacts of a glorious past, that was fine with him. His requirements were far simpler: an office that had at least one wall for his maps, and a phone that worked.

The argument had grown, the two Englishmen standing a few feet apart, Eisenhower sitting between them. He had been caught off guard by the heat that poured out of each man, though Tedder seemed more in control. It wasn't surprising, the man able to weather most storms he had to suffer through at SHAEF. But Eisenhower had already endured a gutful of the blustery temperament of Arthur Harris, the man everyone called "Bomber." More often now, the staff had adopted a new nickname for the British chief air marshal. They were referring to him as "Butcher."

Harris was speaking, a flow of hot words aimed at Tedder through a pointed finger.

"By damn, Tedder, this war is being won, and I am bloody well sick of the backbiting I've had to listen to. If not for the bomber command, this war would continue for another decade, maybe two. You cannot tell me that the heavy bombers haven't been our most valuable asset. Our raids upon the German's most vital strategic targets have cost him much of his vaunted ability to make war. Is that not appreciated by every fighting man in our collective armies?"

The speech did not back Tedder down. He was as angry as Eisenhower had ever seen him. Eisenhower wanted to interrupt, felt suddenly like a referee in a boxing match, but Tedder's furious expression kept him in his chair.

"Strategic targets? Yes, by all means, I completely agree that we should bomb hell out of every strategic target we can find. Take on every transportation hub, every rail line, every gasoline depot, every ball-bearing plant. Erase them all and this war is over. No argument, there, Arthur. But you are quite glossing over the point!" Tedder's voice was breaking, and he stopped, seemed to choke slightly.

Harris rocked back on his heels, seemed always to strut even when he was standing still. He tried to seem bored, a tactic Eisenhower had seen before, the air of superiority meant to disarm anyone who disagreed with him. With a slight sneer, he said, "What point is that?"

Tedder turned to Eisenhower. "Dammit, Ike, you've seen the daily reports from bomber command. Over the past three days, we have utterly annihilated the city of Dresden. *Someone* decided that incendiary bombs would make for . . . what? A more spectacular bonfire? That's precisely what that city has become. I have no idea what *strategic targets* we were able to destroy but the cost in civilian casualties has to be extraordinary."

Harris sniffed. "*German* civilians. Let us not be blind to the cause of this war, and those who have enabled Hitler's armies to take the field. Let us not be blind to all it has cost us."

Eisenhower flinched, eyed Tedder, knew that Harris was dangerously close to crossing a line that might result in his receiving a broken nose. Tedder reddened further, his hands in a tight clench, and Eisenhower said, "Air Marshal Tedder knows quite well the cost of this war."

Harris seemed to understand where he had gone, retreated, nodded slowly. "Sorry, old chap. Of course you understand."

Eisenhower felt the tension cooling, but only a little. Tedder was still under control, and Eisenhower thought, yes, Bomber, you've shot yourself in both feet.

Tedder had already suffered the death of a son in combat, and soon after, his wife had died in an air crash that he'd witnessed firsthand. The tragedies had seemed to stay with Tedder as a heavy blanket that tempered his moods. But his fury was obvious now, and so, that much more unusual.

Eisenhower had never liked Bomber Harris. He agreed with most of his staff, and many of his generals, who considered him somewhat thick-skulled, a rigid and inflexible man who placed far too much weight on his own importance. Eisenhower's only handicap was that he had to be discreet about it.

After a somewhat calmer moment, Tedder said, "What possible strategic advantage have you handed us by burning the city of Dresden to ashes? What will that say about us to the German people? There are Germans who will survive this war, you know, the people who must eventually replace Hitler. There will come a time when humanitarian concerns rule the day. I fear that by such actions as this Dresden mess, we shall have a far more difficult time making the peace. It cannot possibly be of benefit to us if we are hated by every German civilian."

Harris's arrogance returned. "Those, sir, are your opinions. I have assumed the duty assigned to me by carrying out our primary goal: to end this war by any means necessary, including the killing of as many Germans as we are able. By raining hellfire down on every German city, laying them to ashes if need be, we shall convince the German people that their war is hopelessly lost. I have always maintained that we required little else to win this war, and I believe that now more than ever. If we demonstrate our might, and our will to effect the utter destruction of their cities, we shall disembowel their very will to fight."

Harris seemed pleased with his metaphor, rocked back on his heels again.

Tedder looked at Eisenhower, frustrated, and Eisenhower said, "I cannot dictate the strategic goals of your command, Air Marshal. But fire-bombing German civilians will not sit well with *any* civilians down the road, be they German, British, or American. I can imagine the newspapers are already finding out about Dresden, particularly all those reporters who have an ax to grind with the prime minister or President Roosevelt. None of us needs the kind of grief that will cause."

Harris seemed disgusted, shook his head.

"You are suggesting that one of our chief priorities should be to maintain some sort of artificial moral high ground, and thus, we should fight a gentleman's war, a *kind* war. Bombs do not have eyes, General. We seek out targets that have meaning and allow the bombs to do the work. There is chance in that. My people have been roundly criticized too often that our targets are struck with minimal damage, or missed altogether. It is greatly distressing to me that the loss of our planes and crews continues at a horrible rate. We are changing all of that. The long-range fighters have saved many a bomber crew, and my new policy of area bombing will take much of the chance out of the equation. When we blanket an area completely, when we use incendiary bombs, a direct hit is not required. It must be a glorious fright to those on the ground when the firebombs erupt in a virtual carpet of destruction. And that, sir, is quite the point. If you are not comfortable with killing German civilians, then perhaps both of you are in the wrong business. If I may remind you, the German has had no qualms whatsoever about killing the civilians of every country he has engaged in this war, including our own."

The lecture from Harris had gone beyond annoying, and Eisenhower knew it would go on as long as he allowed it. He stood, said, "Air Marshal Harris, I appreciate your taking the time to present your report in person. It is always a pleasure to see you."

Harris took the cue, seemed satisfied that his explanation was understood.

"Very well. I shall take my leave. You can be sure that this war will end soon, and we who serve the bomber command shall claim our proper share of the credit. Good day, gentlemen."

Harris spun around, marched crisply out of the room. Tedder began to pace, still angry. He glanced toward the door, seemed to wait for Harris to be far out of earshot.

"Bloody arrogant moron. He's going to cost us far more than he's gaining us. And not just him, mind you. Quite a few of those damn bomber barons have no conscience and no sense of history. What they are doing is wrong. I don't care who started this bloody war or how many atrocities Hitler has committed. One day in the future, you and I, and every other commander, air, sea, and land, will have to look himself in the mirror and wonder if what he ordered his men to do was acceptable, just a part of war. I have never questioned my role here, Ike. I've never questioned yours, or any of your people's actions. And I promise you, I am not growing soft. If it were possible, I would stick a bayonet into Hitler's entrails myself. But the mass slaughter of civilians . . . no soldier I know signed on for that." He paused, shook his head. "Doesn't Harris recall what we did in 1919? He was there, for God's sake. We decided it was prudent to *punish* the Germans for their bad acts, and that meant punishing *every* German. We crushed them in every way, in the name of revenge. All we did was open the door for a man like Hitler."

He stopped, moved to a chair, and Eisenhower saw sweat in the man's uniform. Tedder sat, continued, "This will be worse than before, Ike. If we obliterate every German city, just because we can . . . how will the German people regard us? How many more Hitlers will we spawn?"

"Dammit, Arthur, I can't be concerned with that. You know full well that my orders are to steer clear of politics, and so far, I've done a pretty damn good job of it. Besides that, I don't have the authority to tell the bomber barons what they can and cannot target. A year ago, before Normandy, we convinced them to accept your plan, to target the transportation hubs, and it worked. By preventing the Germans from moving their railcars and trucks to the forward lines, we probably saved tens of thousand of Allied lives. And despite Harris's sledgehammer attack on German civilians, our raids on the fuel and transportation centers are still effective. The enemy failed to sustain his drive in the Ardennes as much for a lack of fuel as *our* ability to stop him. Credit the air people for that. They're *your* people, for God's sake."

"I'm not like Harris. I don't agree that we're winning this thing just because of heavy bombers. And I will never accept that extinguishing enormous cities is the most effective way to win a war. It's bad enough that I disagree with his strategy. But it helps not at all that I cannot stand to be in the same room with the man. He's nothing more than a swaggering blivet."

"A what?"

Tedder seemed slightly embarrassed, turned suddenly sheepish.

"Um . . . sorry. Not the most dignified observation I've made here. A *blivet* is best described as a one-pound bag filled with two pounds of horse manure."

Eisenhower couldn't help the smile, reached for a cigarette, saw the stack of folders on his desk.

"Arthur, I have too much to think about right now. And one thing I cannot do is weigh the morality of every decision we're making. That *blivet* is right about one thing. The enemy . . . hell, both enemies, the Germans and the Japanese . . . they're waging war with a complete disregard for what we believe is basic human behavior. So what the hell do we do about that? There's no *turn the other cheek* here, Arthur. My job is to end this war as quickly and as completely as I can. That's why Patton still has his job, and why Monty still has his. If we have to answer to some higher authority down the road, so be it. But I guarantee you, Hitler and his pals will be answering first."

FEBRUARY 17, 1945

Churchill had come again, this time after returning from Yalta, an obscure coastal city in southern Ukraine, on the shores of the Black Sea. What had taken place at Yalta was already the source of every reporter's speculation, and the news that flowed westward was a curious mix of joyous political backslapping and dark warnings of what might follow.

Optimism had followed the participants who attended, the leaders most obviously labeled the Big Three: Roosevelt, Churchill, and Stalin. Their purpose was to begin the specific planning for what would follow the inevitable collapse of Germany. Obvious questions had been raised in diplomatic circles for months, the optimism among civilians far more glowing than what Eisenhower knew to be reality on the battlefields. But the leaders did meet, a weeklong opportunity for all sides to have their say on their expectations and, in some cases, demands for what should become of Germany. Topics ranged from the seriously diplomatic to the most mundane, from concern for the disposition of Germany's leaders to concerns about the German economy and the country's future capability as an industrial and military power. The most optimistic returned to their own capitals with the satisfied sense of accomplishment, that what had been contemplated at Yalta would mark the first step in what would become a New World Order. Eisenhower had been curious about just what kinds of plans the heads of state considered so worthwhile, and how much of that would actually be borne out by the events to come. He was, after all, still fighting a war.

Eisenhower poured the brandy snifter nearly full, reached it carefully across the desk. Churchill did not look up, slid thick fingers under the bowl of the snifter, then paused, motionless, seemed completely lost in thought. Eisenhower didn't know what to say, and so he said nothing at all.

After a long moment, Churchill raised the glass, looked at Eisenhower with deep sagging eyes, said, "I suppose we should offer a toast. To the New World Order."

Eisenhower detected sarcasm, heard no enthusiasm in the words. He raised the glass.

"If you say so."

Churchill tilted his head, a piercing stare.

"Why do you say that?"

"No reason. Not sure what you're asking me. Just responding to your toast, I suppose. I meant no offense."

Churchill drank from the glass, leaned back in the chair.

"No, I know you didn't. You're not the type of man to rub salt in the wound."

Eisenhower tried to interpret Churchill's mood, thought, nope, just shut up. He'll tell you soon enough. Churchill seemed less interested than usual in the brandy, lit a cigar, pulled it from his mouth, looked at it closely, set it down in the ashtray.

"Nothing tastes good these days. Not since I got back anyway." He squinted at Eisenhower. "You don't know what the hell I'm talking about, do you?"

"Yalta."

"Yes, for God's sake, Yalta. Don't play with me, Ike."

"No . . . I assure you . . ."

"You know what happened at Yalta?"

"I've seen some of the reports. But you know I try to stay out of those diplomatic minefields. I'm not in charge of anything beyond this theater of the war. I like it that way."

"Apparently, you're *in charge* of a great deal more than I am. I spent a week in the company of your president and Uncle Joe Stalin, and the first observation I could make was that the British Empire has all the political influence of a tick on a dog's backside. I've always tried to be blunt with you, Ike. I believe you're an honest man, and I've never seen you involve yourself in the nasty side of this. All that good stuff that Shakespeare so relied upon, men who carry knives around, hidden away, awaiting that delicious opportunity to plunge the blade into the back of a friend." He paused, still ignored the brandy. "I love Franklin. Truly do. I don't think he would ever betray me. He didn't, actually. But I sat there, with Uncle Joe on one side and your president on the other, and watched them carve out the future of our world. I might as well have been the damn waiter, filling up their vodka glasses. It was a painful lesson, Ike. Painful. I knew better than to take it personally. No, it wasn't intended as an insult to me, no one decided that I shouldn't really be there. The problem is . . . England. It was apparent to me that those two men feel that England no longer has a place at the big table. The decisions made there were horrific, Ike. Horrific and stupid. Devastating to the lives of millions, and no one seems to understand that. And when I tried to tell them, to point out the flaws in what they were suggesting, I was . . . dismissed, ignored. Your president was captivated by Stalin, enraptured, seduced by him. That's such a mystery to me, because, frankly, Uncle Joe isn't anyone's idea of a charmer. But Franklin went to Yalta carrying the advice of your statesmen in Washington, your diplomats, the men who believe that peace will bring . . . what? Happiness for all? Joy and flowers and singing birds? And Stalin knew just how to play that, saying all the right things, boosting Roosevelt's pride. It was . . . distressing to watch." He paused, sipped the brandy. "Hitler is certainly done for, just a matter of time. No one knows that more than you do, of course. Yes, yes, don't give me any protests, General. I know all about your caution. Fine. It's all necessary. God knows that Nazi maniac could still come up with some oddball secret weapon that tosses all our optimism in the dustbin. But I don't believe it, even if you have to. This war will end, and it will end this year. And it will not be pleasant and it will not be glorious, and dammit Ike, we will have no right to be *proud*."

Eisenhower felt overwhelmed by Churchill's unexpected gloom.

"I'm sorry, sir, but I really don't understand . . ."

"I'm not insulting our soldiers, Ike. They will have every right to wear their uniforms and their medals, and go home knowing they kicked hell out of the most evil sons of bitches the world has ever seen. Not here to insult your president either. I'm not stupid, you know. Don't want to make you all defensive. But if you'd have been there, you'd have seen it for yourself. The Russians have an agenda that is far more . . . oh hell, what's the word? Sinister? Yes, that's a good one. Sinister. Uncle Joe went to Yalta knowing exactly what he wanted, and by damn, he got it. Germany will be divided up, carved up like a beef roast. Fine, I can't say I'm terribly upset by that. But Stalin wants so much more, and Franklin did nothing to stand in his way. There are people right now in Washington who believe that when the war ends, Russian troops will treat this great victory exactly as we will, that their armies will do just what *we* will do: They will all march home to grateful families, so many proud warriors who have eradicated the world's evil, and just like in Washington and New York and London, the streets of Moscow will be filled with celebrations, parades and tears and salutes to fallen heroes. Your president believes that. I don't, not for one minute."

"The troops will deserve their parades. I have no patience for anyone who forgets who's doing the fighting. Those men out there are giving more to this war than we have."

Churchill downed the rest of the brandy, wiped a sleeve across his mouth.

"Oh fine, yes, stand up for your men. That's your job, isn't it? I agree, we must build our monuments, and lay out our cemeteries. We must honor the dead and we must not forget them. *Hallowed ground.* That's what Lincoln insisted upon, right?"

He was surprised by the depth of Churchill's anger, far more fury than Churchill usually allowed himself to display.

"I meant that the fighting men deserve their due. Too many generals think they are the reason we are winning this war."

"Forget it, Ike. You said the right thing. No argument there. But make no mistake. The Russians believe their ground is more *hallowed* than ours. They've given a great deal more in lost lives than we have. Woe is them, for they have borne the greater burden of suffering. I heard that kind of speech every damn day. And what does Uncle Joe want in return? The answer to that question put your people to obsequious generosity. I've never seen so much deference paid in my life. No one stood up to him, none of your spineless diplomats, and not your president. Well, by damn, I stood up to him, and all I got for it was a condescending *harrumph* from both of them, Stalin and Roosevelt. They might as well have spent the week holding hands, like two lovers in a flower patch. After a while, it was plainly apparent that I was becoming quite the bother. So they sought to pump me full of vodka, hoping I would shut the hell up. And, in the meantime, among other outrages, they took it upon themselves to determine the fate of the entire Polish people. That's what really punched me, Ike. We have sacrificed the Poles, ceded the control of their country to Uncle Joe's puppets. And Franklin went along with it. Or, worse, he was oblivious."

Churchill stopped, eyed Eisenhower with another tilt of his head.

Eisenhower said, "It's okay. Nothing you say leaves this room."

Churchill leaned forward, one hand wiping his brow.

"That's never true. Ever. No insult intended, but what I say here will be said again, and written about and analyzed and argued over. The British people have not yet absorbed what our place is in this New World Order. We are quite accustomed to being somewhere close to the top of the pyramid, so to speak. Now we are likely to end up down somewhere alongside the French. Excuse the pun, dear boy, but to an Englishman, that is the most *galling* thing one can imagine."

"I wasn't aware the Russians were setting up any kind of government in Poland. I know that Marshal Zhukov's forces have liberated almost the whole country, driven the Germans completely away. I thought that was the idea."

Churchill studied him, seemed to test if Eisenhower was serious.

"You have your head buried in the western campaigns. Your job, I suppose. But last August, the Russians showed us what they intended for Poland. It amazes me that some people still don't understand what truly happened there."

"You mean . . . Warsaw."

"Yes, dammit! Warsaw!" Churchill was shouting now, red-faced, and Eisenhower was suddenly concerned, eyed him carefully. Churchill slapped the desk with a heavy hand, was still shouting. "The Russians marched right up to the gates of the city and gave assurances to the Polish people, to the underground resistance, that they were coming in to do the job, to crush the Germans, drive them out straight away, to *liberate* the city! And then . . . they stopped! The Germans knew they were in trouble, were already planning their retreat, didn't want to try to hold on to such a difficult place to defend. Surely you saw the same Ultra reports I did. As the Germans were starting their withdrawal, the Russians encouraged the Poles to rise up, to join in the glorious fight for their freedom, and it worked. Perfectly! Just when those people came out of their bunkers and cellars and opened up their secret stashes of weapons, the Russians pulled back, stopped fighting, stopped shelling. They just stopped. You know what happened next? The German generals realized that maybe they weren't in trouble after all. And so, they had a truly marvelous time of it. They obliterated the Polish people. It was a massacre. The Polish underground was erased, and every Pole who stood his ground, who attempted to fight for his own city, was promptly crushed under German boots. And still the Russians sat on their perches and waited. We tried to help, air-drops, supplies and munitions, long-range bombers hitting German targets in the city, but those bombers were denied permission to land in Russian territory to refuel. *Denied.* They're our allies, by damn!" Churchill stopped, was breathing heavily, seemed to catch his breath, calming himself. He raised the empty glass toward Eisenhower, the obvious request. Eisenhower poured the remnants of the bottle into Churchill's glass, slid it across the desk. Churchill stared at the dark liquid, seemed suddenly very sad.

"There is so much stupidity in politics. Like your man Harriman, in Moscow. *Ambassador* Harriman. Stalin's friend, because he only sees what Uncle Joe allows him to see. He doesn't understand to this day that what the Russians did at Warsaw was to invite the Germans to eliminate all those Polish leaders who would be there to welcome their liberation by forming a legitimate Polish government, a *non-communist* government. The Russians sat right outside the city and let the Germans do their dirty work for them. That sound a little harsh, Ike? You think I'm being too cynical, that your Ambassador Harriman is accurate in his optimism? Your president left Yalta believing that all is right with the world, that our enemy is about to go down to defeat, and that we shall celebrate the victory with our good friends in Moscow." He paused, picked up the cigar again, rolled it in his fingers. "I love that man, I truly do. We would not be where we are right now without Roosevelt. But I'm afraid for him, Ike. He wasn't healthy. Hell, I'm not in such dandy shape myself. Neither are you, most likely. All of us are worn out by this, tired of carrying such *full plates.*"

"The soldiers are in a little worse shape."

"Yes, yes, fine. Don't scold me, Ike. I'm not pouring out self-pity here. All I'm telling you is that those young men in all those graveyards were once told that this fight was essential, that if we did not win, it might threaten our very survival on this earth. What I'm telling you, and what your president does not seem to understand, is that, yes, we will defeat the Germans. But that will not end the war."

22. BENSON

The thaw had come, warm air that stripped the trees of snow and turned the ground to a glue-like muck. The roads were not much better, the heavy armor crushing what pavement there was to a jumble of cracks and upended rock. The men still dug foxholes, of course, an easier job in the softer ground, though the mud was far more likely to fill your boots now than before, no freezing nights to stiffen the ground where the men might have to sleep. Benson wasn't complaining.

They marched only in daylight, advancing on an enemy who still kicked up a fight, who staged ambushes and laid booby traps with frightening efficiency. At night, the work was left to the artillery, American units blanketing the ground all out in front of their own infantry, what the foot soldiers considered to be a perfect substitute for night patrols. Benson didn't complain about that either.

The mud was not the worst part of the early spring. As the snow disappeared, the ground gave up the bodies of so many who had died throughout the winter's battles, some from well before the German thrust in mid-December. As the soldiers marched eastward, any open field could

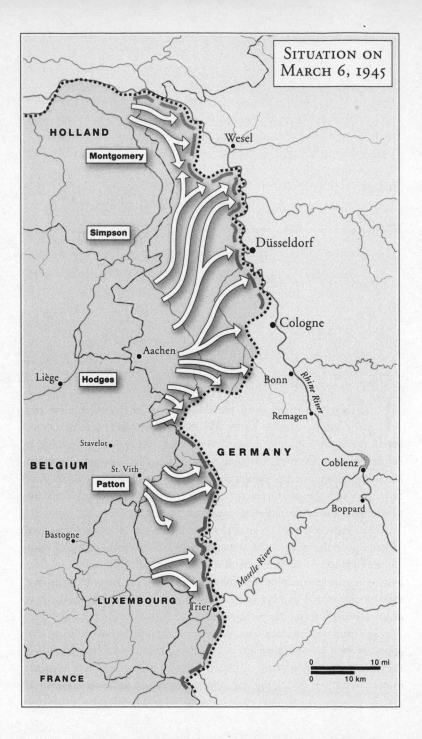

SITUATION ON
MARCH 6, 1945

HOLLAND

Montgomery

Simpson

Wesel

Düsseldorf

Cologne

Aachen

Liège

Hodges

Bonn

Rhine River

Remagen

Stavelot

GERMANY

Coblenz

BELGIUM

St. Vith

Patton

Boppard

Bastogne

Moselle River

LUXEMBOURG

Trier

0   10 mi
0   10 km

FRANCE

offer up a fresh wave of stink, the sickening smell of once-frozen men whose bodies now were opening up to every kind of biological violation. The smells came from other sources too, immense numbers of farm animals, cattle mostly, carcasses upturned, some scattered among the faceless corpses of soldiers. Benson had noticed more of the horrific green skin of the German dead, what someone said was caused by the poor diet of their soldiers. After so many days, the sights failed to sicken, too many to notice, Benson's brain masking it all. But there was no escaping the awful smell, though after a time even that became acceptable, a strange kind of *normal* that infested the muddy German countryside.

But there could still be shock. They had approached a small German village, no danger, the place cleared earlier by patrols that had chased the last of the snipers away. But the German soldiers had left behind a vivid symbol of what could happen to anyone who might have betrayed the cause, any civilian who might have done some good deed, showing kindness to an American, perhaps taking in a wounded GI. No matter how much they had become used to the bodies and the smells, there had been a sight that broke through the numb acceptance. Benson and the rest of Williamson's platoon had passed by a body in the ditch. It was a woman, her clothes ripped completely away, her body violated in graphically obscene ways, and the final obscenity, her corpse slit lengthwise down the center. She had been left beside the road in what was surely a purposeful message, one final act of indecency. The GIs who had grown numb to so many horrors could not pass her by without a response. Anger came first, eruptions of fury, calls for revenge toward anyone whose soul could allow them to commit such an act against anyone, especially one of their own people. Benson had not lingered, one hard look had been all he could absorb. But others did, some of the men defying Williamson's order to move on by burying the corpse where she lay. With the woman's remains set deep into the muddy ground, the talk continued, even as they marched, angry grumbling of what they would do to the men who could commit this kind of atrocity. Benson had stayed quiet, had done all he could to erase her image from his mind. Beside him, Mitchell had been silent as well, but Benson knew him, knew that the woman's grisly death would add one more bit of fuel to the fiery hatred Mitchell could not conceal. Even Williamson seemed affected, a brief conversation with Sergeant Higgins, that it must surely have been one of the SS officers, the troops most rabidly loyal to Hitler. Benson had heard that conversation, tried to understand the lieutenant's logic. It was Mitchell who had spoken up, his own simple statement.

"A Kraut's a Kraut."

They had moved past more of the small villages, some occupied by squads of engineers and the ordnance details, the men who dealt with explosives, called in to sweep away any obvious booby traps or deal with blasted roadways, missing bridges. Benson had been impressed by their work, a scramble of activity on the roads as the engineers laid out wire or rock to repair water-filled craters or washouts, shoring up the wet pathways to allow vehicles to pass that way once again. The engineers seemed to have more information about what was happening to the front, and as infantry moved past the workers, Williamson and the company commander had spoken to the engineering officers, brief meetings, maps spread on the hoods of dirty jeeps. Word had come down from the 106th's command to expect a stiff fight, but the engineers reported something different. Many of the German units in front of them had been weakened, entire battalions of enemy troops just disappearing. Speculation was rampant, some of the men assuming the Germans were simply giving up and going home. But the officers had a different view, Benson overhearing the captain talking about the Russians, noting that far to the east the fight was going very badly for the Germans, and surely they were responding to the Russian offensive by shifting troop strength away from the west. In some of the village bivouacs, there had been mail, and with the mail had come copies of *Stars and Stripes,* the army newspaper confirming what the captain had said, headlines about the enormous power of the Russian thrust, that German commanders had no choice but to weaken the Western Front to help defend against the wave of Russians surging forward into German territory. The soldiers knew very well that that kind of news was spouted out to boost the morale of the Americans, and Benson knew that there was much more going on than *Stars and Stripes* would ever tell them. But they didn't need a newspaper to tell them that the enemy they now encountered was far weaker, with much poorer equipment and a will to fight that was noticeably draining away. Prisoners were common now, entire platoons offering themselves up for surrender to the Americans. But not every German had given up his cause. Whether or not the SS units were responsible for the amazing display of atrocities against their own civilians, those troops were still clawing to every inch of soil. The SS had always been tenacious fighters, and along every part of the advance, in the patches of woods or the wreckage of some village, it took far more effort and cost far more casualties to root them out.

T he road was an oozing trail of slime, deep ruts filled with soupy liquid. The men stayed out on either side, Benson moving behind Sergeant Higgins, trying to guide his footsteps through the patches of grass. The village in front of them had been visible for a while, the terrain not quite as undulating, the villages less likely to be nestled in the bottom of a mountainous bowl. Williamson led them forward slowly, weaving through the only cover they had, low clumps of brush, the occasional fence line. Benson stepped slowly, keeping rhythm with Mitchell beside him. He glanced to the other side of the road, a low stone fence, men moving close, some kneeling, peering out, their sergeant shoving them back into motion. But so far, there had been nothing, no hint of an enemy.

Williamson stopped them with a silent wave, began checking a map, Lane beside him with the walkie-talkie. Benson was grateful for the momentary rest, flexed his toes, his socks hopelessly soaked. Beside him, Mitchell had found a clump of thick grass, sat down, took inventory of his grenades, a habit now. Benson did the same, counted four, never any different. They had plenty of ammunition, the convoys of supply trucks following their advance, depots moving up consistently, a few miles behind them. There were more hot meals now, and more mail, the trucks unimpeded by the muddy roads the Americans had fought for, lost, and fought for again. Mitchell was eyeing one of the men behind them, and Benson glanced that way, saw one of the newer replacements, wiping his rifle with an oily rag. Mitchell shook his head, looked to the front again, impatient, and Benson watched the new man, only two days on the march, tried to remember his name, thought, I should talk to him. He seems like a nice enough guy. Better than some, for sure. Up front, Williamson was talking on the walkie-talkie, and Benson looked that way, saw Lane sitting close to the lieutenant. He caught the man's stare, empty eyes looking skyward. Benson glanced up, nothing, the sun fully up, patches of white clouds. He still had no use for Lane, could not forget how much of a son of a bitch the man had been, even if now he seemed to be missing something.

Williamson called out, waving the men to their feet. "Let's go. Let's get into the village pretty quick. Some of our armor's been through here, but I'm not sure where they are now. Keep your eyes open. The town's not secure."

Across the road, the other sergeants waved acknowledgment, the fifty-man platoon moving again. Out across the open field, Benson could see more of the company, staying in line with them, two more platoons moving toward the village from another angle. Farther out across the road, a ragged orchard blocked the view, some kind of fruit trees. There were signs of a fight, blasted ground, some of the trees broken and uprooted, but Benson tested the air, no stink of explosives, and he thought, whatever happened here happened a while back. Benson couldn't help a shiver, thought of the Tiger tanks. Those damn things *like* orchards. Good place to hide and wait for some idiot ground pounders like us to wander up too close.

The road curved to the right, and Williamson turned to look back, waved the men forward with urgency, said in a low voice, "Farmhouse. Easy!"

Benson moved up, the lieutenant hanging back, allowing Higgins and the squad to move past. Benson saw the windows in the farmhouse, black squares, no glass, movement, a wisp of a curtain. Higgins broke into a run, reached the house, low beside a window, others coming up alongside. Higgins looked back toward the lieutenant, nothing from Williamson, no instruction, the officer just watching them. Higgins slipped around one corner of the house, motioned behind him, Benson following, others with him, staying low and close to the wall. Benson saw the doorway intact, watched Higgins take a deep breath. The sergeant reached out, grabbed the door handle, and the anger on his face told Benson the door was locked. Benson knew what Higgins was thinking, had gone through this before. *What the hell is wrong with these people? They think locking their doors is gonna keep us out?* Higgins seemed to test the door's strength, one hand pressing against rough wood, and he backed away now, pointed his rifle at the handle.

Suddenly a voice came from inside the house. "Hello! *Kamarad!* Surrender!"

Higgins still pointed the rifle at the door, motioned with the barrel for Benson to do the same. The sergeant waved the others back behind him, all raising the rifles, aiming at the door. After an agonizing moment, the door opened slightly, one hand protruding, holding a white piece of cloth, shaking it furiously.

"Surrender! No soldier!"

Higgins moved quickly, kicked the door wide, still pointing the rifle. Benson saw the old man now, tough weathered face, the man's hands rising over his head, wide eyes staring at the muzzle of Higgins's rifle. Higgins pushed past him, Benson following, others coming in quickly, Higgins barking out, "Keep a gun on him! Keep his hands in the air! Okay, old man. Anybody else in here?"

"No soldier! *Landwirt! Landwirt!*"

Williamson was in the doorway now, said, "Farmer. That's what he's saying. The field behind the house is full of dead cattle, some chickens running around."

Higgins continued to move through the rooms, Benson close behind him, and Higgins stopped at a closed door, said in a low voice, "Cellar. Easy now."

Benson stood ready again, Higgins turning the knob, jerking the door open suddenly. There was a glint of light, two faces, an old woman and what seemed to be a young boy.

Higgins shouted down the steps, waving with his rifle. "Up! Let's go."

The boy came first, and Benson thought, twelve, maybe. The old woman seemed unsure on the steps, and Benson said, "Help her out, Sarge. She's pretty damn old."

Higgins did not move, looked instead toward the boy, who stared at both of them with a look Benson had not seen before. Higgins said, "The kid hates our guts. Search him."

"Sarge, he's a kid . . ."

"Search him!"

Benson slipped the rifle onto his shoulder, the old woman standing shakily behind the boy, and Benson motioned her away, said, "Uh . . . arms up, kid."

"Just check his waistband, any pockets!"

"Right."

The boy was wearing a short jacket, and Benson moved close, the boy's stare digging deeply, black hatred on his face. Benson reached to open the jacket, and the boy lunged forward, grabbed for Benson's rifle, kicked him, a glancing blow to Benson's groin. Benson yelped, grabbed the boy by the neck, others there now, one hard punch, Mitchell, the boy crumpling to the floor. The farmer was shouting, pleading, the old woman watching in shocked silence, and Higgins said, "Dammit, I told you! Search him!"

Benson's heart was pounding, the pain in his groin angering him, and he bent low, rolled the boy over. Mitchell's foot came down on the boy's shoulder, holding him tight to the floor, his rifle pointed inches from the boy's face. The young eyes showed fear now, and Benson grabbed the boy's pants, slapped his hands on the pockets, then around the boy's back, felt a hard lump. He dug his hand under the boy's belt, warm steel, pulled it out, saw now, a grenade.

"Holy crap! Look here, Sarge!"

"I told you. Dammit, you listen to me! These aren't Belgians, for God's sake! Pull the kid upright."

The lieutenant was close now, said, "Easy, Sergeant. They're civilians. The kid probably picked it up to protect his family. God knows what these people have been told about us."

Benson studied the grenade, and beside him Mitchell said, "That's one of ours."

"Yep."

Mitchell ignored the lieutenant, grabbed the boy by the back of the neck, lifting him by the collar.

"So, you take this off a dead GI, you little piece of—"

"Enough, Private! Leave these people be."

There was authority in Williamson's voice, unusual, and Higgins said, "Back off, Private. Nothing else to do here."

The lieutenant turned to the couple, who had moved close together, the old man supporting the woman by the arm. Benson saw the fear in the old man's face, thought, this one's not an old soldier. Doesn't act like it, anyway.

There was a voice coming from another part of the house. "Hey, Lieutenant! They got eggs!"

The others reacted with enthusiasm, some of the men moving away. Mitchell still held the boy in a hard grip, said to Higgins, "Not sure we should let this one go, Sarge."

The boy's expression had hardened again, and he seemed to understand that nothing any worse was going to happen to him.

Higgins said, "Lieutenant, we should check the cellar for weapons. What do you want to do with the kid?"

Williamson said, "He's still just a kid. Give him to his grandpa. The old man understands what we could have done to all three of them. They know we don't mean any harm."

Mitchell released the boy's collar, seemed disgusted.

Higgins said, "You two go downstairs, check it out. I'll stay with the family. Be careful."

Mitchell glanced at Benson, said, "Right, Sarge. Let's go, kiddo."

Benson followed Mitchell down the dark stairway, saw a mattress, a stack of clothes, said, "Guess they been hiding out here."

"Don't really care. Look under the clothes, poke around."

Benson moved to the mattress, squatted down, raised one corner, nothing, glanced through the clothing, linens, and suddenly Mitchell said, "Well, lookee here!"

Benson turned, saw a helmet in Mitchell's hand, an American helmet.

"That little bastard's done more than the lieutenant thinks. If he didn't kill our guy, he sure as hell stripped him bare. A Kraut's a Kraut."

Benson felt uneasy now, nervous hands still searching through the family's dusty artifacts. He saw Mitchell poking into a small cupboard, and Mitchell said, "Wine. Guess we oughta take that. Somebody'll thank us."

From above, Higgins called down. "Anything?"

Benson responded, "No weapons."

"Let's go, on the double. Looey got a call. There're snipers in the village. He wants us on the move."

Mitchell tossed the helmet onto the mattress. Benson said, "Wonder who the guy is? *Where* he is?"

"That little son of a bitch won't tell us, and the looey won't let me beat it out of him. Guess we'll never know."

Benson moved up the stairs, heard the clink of the wine bottles, Mitchell following. Upstairs, the others had already moved out, Higgins standing with the three Germans, the boy still watching them with the hateful stare.

The old man pointed to the wine, nodded, tried to smile, said, *"Bitte, bitte. Sehr gut, ya."*

Higgins still eyed the boy, and the old man seemed to understand, put his hands on the boy's shoulders, shook his head. *"Nein. Sehr jung. Kind."*

Higgins looked at the boy. "Yeah, he's just a little kid. Means no harm. We should give him back his *toy*." He looked at Benson now, then Mitchell, saw the wine.

"Let's go. The boys grabbed a basket of eggs, and now we've got something to wash 'em down with. This sure as hell could have been worse."

B enson saw the wreckage and debris, at least half the village blown apart by an artillery barrage he could smell. There was one more smell too, not the usual stink of death, something very different. He moved past the remains of a church, heard a low groan coming from one of the men on the flank, and now he saw what the man was staring at. Behind the church was a cemetery, a gaping crater in the center. Headstones were tossed about like so many dominoes, and among them, shattered pieces of wooden coffins. The smell was overpowering, the contents of the coffins lying about in a jumble of decayed clothing and black flesh and bone. Some of the men had moved that way, drawn by the horror, but not for long. Benson saw one man bend over, throwing up, and Benson moved quickly away, the others doing the same.

Higgins waved them on, said, "Let's go! Nothing we can do there. Thank the artillery boys for that one."

Williamson slowed them down with a wave of both hands, silent, caution in his eyes. Benson could see now, the main street of the village was wide, houses and shops spread out in a checkerboard pattern, piles of rubble alongside some buildings that were mostly intact. The houses were an odd mix, some of them like gingerbread, ornate and childlike, many that had no damage at all.

Williamson pointed to cover, gaps to one side, an alley.

"There! Go!"

The men obeyed, and Williamson moved across, to another squad, the sergeant there doing what Higgins was doing, staring out intently at the windows that lined the street. Benson followed Mitchell into the darkened alley, most of the squad lining up against the side of a stone house, and Benson kept his eye on Higgins, closest to the street, peering out.

Beside him, Mitchell said, "What the hell we supposed to do now?"

Higgins turned toward him, a brief glance, said, "Shut up. We're gonna have to check these damn buildings one at a time. Krauts could be anywhere."

The sound gripped Benson, a low rumbling echo, the others hearing it too, some calling out.

"Tanks! That's tanks!"

Higgins eased out of the alley, looked back from where they had come, said, "Yep. Shermans. Whole damn column, looks like." The sergeant leaned back into the alley, and Benson saw a hint of a smile. "Makes things a bit easier, I'd say."

The tanks were coming in on the same road, close now, and Williamson emerged from the alley across the street, moved out, waving. Benson heard the first tank slow, the grumbling idle of the engine, could see the lieutenant talking to someone, animated gestures, and suddenly Williamson dropped to his knees. Benson thought, what, he's thanking the tanker . . . ? But then the lieutenant rolled to one side, blood on his back, and Higgins said, "Snipers! Son of a bitch! Everybody stay put!"

The tank engine roared to life again, rolled past the body of the lieutenant, the white star moving as the turret spun from side to side. Another tank followed, slowed, stopped in front of the alley, the turret rolling to the side, the barrel of the gun rising, pointing just above the alley. The gun erupted, a blast of fire, smoke, the thundering explosion shaking the stone house beside them. Higgins shouted something, the smoke rolling into the alley, blinding, Benson choking, and in the street more of the big guns opened up, hard thunder, mixed with the rumble of the engines, the ground shaking under his feet. The smoke began to clear, and he saw Higgins ducking low, a hard run into the street, through the black exhaust of the tank. Benson moved out closer to the street, filling Higgins's place at the wall. Another tank rolled past, and Benson could see Higgins on his knees beside the lieutenant, and now another man coming from the other side, a medic. Another tank rolled past, and Benson saw his opportunity, ran out quickly, using the tank for cover, reached the men, shouted out, "Sarge! He okay?"

"Get your ass back into cover! He's got a million-dollar wound, that's all. Tell the others to stay in the alley until I come get you. Stupid idiot."

Benson backed away, saw the medic working furiously, blood on the lieutenant's shirt, a pool of wetness in the soft dirt. Higgins was helping the medic, and Benson saw Williamson's face, ghostly white, bubbles of blood rolling from his mouth.

Another tank moved past now, then stopped, the hatch opening, a voice, "You need some help? Everybody okay?"

Benson felt stabbed by the raw stupidity of the man's question. He turned, saw a helmet and goggles, and shouted out, "Hell no, we're not okay! Our looey's down!"

The man disappeared into his hatch, the tank moving again, and Benson was furious, looked back toward the medic, Higgins suddenly up, grabbing him, dragging him back.

"I told you to get your ass back there! Nothing we can do out here!" Higgins pulled Benson with him, leaving the medic to his work. There was rifle fire now, more of the men moving in from another street, the snipers seeking targets, the Americans doing the same. There was a wave of shouting, a burst of machine-gun fire, and up ahead Benson saw one tank turn to the side, moving closer to a stone structure, a church. He fought against Higgins, broke free, the fear erased by the power of the tanks. The big gun rose up, pointing at the church, and he expected the blast, had to see it, the rush of raw power.

Higgins stopped as well, looked toward the tank, said, "They must have spotted the bastard. Oh hell, this ought to be good."

The tank gun spewed out a fat stream of fire, the flames blowing into the front of the church, up the steeple, the church engulfed, a boiling cloud of black smoke. The fire consumed the entire building in a few seconds, and Benson stared, in shock, thought, something's wrong . . . the tank's gun didn't work.

And then Higgins said, "I'll be damned. Flamethrower. Bad place for a sniper to hide."

Along the wide street, more tanks were rolling into the village, and now a half-track, men at a machine gun, others calling out, "Get the hell out of the way!"

Benson ignored them, watched the fire still, thought of the power of the flamethrower, liquid hell, the church fully ablaze. The men began to emerge from the alleys on both sides of the street, drawn by the armor, all of them seeming to understand that the danger was passing. Up ahead, Benson heard machine-gun fire, the fifty-caliber from a tank, more, another hard thump from a tank gun. Higgins began to move away, putting his own men against the front of the blasted building, keeping them out of the street, the advance on foot beginning again. Up ahead, the church began to crumble from the heat, the tanks and trucks moving past, oblivious, the machine gunners still peppering the open windows. Still another tank moved past, and beyond it Higgins shouted, "Private! Get your ass over here! This ain't a party!"

Benson moved that way, dodged another half-track, and behind it a jeep, four men, brass. He turned back, a last look at the body of the lieu-tenant, but Williamson and the medic were both gone, telltale scrapes in the mud where the lieutenant's body had been dragged away. Benson felt like following, but his instincts knew better, knew to follow the man in charge. And now it was Higgins. He turned, saw Mitchell trot out toward him, one hand grabbing Benson's jacket.

"Come on, dammit. No time to get all mushed up. You can't do any-thing about the looey. Stupid bastard shouldn't have stood out in the street."

"The sarge said he had a million-dollar wound. That's bull. He's dead. I saw his face. He's dead."

"What's the difference, kiddo? Either he goes home with his million-dollar Purple Heart or he goes home in a hundred-dollar box. What mat-ters is us. We're still here. Let's go."

They stayed in the village, the company commander ordering the pla-toon leaders to encamp their men in any cover they could find. De-spite the shelling from American artillery, and the brief assault that cleaned out the last of the snipers, many of the houses were more or less standing. It was one more thing for Benson to be thankful for. Tonight, there would be no foxhole.

The kitchen trucks had come up as well, serving what someone said was pork loaf, a mass of meat that smelled worse than it tasted, and almost no one in the squad could even handle the taste. Benson had long forgot-ten about the eggs, but the men who hauled that particular treasure had been amazingly careful, nearly every egg surviving the afternoon's ordeal. It wasn't difficult to find a house with a stove, and with carefully guarded se-crecy, Higgins's squad was happily scarfing down fried eggs for the first time in weeks. The farmer's wine had been a perfect accompaniment, en-hanced by the discovery of several bottles of cider. Even Higgins suc-cumbed, passing along the suggestion that the water in the village might have been poisoned. Clearly, the wine was the only safe thing they had to drink. No one dared contradict the sergeant by pointing out that the army's own water trucks had come up as well.

NEAR FRAUENKRON, GERMANY
MARCH 7, 1945

The company commander had come to them at dusk, just missing their private banquet, a fact no one offered to the captain himself. If he smelled the delicious scent of fried eggs or detected the wine and cider on the breath of Sergeant Higgins, he seemed not to care. His orders had been simple and direct. The men in the town would be allowed to sleep through the night, and no one was more grateful for that order than Higgins's squad. Their feast had been a luxury that few of them had the stomach for, and the effect on men who had become accustomed to K rations was entirely predictable. Most of the men awoke at various times during the night from an urgent signal in their gut that took them stumbling out into the night, desperate to find a place where relief could at least be hidden, if not dignified. Not all of them made it, and Benson could smell the results. As they awoke to daylight for the first time in many weeks, Benson shared the cursing disgust for the pungent odor that filled the building, not really sure if he was a contributor to the problem or not. For most of the men, the headache they carried into the dawn was punishment enough.

In the streets below, the trucks flowed past, and word had come from the captain again that units of the Sixty-ninth Division were sweeping ahead of them, in what seemed to be hot pursuit of an enemy who was weakening daily. For now the 106th would hold tight to the gains they had made, while in front of them, fresher troops would carry the load. The captain had seemed disappointed at that, as though his men had earned the right to charge once more into enemy guns. Not many shared his enthusiasm. Despite the army's ongoing push that seemed to leave the 106th behind, the captain would not allow his company to occupy a German village without at least taking care of some kind of useful business. Reports from other villages had sent alarm through the division commanders that the Germans were not all escaping toward the Rhine. The villagers made a considerable commotion to the Americans that orders had been passed from soldier to civilian, even as the German soldiers pulled out. The SS officers had been the most brutal with the threats that the citizens were to obey an order from their Führer to begin a guerrilla campaign against the invaders to the German homeland. Whether or not the order was widely obeyed, reports flowed through the town of brief firefights, somewhere to the north, and one of the surviving platoon commanders, a panicky lieutenant, had convinced the captain that patrols were needed to clear out what might become a serious menace along the army's supply lines. Despite their hangovers, Higgins had obeyed the order, putting his squad into the street once more, several of the squads marching out on muddy farm lanes that wound into wooded hillsides, land that the lieutenant insisted was still infested with Hitler's last-gasp resistance.

Higgins kept them moving on the edge of the wooded trail, Benson and Mitchell close behind him, what had become their usual place, the others strung out in single file. Farther out in the woods, another squad had the unenviable task of slogging through the trees, their sole advantage a lack of concern for mines in the road. The lieutenant who sent them out had seemed to melt away behind them, and Benson had been surprised at that. He didn't know the man well, but the face and name were familiar, the officer heading up another of the platoons that had survived the various fights in the Ardennes. The first joke had come from Mitchell, that the lieutenant was another of those *delegate and disappear* officers. But Benson had sensed a strange jitteriness in the man, what must have been the effects of too many days on the line. It happened often to the junior officers, the men who led their patrols and squads straight into the enemy. The survivors of that duty were fewer in each campaign, and Benson had wondered about the guilt of that. But this lieutenant had seemed less like a man carrying guilt than a man about to come unglued. The orders for the patrol had come at Higgins's squad in a spray of chatter that sounded far more like the words of a frightened newcomer than a man who could claim to be *seasoned*. It was no wonder he stayed behind, Benson thought. If he was here, up front, he might suddenly go nuts. It could get us all killed. I'd just as soon follow the sarge.

Higgins was more somber than usual, glanced back frequently, keeping the men spaced apart, less vulnerable to a sudden burst of machine-gun fire or a mortar shell. Benson felt the wetness in his boots again, the mud several inches deep, the squad easing alongside the roadway in a parade of low cursing. Past Higgins, he saw a clearing up ahead, the trail seeming to end at the hill's long crest. Higgins stopped them, seemed strangely unconcerned.

The men gathered closer, and Higgins said, "That jackass lieutenant told us to check out this hilltop, that Kraut infiltrators could be setting up artillery positions. That's stupid as hell. The Krauts hauled their last cannon out of here by oxcart days ago. But we've got to report back on what we found. Spread out along this tree line, and if you can find a dry place to sit, park your ass where you can see across. Any Krauts show up, raise hell. We'll kill an hour or so up here, and we can tell that damn lieutenant we did the job. Where is that jackass, anyway?"

Mitchell said, "He stayed behind, didn't say why."

"Yeah, well, we know why. The word got passed along to all the officers about Williamson, and none of these field officers want to be the next one to eat it. They've lost too many of their buddies to take any risks. So they give that job to us."

Benson thought of the logic of that and shrugged. "I suppose they're right, Sarge. Seems like we always lose a lieutenant first—"

The bullet cracked past his ear, and Benson froze for an instant, the others reacting by scattering out, dropping low.

"What the hell . . . ?"

"Get down!"

Mitchell pulled him hard, Benson falling forward, his rifle jammed under him, punching his ribs. Beside him, a man rose up, firing the M-1, a steady rhythm, emptying the clip. The man quickly reloaded.

Higgins shouted, "What the hell are you shooting at? You see anything?"

Benson saw the wide-eyed stare of the new man, the replacement, searching the field in pure panic.

"Krauts, Sarge!"

The man fired again, eight quick shots, another clip, and Higgins crawled toward him, yanked at the rifle, yelled into the man's face. "Knock it off! You're not even aiming!"

Higgins was red-faced, moved back toward Benson, growling, "Idiots send us these repple-depple rejects." He reached Benson now, said, "Could you tell the direction, which way it came?"

Benson was struggling to breathe, rolled over, then rose up slightly, a quick glance across the open ground. He saw a cluster of low brush, a skirt of cover along the far trees a hundred yards away. He pointed that way. "Maybe there. The brush."

Mitchell peered up, said, "Yeah, maybe so. Those short trees. Good cover."

Higgins said aloud, "All of you, when I give the word, lay down some fire on that brush line! Aim low. If that's where they are, they're lying down!" He looked at Benson now, said, "You don't shoot. Ease over to that tree, get a good vantage point. When we open up, you watch that brush, see if anything moves, any smoke, anything. You got that?"

"Yeah, Sarge."

Benson fought the pain in his ribs, crawled low toward the trees, the closest one a fat pine. He slipped behind it, sat up, thought, I sure as hell hope that's where it came from. If it's a sniper back here in this timber . . . I'm a sitting duck. Higgins was waiting for him to get into position, and Benson took a deep breath, nodded, timed his movements for Higgins's command.

"Fire!"

Benson rolled around, stared out past the tree, the chorus of rifle fire slicing through the brush, thin branches cut, the brush shuddering from the impact. He stared, searched, and now the cry came, the man rolling out, a stumbling crawl, one hand in the air.

Higgins shouted, "Nobody moves! We hit one of them. But they could be setting us up."

Benson watched the German crawling toward them, no weapon, another sharp cry, but Benson stared past, kept his gaze on the brush line. He heard voices behind him, men coming up through the trees, the sergeant from the other squad, responding to the firing. Higgins explained, and the sergeant pulled his men up closer, spread them along the tree line, added power to deal with whatever enemy might be across the field. Benson kept his stare to the front, the German still crawling toward them, and there was a single shot, the man suddenly collapsing, lying flat. Benson turned, saw Mitchell aiming, smoke from the rifle barrel. He felt a shock, wanted to say something, the sergeant speaking first.

"What the hell was that for? He was giving up!"

Mitchell lowered the rifle, no expression, and Benson saw the man's dark quiet eyes. "Don't think so. I thought I saw a grenade."

Higgins said nothing, looked toward Benson. "Anything?"

Benson searched for movement again, any sign of something besides brush. Suddenly a hand appeared, waving, another, shouts, and now, the pop of a rifle, the bullet cracking past Benson's tree.

Higgins shouted, "Dammit! Give it to 'em again!"

The men responded, more now, supporting fire. Benson watched the brush, saw one man roll out into the open, another.

Higgins called out, "Cease fire! Enough of this crap. Sergeant, can you move some of your men to the left, that low ground, come up behind them? God knows how many there are. Watch it. They could be on the move."

"Got it."

The other squad leader was gone quickly, some of the soldiers in the woods shifting that way. Higgins said, "There can't be too many of 'em. Gotta be a scattered bunch, cut off, hiding out, trying to get the hell out of here. That looked like somebody was giving up, and somebody still wanted to fight. Let's not give them time to argue it out."

"It'll be a short argument," Mitchell said.

Benson saw the sergeant looking at Mitchell, no response, and now there were shouts, out in front, commotion at the brush line. Benson saw the other GIs, one man waving them forward.

Higgins was up quickly. "Let's go! Party's over."

They scampered across the open ground, and Benson saw two men, hands in the air, and then, two more, smaller, younger. The faces showed terror, an M-1 pointed at each man's head, the four paraded out into the open. The two adults had uniforms, the boys in ragged civilian clothes, and Benson saw the faces, focused on the young, felt a sudden jolt of recognition.

Mitchell had seen as well. "Well, look what we got here. It's an old friend of ours, Sarge."

It was the boy from the farmhouse, the boy with the hidden grenade. Behind them, the other sergeant was shouldering his rifle. "I wouldn't call them much of a threat. Only two weapons in the lot of 'em. These two are just kids."

Higgins said, "Search them carefully. Start with this little bastard. We've met him before."

The other sergeant backed away, said, "I think we found all the *guerrillas* that are up here. And they're all yours, as far as I'm concerned. Congratulations, Higgins. You'll make the lieutenant proud. Mission accomplished. I'm taking my squad back to the village. You?"

Higgins watched as two of his men rummaged through the pockets and waistbands of the four Germans, said, "Yeah, right. We'll be there, right behind you."

No one else was speaking, and Benson felt a strange mood in the others, stared at the boy, saw the hatred dulled by the fear in the others. The soldiers stepped back, and one man said to Higgins, "Clean. That's all they had, two rifles."

Higgins looked at the fallen men. "Seven all told, and only two weapons? And they still tried to make a fight of it. Crazy damn people."

Mitchell said, "Hey, Sarge. Look at the insignia on the soldiers' collars. They're SS."

Benson saw what Mitchell was pointing to, the small jagged symbols, like two lightning bolts.

"Well, I'll be damned," Higgins said. "Look here, SS man. I'm your mongrel swine of an enemy. Guess I should be impressed how damn tough you are. How much did it take you to scare these kids into trying to kill us?" He turned away, said, "Let's move out."

Higgins started across the field, then stopped, watching as the men guarding the prisoners prodded them forward.

Benson saw Mitchell hanging back, and he stayed with him as Mitchell said, "I'll guard 'em. You boys go on ahead."

"Fine with me."

"All yours."

The other men moved away, and Mitchell motioned with the rifle, the prisoners all watching him. They followed the GIs out in single file, hands still up on their heads, the farmer's boy last in line. Benson saw the black stare in Mitchell's eyes, the same look he got from the boy, and he felt the uneasiness stirring again.

"Kenny, don't do nothing. Let the army handle 'em."

Mitchell moved in behind the Germans, his rifle pointed at the back of the boy. "Don't worry, kiddo. Somebody's gotta watch 'em. You know how these bastards are. One of 'em tries to shag ass, we need to be ready."

Higgins had waited for them, the others moving back down the road, and Higgins said, "We're gonna make some good time going back. Gonna be dark soon, and I don't wanna get caught out here. One guard's not enough. I'll help you out, make sure we bring 'em in as quick as we can. Right?"

Mitchell nodded, kept his stare on the Germans in front of him. "No sweat, Sarge."

Higgins looked at Benson, said, "Get up front, Private. Take the point."

Benson saw the look between the sergeant and Mitchell, felt a raw stab of cold, and Higgins had him by the arm, gave him a soft shove.

"Get up there and take the point."

Benson felt paralyzed, the others moving away, and he started to speak, saw a hard stare from Mitchell, a brief shake of his head. Benson said, "You . . . can't do it."

"Take the damn point, Private! Get going!"

The rest of the squad were strung out on the trail, watching, and Benson felt helpless, quivering in his hands. He obeyed, moved up past the others, heard low mumbles, still felt the cold in his brain. The squad followed him out into the muddy roadway, and Benson stayed to the side, out of the deeper mud. The road curved away downhill, and Benson felt the old panic returning, but different this time, no fear of what was ahead of them, no enemy guns, no artillery, no Tiger tanks. He was moving quickly, trying to get away from the prisoners. He ignored the others, thought of the town, where the officers would be, command and order. Behind him, the rest of the squad was moving quickly to keep up with him, no one objecting, opening up space between themselves and the Germans who trailed behind, and the two men who guarded them with their rifles. Benson tried to think of the lieutenant, that they would have to report to him on their accomplishment, flushing out the soldiers. No, that's not your job. That's for the sarge. Nothing for me to do but find some chow and make like this day's over. He knew the sounds were coming, pushed himself faster, thought, it's war, dammit. It's war. But . . . no, it's up to the sarge. Whatever he says is what happened. He sensed the strange fear in the others, some moving up beside him, hurrying to get away, and Benson knew, no one would speak of it, no one would recall anything, no matter what was going to happen in the woods behind them.

23. PATTON

The Allied push continued all across the rugged terrain, through villages and small cities, the patches of open land between Germany's borders with Belgium and Luxembourg, and the Rhine River. Despite Hitler's rabid calls for an unbreakable defense across every inch of German soil, the soldiers of his army had accepted the reality they faced. Outgunned in every way, the German forces had no choice but to withdraw to the safety of the Rhine's defenses, making the best use of the tall peaks on the eastern shores that allowed German artillery to hold off the advancing Allied tanks and infantry. As the Germans sought the safety of the river, they were predictably proficient in destroying the remaining bridges that spanned the waterway. The Allied commanders continued to press forward, driving their troops closer to the river itself, but every soldier and every engineer who gazed at the river understood that without a bridge, they would have to force an amphibious crossing. With so much German strength regrouping on the far side, that kind of operation, even in darkness, could be a murderous disaster.

In the mists of a foggy dawn on March 7, one company of the American Ninth Armored Division drove into the hills along the western banks of the river near the town of Remagen, and with the first hint of daylight discovered to their utter amazement that a stout stone-and-steel railway bridge was still intact. Across the bridge itself, German troops were making a rapid retreat, while on the far side, German engineers worked frantically to complete their wiring of demolitions that would destroy the bridge completely. The first American officers to absorb the sight debated whether the bridge should be shelled, cutting off the German retreat, but they understood that such a decision had to come from higher up. That authority was Brigadier General William Hoge, who ended all arguments by issuing the order that, instead of destroying the bridge, the Americans should make every effort to cross it. Led by Captain Karl Timmerman, a company of armored infantry scampered frantically across just as German demolitionists were completing their wiring of explosives. Though minor blasts rocked the Americans in their tracks, the primary charge, a five-hundred-pound block of TNT, failed to ignite. Timmerman kept pushing, some of his men climbing up into the bridge's steel superstructure to fire at the Germans who tenaciously held to their positions. After tense minutes on both sides, the Germans finally retreated. The sole remaining bridge across the Rhine River had fallen into American hands.

Though American engineers worked feverishly to strengthen the span, the bridge was now a target for the Germans. After repeated assaults from German dive-bombers and artillery strikes, the good work of the American engineers came to a costly end. Ten days after Captain Timmerman's crossing, the weakened bridge collapsed into the river, killing twenty-eight engineers who were doing all they could to keep it intact.

The bridge at Remagen did not give the Allies a massive breakthrough across the Rhine. As Eisenhower knew, the primary crossings would still have to come from Montgomery's sector in the north, and from Patton and Devers in the south. Strategically, the Remagen crossing was only a minor victory, but the meaning of that success was not lost on the men of either side. Not only had the Germans failed to stop the Allies from continuing their drive into German territory, but at Remagen the Americans had breached the artery that symbolized Germany's lifeline.

TRIER, GERMANY
MARCH 14, 1945

"What do you think, Colonel? Old Courtney redeem himself?"

"If you say so, sir."

Patton knew that tone in Codman's voice.

"Don't patronize me, Charlie. Hodges deserved every bit of the grief he got. He was caught with his damn pants down, and damn near gave

Antwerp back to Hitler. Nobody knows how he screwed up more than he does. So he's allowed to strut a little for putting his people across the Rhine before the rest of us. I don't need to remind Brad or Ike that it was my boys who yanked his sausage out of the fire. Hodges can have his little parade at Remagen, or whatever Ike thinks he's entitled to. We've still got the big job, right in front of us."

"I should think, sir, that Monty would say the same thing. He's making quite a bit of noise about driving across the Rhine, still thinks Berlin is his own private plum."

Patton caught a glimpse of a smile from Codman, unusual.

"I don't give a donkey fart what Monty thinks. But I tell you this. If we don't get our people punched across that damn river before Monty does, I might as well go home and teach nursery school. I guarantee you, right now Monty's up there *preparing*. He'll still be *preparing* after I've ended this war, after Hitler's been strung up by his own people, after Ike has been elected king of France, and God knows what else. But by damn, Monty will *prepare*. You hear me? If Monty makes it over that damn river before we do, it won't be because he did anything at all. It'll be because we sat on our asses and gave him the glory. Not going to happen, Charlie. Not in this command. I don't care what Ike thinks, or Bradley or Devers either. We're getting across that damn river if it kills . . ." Patton stopped, knew he had gone too far. "Well, you know what I mean. No excuses allowed. Ike doesn't want to hear 'em from me, and I won't hear 'em from Gaffey or Walker or anybody else in my command."

"Yes, sir. I'm certain that has been communicated throughout the Third Army."

Patton knew Codman was right. No one in Patton's command had to be reminded that to Patton, the enemy included commanders who weren't necessarily German.

Patton paced the wide office, said, "Any idea who had this place before?"

Codman seemed unsure of the question. "You mean, this building?"

"Yeah. Some Nazi official, looks like. One of those iron-thumb kind of jackasses, terrorizes the whole city, then runs like hell when we show up. Like to meet the guy, have a little chat about how much *fun* he had abusing his own people."

"The local officials had pretty much cleared out when we occupied the city, sir."

"Yeah, my point exactly. Scrammed right on out of here. What about that general? What's his name?"

Codman pulled a pad from his pocket. "Well, according to the G-2, his name is . . . Major General Ernst George Edwin Graf von Rothkirch und Trach."

"Good God. No wonder they're such good soldiers. Look at the names they have to live up to. What the hell do I call him? Ernie?"

"How about . . . General, sir?"

Patton laughed, had rarely seen Codman in such a lighthearted mood. Victory will do that, he thought. Capturing a place as important as Trier puts everybody in a good mood.

"Fine. At least he doesn't outrank me. Let's go have a chat."

The German was short, thin, gray-haired, with a face that showed more age than the man's years. Patton studied him for a few seconds, thought, I bet that's how most of them look right about now. How much more of this can they take?

The German was standing, respectful, guards in each corner of the room. Patton noticed a lack of medals, thought, some GI souvenir hunter probably grabbed them. Damn shame. The man deserves to keep his mementos. All he's got left. Doesn't seem the type to have groveled his way to the top.

Patton eyed his interpreter, said, "It's a pleasure to make your acquaintance, General. I'm General Patton."

"Yes, I know who you are, sir. It is my honor to be in your custody."

Patton couldn't help feeling the flattery, sensed something sober in the man, an air of intelligence. Patton had prepared a brief speech, a dressing-down to this man who would dare to follow the scourge that was Hitler. But the German's quiet humility disarmed him, any browbeating suddenly inappropriate. Patton searched the man's eyes, saw no arrogance, none of the chest-puffing superiority that so many of the captured German officers carried with them, as though their captivity were all part of their greater plan. Patton still watched him, the German staring past him, a hint of sadness seeping through his show of dignity.

"You commanded a corps, is that right?"

"Yes, sir. Fifty-third. I was part of the Seventh Army."

"I understand you were involved in the assault on Bastogne. Messy little affair. Took some doing for our boys to pull that one out."

"We made many errors, General."

"We made a few. Fewer than you."

Patton waited for something else, but von Rothkirch was clearly conceding the stage.

"I'll not ask you for your secrets. Waste of time for both of us. You don't have much left to hide. A good many of your people are either rounded up or dead, and more are coming in that way every day. Sorry, don't mean to be disrespectful. It's just war. Under different circumstances, I might be the one who had lost his medals. I sure as hell wouldn't be squawking to you if these guards were Germans."

Von Rothkirch did not react.

Patton said, "I have to ask you one thing. You faced us in the Ardennes, and maybe before. You had your chances, many of 'em. Some of 'em against me, some against . . . well, other people. Hell of a fight, sometimes. But all that changed. We've got you, got your people, your whole army is falling backward. By now you know damn well what we bring to this fight. You know that your people cannot possibly hold us off for long, not with your losses and our superiority in numbers, our superiority in the air. Why in hell do you continue to fight? You cannot believe for a second that you can still win this thing. Not for one second. But still you fight. It makes no sense, none at all."

Von Rothkirch tilted his head, absorbed Patton's words.

"I would not use that term, General. What we do on the battlefield makes plenty of *sense*. I am an officer in the Wehrmacht, and I have lived my entire life by following orders. I can do nothing else. My personal opinion about our chances for victory, if I had one . . . cannot matter. My personal beliefs have no place on the battlefield, or even in my headquarters. I am no different from any of my superiors, or my subordinates. We are all under orders. As long as the orders instruct us to carry on the fight, we will."

It was the perfect answer, and Patton knew he had nothing left to say. He made a quick short bow, said, "General, despite your orders, your war is over. You shall be treated with respect due your position. But you are a prisoner of war. The only orders that matter to you now will come from me."

Von Rothkirch lowered his head in acknowledgment, still none of the arrogance, no defiance. Patton felt a strange respect for the man, had not expected humility. He spun on his heel, motioned to the door, the guard pulling it open. Outside, Codman was waiting, held out a cup of coffee. Patton shook his head. "No, not now."

"I'm curious, sir. What was he like?"

Patton led Codman toward the outside door, saw the car waiting. The guards stood stiffly along the walkway, white helmets and perfect neckties, rifles held upright. Patton ignored them, moved toward the open car door, then stopped, thought a moment.

"They're a great people, Charlie. And they're fools. It's a damn shame we have to kill so many of them to prove it."

He had been excited about walking through Trier, knew too much of the extraordinary history of the place not to be curious. It wasn't the facts and historical monuments that attracted him, but more the feel of the place. He moved past a small shop, a bakery, most of it destroyed. He tried to ignore the wreckage and debris, the streets themselves fairly clear, the good work of the engineers, making way for his army's continuing push eastward. Codman was just behind him, followed by several MPs, nervous and efficient men, eyeing the destruction and what might lie beyond, in some hidden place. There had been no sign of snipers for more than a week, but Patton knew he could not order the MPs away, that both Eisenhower and Bradley would erupt at him if they knew Patton took a stroll through anyplace where someone could pick him off from a rooftop. He stopped, shuffled his feet in the muddy earth, looked down.

"Caesar was here, you know. Walked these streets. *This* one. Scrape away some of this muck and crud, and I bet you'll find out this roadbed is Roman. He probably marched through here leading his legions, flags flying, trying to find the best way to kill as many of his enemies as he could." He looked at Codman. "I rather appreciate that, you know. I'd love to give him a ride in a tank. That'd be a damn sight more impressive than a chariot. A few armored cars, a half-track or two . . . that would have sent those damn Goths or whoever else scurrying back into their caves."

A screaming whistle split the air overhead, and Patton looked up, flinched from instinct. He caught a glimpse of silver ripping past, a faint trail of smoke, the sound rolling over him, then, just as quickly, gone.

Codman said, "What in hell was that?"

The sound rumbled still, distant, fading, and Patton stared that way, gray skies, nothing left to see. He had seen the V-1s before, but this was very different, nothing like the low-pitched whine of the flying bombs.

Codman said, "Wasn't a V-2. You never hear them at all."

Patton heard men calling out, others who had heard the sound, who had caught a glimpse, and now he understood.

"I know what it was. I've seen the reports, Ike mentioned them. That, Colonel, was a damn Nazi jet airplane."

"What? You sure, sir?"

Patton stared at empty sky, waited for another, wanted a better look.

"I'm sure. G-2 has been spewing with reports from the air boys. Those things have started coming after our bombers, and the fighter escorts don't have the first idea what to do about them."

"Jets? How fast?"

Patton shrugged.

"No idea. We'll get one sooner or later. Figure out all the secrets. Supposed to be one more of Hitler's secret weapons. Their propaganda's spitting out this stuff even now, how the war is about to change, how they're cooking up something that's gonna throw us back into the sea. Hard to believe anybody in Germany believes this stuff."

"I believe what I just saw, sir. Pretty frightening impression. They could play hell with our aircrews."

"For a while, maybe. But get hold of it, Colonel. We heard this crap before, remember? The V-2s scared hell out of us for a while. All that talk about bombs that could wipe out whole cities. It's never as bad as the propaganda people say it is. It's like Hitler enjoys being the bogeyman, finding some scary new toy to toss our way. Well, I'm not scared of any of it. Doesn't change a damn thing. We've still got a job to do, and so far Hitler hasn't shown me he can stop us."

Patton still looked skyward, searched, only silence. "Hope I see another one of those things. I bet those sons of bitches are fun to fly."

24. VON RUNDSTEDT

The call had come first from Siegfried Westphal, von Rundstedt's chief of staff. Westphal was the most loyal and efficient officer von Rundstedt could name, and others had felt the same way, especially the other commanders Westphal had served. Throughout the war, the young man's assignments had reflected the enormous respect that came his way, even from the High Command, those officers close to Hitler who seemed incapable of offering respect to anyone who might be a rising star. Though it never seemed to affect Westphal one way or the other, his various superiors—Rommel, Kesselring, and now von Rundstedt—all recognized that a wave of Hitler's hand might take Westphal straight to Berlin to occupy a seat held now by one of the maddeningly mindless yes-men the field commanders had to endure. So far, Hitler's own staff, who were expert at protecting their own lofty perches, had been successful at keeping Westphal in the field. So much the better for those he served.

Von Rundstedt had always known that his command existed at Hitler's whim, and when the need came for a scapegoat, von Rundstedt would fill that role perfectly. Though disdainful of Hitler, he knew the wisdom of keeping his disrespect at least somewhat discreet. In July, when

Claus von Stauffenberg had nearly succeeded in assassinating the Führer, von Rundstedt had been outraged that an army officer could have carried out such a plot. No matter how much rationalization had fueled the conspirators, how *necessary* the death of Hitler, an attack on the nation's supreme commander was the kind of treason von Rundstedt could never accept. He had reacted by loud condemnation of the plot, and had served on the army court that ultimately sentenced many of the plotters to death, whether the evidence supported such a drastic fate or not. It was a show in part, for the benefit of those close to Hitler, particularly the Gestapo, who were now suspicious of every officer in the army. Even though he had to accept the blame for the failures to hold the enemy away from the beaches at Normandy, his show of loyalty kept his name prominent among the army's hierarchy. Though Hitler knew von Rundstedt was no friend, the Führer also knew he could still be of value. Now von Rundstedt's predictions were being fulfilled. Once again, Hitler needed a scapegoat, not only for the complete collapse of the Ardennes offensive, but for the enemy successes that had followed. The final straw had now come as word reached Berlin of the failure to destroy the Remagen Bridge. Von Rundstedt knew little of the specifics, which field officer or engineer should have been blamed, whose neck should have gone into Berlin's noose. The High Command had reacted to the loss of the bridge with predictable venom, executing three officers virtually on the spot, men who may or may not have been culpable at all. The importance of the enemy's new bridgehead had been emphasized by Field Marshal Model, who had taken it upon himself to command the defensive efforts around Remagen, what von Rundstedt knew was yet another futile effort to hold back the Americans. Even with the army's failures of December and January, von Rundstedt knew that blame would slip past Model. Hitler simply liked the man, and usually, in this army, that was enough.

Von Rundstedt had stayed away from Berlin as much as possible, had no need to hear Hitler's furious tirades at the failure of those generals who commanded an army that Hitler still considered invincible. Not only had the old man avoided the screaming directed toward his own failings, he would not give Hitler the satisfaction of relieving him face-to-face. With the loss of the bridge at Remagen, Hitler needed his scapegoat, and used the old man exactly as he had planned. If an important bridge had been captured, it meant that a disease had infected that part of Hitler's army. Von Rundstedt had fulfilled the destiny assigned to him.

The man assigned to replace him had been something of a surprise. Von Rundstedt had expected the job to go to Model, but Model was at his best in the field, and with enemy pressure mounting all along the frontier west of the Rhine, Model was exactly where Hitler needed him to be. Instead, Hitler would bring to western Germany the only man who had thus far succeeded in giving the enemy as good a fight as he had received. For nearly three years, Albert Kesselring had commanded German forces in North Africa and Italy, and though the Italian campaign had become something of a sideshow to Hitler's concerns, Kesselring had kept the Allies bound up in a vicious stalemate there for more than a year. But Italy was no longer a priority to Hitler, and Kesselring had shown not only that he could effectively manage an entire theater of the war, but that he had the unusual ability to handle difficult subordinates, most notably, Erwin Rommel.

Kesselring was in fact Luftwaffe, presumably answering to the authority of Hermann Göring. But for the past several months, no one in the German High Command seemed to be concerned with Göring at all, Kesselring included. If Hitler wanted Kesselring to take command of OB West, Göring would have little to say about it.

They called him Smiling Al, an unfortunate label that had stuck to Kesselring since his earliest days in the service. Von Rundstedt always respected the man, ridiculous nickname notwithstanding, and he never really believed that Kesselring spent much time smiling at anything. When word came from Westphal that Kesselring was on his way, the old man was more curious than fearful.

S o, you did not come here to execute me?"
     Kesselring seemed alarmed at the question, realized now that von Rundstedt was teasing him. He laughed, still uneasy, said, "No, Field Marshal. Your service to the Reich has run its course, that's all. The Führer felt that some fresh perspective—"

"Stop. Don't speak to me of perspective, don't even speak to me of the Führer. You might also temper your happy thoughts about this *Reich* we have all given so much to create."

Kesselring looked toward Westphal, who stood at attention against one wall.

"Tell me, Siegfried, is the Field Marshal always so . . . blunt?"

"Yes, sir."

Kesselring lowered his head, a long deep breath.

"More blunt than Rommel?"

Westphal hesitated to respond.

Kesselring let out a small laugh. "Never mind, Siegfried. You have suffered under some of this army's most accomplished grouches. There should be a medal for that." He looked at von Rundstedt now, said, "My apologies. I do not intend to insult you. My presence here is sufficient insult."

Von Rundstedt could see Westphal's discomfort, but there was nothing for him to say, no energy for polite conversation. Kesselring was stirring in his chair, and von Rundstedt thought, he wants me to be at ease with this, wants to say the right thing. It truly doesn't matter, but I'm not sure he should hear that.

After a moment, Kesselring said, "I am fortunate to be in this command, Herr Field Marshal. I know very well that Berlin often has difficulty separating fantasy from fact. The best men in this army are the men who do not accept fantasy at all. Dreams make for wonderful novels, but they do not serve military men well. I have tried to dance my way through minefields of dreams, not always with success, Field Marshal. In North Africa—"

"Please, you may call me Gerd. I do not believe the title *Field Marshal* is appropriate any longer. Berlin will say otherwise, and certainly, someone there is already preparing me some sort of honor, one more medal for my aching chest. But your presence here is a death knell for me. My particular dream has concluded. I am no longer in the service of the Führer."

Kesselring seemed to relax, nodded slowly.

"I have spent several days in Berlin, among men who would rather shoot themselves than admit such an honest thought. You are . . . refreshing, Field Marshal. Excuse me. Gerd."

Von Rundstedt tried to stretch his back, the stiffness holding him uncomfortably in the soft chair.

"I have been looking forward to this actually. I had feared that the Führer did not believe an old soldier should ever retire. These days, I thought it possible that he would order my final service to this army to come in front of a firing squad. Or perhaps I should be planted on a meat hook, as was done to so many of those assassins. I might not be in the best of health, but still, I have some time. My rosebushes have missed my attention. It is one of those pleasures an old man is equipped to enjoy. Sitting in dirt. Call it . . . preparation for what is to come."

"Please, sir!" Westphal stepped forward, obviously upset at the old man's analogy. He leaned close to von Rundstedt's desk, said, "I cannot hear such talk, sir. You have many years. I would rather see this day as a change of administration, and not the end of your life."

Von Rundstedt laughed, pointed to a chair in the far corner of the room.

"Sit down, young man." He looked at Kesselring, shrugged. "You see? There are still officers among us who dream. Tell me, Siegfried, what did you hear in Berlin? What reasons did someone confide in you, the reasons why I am being replaced by my friend Albert?" Westphal did not sit, seemed uncomfortable with the conversation. "Go on, Siegfried. You have no fears here. I know the kind of mud that flows through the High Command, the sort of fantasies they force themselves to believe. Entertain me, one last time."

Westphal hesitated, glanced at Kesselring, who nodded in approval.

"Sir, General Keitel told me that, among your other indiscretions, you have been in contact with the enemy, specifically the British. The Führer was outraged that you would betray us so. I did not believe any of it, but I could not protest. I hope you understand, sir."

Von Rundstedt looked at Kesselring again, raised his hands, a gesture of surrender.

"You see? I too am a conspirator. Be careful, Albert. They will find some conspiracy to hang on *you*."

Kesselring turned toward Westphal. "Keitel actually said that?" He shook his head, rubbed a hand on his chin. "What he told *me* was that we should somehow find the means to bring the British and Americans into the war on our side. I interpreted that as a hint that there are some among the High Command who hope I will find a way to make discreet contact with the enemy." He laughed. "You should know, Siegfried, that the winds blow in odd directions around Berlin. But there is fear there now, more than I have ever observed. The Russians have shattered more than our borders, they have shattered some of the High Command's delusions. I was told of a message being prepared that might somehow be communicated to Churchill in particular: The communists have succeeded in infiltrating our army, and this infiltration is meant to continue westward, into the English army. I cannot speak for Jodl, but I am fairly certain that Keitel believes the Russians cannot be stopped."

Westphal seemed intrigued by Kesselring's frankness.

"But they have been stopped, have they not? I saw the maps."

"A hundred kilometers from Berlin. The Führer considers that to be a victory, insists that our army has found its spirit and we are rising to the fore, inspired by our hatred of the communists. He told me it is only a matter of time before their filthy hordes are tossed back out across the Polish frontier."

"And what do you believe?" von Rundstedt asked.

"I believe the Russians have stopped because they have exhausted themselves, and have stretched their supply lines too far too quickly. Marshal Zhukov is not to be turned back, I am confident of that. The forces that were taken from your command are being sent east to be fed into a meat grinder. It *is* only a matter of time, but not the way the Führer describes. It is a matter of time before the Russians are in the streets of Berlin." He paused. "Forgive me for my dreams, Gerd. But I share the hope that we can somehow convince the Americans and the English to see this war for what it has become. We can persuade them to join us in a fight to keep the communists out of Germany. If Germany falls to Stalin, France could be next."

There was no enthusiasm in Kesselring's statement. Von Rundstedt saw the obvious gloom on the man's face. After a silent moment, he said, "The Americans will not fight a war with the Russians. *We* are the enemy here. Our enemies seek our destruction, and no American and no Englishman will dare to stand up and say, well, this part of the war is over, so now, we must join Hitler's people in a *brand-new* war. No, Albert, they have made it very clear that *unconditional surrender* is the rule that guides them. That, they share with the Russians."

Kesselring did not respond, and von Rundstedt watched Westphal sitting slowly, the young man allowing his own pessimism to seep through.

Westphal said, "The Führer insists that we are close to our final victory. He insists that the Russians have destroyed themselves against our defenses, and that the English and the Americans have tired of fighting. He sees opportunity before us. I heard him myself. Is it wrong to believe him? If we do not have faith in him, are we disloyal?"

Von Rundstedt realized how much affection he had for the young man, felt suddenly sad for him. I shall not live so long, he thought, that I must endure what follows this war. But he . . . deserves to see a better world. We have not given him one, none of us.

"There is always hope, Siegfried."

Von Rundstedt injected as much energy into the lie as he could. Kesselring seemed to read him, but Westphal spoke up.

"There *is* hope! We have squandered so much of our strength, and we continue to squander it. The Führer has ordered us to maintain far-flung outposts, from Scandinavia to Greece, just so he can claim those places on a map. If assembled here, that troop strength can become a formidable fighting force, and can add considerably to our efforts at keeping the Russians away. It is not my place to make such a suggestion, but you can! In Berlin, I was told of the weapons, many being tested even now. Any one of them could turn this thing, or at least convince the Anglos to speak with us, treat with us. Admiral Dönitz has assured me that our strength in submarines has never been greater."

Von Rundstedt could not respond, did not want to erase the young man's last glimmer of optimism. He looked at Kesselring. "General Westphal has served you well in the past, and he will do so again. As you can see, he has lost none of his energy."

Kesselring smiled, said, "Yes, I know. I welcome his service." There was a silent pause, awkward, and after a moment, Kesselring added, "On my journey here, I tried to imagine how different this war might have been if the Führer had enjoyed the counsel of men like Siegfried. Or you. If Rommel had been given what he required in Africa, if Paulus had been allowed to wage his own campaign at Stalingrad, if Göring had not wasted our air resources. So much could have been different."

Von Rundstedt shook his head.

"If Stalin had tripped and fallen under a truck, if Churchill had choked on a peach pit, if the sky itself had fallen onto Patton and Montgomery . . . yes, yes. But I have heard too much of this. You are still a dreamer, Albert. That may serve you well here. This entire war, everything that has happened and everything that lies before us is all a wellspring from a mad little corporal's tortured imagination. No dreaming will change that." He pulled himself up slowly, fought the pains in his back, the dull ache in his chest. "Your authority is recognized, and I relinquish my command to you, Field Marshal. You must continue your fight with those things that fate has provided you. And fate has provided you with Adolf Hitler."

25. PATTON

After a vigorous fight by what was now Patton's Eighth Corps, led by Troy Middleton, the city of Koblenz fell into American hands. All along the Rhine River, the story was similar, Allied troops slugging their way forward, German resistance either falling back across the river or collapsing altogether, vast numbers of prisoners flowing back through the Allied lines.

Gotta hand you one thing, Troy. You're the only commander I have who I haven't cussed out."

Middleton walked beside him, looking down, said nothing. He walked with the familiar limp, favoring the arthritic knee that had bothered him for years. Patton never saw the limp without thinking of George Marshall, the chief of staff assigning Middleton to a field command when others in the War Department thought him too crippled for action.

I'd rather have a man with arthritis in the knee than one with arthritis in the head.

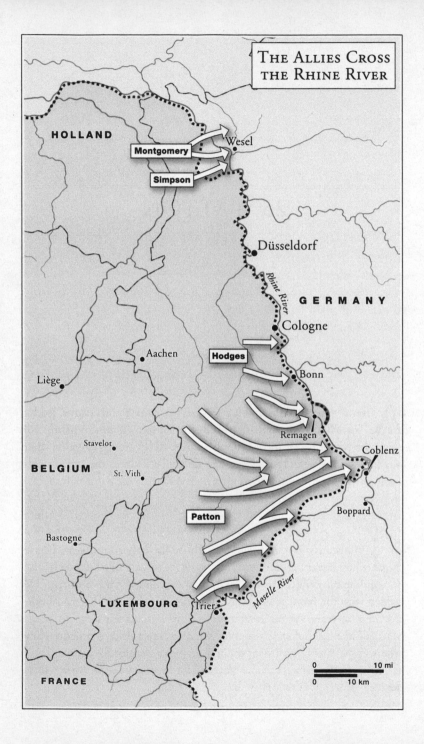

Patton could not have agreed more.

They walked past a line of troop trucks, supply vehicles, men all in motion, the Eighth Corps gathering strength along the west bank of the Rhine River, preparation for the inevitable crossing.

Patton had hoped for more of a response to his compliment, said, "I mean, you've done the job. The Krauts can't swim their way fast enough, and we keep scooping them up in trainloads. Nice job here."

"Thank you, sir."

Middleton's Mississippi drawl was unmistakable, the man's thick glasses and deliberate gait giving him the appearance of a mild-mannered college professor who would more likely be strolling through dogwoods and magnolias. In fact, Middleton was exactly that, or close enough for Patton to tease him about it. Middleton had served as vice president and dean of admissions at Louisiana State University before the war. It was a scholarly description that disguised the reputation he had earned in the First World War when, at twenty-nine, he had become the army's youngest colonel.

All through the Normandy campaign, Middleton had served under Bradley, had done much to clear the Cotentin Peninsula of German resistance, and then had become a part of Patton's now legendary breakout, the final nail that would eventually seal the coffin on Germany's occupation of France. When the Battle of the Bulge began, it was Middleton who had recognized and then reacted to the vital importance of the town of Bastogne where, by a stroke of fate, the Eighth Corps had its headquarters. Unlike several of the higher-ranking commanders, who reacted to the German punch in the Ardennes with what Patton considered panic, Middleton held his ground at Bastogne long enough to allow the 101st Airborne Division to move in and set up their defenses. Patton knew that Middleton was due for some serious recognition for that, though, for now, he still wore only two stars on his collar. Patton glanced over at Middleton, saw him wiping his glasses, a constant chore with so much mud and debris in the air from the moving vehicles.

"You need a third star, dammit. Doing all I can about that."

"Thank you, George. Not truly necessary. I'd trade all this décor for a victory."

"See? That's why I can't cuss you out. I tried in Africa, I tried in Sicily, and by damn, I tried in France. You just won't give me the satisfaction. I've given Ike more lip than I've given you. It's not natural, you know. You need to screw up once in a while, let the men know what kind of a son of a bitch they work for. Keep them on their toes."

"If you say so, sir."

Patton laughed to himself, knew he couldn't get a rise out of Middleton. He was so very different from Manton Eddy, who commanded Patton's Twelfth Corps. Eddy spent most of his time as an agitated wreck, though even when he gave Patton cause to bathe him in swear words, Eddy would eventually get the job done.

Patton slowed his steps, didn't want Middleton to strain the leg. They passed beside a cluster of supply trucks, a team of men unloading heavy wooden crates, some kind of machine parts. The men were covered in grease and sweat, and no neckties. Patton flinched at that, the temptation to explode in their direction, but their good work held him back. No one was wasting motion, no stopping to gaze at the passing brass. Sometimes, he thought, you need to let the boys do their jobs. And right here, we're doing a damn good one. He continued walking, said, "You hear about my press conference?"

Middleton put the glasses back on, adjusted them. "Can't say I did. You get in trouble again?"

"No, dammit. My staff had come up with our prisoner count. I just told the reporters what my people told me. The Third Army has been operational for two hundred thirty days. In that time, we've captured two hundred thirty thousand prisoners. *A thousand a day.* Pretty damn impressive, I thought. Figured the reporters ought to be impressed too, give them something they can say about me besides the usual bitching. Actually, they haven't been writing much of anything lately. Hodges has been getting the headlines, all the Remagen stuff."

"He earned it."

"That's what I told the reporters. He finally got a chance to stop licking his wounds and kick the enemy in the ass. How quick can you get your people across the damn river?"

The question stopped Middleton in his tracks, and Patton was past him, turned, saw a smile.

"When would you like?"

Patton pretended to ponder Middleton's question.

"Well, it's a little late to get started today. But Brad knows all three of my corps are pretty much in place. He's got Ike on his back pushing Hodges to jump over the river around Bonn and drive like hell for Kassel.

I think Brad's a little nervous about that, because he wants me to head that way too, join up with Hodges at the same place, Kassel. Brad thinks that if we can pull that off, we'll trap what's left of the German Seventh Army in a pincer move. That's the official explanation anyway. Brad knows if I send any of you up that way, you'll move a hell of a lot faster than the First Army on its best day, and beat Hodges there by a long shot. I bet he's using that to give Hodges a kick in the ass, like we should make a damn race out of it. It might be the best way Brad has of keeping Hodges from bogging down and screwing everything up."

Middleton seemed to cringe. "You didn't say that to the reporters, did you?"

"Oh, hell no. Can't risk hurting Hodges's feelings." Patton couldn't help the sarcasm. "Heaven forbid we should have any bruised feelings in this army. Nope, we're going to be equal partners, share the spoils. A couple hundred thousand Krauts would make everybody happy. If Devers gets over the river down south and Simpson does the job up north, it's all but over. That's what Ike is thinking, anyway. Everybody's gotta share, though. I can hear that crap being tossed around Ike's headquarters from here. Can't have anybody getting their toes stepped on, and Ike knows that if Brad turns me loose, we won't stop until we get to Berlin. Heaven forbid."

He knew he was treading on sticky ground, but Middleton never reacted to the politics that seemed to swirl around Patton's feet like so much molasses. "You didn't answer my question. How quick can you jump off here?"

"Rather not jump off *here* at all. Difficult ground on both sides of the river."

Patton knew that Middleton had more on his mind than he was saying.

"All right, if it's not Koblenz, where's the best place?"

"My engineers are advising south of here. Boppard. The river current isn't bad at all, and we can send a good number of people across in boats after dark. We establish the bridgehead, it'll put us on a straight shot toward Frankfurt. That'd be kind of a nice trophy. I'm hoping that any crossing we make will be a quiet one, no fanfare, nothing to give the enemy a heads-up. Eddy and Walker both agree with me. But . . . that's your decision of course. You want some kind of *rockets' red glare,* that's what we'll do."

"Already thought it over. No artillery, no advance warning we're coming, or where. Let's just get there, and make it damn quick, even if it's one company. You sure you'll need the twenty-fourth?"

"Can't be helped, George. We've got people strung out way the hell back. If I was to send a small operation across the river just to make headlines, they could get butchered. Not worth it. Sorry, George. I need a couple days. Walker and Eddy are both in better shape. You already know that, I guess."

Patton didn't answer. He knew he could count on Middleton for complete honesty, but he didn't ever want to ask Manton Eddy how ready *he* might be. If Patton wanted Eddy to move, he simply ordered him to move. Patton had more faith in Walton Walker, the third of his corps commanders. One way or the other, Patton would get somebody from the Third Army across the river before anyone on either side knew what was happening. He had endured all the *passive defense* he could stand, that peculiarly ridiculous order Omar Bradley had insisted on, the order Patton had obeyed by attacking at every opportunity.

"All right, get your ass across the river on the twenty-fourth. I'll tell Walker to put somebody over there as quick as he can. Maybe quicker."

"So, when's Monty jumping off?"

Patton hated hearing the name, but he couldn't fault Middleton, knew exactly why he asked the question.

"Same day as *you,* dammit. According to Ike, Monty's grand plan is to make his move by the twenty-fourth. But first, he has to make sure every truck in England is parked in a straight line, he has to put every man in a perfect new uniform, oil every damn rifle, and make sure King George has had his breakfast. Then, he might attack. Unless somebody shoots at him first. Then he'll have to start all over."

Middleton kept his laugh discreet.

"Don't worry about us, George. We'll be across before Monty."

Patton rested his hands on his pistols, saw one of the men taking his picture, standing tall in the back of a large truck. Others had noticed Patton, were cheering him, and to one side a young lieutenant stood at the rear of a kitchen truck, staring with an open mouth. The officer held an enormous ladle in one hand, snapped a salute, still holding the ladle. He seemed paralyzed with intimidation, food dripping on his open-collared shirt. Patton felt a slug of disgust, said to Middleton, "Fine that jackass fifty bucks. Next time I see him, he'll be in a proper uniform or you'll bust him to corporal. And for God's sake, tell him an officer shouldn't be dishing out the oatmeal."

Middleton motioned to an aide trailing behind them, the man overhearing Patton's order, moving quickly toward the dumbstruck lieutenant. Patton turned away, the matter settled, already gone from his mind. There was an intersection ahead, the traffic moving slowly, and he saw a howitzer towed by a truck, another, following behind. He loved watching the artillery moving forward, knew that the big guns wouldn't go unless the ground was already in his hands. But there was traffic coming the other way as well, ragged civilians, two children leading a small dog, one old man hauling a two-wheeled wagon by hand. Patton kept walking, stood beside the remnants of the paved road, heard the artillerymen shouting his name. He ignored them, saw the old man looking at him, no recognition, dull despair in the man's eyes. On the far side of the road, a group of refugees had gathered on a small knoll, the road becoming too congested with heavy vehicles. Patton saw a cart, heavy with clothing, half a dozen women in filthy dresses, one carrying a baby, wrapped in a rag of a blanket. Patton stared at them, the details, some without shoes, others wearing what must have been expensive clothes. One woman's beauty showed through the dirt and misery, a child clinging to her, the young face staring wide-eyed at the passing cannon. But the adults kept their gazes to themselves, ignored the convoy, paid no attention to the guns, or the generals who stood only a few feet away. He tried to feel sadness, remembered how this scene had played out everywhere the wars had taken him. Not so different, he thought. They might as well be French or Belgian or Sicilian, that same look, the dull shock, people who've lost everything in their lives.

Another man came past, older still, pushing a wheelbarrow, piled high with whatever possessions he thought worth saving. He stopped beside the women, low greetings, people who knew one another, neighbors perhaps, people who shared the misery. Patton saw one woman crying, the mother and baby moving closer, comforting, anguish and tears spreading through them all. More of the big artillery pieces moved past him, blocking his view, and Patton tried to focus on the guns, heard more cheers from his men, but his eyes went back to the refugees.

Beside him, Middleton said, "Terrible. War always hurts the innocent."

Patton shook his head.

"They're not innocent of anything. This is *their* war. You expect me to feel bad about that? Hell, General, I did this to them! I blasted their homes to rubble and erased their villages from the map. And if they can't get out of the way, I'm going to do it some more. I won't feel sorry for Germans, you hear me? Let's get across that goddamn river."

In the pitch darkness on March 22, Company K, the Eleventh Regiment of the American Fifth Infantry Division, part of Walker's Twentieth Corps, paddled their way across the Rhine River in small boats, reaching the east bank without arousing any response. The German forces that stood to oppose them had been caught completely off guard. Throughout the following day, the remainder of the Fifth Infantry crossed by boat, while engineers began to lay dozens of pontoon bridges strong enough to support vast columns of tanks and heavy artillery. The bridgehead was expanded, the Americans driving away the disheartened enemy forces, who knew with perfect certainty that their last great barrier had been breached.

Patton had made his crossing of the Rhine without any direct orders from Omar Bradley to do so. Despite the overwhelming number of heavy artillery pieces available, the crossings by each of Patton's corps commanders were made at night, in silence, with no artillery bombardment at all. Thus, without advance warning that the Americans were coming, every crossing was successful, with minimal casualties, utterly surprising the Germans who waited on the other side. Given the rapid construction of the bridges, the engineers paved the way for the rest of Patton's mechanized forces, and within three days the Third Army was driving into the outskirts of Frankfurt.

On March 24, Patton could not resist a typical stunt that would put his name back in the headlines. Walking across one of his bridges, he made great ceremony of stopping his entourage in midstream. Undoing his trousers, Patton urinated into the river.

To the north, Montgomery pushed across the river on the schedule Eisenhower had been promised. Montgomery's operation began with a parachute drop that included twenty-three thousand men, the largest airborne assault of the entire war. Dropping close to German lines in daylight, the paratroopers and their transports endured heavy losses from German ground fire, but support from two thousand Allied fighter planes helped drive the enemy away. Joining the paratroopers as a preliminary to the main assault, Montgomery employed hundreds of heavy artillery pieces in a spectacular show of strength, a massive bombardment that preceded a crossing by eighty thousand British and Canadian troops. As had happened all along the Allied front, the Germans backed away, overwhelmed by the power they faced. Despite Montgomery's extraordinary display, which was trumpeted loudly in the British newspapers, once more Patton had won the race.

With the bridgeheads quickly secured, six Allied armies crossed the Rhine River. To many of the Allied generals, the next logical target should have been Berlin. But that decision had been made weeks before, at the Yalta Conference. Despite the rapid collapse of organized German opposition, the Allied forces were ordered to extend their advance only as far as the Elbe River, some forty miles short of the German capital. No matter how vehemently Patton and Montgomery hoped to wage war against both the enemy and each other for the great prize, President Roosevelt had already promised that prize to the Russians. Eisenhower continued to hear grousing from Winston Churchill, objections to the Yalta agreements that carried no weight. Directed by the politics he tried to avoid, Eisenhower had no choice but to focus his advances more to the south, rolling over crumbling German resistance on a path that would push into southern Germany and beyond, bypassing the Berlin area altogether. Eisenhower had accepted the same political realities as Churchill. At Yalta, Joseph Stalin had demanded that his army alone would take Berlin. No one but the Germans would stand in his way.

PART THREE

REPORTER: Will the Nazis go underground when the
  Allies get to Germany?
PATTON: Six feet.

26. BENSON

Near Nantes, France
March 31, 1945

On March 14, the remnants of the 106th Infantry Division were pulled back from the fighting on the Rhine River front and transferred west, to assist in dealing with an annoying problem. Throughout the great push inland from the Normandy beachheads, the Germans still maintained strongholds along the Atlantic coast in Brittany, the territory that Patton had first swept through on his breakout in August. But clearing the Germans out of the fortified seaports of Saint-Nazaire, Lorient, and La Rochelle would have required considerable time and possibly casualties that weren't worth the prize. Throughout the late summer and fall of 1944, as the Allied armies pushed eastward, the German ports were hemmed in both on land and at sea and essentially ignored. The only advantage the Germans had were their fortifications, but there was little chance that they were going anywhere, even if Hitler had ordered them to break out. None of the German commanders had sufficient strength to try such a move, and Eisenhower knew that if the war was won in Germany, those strongholds would surrender anyway. There was no reason to charge the battlements at the cost of American lives.

Still thought of as orphans, the men of the 106th were attached to the

66th Division, who were part of the forces keeping watch on the Brittany ports. Word had come that a vast new wave of recruits was soon to rejuvenate the 106th, but since those men would be as green and untested as any in the army, it was highly unlikely that the newly re-formed division would see combat again, unless the war continued long enough to drain away American strength on the front lines, something Eisenhower did not expect to happen. Rather than have a newly strengthened 106th sit idly by, accomplishing little more than the consumption of rations, SHAEF determined that the division could fulfill a job that was becoming more essential every day. The inflow of German prisoners of war was overwhelming the small contingents of military police and other troops who had been guarding them. Enormous compounds had to be constructed, and quickly, and an organization had to be assembled to offer medical assistance, food, and shelter for what had already become hundreds of thousands of POWs. The order soon came: The 106th Division would become the prison guards.

T hey are out of their damn minds! No way in hell I'm gonna stand around and poke a bayonet at prisoners!"

Benson had seen Mitchell angry before, but this was different, a fury bordering on panic.

Higgins looked at the captain, said, "Sir, my apologies. If you'll allow me a minute or two with my men."

The captain had not expected this kind of reception to his news, held up both hands, backed away.

"They're your men, Sergeant. I've got three new lieutenants to check on, make sure their baby bottles are full. I've got no time for this kind of bitching."

The captain moved away, and Benson could see the rest of the squad looking at Mitchell like he was far stranger than they had thought.

Higgins turned toward him, hands on his hips, said, "What the hell is wrong with you? You mouth off like that, you're lucky the captain didn't toss you in the stockade. We're being given a noncombat assignment. Every damn unit in this army would jump at that. Besides, once the Four Two Two and Four Two Three are re-formed, they're gonna need veterans."

"Why? To teach them how to do what? Stand outside a fence? Even those new lieutenants can handle that on their own. Dammit, Sarge, I want to fight."

Higgins looked at Benson. "What about you? You as nuts as your buddy?"

"I don't know, Sarge."

Benson had wondered if this would happen, if Mitchell would explode from the gloomy boredom that Benson had felt for weeks now. He had never been as manically driven to killing Germans as Mitchell, but he knew exactly why Mitchell was upset. He looked at the others, saw surprise, heads shaking.

To one side, one of the new men spoke up. "You *are* nuts. Going home in one piece makes a whole lot more sense than trying to find a way to get your brains blown out. I got a wife waiting for me."

Mitchell kept his stare on the sergeant, said, "I don't intend to get anything blown out except this damn rifle. Dammit, Sarge, I want to volunteer for some other duty, something besides nursemaiding POWs. I've seen too many guys get hit, too many guys get hauled away, not to do something about it. Hell, this unit spent lieutenants like pennies at an arcade. I'm just not done yet, that's all."

Benson could feel the emotion in his voice, the man's words driving into him. He looked down at his boots, a growling nervousness in his stomach. He thought of Yunis, the helpless soldier curled up in a mass of fear, left behind in the frozen foxhole. The image of that had risen up late at night, and Benson gripped hard to the fantasy that maybe Yunis had survived. But what then? Would he go home to some kind of hero's welcome? Would Yunis be one of those old bigmouthed soldiers at family gatherings who spouted off all kinds of stories about exploits that none of them had ever experienced? And what about these guys, right here? Most of them are new, and they'll never even see a German who's not already done for. The rest of us spent most of our time running for our damn lives. Nice thing to tell your grandkids.

He knew that the others thought Mitchell was a fanatic, had already heard low talk about keeping their distance from the man who might go off like some kind of human grenade. But dammit, he's my friend, and he saved my ass more than once. Maybe I need to return the favor.

"Me too, Sarge. I wanna volunteer to go back. Maybe we're both nuts, but Kenny and I been through everything together. When they pulled us out of Kraut land, I thought I'd be ready to quit, to go home, or whatever else. But there's something we haven't done yet."

"What the hell are you talking about?"

Mitchell nodded toward Benson, said, "Yep. He's right. Look, Sarge, we came over here to do a job, a job every damn one of us knew was important. We spent months learning how to fight, all that baloney the officers fed us. And for what? All we did was get our asses kicked. We didn't start moving in the right direction until somebody else had bailed us out. We took more losses than any division in the army, far as I know. Our whole damn regiment disappeared! There's something to be proud of! I can't just go home and pretend I left here a soldier. I've gotta do my part, and damn it all, if that makes me nuts, fine. But there's a pile of Krauts out there who are still trying to kill our guys, and I need to do something about that." He looked toward Benson, a quick nod. "Thanks, Eddie."

Higgins looked at the others, no one else joining in Mitchell's enthusiasm, and the sergeant thought for a long moment.

"Tell you what. I'll talk to the captain. The repple-depple is crawling with orphans, mostly brand-new guys. There's gotta be someplace they'd want veterans to go." He looked at Benson. "You sure you wanna do this? So far, you've both been lucky as hell. We made it out of this stinking mess alive, two arms and two legs."

Mitchell looked at Benson, then at the others, no one else speaking up.

"I'm not saying everybody oughta feel this way. And I'm not calling anybody a coward. But from what we hear, the Krauts are still kicking up a fight. I need to be there. I joined up to help win a war. I feel like I've done a piss-poor job so far."

Higgins turned away, said, "I'll be back. You two are either heroes or morons. It's a toss-up."

Benson had boarded the truck last, as he always did, still carried the embarrassing fear that he would get motion sickness. But his stomach was calm, even if his brain was racing with thoughts of what they had volunteered to do. His mind flashed to Higgins, the last handshake, the sergeant offering them one more chance to change their minds. Higgins had done as he'd said, and the captain had agreed to allow any volunteers who wanted to transfer to the replacement depot, where there was still the urgent need for experienced riflemen. Benson and Mitchell had been the only two to volunteer from the entire company. Benson was surprised by that, but many of the others were veterans of the 424th, the only organized combat regiment that still existed from the 106th. Those men had fought tenaciously throughout the Bulge, had not been as scattered, had not lost their leadership and most of their numbers, and Benson could find no reason to fault them for feeling that they had done enough. Benson had been disappointed that Higgins didn't join them, but the sergeant owed them no explanations. Before the transfer orders came, Benson heard talk that Higgins might be promoted to lieutenant. That's gotta be worth something, Benson thought. Not just the prestige, or whatever those ninety-day wonders think about. He knows how to lead people, and he knows what he's doing, and he ought to go home with something besides a combat infantry badge. The sarge knows that all those replacements are gonna need their butts whipped pretty often, and he'll be a good one to do it. I'll bet the captain knows that too. No way the brass would have let Higgins come with us. And I bet he wanted to, no matter what else he said.

Mitchell's urgent need to keep fighting was no surprise at all to Benson, but his own decision had given him waves of second thoughts. He carried the same horrors as Higgins and Mitchell, had escaped the same disasters, had survived a fight too many had not.

They rode in a convoy of trucks, the deuce-and-a-half one of several dozen, mostly supply trucks. The roads were better than any Benson could recall, the good work of the engineers, bomb craters repaired, mud holes filled. Across from him, Mitchell had been quiet, staring out through the canvas covering, the calm vacant stare, the M-1 resting against one leg. Benson followed his gaze, out past the truck in line behind them. The sky was a dull gray, a smattering of rain, and Benson thought of the first time they had done this, frozen misery through Belgium, vomit and ridicule. We had no idea, he thought. I was terrified and didn't really know why. Those guys with the big mouths, Lane, the others, they're happy as hell to go do guard duty, aim all their big talk to German POWs. And they will. Talk.

He glanced down at his rifle, caught the smell of gun oil, a slight turn in his stomach. Stop that, dammit! He looked out the back of the truck again, his mind racing with memories, flexed his fingers, no stiffness, a mild chill in the air. Thank God for spring. The truck slowed, a rumble beneath him as the truck eased one side off the road's edge, crawled to a stop. He heard shouts, saw trucks moving slowly past, going the other way. They were open-topped, no canvas, filled with filthy bareheaded men. The driver began to yell curses, others from the convoy joining in, and Benson saw jeeps following, a man standing at a machine gun, two more jeeps, another truck. He saw more of the uniforms of the passengers, gray, some wrapped in rags of blankets, bandaged wounds. *Prisoners.* He felt his heart jump, tried to see their faces, but they were past, their war over. He curled one hand hard around the stock of the rifle, tried to breathe, calming himself, saw no expression on Mitchell's face. He leaned back against the railing of the truck, felt a rush of energy. *That's why I needed to do this. I hate those bastards, I hate what they did to our guys, what they did to the civilians.* He felt a shiver, the image in his mind that was never completely gone. It had been there in his nightmares, one awful memory, the rows of Belgians, old men and children simply executed, and then, the body of the woman, violated beyond description, the kind of horror that has no explanation. He looked at Mitchell again, still no response, thought, *he remembers that too. That's why he's here. But, I gotta admit, he is a little strange. The sarge was right about that.* He spoke to Mitchell in his mind. *Don't you go and do anything stupid, Kenny. I still want us to get home in one piece. I'm not sure you care one way or the other. Guess that's why I came along, to keep an eye on you.*

The truck lurched into motion again, the other men adjusting to the movement, shifting in their seats. Benson heard the groans, didn't know much about them, except that they were all replacements, green soldiers. He looked at the man beside Mitchell, saw youth, wide eyes, pimples and pale skin. Eighteen, maybe. *You have no idea, kid. You guys must be draftees, somehow got caught up in that mess of army paperwork that put you in the repple-depple. No loyalty, no rah-rah of those idiotic pep rallies we had in Indiana. Yeah, the 106th is the* best. *Sure we were. Ask the Krauts about that.* Benson knew little else about the dozen other men who rode with them in the truck, no names, only bits of small talk among them as they gathered to load up. They were a part of several detachments being sent eastward, plugging holes in some of the units where the fighting had been hot. Benson had heard some of the unit designations, meaningless to him now, no identity that mattered. Except one. This time, they would be fighting under Patton.

27. BENSON

They rode on a tank, what seemed at first to be one more grand adventure, the tank commanders offering the invitation as though these foot soldiers were among the very privileged. Despite the rapid progress along the roads, a far cry from the usual march, Benson was regretting his own stupidity. The convoy of armor rolled along a narrow farm road, stirring up vast clouds of dust, the half dozen men huddled around him doing what he was doing, pulling his jacket over his face, trying to breathe something besides a fog of German dirt. With every lurching dip on the uneven road, the men would fight to hang on, hands gripping every kind of hardware, coils of rope, grease, and gas cans. There was no need for extra warmth, but it was there anyway, swirling around them in a stink of black exhaust. Benson bounced high, came down hard on solid steel, his rifle barrel slapping his helmet, nearly dislodging it. He glanced at Mitchell, saw the man's face buried in his jacket, thought, boy, this is some fun, huh, Kenny? I wonder where in hell we're going. I guess having a Sherman for a companion might be good, no matter where we end up.

The tank began to slow, then stopped, the cloud of exhaust giving way to a soft breeze that cleared away the smoke. The tank's engine was idling and Benson peered up, saw the hatch coming open right in front of him, avoided a broken nose by ducking to one side.

The Sherman's commander appeared, said, "Everybody off! There's a village up ahead, Waltherhausen, or something like that. Our orders are to fan out, hold a line to the south. The brass wants you guys right here."

The infantrymen slid off, groans of relief, clouds of dust rolling off each man, some slapping at their pants and jackets, some coughing, one man, a sergeant, saluting the tank commander.

"Thank you, sir. We appreciate the ride."

"Don't call me sir, sergeant. I'm not an officer. But there's supposed to be a command post moving up here behind us. You'll find all the officers you need."

The tank commander spoke into a radio, something Benson couldn't hear, then gave a command to his driver, the tank spewing out a hard belch of smoke, the treads throwing clods of dirt back toward the foot soldiers.

Mitchell was close to him, said, "Cocky son of a bitch not to be an officer."

Benson spit dirt from his mouth, checked his rifle, said, "You'd be too if you had a cannon and half a dozen machine guns to play with."

"Not me. I ever run up on a Tiger tank, I'd whole lot rather hide in some hole than in some tin can. I'm not so keen on fighting a duel with somebody bigger than me. Done too much of that already."

Benson looked at the sergeant, another of the new men, who had probably earned his stripes in some stateside training camp. The sergeant watched the tanks pull away with what seemed like sadness, and Benson said, "Hey, Sarge. What you want us to do now?"

The sergeant shrugged, clearly had no idea, turned and watched as the others gathered, a full platoon of men. There were more coming up the road behind them, more passengers from the armored column that had already disappeared across flat fields and two-rut roads that ran to the south. Back along the columns of foot soldiers, Benson heard a voice, an order.

"Two abreast! We need to make sure there're no straggler Krauts out here. Move into the houses, check 'em out. No screwing around!"

It was the first time Benson had heard an order from the officer in charge, a lieutenant who seemed angry at the world, more angry at the men he now commanded.

Mitchell said quietly, "What's his problem? Wonder if he's ever done this before."

"Maybe that's his problem. He probably hasn't. But I bet he's heard all about the life span of lieutenants."

The officer moved past them, shouldered a carbine, a map in his hand, said nothing else, the others falling in behind him. Benson and Mitchell fell into line, marched through an intersection, heavy churned ruts where some of the tanks had turned off, but the infantrymen were moving straight ahead. They climbed a slight rise, the lieutenant leading them forward with seemingly no concern for what might be on the other side of the hill. No, Benson thought, I don't think he's done this before. Benson crested the hill at a much slower pace than the men in front of him, Mitchell slipping more toward the edge of the road, close to cover. Benson could see the village, wondered if anyone else had been there first, if the place had been secured. The lieutenant hadn't said a word about it. Benson could see more of the rooftops, a small village, mostly intact, and from every house something white was hanging from a window, makeshift flags of sheets and tablecloths.

Beside him, Mitchell said, "Wonderful. Either we're about to be smothered in kisses and sauerkraut, or it's the perfect ambush. Watch yourself, kiddo."

The lieutenant led them past the first of the buildings, a small house, and the officer pointed that way, two men responding by moving to the door. Benson stared at the windows, mostly open, curtains flapping, and now, across the street, other doors began to open, people emerging. Benson raised the rifle, nervous instinct, watched one old man moving toward the lieutenant, speaking in a rush of German, gesturing down the street. More people appeared, civilians from every building, moving out in small groups, some staying close to their homes, others approaching the soldiers. Benson focused on the women, clean dresses.

Mitchell said, "They've dressed up in their Sunday best. No accident there. See all that face paint? A whole new kind of ambush."

The army had issued orders against fraternization, was levying fines, though few were sure just how anyone would enforce that. Benson had endured the usual lectures at the replacement depot about all the *dangers* they might find in the women they encountered, German or otherwise. After one particularly graphic and unpleasant film, Benson had no interest in testing if what the army was telling them about German women was just propaganda. Already rumors were flying, tales from other advanced units that the women were as likely to be carrying a knife as a venereal disease, and Benson had already given himself a lecture about his own behavior. Mitchell never seemed to care one way or the other about civilians, except the ones who wanted you dead. It was a lesson in priorities Benson had taken to heart.

The lieutenant held up the column, moved back toward them, said, "Anybody speak Kraut? This old guy's trying to tell me something, and he's pretty damn excited about it."

Mitchell said, "Why don't we just let him show us the way, sir? He's obviously got something he wants us to see. He might be out to pull some crap, but he can count rifles, and I bet he heard those damn tanks. Just keep him right in front of us, in case there's a sniper. If the old guy starts to backtrack or act squirrelly, shoot him and take cover."

The lieutenant stared at Mitchell, then nodded slowly.

"Yeah, good idea. All right, let's see what he's up to. Why don't you and your buddy take the point."

Mitchell moved closer to the old man, pointed his rifle into the German's stomach, the old man's enthusiasm turning to uncertainty, then anger. He began to speak again, pointing farther into the village.

Mitchell glanced at Benson, then said to the old man, "Okay, okay, I'm not going to shoot you yet. Go on! Let's solve this big mystery." He looked back toward the lieutenant. "Sir, you best stay back behind the first dozen guys, where it's safe."

The lieutenant said nothing, was fumbling with the radio, didn't seem to catch the sarcasm in Mitchell's voice. Benson moved up close to the old man, who was still waving them on furiously, a cascade of words. Mitchell motioned down the street, and the old man glanced nervously again at the muzzle of Mitchell's rifle, began to move in short quick steps.

Benson kept pace, searched the windows, nervous now, some of the larger homes and buildings with second stories. Behind them, the others had moved up, still two abreast, the only talk coming from the German civilians who continued to gather in small groups along the side of the street. Benson scanned them, focused on their hands, searched for some hint of a weapon. Most were waving, calling out, smiles, but there were others, grim silent stares, the message unmistakable. Benson said, "Not everybody's happy to see us. These ain't Belgians."

He heard a woman's voice above, one loud word, and behind him a hard grunt. Benson turned, saw the man go down, his helmet lopsided, a brick tumbling to the street beside him. Benson caught the movement in the window above, saw an old woman, her raised fist, more cursing, another brick in her hand, and now a shot, the muzzle blast just behind him, deafening, the woman punched back into the house. Benson put a hand over his ear, turned, saw Mitchell aiming, a wisp of smoke from his rifle. Other soldiers were kneeling around the fallen man, the lieutenant scampering up.

"What happened? Sniper?"

The injured man was up quickly, one hand nursing his shoulder.

"The bitch hit me with a brick!" The medic was there quickly, but the soldier shrugged him off. "I'm okay. Sore as hell. Bruised up, that's all. Damn, I never saw her, until . . . he shot her."

They were looking at Mitchell now, the lieutenant's eyes shifting from his rifle to the window above.

"Somebody needs to go check her out. Medic, take two men, see if she's dead." The officer paused, said to Mitchell, "Hey, soldier. Don't you check something out before you blast away?"

Mitchell didn't respond, stared up at the window, obviously prepared to shoot again.

Benson said, "No, sir. Not a good idea to take chances. All we knew is a German threw a weapon at us. If that'd been a grenade, we wouldn't be talking about it."

The lieutenant seemed unsure how to respond, kept his stare on Mitchell.

"Fine. Good job, I guess."

Benson saw faces in the window above, the medic.

"She's dead, sir. No one else here. There's a photograph on the wall of a Kraut soldier."

The lieutenant waved them down.

"Let's go. Where's that old man?"

Benson saw the man, staring up at the window, horror on his face, sadness, words coming again, angry, aimed at the woman's house. Benson thought, he's cursing her. Yep, pretty damn stupid, no matter how much you love Nazis. Unless you've got something better than a brick. The old man seemed to gather himself, the talk coming again, waving them forward. Benson scanned the windows, his hands shaking, the old annoyance, a sick stirring in his stomach. Across the street, the faces of the people had changed, wide-eyed shock, no more smiles. Mitchell didn't wait for the lieutenant, began to move again, prodding the old man forward. The civilians were hesitant, but slowly, they began to respond, some talking to the old man, sounds of encouragement, some moving with the soldiers. Benson kept his eyes on them, saw some raising their hands, palms out, a clear sign that they had no fight to make, that they were no threat. Yeah, he thought, this isn't a damn parade.

The old man was hurrying now, and Mitchell kept pace, Benson hustling to keep up. The old man turned a corner, and Mitchell hugged the wall, eased around, motioned to the others to follow. Benson saw a beer hall, more shops, the doors wide open, faces behind glass, more waving.

Mitchell said, "Word's passed pretty quick. Now they all wanna be our pals."

The old man stopped now, pointed to a large house.

Mitchell pulled him back by the shoulder. "Okay, far enough. What do you think, kiddo? Guess we oughta take a look."

Benson moved up toward the door, and the lieutenant was there now, said, "You want to do it? Well, okay then." He looked at Benson. "Maybe grab a grenade. Anybody tries anything funny, toss it in. No screwing around! The rest of you, watch the crowd, watch the windows!"

Benson saw the look from Mitchell, a hint of annoyance with the lieutenant who had no idea. Mitchell's rifle came up, aiming at the door, and Benson eased forward, his heart pounding, stared at the door's handle, thought, don't be locked . . . and the door suddenly opened. Benson jumped back, startled, Mitchell's rifle pointing past him, and Benson saw a woman, her hands moving out to the side, a look of sad resignation.

Benson said, "No! Don't shoot."

Mitchell moved up to the door, a small laugh.

"Don't worry, kiddo. I'm not trigger-happy."

The woman motioned with her hand, no fear in her eyes, stepped back, an invitation.

The lieutenant said, "Follow her. But be careful."

Mitchell moved past Benson, the rifle pointed at the woman, and Benson saw now that there were bloodstains on her dress, her hands crusted with dull red. Benson pushed in close behind Mitchell, saw her gesture silently toward the basement door. It was open, and Mitchell led the way with the rifle, started down the steps, and now the voices.

"Thank God!"

"Don't shoot! Americans!"

Benson saw now, the floor of the basement was lined with half a dozen men, lying flat, all with bloody uniforms, bandaged legs and chests and heads. Benson called out, "Medic! It's okay, it's our guys!"

He scrambled down the steps, knelt low, talk coming from several of the men, grateful relief. The lieutenant came down quickly, said, "What happened here? Who are you?"

Benson saw sergeant's stripes, the man with a heavy bandage around his chest.

"We were ambushed, sir. Our patrol . . . they got a bunch of us. The ones who could walk . . . the Krauts took with them. Pretty rough, sir."

Mitchell said, "Where? The town? We'll level the damn place."

"No, no. The road to the east. We were the advance for the artillery, following behind the armor, a tank platoon from the Fourteenth. We did something stupid, wandered out through an orchard, ran slap into a Kraut armored column. They were pulling out of here, and we stumbled right into their path. We didn't have a chance. The townsfolk . . . helped us. The woman here, she's something of a nurse, I think. We're lucky to be alive. The Krauts were in a hell of a hurry to leave, or they'd have finished us off, I'm pretty sure of that."

The medic was moving from man to man, checking the bandages, and now the woman was down beside him, a flurry of German, pointing to the bandages, her own handiwork.

Beside Benson, the lieutenant said, "Well, it's good to see you boys. We'll get you out of here, get you to an aid station."

"Sir, we heard a shot. You find a sniper? The nurse acted like the bad guys had all gone away."

The lieutenant glanced at Mitchell, who moved away, began to climb the steps.

"We had some trouble. Took care of it. Where's my radio?"

"Here, sir."

Benson watched the lieutenant fumble with the radio, reporting what they'd found, giving an all-clear to a place that might still have an enemy close by. Benson followed Mitchell up, back out into the daylight, saw the old man there still, all smiles, nodding, more fast words, obviously pleased with himself.

Mitchell moved past him, and Benson said, "Yeah, thank you. Thank you for your help. I guess you're not all butchers."

More soldiers were fanning out through the town, some in jeeps, and Benson followed Mitchell back out to the main street. Trucks were coming in, officers, the command post, men with radios, a kitchen truck. The civilians were still there, watching it all, watching the Americans occupy their town, a few starting to cheer, others just staring, cold silence.

Mitchell seemed to move aimlessly, nothing to do, and Benson stayed close to him, said, "Good work, Kenny. You mighta saved our asses back there. That old lady coulda had a grenade."

Mitchell looked at him, shrugged, watched the officers spitting out their commands, radios carried into one tall building, one truck moving up close, then another, an ambulance. Medics scrambled out, moved past them toward the house where the woman had made her own hospital.

Benson said, "I guess the lieutenant got these guys on the radio. Those GIs are damn lucky."

Mitchell shouldered his rifle.

"Yeah. But that sergeant said there were more who didn't make it. This ain't a picnic, kiddo, not yet."

"You! Soldier!"

Benson turned, saw an older man, the unmistakable aura of brass. "Where's your lieutenant?"

Benson pointed back toward the woman's house, said, "There, sir. We found some wounded—"

"Forget that. Get him, get your unit in gear. You're moving out. We've picked up some displaced persons, a bunch of Armenians, said there's a prison camp down this road. The enemy is hightailing it, and the prisoners are wandering all over hell."

Benson heard the lieutenant coming out from the side street.

"Sir! We've found—"

"Never mind, Lieutenant. Put your men on these trucks. Take this road, a few miles south, see what the hell's going on. Reports are sketchy, but it's not hot. The enemy is pulling back, and we've got armor chasing them. But the lead tanks say that things are a real mess down there. Get going! We'll have some people right behind you. I'm sending Charlie Company on a parallel road."

"What's our objective, sir?"

Benson cringed, the question straight from a training manual. The older officer turned away. "All I know is what the map says. And what those Armenians said. Place is called Ohrdruf."

OHRDRUF, GERMANY
APRIL 4, 1945

They climbed down from the truck, rifles ready, the field along the road suddenly erupting with men moving toward them in a mad scramble. Behind Benson, a jeep rolled up close, one man high on the fifty-caliber, an officer in the front standing as well. The officer shouted out, "Hold your fire! They're not armed!"

Benson moved out across the road, stood on the edge of the field, more GIs coming up beside him, some dropping to one knee, rifles ready. In the field, the wave of men drew closer, some stumbling. Beside him, Mitchell said, "They're all wearing uniforms. Looks liked striped pajamas."

The men began to reach the soldiers, and Benson saw the faces, realized the men were bone-thin, emaciated, hollow eyes and cheeks. They were speaking, not German, but some language Benson had never heard. One man dropped to his knees in front of Benson, crying, heavy sobs, the sounds growing, desperate and pleading.

Behind Benson, the officer said, "Get these men some rations. Anything you've got."

The officer returned to the jeep, began to talk into a radio, and Benson felt one man's hands on his leg, bones for fingers, the man choking, out of breath. Now another man spoke, pieces of English.

"Go! Go! This road! Many more! Please!"

Behind Benson, the officer called out, "On foot! Move out on this road."

Benson was still in the grip of the man, stared down at the man's strange clothes, filthy pajamas, and he caught the smell now, sour and sickening. Others were moving close, some pointing the way, the way the officer had ordered them to march. Benson stepped back, the man's fingers giving way, and he wanted to say something, felt overwhelmed, too many questions. Who are these people?

He felt a hand on his arm, Mitchell, who said, "Let's move out. Sounds like there's a bunch of these guys."

They marched for a short way, the brush falling away, the grounds flat, and Benson saw a vast spread of wooden buildings, surrounded by tall wire. The road led straight toward a wide double gate, the gate open, more of the men in the striped pajamas standing there, motionless, watching the GIs come. Around him, men began to comment, low voices. Benson felt his heart racing, but it wasn't fear. Beside him, Mitchell said, "Good God. What's happened to these people?"

"They're prisoners, Kenny. The Krauts took off, I guess."

Prisoners emerged through the gates, more of the tearful greetings, desperately thin men, some barely able to walk, some not moving at all. Behind him, Benson heard the officer, "Keep moving! Get inside the wire! Keep your eyes out."

Mitchell said quietly, "No Krauts here. They're gone. They knew we were coming and didn't have the guts to stick around and explain this."

The soldiers moved past the gates, and Benson saw many more of the stripe-clad men stumbling forward, some sitting, leaning against the wooden buildings, unable to move. Some were waving to the soldiers, motioning them in one direction, and Benson felt a sudden dread, caught a new smell, the air thick and foul, like dead animals or rotten garbage. The smells grew, sickening waves, much worse, and Benson forced himself forward, one hand across his face. More of the soldiers followed the prisoners, and past the first building Benson stopped, weak-kneed, stumbled, unavoidable sickness, hands hard on the dirt, the smells overpowering him. He fought against it, spit hard, wiped his mouth with a sleeve. He stood again, followed the soldiers moving along the fence, some staying back, others moving into a barrack-like buildings. A group of soldiers had gathered out on the open ground, some turning away, tears, raw anger, much more sickness, and he moved past them, stopped suddenly, shocked by a new grotesque horror. Spread out across the hard dirt were several dozen dead men, the pajamas stained red, the wounds not so old.

Mitchell said, "Holy Christ. They shot them . . . and pulled their pants down. What the hell?"

More of the prisoners were calling out, feeble voices, some English, pulling soldiers toward the horrific scene.

"See! See what they did!"

"Guards ran away!"

Benson tried to move close, but his mind could not see anymore, and he backed away, heard the soft shouts, feeble cries, hard angry voices, officers trying to find some order.

"Sick men here! Medics, over here!"

The GIs were spreading out past the barracks, some officers taking command, medics scrambling among the prisoners. Benson moved with slow automatic steps, saw men at a closed door, rifles ready, and he felt

NO LESS THAN VICTORY   343

helpless, didn't know what else to do, moved up close to them, Mitchell beside him. They pushed the door open, and there were grunts, most of the soldiers backing away, reflex, the odor enormous, pushing them away. Benson fought it, his eyes searching the darkness, saw the room stacked high with corpses, a hundred or more, five or six deep. There was a thick white powder spread over them, and behind him, someone said, "Lime. To get rid of the smell. Couldn't have been more than a day or two ago. This just happened."

Benson felt blinded, the smells and the sights too overpowering. He stumbled, heard a crack, fell backward, landed hard, saw the striped cloth, the man's eyes gone, his back against a fence post. Benson had stepped on the man's leg, crushed the fragile bone, but it didn't matter. There was nothing left of the man but skin and skeleton. Mitchell was there, helped him up, Benson's legs weak, barely holding him. More GIs were coming into the camp, officers and medics, trucks, ambulances, the most able prisoners surging forward, a chorus of pleading, the soldiers responding by tossing out packages of food. Benson wanted to cry, to be sick again, but his body was numb, too many sights, too much of the worst of anything he had ever seen. He tried to speak, confused words, saw Mitchell suddenly collapse, bending over, sick, and then, again. Benson knelt down, put a hand on his friend's back, felt the convulsions, tried to speak, but his thoughts were chaotic, and he followed the motions of the soldiers, saw more men down on their knees, helpless against so much horror. Prisoners were down as well, some praying, crying, begging, some dying, their last breath preserved for the day when their captors would be gone, when liberation would come, when the nightmare would finally end.

The forced-labor concentration camp at Ohrdruf still contained nearly three thousand prisoners when the Americans entered the gates. Two days prior, on April 2, as the Germans realized the Americans were closing in, they had forcibly marched another nine thousand men out of the camp, a thirty-two-mile journey to the primary camp in this sector, Buchenwald. For reasons no one could explain, before the Germans left, they executed some three dozen men and left them as the grotesque display the Americans had found, each man shot and his pants pulled down, an astounding act of humiliation and inhuman contempt. In the barracks, those remaining prisoners who could speak told the Americans that those who were left behind were thought to be too sick to march, and the murdered men had been pulled aside as a random act, a vengeful message to the remaining prisoners. By the time the Americans arrived, the weakness of so many of those had ended their suffering. Hundreds lay dead, succumbing before the medical help could save them.

What began as an act of kindness by so many of the GIs, handing out chocolate and ration packs, resulted in a new and unexpected horror that only the doctors could explain. The prisoners had been so deprived of nourishment that the sudden intake of food overpowered their ability to absorb it, and through no more than a gesture of goodwill the GIs unwittingly caused the deaths of many of the weakest survivors.

Ohrdruf had not been the first concentration camp the Allied troops had discovered. That was in Alsace, the camp at Natzweiler, which had been liberated five months prior. But those gates had been opened as well, the Germans relocating their prisoners before the Allied troops could actually witness what the prisoners had become, how they had been treated by their German captors. That discovery was made first at Ohrdruf.

Though many of the GIs who wandered through the camp were helpless to give the kind of aid the survivors required, they provided a different kind of assistance that few of them could yet understand. They became witnesses.

28. EISENHOWER

Eisenhower listened in silence, Bedell Smith to one side, doing the same.

"General Patton insists in the strongest terms, chief. He's hoping you'll bring General Bradley as well, but I would expect he's already given General Bradley that invitation himself. The find is truly extraordinary. The general believes he may have discovered the entire Nazi treasury. Or at least, the part they hoped to hide. He insists that if you do not at least take stock of the riches yourself, he may have no choice but to find the means to transport the entire batch home. I suggested to General Patton that it could be the souvenir of a lifetime."

Eisenhower found nothing funny about Butcher's attempt at humor.

"What about the camp, Harry?"

"Oh yes. General Patton was also quite insistent that you visit Ohrdruf, see it for yourself. He wouldn't give me much in the way of reasons, said you'd understand."

Eisenhower looked at Smith, said, "Understand what? Okay, fine. If I know Georgie, he'll be punching walls if we keep him waiting. Sounds pretty damn intriguing."

"Which, sir?"

"The gold, Beetle, the damn gold. The concentration camp is something else. I want to see that for myself, make damn sure the reporters don't blow this stuff up to more than it is. Anybody in the States asks me about it, I want to be able to give them an accurate picture. G-2 says the enemy is shifting people out of these kinds of camps all over the place, pulling some of them back out of the way of the Russians. General Strong is coming for a briefing shortly, and I want to hear what he's learned about our own boys. We've had too many fliers go down, and I won't believe the Germans have just executed them. I expect a hell of a load of liberated GIs before this is over. Patton said that this Ohrdruf camp was full of slave labor, none of our boys. Get on the stick, Harry. Tell Brad to join us down there tomorrow."

"Right away, chief."

Butcher moved out of the office. Smith said, "Leave it to Patton to make a fuss over a pile of treasure. Not sure what this has to do with fighting a war."

"I'll find out. George isn't about to take a vacation from the matter at hand. If he wants me down there, he's got more than one good reason."

Strong was pacing, as angry as Eisenhower had ever seen him.

"It was highly uncalled for, sir. Inappropriate, insubordinate, and damn well dangerous. As far as I can tell, from all reports, the mission was a complete failure. Admittedly, facts are in short supply. No one around Patton is especially interested in pouring out his guts, as it were. I think they'd rather face a court-martial than have Patton as an enemy. Consider, sir, that it took nearly two weeks for us to even learn of this little misadventure. I understand you're visiting him tomorrow. I should think you'd want to get to the bottom of this yourself, sir."

Eisenhower, who trusted his chief of intelligence as much as any man on his staff, Bedell Smith included, absorbed his report with deepening despair.

"Go on, Ken."

"As you can see on page four, sir, casualties amounted to at least two dozen men, plus an unknown number of the American prisoners they were sent to liberate. Patton's own Major Skinner is missing and presumed captured. From what I can determine, General Patton instructed Major Skinner to accompany the mission as the general's eyes and ears."

Smith crossed his arms in front of him, had the look Eisenhower had come to expect from his chief of staff. He knew Smith's energy wouldn't allow him to just listen without jumping in.

Smith said, "General Strong, do we know why Patton did this?"

"According to the people I have spoken with, few of whom are willing to testify for the record, General Patton ordered this excursion knowing that the Hammelburg POW camp housed his son-in-law, Colonel John Waters. It is not difficult to speculate that General Patton's plan was the rescue of his daughter's husband, no matter what it might cost in men and equipment."

Eisenhower let out a breath, shook his head.

"I'm not interested in anybody's speculation, Ken, not even yours. I just wonder why in hell George didn't feel the need to run this by Bradley, or me? Why in hell didn't he ask first?"

"You will have to ask that of *him*, sir." Strong pointed to the papers on Eisenhower's desk. "That bit of information is not in my report. I know that General Bradley was just today informed of this mission, sir, and he says in most definite terms that he would not have authorized it. I think we can infer that General Patton took this upon himself, knowing that had he asked, he would have been refused."

Smith's voice rose, the man red-faced. "So, because George knew we'd say no, he decided it was best not to ask? Ike, here we go again!"

"I told you, I'm not interested in speculation. From either one of you. Damn him anyway." Eisenhower felt the old anger, his mounting frustration with Patton's unique way of running his own private war. "Okay, enough. None of this leaves my office, you understand? General Strong, there will be no further inquiries into this matter until I have spoken to General Patton myself. I want to make damn sure we have our facts straight before someone beyond our reach launches another full-out attack on the man. How in hell do *we* know that Colonel Waters was in that camp? The Red Cross has been vague at best."

Strong pointed to his report again. "Sir. Forgive me, but my conclusion explains that in fact, Camp Hammelburg was liberated two days ago, by units of the Fourteenth Armored Division. It seems that Colonel Waters was severely wounded at some point during General Patton's . . . um . . . commando mission. He is in our hands now, hospitalized, as best I know."

Eisenhower leafed through the report.

"Until I know more facts, I don't think we should be referring to this as a commando mission. I see here . . . he sent fifty-seven vehicles, including tanks, half-tracks, and armored cars? How far did they have to go?"

Strong pointed to the papers again.

"Page three, sir. Camp Hammelburg was approximately fifty miles behind enemy lines. Not even General Patton could have assumed the mission would have been successful."

"You're wrong there, Ken. Patton thinks he can pull off anything. He's got nine lives, like a cat. He's used up half of 'em, but dammit, I would have thought he was through pulling stunts like this. Never mind. I don't want this in the papers, you understand me? Not a word!"

"Not a word, sir."

"I've got your report, I'll go over it in detail. Tell me about what you've learned about Hitler's stronghold in the Alps."

Strong seemed grateful to shift gears, to focus on something that suited his role as intelligence officer.

"They're calling it their National Redoubt. Indications are that Hitler intends to abandon Berlin and withdraw his last and best fighting troops to the area around Berchtesgaden, which will encompass some of the most difficult mountains and high passes of southern Germany, Austria, and northern Italy. We anticipate that many of those forces that would accompany him would of course be the most fanatically loyal, thus, the Gestapo, the Hitler Youth, and so forth. We do not know how extensive the fortifications are in those mountains, networks of tunnels, anti-aircraft positions, and so forth. Aerial reconnaissance has not been particularly useful, and with the Germans still in tight control of the area, we haven't been able to send anyone in on the ground. Perhaps we should offer such a mission to General Patton." Eisenhower started to protest, but Strong knew the line he had crossed. "Sorry, sir. No more about that. In my opinion, sir, we should continue to occupy as much German territory as we can, in an effort to block any large-scale enemy withdrawal to the south."

Eisenhower pointed toward the map on the wall.

"That is precisely what Patton is doing. Give him credit, once he kicks into gear, no one moves faster. I want him to get across to the Czech border with all speed, and he knows that. It will take one hell of an effort for Hitler to move a sizable force into Bavaria if George is blocking the way. Knowing George, he'll hope Hitler tries it anyway." Strong waited for Eisenhower to finish, and Eisenhower sensed the man's impatient need to complete his report. "Go on, Ken."

"It is fairly obvious, sir, that considerable airpower should be brought to bear on any such fortifications as we locate them. There is also one other matter that has come to our attention. In various locales, German commanders are issuing a call for what they are labeling *werewolves.* Simply put, sir, the Germans are going to attempt guerrilla warfare in every practical place for such a tactic. The most disturbing aspect of this is that the orders are going out to the German populace, with emphasis on the young. They are recruiting children, sir. Whether they can put up any kind of serious obstacle to our forces is not a question I can answer, of course."

Eisenhower slapped a hand on the desk.

"Dammit! I hate that, purely hate it! Don't sell the idea short, Ken. Think about it. Any German kid born since 1930, all they have known in their lives is Hitler. They haven't been taught anything else. He's been dictator since 1933, but that's just a title. To the children, he might as well be God. We've already captured a considerable number of teenage boys who've been shooting at us, and some of them were getting good at it. We've got to snuff out this kind of thing as quick as possible. The only way to handle that is to grab as many towns as we can, as soon as we can. We have to occupy every square inch of that damn country. I sure as hell don't want it going back to the newspapers in the States that we're killing whole flocks of children. But to every GI, there's a reality to this. If a thirteen-year-old is shooting at you, you shoot back. That doesn't translate into a patriotic pep rally back home. Put the word out, Beetle. I want every commander to know the danger of this."

"Yes, sir."

Eisenhower looked at Strong again, said, "That's all for now, General. Keep your ear to the ground."

The English intelligence commander had never seemed to grasp the meaning of Eisenhower's Old West slang. Strong said with a smile, "Wouldn't do for the men to see me in that position, sir. But we'll be listening to every word we can pick up."

"That's all, General."

Strong snapped to attention, made a quick nod toward Smith. He backed away, then moved out, closing the door behind him.

Eisenhower could tell that Smith was still angry about Patton. The two men had never been close, and would likely never be. As usual, Smith wouldn't just let it go.

"Not a word about George's little maneuver, Beetle. Not one word."

"I know. I agree. But dammit, Ike, how in hell does he think he can get away with this stuff? How'd you like to be the poor captain, what's his name, Baum? This poor sap gets the order from Patton to lead three hundred men straight into German territory and bust open a POW camp. No intelligence, no preliminary planning to speak of, no idea what kind of force is waiting for them. They end up fighting their way in, and then, when they find out the enemy knows every move they've made, they end up fighting their way out. This isn't some backyard kids' game, Ike! We don't even know what happened to the poor guy, and Patton's own staff officer is gone too. All they accomplished was adding to our casualty count, and as far as we know, every damn one of those American prisoners was still stuck in that camp."

"Apparently, not anymore."

"No, fine, you're right. We liberate them anyway. If George had just waited a week or two, he'd have gotten his son-in-law in hand, with no problems."

"All right, Beetle, we've beat this horse to death. You've got other things to worry about, and so do I. I'll deal with Patton when the time is right, and that might be tomorrow. For now I need him grabbing as much countryside as he can. Children, for God's sake. How do you think George would treat a ten-year-old girl who killed one of his men?"

Smith lowered his head.

"I'd rather not think about it at all. Don't worry about the staff, though. We'll keep this whole Hammelburg thing buttoned up." He moved toward the door, paused, said, "When you see George, tell him I hope Colonel Waters recovers. He's a good man."

Eisenhower was grateful for Smith's deflating temper.

"Tell him yourself. But later."

Smith was gone, the door closed again, and Eisenhower felt a burst of energy, a mix of relief and fear. At least we liberated the damn POW camp. That's the important thing. He scanned the papers, General Strong's report, thumbed to the last pages. Here it is . . . fifteen hundred Americans, plus hundreds of foreigners, Serbians mostly. Thank God for that. Dammit, George, what in hell were you trying to prove? Word gets out that you sent a task force to the one camp in Germany that just happened to house your son-in-law . . . what did you think was going to happen? He could see Patton in his mind, the man's self-righteous strut. Yeah, you thought you were gonna get your name in the papers again, for all the right reasons. Instead, your Captain Baum gets the crap kicked out of him, and for all we know he's dead. Sometimes you make your plans like you're writing a comic book, for God's sake. You owe the commander of the Fourteenth Armored Division one hell of a gift. The Krauts could just as well have machine-gunned every damn prisoner, all because of your Task Force Baum, and by God, there'd be blood on your hands.

Eisenhower rose, moved to the map wall, scanned, located Hammelburg. The pins had been shifted continuously, marking the position of the Allied forces, bulges pushing eastward, the larger cities starting to fall, Frankfurt, Würzburg, the lines extending close to Nuremberg. In the north, Montgomery was driving hard not only to reach the Elbe, capturing the vital port cities of Bremerhaven and Hamburg, but then to slide northward, cutting across Germany's border with Denmark. The official reports insisted that the move was a necessity, a means of cutting off the German forces still in that country, which would also cut off German troops still occupying Norway. But unofficially, Montgomery's mission to put himself between Denmark and the advancing Russians was a strategy no one would discuss publicly. The agreement with the Russians had called for the Elbe to be the boundary between the two sides of the great Allied vise, both driving toward a junction that would put them face-to-face, crushing the Germans between them. But the Elbe emptied to the North Sea only miles from the western fringes of the Danish border. Eisenhower knew there was concern in Washington that once the Russians reached the river, it might be tempting for them to offer a military excuse for punching northward and occupying Denmark. Montgomery might be sulking over his lost opportunity to drive on Berlin, but Eisenhower had no time for Montgomery's complaints. *Whether Monty likes it or not,* he thought, *this mission is important enough, even if it can't be trumpeted to his beloved newspaper reporters. The Danes are certainly aware that the British might be the only thing standing between two very different definitions of* liberation, *something the Poles, Czechs, and Hungarians are already finding out.*

Stalin had made every pretense of establishing homegrown governments in every country his troops had *liberated,* but no one in the West had been fooled. The men now in charge in eastern Europe answered first to Stalin.

The Russian offensive that began in January had been enormously successful, and along the Polish border, Marshal Zhukov's troops had heav-

SITUATION ON
APRIL 10, 1945

SWEDEN

DENMARK

North Sea

Baltic Sea

HOLLAND

Elbe River

Berlin

POLAND

The Ruhr

G E R M A N Y

Oder River

Prague

CZECHOSLOVAKIA

FRANCE

Rhine River

Nuremburg

Munich

Vienna

AUSTRIA

SWITZERLAND

ITALY

Venice

Trieste

Bologna

YUGOSLAVIA

Adriatic
Sea

0   100 mi
0   100 km

····· Approximate
       front line
▭ Allied position
▬ German position

ily lined the banks of the Oder River, only thirty miles from Berlin. But Zhukov had been stalled by the exhaustion of his armies and the contracting of German defensive lines. Having their armies pushed backward in an ever-tightening circle was a benefit to the Germans. Now, with the Russians spilling into Germany itself, the Germans had been driven back into the very defensive positions their generals had hoped for, which allowed them to shorten their supply lines and make the best use of their rapidly declining strength. Eisenhower knew that Zhukov was too capable a commander to sit still for long, and Stalin was too dedicated to crushing Hitler and his army to tolerate much of a lull. Like the Americans, the Russians had what seemed to be an endless supply of men and equipment, a wave that the Germans could not stop for long.

All along the Western Front, Eisenhower's generals were seeing firsthand the collapse of the army that had once inflicted so much vicious damage, a great beast growing slowly toothless. It was clear that many of Germany's best armor and infantry were being sent east, Hitler and his High Command far more concerned with holding back the Russians than they were the Americans.

In the south, Patton and Devers were continuing their push toward the Czech border, a snout of land that jutted into Germany from the east. In the center, the rest of Bradley's forces under Hodges and Simpson were doing as Montgomery was doing, driving relentlessly toward the Elbe River, after first swarming around and through the Ruhr, one of Germany's most critical industrial regions. The number of German prisoners captured in the Ruhr pocket had been extraordinary, and one by one the factories and other crucial tools for Hitler's war machine were being shut down or obliterated.

As he studied the map, Eisenhower couldn't keep his eyes from Berlin. The Russians will be putting everything they have toward crushing the place, he thought. Zhukov has Stalin on his back every day, and Zhukov is not a man who will disappoint his boss. Surely Hitler knows that. Surely Hitler has a map just like this one, and even if his own staff lies to him, or deludes him, Hitler must know what the Russians are capable of doing. Will Hitler risk the complete destruction of his capital? We've already bombed parts of the place to rubble. Will Hitler fight on to his last soldier? Who will fight beside him? Why in hell won't the Germans give up?

29. EISENHOWER

MERKERS, GERMANY
APRIL 12, 1945

Bradley had flown with him in a small plane, the two men reaching the airstrip selected by Patton, who had met them when they landed. They drove mostly in silence, Eisenhower passing the time in silent concentration on what he might still say to Patton, all three men aware of the tension. There was no chatter, none of the mindless gossip or bellyaching that Eisenhower was so used to. Beside him, Bradley was his usual stoic self, seemed content to keep his conversation to a minimum, and Eisenhower wondered if Bradley had his own speech prepared for Patton, if there was a good blasting yet to come for Patton's astonishingly ill-advised commando mission. It had to be the primary reason Patton was keeping quiet. He had to know what was coming.

They passed through the small village with an escort of armored trucks, and Eisenhower saw the MPs working the crossroads, directing the flow of traffic from Patton's Ninetieth Division, as they passed through on their way east. Eisenhower had heard no criticism of the Ninetieth since Patton had put them into line, a testament to Patton's ability to whip any unit into shape. The Ninetieth had been one of the great disappointments in the early days of the Normandy campaign, untested soldiers crumbling completely at their first confrontation with the Germans. Bradley had cleaned out the division's problem officers from top to bottom, and once the unit had become a part of Patton's Third Army, the soldiers had seemed to find something new in their backbone. In the nine months since, they had performed as well as anyone could hope. Now, by an act of chance, they had occupied a town that happened to be sitting on a treasure that no one even knew existed.

The troops had been led to the enormous hoard of gold bullion, coins, currency, and artwork purely by the innocent comment of a local civilian, a woman who matter-of-factly informed two patrolling GIs that among the local salt mine shafts, one in particular happened to be the one *where the gold could be found.* Her nonchalant description had turned out to be an extraordinary understatement.

They descended in a shaking uncertain elevator, and Eisenhower was crowded in with four other men, Bradley among them. Above them, Patton rode in a second car. The elevators were operated by the same German civilians who had labored in the salt mines for years. At the mine's entrance, Eisenhower had been selective, testing the hospitality of several workers, had chosen a cordial ruddy-faced man to handle the controls of the elevator, a man who seemed pleasantly impressed that his place of work would suddenly receive so much attention. The man's quiet sense of competence had been the assurance Eisenhower required before he actually stepped into the elevator car. The car was supported by cables that extended two thousand feet into a hole that Eisenhower had to imagine would be a German general's idea of a perfect tomb for three of the American army's highest-ranking commanders.

When they reached the bottom, Eisenhower's fears abated immediately. The mine was in fact a vast series of tunnels and chambers, fully staffed now by MPs and officers. Every precaution had been taken to ensure that the extraordinary find would be preserved intact, at least until some higher authority should decide what to do with it. Once Patton began their tour, Eisenhower understood why he had been so enthusiastic about Eisenhower's visit.

The gold was the most obvious draw, a tunnel lined with cloth sacks that contained, by some officer's knowledgeable estimate, $250 million worth of bullion, which included both bars and coins. Among the hoard were bundles of currency, primarily German, with a significant amount of American dollars, and lesser amounts of currency from several other European nations. In yet another tunnel were heavy wooden crates containing paintings and other works of art. Eisenhower had to wonder if these were German art treasures placed far belowground for safekeeping, or if they had been looted from various museums and cathedrals all over German-occupied Europe. Patton had been eager to point out that the entire display could fund a midsized nation's treasury for years. The question in Eisenhower's mind had been, which nation? For now, the entire hoard was secure in American hands. Where it would go next was a decision to be made by politicians.

P atton was facing him from the front of the staff car, a wide grin on his face.

"Pretty amazing, wasn't it, Ike?"

"I'll give you that. I'd hate to be in charge of figuring out who really owns all that artwork."

Bradley laughed, said, "You know, George, in the old days of warfare, loot was considered the property of the man who found it. Either you or one of your boys could have gone home one of the richest men in the world."

Patton feigned seriousness. "I guess that did occur to me. Gave a brief thought to keeping my mouth shut, sealing the damn hole up with a few well-placed charges, and then maybe come back here after the war. Bribe some of these locals to help me out, and then I'd set up shop, my own bank, maybe a good-sized castle. Call my country *Pattonstine*. Nice ring to it."

Eisenhower laughed, said nothing, thought, I bet he did think about it too. He glanced at Bradley, who caught the look. Best to let some things lie quietly.

Patton continued, "Actually, I had a better idea. Melt the whole she-bang, have medals made for every man in the Third Army. That would really piss off . . ." Patton seemed to catch himself, and Eisenhower completed the sentence in his mind. *Montgomery.*

Eisenhower appreciated Patton's minor show of discretion, an opportunity to change the subject. "How much farther we have to drive, George?"

Patton's mood abruptly changed, and he glanced out through the front windshield, looked to his driver, who said, "We're close now, sir. Ten minutes."

Patton turned to Eisenhower again, said, "I knew you'd want to see this. We knew the Germans were doing some of this stuff, slave labor, locking people up just for being . . . different. We heard stories from some of the civilians in the cities, all those hotshots bending over backward to curry favor with their new conquerors. Funny, Ike, in every city I've been through, no one has ever called me a *liberator*. I guess these people are used to being under somebody's thumb. It's normal to them. We're just . . . one more thumb."

Eisenhower saw troops gathered, rows of parked trucks, tents with red crosses.

Patton said, "We're here, gentlemen."

The car stopped, and Eisenhower prepared to exit, saw Patton not moving, heard an audible breath, Patton obviously hesitating. Bradley was out of the car, the guards from their escort vehicles moving quickly, spreading out into a perimeter. Officers began to appear from the tents, the word already passing from Patton's staff that the generals were coming. Eisenhower rose up from the car, saw recognition from the soldiers, men gathering. He waved, smiled, his usual greeting to men in the field, but there was something different in these men, no cheering, just respectful nods, salutes. To one side he saw a road sign, noticed that someone had tied a black ribbon on the post, a strange adornment. But the sign told the story. It was Ohrdruf.

Y ou go on ahead, Ike."
The words choked off, Patton slipping away quickly, and Eisenhower was surprised, could see now that Patton was obviously sick. Eisenhower said nothing, understood, the powerful smell of death and decay swirling around all of them.

Patton had ordered every soldier in the general vicinity to march through the camp, unit after unit, had insisted that every commander and every subordinate be made aware what had been found, what kind of enemy they were fighting. As he moved farther inside the wire, past the first rows of buildings, Eisenhower saw dozens of men, some older officers, MPs and medics, office aides and rifle-toting GIs. He was recognized again, but again, there were no cheers. He could feel it immediately, an odd sense that this place required silence.

The survivors of the camp were mostly gone, moved to hospitals or other makeshift facilities, vastly overworked doctors and medics trying to find the most humane way to restore the health of the most brutalized prisoners. But in every barracks, and across the open ground, the dead still lay, the victims of the last massacre still spread out close to the wire. He saw the open doors of the one barracks he had heard about, where the stacks of corpses had been coated with lime. He moved that way, fought through the obscene odors, stared at the sickening sight, then forced himself to keep going. No matter the sickness or the nightmarish sights, Eisenhower had already told himself he would make absolutely certain he saw it all.

For the next hour or more he walked down every alleyway, through every barracks where there was something to be seen, past the corpses that filled every dark corner. In the open fields, army engineers had unearthed enormous mass graves, bodies only partially covered, hasty burials by German guards who knew their time was short. Some of the dead who were not buried were piled high in a funeral pyre, someone's effort to hide their crime in heaps of ash. But again, the Germans had abandoned the camp without the time they needed to complete the job, and so the bodies were only partially burned, blackened skeletons that curled among themselves in a twisting tangle of bare bones and seared flesh.

Most of the medics who moved through the barracks wore masks, but masks could not prevent the senses from absorbing what Eisenhower saw and smelled and felt. In one barracks, he slowed the pace, moved toward a doctor, the man kneeling beside a near-naked man, applying some sort of salve to an open wound on the man's chest. The doctor stood, saw Eisenhower, offered no salute, no reaction at all.

Eisenhower said in a low voice, "Will he survive?"

He felt foolish, the question meaningless, and he realized that his voice had broken the sickly silence. Dead men were scattered to one side, dead where they had fallen, eyeless faces staring into nothing, lice and maggots swarming on their yellow and black skin. The doctor seemed to search for words, seemed confused, lost, looked at Eisenhower, tearful sadness in his eyes.

"He says they ate the dead. They ate their own dead. What do we do about that? How do we treat that?"

The man turned away, sobbing, and Eisenhower fought his own emotions, the shock of all he was seeing soaking through him. He had no answer for the doctor, no answer for any of it. He moved outside, had to escape the barracks, move away from the hollow eyes. The security men were shadowing him, keeping their distance, no one speaking. He stared at the fence wire, some of it gone, ripped down by tanks, broken posts, more corpses, blending in with the splintered wood, splintered themselves. He closed his eyes, tried to see Hitler in his mind. Who would do this? Has he been here? Has he seen this? Why? These were not . . . animals.

He opened his eyes again, fought for logic, fought for the energy to do his job, thought, there is a reason Patton needed you to see this. He wants justification, he wants a free hand to crush the enemy wherever he finds him. But there are reasons why I had to be here that even he might not understand. Eisenhower thought of his first reaction to the news, word of *concentration camps.* Horrible thing, certainly. Penning up people like so much cattle. Imprisoning your enemies, imprisoning anyone who could be a threat. It is war, after all. We penned up the Japanese, our own citizens, because we thought they were dangerous. Pearl Harbor scared hell out of us, and we believed they would be sympathetic to their home country more than they would be to us. Milton ran the program, my own brother convincing me it was necessary, that it could not be helped. But that's over now, the Supreme Court, someone there who must be wiser than so many of us . . . realizing that just because a man is different doesn't mean he is the enemy. But that cannot compare to what has happened here. Hitler did not fear these people, this was not about hysteria or mob rule. This is slavery and butchery and the worst kind of crime. War brings out the worst instincts of man, and we've already seen the atrocities, what the Germans have done to civilians. I know our boys have done their share, some things I'll never hear about, things that will go unpunished, that dark need in some men to take revenge. *But that's not what happened here.* This has nothing to do with war. Hitler set out to use these people in the most brutal ways imaginable, and when he used them up, he just brought in more. Slave labor. A kind euphemism for mass murder.

He looked for Bradley, saw a cluster of officers, moved that way. There is one more reason I had to be here, he thought, something far more important than anything that would occur to Patton. I was so afraid the newspapers would play this up the wrong way, sensationalize this so it became nothing more than our own brand of propaganda, blowing our own horns. Hey, we're the good guys. But I was so damn wrong. I want every reporter in this theater to see this, to write about it, to describe every horrible detail. When I go home, if someone, whoever, some congressman, some local reporter asks me if these reports were blown up, were so much bull, I can tell them, dammit, I was there. I *saw* it. And every horror story, every atrocity you read about is true. And Hitler . . . God damn that Nazi son of a bitch to hell.

HEADQUARTERS, THIRD ARMY, HERSFELD, GERMANY
APRIL 12, 1945

Patton had insisted they stay, and neither Eisenhower nor Bradley had objected. Dinner had been a subdued affair, no one particularly in the mood to eat anything. Patton had recovered, seemed embarrassed by his show of weakness at the camp, something no one would mention to him at all.

"I'm going to bed. Hell of a day."

Bradley nodded silently, pulled himself up, made a low wave with one hand.

"Me too. Thanks for the hospitality, George."

Bradley was gone now, and Eisenhower felt the aching weariness in his legs, saw Patton thumping on his wristwatch.

"Damn thing. Quit on me again."

Eisenhower had avoided the subject all day, wanted to avoid it now, but he knew there would be no sleep if he didn't at least ask.

"Why'd you do it, George? Three hundred men, fifty miles into enemy territory. What did you think you'd accomplish?"

Patton seemed relieved to talk about it, his energy increasing.

"I heard about the Hammelburg POW camp. Nine hundred of our guys, a good percentage of them officers. I thought it would be a hell of a thing if we could spring them. I honestly thought we'd catch the enemy completely by surprise, that no one would ever suspect that kind of move. We'd go in, grab our boys, haul our asses back before the Krauts knew what hit 'em."

"Did you know your son-in-law was there?"

Patton looked down, stared for a long moment.

"No. Not until it was over with."

"That's not what the reports are saying. It's not what some of the officers around you are saying. They're saying it's the reason you sent your Major Skinner along, because he knows Colonel Waters, would be able to recognize him."

Patton seemed to inflate, prepared for an argument, an argument Eisenhower did not want. But as quickly as he bowed up, Patton seemed to change his mind, his expression calming, and he said in a low voice, "What *I'm* saying, Ike, is that I didn't know he was there. I just thank God that Colonel Waters is alive now."

Eisenhower could feel the brew stirring—this could be one more mess that would trap Patton in a ridiculous controversy the army didn't need. He knew Patton too well, saw the man's eyes staring at the floor, knew that what Patton was telling him wasn't entirely true. But the day's events had sucked every ounce of energy from Eisenhower, and he sat back in the soft chair, thought, dammit, we have bigger priorities than this kind of crap. March someone through Ohrdruf, then tell them how important it is to make a stink about an idiot raid to Hammelburg. Not while I'm in charge.

"Let's go to bed, George. I'm beat."

Patton stood quickly, and Eisenhower could see he was grateful.

"Right through there, Ike. Hallway, second room on the right. It's all set up for you."

"Right. Thanks."

Eisenhower moved away, looked back at Patton, saw him thumping the wristwatch again, low curses, and Eisenhower moved into the dark hall, thought, he might be the biggest pain in the ass in this army, but I don't know how we would have done anything without him.

H e lay in the dark, fighting for sleep, the images of the camp slipping through his exhaustion. Damn this, anyway. Shoulda had a good stiff drink. Churchill probably sleeps like a baby. There's a lesson there.

He heard a tap at the door, Patton's low voice.

"Ike! Ike!"

Eisenhower sat up, said aloud, "What is it, George? Door's unlocked."

Patton opened the door, his shadow filling the doorway, and Eisenhower could see Bradley standing behind him.

"What's up? Something happen?"

Patton seemed to stumble, soft words, then caught himself.

"I went outside, to check the time. This damn busted watch. Used the radio in my HQ truck, thought I'd get a time signal from the BBC. There's news, Ike. The president . . . President Roosevelt is dead."

Eisenhower sat frozen, saw Roosevelt in his mind, thought, months ago the man was sickly, frail.

"You sure?"

"The BBC was pretty specific. A stroke, at Warm Springs, Georgia."

Eisenhower lowered his head.

"They wouldn't get that wrong."

Patton moved into the room, Bradley in the doorway. Patton said, "What does this mean, Ike? What do we do?"

Bradley eyed a chair in one corner, moved that way, sat. He looked at Eisenhower with the same stoic stare he seemed to carry through every catastrophe. Bradley said, "We don't do anything except what we've been doing, George. We keep fighting until the German is licked."

Eisenhower shifted to one end of the bed, motioned for Patton to sit down.

"That's all we can do. Washington will have their own problems, but they can't be ours, not yet anyway."

Patton said, "The new president is Truman. What's he like?"

Eisenhower sagged, leaned back against his pillow.

"God only knows, George. God only knows."

30. SPEER

The shouts of the people told him to follow the flow, a quickly organized scramble toward the shelters. He hesitated, stared upward, clear blue skies, no sign of the danger, but someone had seen the bombers, an outpost beyond the city perhaps, and the air raid alerts had been sounded. The civilians were responding as they always responded, people accustomed to the raids and the damage they would do. There was mostly silence from the crowd, no one screaming, a strangely controlled panic, people merging into lines, moving through the doorways that would take them below street level. The children seemed oblivious to any danger, and Speer heard laughing, saw a spontaneous game, two boys chasing each other up and over a debris pile, ignoring the risk from jagged concrete and sharp steel beams. He saw the mother, a stout bear of a woman who spit out a harsh command, an order obeyed with some reluctance, the boys joining the others in one of the lines, the fatherless family quickly disappearing into the shelter. Everyone was on foot, no cars at all, those few among the elite who had gasoline saving it for journeys more important than running errands in the city. There were no military vehicles, a surprise, none of the usual staff cars that roared past the civilians who had learned to ignore them. Speer thought of the officers who had commanded the shelters, the home guard, the men who were charged with protecting the civilians. For the past several days, they had seemed to vanish well before the bombers came, as though their jobs had suddenly become less of a priority. Speer hadn't given them much thought until now. But he had been in the streets by chance, an unusually long walk from the Chancellery to the home of a friend who had been wounded in one of the raids. He had never been outside during an air raid, found the organized urgency of the people reassuring, the utter lack of chaos, people moving in their predetermined routes to the many shelters, what had been simple basements, now the only protection the civilians had against the increasing numbers of daylight raids from the vast flocks of bombers. The crowds flowed by, but Speer did not move with them, not yet, still stared up, wondered how many, how long the raid would last, how bad it would be. Finally, he gave up, no sign of anything, and he fell into line, followed the civilians into their shelter.

The room was dark and musty, dampness on the floor, one lightbulb hanging above, a harsh glare on the dull faces who sat quickly and quietly, pushing gently against one another, making room for as many as could fit. Speer stayed by the entrance for a long moment, felt a responsibility, thought, no one is in charge here. I should do something, let them know who I am. But the people were calm, were familiar with their routine, and Speer began to feel faintly ridiculous, as though he could be *in charge* of anything that was happening. These people were managing for themselves. And who am I, anyway? What authority do I have in a bomb shelter in the middle of a city that has already endured such brutal indignity? What can I say to make any of this better?

There was machine-gun fire, barely audible, and a sudden eruption of thumps, the anti-aircraft batteries going to work. Speer listened intently, no other sounds, the people around him silent, no whimpering fear, no talk at all. He ached to see, if only for a moment, the formations of silver birds, the flashes of black smoke, the lucky hit, the enemy plane falling in fiery pieces. The city was surrounded by enormous batteries of flak guns, a curtain of fire, and more, the eighty-eights hidden in parks, sheltered by walls of sandbags and concrete. The best we have, he thought. That's what they say, anyway. But they haven't stopped the bombers, so, clearly, they aren't as good as they might have been. Perhaps nothing we have done is as *good* as we have been told.

He thought of the argument, Hitler loudly dismissing the suggestion that all that energy and manpower devoted to the V weapons had been wasted. Speer didn't know the answers, had not dared to insert his own opinion, but someone else had, a physicist who knew something of rockets and explosives. For all of Hitler's noisy pride in the weapons, particularly the V-2 rocket, the enemy had seemed completely unaffected. There were casualties to be sure, random devastation across England, but nothing like Hitler had predicted, nothing to drive the British out of the war. The generals had pleaded that the new weapons be targeted toward military targets close at hand, the occupied seaports, Cherbourg and Antwerp, or toward the Allied supply depots and troop assembly points. The argument the scientists had waged was over priorities, that the technology and labor should be devoted first to a land-to-air anti-aircraft missile, specifically targeting the enemy's bombers. Speer had agreed with both those points of view, had been especially attracted to what the scientists had insisted was a much more effective weapons system. The scientists pleaded their case that the anti-aircraft missiles would be cheaper to build than the V-2, and could be produced in massive quantities. Hitler's physicists had the technology in hand for precise targeting capabilities, which would devastate any Allied bombing raid. But Hitler had been dismissive, shouting down the men who knew the technology. He loved his V-2, and he never stopped insisting that, in time, the V-2 would win the war. There was no other argument to be made. The helpless anger of the scientists had done nothing to change anything, except to send them back to their manufacturing facilities in a haze of hopelessness. It had been a lesson for Speer. German technology was thought to be far superior to any in the world. But if the Führer was not enthusiastic about a project, that project would simply be ignored, no matter how extraordinary the scientists thought it to be.

The same argument had erupted over the Messerschmitt 262, the jet fighter plane that so excited the air commanders. Even Hermann Göring became the jet's champion, insisting that a thousand jets could completely turn the air war to Germany's favor. Göring's own subordinates had been surprised by his outspoken advocacy of the jets, mainly because Göring had ceased to be actively involved in almost anything to do with the war. Worse, he had fallen completely out of favor with Hitler and the High Command. But Göring persisted, advocating that the jets were a marvel, something that Hitler could surely cling to as one of his precious *secret weapons*. To the enormous dismay of Göring and his Luftwaffe commanders, Hitler believed the jets should best be used as small-scale bombers. Hitler's argument was that the jets were unstoppable by enemy fighter planes and could drop bomb loads without any serious threat from enemy anti-aircraft fire. Hitler seemed not to understand, or chose not to hear, that the bomb-carrying capability of the ME-262 was minimal. Göring had been passionate about the advantages of using the jets to attack Allied bombers, since their speed would obliterate the advantages enjoyed by the American fighter escorts. But Hitler tossed that idea away completely, and Speer had to wonder if it was only because Göring favored it.

The rumble of the anti-aircraft guns was growing more intense, and Speer stared at the door that led to the street, tried to sort through the sounds. He had never seen a bomber blown out of the sky, imagined the intense thrill of that for the gunners, the only kind of success they could have. But now there were new thumps, then many more, a heavy rumble, the room vibrating, a low groan rising from several of the old women. Speer felt the concrete beneath him shivering, heard creaking from the beams overhead, thought, *bombs.* All right, you can stay right here. These people know exactly where they need to be. Pay attention to that.

The rumble grew louder, hard thunder, one woman crying out, another comforting her, hands grasping the woman's shoulders. Most of the people sat with heads bowed, staring at dark nothing, just enduring, passing the minutes in their own minds. Speer watched them, the lightbulb starting to swing slowly, shadows weaving back and forth, the light suddenly bouncing with a jiggle from a heavy impact close by. He flinched from the sound, but the people around him stayed mostly silent, no movement. He began to be afraid, thought of the building above them, an architect's mind appraising, the beams old but solid. If there was a direct hit from one of the larger bombs . . . we wouldn't even know, probably. It would just be over, a flash. Or worse, the place would collapse on top of us. Some would survive in the rubble, at least for a while. Someone must be in charge of rescue crews, but I saw no one in the streets. He continued his search, examining every foot of the low ceiling for signs of weakness. Dust drifted down into his eyes, and he wiped furiously, felt a tugging at his side. He looked down, saw a small boy, pushing close, seeking the tall man's coat. Speer put an arm around the boy's head, pulled him close, wanted to say something comforting, but there was no fear in the boy's eyes, no panic, no tears. The boy looked up at him with no expression at all, said, "Are you a Nazi?"

Other faces rose, looking at him now, and Speer saw the sharp blue eyes, said, "Yes, I am."

The boy looked away, his curiosity satisfied, still clung to the heavy coat. The others watched him still, nothing in their faces but silent acceptance. After a long moment, the rumbling faded, the chatter of anti-aircraft guns growing quiet. Close to the door, an old man rose, pulled open the door, dusty light flooding the room.

"All clear."

The people began to rise, the old stretching their stiff joints, the children clamoring up the stairs, pent-up energy launching them out into the daylight. Deep in the shelter, the line formed again, the people keeping their good order, making their way to the steps, and Speer stood aside, let them pass. He began to feel an urgency, imagined the damage, what the bombs might have done, thought, we need to find out if there are casualties. Of course there are casualties. Maybe there's a fire. Let's go!

But the line kept its order, the people stepping up through the doorway in single file, and finally Speer was there, impatiently pushed past them, the sunlight shrouded by thick clouds of dust. He scanned the street, saw black smoke rising a block away, more smoke far beyond, the sound of one siren, but around him the people moved away in calm order, returning to their homes or their shops. Speer looked up, the blue sky clearing, still nothing to see, the great flocks of silver planes long gone, or most of them certainly. There were always successes for the anti-aircraft gunners, blasted heaps of wreckage, the fallen bombers drawing the soldiers and civilians both, souvenir seekers, or those who just needed to see some proof that the enemy could be defeated. But Speer saw nothing like that here, thought, the targets must have been to the east, the oil plant perhaps, or the rail yards. I should go there, see what needs to be done. He began to move, feeling the urgency, but there was no car, and the worst of the smoke was many blocks away. He felt helpless, ridiculous, saw the children, the two boys playing again on the rubble, chasing each other through the wreckage of war. He felt a tug on his coat, turned, saw the small boy again, the mother standing back, wary.

The boy said, "Do you know the Führer?"

Speer looked at the mother, saw a hint of anxiousness, but the boy tugged again, perfect innocence, his eyes digging into Speer's conscience.

"Do you know the Führer?"

"Yes, I do. I will see him . . ."

"Tell him that we want this to stop."

Speer looked at the mother, saw the first tears, and she stepped forward, took the boy's hand, said, "Very sorry. Please, I beg you not to report us. He doesn't understand."

The woman pulled the boy away, moved quickly through the people who made their way along the wide street. Speer watched them until they were gone, disappearing around a corner, past more debris, more shattered concrete, more buildings reduced to rubble by the Allied bombers. Around him, the people continued their routine, a car appearing, small, sputtering past him, filled with soldiers, one officer glancing in his direction, no recognition. Speer looked down at his uniform, the sharp gray adornment he had insisted upon. He had wanted so much to feel the importance of that, something to give him an identity among the circle of men who kept Hitler's company, those men who were *in charge*. It was arrogance, and he knew that now, felt foolish, thought of the boy, the sharp blue eyes, the innocent demand, the mother who was afraid. *We want this to stop.* Yes, boy, we all do. But it will not stop until it is *over*, and it will not be over until all of this . . . everything you see around you . . . is gone. And none of us can change that.

THE CHANCELLERY, BERLIN
APRIL 13, 1945

Speer stood among the models, his models, the glorious buildings, one topped with a magnificent dome. They spread out across large tables, vast magnificence, a city of the future, and he moved between the tables, scanned the details, his sharp eye catching a flaw, one tiny window not quite square. He frowned. No reason to change it now, he thought. These are, after all, only models. And very likely, this is all it will ever be. He knew how much Hitler enjoyed this display, the grand plan that was to have transformed Berlin into the architectural showplace for the entire world. That was the seduction, he thought. That is why I am here. It is all I ever wanted, and he gave life to my dreams. Like Faust, I have sold my soul to the devil. The thought jarred him, and he felt a strange guilt. Hitler is not the devil, after all. He is our leader, and we have sworn . . . the thought drifted away, had been repeated too many times. So now look at you, young architect. You have been the chosen one. The Führer is impressed by you, because you understand what he wants. And so, *you* will build all of this magnificence, if we succeed in this war. Dream about that. Plan for that. It's your duty.

He moved slowly past more of the miniature buildings, stopped at the imposing figure of the arch. It was Hitler's idea, a dismissive slap at the famous arch in Paris, but the design was Speer's, something much more grand than the Arc de Triomphe, much more elaborate, a design to thrill the Führer. Speer had used the same name, the Arch of Triumph, another slap that had delighted Hitler. But Speer's arch would be more than three times as large as its French namesake, a massive monument to the destiny Hitler still believed in, still cherished above everything else.

He heard a voice, at the far end of the room.

"Marvelous display, Herr Speer."

He turned, saw the familiar face of Kesselring, the white hat clamped under his arm, the genial face. Speer moved that way, Kesselring extending a hand, a far friendlier greeting than Speer was receiving from most of Hitler's inner circle. He took the hand, felt Kesselring's warmth, the man's words genuine, something else that had disappeared long ago from any meetings in this building.

"It is a delight to see you, Herr Speer. Admiring your own work?"

"Admiring my dreams, Field Marshal." He felt suddenly self-conscious, the spontaneous show of emotion he would reveal only rarely. "I am biding time, sir, awaiting the invitation to join the Führer. He requested a meeting."

"Yes, I am a part of that as well. I thought I was late, so it is fortunate for me there is a delay. I have not enjoyed those times when the Führer's foul temper is caused by something I could have avoided. Tardiness is not a virtue in this place."

"He has been meeting with Dr. Goebbels, so that could last awhile longer. When I have to wait, I usually spend my time here, among the models. Vanity, I suppose."

Kesselring lowered his voice, motioned to the model of Speer's arch. "A perfect symbol, you know. Our Führer has raised himself up so high, he believes himself to be beyond the reach of fate. Perhaps he is correct. It is certainly not true for the rest of us. Guderian is gone, have you heard? Well, yes, of course you would know that. You are the Führer's friend after all. Do I speak unwisely here, Herr Speer?"

"I know of Guderian, yes."

Kesselring was studying him, said, "So, you did not approve either. Officially, the Führer ordered him to go on leave, to take a vacation. No one has illusions about the meaning of that, do they? Heinz Guderian nearly won the war, but that was five years ago. Memories are short in the High Command, and our Führer does need his villains, perhaps now more than ever. One wonders how long he will keep *me* in this lofty position."

"Oh, please allow me to congratulate you, Field Marshal."

The word had gone out a few days before that with so much *change* taking place on both fronts of the war, and with the German army contracting, Hitler had decided to place the entire military under two primary commanders, dividing their authority by geography. Kesselring would command all troops to the south, from Bavaria all the way to the outposts in Greece and Yugoslavia. The forces to the north would be commanded by Admiral Karl Dönitz. Dönitz had risen to command of the German navy primarily on the strength of his remarkably successful U-boats and the wolfpack tactic that had devastated Allied shipping in the Atlantic. But the Allies had adapted, and by 1944 Dönitz had to concede that the U-boat war had been lost. For the past few months, he had preserved most of the surviving U-boats by keeping them out of harm's way. It was Speer who gave new importance to Dönitz, by providing the facilities to construct what might prove to be the next phase of the war at sea, a submarine that could remain submerged for days at a time, recharging batteries and air supply with a technology that even Hitler seemed to appreciate. Though Hitler never considered the German navy to be a priority, Dönitz's successes had long ago earned the Führer's admiration. Command of half of Germany's remaining armed forces seemed to Hitler to be a fitting reward to a loyal and competent servant of the Reich. To some in the army, the selection of Dönitz made no sense at all. The field generals who still struggled to hold the enemy away considered Admiral Dönitz precisely what Speer knew him to be: a figurehead.

Kesselring seemed to purposely examine the models, leaning low, studying detail, and Speer felt suddenly self-conscious, thought, he is only being polite.

"Sir, would you prefer to wait in my office?"

"Only if you will join me. I should enjoy some brandy, if you have some. I prefer to imbibe behind closed doors, beyond the Führer's reach, so to speak. One usually requires some fortification before a meeting."

Speer had always liked Kesselring, appreciated the man's frankness, so rare in Berlin. He pointed the way.

"I believe I can offer something useful. After you, Field Marshal."

They moved along the hard stone of the corridor, Kesselring's boots echoing past the open doors of other offices, eyes glancing their way, secretaries and men in uniform, the vast machine of Hitler's government. Speer had other offices outside the Chancellery, most often preferred to keep his distance from the other machinery that surrounded Hitler, politics and backstabbing, those who continued to fight for favor at the expense of anyone who stood in their way. But gaining Hitler's favor had come with the usual cost: enemies, something no one who lingered close to this much power could avoid. Today he had been invited to discuss Admiral Dönitz's new submarines, a meeting Speer had thought would be with Hitler alone. But as was always the case, those plans were subject to change.

Speer followed Kesselring into his own office, closed the door, said, "Please, be comfortable. Take my chair, it is better."

"Sit in your own chair, Herr Speer. I am the guest. And as far as I know, I hold no rank over you. Not one that matters anyway. Your deference is appreciated, however. Respect is a rare commodity around this place. About that brandy?"

Speer reached into a small cabinet, two glasses and a bottle that never sat long enough to gather dust. He poured both glasses, handed one to Kesselring, who sat across from him. The walls were a patchwork of drawings, some of Speer's designs for other works that Hitler had encouraged him to pursue.

Kesselring scanned them, said, "Your love of architecture is admirable. But I see something more in your work. You are an artist, truly. I admire that. I admire that you still have . . . dreams. You did not expect to be running factories."

"No."

"Ah, but you are gaining one advantage. Every day, there are fewer of them for you to be concerned with. We have lost the Ruhr, and that, I'm afraid, is a process that will continue."

Kesselring sipped from the glass, and Speer wondered if Kesselring would make such a direct observation to Hitler. It was part of the cloud of depression that hung over Speer every day. He had made too many arguments, too many speeches, and yet, despite his position so close to Hitler, Speer knew he had very little *power,* and almost no discretion at all. He thought of Kesselring's description, that Speer was the Führer's friend. No, that will never be true. Hitler has no friends. There is no one he trusts enough to admit his failings, his fears. Perhaps he does not have them. Speer sipped from his own glass. If he does not fear, and does not believe in his own fallibility . . . he has no need for friends at all.

After a silent moment, Kesselring said, "I attempted to reach Berlin by using the autobahn. Last night, of course. No one attempts to drive anywhere on a major roadway during the daylight, unless you wish to provide the enemy with a convenient form of target practice. But the enemy has done to the autobahn what he has done to our railroads. And what he continues to do to your factories. The roadway is nearly useless, too many bomb craters, too many detours. I thought of you as I drove past the wreckage. Just how much concrete and steel was required to build those incredible roads? Have you ever wondered what sort of use we could have made of that, in other places? Have you given any thought to that?"

"I was not involved in the construction."

Kesselring laughed, surprising him.

"It is not an accusation, Herr Speer! I know very well why the autobahn was built. The Führer told us many times! In war, it is essential to have rapid transport, from one zone of combat to the other. It is one of the rules of war prescribed by Clausewitz. Our Führer agrees with those rules, when it suits him. But Clausewitz knew nothing of the B-17, or the P-51. Apparently, Reichsmarschall Göring knows little of them either, since he seems blissfully unaware that we have any problems at all controlling the skies."

"That is not true, sir. I was at a meeting when—"

"Yes, yes, I know all about Göring. Surely you know that in this place, the Reichsmarschall no longer has a voice. It saddens me, truly. If anyone else besides Göring had been given control of the Luftwaffe, or if Göring had used it properly, we would not be in our current predicament. Though he still considers himself my superior, I am no longer afraid of him. Hitler has taken away his claws. If you want to raise laughter in our meeting, just mention the *fat man.* Hitler takes great pleasure now in his boisterous dismissal of Göring. It took a while for those clouds to part, so to speak. The tragedy is that for years, Hitler did not see Göring for the drug-addicted fool that he is. Finally, he has come to realize that Göring might actually be a threat, that he is a man driven by his own ambitions, puts his personal desires before the interests of the Führer. For all I know, the man is planning to start his own country once this war is over. He has looted every museum outside of Switzerland, and probably has more gold than the German treasury. For too long, Hitler would hear none of that. Fortunately that has changed. As I said, the clouds have parted. Unfortunately, along the way, the magnificent Luftwaffe has dissolved into a courier service."

Speer didn't know what to say, would not argue any military point with someone like Kesselring. He was surprised by Kesselring's openness, looked at the door, thought, well, of course. The door is closed.

Kesselring sipped again from the glass, examined the dark gold liquid, nodded in approval.

"Very nice. Tell me, Herr Speer, have you any sense of the morale of the people?"

Speer thought a moment, said, "The civilians? They are . . . accepting."

Kesselring pointed at Speer, as though his point had been made.

"You're right, of course. But think about that. No matter what has happened to their soldiers, to their borders, to their cities, they still follow the Führer. Does that not amaze you? What is it that holds their loyalty? His *aura*? You spend more of your time among civilians than I do, certainly. But you see it, don't you? Look at your history. Where has there ever been so much destruction, so much oppression of a population, while at the same time, there is no hint of discontent."

Speer frowned, shook his head.

"Wouldn't you call an assassination attempt *discontent*?"

"Ah, but it failed! And so, what followed? The very tools that gave Hitler his power only grew stronger. Anyone who could have had the slightest tie to the conspiracy was eliminated, and the Gestapo pushed their tentacles even farther into the lives of the people. Who would dare a conspiracy now? And since last July, Dr. Goebbels has raised the volume of his speeches, pointing out that the assassination attempt only proved how strong, how invincible their Führer truly is. How have the people reacted to that? Your word, Herr Speer. *Acceptance*. Amazing, is it not?"

There was a knock at the door, sharp, rapid. Speer jumped, a stab of nervousness.

"Yes! Come in!"

The door opened, and he saw the fat face of Martin Bormann.

"Well, here you both are! We wondered where you might be hiding. The Führer cannot be kept waiting, you know."

Bormann turned, was gone, heavy clicks of his boots in the corridor. Speer felt his heart racing, a child caught in some naughty game.

Kesselring was watching him. "He is not your best friend, is he?"

Speer rose slowly, staring at the open door. He said in a low voice, "I despise the man. If I was to suddenly disappear, Field Marshal, begin your inquiry with *him*."

Kesselring laughed, another surprise.

"One day, Herr Speer, we shall all disappear. The rats will find us no matter where we hide. There is nothing to be gained by worrying about them now."

The music blared, Hitler standing by the window, staring out, lost in a thunderous flood of Wagner pouring from a phonograph. To one side, Goebbels sat, patient, obedient, motioned silently for Kesselring and Speer to sit. The music was reaching a crescendo, and Hitler's right arm rose, his fist curled tightly, a last stab in the air with the final note. He spun around, faced them with a broad smile.

"That's what we're doing here! That's why we will win this war! Did you hear that? If Wagner were alive, he would be sitting right here, right by my side. That man understands all that I believe in. He is our greatest genius." Hitler paused, seemed emotional, searched for words. "It is the failure of our educators that so often dooms us, takes away our lack of understanding, weakens our culture. Wagner understood the inevitability of history. Teachers do not. They teach the lessons of the past as though they are merely written in books for our amusement. And yet, history is all around us, a part of us. We make that history, and we shall continue to live out the design that has been evolving for thousands of years. There was a time when I felt ashamed of Germany's distant past, but I have come to new conclusions. In the ancient world, the Romans and Greeks had their finest glories, while our people lived in mud huts and killed animals with sticks. It is one of those annoying traits that I must endure from Mussolini. He believes that because he is Italian, he is somehow superior, because his history is superior. He misses the point. Rome and Athens are gone, finished, obliterated into modernity. But over the centuries, Germany's greatness has grown. It is a slow and deliberate process, men like Frederick the

Great and Bismarck taking their lessons from those who came before. We embrace those things that made those empires great, while we avoid their mistakes. Teachers are mostly stupid. The instructors I had in Vienna had no grasp of history, of the arts, of the greatness of Wagner. I should like to reconstruct our school system, once we have completed our current task. I should write the lessons myself."

Kesselring was listening with one hand propped under his chin.

"My Führer, may we turn our attention to that task?"

Hitler seemed annoyed by the interruption, moved to his chair, did not sit, paced again toward the window. Speer had seen this before, Hitler seeming to overcome the physical agonies he carried. His left arm was mostly limp, and he walked with a slouch, seemed always to be exhausted. But Speer had learned to notice the stimulating effects of the drugs, assumed that Hitler's doctor had been there not long before. He glanced at Goebbels, who sat back with a stoic stare, infinite patience for whatever behavior Hitler would display.

After a long moment, Hitler turned toward Kesselring, said, "If you have come here to complain, I will not hear it. I have given you complete control, all you could possibly ask for." He paused. "You have not heard! You do not know the news, or you would have said something!"

Kesselring glanced at Speer, said, "What news, my Führer?"

Hitler slapped one hand against his chest.

"The American president has died!"

Speer said, "Roosevelt is dead?"

"That's what I said! Is that not wonderful news?"

Speer rolled the thought over in his mind, the question looming up silently in his brain. Why is that wonderful?

Hitler seemed disappointed at their lack of celebration.

"One of the world's great war criminals has met his fate! That is a sign, gentlemen! To all the doomsayers, those who speak only of defeat, those who spit out their bad news to me, as though I am an ignorant child . . . I say to them, to you, to the entire world . . . our enemies have become weaker. Leadership drives the machines!"

Goebbels was smiling, nodded, silent applause for Hitler's revelation.

"You are certainly correct, my Führer. Field Marshal Kesselring will be quick to seize that advantage. Is that not true, Field Marshal?"

Kesselring knew the cue, said, "Most definitely, Doctor. I shall see that the army is informed immediately."

Goebbels nodded approvingly, and Hitler seemed to move away from the thought, moved to the phonograph, eyed the record.

"I should play another one for you, Wagner's next in the series."

Kesselring said, "My Führer, I wonder if I might inquire. In Admiral Dönitz's absence, I had wondered if you would inform me of your plans for the defense of Berlin? Surely I can be of assistance in moving troops to the most advantageous positions."

Hitler turned away from the phonograph, seemed surprised at the question.

"Do you believe we are in danger here?"

Kesselring stared at Hitler for a moment, and Speer thought, he is trying to find the right way to answer that. There is none.

"My Führer, the Russians believe they will destroy this city, and all who stand in their way."

Hitler shook a finger at Kesselring. "Yes, they do believe that! But they will find a surprise here, Field Marshal. When we stood at the gates of Moscow, we believed the city would crumble into pieces by our very presence there. It was but one of the catastrophic errors my generals made in that campaign. But Moscow would not fall merely because we hoped it would. Now the roles are reversed, and the savages who fight for Stalin will learn the same lesson. There is no danger here, Field Marshal. Berlin is protected by the will of the German people, and that will is fortified by my own. You should concentrate your efforts against the Americans in the south. I want them removed from German territory with all haste. They dare to cross the Rhine and violate our land. Make good use of the river, and drown them in it. Yes, drown them."

Hitler seemed to notice Speer for the first time.

"Why are you here?"

"You sent for me, my Führer. I have the production numbers for the new submarines."

Hitler appeared to wake to the memory, sat down in his chair, then abruptly stood again.

"That will change the war. Admiral Dönitz has assured me, and I believe him. We will once again destroy the enemy's shipping lanes, we shall sink his transports before they leave their ports. He will no longer be able to supply himself on this continent. I am not a sailor, you know. I left the sea war to others, and that was an error. Admiral Raeder was a stupid fool, a traitor. He did not understand that launching a battleship against another battleship is not how a war is won. Dönitz understands, and that is why he still serves the Reich. How many submarines can you produce in the next six weeks?"

Speer was prepared for that kind of question, said, "Dozens will be rolling off the lines very soon, with hundreds more in the next few months. We will have a thousand in service by the end of the year."

He knew he hadn't answered Hitler's question, but Hitler seemed to chew on the word.

"A thousand. Yes, very good. I knew I could depend on you, Speer."

Goebbels spoke up now. "My Führer, I should leave. The speech is tonight, and it could take me a while to reach the studio. I must be sure the correct preparations have been made. We have every broadcast channel involved. It should be most effective."

Kesselring said, "Excuse me, Doctor, but are you speaking publicly? I should like to attend."

Goebbels looked at Kesselring with a tilt of his head, a man who knew when he was being patronized.

"You are gracious, Field Marshal, but your presence would be more valuable elsewhere, certainly. I will be in a studio. No crowds."

Speer thought of the great rallies that Goebbels had engineered, massive spectacles of lights and flags, inspiring so much energy in the people, the energy that had fueled Hitler's power. There can be none of that now, he thought. One nighttime bombing raid . . .

Hitler focused on Goebbels, said, "You will emphasize a timetable?"

"Not at this time, my Führer. It should be sufficient to tell the people that we are continuing to destroy the enemy on every front. Victory is within our grasp. It is not so important to tell them when."

Hitler seemed to accept the explanation, and Goebbels looked toward Kesselring as though expecting a protest. Kesselring stayed silent.

Goebbels said, "The larger the lie, Field Marshal, the easier it is for the people to believe it."

Hitler seemed not to hear, turned away, moved again to the window.

Goebbels rose, said, "Heil Hitler!"

Hitler acknowledged with a silent gesture, a quick wave of his right hand, and Goebbels was gone. Hitler turned, looked at Kesselring, and Speer saw a strange calm on the Führer's face.

"Field Marshal, if the enemy is not to be driven away quickly, if he insists on defiling more of our soil, then you will carry out a new order. I am confident that every German is willing to fight and die for his country. We shall see that he does. If the enemy cannot be stopped, you shall create a desert in his path. Every factory, every home, every town shall be destroyed. We will eliminate the means of gas and electrical production, all bridges and roadways, croplands, all food and cloth stores." He looked at Speer, continued. "Every factory shall undergo self-destruction. There shall be no means of manufacture, no facility shall remain standing. All of this shall be accomplished without consideration for our own population."

Speer was shocked, stood, surprising Hitler, who backed up a step.

"My Führer, you cannot do this! There can still be peace on terms that will benefit Germany."

"Herr Speer, I am of two minds on this subject. Study your history. Great men are known by the failures they overcome. Yes, we can defeat this enemy. Even now, our scientists continue their work on weapons that will unleash great terror. Should we prevail, I will have proven to the world that I stand beside the greatest conquerors of history. But I cannot control the failures of others, and this war has so often been decided by those who have betrayed me, the weak and the incompetent. I will not subject the German people to the humiliation they endured after the last war. If this war is lost, the German nation will also perish. No German will suffer under another's boot heel. The German people will accept this as their destiny."

Speer stood with his mouth open, felt a hand on his arm, Kesselring pulling him back down into the chair.

Hitler seemed satisfied at his pronouncement, said, "Enough for now. Field Marshal, I shall meet with you again tomorrow. Herr Speer, you will return to your office and expedite the submarine production. A thousand is satisfactory, but I would prefer to see that many in service by July."

Speer nodded, stared at the floor.

"Yes, my Führer."

Kesselring was up, and Speer followed, the two men moving outside the office. Bormann was there, the usual smirk that Speer detested.

"Sorry I could not attend the meeting. The Führer instructed me to send a disciplinary message to several of your factory managers. They have been too slow in effecting repairs. We cannot have that."

Speer knew Bormann was purposely intruding into his authority, a practice that gave the man particular joy. But Speer ignored him, followed Kesselring out into the corridor. Kesselring led him to a narrow hallway, darker, no offices, pulled him aside. Speer felt the usual exhaustion, the effect of every meeting with Hitler, his clothes wet with sweat.

Kesselring had him by the arm, said, "Get hold of yourself, Speer. He cannot possibly carry out such an order. Even if Bormann spouts all of those same absurdities to your factories, you can contradict the order. The factory managers will listen to you. Just as the *burgermeisters* and military prefects will listen to me."

Speer felt a wave of weariness, the depression returning in a black flood. He tried to draw strength from Kesselring's certainty.

"I cannot defy him. None of us can. What do we do?"

Kesselring stood back, still had the hat clamped under his arm.

"We do our jobs. Repair your factories, produce your submarines. I shall maneuver my armies, defend our cities. It is the one great advantage, Herr Speer, to all that we do here. The Führer has made our lives simple, our duty has been made clear. We have been relieved of the need for *thought.*"

31. SPEER

On April 14, the Russians began their massive assault, their objective first to surround Berlin, and then to crush the army that defended it. With hopelessness spreading through the field commands, some German generals accepted that the only salvation for Germany would be an armistice with the western Allies, who might be persuaded to stand up firmly to the Russians, preventing the destruction not only of Berlin but also of the rest of eastern Germany. It had become apparent, from the panicked retreat of German soldiers and the vast streams of refugees desperate to escape the Russian advance, that no German general could expect the Russians to accept any requests for a cease-fire or a peaceful conclusion to the war that would allow Germany some kind of stability for its people. But hopes for some communication with the West had been severely condemned by Hitler, who continued to insist that German soldiers would fight to the last man. Any general who dared to risk a communication with his American or British counterpart did so at the risk of his own life.

Already, reports had spread through the villages close to the Russian advance that the Russians were treating German soldiers and civilians with astounding viciousness. To the horror of many in the German High Command, many of the reports were graphically accurate. As the Russians continued their drive through German villages, over rivers and around Berlin itself, they produced a hysterical panic. Along the front lines, German soldiers were deserting en masse, not into the hands of the enemy in front of them, but away, a desperate escape toward the west. The consensus among the fleeing Germans was clear. If they were to fall into the hands of a captor, it would be an American captor.

As the Allies continued their pressure from the west, the last pocket of resistance in the German Ruhr Valley finally collapsed, resulting in the capture of more than three hundred thousand German troops, many of them the same troops who had fought so well under Field Marshal Model in the Ardennes. The loss of the Ruhr erased much of Germany's capacity for producing the tools of war, and Model himself understood that he would be blamed for failing to keep the Allies away. On April 21, before a furious Hitler had the opportunity to either replace or condemn yet another of his commanders, Walther Model took a pistol from his command post, walked into a nearby patch of forest, and killed himself.

With Russian artillery now impacting the city, Berliners reacted with a mix of panic and an astounding commitment to put up the best fight they could against what they believed was the brutal savagery of the Russian soldiers. Despite their passion, Berlin's defenders had one major disadvantage. In an amazing display of overconfidence toward his Russian enemy, Hitler had never ordered any kind of defensive barrier to be built in the east, nothing similar to the West Wall, which had been somewhat effective in slowing the Allied advance in the west. Thus, as the Russians pressed their way closer to the outskirts of Berlin, the Germans had few if any defensive works to protect the city. German soldiers could only rush piles of debris and any other makeshift barrier they could find in a feeble attempt to slow down the approaching columns of Russian armor and infantry. Seeing the best efforts his men were making, one German general observed that his barricade would hold the Russians away for a single hour: fifty-five minutes of Russian laughter, followed by five minutes of actual fighting.

It quickly became apparent to the German High Command that the Russian strategy was to surround Berlin completely, cutting off any troops in the city from escape and trapping the hapless civilians who had sought safety in the city's cellars and thick-walled buildings. Only ten days after their massive assault began, the Russians had nearly closed the ring. For once Hitler seemed to acknowledge the desperation of his army's position. In response to the Russian successes, Hitler ordered the German Twelfth Army, the primary force still opposing the Americans near the Elbe River, to turn around and drive eastward toward the capital. In the city itself, the

German Ninth Army was fighting for its survival. Hitler's hope was that the Twelfth could break through the Russian ring to unite with the Ninth, and that the combined forces would be strong enough to drive the Russians completely away. There was one obvious cost to Hitler's strategy. The Americans, who were already making extraordinary progress driving deeper into Germany, suddenly had a much easier time of it.

HITLER'S BUNKER, BENEATH THE CHANCELLERY, BERLIN
APRIL 23, 1945

"I am surprised to see you, Herr Speer. Pleased, but surprised."

Speer made a short bow toward Goebbels, said, "Thank you, Doctor. I have been visiting with the Führer, but he had a considerable number of details to attend to, many people waiting to see him, so it was appropriate for me to cut short my visit. I hope to meet with him again before I leave."

"How did you get here, if I may ask?"

"Small plane, a Storch. My pilot is Colonel Posen, and he made use of the runway constructed on the city streets. Perhaps you know him?"

Goebbels shook his head. "Sorry, no. But if he chanced a landing at this time, he is a brave man indeed."

Speer was impressed by Goebbels's patience for this kind of small talk, wasn't sure why Goebbels was even there at all. The bunker was far more subdued than Speer had ever experienced, the obvious sign that many of the staff had simply gone.

Goebbels seemed to read him, said, "My family has decided to move in here, so that we may be united through our darkest hour. Regrettably my wife is not in good health."

"I am sorry to hear that. I should like to visit with her, if there is time."

"Yes, perhaps. Herr Speer, have you been told of the Führer's instructions to Field Marshal Kesselring? Our forces in the west have been ordered to withdraw, a signal to the English and Americans that we will not oppose them if they will occupy the city. It is thought that this will be the best for everyone, wouldn't you say?"

Speer knew of the effort to break through the Russian encirclement, but had not heard anyone express it in such a positive way. Goebbels waited for a response with that thin-lipped smile, the counterfeit cheerfulness that now seemed utterly out of place. Speer thought, do they believe it will happen that way, that the Russians will just . . . back away? But he knew not to disagree with Goebbels about anything. No one but Hitler could suggest any idea that did not fit into the *plan*.

After a moment, Speer nodded, tried to sound thoughtful. "That would be best, yes. For Berlin and for all of Germany."

Goebbels seemed satisfied that Speer had responded appropriately. He looked away for a moment, then said, "We have always believed that the German people have much in common with our western friends. It is only logical that we stand united against a common foe. No one wants to see the stain of Bolshevism spread across Germany. Certainly not Mr. Churchill. We know little of the new American president, Mr. Truman, but we must assume he will curry the favor of the American people by making a strong stand against the spread of communism. There is opportunity for him to cast away the mistakes made by his predecessor at their Yalta Conference. We are aware that Mr. Churchill was vigorously opposed to the agreement that Stalin coerced from the Americans, and the Führer has been surprised that the English in particular have not been more forceful in their opposition of Stalin's brutish ways. If they allow us to fall under Bolshevik boots, there are many here who do not wish to remain alive. That is one reason my family is here. If this bunker falls into Russian hands, they will inherit only our corpses." Goebbels paused, seemed to want the meaning of that to sink in. "The Führer knows that Stalin wants him alive, which is the primary reason the Führer will not allow that to happen. Can you imagine the horrible spectacle of the Führer put on public trial for the imaginary crimes that Stalin would conjure up? It sickens me to think of our beloved Führer paraded out in a humiliating display, a circus act for the benefit of the most savage of entertainment. It will not happen, not to the Führer, not to any of us."

Speer saw no emotion from Goebbels, absorbed what the man was telling him.

"Of course, Doctor. It must not happen."

"Consider your own fate, Herr Speer. Just a thought."

There was an oily seduction in Goebbels's voice, what the man had used so well to sway people to Hitler's cause. Speer had always understood the appeal of Goebbels's oratory, felt the weight of that now, a small speech directed solely at him.

"Thank you, Doctor. I am hopeful your wife recovers. I do hope I will see her before I leave."

"Perhaps." Goebbels turned away, then stopped, spun around, cold steel in his stare.

"Heil Hitler."

"Heil Hitler, Doctor."

S peer had spent an uncomfortable hour with Eva Braun, Hitler's mistress, who was now a full-time resident of the bunker. He never had particularly strong feelings about the woman, but he had been somewhat close to her throughout the last year, primarily because she despised Martin Bormann as much as he did. If she seemed relatively oblivious to politics, she knew very well that Bormann was a snake to be watched carefully, that Bormann jealously guarded his closeness to Hitler. Thus even Hitler's mistress was something of a threat. If Bormann spent any of his energy contemplating some treachery toward Eva Braun, it meant Bormann was preoccupied with something other than removing Speer from the inner circle. It made Speer and Eva Braun natural allies.

But the talk was always there. In those indiscreet moments, fueled by the long nights of flowing alcohol, he had heard low comments, few of them positive. She was thought to be something of an opportunist, a fairly selfish and dim-witted woman with a flair for attention. She was pretty in a plain sort of way, enjoyed athletics and a partying life, which Hitler most definitely did not. Oddly, Hitler would not allow her to be seen in public alongside him, and as far as Speer knew, the German people had no idea she existed. Hitler was more than twenty years her senior, and had never seemed healthy or energetic beyond his manic obsession with politics. The talk was often more prurient than Speer wanted to hear, observations among Hitler's circle that Braun's attraction to Hitler must have been inspired more by a lust for power than lust in general. Yet Eva Braun was never a part of the military meetings and planning sessions. She was never included in any official capacity, had no title, no duties. If she had any influence over Hitler's decision making, Speer had seen no evidence of it at all. He imagined that she was simply the Führer's plaything, and she had accepted her role willingly, if not with some occasional complaints. It was also clear that on occasion, her restlessness had caused harsh whispers in the High Command, that too often the Führer's mistress was engaging in distinctly inappropriate behavior, behavior that Hitler seemed to ignore. Speer had known Hitler to show far more affection to his dog Blondi than he ever demonstrated for the woman who was supposed to be his beloved companion. Yet it defied anyone's imagination that Hitler was blind to her blatant flirting, or worse. For some time, it was a poorly guarded secret that Braun had kept up an intimate relationship with a Gestapo officer named Hermann Fegelein, an indiscretion that was known to almost everyone in the inner circle except perhaps Hitler himself. Speer could only assume that Fegelein was the stupidest man in the German army.

Tonight's request that he visit her private chamber had come to Speer through an invitation handed him by a young Gestapo officer. Speer had responded the only way he could. No matter how hesitant he might have been, he knew that incurring the wrath of Hitler's mistress was a truly terrible idea, and given her aggressive approach to many of the men who swirled around Hitler, wrath from Eva Braun was not a challenge Speer wanted to accept.

Her mood had been amazingly buoyant, with an offering of food and champagne, which Speer had nervously accepted. But to his relief, Braun was more interested in talking than she was in Speer himself. As the champagne flowed, it had become obvious that she merely wanted someone to talk to. For the first time, Speer understood that even this flighty young woman grasped the inevitable and was resigned to ending her life alongside the Führer. She spoke openly of suicide, with none of the regret or sorrow that Speer could feel in every other corner of the bunker, a darkening mood he sensed even from Goebbels.

When word came that Hitler was at last alone and willing to see him, Speer was able to extricate himself from her one-woman party. Her farewell was breezy and positive, and he marveled at her cheerfulness, a gaiety he simply could not understand. As he made his way toward Hitler's office, Speer rolled the thoughts over in his mind. Was her life so confining and miserable that suicide was something to be relished? And if somehow, Hitler's army performed a miraculous recovery and tossed the Russians out of Germany, would she be disappointed? In front of Hitler's door, he composed himself, thought of the champagne on his breath, something Hitler would not approve of. Speer scolded himself, thought, you know all about buildings. You don't know a damn thing about people. He looked at his watch. Three o'clock. I suppose . . . it's time.

It had been Hitler's habit for many months that well after midnight, long after his generals had exhausted themselves and drifted away to their quarters, he would seek out someone to engage in conversation, a quiet

time that would sometimes last past dawn. Speer had fulfilled that role
many times, understood that he was there primarily to serve as the recep-
tive audience to Hitler's musings and pronouncements. The conversation
was rarely two-sided, though the Führer still respected Speer for his knowledge of things so unfamiliar to Hitler himself. It had been a saving grace
for Speer, and one reason why Bormann had been unable to supplant
Speer as Hitler's intimate. Bormann could be a listener as well, but he had
very little to say that did not involve politics or his own ambition. Even
Hitler had grown weary of that.

Speer glanced at the guard, standing rigidly to one side, gave a brief
nod, the man expressionless, watching him, as the guard watched everyone
who came close to Hitler's private office. Speer felt a rumble, a sudden
thump, and he froze, listened.

The guard said, "Russian artillery. It has come closer in the past two
days."

Speer saw the guard looking up, betraying his nervousness, and Speer
said, "It's all right. There are several meters of concrete above us. There is
no danger here."

"Thank you, sir. But we must be prepared to fight."

Speer had no answer, knocked gently at the door, waited, heard
Hitler's usual greeting.

"You may enter."

Speer pushed the door open, moved inside the room. The light in the
office was dim, the walls spare and dull, a dismal stench to the stale air. It
was always a problem throughout the bunker, something that could not be
helped with the limited ventilation from the outside.

"Herr Speer, come. There is tea."

Speer slapped his heels together, stood stiffly at attention, the habit.

"My Führer, it is good to see you again."

Hitler said nothing, pulled himself up from the chair, a groaning effort, and Speer thought, you should help him. But no . . . he hates that,
would rather believe we notice nothing of his ailments. Hitler retrieved a
pot from a small stove, turned, moved back to the chair, and Speer saw the
limp, more pronounced now, Hitler walking with increasing difficulty. His
hair had grayed considerably, and Speer saw the twitch in Hitler's left
hand, always there. Speer wouldn't sit until Hitler approved it, watched in
silence as the hot water flowed into the cups. Hitler sat, pulled his left leg
over his right with his hand, another strain. Speer knew Hitler might not

even notice him standing at attention for some time, but he was very tired, the effects of the champagne.

"Are you feeling well, my Führer?"

"Do not concern yourself with my health. I have banished Dr. Morell from this place. I finally realized what that man was trying to do. He insisted on administering a hypodermic, claimed it would energize me, but I know it was morphine. He was attempting to drug me so that they could remove me from here by force. That's what they want, you know. I hear that barking from every one of them. 'Get out of Berlin!' It is the most traitorous decision anyone could make, and I will not hear it." He cocked his head, stared at Speer with black eyes. "Is that why you are here? Have you come to annoy me with all those *good reasons* why I should abandon the capital? Sit down. You are making me tired."

Speer obeyed, sat across from Hitler, a small table to one side, the cup of hot water steaming. Speer reached for the tea, scooped a spoonful into the strainer, set it in the water, noticed that Hitler was watching every move with keen interest.

"No, my Führer. I have no such wish. I flew here this afternoon to offer you . . . support."

"That is a lie, Herr Speer. You do not need to be here at all. You should *not* be here. My own staff are abandoning me, and with things as they are, I no longer require your loyalty, or your services. I am astounded to find how many cowards there are, all those men I trusted for so long. And if they are not cowards, they are traitors. General Jodl has been begging me to leave the city. He says that plans have been made for a safe passage to Berchtesgaden. *Plans.* They have thought this through, taken every precaution. For how long? Weeks, months? They have *planned* to abandon Berlin. I ordered them away, told them they could go anywhere they please, that I will give them no further orders. I will remain here for one reason, a reason no traitor can understand. The soldiers will fight if they know I am *with* them, that the fight is being directed from *here,* by my hand. I will die before I allow the Bolsheviks to take my city."

Hitler seemed to slump in the chair, stared at the tea, raised the cup with his right hand.

"This does not taste good. Are they poisoning me again?"

Speer looked at the tea, hesitated, thought, no, don't do that. Don't hesitate. He drank, a long hot sip, said, "It is a little bitter. Perhaps the water is not good. But . . . I do not feel any effects of poison."

Hitler looked at him, blinking hard, as though trying to focus.

"I am glad you are here, Herr Speer. Be assured, my faith in you is un-tarnished. Your plans, all those marvelous structures, all of that will come to pass in time. There is an inevitability to history, and our destiny is certain. History will vindicate us all, no matter what happens in the months to come." He paused. "I used to enjoy Vienna, you know. In my younger days, it was a wonderful place. But there were too many Jews, and they controlled the arts. My talents were not appreciated because I was not one of *them*. I despise the place now. I despise . . ." He paused, seemed to lose the thought. Speer eyed the tea again, took a small sip, and Hitler said, "The English cannot be happy with our state of affairs. But even so, they have betrayed us. They know they should be fighting beside us, they should be helping us drive the Bolsheviks back to their caves. It was my mistake to believe that the West would understand what our *real* catastrophe will be. It is why our soldiers will die to save this city. They know they will become Russian slaves if they are captured. The German is too proud to ever accept such a fate. I have seen reports of mass desertions by some of our troops. It sickens me, but I understand that when there is hopelessness, when there is despair, men can do the wrong thing. The Russians are beasts, and they will not prevail, because they do not understand our will. The German people know that our lives will not be worth living if we fall into their grasp. The desertions are shameful, and I know it is the fault of our generals, that they do not know how to inspire my troops. I have the solution, though. I will order the execution of all prisoners of war, all the foreign soldiers we hold in our stalags. Our enemies will have to reciprocate by doing the same. That will end the desertions. Even our weakest soldiers will understand that it is far better to die fighting than to die a prisoner."

Speer felt a cold stab in his stomach, the same feeling he had endured when Hitler ordered the destruction of Germany's factories. Speer had been able to go about his business with some quiet discretion, the local officials and industrial managers understanding the careful tightrope he had to tread to ignore that order. It had been enormously helpful to him that Kesselring, and thus the army, had ignored it as well.

The thump of artillery came again, then more, close by, and Speer flinched, instinct, wondered if there had been an explosion in the Chancellery.

Hitler seemed to ignore the sounds, said, "It is not necessary for you to remain in Berlin."

"Yes, my Führer. You have told me that. I am grateful. I should like to be with my family, to do what I can to keep them safe."

There was a sharp rap at the door, and Hitler seemed annoyed. "I ask for a *moment's* peace. What is it?"

The door opened slowly, and Speer saw Bormann, holding papers.

"My Führer, we have received a wire from Reichsmarschall Göring at Berchtesgaden. It is important that you see this."

Hitler shrugged. "Yes, so what does the fat man want now? Has he exhausted his supply of prostitutes? Go on, read it. My eyes are tired."

Bormann glanced at Speer, seemed uncomfortable sharing a high-level communication.

"If you wish it, my Führer."

Bormann cleared his throat, read.

My Führer,

   If you are in agreement after your decision to hold out in fortress Berlin, in accordance with the law of 29 June 1941, I now take over leadership of the Reich with all powers internally and externally. If I have received no reply by 2200 I will assume that you are no longer free to act and will therefore consider the conditions of your law as having been met and act on my own responsibility in the best interests of our country and our people. What I feel in this most difficult time of my life cannot be expressed. May God protect you and I hope that you will still come here from Berlin.

                                     Your Loyal, Hermann Göring.

Hitler sniffed.

"So, what am I to do about my good friend Göring? He has made good his escape, and though he has much *sorrow* for our situation here, I should be comforted that he is safe and fat and happy."

"My Führer, there is more. The Reichsmarschall also sent a wire to Foreign Minister Ribbentrop, informing him that Reichsmarschall Göring is presuming to be Germany's new authority. It is apparent, my Führer, that the Reichsmarschall is inviting Herr Ribbentrop to join him in his new . . . government."

Speer saw the eruption in Hitler's eyes, the fury boiling over.

"Ribbentrop is a traitor, always has been! I knew that! I knew that he was making entreaties to our enemies, going behind my back to seek a cowardly armistice. Now the fat man will do the same! This is how my most trusted . . ."

Hitler's words choked away, his right fist slowly pounding the table, a steady rhythm, the sounds blending into a new barrage of artillery above. Speer saw the satisfaction on Bormann's face, the message delivered, the response exactly what Bormann had hoped for. Yes, Speer thought, he wants to be the last man standing, the last loyal servant to the Führer. If he could shoot me right now, as I sit here, he would do so.

The artillery barrage continued above, but Hitler seemed to calm, made a quick gesture with his hand, waving Bormann away.

"I have more important things to do than concern myself with the fat man's dreams of glory. Leave us."

Bormann looked at Speer with a hint of anger, and Speer tried to ignore it, thought, wonderful. He will certainly believe I am plotting against *him*. Bormann marched out of the office, closed the door with an efficient thump.

Speer said, "My Führer, is there something . . . anything you wish me to do?"

"Yes. Leave. You have been loyal, and I admire you for your skills and your artistry. But there is no place for you here."

Speer couldn't avoid the feeling of relief, tried to hide it. He stood, began to move toward the door, stopped. He looked back at Hitler, saw the sickliness, the weakness, remembered Eva Braun, all the talk of suicide. Speer realized, this is the last time. If I escape Berlin, I will never see him again.

"Good-bye, Speer."

There was nothing more to say. Speer opened the door, stepped into the damp hallway, the air just as stale, the faint glow from the lightbulbs casting long shadows. He moved past a guard, past the open doors of the empty offices, a brief glance, no secretaries at work this late, no one at all. He climbed the steps, past more guards, one man holding open the door. The night was cool, and Speer felt a sharp breeze, saw a massive red glow to the east, a spreading fire. The thumps of artillery were much louder now, and he thought of the plane, his fragile escape, the wide avenue close by that had been transformed into a makeshift runway. He began to walk past the tall dense walls of the Chancellery, had a sudden urge to go inside, to pass through the hallways of the grand structure he had built. But there was no electricity aboveground there, the hallways impenetrable in the darkness, a darkness that drove through him, that drained away his energy. He thought of the models, the magnificence in miniature, his dream, his future. He knew now, as he had known all along, that it was the *dream* that had pushed him to ignore so much, to deny so much. He looked toward the glow, more artillery shells landing blocks away, thunder beneath his feet. There will be no miracle. No matter what Hitler claims to believe, the army cannot survive. We cannot survive.

The shelling slowed, stopped, a strange silence in the chill around him, the night seeming darker now. He knew it would be dawn soon, that if the sun rose, he could not escape by air, would be an easy target for enemy gunners or the swarms of fighter planes. He quickened his pace, thought of his pilot, Colonel Posen, the man more loyal to Speer than to the army he served. He will be waiting, just as he said. And we shall leave this place. The argument rose up in his brain, the guilt he had tried to avoid. Should I stay? Perhaps that is the right thing to do, the only thing to do. Pick up a rifle, and fight. But he saw his wife now, the image of his children. That is the only future. You have been arrogant, a fool. And those who stay here and believe we have something to fight for . . . they are all fools. Hitler will die . . . all of this will die. Perhaps if I survive, I can do something to preserve Germany, to help keep something alive. Or is that arrogance as well, another of my foolish dreams?

He pushed himself through the cold, his heart pounding, the click of his boots on broken concrete. He rounded a corner, saw the rows of faint red lights on the avenue, the manufactured runway, barely lit, just enough to allow a pilot to see. In the distance, Speer could see a glow from distant fires reflecting off the imposing monument, one of his favorites, a piece of Berlin's history for nearly a century. The monument was a beloved symbol, a celebration of Germany's successes in war, of conquerors and gallant soldiers and the crushing defeat of their enemies. It was called the *Victory Column.*

O n April 25, the Russian ring around Berlin was sealed. Inside the ring, the German Ninth Army waged a last-gasp effort to defend the city, an effort that resulted in its virtual annihilation. Outside the ring, the German Twelfth Army made a valiant attempt to break through, but opposing them was an overwhelming number of Russian tanks, boosted by the increasing confidence of Russian troops. No matter how dedicated the German commanders were, there was a solid awareness that their cause was hopeless. Among those was Alfred Jodl. He and Wilhelm Keitel had been the senior officers in the German High Command. Now both men had made their escapes from Berlin, and though they maintained whatever communications were possible with Hitler's bunker, they did so from locations far removed from the disaster in Berlin. In the field, Kesselring and Admiral Dönitz gathered troops and fortified their defensive positions with what dwindling strength they could muster, but neither man expected the tide to be turned away.

To those few who remained in Hitler's bunker, the military realities finally crushed the illusions that Hitler continued to foster. The stale air in the bunker was becoming more foul, polluted by the smoke from incoming Russian artillery. It was the first clear sign that the Chancellery itself had become a major target for Russian guns. The massive structure that had given Albert Speer so much pride was being demolished. Far beyond Berlin, there were political realities as well. Heinrich Himmler had served alongside Hitler since the Nazis' first rise to power, and in the early 1930s, as Hitler's government asserted itself, Himmler's Gestapo had given Hitler an efficient machine for both terror and muscle. Despite what Hermann Göring had believed, Himmler was the second most powerful man in Germany, and was the man who carried out Hitler's order for the construction of the concentration camps, which led to the execution of countless millions in the gas chambers and slave labor camps all across German occupied territory. But Himmler had escaped Berlin as well, and as he accepted the dire hopelessness of Hitler's situation, Himmler did the unthinkable. Using the Swedes as intermediaries, Himmler made his own entreaties to the West, his own call for some kind of armistice. Hitler learned of Himmler's efforts from Swedish radio reports, through broadcasts over shortwave that had become Hitler's only means of communication with the outside world. Predictably outraged, Hitler now branded Himmler as yet another of Germany's traitors, and issued a decree that the man be imprisoned and executed. But the order was only a fantasy in Hitler's mind. There was no one left in the German command outside of Berlin who had the means or the will to carry it out.

To Himmler's dismay, his entreaties to the western Allies met the same response as those of Ribbentrop or the many generals who had made the same attempt. He was flatly refused.

With Russian troops driving to within several city blocks of the bunker, Hitler's slippery grasp of reality had given way to a solemn determination to deny the Russians the satisfaction of capturing him. The decision was made that those who remained in the bunker would die by their own hands, a pact that no one dared to dispute openly. On April 28, near midnight, in a ceremony marked solely by gloom, Hitler married Eva Braun. In the hours that followed, Hitler dictated his will, as much a political harangue for the causes of the war as any personal bequest. In the decay of Hitler's mind, the blame for the war had to be laid squarely on the shoulders of the Jews. Hitler's rage brought forth yet another call for extermination, an order that all Jews still remaining in concentration camps would be put to death at once. What Hitler could not grasp was that, again, there was no longer anyone outside of Berlin loyal enough, or dedicated enough to his cause, to carry the order to its conclusion.

On April 29, the street fighting close to the wreckage of the Chancellery was pushing in on the bunker from three sides. Faced with the total collapse of the world around him, Hitler seemed to withdraw from any role in his own government. He focused instead on his dog, the German shepherd Blondi. Hitler ordered the dog poisoned rather than have the dog fall into Russian hands. The death of the dog created an eruption of emotion in Hitler, a strange bit of illogic for those who observed the master ordering the animal's death. Hitler had killed what even he knew was the most loyal member of his family. What most of the staff did not know was that Hitler was using the dog as a test of the effectiveness of the poison ampoules, containing prussic acid, brought to him by his new doctor, Werner Haase, the same ampoules that were distributed to the others around him. Hitler now trusted the doctors least of all.

Near midnight on April 29, Hitler learned of the execution of his sole remaining ally, Benito Mussolini. Though Mussolini had been little more than a symbol to the fading hopes of Italians fascists, his execution by machine gun had been followed by a shockingly gruesome display. The once all-powerful Italian dictator was hung by his feet in a square in Milan, alongside the corpse of his mistress. For hours, Italians reacted to the spectacle by abusing the bodies with rocks and sticks, a public display of disrespect and revenge that shocked Hitler, and strengthened his own resolve that the leader of Germany's Reich would not be captured.

The next day, April 30, Hitler issued his final order, sent by hand to the senior officers still engaging the Russians short blocks from the bunker.

The order granted permission for any soldiers who had exhausted their ammunition to break out of Berlin, with a further order that they continue the fight in the forests beyond the city. Whether there was ammunition or not, those few soldiers still participating in the incredible viciousness of what was now house-to-house fighting seemed to care nothing at all about escape.

At three thirty P.M., after a quiet farewell to those who remained in the bunker, Hitler retired to his private room, accompanied only by his new wife. Within minutes, a single shot was heard. Hitler's adjutant Otto Günsche and his valet Heinz Linge entered the room alongside Martin Bormann. The couple were seated at either end of a couch, Eva Braun dead from ingesting a prussic acid ampoule. Hitler had shot himself, a single wound to his right temple. Within short minutes, Günsche, acting on specific orders he had received from Hitler, supervised the movement of both bodies up and out of the bunker, to a shallow pit only a few feet from the bunker's entrance. With Russian mortar and artillery shells impacting close by, the bodies were doused in gasoline and cremated.

As paralysis spread through the bunker, one man performed an act of loyalty that Hitler would have certainly approved. Joseph Goebbels had moved his entire family into the bunker as a show of unity with his Führer, and there was only a final act to perform. His wife, Magda, had accepted the necessity of what was to come, but had become too incapacitated by grief to carry out the duty alone. In her stead, Dr. Ludwig Stumpfegger obeyed the orders of Dr. Goebbels, and, accompanied by the children's mother, Stumpfegger administered morphine to put each of the children to sleep. Then, as Magda Goebbels hurried from the room, the doctor placed a poison ampoule into each child's mouth and crushed it by his own hand. Within seconds, all six children, aged three to fourteen, were dead. Joseph Goebbels carried out the final part of his plan. Accompanied by his grief-stricken wife, he stepped up into the open air outside the bunker, where a Gestapo orderly obeyed Goebbels's final order and shot Goebbels and his wife in the back of their heads. Then, in the open shell-pocked grounds of the Chancellery, their bodies were cremated as well.

On May 2, the Russians seized control of most of Berlin. The two armies had each struggled in a desperate race to exterminate the other, as two vicious animals locked together in a cage. When the fighting began to quiet, the Russians rolled over and through the remains of Hitler's stronghold, past the charred corpses that someone had the curiosity to grab up and hustle away. The German soldiers who survived the fight were marched out of the city, prisoners of a hell they had fought desperately to escape.

As a sickly peace settled over Berlin, it began to rain. Through the debris and carnage that covered the streets of the once-grand city, the water gathered in shell craters and pits of destruction. The muddy water grew deeper, spilling and flooding into the cracks and crevices, carrying the blood and filth of the soldiers and, with it, the mad and vicious fantasies of a twisted little man who destroyed lives and dreams and all he touched.

32. PATTON

In the weeks that followed the liberation of Ohrdruf, more camps were overrun and exposed to the eyes of the Allied command. The names were already becoming known throughout the army, and in newspapers across the Atlantic: Buchenwald and Dachau, Bergen-Belsen and Mauthausen. The Russians liberated camps of their own, including the largest camp at Auschwitz in Poland, where more than a million prisoners, most of them Jews, had been either starved, gassed, or gruesomely exterminated by what German doctors described as *medical experimentation.*

Ohrdruf had been a satellite of the much larger Buchenwald camp, and it was Patton's men who continued to bring the light of day to so many more of the horrifying atrocities they had witnessed at Ohrdruf. The fury that Patton had always carried to the battlefield had grown into a raging fire for this particular enemy, an enemy he was still trying to comprehend. For the first time he had experienced something far beyond his passion for war, the clear and poignant need to kill his enemy. At the Nazi camps, he had come face-to-face with the raw concept of *hate.*

In Patton's world, war did not involve civilians. But the atrocities he had seen raised a new and infuriating question, a fierce curiosity to know how much the German civilians knew of the camps, if they knew anything at all. It defied logic to him that civilians in the towns around Buchenwald had no idea what their soldiers and the SS guards were doing there. With those camps still within his jurisdiction, he would at least try to answer that dilemma, if only for himself. Whenever possible, he had ordered that his soldiers march through the various camps. Now that same order was issued to the towns and villages that spread out around those places like Buchenwald. Patton would hear no excuses, no explanations. Before he moved on to completing his drive into Czechoslovakia, he would see that the German civilians who lived nearby toured the camps as well. If the MPs needed bayonets to persuade them, that was fine with him.

He ordered his MPs to round up as many civilian officials as they could locate. Some of those were obvious, the men who still occupied civil offices, controlling utilities or some other function of the German government. Others had to be ferreted out, many of those given up by their own people, local citizens finally able to strike back at the Nazis by pointing out those men who had exercised some local role in party politics. Even the lowest-level Nazi officials were not eager to be found by the Americans, and most insisted they had no knowledge of what went on behind the wire. They certainly accepted none of the blame. Patton didn't care. Despite the occasional protest by civilian officials outraged to be lumped together with the military in their supposed crimes, Patton ordered the tours to begin. More than fifteen hundred Germans would be guided through the camps, forced through every nook, every building where some of the most gruesome sights could still be seen.

Buchenwald Concentration Camp
May 2, 1945

Patton stood up on the turret of a tank, made very sure that his MPs saw that he was watching them do their jobs. The tank had parked just inside the main gate, and his vantage point allowed him a view of most of the enormous spread of buildings and barracks. Even now, the smells found him, sickening, inescapable, his eyes watering from the powerful odor of burnt flesh and chemicals. He forced himself to stand tall, crossed his arms over his chest, waiting. From the road behind him, he could hear the engines of the trucks, didn't need to see them, knew they were escorted by men in jeeps with machine guns. The brakes were squealing, the trucks parking to one side, behind him, and he turned slowly, said nothing, watching as men in rumpled suits climbed out, helping their women, who had dressed for the occasion with surprising formality, as though they had been escorted to some sort of festivity. But there was nothing festive in their mood. Patton watched them milling about; then, as more of the trucks arrived, the MPs put them into line, and directed them through the gate.

They passed right below him, orderly, no talking, the German way, a perfect show of ignorant efficiency. Some looked up at him, no acknowledgment of his rank, no smiles. Most of them seemed to be curious, glancing around, as though seeing the barracks and the guard towers for the first time. He marveled at that, thought, is it possible . . . they really didn't know? What about the *smell,* for God's sake?

The guards led them farther into the camp, more of his soldiers standing beside open doors of various wooden buildings, the guards guiding the civilians that way, marching them through every place that mattered, every building where the sights would make the point. For the first time, they began to show some reaction, the women first, some turning away, soft whimpering cries. One man surged away from the line, was sick, dropped to his knees, some words Patton couldn't hear. The MPs were relentless, the man dragged up by the coat, Patton's orders obeyed. He watched the man, saw him glance back toward Patton, and the tank, and Patton thought, it gets worse, you Kraut son of a bitch. I want you to see every damn horror there is to see. Then go home and tell your children how much glory there is in your goddamn Hitler.

The reports came back to him from some of the liaison officers, the men who were already engineering the protocols for an army of occupation. Patton's organized tour through the death camp had produced a graphic result, which was, to him, the best possible outcome. Several of the civilian officials had reboarded the trucks, returned to their homes, and committed suicide.

Patton tapped the pilot on the shoulder, the plane banking sharply, moving low, a casual flap of the wings, the sign for any idiotic antiaircraft gunner to pay attention to the plane's markings. He knew the staff hated it when he did this, when he took the opportunity to make a brief flight over some piece of the battlefields. Codman had been stern with him, as stern as Patton would allow, but Patton had faith in his own officers to keep control over their gunners. The argument from Codman had been futile, the colonel finally giving up, no one more familiar with Patton's stubbornness. Patton would never give in, but even now he knew that down below there were many itchy fingers among those who manned the anti-aircraft guns, who had yet to shoot down what was a nonexistent German air force.

"That's the extent of it, sir."

Patton didn't need the pilot telling him what he was seeing. The ground beneath him was a vast sea of debris, shattered buildings and wrecked streets, fires and black smoke. It was the city of Nuremberg. But it was no city at all. It was a wasteland. He had expected to feel the usual rush of satisfaction, gloating to himself over the devastating conquest of one more enemy stronghold. But he knew enough of history to know that destroying such a place did very little to end the war beyond killing those few Germans who remained to defend it. He turned away, had seen enough, a quick motion to the pilot with his hand. *Home.* The plane banked again, the pilot obeying, and Patton sat back in the small seat, stared ahead into blue sky. It's the price they have to pay, he thought. All that history down there, the entire city like a big monument to past glories. Gone. Bombed to hell. No other way to do it, I guess. He knew he was making excuses for himself, that no one else would say anything about it, not Eisenhower certainly, not the newspapers, who covered their front pages with the sought-after photographs of massive destruction. He knew the bomber barons had a bloodlust of their own for this kind of obliteration, had been practicing it for more than two years now. The targets were big and obvious, and the high-flying heavy bombers had laid carpet after carpet of their bomb loads on anything standing. Stupid waste of explosives, he thought. Always was. They'll claim they won this war, but all those stupid bastards did was make work for our engineers. Every main road has to be repaired now, clearing away all that busted-up junk so I can get my people where they need to be. If I'd been in charge . . . he let the thought drift away, had been through that exercise too many times. Yeah, maybe we'd have won the war a hell of a lot quicker. And somebody in the British chief of staff's office would have had me shot. At least they're still letting Ike do his job.

He stared at the sky, the plane drifting lower, close to his new headquarters. He could see the massive structure, thought, a full-grown palace.

There's more useless crap in that place. I oughta let my boys grab it all up, ship it home for souvenirs. He knew that would never go over with SHAEF, that the army had been adamant about the theft of German artifacts. No, I'll just live with it. Not bad for a headquarters, but by damn, if I stub my toe in the middle of the night over some idiot statue, I'm hauling it out for target practice.

THIRD ARMY HEADQUARTERS, REGENSBURG, GERMANY
MAY 4, 1945

"Sir! It's official! They printed it in *Stars and Stripes,* can't get much more official than that!"

The aide slowly slid the paper toward him, and Patton pretended to ignore it.

"That damn paper is useful for one thing: the bottom of a birdcage. We don't have a bird, do we?"

"Uh, no, sir. But, sir! They printed news of your promotion!"

The man seemed to ache for Patton to pay attention, and Patton was already tired of the joke. He glanced at the article, said, "I guess maybe the new president has something on the ball. About damn time, though."

The sergeant was utterly exasperated with Patton's lack of enthusiasm, and Patton could feel the energy of the man's frustration, trying to keep his mouth in line with his position.

"Sir! At least . . . permission to congratulate you, sir!"

Patton looked up, allowed a smile to slip through.

"Fine. Congratulations accepted. Now get out of here. You've got work to do, right?"

The man was satisfied, his mission complete.

"Yes, sir! Right away!"

The sergeant disappeared through the office door, and Patton sat back, picked up the army newspaper, read the article. He caught motion from the door, heard Codman.

"Ah, good, I see you've read it. Nice of them to give you that kind of press."

"Oh for chrissakes, Colonel. You too? I knew this was coming, sooner or later. It's not like we should have a damn party."

"I'm not sure I agree with you, sir. Four stars. That's saying something in a man's career, especially . . . um . . . *your* career."

"Just what I need, a wise guy. The best news about this is that my promotion dates two days before Hodges's. About time those idiots in Washington got something right."

Codman said nothing, no response required, and Patton turned the page, made a loud grunt.

"Dammit!" He tossed the paper to one side. "Well, I lost *that* war! They're still going to print that idiot cartoon. Son of a bitch. This was Ike's doing."

"What, sir?"

"*Willy and Joe.* That damn cartoonist, Mauldin, first time I saw his piece of crap, it boiled my blood. This army doesn't need its soldiers portrayed as slobs and misfits. I insisted I wouldn't put up with it, told *Stars and Stripes* I was gonna ban the paper from the whole damn Third Army if they didn't stop printing that guy's scribbling. Turns out I'm the only officer in the whole damn theater who feels that way. Even Ike thinks it's just fine to encourage a lack of discipline, as though these damn cartoons represent our boys in action. Pissed me off then, pisses me off now. If it wasn't for Harry Butcher . . ." Patton paused. "Gotta give Harry credit. He's the hardest damn worker on Ike's staff. Does a hell of a lot more than Beetle Smith, but you can't tell Ike that. You were off somewhere, Paris, I think. Butcher actually brought Mauldin down here, planted him in my office, tried to make peace. Here I am face-to-face with a damn sergeant, and Butcher's got the guts to tell me we should be pals. I would have tossed that bastard in the stockade, but Butcher knew what the hell he was doing. It turns out this Sergeant Mauldin's been wounded in action. I never have an easy time knocking teeth out of a guy who's earned a Purple Heart. Mauldin stands there looking at me with his jaw dangling, but at least he dressed for the occasion. I expected him to look like his damn characters, and I'd have had to fine him or shoot him or something. Of course, it didn't hurt Butcher's case that he had already told Ike the whole story, so sure as hell, Ike gives me his standard speech about army morale, that the GIs like *Willy and Joe.* Fine. Ike's got nothing better to do than go to bat for a guy who draws cartoons. So, yeah, I lost that war." Patton chuckled. "But . . . if Sergeant Bill Mauldin ever shows his face around the Third Army again, you make sure the MPs know to throw him in the stockade. I'll figure out a reason why." Patton looked up at Codman, who was stifling a smile. "Yeah, go ahead and laugh. You know I've got the best damn staff in Europe, and you're part of it. But I better not see anybody in this HQ laughing at *Willy and Joe.*"

As the Third Army pressed closer to the Czech border, the Germans in their path were surrendering in massive numbers, entire regiments laying down their arms, greeting the Americans like liberators. Patton had been amazed by that, had always respected the German fighting man as a warrior even more than he had his own troops. It was one of Patton's particular complaints about American training, that the foot soldier wasn't given whatever the ingredient was that made a man a ruthless killer. Eisenhower had believed that as well, that the American soldier would never prove as vicious as the enemy he faced. But now the Germans had changed completely, the officers who brought their men into American lines desperately relieved that they had escaped the Russians.

PRISONER OF WAR COMPOUND
NEAR REGENSBURG, GERMANY
MAY 5, 1945

He stood on a grassy rise outside the wire enclosure, stared out over a sea of humanity. Troops outside the wire were cheering him, the same shouts he heard everywhere he went. Close to one side, he saw a man with a camera, and Patton turned that way, a brief accommodation, stood tall with his hands resting on the butts of his pistols. Behind the wire, the Germans were staring as well, a strange openmouthed awe, which surprised him. He puffed out his chest, thought of the four stars on his shoulders. The same promotion had already gone to Bradley and Devers, and to others, including Mark Clark, the American commander who was finally wrapping up the campaign in Italy. Patton had no idea if any of the others were actually wearing their stars yet, and he didn't care. He glanced at the jeep, the red four-starred flags, thought, gotta make sure I take that home. Beatrice will enjoy that, maybe put it over the mantel, or frame it. It's as high as anyone will get in this army, and the way things are going, the army's not going to need a whole flock of four-stars wandering around Washington.

He turned slightly, tried to aim the reflection of the sun on his helmet, trying to make a display for the POWs. I wonder if those Krauts have the slightest idea what these stars mean? He felt a little obnoxious for the preening, thought, even if you don't have any idea, you know that I'm the guy in charge. A German understands how to spot authority. It's part of how he's bred. That's right, boys. This is my command, and my camp and

FINAL TROOP POSITION—
MAY 8, 1945

SWEDEN

North Sea

DENMARK

Baltic Sea

Elbe River

Berlin

POLAND

GERMANY

Rhine River

Oder River

Frankfurt

Prague

Nuremburg

Pilsen

CZECHOSLOVAKIA

FRANCE

Munich

Vienna

Berchtesgaden

Salzburg

AUSTRIA

SWITZERLAND

Venice

Trieste

Bologna

YUGOSLAVIA

ITALY

Adriatic
Sea

0   100 mi
0   100 km

Held by USSR

American/British
position

In German hands

my damn army. And for now, until somebody signs one big pile of papers that spells out how this mess is going to end, you belong to me.

"Sir?"

Patton felt interrupted, annoyed, saw Codman beside the tank holding a paper.

"What the hell is it?"

"Message from SHAEF, sir. They've established the forward limits of our advance. They insist that you establish our forward position along the Elbe–Pilsen line."

Patton was more than annoyed now, knew something like this was coming.

"Do they say *why*?"

"Because that's the line agreed upon with the Russians, sir."

"Are the damn Russians there yet?"

"I'm not sure, sir. I could call the forward observers. We've got people close to Pilsen right now. Since we've hit the Czech border, we've been pushing ahead pretty much unopposed."

"Never mind. I hate this, Charlie. Absolutely hate it. We should be drawing that damn *line* ourselves, with tanks and artillery positions, not lines of a map. This is the only part of the entire theater where our boys can still push ahead, and Ike is ordering me to halt. We should be telling the damn Russians where *we're* gonna stop, and let them come up and meet us at the spot *we* choose. No reason why we can't be sleeping in Prague tonight."

"There is one good reason, sir. It's against our orders."

33. EISENHOWER

For several days in late April and early May, Eisenhower had been receiving reports of requests for armistice, separate attempts by various German commanders to surrender their armies. It made perfect sense that if a local commander knew his men had no hope, the logical move was to put up the white flag. But the entreaties were coming in from strange corners of the Western Theater, passing through Sweden and Switzerland, some coming directly from the most senior commanders themselves. Eisenhower had received a message directly from Kesselring, offering to end the war in the west, the same sort of message Churchill had received from Himmler, by way of the Swedes. Despite the excited optimism that spread through the Allied commands, Eisenhower knew he could not accept any offer that did not include one simple condition: unconditional surrender from every front where the Germans were engaged. That policy had been publicly announced more than two years earlier by President Roosevelt, and Roosevelt's death had not changed what had been declared the official policy of the Allied forces. Confirmation of that had come from General George Marshall in Washington. The new president, Harry Truman, would not alter the terms that his predecessor had set down. There was no other consideration, no other negotiation that Eisenhower could offer. Thus, no matter how many entreaties flowed westward, Eisenhower would not entertain any offers of surrender that did not include those Ger-

man forces still opposing the Russians. Kesselring had no authority over
those troops, and the authority Himmler possessed was a complete mystery. In either case, no official surrender could take place.

As word filtered through to the Allies that Hitler was in fact dead,
Eisenhower had to believe that the German High Command had been
thrown into chaos. Berlin was in ashes, and the various German field commands were certainly being controlled only by their local headquarters.
The German army itself was a complete shambles. By the third week of
April, more than a million German soldiers had surrendered into American and British lines. That number was increasing daily, and Eisenhower
knew that the facilities for handling the prisoners were enormously overwhelmed.

Finally, on May 5, much of the mystery about German authority was
cleared up. Reports were received directly through the offices of Admiral
Dönitz that Hitler's last will and testament had named Dönitz as the
Führer's successor. Eisenhower knew very little about Dönitz, and at first
his claim of authority was a surprise. Dönitz was certainly a capable commander, and had earned respect for his brilliant tactical use of the U-boats.
But Eisenhower had always assumed that if Hitler was removed from
power, dead or not, someone with far more visibility to the German people would have stepped in to assume power. Hermann Göring seemed to
be the most obvious choice, or Heinrich Himmler. But the intelligence officers under General Strong had been thoroughly sifting through the
chaotic German communications, and so had learned a great deal about
Hitler's own bizarre collapse, the mistrust and paranoia that seemed to
erase once-prominent commanders from any role at all. Von Rundstedt
had virtually disappeared, and Eisenhower had received confirmed reports
that Field Marshal Model was dead. In the Ruhr pocket, the Allies had
captured not only a larger German force than had been lost at Stalingrad,
but also thirty German generals. Every one of those had his own story to
tell, and though most seemed to accept their defeat with stoic relief, there
were those who expressed unabashed honesty, intense regret that such a
skilled and dominant army had been crushed not by any superior enemy,
but by the insane manipulations of the madman they had served.

Eisenhower also began to understand that the messages coming from
various German commanders were having another effect. With Germany
squeezed between the Russians and the western Allies, it had become obvious that the flow of refugees, military and civilian, was moving west.

Every day that the Germans could drag out the surrender process allowed that many more Germans to escape capture, or worse, by the Russians.

Throughout Europe, the pieces of the pie were sliding together. On May 2, German troops in Italy capitulated. By May 3, Montgomery had captured the city of Lübeck, which sealed off the Danish peninsula and the German troops who were stranded there. In Holland, the Canadian First Army had hemmed in the remaining Germans who had held out in a corner of Europe that, for the time being, the Allies had simply bypassed. In other strongholds, including the Brittany peninsula in France, Germans simply had nowhere to go. Then, on May 5, Jacob Devers's Sixth Army captured Salzburg, Austria, which allowed them to link up with the American Fifth Army moving north from Italy, effectively ending the fight along the entire Western Front.

On May 5, as the confusion over German authority cleared, Eisenhower received a representative who had come directly from Admiral Dönitz. But Dönitz's man was only authorized to surrender to the western Allies, a diplomatic booby trap Eisenhower knew he had to avoid. If the Germans intended to accept unconditional surrender, they would do so everywhere, to representatives of all the Allied powers. Only after representatives of the Russian and French armies were present would Eisenhower permit any kind of official documents to be signed. Dönitz had no choice but to agree, and he informed Eisenhower that he was authorizing Alfred Jodl as Germany's official signatory. Jodl had been Hitler's closest military adviser, and Eisenhower knew that Jodl was regarded by the best German field commanders as nothing more than Hitler's puppet. Eisenhower didn't care. If anything, that description made Jodl the logical choice as the German most suitable to surrender their army.

SHAEF, RHEIMS, FRANCE

MAY 7, 1945

It was well after midnight, and the men were gathering in what had been Eisenhower's War Room, walls plastered with maps that were still alive with the various colored pins that designated troop positions. He purposely stayed out of the way, confining himself to his office to the side of the main room. He felt uneasy about participating in a ceremony that did not include Germany's highest-ranking military official. Dönitz had of course stayed away, what Eisenhower assumed was either a show of defiance or a problem with logistics. Regardless, since the Germans were sending their chief of staff, the Allies would do the same. The ceremony would be handled by Bedell Smith. The British were represented by Eisenhower's second in command, Air Marshal Arthur Tedder. Tedder was accompanied by another Brit, a man Eisenhower felt should be included in any kind of ceremony as significant as the German surrender, General Frederick Morgan. Morgan had created most of the original plan for the Normandy invasion, and was now a well-respected and well-liked member of Eisenhower's staff. The air forces were represented not only by Tedder but also by American general Carl Spaatz, the navies by British admiral Sir Harold Burrough. The French had sent General François Sevez. Already there was a stickiness brewing with the Russians, messages from Moscow that the Russians insisted on a separate ceremony to take place in Berlin. Eisenhower had learned enough about Russian pride to understand that if Stalin could not enjoy humiliating Hitler, he would find some way to humiliate the Germans who remained in power. But the diplomatic minefield that Eisenhower faced with the signing of the documents at Rheims was solved when the Russians agreed to the participation of their liaison to their French mission, General Ivan Susloparov. The wrangling caused grumbles in both London and Washington, but Eisenhower had no objection to the Russian maneuver. He respected his Russian counterpart, and Eisenhower believed that Marshal Zhukov had earned the right to have the Germans capitulate to him any way he saw fit.

The room was thirty feet on a side, and the principals who were directly involved in the ceremony were accompanied by a flock of aides and other senior staffers, who jostled one another for some view of the rectangular table, a tense scramble that also included selected photographers, who were kept against one wall. The packed crowd was an unwieldy situation, but Bedell Smith had taken charge, and any controversy over who had the better view was settled without discussion. Smith understood the role he was playing, and Eisenhower's chief of staff had never been known for his patience. Once Eisenhower was comfortable that Beetle had everything under control, Eisenhower finally accepted that the best thing for him to do was stay out of the way.

The actual negotiations, the examination of documents, were dealt with privately, away from the reporters. Eisenhower knew that any hitch or last-minute controversy could get blown into a major explosion if the various governments suddenly felt their interests weren't being properly represented. In the War Room itself, the ceremony represented Germany's official capitulation, but the signing of the documents would be a formality. Unlike the chaos of the Versailles Conference in 1919, this time the Germans would not be handed a surprise.

As the packed crowd waited nervously, the Germans were ushered in last. Jodl was led to a seat directly across from Smith. In forty minutes' time, the documents that ended the war in Europe were signed. It was two forty-one in the morning.

For one tense hour, Eisenhower had waited in the office, agonizing through every minute by wrestling with the details, second-guessing himself in tense silence, the ridiculous menu of minutiae that had presumably been handled by Smith and the men he had assigned. He could hear the popping of flashbulbs, a rising volume to the hum of voices, and he stared at the door, his brain focusing on the idiotic mistakes that could still happen, all those things that could go wrong. His brain had fixed itself on one detail, what he knew was an irrational fear. It had been handled, he thought. It *was* handled. Forget about it. But his mind gripped tightly to the thought, and he rehashed the moments yet again. The fantasy would not leave him: that the moment would come and history would pause, the entire world forced to hold its breath while someone suddenly scrambled to find a working ballpoint pen. He knew he was being ridiculous, but the thought of that kind of hitch in the proceedings, one absurdly stupid moment in history, had festered through the agony of the slow passage of time. He replayed the scene one more time, knew that he had provided the pens himself, two of them. One was solid gold, one gold-plated, gifts from an old friend. He recalled the moment, giving the pens with hand-quivering nervousness to Harry Butcher, who tested them on blank paper, making sure they would actually write. He tried to laugh it off, to scold himself for being an idiot. But the humor wasn't there. No thoughts invaded his mind but raging impatience that the ceremony be concluded. And, he thought, will someone please remember to come and tell *me*?

He looked again at his watch, nearly three o'clock in the morning. Outside the office, he could hear a rising hum of activity, and looked again at his watch, had done so at least four or five times for each minute that passed. This is a hell of an hour to end a war. I should have been in there, he thought. I should have seen this. They'll ask me about that, those damn reporters. But no, it's protocol, and protocol matters. Not to me, but to someone, somewhere.

The tension was swirling through him, and he thought of going to the window, counting stars, counting anything he could see in the darkness. No, I should just go out there. But I can't. Dammit! He was jolted by a soft knock at the door, his response immediate and far too loud.

"Yes. What is it? Come in."

He saw Smith, a hard clench to the man's jaw, a slight wink of his eye. Smith stood aside, and Eisenhower saw the uniform behind him, splendid with medals, the man tall, regal in his walk, a monocle in his eye. It was Alfred Jodl.

Behind Jodl came Kenneth Strong, Eisenhower's intelligence chief. Strong was there for one very specific reason. He spoke German. Eisenhower looked at Jodl for a long silent moment, saw a hint of sadness in the man's eyes, camouflaged by an unmistakable curtain of arrogance. Eisenhower kept his seat, measured his voice, held a tight grip on his words.

"Do you understand the documents you have signed?"

Strong repeated the words, and Jodl looked directly at Eisenhower, studied him, a slip of curiosity. Jodl made a brief nod.

"*Ja.*"

"Good. Then understand this. You will be held personally and officially responsible for any violation of the terms of surrender. That will include the provisions for German commanders to appear in Berlin before the Russian High Command to accomplish your formal surrender to that government." He paused, angry he had not thought of more to say. But Jodl had no real purpose there, a courtesy that meant nothing to the ceremony. Jodl remained silent.

Eisenhower said, "That is all."

Jodl clicked his heels together, kept his back stiff, stared past Eisenhower through the monocle. He said nothing more, made a simple salute. Then he turned and, followed by Smith and Strong, left the office. Eisenhower slumped back, his heart racing, allowed his hands to release the arms of his chair, sweat running down the inside of his shirt. The surge of energy was overwhelming him, and he stood, moved out to the sea of activity in the War Room. He slipped through the crowd, acknowledged no one, moved to one of the chairs that lined the long table, sat. Gradually the room grew more quiet, men suddenly aware of his presence. Smith was beside him now, put a hand on Eisenhower's shoulder.

"It's over, Ike."

He heard the quiver in Smith's voice, emotion he had never seen before.

"Good job, Beetle. Thank you."

"The reporters are waiting to hear from you. It's all been set up."

Eisenhower had known that, felt suddenly nervous, never enjoyed the press conferences.

"It can wait . . . just a minute. First, I think somebody ought to find a bottle of champagne."

They walked without security guards, the first time Eisenhower could remember being unescorted. The guards were there, of course, watching from distant perches, making sure no renegade sniper, no spy with some unfulfilled mission, found his way into the headquarters compound. Patton was calm, subdued, and Eisenhower could sense the man's dark mood, something he had expected completely. Patton's war was over. At least for now.

"You sure he's dead? I'd be happy to go up there and check it out myself."

Eisenhower had expected that as well.

"The Russians found bodies outside Hitler's bunker. They say there's no doubt one of them is Hitler. They're a little cagey about details, but that's nothing new. The rest of the German command is being rounded up, most without any problem, though the Russians aren't saying much about that either. I'm guessing it's the reason so many generals are finding their way into our lines. They try to hide out, there's the chance it'll be the Russians who finds them. And from what I've heard, no one is calling seriously for guerrilla warfare. Some of the top Krauts will blow their own brains out. It seems to be the German way."

"Too damn bad. I really wanted to be there when we nailed Hitler. Really wanted to see the place, to move in there with a flock of tanks and blow the whole place to bits."

"Berlin's not much to see, George. Whatever the bombers didn't flatten, the Russians did. I've heard it was a bloodbath. It'll take years to clean that place up."

They walked for a few more paces, Eisenhower feeling strangely lost. He had fought the nagging hints of depression, told himself it was normal. Shouldn't be, he thought. We oughta be dancing out here, celebrating that after six years, nobody's being shot at today. Well, almost nobody. There's always some jackass who won't accept that he's beaten, that his side lost. He glanced sideways at Patton. Might be a few who won't accept winning. He kept walking, his brain curling toward the mountain of work waiting for him, the extraordinary task of organizing the occupation forces, all the incredible details that had to be dealt with before the diplomats would take over. That's why George is so blue, he thought. This will be no place for a soldier.

Patton said, "The undersecretary left this morning. Patterson. On his way . . . hell I don't know, Salzburg maybe. Nice sort of fellow. For a government man."

"We're all government men, George. GI. Government Issue."

"I had a good talk with him last night. Surprised me. He actually had a brain. I'd met him before, somewhere, and damn if he didn't recall every detail. Gift for faces, he says. We spent the evening at the horse stables at the Imperial Riding Academy. Impressive place. You'd never know those people just lost a war. They were a real whizbang at teaching those horses to do tricks. I miss the cavalry, always have. Tanks don't do tricks."

Eisenhower was getting impatient, knew there was a reason Patton wanted to talk to him. "What's on your mind, George?"

Patton rubbed a hand on his face, thought a moment, said, "I'd hate to see you dismantle what we have here. We need to keep up the flow of replacements, keep pushing the training."

Eisenhower stopped walking.

"Why?"

"That's what the secretary asked me. I'll tell you what I told him. We need to show the Russians how strong we are. Sharpen the bayonets, polish the boots. It's the only way we'll get their respect, and if we don't have their respect . . . we haven't won this war."

Eisenhower saw the familiar gleam in Patton's eye, knew there were wheels turning, wheels that might run completely off the track into yet another minefield.

"Watch it, George."

"Dammit, Ike, we could drive those people all the way back to their border in five days. They've overstretched their supply lines, they're beat to hell. They survived by stripping the countryside when they made their advance, and they'd have to go back the same way. It wouldn't be a fight, Ike, it would be a stampede! If we give them time to build up their supplies, to refit and rearm—"

"You want to start a war with the Russians? George, are you out of your damn mind?"

Eisenhower glanced around, realized his voice had risen. No one was close, the streams of activity moving past mostly in the steady rumbling of trucks.

Patton seemed to absorb the scolding, his gloom deepening.

"War is about power, Ike. Moscow knows that. I don't think Washington does. If we claim we won this war, and then we let half of Europe fall into communism . . . we haven't won a damn thing. My job was to knock that Kraut son of a bitch on his ass. Okay, mission accomplished. But there's a Russian son of a bitch who is stepping in to take his place."

"Stop it. Enough of this. You talked like this to the undersecretary of war? That wasn't too smart, George. That kind of talk gets back to Washington, and you're the one out on your ass. The Russians depended on us for supplies and we depended on them to punch in Hitler's eastern flank. That's what allies do, dammit. And even if I thought they were going to be a problem, it's not for us to decide. President Truman tells me to attack Zhukov's army, that's what I'll do. But that's not going to happen, and you know it. You said that to Patterson? George, that was just plain stupid."

Eisenhower was angry now, the stress and anxiety of all he had to do releasing itself in a wave of temper. He fought the urge to scream into Patton's face, stared away, couldn't look at the man's self-righteous smugness. "You think you have the answer to every problem. You think your fists are a cure for everything." He paused, forced down the volume of his voice. "This war is over. Get that through your skull. You want to fight? Good! I heard you were asking about China. Fine, sounds like a swell idea. I'll start working on that, talk to General Marshall about it. Marshall is already suggesting that Hodges be assigned to MacArthur. Courtney's happy as hell, can't wait to get to the Pacific."

Patton grunted, and Eisenhower knew the meaning immediately.

"Don't worry, George, I wouldn't dream of putting you and Mac in the same room. One of you would end up hanging from the gallows, and it wouldn't be MacArthur. But that's where you need to be aiming all those sharpened bayonets, George, the Pacific!"

Patton was obviously subdued, nodded slowly.

"China is the place for me. Al Wedemeyer's a good friend. I'll be happy to serve under him."

"You outrank him, George."

"Doesn't matter. I outranked Bradley, and, if I recall, there was a time when I outranked *you*. I'll go where the fight is."

"We'll see how this plays out. There's too much to do here before I can lose you."

"Oh, I know. I want to prepare a general order for the Third Army, give my boys some credit for what they did. The press is waiting to hear from me, so I need to scoot back down to my HQ. Tomorrow, I'm supposed to tour the Škoda munitions plant. Might be pretty interesting. Yep, plenty to do."

Patton was suddenly too agreeable, and Eisenhower knew when he was being patronized.

"Leave this Russian thing alone, George. Especially to reporters. You got that?"

Patton stared up at the sky, hands on his hips.

"You're the boss, Ike."

On May 9, the Germans dutifully attended a second surrender ceremony in Berlin. Eisenhower was told that the event had been designated by the Russians to serve as a symbol of the unity of all the Allies, to make clear to the world that the Germans had capitulated completely to all their enemies. Eisenhower was invited to participate, but his duties were mounting, and though he appreciated the gesture from Marshal Zhukov, the logistics of his attendance just weren't practical. Arthur Tedder went in his place, accompanied by two planeloads of staff officers, including Harry Butcher. There were reporters as well, and Butcher's job was to keep everybody in line, to make sure no one stepped on any Russian toes.

The Russians made considerable effort to glorify their ceremony, and produced a film of the event, a lavish production that emphasized in definite terms that it was the sacrifice of the Russian soldier that had made possible *their* victory over the brutal savagery of the Germans. The surrender ceremony at Rheims was never mentioned.

34. BENSON

The army of occupation had taken shape, and many of the battle-weary divisions were assuming a new role: manning the front lines along clearly defined boundaries that marked the territories agreed upon between the western Allies and the Russians. The two armies faced one another along distinct geographic lines, including rivers, but other lines existed only on maps. The American forces whose forward motion had been halted by the dictates of politicians were now staring across at a Russian army that returned the stare with the same growing anxieties that their ally was not completely trustworthy. The animosity had been stoked by the exchange of prisoners. The British and Americans had worked to expedite the return home of those Russian soldiers who had been liberated from German camps. On the other side, American POWs were being held by what seemed to be Russian hesitation, and, according to some of the GIs who were finally returned, American troops were being interrogated, or treated in other ways as though they weren't exactly on friendly terms with the Russians who held them. No one suggested that the American POWs were being especially abused. That abuse was reserved for the German troops now in Russian hands. Word was sifting through the Allied lines that Russian treatment of German soldiers and former Nazi officials was everything the Germans had feared. But the Russians were surprisingly suspicious of their own, Russian soldiers, who had been passed over through American lines. More reports were received that the Russians were regarding their captured brethren as potentially dangerous, as though by allowing themselves to be captured, the Russian troops had somehow co-operated with Hitler's forces. Nearly every prisoner was suspected of being a deserter, whether there was any proof of that or not. Even worse, Russian soldiers of non-Russian ethnicity were being treated with the same brutality as the Germans.

The outrage over delays in releasing the British and American POWs began to jeopardize what Eisenhower knew was a fragile cordiality. Finally, after considerable noise behind the scenes, the Russians succumbed to the pressure to expedite the release of western POWs. The Russians offered no apologies, and no justification for the hostile treatment of their allies. To many, it seemed they were delaying the release of friendly POWs just because they could. And there wasn't much Eisenhower, or anyone else, could do about it.

The Allied army for the occupation of Germany did not require the enormous numbers of troops that had been poured into Eisenhower's command. Some of the units who had endured the toughest assignments were designated to be sent home. Others were selected to return to facilities in the States to begin training for what the army described as *jungle training*. No one was confused by the meaning of that. Even the troops who were designated for discharge from the service were wary of an increasing tide of rumors. All through the encampments, the orders came for the men to prepare to travel once more, this time toward the seaports on the French and Belgian coasts. But the celebrations were more often muted by the nagging fear that *going home* was the army's euphemism for a brief visit to the States, a quick glimpse of family and friends, before new orders would arrive. Everyone understood that a war of extraordinary viciousness was still being waged in the Pacific. No matter the army's assurances that many of these infantrymen had done all the army would ask of them, the rumors continued to fly. Their visit to the States was only a stopover on their way to face the Japanese.

PILSEN, CZECHOSLOVAKIA
MAY 24, 1945

Benson was amazed that, for reasons no one could explain, his duffel bag had been delivered to him. He had not seen the bag or its contents since he'd left Le Havre six months earlier.

"Hey, here's my damn razor! And the photo of my mom. I forgot all about this stuff."

Beside him, Mitchell was shaving from water in his helmet, leaning close at a small framed mirror.

"Yeah, good for you. You can finally get a good shave, and then kiss your momma all the way home."

Benson ignored Mitchell's sarcasm, fished through the clothes, the extra socks, a pair of boots.

"I could have used this stuff. I don't believe this. A whole box of candy bars. Oh God, they're all melted. What a mess."

He fought the urge to empty the entire bag out on the ground, knew there was little time. Mitchell continued to shave, said nothing, and Benson looked out past the small house they had used as a bivouac.

"Not gonna miss this place. Not one bit." Mitchell didn't respond, and Benson closed up the heavy bag. "I'm just gonna leave all this the way it is. We get on a damn ship, I'll mess with it then."

"No you won't. They'll take it from you before we get on the trains, and you won't get it back until we get stateside. Take a good look at your momma, then say good-bye. You'll see *her* before you see that picture again. This is the army, kiddo. Nothing makes sense. Here, shave. This water's okay. Use my razor. No need to waste your fancy one."

Benson smiled, pulled his own helmet off his head, stepped over to the water jug, filled it.

"I'll make my own, thanks. How about the soap? Or did you use it all up?"

Mitchell stepped aside, made room for Benson, who smeared the last scoop of shaving cream on his face, staring down into the mirror. He began to scrape his beard, Mitchell's razor blade just dull enough to pull each hair out individually, and he grunted, saw the nick, a small smear of blood.

"Damn! When was the last time you changed blades?"

Mitchell laughed, said, "You gotta be tough to use my razor, kiddo. You still got peach fuzz. Go on, it'll work."

"Hey! You guys give me a hand with this, right?"

Benson looked up toward the voice, a smear of white soap still on his chin. Beside him, Mitchell was wiping his face with a small green towel, and Benson saw the lieutenant, said, "Right now, sir?"

"Yes, right now. This damn thing is heavy. Get it up into the truck over there."

Mitchell said something low under his breath, and Benson wiped his face, dumped the soapy water out of his helmet, followed Mitchell. The lieutenant was standing beside a large trunk, civilian issue, brass buckles and old brown leather. Benson could feel the officer's jumpiness, the man glancing around. Benson moved to one end, grabbed a thick leather handle, Mitchell on the opposite side. Mitchell nodded, and they lifted in one motion, the trunk far heavier than Benson expected. His hand slipped from the handle, the trunk thumping down hard on the ground.

The lieutenant seemed to erupt. "Watch it! That's a bunch of valuable . . . good stuff! You break anything, and I'll put your asses on latrine duty for a month!"

Mitchell stood straight, adjusting his back.

"What's in here, sir? If you don't mind me asking."

"None of your damn business, Private. Put it in that truck. Now!"

"What's going on, Lieutenant?"

The voice came from the larger house across the road, and Benson saw an older man, brass, knew only his name, Major Steele. The major seemed to know the answer to his question already.

The lieutenant stood straight, nervous, said, "Just helping these boys get some of their stuff loaded up."

Mitchell's eyes narrowed, a hot stare at the young lieutenant.

The major said, "You know there's a law about looting from the civilians, don't you, Lieutenant? I'm not questioning you. But whatever's in that trunk better have come from enemy soldiers."

"Yes, sir! Most certainly, sir. I've told these boys that."

The major kept his eyes on the trunk for a long moment, then turned away, moved off down the road.

The lieutenant seemed to deflate, said in a quiet growl, "Get this thing on that truck, and do it right now!"

Mitchell glanced at Benson, the two men leaning down, grabbing the straps, Benson preparing himself for the weight. They hoisted the trunk just clear of the ground, shuffled quickly toward the truck, and the lieutenant moved in now, a third set of hands needed to make the final hoist into the truck. The trunk slid in heavily, the lieutenant breathing hard, relief and guilt.

"Thanks, boys. You boys . . . there's no need . . ." The officer was still looking around, seemed to search for the major. "Look, boys, I just picked up some stuff . . . gifts for my wife. Hell, these people don't need any of this crap. We're feeding them, giving them medicine. It's the least they can do."

Benson started to say something, but Mitchell cut him off. "I wouldn't worry about it, sir. If nobody asks us, we probably won't say a word. Gotta say, though, I never flat-out lied to an MP before."

The lieutenant seemed to grit his teeth, a hard stare at Mitchell.

"All right, look. I heard that somebody in the command post rounded up some steak. Go on over there and tell them I said you could have some. Just . . . don't spread the word around."

Benson saw the disgust on Mitchell's face, but breakfast had been hours ago, and Benson put aside his own moral outrage.

"Where exactly would that be, sir?"

"Check inside that big house over there. The company CO said some cow stepped on a mine. The farmer bitched like hell, but wasn't much he could say about it. Not our fault. At least . . . nobody actually shot the damn thing."

Benson realized there was as little truth to that as there was to what the lieutenant pretended was in the trunk.

"Thank you, sir. We'll check it out."

"You've got about an hour before we move to the trains. Make sure your gear is all packed up."

Mitchell arched his back, still feeling the strain.

"You going with us on the train, sir?"

"No, I think I'll be in the truck here. Give you boys some more room."

"Kind of you, sir."

The officer moved away, one last glance toward the truck's new cargo.

Benson watched him with relief, hadn't liked the man since the lieutenant had come to the platoon. He said in a low voice, "Wonderful little game they play. No looting, unless you can keep from getting caught. Anybody like us figures out you're stealing half the crown jewels, toss a bribe our way."

Mitchell slapped Benson on the back.

"Yeah, he's a jerk for sure. But I don't see *MP* on your helmet. He said steak. Let's get some steak."

The meat was cold, the bread thick and hard, and Benson had never enjoyed a meal more. The officers who guarded what was left of the unfortunate cow seemed to resent their fellow lieutenant revealing the secret, but Benson and Mitchell had shown just enough knowledge of the beast's demise to be included among the select few.

They sat in a corner, on the floor, Benson stuffed with the agonizing pleasure of real meat. The large house was a communications center for the entire regiment, but the two GIs were ignored by the men who swarmed past them, and no one seemed to care that they occupied an unused corner of the front room. The house was alive with activity, mostly officers, the rooms on all sides humming with telephone conversations and the steady clack of Teletype machines. Benson could see up a long stairway, men in clean uniforms passing one another with that look of the *Important.*

Beside him, Mitchell said, "What do you think was in that trunk?"

"Stuff. Who cares?"

"Heavy stuff. Probably silverware. That looey was too jumpy, so it musta been pretty hot. I bet he gets nailed somewhere along the line. He's gotta get on the same ship we do, sooner or later."

Benson felt a sudden itch on the back of his neck, scratched.

Mitchell said, "You forget that lice powder? Dammit, don't you scatter those little turds on me. Here."

He reached into his pocket, pulled out a small tin, handed it to Benson, who shook some into his hands. The powder was gray and stinking, ruining the happy glow from the meal. He rubbed it on his neck, opened his shirt, spread it on his chest, the smell turning his stomach. He coughed, said, "Damn, I hate this stuff."

Mitchell slid a few feet away from him.

"Yeah, but I hate cooties worse. You took a shower, you're supposed to use that stuff afterward. Every damn time."

Benson closed his shirt, muffling the stink, handed the tin back to Mitchell.

"Showers. I never thought I'd see that. Big damn tents, pitched right down the street. I guess they figure the Czechs don't care about modesty."

"As dirty as I was, I didn't care who saw my bare ass. That cold water was just fine. I still had crud on me from December. You too. Flies were making a home in your boots. They didn't get those showers up here soon enough. Only thing smelled worse than us were those prisoners."

Benson laughed, was relieved that Mitchell's griping had changed, the dangerous edge dulled by the end of the fighting. He thought of the prisoners, a long column that had marched through the town on foot. They wore German uniforms, but they weren't German at all. The men were ragged and happy, and Benson had learned they were Armenian. No one was certain if they had volunteered to fight for Hitler, or if they had been grabbed up and stuffed into German uniforms. For the prisoners, it didn't seem to matter. They were marching away from the Russians.

"Hey, you two! Just who I'm looking for!"

Benson searched for the voice, saw the man coming out of a side room, a civilian, a camera hanging from his waist. The man knelt down in front of them, held out a hand, his face curling slightly from the stink of the lice powder.

"Uh . . . hi. I'm Jack Burgess, United Press. I'm here talking to GIs, guys in the field. Are you fellows combat soldiers? Did you see any action?"

Mitchell had the look Benson knew well, a hard scowl, the reporter utterly oblivious. Benson said, "Yes, sir. We've been in action since the fight in the Ardennes. We were in the One Oh Sixth."

The reporter's enthusiasm poured out in a gush.

"Veterans! Combat veterans! Excellent! I understand you boys are heading home. That's what I want to write about. You've gotta be looking forward to a whole lot, right? I want to hear about it. You got gals waiting for you? Families? I bet you can't wait to chow down on a good old American hot dog. Where you from?"

The man's energy was crushing him, all the enjoyment Benson felt from the meal wiped away. He said, "I'm from Missouri. I'm hoping to find a gal, I guess. Nobody waiting for me . . ."

The man forced a counterfeit laugh, scribbled on a piece of paper.

"Cardinals fan then? Or maybe the Cubs? Bet you can't wait to see a ball game. This'll probably get into your newspaper before you get home. You could end up a hometown hero! What you think of that? Maybe a parade, right? You sent old Fritz running for home, you boys did. That had to be *great,* blasting holes in Hitler's Heinies. So, when you get home, what's the first thing you're gonna do?" He reached out, slapped Benson's arm. "Or do I know the answer to that already? Right? Better stay away from these foreign girls, though. I've heard some of *those* stories." More laughter, the man winking, and Benson wanted to crawl straight under the floor. "So, tell me some of your adventures. Don't leave anything out. I want to hear how great it felt to knock hell out of old Fritzie—"

Mitchell was up suddenly, grabbed the man by the front of his shirt. The reporter fell back, held up only by Mitchell's grip.

"Hey! What gives?"

"Listen, you son of a bitch, you go somewhere else and talk to guys who think this was *great*."

Benson reached out, but Mitchell was immovable, and he pulled the terrified reporter up close to him, their faces inches apart.

"Have you seen what these Kraut bastards did to people? Have you smelled it? That's your story, you stupid asshole. There's millions of us over here, and nothing we say matters one damn bit. Go to Ohrdruf or one of those other camps and take a deep breath, run your hands through the dirt, take some pictures of the bones. Or go find the grave where we buried our lieutenant, take your pictures there. *Then* you can write a story. But don't you dare tell anybody that this was *great*."

Mitchell shoved the man away, the reporter rolling back onto his rear. He scrambled quickly to his feet, backed away, his eyes locked on Mitchell.

"Whatever you say, soldier. You don't want to talk, I've got no problem. You boys have a good trip home."

The man was gone quickly, a mad escape out the door of the house. Mitchell sat back against the wall, the hum of activity around them resuming, no one paying them any attention at all. Benson felt the familiar fear again, that Mitchell was very close to doing something supremely stupid, that glimmer of madness Benson had seen too often. But Mitchell closed his eyes, no words between them, and after a long moment, Mitchell said, "You think they got any of that steak left?"

MAY 25, 1945

They rode in the railcars that had carried thousands before them, the strange boxes made by the French, the faded signs hanging beside the wide-open doorway, *Hommes 40 Chevaux 8*. The translation was old hat to the men who had ridden these before: forty men or eight horses. Many of the men around Benson had ridden in these same cars only weeks before, the most efficient transportation available to carry them from the port cities eastward to the front lines. They had been replacements fresh from the training centers and troopships, had come well after the vicious fighting in the Ardennes was over. By the time many of these men had come to the war, the rail lines were completely safe, no danger from German air strikes. As they rode on the undulating rhythm of the rails, some were sharing their complaints, stories about their first ride in these cars, the oh-so-miserable experience. Mitchell had withdrawn inside himself, ignored them all. Benson tried to do the same, but he couldn't escape, suffered through their bragging, the competition over whose train ride had been tougher. They spoke of sardine cans, how tightly packed they had been, with no room to lie down, men sleeping only while sitting against one another in rows like so many dominoes. Benson kept his own stories quiet, couldn't help feeling annoyed that most of these men had never suffered through the brutal ride over snow and mud. They had never been cramped in the back of a deuce-and-a-half while shellfire bounced through the dark woods around them. They had never fought in a frozen foxhole or slept in mud. If they had been in the trucks at all, it was mostly on the flat serenity of the autobahn.

No matter the ridiculous griping from the others, Benson appreciated the luxury of a thick straw matting that had been shoveled into each car. He knew Mitchell would feel the same way, though Mitchell was still silent, lost in some place that Benson knew was best left alone. Benson laid back, adjusted himself, wiggled his toes inside clean boots and dry socks, thought, this'll do just fine, no matter how long we gotta ride. The lack of crowding was another luxury, enough space for each man to lie flat. For the first several hours, not even the talkers could keep Benson from the nap, made more comfortable by the rhythmic rocking of the train.

Twice a day, the trains had stopped somewhere in open nowhere, the men disembarking for fifteen minutes or more. The stop was a courtesy, allowing the men some personal relief, and Benson had joined the lines of men standing along the tracks, offering their own kind of salute to the German countryside. The rations came regularly as well, the trains pulling into stations, surrounded by towns or villages that barely existed now. But the army was there, kitchens and hot food and fresh water. The engineers had repaired the rails, but Benson assumed that any repair of the villages would come from the hands of those who might one day return to reclaim a home.

In some of the stations, other trains appeared, moving the opposite direction on parallel tracks. Most were filled with refugees, civilians being relocated, either homeward or to some new place. When the trains were stopped, they sat only a few feet apart, and Benson would join the troops around him in a strange staring match, soldiers looking into the eyes of people who stared back with what seemed to be a desperate aching, men and women who seemed utterly lost. The smells rolled out of the railcars, no luxury there, no clean straw, no room for sleeping. But they were always curious, staring back at the Americans, searching them with hollow eyes and thin faces. Benson couldn't help thinking of the camps, though these people wore actual clothing, and not the obscene striped pajamas. The trains didn't stay alongside long enough for anyone to talk, the MPs and guards on the platforms offering no word about who these people were. But their faces brought him back to the memories he had tried to hold away, the camps, and he searched their eyes, wondered if they were *survivors*. Now, he thought, they're going back home, to whatever home they might still have. He marveled at the variety of their clothes, some of the men in ragged suits, women in thick fluffy dresses, fancy embroidery, most with some kind of hat. If there were smiles, they came mostly from the children, and Benson felt a hard pain staring into their faces. The word had passed that many of the people on the trains were Russians, or eastern Europeans who had not been in camps at all. They were simply refugees who had fled westward to escape the fighting that had torn across their land. Now they were going home, to places that seemed as exotic as Benson could imagine, ancient cities like Budapest and Prague, or their small farms, where animals did the work and a man made his own tools. But Benson's imagination didn't seem to match the faces he saw. There was no joy, no sense of celebration, just the dead stares. Benson tried to understand that, tried to guess what these people had seen and endured, and how many just like them had not survived. He watched the children, their smiles innocent and curious, some of the soldiers tossing chocolate bars over, candy that the adults grabbed first. At least, he thought, they have the children. But how many do not?

The railcar was moving again across open countryside, its wide door kept open, the weather warm, high sunshine, the movement of the train its own breeze. They rolled past deep forests, over bridges crossing narrow streams, mountains in the distance, mountains that Benson suspected he had seen before. The farms they passed were mostly intact, neat squares of geometric perfection, stone fences and livestock, old men and women and sometimes their daughters standing in the doorways of rugged little houses, watching the trains go by. Not all the rail stations were surrounded by the debris of war, and in the towns that had survived, the young women were there, waiting. The soldiers knew it was no accident that the German women seemed to know when the next train would arrive. At each stop, there was a flurry of bright dresses, cheerful greetings, the MPs keeping the women back across the tracks. Benson had watched them with virtuous curiosity, but there was no virtue in some of the men around him. The MPs would allow no fraternization, the train not stopping long enough for any kind of social mixing. But for the brief moments until the train moved again, the MPs allowed the women to offer whatever barter they could, the women speaking broken English, the few words that mattered, tossing over garters and other bits of clothing for cigarettes and chocolate. The soldiers accepted that the show was exactly that, the women parading legs and a shifting bottom, sometimes too much leg and more shift than Benson could ignore. The talk was loud and boisterous, the catcalls and shouts, soldiers bragging to anyone who would listen what would happen if they had just one night in that town.

They passed other trains as well, filled with men in rags of uniforms, prisoners of war, many of them Russian, returning to their army in the east. When the trains parked close together, an active marketplace would spring to life, brisk trade in American cigarettes and wristwatches for Russian weapons or anything else that seemed exotic to the GIs. Benson saw a man holding up an officer's sword, spitting out his sales pitch in manic Russian, trying to make his deal before the trains parted. Benson had been tempted, but another GI had jumped in, offering the Russian an American .45. The Russian had grabbed the pistol with the careless lust of a man who knows he has gotten the better of the deal, but the GI climbed back into the railcar, holding his trophy aloft, a hearty cheer from the men around him.

As the trip lengthened into long hours, the men in the railcars created their own sport, card games breaking out, word passing among the most avid poker players which car had the better game. With each hour, they knew they were closer to the seaports, and with the change in scenery came a change of conversation, the inevitability of rumors. Benson had the orders that told him he was going home, and he had already written his mother, a letter that might be somewhere in the cargo car of this very train. He had already begun to think of school, if he would try to go to college, study something meaningful, exciting. He always admired the engineers, the most difficult of jobs that so many soldiers took for granted. His alternative was to stay in the small town, Sullivan, but he had already decided that the future was in the cities, St. Louis or maybe Kansas City. The thought of college, of big cities, had always been frightening to him. But he ignored that now, knew that no matter what choices he made, he would never be *frightened* again.

The impatience of some in the railcar brought out the loudest mouths, and Benson stayed close to Mitchell, tried to mimic the man's grim silence, avoiding the absurd talk from those who seemed to have nothing else in their brains. The loudest mouths began to embrace the rumors that the army had lied to them all, that no matter what the officers or the papers said, they would end up in Le Havre or Antwerp only to board ships sailing straight for the Pacific. Benson could not fathom that the army had simply lied, not to the men who had already done their job. The big talkers kept it up, some men absolute in their claims that rather than face the Japanese, they would desert, slip out through the French countryside, or, if they made it to the States, hauled to a new training camp, they would disappear from there as well. The talk was dangerous and nasty, but Benson saw through the anger to the fear, that same fear that had caused so many self-inflicted wounds. He knew that some of the biggest talk came from the men who might never have seen a German soldier, but there were others, and Benson could see it in their faces, the blank stares, the quiet resolution that surprised him. It was the veterans who absorbed the talk of desertion and acknowledged it with a subtle nod. Benson tried to erase that from his mind, would not believe any of these men would run away from a fight. He had never thought of the Japanese as anything but a name, strange people that the Marines were confronting, the navy, small islands and beach landings that seemed no more real to him than some Hollywood movie. But he also knew that some of the men who rode beside him had seen the worst side of man, and some carried memories of things they could never tell anyone back home. As the skies grew darker, he could not help thinking of Mitchell and the sergeant, Higgins, marching off with the German prisoners, that boy who had tried to kill them. Benson had swept that away, tried to convince himself that he didn't really know what happened to them. He hadn't actually witnessed anything. But he knew Mitchell carried that somewhere inside him, a memory of that young boy and what he had done to him, a memory that he would never escape.

On the second morning, the men awoke to a breakfast waiting in a row of kitchen trucks parked alongside a broken concrete platform. There had been pancakes and oatmeal and toast, and gallons of coffee, and Benson knew that with the dawn, they were that much closer to the end of the trip. When the train moved again, he was energized by a new thought, a sudden need to see it all, every sight. The men around him were doing what they had been doing all along, some talking among themselves, one card game in a corner. Benson ignored all of that, began to realize that he was actually leaving this place, that for the next few hours, or maybe days, he was still in *Europe*. This is a different place, he thought, different from Missouri, different from any other place I'll ever be. I won't come back here, probably. Why would I? Why would any of us? He had seen magazines about Europe when he was a boy, fantasies of the very rich who could ride the vast ocean liners, vacationing in the glorious cities, cities that now might be great fields of debris, stinking of fire and death. Who would come to see that?

He stared out across an open field, yellow with wheat, could see the farmhouse, a thick decaying grass roof. That was a surprise, the German farms almost all perfect and clean. Now the fences were uneven and sagging, the roads mostly weed-choked trails that ran out across the tracks. There was none of the neat grooming, the flower beds and tightly rowed gardens. Around the farmhouses were clusters of weeds, unkempt, crooked barns, a broken windmill. The change was strange and obvious and he searched the small roads, saw a carriage, an ox pulling an old man in a wagon filled with dirt. He saw a road sign, the name of a town, and now he understood. They were not in Germany anymore. They were in France.

Benson sat at the edge of the doorway, his legs curled under him, the sun gloriously warm. He tried to see every sight, logging it away, remembering. He began to nod off, the *clack-clack* rhythm of the train lulling him to a nap, but Mitchell was there suddenly, sat down heavily beside him. Benson was wide awake now, glad for Mitchell's company. He had felt a growing sadness that Mitchell had drifted far away already, leaving him behind. Benson had never had a friend he felt as close to as this eerily dangerous man who seemed eager to put himself at risk.

"How ya doing, Kenny?"

Mitchell shrugged, stared out at the passing farms, kept his thoughts quiet. After a long while, he said, "You think we'll go to the Pacific?"

"I don't know. No. The army wouldn't tell us we're going home, that we're going to be discharged, and then just . . . lie. I don't care what some of these guys are saying."

"What you gonna do?"

"School, maybe. Maybe Saint Louis or Kansas City. Find a good job. I'm kind of excited about that." He paused, Mitchell still staring far away. "What about you?"

Mitchell shrugged.

"My old man wants me to come to work in his mill." He motioned out to the golden fields moving past. "He buys grain from the farmers, makes pretty good money."

"Sounds pretty good." Mitchell kept his stare, said nothing. Benson felt a nervousness, looked at Mitchell's eyes, had seen the look so many times. "You're not gonna do that, are you?"

Mitchell shook his head.

"Can't. Not anymore. Can't. We're supposed to muster out, but I'm gonna talk to somebody, see what they'll let me do."

"Like what? You wanna go to the Pacific? You nuts?"

Mitchell shrugged again.

"Not sure. We'll see."

"You gotta find something to do, Kenny. You can't be a soldier forever."

Mitchell looked at him, the cold clear eyes.

"Why not?"

Benson had nothing else to say, felt a hard sadness, thought, I knew he would do this. I knew he couldn't just . . . go home. He *misses* it.

The train climbed a slight rise, then rolled around a curve, the car leaning, the wheels beneath them squealing. The hill gave way to another open field, more wheat, more farmers, a horse dragging a plow, another horse pulling a small wagon, men with shovels and pitchforks. Benson watched them, no one looking at the train, no one seeing the soldiers as they passed, the farmers already busy with their own lives, as though the soldiers had never been there at all, the war had never happened. Out beyond, in the vast golden field, Benson saw flecks of red, the wheat field dotted with thousand of flowers. They were poppies.

AFTERWORD

... This was a holy war, more than any other in history, this war has been an array of the forces of evil against those of righteousness. It had to have its leaders, and it had to be won—no matter what the sacrifices, no matter what the suffering to populations, to materials, to our wealth—oil, steel, industry—no matter what the cost was, the war had to be won. In Europe, it has been won.

—DWIGHT D. EISENHOWER

Peace is going to be a hell of a letdown.

—GEORGE PATTON

THE GERMANS

A thousand years shall pass and this guilt of Germany shall not have been erased.

—HANS FRANK, HITLER'S GOVERNOR OF POLAND

KARL RUDOLF GERD VON RUNDSTEDT

Captured by American troops near his home at Bad Tölz, Germany, on May 1, 1945. Through the last year of the war, his health slowly fails, and shortly after his capture he suffers a heart attack. But the Allies show little mercy, and he is held for trial as a war criminal. He is first sent to the holding facility for high-ranking German commanders at Spa, Belgium, and then relocated to various prisoner-of-war camps in England. He doggedly endures delays in his trial, and reluctantly Allied prosecutors concede that they cannot bring formal charges against him that have any merit. He is released in 1949. Roundly criticized by other surviving German commanders, he is an obvious scapegoat for those Germans who insist on believing that their failings came on the battlefield, and not from the madness of their leadership. Nevertheless, von Rundstedt receives considerable respect from his former enemies, if not from those he served.

He contributes to and supports an exaggeratedly positive biography of himself, which is never published in German, and dies in Hannover, Germany, in 1953, at age seventy-seven.

ALBERT SPEER

Hitler's architect, and one of his most trusted subordinates, is captured on May 23, 1945, at Glücksburg Castle, near Flensburg, in northern Germany. In the days following Hitler's suicide, Speer actively consults with Admiral Dönitz to seek some preservation of the German nation, though Speer agrees with Dönitz's orders that the German military should engage in no further hostile acts against its enemies.

As Hitler's intimate, and since he holds the official title as Reichsminister for arms and munitions, Speer cannot avoid a trial for war crimes. He cooperates with prosecutors and offers lengthy testimony, providing a significant window into the workings of Hitler's inner circle, but his conviction is a foregone conclusion. Speer is sentenced to twenty years in prison. He accepts the sentence as an act of justice, and does not appeal.

His testimony during his trial also provides a vivid illustration of a thinking man's susceptibility to the seduction of Hitler's aura, and Speer accepts complete responsibility for his role in the Nazi regime. He serves the full term of his sentence, and is released from Spandau Prison in Berlin in 1966.

His memoir is published in 1969, from notes Speer has smuggled out of prison throughout his incarceration. Titled *Inside the Third Reich,* it is widely considered the most accurate and unaffected memoir of anyone close to Hitler, and is thus an invaluable tool in understanding the inner workings of Hitler himself, as well as the swirl of intrigue that surrounded him.

Though Speer admits to having harbored his own plot to kill Hitler, a plot that was never carried out, he also admits to a loyalty and a devotion to service that even he cannot excuse. In a letter to his wife, Speer writes,

> I am glad to accept my situation if by so doing I can still do something for the German people.

Describing his first awareness of Auschwitz, Speer says,

> I did not investigate—for I did not want to know what was happening there. . . . As an important member of the leadership of the Reich, I had to share the total responsibility for all that had happened. I was inescapably contaminated morally; from fear of discovering something which might have made me turn from my course, I had closed my eyes.

In 1981, he suffers a stroke in London, and dies at age seventy-six.

HERMANN GÖRING

He surrenders himself to the Americans near Berchtesgaden in Bavaria on May 7, 1945. Charged with war crimes, he is tried at Nuremberg. In October 1946, he is convicted and sentenced to death. Rather than allow his enemies to have their final revenge, Göring somehow secures a capsule of cyanide, and poisons himself the day before his scheduled hanging. He is fifty-three.

Göring's body is taken to Dachau, where he is cremated, and his ashes are disposed of in a garbage can.

HEINRICH HIMMLER

The man who has stood beside Hitler since the earliest days of Hitler's insatiable quest for power, Himmler is arguably the second most powerful man in the Reich. As the founding force behind the SS, Gestapo, and the Waffen-SS, Himmler has acquired a well-deserved reputation for cold-blooded viciousness. Like Hitler, Himmler bears no resemblance to the Aryan ideal of the strapping blue-eyed blond—those people who in Hitler's eyes carry the genetic perfection that entitles them to rule the world. Himmler is short of stature, with a crippled foot and chronically poor health, but appearances are deceiving. The mouselike man has carried out Hitler's orders for the imprisonment and execution of several million Jews and other ethnic Germans and non-Germans through the astonishing reign of terror that began with Hitler's dictatorship.

As Germany's defeat becomes increasingly apparent, Himmler seems to violate his own principles and seeks favor by offering an armistice with the West, which is flatly refused. On May 6, 1945, he is removed from all power in the German government by Hitler's titular successor, Admiral Karl Dönitz. As early as February 1945, for reasons never adequately explained, Himmler begins releasing Jewish concentration camp prisoners to the Swedish Red Cross, thus preventing the extermination of tens of thousands whose names would otherwise have been added to those of the victims of the Holocaust.

Heavily disguised and seeking escape from Germany, Himmler is captured by the British near the German seaport of Bremen on May 22, 1945. He commits suicide by poison three days later, at age forty-five.

KARL DÖNITZ

Surrenders to the British on May 23, 1945. No one is more surprised than Dönitz that Hitler has named him successor in control of the German government, and he accepts that responsibility not by continuing the fight Hitler would have wanted, but by engineering the arrangements for the formal end of the war. He is convicted of war crimes at Nuremberg, but the death sentence that the court deems appropriate is negated after a stunning show of support for Dönitz from British and American naval officers, including American admiral Chester Nimitz. The Nuremberg court reluctantly reduces his sentence to ten years in prison, which he serves at Spandau. He is released in 1956 and retires to a small village in northern West Germany, where he writes his memoirs. He remains unapologetic for his service to Hitler, accepts that a military officer should, above all else, do his duty. It is a position that forces the German government to keep him out of any limelight, although Dönitz continues to garner respect from naval officers around the world. He dies of heart failure in 1980, at age eighty-nine.

MARTIN BORMANN

The man most despised by Albert Speer as a vicious master of intrigue, Bormann is regarded by most, Speer included, as little more than Hitler's political buffoon. Officially, Bormann is designated Hitler's chief of the Nazi Party and deputy Führer, though none of the German military ever accept his authority in military matters. In reality, his duties seem more like those of a doting private secretary, whose insecurities cause him to distrust and plot against anyone who gains Hitler's favor.

Immediately after Hitler's suicide, the forty-five-year-old Bormann attempts to slip through the Russian cordon surrounding Berlin. Rumors of his survival and escape abound for decades after, including speculation that he has reached either Argentina or Paraguay, which provides considerable fuel for conspiracy theorists, who suggest he has founded an underground colony of former Nazis. However, those sensational rumors have no foundation in fact, and are finally put to rest in December 1972, when, during an excavation in Berlin, a skeleton is unearthed that proves beyond all doubt to be Bormann.

ALFRED JODL

Hitler's titular chief of staff, the man closest to Hitler in the execution of military decisions, surrenders himself on May 23, 1945, in Mürwik, Denmark. He is convicted of war crimes at Nuremberg and sentenced to death. Jodl is hanged in October 1946 at age fifty-six.

WILHELM KEITEL

The man best described as "Hitler's office manager" is the signatory authorized by Admiral Dönitz to attend the ceremony in Berlin that the Russians demand in order to officially end the war. Thus, on May 9, 1945, it is Keitel who fulfills the same duty in Berlin that was performed by Alfred Jodl at Rheims two days prior. The Russians allow Keitel to return to his own headquarters at Flensburg, Germany, where he now serves Admiral Dönitz. As Dönitz's staff dismantles the last remnants of Nazi command, Keitel surrenders to the British on May 13, 1945. Convicted of war crimes at Nuremberg, he is sentenced to death, though in his defense he offers what has become a grotesquely infamous excuse: "I was only following orders."

After his conviction, he denies any attempt by his supporters to appeal his sentence, requesting that he be allowed to "die like a soldier" and face a firing squad. His request is denied, and he is hanged the same day as Alfred Jodl. He is sixty-four.

ALBERT KESSELRING

The man cursed with the moniker *Smiling Al* is nonetheless regarded as one of Germany's premier battlefield commanders. He turns himself and his staff over to the custody of American troops near Salzburg, Austria, on May 6, 1945. Treated with respect by General Maxwell Taylor, commander of the 101st Airborne Division, Kesselring expects to be allowed to return home, a beaten warrior. Photographs are taken of Taylor hosting Kesselring in what appears to be a scene of social pleasantry, which causes some controversy for Taylor. Kesselring does not expect to be included among those minions of Hitler who are charged with war crimes at the Nuremberg trials, and the prosecutors at Nuremberg agree. But the British do not. Thus, Kesselring is surprised to be charged with war crimes that occurred under his command in Italy, and in May 1947 he is tried before a British tribunal. He is convicted and sentenced to death, but there is strong sentiment that Kesselring is not the villain the court says he is. Pressured by Winston Churchill and various British commanders, including Harold Alexander, the court commutes the sentence to life imprisonment.

He serves most of his sentence in Werl Prison, Westphalia, Germany. Like Albert Speer, Kesselring writes his memoir by smuggling scraps of paper out of the prison.

Diagnosed with throat cancer, Kesselring is released from prison in 1952, both for humanitarian reasons and because of a vigorous public relations campaign on his behalf by the West German government. His memoir is published in Germany in 1953, and translated into an English edition in 1954.

Though he actively supports organizations that seek to assist German veterans, it is not a cause that is politically popular, and Kesselring lives out his life unable to shed his connection to the Nazis. He dies in 1960, at Bad Nauheim, Germany, at age seventy-four.

HASSO MANTEUFFEL

Manteuffel is considered the most capable of the field commanders who carry out Hitler's great assault in December 1944, and his reputation is justified. His troops achieve the greatest penetration of the American lines during the Battle of the Bulge. But as Manteuffel knows, it is not a fight that could have succeeded. Pulled away from the Western Front in March 1945, Manteuffel is assigned to command the German Third Army, in a futile attempt to hold the Russians away from the eastern German border. Beaten back, Manteuffel withdraws westward while making extensive efforts to allow German civilians to flee the Russian advance. He surrenders to the British on May 3, 1945. Never charged with war crimes, Manteuffel serves as a distinguished POW until Christmas 1946, when he is released.

Returning to civilian life, Manteuffel enters banking and becomes an industrialist; in the mid-1950s he serves as a member of the German Parliament. He retires with his wife to a quiet life at Lake Ammersee, Bavaria, and dies in 1978, at age eighty-one.

THE BRITISH

WINSTON CHURCHILL

> Never give in—never, never, never, never, in nothing great or small, large or petty, never give in except to convictions of honor and good sense. Never yield to force; never yield to the apparently overwhelming might of the enemy.

No single figure in the history of the Second World War deserves credit for inspiring his people to their cause as much as the British prime minister. With all of Britain still reeling from the horrific effects of World War One, during which they lost much of a generation of young men, the Second World War has inflicted on that nation the same horror. Though the British military suffers extraordinary losses, especially among frontline officers, it is the British civilian population that has enabled the British government to carry on. Churchill is singly responsible for strengthening the morale of the people whose sons, husbands, and fathers are sacrificing their lives to keep Hitler at bay.

Many suggest that one of Hitler's greatest errors was not following through with plans to invade England in 1940, once the British army suffered the catastrophic defeat that drove them into the sea at Dunkirk. But often overlooked is that Churchill actively prepared the British people for such an invasion, and despite what may have been Germany's superiority in troop strength and accompanying airpower, Germany's success in conquering the British Isles was never a foregone conclusion. Credit for that must go in large part to the inspiration Churchill provided to the British people, a show of resolve that contributed to the seeds of doubt planted in Hitler's mind.

At the war's end, Churchill's leadership seems to fall into irrelevancy, and the world is amazed when, late in 1945, the British vote his party out of office, thus costing him the role of prime minister. He returns to power in 1951, and serves as prime minister until 1955 when he retires from that office, but continues to serve in Parliament until 1964.

Though his colorful and inspiring speeches fill volumes, it is his keen ability to predict the political future that is often overlooked. His strenuous objections to the outcome of the Yalta Conference are borne out, as Stalin's Soviet Union seals off most of eastern Europe, including East Germany, from western influence—and in many cases contact of any kind. It is Churchill who describes the Soviet action as the "dropping of an iron curtain." This antagonism, which was predicted by Churchill (as well as George Patton), results in decades of Cold War between East and West, and the subjugation of nations that resembles in many ways the very conquest Hitler had intended.

A staunch ally of the United States, Churchill befriends every American president and is a welcome guest at ceremonies and official functions in the United States. In 1963, Congress authorizes President John F. Kennedy to declare Churchill an honorary citizen of the United States.

But Churchill's health fails rapidly, and in January 1965, he suffers a stroke. He survives for nine days, and dies at age ninety. His funeral is the largest of its kind in British history.

Upon this battle depends the survival of Christian civilization. Upon it depends our own British life and the long continuity of our institutions and our empire. The whole fury and might of the enemy must very soon be turned on us. Hitler knows that he will have to break us in this island or lose the war. If we can stand up to him, all Europe may be freed, and the life of the world may move forward into broad and sunlit uplands. But if we fail, then the whole world, including the United States and all that we have known and cared for, will sink into the abyss of a new Dark Age made more sinister and perhaps more prolonged by the lights of perverted science. Let us therefore brace ourselves to our duty, and so bear ourselves that if the British Empire and Commonwealth lasts for a thousand years, men will still say, "This was their Finest Hour."

—To the House of Commons, June 18, 1940

BERNARD LAW MONTGOMERY

As soon as I saw what was happening in the Ardennes, I took certain steps myself to ensure that if the Germans got to the Meuse, they certainly would not get over that river . . . This battle has been most interesting, I think probably one of the most interesting and tricky battles I have ever handled.

—Montgomery, press conference, January 7, 1945

Montgomery's self-proclaimed heroism for rescuing the Americans during the Battle of the Bulge is a pill that no American and few British commanders can swallow. Forced by the influence of those close to him, including his chief of staff, Freddie de Guingand, and British Chief of the Imperial General Staff Sir Alan Brooke, Montgomery concedes to offer Eisenhower an apology for his statements at the press conference. But the damage has been done. He continues to demonstrate a remarkably oblivious sense of his own importance, which, unfortunately, negates his reputation for accomplishments in the field. Throughout the remainder of the war, Monty's actions and pronouncements create animosity among even those who had long given him the benefit of the doubt. Though Eisenhower continues to maintain authority to remove Montgomery from his command, he recognizes Monty's value to the British forces, a political reality Eisenhower despises, as much as he begins to despise Montgomery himself.

Throughout the final year of the war, Montgomery continues his standard practice, insisting on absolute preparation before launching any attack. In fairness, Montgomery is acutely aware that the British and Canadian forces under his command have suffered losses the Americans cannot fully appreciate, losses that have become nearly impossible to replace. If Montgomery is to be blamed for excessive pride and a loud championing of nationalism, he must be credited with maintaining an army in the field that, by 1945, is a shadow of what it had been five years prior. Despite the hostility he engenders from men such as Bradley and Patton, the British soldiers love him, and it is this affection that enables the British to contribute to the final drive that defeats Hitler's army in the west.

After Germany's surrender, Montgomery serves as commander in chief of the British army of occupation and is awarded a peerage, thus becoming "First Viscount Montgomery of Alamein." The American shorthand becomes "Sir Bernard," which, coincidentally, is a derisive label George Patton had used to describe Montgomery throughout the war.

In mid-1946, he succeeds Sir Alan Brooke as chief of the Imperial General Staff, but his personality will never win him friends, and when he steps down two years later, no one in the British High Command is unhappy.

In 1951, Montgomery becomes Eisenhower's subordinate once again during the creation of the North Atlantic Treaty Organization (NATO), but the two men are never close. He serves as inspector general, but negotiating the political minefields in the halls of NATO is a far more complicated exercise than Montgomery had endured at SHAEF, and once again he creates more controversy than goodwill.

He publishes his memoirs in 1958, which results in outrage, particularly among the American military, for his blithe dismissal of Eisenhower's skills as commander, and he specifically blames Eisenhower for lengthening the war by at least a year. It is not a view shared by many who were there. Though Montgomery's memoir is an extensive and detailed account of his experiences, his arrogant tone and casual, unmerited claim of credit for successes become the final straw for many who still attempt to support him.

Instead of mellowing into old age, Montgomery becomes abrasively outspoken on sensitive and controversial issues of the day, including apartheid in South Africa, which he vigorously supports. He also expresses support for the regime of Chairman Mao in communist China, which to many lowers him into the role of senile curmudgeon.

He grows more feeble throughout the 1960s, and dies in 1976 at age eighty-eight.

Monty is a tired little fart. War requires the taking of risks, and he won't take them.

—GEORGE PATTON, DIARY, DECEMBER 27, 1944

ARTHUR TEDDER

Eisenhower's second in command serves as chief air marshal of the Royal Air Force through the end of the war, when he is awarded the more prestigious title of marshal of the Royal Air Force. He continues in that post until 1950, when he retires from the service. Always a student of military history, Tedder contributes to a historical study of the British Royal Navy, and later, he continues his close ties to the American military by serving in Washington as chairman of the British Joint Services Commission, the liaison between the British and NATO. He returns to England when he is named chancellor of the University of Cambridge in 1951. He serves on the board of directors of the British Broadcasting Corporation and writes his memoirs, considered a fair though slightly pro-American view of the war years. Of all the British commanders who serve Eisenhower, Tedder has the greatest dislike for Montgomery, and endures a feud with Montgomery that lasts until the end of his life.

He dies in 1967 in Surrey, England, at age seventy-six.

ARTHUR "BOMBER" HARRIS

The man whose tactics were chiefly responsible for the utter devastation of every major German city remains at his post until September 1945. He is then promoted to marshal of the Royal Air Force, and promptly retires, raising speculation that the promotion is the carrot that allows him to leave the service with his dignity intact. He writes his memoirs, in which he champions the brilliance of his carpet-bombing strategies, and continues to state publicly that it was his bombers who made possible the defeat of Hitler.

In the postwar years, the British press and public begin to wrestle with the morality of wartime horrors such as the Dresden firebombing and the deaths of so many German civilians, and thus, Harris's position becomes distinctly out of fashion. Bruised by the lack of credit and respect, Harris moves to South Africa. In 1954, he is persuaded by Winston Churchill to return to England, and is awarded a baronetcy, which only Churchill's influence can provide. Harris dies in Goring-on-Thames in 1984, at age ninety-one.

Those who condemn Harris and his strategies as inhumane often compare them to the sins of Hitler's Germany, as though both sides commit equally reprehensible acts of slaughter.

> Some Germans today brand the bombing of their cities a war crime. This seems an incautious choice of words. . . . For all its follies and bloody misjudgments, the strategic air offensive was a military operation designed to hasten the collapse of Germany's ability to make war. It stopped as soon as Hitler's people ceased to fight. Most of Germany's massacres, by contrast, were carried out against defenseless people who possessed not the slightest power to injure Hitler's empire. They were murdered for ideological reasons, devoid of military purpose.
>
> —HISTORIAN MAX HASTINGS, 2004

KENNETH STRONG

Eisenhower's chief of intelligence endures much postwar criticism for the failures to detect the German plans that resulted in the Battle of the Bulge, but the greatest criticism comes from British commanders, who use the opportunity to lash out at Strong because he has displayed what they feel is a pro-American bias. Always respected by Eisenhower, Strong is instrumental in gleaning as much advantage as possible from the top-secret Ultra program, which has broken the German Enigma codes. What Strong cannot know is that, during planning for the Ardennes offensive, Hitler himself became distrustful of his own Enigma system and avoided using it, thus depriving the Allied intelligence network of critical information. Despite these problems, Strong's intelligence-gathering network succeeded in thwarting German planning throughout much of the war.

After the war, Strong continues in his role as chief of British intelligence, though his focus is more on political intrigue than military. He retires from the military in 1947, but continues to serve the British government as a valued adviser. In 1952, he becomes "Sir Kenneth" when he is knighted by King George VI.

He writes his memoirs as well as books that examine the role of intelligence in military operations, and he remains highly respected on both sides of the Atlantic. He dies in 1982 at age eighty-two.

THE AMERICANS

DWIGHT DAVID EISENHOWER

With the conclusion of the war in Europe, Eisenhower accepts the position of military governor of the German Occupation Zone. His experiences, particularly as a witness to many Holocaust atrocities, steel him in his anger toward the Germans who blindly followed Hitler, and he advocates the complete dismantling of Germany's industrial abilities. Because he never enjoys his role in the war's aftermath, his stay in Europe is not as lengthy as those of many of the troops he commands. In November 1945, he is named to succeed George C. Marshall as army chief of staff, a position many had thought he would have assumed much earlier in the war. He serves until 1948, when he accepts the presidency of Columbia University in New York. While still maintaining that position, he takes a leave of absence and returns to Europe to serve as supreme commander of the new alliance called NATO, which is created as a unified front to deter Soviet expansion in Europe.

In July 1952, Eisenhower officially resigns from the army, resuming his position at Columbia. But Ike is a beloved American hero, and political advisers begin to surround him, encouraging him to seek office. It is a temptation he cannot avoid. He accepts the Republican nomination and in the election of November 1952 handily defeats Democrat Adlai Stevenson. Thus, Eisenhower becomes the thirty-fourth president of the United States. At age sixty-two, he is at that time the oldest man elected to the office. He overwhelmingly defeats Stevenson again in 1956.

As president, Eisenhower continues most of the social programs set forth by Franklin Roosevelt's New Deal, and is a witness to the destructive effects of McCarthyism. Before the terms *liberal* and *conservative* so actively define the political landscape, Eisenhower seems to take a conservative stance on issues regarding foreign policy, and is chastised severely by Harry Truman for not speaking out against Senator McCarthy's obvious abuse of power as a rabid anti-communist, whose dragnet unjustly drags down the reputation of many prominent and patriotic Americans. In contrast, Eisenhower appoints Earl Warren as chief justice of the Supreme Court, a court that hands down the momentous *Brown v. Board of Education* ruling in 1954, which declares segregated schools to be unconstitutional, thus beginning this country's inexorable push toward what will become Lyndon Johnson's Civil Rights Act of 1964. Eisenhower surprises some of his supporters by his virulent antipathy toward segregation, and in 1957, he directly confronts Arkansas governor Orval Faubus by ordering National Guard troops to Little Rock to forcibly integrate the public school system, which Faubus has refused to do.

In 1961, he retires from public life and settles in Gettysburg, Pennsylvania, on a farm he purchased a decade earlier, which sits adjacent to the battlefield. In 1967, he donates that farm to the National Park Service, and it is today a major tourist destination.

During his presidency, and after, Eisenhower suffers from heart ailments, and he dies in March 1969 at Walter Reed Army Hospital in Washington. He is buried beside his young son Doud in Abilene, Kansas, on the grounds of the Eisenhower Presidential Library. His wife, Mamie, dies in 1979, and is interred alongside him.

In any examination of his career as commander in chief of Allied forces in Europe, a case can be made that Dwight Eisenhower is possibly the only man at the time who could have performed that job with the skills and excellence it required. His efforts put to rest the claim made by Napoleon that "there is no easier enemy to defeat than a coalition," a notion Hitler would have taken to heart. In uniting the Americans alongside their British, Canadian, Polish, and French allies (among others), Eisenhower created a fighting force with a single focused goal, and in the process overcame the jealousies, egos, personality clashes, and animosities inherent in all of those relationships. By never tolerating the nationalistic backbiting that lay under the surface, he guided the energies of his subordinates toward their common goal instead of myriad individual ones, something Hitler could never accomplish. Eisenhower's ability to relate to the soldier in the muddy field, as well as the field marshal in his palatial headquarters, made him a leader who, during that period in world history, was unequaled. More amazing is that, in his long military career, he never actually led troops on a battlefield.

In our history, there are many examples of hero-worshipping American voters who enthusiastically elevate a general to the office of president. From George Washington to Andrew Jackson, Zachary Taylor, and Ulysses

Grant, no one else except perhaps Teddy Roosevelt proved to be as competent a president as he was a military commander. And while Dwight Eisenhower has his detractors, and while he most certainly made mistakes, there is no other individual among the western Allies who can claim more responsibility for defeating the armies of Adolf Hitler.

> Not only did he take the risk and arrive at the fence, but he cleared it in magnificent style.
>
> —WINSTON CHURCHILL, JUNE 1945

GEORGE PATTON

The man who engenders either reverential respect or dismissive loathing is, in terms of accomplishment against the enemy, the finest battlefield general of the Second World War.

With the war in Europe concluded, Patton is named military governor of Bavaria, a political post that is completely inappropriate to his personality. In September 1945, he once again invites a circus of controversy by publicly comparing "this Nazi thing" to a political election in the United States, equating Nazis to Democrats. The Democrats in Congress are not amused, and Patton's career in postwar politics is brief. He is replaced in Bavaria by General Lucian Truscott.

In June, Patton allows himself a brief visit to the States and, alongside another war hero, Jimmy Doolittle, is received in Los Angeles by enormous crowds in a parade and public appearances, which include an event at the Rose Bowl. Patton addresses a crowd estimated to exceed one hundred thousand people, and his remarks are laced with the same astounding variety of profanity he has always used on his troops. Though somewhat shocked, the civilian audience nevertheless regales Patton as the hero he is.

Despite Patton's urgent desire to continue fighting in any capacity open to him, including especially the ongoing campaigns in China, he will never again see combat. In August 1945, when the war in the Pacific comes to a close, Patton becomes a warrior without a war, and grudgingly accepts that his only option is retirement. On December 9, 1945, he embarks on a pheasant hunt near Mannheim, Germany, with his chief of staff, General "Hap" Gay. Patton and Gay ride in the backseat of a Cadillac that is struck head-on by an American deuce-and-a-half truck, near a railroad crossing at the town of Neckarstadt. Both vehicles are traveling at slow rates of speed, and at first the accident seems minor, but Patton's head strikes a steel bar, part of the partition that separates him from the front seat. Though the others in the car are virtually unharmed, Patton's scalp is split open, and he labors to breathe. True to his personality, he responds by cursing, but it becomes immediately apparent that he is paralyzed. He is rushed by MPs to the army hospital at Heidelberg, and as the doctors begin to treat him, he remarks, "Jesus Christ. What a way to begin a leave."

The doctors quickly determine that Patton's spine has been dislocated, but the question remains how badly his spinal cord is damaged. Contact is made immediately with Washington, and on the recommendation of the American surgeon general, a neurosurgeon at Oxford University, Dr. Hugh Cairns, is contacted, and agrees to fly to Heidelberg. Notified of her husband's accident, Beatrice Patton is provided a plane by Eisenhower himself, and within forty-eight hours of the accident Patton's wife has crossed the Atlantic and is at his bedside. Accompanying her is Colonel Glen Spurling, an American army doctor specializing in neurosurgery.

Patton remains awake and cognizant for the next several days, though his paralysis improves only slightly. When the two men are alone, Patton requests that Dr. Spurling give him an assessment of his chances for survival. Patton demands honesty, and Spurling provides it. Patton's responds to the grim diagnosis, "I'll try to be a good patient."

During Patton's stay, the hospital is deluged with letters from around the world, most notably from President Truman and, of course, Eisenhower. Though Dr. Spurling maintains a glimmer of optimism, Patton's condition does not improve, and his breathing difficulties begin to worsen. During the evening of December 20, Patton's breathing nearly stops, the effects of a pulmonary embolism. He manages to survive until the following afternoon. The official cause of death is pulmonary edema and congestive heart failure. He is sixty years old.

Patton is buried at the American Military Cemetery in Hamm, Luxembourg. Two years later, his body is moved so that Patton is placed at the head of his troops also buried there, who lie before him.

There is no doubt that Patton's viewpoints are more often than not controversial, creating severe disadvantages for his own career and severely straining the patience of those he serves, but his legacy cannot be overlooked. He is often charged with racist attitudes, and yet it was Patton who agreed to deploy a black unit, the 761st Tank Battalion, into combat alongside white troops. To them, Patton said,

Men, you're the first Negro tankers to ever fight in the American army. I would never have asked for you if you weren't good. I have nothing but the best in my army. I don't care what color you are as long as you go up there and kill those Kraut sons of bitches. Everyone has their eyes on you, and is expecting great things from you. Most of all, your race is looking forward to you. Don't let them down, and damn you, don't let me down!

His attitude toward the Soviets made him unpalatable to those among the Allies who were trying to forge the uneasy alliance that divided postwar Europe. He referred to the Russians as "Mongols" and said publicly, "They have no regard for human life, and they are all-out sons of bitches, barbarians and chronic drunks." Despite the unwise bluntness of his words, his distrust of the Soviets spreads throughout the western world, a distrust that is very mutual, which results in four decades of Cold War.

The German attitude toward Patton was perhaps summed up by Lieutenant Colonel Freiherr von Wangenheim in spring 1945:

The greatest threat . . . was the whereabouts of the feared US Third Army. General Patton is always the main topic of military discussion. Where is he? When will he attack? Where? How? With what? Those are the questions that raced through the head of every German general. General Patton is the most feared general on all fronts. He is the most modern general and the best commander of armored and infantry troops combined.

Another war has ended and with it my usefulness to the world. It is for me personally a very sad thought.

—PATTON'S DIARY, AUGUST 10, 1945

THE BOMBARDIER

Lieutenant John Buckley is taken by his German captors to Stalag Luft III, near Sagan, Poland, a prisoner-of-war camp designated specifically for downed fliers, though by 1944 the camp houses a variety of Allied prisoners. In early 1945, as the Russians press forward across the Polish countryside, the camp is vacated by the Germans, who force their prisoners to march westward. Buckley is eventually housed at Stalag VII-A at Moosburg, Germany, until the camp is liberated by the American Fourteenth Armored Division in late April 1945.

After a brief hospital stay, primarily for rehabilitation, Buckley returns to the States and resigns his commission. He returns home, near Kansas City, then settles in Chicago, where he works for a radio parts manufacturer. He eventually acquires considerable skill as an industrial electrician. He marries Galinda Jessup in early 1948, and they have four children.

He retires in 1991, and lives today with his wife in Bradenton, Florida.

EDWARD BENSON

The train that carries him to the French coast arrives near the port of Le Havre, but instead of boarding an ocean liner, Benson is ordered to Camp Lucky Strike, one of several "cigarette camps" (so called because of their names) that serve as clearing grounds and rehabilitation sites for various American military units as they prepare to leave Europe. Like those who serve with him, Benson is victimized by a steady flood of rumors, especially those involving his unit's imminent departure to the Pacific. But as is so often the case, the rumors are fiction. Benson receives his orders in September 1945, and gratefully boards a troopship bound for the States.

He returns to his family's home in Sullivan, Missouri, but cannot settle into the quiet rural life. Benson applies to the University of Missouri, in Columbia, where he begins the study of journalism and broadcasting, and graduates with a degree in communications. He secures a job in St. Louis at a radio station, but is drawn to the new adventure called television. In 1954, he joins the staff of fledgling KWK-TV and becomes an on-air newscaster. When the station becomes a CBS affiliate, Benson pursues a climb up the corporate ladder, and moves to New York. He becomes producer of several locally broadcast programs on WCBS-TV, and during the 1960s is awarded two Peabody Awards for stories that follow the unfortunate lives of Vietnam veterans who cannot make the adjustment to civilian life.

In 1960, he meets and marries New York writer Roslyn Baker, but the fast-paced life in the city takes a toll, and they divorce in 1966. In 1970, he marries Suzanne Gilder. They have no children. Suzanne dies of cancer in 1997, and Eddie settles into life as a widower. He lives today in a retirement community in New Jersey.

Kenneth Mitchell

The man who seems reluctant to befriend anyone leaves Europe as Eddie Benson's best friend. Though Benson returns home, Mitchell fights the army's efforts to discharge him, and when that fails, he attempts to enlist in the navy. But the armed services are downsizing significantly, and Mitchell struggles to find his calling as a civilian. He has no interest in his father's grain mill in Ohio, and moves periodically to new cities, including Detroit and Cleveland, seeking some inspiration for a career. Helped financially by his friend Benson, Mitchell is finally rescued by the start of the Korean War. With the army seeking recruits, Mitchell enlists and is sent first to the Philippines. He then participates in Douglas MacArthur's extraordinary landing at Inchon, which rescues UN forces hemmed into a desperate situation at the nearby Pusan Perimeter.

Since he has combat infantry experience, Mitchell is quickly promoted to sergeant. From September to November 1950, he leads his squad into several difficult fights against North Korean forces. Fulfilling Eddie Benson's predictions that Mitchell is likely to do "something crazy," Mitchell is killed on November 28, 1950, leading an attack on a well-defended North Korean position. Mitchell is posthumously awarded a Silver Star. He is twenty-six.

Bruce Higgins

The sergeant who is ultimately responsible for saving the lives of both Benson and Mitchell serves out the final weeks of the war, and several weeks after, as a prison guard. The army is caught totally unprepared for the massive influx of German POWs, and Higgins assists in managing a compound where fifteen thousand German soldiers are housed, a facility meant for a tenth that number.

He returns home in October 1945, to Camp Shanks, New York, where the 106th Division is inactivated. Higgins seeks to continue his army career, but is thwarted until July 1947, when he is allowed to reenlist and assigned to the Twelfth Regiment, Fourth Infantry Division in Fort Ord, California. He is quickly promoted to first sergeant, and is encouraged to enter Officer Candidate School. He emerges in March 1948 as a second lieutenant, and within two years reaches the rank of captain. Throughout the 1950s, Higgins serves as a company commander with his unit in Germany, as part of NATO forces. In 1963, the regiment is re-assigned to Fort Carson, Colorado, but the Vietnam War reenergizes the army's emphasis on combat infantry, and in August 1966, Higgins is de-ployed to Dau Tieng, Vietnam. His unit receives the Presidential Unit Ci-tation and participates in ten major engagements. He returns home in October 1970 and retires a lieutenant colonel, settling in Vancouver, Washington.

His marriage to Louise Barrett Higgins endures throughout his many years of overseas assignments, and he fathers two children. He dies of lung cancer in 1994, at age seventy-three. His widow lives today in San Diego.

OMAR BRADLEY

Demonstrating that he is well deserving of the title "the soldier's general," Bradley returns home in June 1945 to head up the Veterans Administra-tion. He serves in that post until 1948, when he is named to succeed Eisen-hower as army chief of staff. A year later, President Truman selects Bradley to become the first chairman of the Joint Chiefs. In 1950, at age fifty-seven, he is the youngest general in American history to be awarded his fifth star, a rank reserved for a very select few. No one since has been pro-moted to that rank.

In 1951, his memoir is published. *A Soldier's Story* is widely regarded as one of the most self-effacing and accurate accounts of the command de-cisions of World War Two, and is to this day a highly regarded reference on the subject.

During the Korean War, Bradley is an outspoken opponent of the strategic views of Douglas MacArthur, and has a role in President Truman's decision to remove MacArthur from command in Korea, a decision that continues to invite controversy.

Bradley retires from the service in 1953 and settles into civilian life as an executive with the Bulova Watch Company. By 1958, he is that com-pany's chairman of the board, a position he holds for twenty-five years. During the 1960s, he serves as a civilian adviser to President Lyndon John-son.

His first wife, Mary, dies in 1965, and a year later he raises some eye-brows in Washington by marrying Kitty Buhler, who is thirty years his jun-ior. He dies in 1981, at age eighty-eight, and is buried at Arlington National Cemetery.

COURTNEY HODGES

In May 1945, Hodges is transferred to the Pacific theater to command those forces who will embark on the planned invasion of the Japanese mainland. The dropping of the atomic bombs on Hiroshima and Nagasaki preempts the need for that invasion.

Hodges continues in command of the American First Army until 1949, when he retires from active service. He spends most of his career overshadowed by George Patton, and often receives unfair condemnation for his lack of preparedness, which allowed German success during the Battle of the Bulge. But Hodges is highly regarded by Eisenhower and Bradley, and his reputation was likely damaged by the positioning of his First Army in the one area along the Ardennes Forest where no one in the Allied command expected any sort of offensive action by the enemy.

He dies in San Antonio in 1966, at age seventy-nine.

We may allow ourselves a brief period of rejoicing; but let us not forget for a moment the toil and efforts that lie ahead. Japan, with all her treachery and greed, remains unsubdued. The injury she has inflicted on Great Britain, the United States, and other countries, and her detestable cruelties, call for justice and retribution. We must now devote all our strength and resources to the completion of our task.

—WINSTON CHURCHILL, MAY 8, 1945

JEFF SHAARA is the *New York Times* bestselling author of *The Steel Wave*, *The Rising Tide*, *To the Last Man*, *The Glorious Cause*, *Rise to Rebellion*, and *Gone for Soldiers*, as well as *Gods and Generals* and *The Last Full Measure*—two novels that complete the Civil War trilogy that began with his father's Pulitzer Prize–winning classic *The Killer Angels*. Jeff was born into a family of Italian immigrants in New Brunswick, New Jersey. He grew up in Tallahassee, Florida, and graduated from Florida State University. He lives in Sarasota. Visit the author online at www.jeffshaara.com.

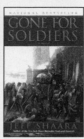

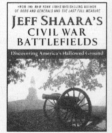